www.fast-print.net/store.php

The Threshold
Copyright © Marcus J. Goodman 2012

All rights reserved

No part of this book may be reproduced in any form by photocopying or any electronic or mechanical means, including information storage or retrieval systems, without permission in writing from both the copyright owner and the publisher of the book.

All characters are fictional.
Any similarity to any actual person is purely coincidental.

ISBN 978-178035-384-5

First published 2012 by
FASTPRINT PUBLISHING
Peterborough, England.
Printed by Printondemand-Worldwide

*My grateful thanks to Diane F. for her insights,
and to Petra for her love.*

The Characters

The Pessimist (Stefan Falk) – business consultant, master of the ironies, prisoner of the past. Wears memories and old friendships like a stone around his neck. Small, wiry and divorced. Strangled his marriage with indecision and has regretted it ever since. Lonely and disillusioned, he's given up looking out for love or sense of purpose in his life.

The Temptress (Annabelle Goldberg-Binoche) – redhead with eyes as green as the sea, initiated queen in the holy rites of temptation, heiress to the great fortunes of life. Young widow, number 3 on Munich high society's list of eligibility. The goddess of independence who plays with men like a rubber ball.

The Extremist (Matthias von B.) – brilliant as a child, in private school stole the chalice from the unworthy and the golden goblet from the gods. Product of the student uprisings of '68, disappeared in the 70's. Lawyer by profession, Stefan's charismatic boyhood friend, the one who comes back to light a fire.

The Mystic (Estella) – mother Irish, successful painter and poetess, lives with her Danish lover. The keeper of the mysteries, the lady of the doors. Platonic girlfriend of Stefan's despite the best of his efforts, and the lamp who lights his dark.

The Journalist   (Christian Beck) – intellectual, the frail sword of democracy, one of a dying breed. He who moves between the networks of the establishment amongst the garbage and the greed, helps keep the powerful on a leash and the elected on their toes. A lifter of stones which it's safer not to lift, a close colleague and friend of Elijah Goldberg.

The Englishman   (George Sunday) – Customs & Excise officer, gangly chinless Casanova, blessed with an Adam's apple the size and speed of a golf ball. A man of bottomless libido and wit, friend of Stefan. Mother German, a pretty little Hamburg stripper back in '46, father a British Army de-nazification officer so impressed by her credentials he made them his permanent home.

The Chameleon   (Hermann von B.) – father of Matthias, ex-Nazi judge fondly known as Hanging Herman in his prime. Indispensible fish who slipped through the net and deftly changed his robes from black to red. A founding father of the post-war German democratic process. Now resident in exclusive private care-home.

The Nazi   (Elisabeth Falk) – mother of Stefan, of humble origins but noble proportions, who married into money. Fondly known as Easy Lizzy in her prime. Proud Arian matron, denier of truths, still praying for Adolf's resurrection. Found covert solidarity in bed with her neighbour Hermann von B. as often as he would but far less often than she could.

The Jew   (Elijah Goldberg) – publisher of rough reputation, small and stocky and tough, standard bearer of Old Testament truth. Hated, respected and feared by the big boys. Only Holocaust survivor of the Munich family Goldberg. Met wife Monique on a sofa in Bedford Square, London, in the 50's. Father of only child Annabelle, the apple of his eye; guards her like a knight of old with a lance which cannot break.

The Hypocrite   (Tobias Falk) – eldest brother of Stefan, Catholic, insurance CEO giant with size 47 feet of clay, pompous defender of dwindling faith. 5 children, 2 consuming passions: his 'cello in an amateur string-quartet, and being led into temptation by the slinky female 2nd violin.

The Catholic (Mathilda) – wife of Tobias, indestructible pillar of the Holy Roman Church, a prickly prudish lady whose own passions are restricted to rosaries and incense and lighting endless candles to illuminate her dark.

The Call-girl (Rosi) – abused by both father and nuns as a child. Tough as a nut, with language to make a bricklayer blush, but born with a soft and lucrative spot. The darling of the big boys. Rosi works out of a penthouse suite above the bar near Stefan's appartment. Their relationship is truly exemplary.

The Realist (Heinrich) – successful architect, son of a village blacksmith who's climbed to the mountaintop. Builds palaces for the Munich new rich, works 16 hours a day. Muscular, handsome and determined, a leader of the pack. Married to Margareth, Stefan's dominant eldest sister, but the marriage is seriously on the rocks.

The Rebel (Eva Falk) – youngest sister of Stefan, business executive, single. Small tough and attractive, queen of emancipation. In her teens fell in love with Matthias, the rich boy from next door. The constant source of her frustration is being born an ambitious woman in an incompetent male world.

The Gossip (Mrs Maußer) – wife of the alcoholic caretaker where Stefan lives, takes care of everybody else's business. Busy, buxom, with uncanny powers of observation, wearer of amazingly gaudy smocks and the permanent carrier of a broom. Suffers from verbal diarrhoea, has eyes in the back of her head, is the thorn in Stefan's side.

The pragmatist (Dr. Gustav Breitenbach) – Bavarian Minister President, gravelly gruff and direct. The one with the bodyguards who comes to the party, good friend of Elijah Goldberg. He who talks about mice and men, and means it. Brilliant blunt and incorruptible, an exception proving the German rule - a flower amongst so many weeds.

The Theologian (Professor Dr. Krister Skell) – the Alpha and the Omega, explainer of the stars and the flower. Guardian of the Gate and the Soul, the one who opens the doors. He who Stefan encounters in Florence. He's the wise old man moving amongst us, invisible to most, the one smiling down from on high.

Chapter 1

I crouched, concealed, just the way we'd planned. On the plateau, high up.

The two of them were coming nearer. There he was, I caught a brief glimpse – he, the one they were after but hadn't yet captured. I could hear Eva's words now, louder, every single one, speaking to him – they were like a laser painting its target, like a searchlight guiding me in.

They came closer and closer.

I crouched lower, panicking. Could hardly breathe at all, everything cramped. Oh God... this is it. I hunkered behind the thick bushes of broom, full of fear. My brain seized up. I couldn't do it – I simply couldn't. But my hands... they were moving, as if of their own volition... they weren't really my hands, were they? I watched them fascinated, horrified, half-mesmerised: they picked up the gun.

I remember the intense scent of the yellow broom, like warm honey-almond, and the luscious green needles against the blue sky. Larks were singing, there were bees humming, a beetle crawled near my knee.

They were stationary now, less than a dozen paces away. Words of affection, words of remorse, she was preparing the way, her sentences hung motionless in the warm air. He had his back to me.

Petrified I rose, came round the bushes. I had both hands lifted, a fist and a gun... in four or five seconds it would all be over – would he go like a skittle bowled over the edge, would he be badly hurt... would he die? Oh God, oh God...

"Hello Stefan," he said.

Said quietly, it was just a whisper, it hit me like a club... he'd said it before even bothering to turn his head.

I went into spasm, I was six yards from him, his back still to me. I stopped dead, terrified. How had he known?

Slowly he twisted, no surprise in his movement. How could he turn so unhurriedly? He was facing me now. There were his eyes, steady and pale blue. They radiated the animal in him.

He watched me, he stood there lean and relaxed hardly five feet from the edge. A dreadful silence. He wore jeans and a T-shirt and a light summer jacket unbuttoned, it was open, hung loose. His hands were empty, his arms hanging at his sides. Everything told me he was in his element, he was in control; oh my God he looked so good.

"Stefan," he repeated. He said it so calmly, so quietly, there was no rebuke. That's all he said.

I stood there shaking like a child, raised the gun again. Held it with both hands to try to steady my aim, the way they do in the movies, the way he'd shown me long ago.

With unconcern he glanced down at it, didn't react – looked back at my eyes. But he was calculating, wasn't he? He must know that we were serious. Then Eva sprang, she was like a cat...

He let out a brief laugh, it was soft as a sigh... dropped to a crouch, quick and sure and cool – he always was so quick. He was ducking, weaving, avoiding the aim of the gun, hands free and prepared, arms suddenly stretched ready, twisting towards the cliff...

It happened so fast, it was just a glimpse, but it comes back to me now in the dark of the night in nightmares over and over, and the image is there clear and fixed like a photograph: a sandaled foot unexpectedly caught in tough heather, a thin sinewy sunburnt body suspended for a second in the air. Then he was gone; he went head forwards over the edge.

There were horrible sounds – a body falling, crashing through branches, rocks and stones rattling. Eva and I were at the edge, peering. Treetops, the valley floor far below, I felt quite sick. Nothing to be seen of him though, except a ghost of dust to mark the passage. Above the distant roar of the traffic, birds screeching their warnings. That was all.

x x x

I had a strange dream the other night. I was in a building I'd never been in before which contained a maze of corridors and staircases and rooms, and I was searching for something but didn't know what. Doors opened, doors closed, there was sometimes light, sometimes dark – and the longer I searched the stronger grew my sense of being lost and confused. Then, unexpectedly, in one of the rooms an old friend of mine who I haven't seen for many years materialised. He stood in my way, confronting me. I tried to speak to him but no words came. I remember thinking: it's good to see him again – perhaps it is he I've been searching for.

The dream continued, a profusion of disconnected scenes in which this old friend was sometimes present, sometimes not, and sometimes in disguise; it was a vivid and haunting dream, one of those which remains in the memory, but it wasn't precisely what I'd call a nightmare. It left an unpleasant taste, though.

And, to my surprise, two days later part of it came true.

Out of the blue he wrote to me – after twenty long years of silence. That was weird too because I'd presumed he was dead. It was slightly disquieting – somewhere inside me I think I was still a little afraid of him and would've preferred to let sleeping dogs lie. We had once been very close, yet there'd always been a side of him I couldn't quite reach. And the influence he'd had upon me in my youth hadn't completely faded either, it leaves a mixed print even now. It's like a feeling of remorse that can mar the sense of gain, or the seal that's got broken on a vintage bottle of wine. Or like a scar which never quite heals.

He sent me a postcard.

Not a more modern form of communication or messaging; just an old-fashioned postcard. But it was somehow symbolic of our past, I suppose, as if technology and time had stood still. Knowing him, he surely did it intentionally. He had always done everything with intent. At any rate, it shook me; it tipped a few memories from the lip of that forbidden jar I'd hidden away safely many years ago. And again I recalled the dream. Yes, it was rather weird.

At first glance, as I'd leafed rapidly through the post from my letterbox, only the picture on the postcard of a path winding up to green hills and sky caught my eye for a second. I was late – for a seminar I had to hold. Just time to flip the card over, see who it was from; I abhor unpunctuality. In that brief instant all I registered were a few typewritten lines. No signature. I rushed through the rest of the post in case of anything urgent, thrust the bundle back in the letterbox because I wouldn't have time till late evening.

But as I hurried up the steep cobbled street with leather laptop case in one hand and bulky briefcase in the other, heading for the underground garages where I rent a parking space, the image of the postcard remained pinned in my brain. It was seldom I received one nowadays, maybe two or three a year at most. I caught myself playing with the thought, who could've sent it? I suppose it was only a sign of loneliness, though: I'm in my mid-forties and since my wife Judit left me six years ago life's become a monotone. Apart from work nothing has been going my way. Even a postcard can present a little highlight...

Yes, I remember a foolish thought flashed – maybe it's from Isabelle in Provence, my first girlfriend, or seductive Claire from the London days. Is one of them divorced now, wanting to renew our old romance? My heart lifted, made a sudden little jump.

Then I stopped. My God, how pathetic...

Waiting impatiently for the lift, I frowned at the lord of indulgence and I took myself sternly in hand. More likely the card was as banal as life itself had become, simply holiday greetings from one of them: 'Hi Stefan, weather's gorgeous, we're both fine, the kids too, and when're you coming to stay?' And probably discreetly wearing a bikini now, too, no longer naked and enticing as in the old days, no longer a holy body like an altar on which I'd lain down my offerings.

But why typed, then, not handwritten?

It was pleasantly cool there in the lobby, waiting for the lift; realism kept creeping on through. I thought more sensibly: I suppose it could also be from Klaus, couldn't it, still on the road in some exotic foreign land on his old motorbike still searching for that answer, suddenly remembering our earlier travels and trying to invoke my envy. Ah yes... for an instant I could smell warm dust and wild thyme, hear the throaty roar of our bikes – there was the hot wind in our hair, sun flickering through pines, we were young, we were free as birds. Did I ever tell him I thought I'd found the answer in Judit till I lost her?

The lift doors were opening – I stepped in. A shadow... I'd only half-turned to press the button but... hadn't that been a shadow of a movement at the corner of my eye? I glanced over my shoulder. The cabin doors were closing... the lobby was empty, and beyond it, outside, the light was very bright. I could see no-one, however, no movement. So I must've been mistaken.

The lift shuddered, began descending.

Ah, Klaus and his eternal searching – he had become a journalist later. Would he have the time, though, to get around to sending a postcard? I shook my head. On consideration, I supposed the card could be from any one of my few good friends, male or female, scattered around Europe and the world with whom I've carefully maintained contact down the years – friends who I surreptitiously like to think, despite my close friend Estella's recent unworthy remarks, are akin to a small string of pearls which helps enrich the corridor of my life...

On this deeply unspectacular morning, therefore, I'd simply presumed the postcard might've been from anyone except him. That evening, upon my return from the seminar, and having established its author, I had left it, half-disbelieving, lying on my kitchen table.

Now, three days later, it lay there still.

It was like a ticking clock whose hands won't stop turning, or like a cobweb, perhaps, that's caught in my face. Just an ordinary harmless postcard, with that pretty picture of the path and the hills. What disturbed me was the communication on the back. It awoke old ghosts.

I stared at it.

I was waiting, procrastinating. And listening. I knew I was waiting for the bell. Yes, the card disturbed. I have to confess. It put a spanner in the works. And for the umpteenth time I thought: strange that I'd dreamt about him just before it arrived, it was a bit like a premonition. But I don't believe in premonitions, or anything of the kind. Didn't Estella broach this subject a while ago in one of our conversations? I'd casually let slip the sentence that life is full of coincidences.

"There's no such thing," she'd said quickly, in her certain and sensual way. To my chagrin she then added, as if any fool should know: "What people call a coincidence is, in fact, an insight, Stefan. It's a sort of hint to increase our awareness and help us. It comes to tell us something."

Well I have great regard for Estella, she's like a lamp in the dark on a winter night and her wisdom goes on and on – but in my heart I'm a realist, and with respect to such things I'm a true disbeliever. We were sitting beside the river and I sat on my sarcasm, simply answered that doesn't one read into things what one wishes to read like Tarot cards or lines on the palm, and why not if it fulfils an inner need?

And who's to tell, anyway? Maybe I'm right. Or maybe Estella's allowed to see things I'm not. The river flowed slowly by, light sparkled, there were dragonflies near our feet, and her dress showed a lot of thigh. The response I expected didn't come. Her only reply was a quiet smile – like the smile of the initiated. My God, though, she had enticing thighs.

Estella's my closest and only true female friend here in Nuremberg. She's been living with a Danish guy for some while, therefore, despite wishing otherwise, our relationship remains platonic; I simply have to accept it, she found the better man. We enjoy each other's company, however. I feel when I need to get under the surface I can talk to her the best. My good friend George Sunday from Customs and Excise, who is half-English, although highly intelligent tends to display his poverty – except on the subjects of politics and women and sex. So when I'm down or feeling a bit philosophical, I go to her; I guess I'm the moth around her flame.

The postcard had arrived the previous Monday.

My first objective reaction was: why the devil's he written? Why now and not before? And since he's written to me, has he made contact with the others from our student days too? We'd all presumed he was dead because none of us who'd known him well had ever heard from him again.

Subjectively, though, my reaction was of a different kind. The card had awoken something not quite definable deep in my gut. What was it? Insecurity, foreboding? Or was a perverse kind of curiosity mixed in there as well? I'd dug about – but couldn't put my finger on it. So I'd given Estella a tinkle from my office on the Tuesday and briefly told her about the postcard; I'd felt the need to share, to shed myself of part of the burden. I didn't mention that I'd dreamt of him, though – no sense in confusing the main issue with fanciful thoughts; no point pouring oil on the tiny flame of a fire she'd tried to kindle which I didn't wish to fan. Her advice had been exemplary and I followed it to a tee. That's why, in spite of a tight work-schedule, I was here now at home in the middle of the working week.

My God, why didn't the bell ring?

I stared blindly across the kitchen... Matthias... My mind was wandering. I glanced down at my hardly-read *Süddeutsche* newspaper near the laid-aside breakfast, glimpsed the headlines: 'PROPOSED GOVERNMENT TAX RISE PROMPTS UNIONS TO THREATEN GENERAL STRIKE' and 'TOP MANAGER KIDNAPPED FROM VILLA ON STARNBERGER LAKE'. I considered continuing reading while I waited. But I'd lost all interest. I looked up at my clock. Just turning nine. Try the radio then. Half-heartedly I stretched across to the portable at the far end of the table, switched it on. The familiar voice of the *Deutschlandfunk* newscaster filled the kitchen...

"*...a.m., Thursday the thirteenth of May. First the news in brief. The Starnberger abduction: a spokesperson for the Munich police confirmed that to date no arrests have been made. Following last month's abductions in Stuttgart of a hedge fund manager, a cardinal and a judge, this now brings the total number of kidnaps since January to six. Berlin: Union chief Bertolt warned last night of the catastrophic effects...*"

Switch it off, I told myself. My thoughts were jumping. There were memories intruding. Matthias was intruding; the jar was tipping, beginning to spill its contents.

"*...rise in profits for the previous quarter to one point four billion. The chairman of the board warned simultaneously of further unavoidable price increases for electricity and gas as from the end of...*"

I turned the radio off. Silence all around me again.

They were very old memories. They came creeping out of the past – out of the dust of those times when we still used to dream dreams together. For an instant I could see him...

He was climbing wooden steps to the stage, at eighteen at graduation in the *Internat* near Munich, seemingly oblivious to the applause. One of those guys who excels at almost everything without effort – he casually crossed to centre stage looking like the golden hero of old, quietly offering unwilling hands to receive gifts reserved for the gods...

I blinked.

And the auditorium was gone... instead there were high cliffs of an abandoned quarry with trees at the top showing their roots – he stood there motionless, arm stretched holding the heavy revolver he'd removed from his father's desk. Holding it like a feather, like a natural extension of his hand, firing calmly, coolly at the cardboard target, blowing out the black bull at twenty yards.

His thin image faded.

Then was there again – a student now, running, dodging the water-cannon and burning cars and torn-up cobblestones, his face masked by a scarf while I hung back... I saw him through my knot of fear and the tear gas and shouts and the smoke clouding the Berlin skies – he was up ahead with the bravest, breaking through the armed police cordon with his hands, using the banner like a flag, like a hammer and there was fury in his throat, anger in his eyes...

I frowned. Had to stop.

And I thought: for God's sake look for a different memory – one of the better ones. Hadn't there been enough of those too, back in the post-war years, in our childhood and teens? What about the pranks and the games we'd got up to? And later the drinking and drugs, our long conversations through the nights, questioning things, our hungry search for the purpose of life? Take a look there in the innocence of our youth, the stuff that succoured, all the good things we shared...

I looked. And I saw mountains.

We were high up, surrounded by sky, climbing boots heavy as lead – no fights, no Commies, no closet Nazis here. Leather and sweat, the Alps at our feet, life at our feet, at our beck and call, the sun through rarefied air hot on our heads. We'd made it, we were grinning. The view was fantastic. We were schoolboys, alone together – he sat beside me, his shoulder touched mine, back leaned on his rucksack, notebook on knee, one of his magic moments composing a poem about things only he could feel and see...

Yes. I'd loved his comradeship, and his poems – they were part of him too. And his physical closeness. The animal in him.

I closed my eyes.

And when I closed them I suddenly caught sight of me peeping at my youngest sister Eva as a teenager in our orchard secretly touching his long artistic fingers in a patch of sunlight between green shadows when she thought nobody was looking...

What really happened to him, Eva? The three of us were very close but you were closer. You fell in love and gave him your body so you're the one who should have a clue. I remember: the last time I saw him he was standing in front of me yet he was far away, and he made me understand events were going in the wrong direction and he was aiming for higher things but he didn't put it clearly in words. When you were lying beside him sharing sex and cigarettes, didn't he at least give a hint?

You recall? A year after he'd disappeared and I was leaving Munich for good, we spent that evening together and you denied you knew. But did you lie? Did he maybe go abroad somewhere still carrying the old banner with just the colours changed? When I pressed you, all you said was: "He told me to forget." You never were one to waste words, sister – you're more than a bit like me.

I took a breath: there were other images rising up, good and bad, beginning to burst through the surface, like bubbles of gas in a swamp. I suppressed them, took a hold on myself. My God, life is so full of memories, I can't seem to let them go. Is that why I've got so isolated – or is it the other way round?

I raised my eyes.

I was back in the present. Back with the postcard. I stood there beside the scrubbed pine table in my large working kitchen – in the apartment I'd been renting through the years. It occupied the top fourth floor in the town house they say is nearly four hundred years old. It's up the hill near the castle inside the medieval city walls, one of the few not hit by the bombs. There are beams and rafters and rooms reaching into the roof; even here in the kitchen I have space to breathe.

I lived here alone, now. My wife had taken our daughter and gone now. But I liked the apartment; I felt secure here, like in a nest, in a womb – along with my possessions, familiar things, and the crumbs of my life she'd let fall when she left. Why the hell couldn't you accept, Judit? One can't change people. You can't change a man like you did your underwear or your thousand skirts that kept going out of fashion.

I stared into space. In the back of my mind I was still listening for the telephone bell. It irritated me not having a number I could call. It made me feel somewhat helpless, like a mouse with one paw in a trap.

My gaze alighted on the big pinboard on the wall next to the table. But that too was full of the past. Look somewhere else, I ordered myself – it won't be long now...

Too late. As my eyes turned away I recalled: there was a photo of Matthias here somewhere. I began searching for it, amongst the notes and the cards, amongst all the cut-out quotes and everyday things I pin there when the whim takes me. God, the pinboard was so cluttered – like a fruit tree gone wild that needs pruning, like a flowerbed full of weeds. Where the hell was it? I scrabbled about, thinking: suppose I ought to chuck half this stuff away, really... maybe I... but... I'm just one of those people who clings to things, can't let them go. Separation causes me pain.

Then, half-hidden by a large newspaper cutting, next to the poem Estella had recently dedicated to me to help replenish my faith, I found the old photographs. My God, I hadn't looked at them for years...

The first I'd removed from one of our family albums, a small snap with crinkly edges that only my mother had noticed was gone: from the war, my parents entertaining SS officers in one-oh-three Ferdinand-Maria Straße, before I was there to remember. There was candlelight caught on cropped blond hair, white laughing teeth and silver-skull insignia. And a cold mask captured for ever on the photographed face of my father, because his guests had perverted his printing presses but he hadn't had the courage to say no – and an entranced expression in my mother's eyes...

Lifting the article higher with a wary hand, in search of Matthias, I stood there staring. I should've taken them down long ago, I suppose. But when the present holds little future one tends to fill it with the past – perhaps I need something to cling to which I know won't disappoint. How often in life we grasp at straws.

Above the crinkly-edged one there was a fuzzy, faded black-and-white photograph of Uncle Heiner in Hitler Youth uniform from the late nineteen-thirties that someone had taken very badly, with the sky in his eyes and a smile which suggested he'd at last found a meaning in life. And beside it another of him forty years later, looking fat and prosperous but lacking something fundamental, in tinted glasses and businessman's Sunday best at someone else's wedding. At Margareth's, I think – my eldest sister. He'd survived the war without a wound then profited from the peace; why is it ones like my father didn't make the grade and so many Heiners came through unscathed to rebuild our sentimental and subservient land? Is there nothing we can do to turn the tide?

Where was Matthias?

I couldn't help it – my eye caught for a second on that photograph of my ex-wife Judit, a close-up of her face, the last one

I'd taken of her a week before she flew off to the States with seven-year-old Andrea. But I didn't have to look twice, the image of it had been imprinted indelibly in my brain since the day I snapped it – that sultry, hungry face which I would sometimes peep at, making secret comparisons, if I chanced to meet someone new.

My gaze slipped. For Christ's sake don't start thinking about her now. You were looking for Matthias. I lifted Estella's short poem on its generous sheet of blue... how could it have been anywhere else? There it was – the snapshot with Matthias.

I bent close, stared in silence. He looked so young here. He was standing on the stone steps to our old home in Ferdinand-Maria Straße in Munich with my two sisters and elder brother; I must have taken the photo in the early sixties, just after they built the Berlin Wall and we were coming into our teens. They were looking at me at the camera, at the cherished *Leica* my father had given me to quench a thirst he'd seen in my twelve-year-old eye. All of them were looking except little Eva – she had her curly-haired head turned, her small face lifted. Even at eleven years old she was gazing up at Matthias.

Stooping, I peered closer. The snap was small, also black and white. I scrutinised the faces: gaunt and fair-haired Matthias, with generous lips which were able to smile in those days; my eldest sister Margareth dark-haired and dominant; my older brother Tobias already at sixteen towering and powerfully built with thin hair slicked down straight and that pompous, asinine air... but my eyes kept coming back to Matthias. His arms hung languidly, his blond hair was long and his eyes ingenuous; he looked so innocent.

I stood there gazing at him. Matthias – my first, my closest boyhood friend, the rich boy from next door. His parents had been our neighbours since long before I was born. His father in the war a prominent judge who, like many of his ilk, had slipped through the de-Nazification net and neatly donned a gown of red over the soiled black. Matthias was an only child; we were inseparable in those days.

Gazing at him, I felt my heart stir uneasily: I was wondering if he ever looked back at those days before he jumped over his shadow and, if he did, whether it would embarrass him now.

I let the blue sheet of poem go and it covered up my past again. I dropped my eyes to the table, to the cause of my nostalgia. The postcard was typed, not signed, but it could only be from him. Even without Estella's recommendation, probably I would've taken the rest of the week off anyway. I'd brought my laptop home with me, I wasn't tied to a desk. Business consultancy is concentrated stuff consisting mostly of seminars over long weekends and bouts of lectures and preparations in between. My next big one was in eight days.

I leaned over the breakfast things, turned the card round with a fingertip in order to read it again. The words were brief and to the point. Matthias used to be good at seducing, at surprise – I could see he hadn't lost his touch. As a student he'd had enough practice, he was one of the leaders, so charismatic, the master of persuasion, the weaver of dreams. Up till the seventies in Munich, that is, when he faded from the scene. He simply walked out of my life, left me hanging in the air – he was like a crossword puzzle unfinished, or a book one never read to the end. There was so much we could talk about, so many threads to pick up and discuss. He'd never visited me here in Nuremberg, for example, never met Judit – would he have approved? Strange, here he was now, suddenly reaching out across the void.

I read his brief words over again. They brought him so close. But why had he chosen these particular ones? I could almost hear his whisper in the wind, feel his breath on the nape of my neck. His message haunted; yes, it made me uneasy. And yet... yet it also fascinated. I knew I was praying the phone bell would ring, I was hoping for his call.

x x x

The minutes passed – it was like a watched pot that won't boil. My old clock hanging on one of the timber beams already said ten past nine.

'Remember?' the message began simply.

Yes, he'd used a typewriter. My God, who possesses such a thing nowadays – had he procured it in a junk shop, or in some jumble sale?

'One bond, one blood, our song of praise...' he wrote.

I remembered. So he wanted to meet me.

'...On the chosen path, let the trumpets sound and the hills rejoice...'

Long ago. But I remembered that too.

And in conclusion: 'Will endeavour to ring you at home this Wed or Thurs between 8 and 9 am...' was typed concisely '...otherwise check top of steps at one-oh-five should you wish to indicate interest. Sincerely.'

Well, he hadn't rung yesterday. I'd had to leave early, long before seven, and returned from work to find no message on the answering machine. And now it was after nine on Thursday already. Had his endeavour not got deep enough? Or was he playing cat-and-mouse? And if he didn't ring now, what then?

The steps at one-oh-five. He didn't mean five-past-one. I knew what he meant: it was a house number. And the only one familiar to us both was his parents' old home. But his mother was dead, his father in a private care home and the house had been sold so could he really mean it — really mean Munich? Why didn't he suggest somewhere in Nuremberg? If his enquiries had been thorough enough to procure my unlisted private telephone number, then he'd presumably also discovered that my work schedule allowed me little free time. It would've been simpler to have rung my work mobile or my office, he could reach me or my mailbox any time — but then Matthias never did the obvious. Was he testing my resolve?

I stood pondering: would I really want to drive down there on such a flimsy chance?

No. Just wait another five minutes, I thought — give him the benefit of the doubt, the academic quarter-of-an-hour. Could feel my impatience. I hated inactivity. My daily paper still lay there abandoned, virtually my only contact with Munich nowadays. But I couldn't read another word now; my concentration had gone to the dogs. I stared into space. Think about what you'll say, then, if he calls. What to say? A thousand things. Would a thousand questions quench the thirst?

What had he been doing all these years? Spent them all abroad? Doing what? Was he in Germany again now? For good? Maybe in Munich? My God, he'd hate it here — the corruption and greed in high places and the growing gulf between rich and poor. Isn't there a dangerous loss of life values, Matthias, aren't morals dead and elbows king? Is society going down the drain? What d'you think? Wasn't preventing this what the demos in the old days were all about — what's your opinion? Is the old enemy back, isn't anyone out there any more to fill up the hole with real meaning? And you, Matthias? Did you give up, too?

My senses contracted, my heart laboured for a second, then bumped...

I could hear something, indefinable, far away. I tensed, suddenly alert. But – no – it wasn't my living room phone. It was something else.

The sound grew in volume. I lifted my eyes, listening. The sound was becoming a noise.

Seconds passing...

It was getting louder and louder. It began to penetrate my brain, bursting in on my thoughts – getting so loud it was like someone hammering my head. I knew what it was, but that brought no relief. I glanced up at the big sloping iron skylights. Beyond the spreading chestnut tree the sky was blue, was very intense, and the tiled roofs and medieval towers of the old city centre of Nuremberg were hot and red-brown and shimmering in the morning sunlight. Again helicopters were flying over the city, but today there were three in a line and they were lower and seemed to be making straight for my windows.

They came closer and closer.

Then one of them was directly overhead, shredding the sunlight, rattling the old panes of glass, setting my nerves on edge. For an instant it filled the whole skylight with grey-green and there was a black German cross stencilled on white, and its body was the shape of a shark. I screwed up my eyes, waiting for it to pass.

And although my eyes were closed I could still see, it was as if a door in a dark room had burst open: an unexpected clutter of images shot tumbling through. There was noise here too, but different, a mechanical rattling... I was at primary school again in Munich not far from the Nymphenburg Schloß, it was dark, the projector rattled, the teacher intoning it was obligatory to watch. What on earth did obligatory mean? There were tanks with white stars close up clattering on the cobbles on the screen, and flowers being strewn, and crowds waving, and then there were rows of emaciated people standing naked, staring, with bushes of hair between their legs where I didn't have any and white rubber bodies being bulldozed like rubbish into pits in the ground and dead German soldiers with children's faces and flies, and someone was crying out and another moaning and the teacher's voice was ordering us to keep on looking but I couldn't look away.

Then the film was flapping, it had come to an end. Sunlight blinded from curtains drawn aside, but the teacher went on talking – about camps called Buchenwald and Auschwitz and another with the name Dachau not far from Munich, right on our doorstep, which he said wasn't a camp like the summer-holiday ones we knew, where he'd been interned and nearly died. He continued on for a quarter of an hour till the ray of sun had crossed my inkwell – continued on about all the evil things we Germans had done that must never be repeated. And I was going home alone in tears with my satchel on my back and telling my mother and nanny Helga, over lunch of *Pfefferminztee* and milk soup with bits of black bread floating which stuck in my throat, that I couldn't understand and didn't want to be a German – and there was a sense of being somehow cheated and feeling old at eight...

There was a phone ringing.

Or was it just another memory playing tricks with me? My mother was screaming there'd be consequences, whatever that serious-sounding word might mean, and next day she had gone to the school and Matthias's parents too and suddenly our teacher wasn't there any more, the man with the limp who'd never once smiled. There were spring days again that still smelled so good and I watched me strutting with Matthias and Eva on the way to our schoolhouse that had lost all but its clock tower and the north wing. But a shadow followed me and something was wrong, the man from Dachau had given me something I couldn't forget, or in the silences which took his place had he maybe taken something away? We sat, now, in our polish-reeking classroom being taught instead by a white-haired old man about geography and algebra and history that stopped with Bismarck and no-one spoke of Dachau or drew the curtains any more...

Yes, wasn't that a phone?

I was standing in the kitchen again, alone again; the sounds of the helicopters were fading. The skylight was once more a peaceful sheet of summer and the chestnut tree had leaves like green hands pressed on the panes of glass.

I tipped my head, tensing again, suddenly nervous, listening the way birds do; the ringing was still there. Yes – it was my phone. A rapid glance upwards: twenty-past-nine.

Turning, I hurried into the hall. Sunlight flooded from the small glassed openings between the rafters above. My stomach was contracting, panicking. I thought: I'm not prepared – I've been waiting all this time and now I don't know what to say.

The open doorway to the big living room was bright from the sun, was a frame of gold. I rushed towards the phone standing on its base on the chest between tall windows that looked down on the street.

I lifted the receiver, I had reached it in time. I stood there, holding it to my ear. For an instant I couldn't speak. My throat was tight, like the nervousness going to an exam, or like a teenager in love before the first touch, afraid she won't reciprocate.

"Hello?" I said.

Chapter 2

"It's me," said a ponderous, penetrating voice.

It wasn't Matthias. I shut my eyes and took a breath, leaned on an arm on the wall. My disappointment was like a damp cloth. I needed a moment to adjust.

"Hello, Theo," I said.

I was slightly surprised to hear his voice again so soon. Late the previous evening, after hours of ruminations, I'd searched for and found Theo's Munich number on the Web and called him because he used to know Matthias as a student – they'd been ideologically on a par. I'd hoped maybe Matthias had renewed contact with him too and given him more details, and he could tell me Matthias's whereabouts. But he hadn't heard anything for many years either.

Or so he said.

He had seemed to be more interested in why I was enquiring than to try to help – and something made me calm his inquisitiveness with an off-hand comment about my merely wanting to pick up contact generally with a few old Munich friends. When we had ended the call I thought, that's that.

And yet here he was again.

Theo was a fox, and a highly intelligent one. Talking to him in the old days used to be like grasping onto fog or walking into a wall with no options in between – now he appeared to have reduced his range to the thorny denseness of a thicket.

I stood, receiver to ear. He was speaking – in crisp brief sentences, he didn't waste words. Gone was his fire, his hot rhetoric; he was a lawyer now with his own *Kanzelei*. Theo had joined the establishment. In the sixties he was the manufacturer of Molotov cocktails; I could picture him nowadays in bars with the chicky-micky Munich clique with more exclusive kinds of cocktails in his big, steady, fat hand. Theo had come of age...

"I've checked, Stefan. He got out in the spring of seventy-three. Flew to the Middle East – Lebanon. After that there's nothing." His tone was flat, impartial, professional. But was it guarded too?

I thought: has he phoned back simply to say that? I said nothing, waited. Perhaps silences could goad even a lawyer into giving a morsel away. But he just waited in silence too. So I said: "Where do *you* believe he went after that?"

"No idea."

"But you were one of the closest to him."

"Only politically."

"That's what I meant, Theo." For Matthias, politics would've dictated the direction. There came no reply.

"You two were together up to the last. You must've got some hint where..."

"Incorrect. We split in seventy-two."

I shook my head. "Make a guess," I pressed. Theo was my only chance, my only thread to Matthias; I was loath to let it go.

Again he didn't answer.

"Think back, Theo, and put yourself in his place. Where was he heading to? Or would he have stayed in Lebanon?"

"No chance."

"The West Bank then, or Jordan? The Palestinians?"

"That wasn't his war."

"But there was solidarity."

"Yes, but mostly..." there was the slightest hesitation "...the camps." He stopped. I knew he meant to say training camps; I'd seen them at a screening and in documentaries long ago. Then he abruptly concluded: "No circumstantial evidence even – wasn't his metier," and for an instant his guardedness was tangible, was like a trapdoor closing, giving him away. He'd let fall a crumb.

I felt him preparing to put down the phone. So I picked up the crumb, tried a provocation: "You're wrong, Theo. I believe he changed sides, to the Arab cause."

"Fallacious assumption."

"I don't think so."

"Objection. Had that been the case, he'd either be dead or on a CIA list. The Americans aren't fools. Nor is he."

Is?

I paused, deliberating. Then I said: "Isn't he dead then, Theo? None of us've heard from him since then. Have you?"

And there was another silence down the line. There it was again; I recognised a second crumb. He knew something. "I want to know," I said. "He and I were good friends."

"I know nothing." Again he stopped.

Again I waited.

"Listen," he said, "his cause was always rooted in the West, not in the Arab world. And times have totally changed. What we started is pure old hat today. He got out for good, that's certain."

"Then why escape to Lebanon?"

"Don't be naïve. That was simply a stepping stone."

"But to where?" I felt frustration, like claustrophobia, like being caught in a cage – the conversation had become a vicious circle. Was I so naïve?

"To disappear, Stefan. Before it was too late he opted to get out. No traces. In those days Beirut was a good springboard."

"Hide from whom, Theo? He wasn't in deep enough."

"Incorrect."

Incorrect? No – no, I didn't believe that. "No, not true," I said.

"Yes, Stefan."

Unhappily I rejected the thought, cast about, seeking a different possibility. Again that claustrophobic feeling – like the damp skin of a drum drying in the sun I felt myself contracting. "But he wasn't on any of those lists."

"Not from theirs. From his side."

His words pierced my ear, entered my brain, and my brain weighed them up, considering. I was hoping for flaws, looking for holes. But put that way it was possible – that I had to admit. Slowly I said: "I suppose that would explain things."

I stood there, still leaning on the wall, staring. But I wasn't seeing with my eyes, I was watching Matthias, trying to get inside him and see how he ticked, wondering where he'd gone – and what he was doing now.

It was very still down the phone to Munich. Into the silence I asked: "So where is he now? There's no longer a threat." It seemed the most logical thing to say.

Theo paused. Or was it another controlled hesitation? "That you asked me last night and I told you I didn't know." He said it with perfect neutrality.

"I'm asking you again."

Again that slight pause. Then: "I reiterate. The answer's the same."

I think I only exhaled, but it sounded like a sigh. "Theo, don't tell me you've phoned me back just to tell me that."

"Yes and no. You made me inquisitive so I enquired. Met a blank, though. Wished to inform you. Thought I owed you that."

I stared at the wall. There were cracks in the old plaster, fine as hairlines. I concentrated; I could sense it once more – he was on the point of ending the call.

I stumbled back to one of the crumbs, said: "You're lying, Theo."

He coughed. Didn't answer. It was a polite professional cough.

"Stop beating about the bush. Yesterday you weren't certain, today you know he's not dead. Where can I contact him?"

Still no answer. At least, not at once. I could almost hear him thinking. Then he said quietly, resignedly: "Planning on a trip to Munich in the near future?" and there was a slight tightness in his tone as though speaking unexpectedly caused him pain.

Was I? Wasn't I? I considered rapidly. Obviously Matthias wasn't going to ring now.

"Yes," I said.

So now I'd decided. In that instant it was almost a relief, like a load off my back. And straight afterwards, in my stomach, there was a queasy feeling. Was it nervousness? Or anticipation?

"When?" he asked.

"Today. Or tomorrow." I shrugged to myself.

"For how long?"

"Not long. Maybe twenty-four hours..."

I heard a page being leafed.

"This afternoon, five-thirty? For half an hour. Or... tomorrow, Friday. Early – eight till eight-thirty before I go to the courts. Later isn't possible, have a flight to Brussels."

Eight tomorrow morning, I thought – not so good. I'd have to go today, then, and stay overnight. And too early to be fully on my toes.

Five-thirty... I glanced over to the gable wall going up into the roof where I'd torn out the gallery after she'd gone – the antique clock on top of my big writing desk said nearly nine-twenty-five. Well – I'd have plenty of time.

"Let's say today," I said. The clock stood crooked, I must set it straight...

"Have you my address?"

"No." I hadn't noted it from the Web.

"Pen?"

He told me; I memorised it.

The writing-flap was open as always – I'd jot it down when he'd said goodbye. I gazed over at the sturdy old *Biedermeier* desk standing proud and six feet tall, with its many little drawers and nooks and crannies, and the secret recess in which later I would lay the object of Matthias's modern gospel.

Theo said curtly, "Till later," then I heard the line go dead.

x x x

I decided: I'd leave at once. Just tidy away the breakfast things, check my e-mails, drive down to Munich. Would be there by midday. Before calling on Theo I'd have plenty of time, I'd go over to number one-oh-five, Matthias's parents' old house on the outskirts, just on the off-chance, just like he'd hinted. Why the devil was he trying to entice me there? Whatever – after Theo I'd simply return again, maybe have a spot to eat on the autobahn on the way, be back in Nuremberg by 10pm at the latest. That, at least, was my plan.

Just for a moment I opened the window I was standing beside – a breath of fresh air. It was so stuffy in the room. A sense of disappointment: why the hell couldn't Matthias simply have rung? I shrugged. I was like a child with its toy taken away.

I stared out at the morning. I remember the sky: hazy Bavarian blue and a few small fluffy white clouds, there was a special light that day. Only 9:30. A curious feeling. It was Thursday – normally I'd be at work, planning, researching, telephoning, or on the road holding seminars in hotels or conference centres – always busy, often in stress, six days a week, sometimes seven. I glanced across the street at the old houses opposite, but I was only gazing into space. If Judit were still here we could've driven down together...

There. It was growing again – that sense of emptiness; again there was a hole starting to puncture my head. I tried to contain it. But the loneliness kept breaking through. I cast about. Would've liked to ring Estella, it was always a comfort hearing her voice, she always managed to say the right thing.

But I didn't. Ought to be moving.

I jumped. A loud noise interrupted my thoughts – tyres screeching on cobbles down in the street, and a car horn hooting loudly. I leaned out of the window, in case there'd been an accident, in case I should help. The old copper sill was already warm. I peered down the four storeys to the steep narrow street. But it was nothing, just a ball from a child rolling away. Few pedestrians around – a man with briefcase, a young woman crossing the cobbles, a small crocodile of Chinese tourists following a flag going up to Albrecht Dürer's house beneath the medieval city wall. No traffic, just one or two parked cars; the neighbourhood was quieter now the council had chained off half the street at the bottom of the hill.

Idly I watched the young woman for a second. She was climbing the steps to the old raised pavement opposite. Battered wrought-iron hand-rail, stone worn into dips by feet; she went up those steps like a symphony. Nice hair, auburn, thick and wavy, nice body too. Had a similarity with the new assistant at the bookshop I'd recently shared a good conversation with but hadn't dared invite out. Maybe I...

Still I leaned out over the sill, a sneaky voyeur, safe on my secret perch up on the fourth floor – she was turning at the top, I got a glimpse of her profile now. Yes, nice breasts, neat bottom, rather sexy...

"Herr Falk?"

... ah God, we men are all dogs. I gazed, distracted...

"HERR FALK!"

I started, I sweated. Someone had called – had someone seen me? Hurriedly tore my eyes away. The voice was penetrating, almost a shriek. Oh God, I'd know that voice anywhere. Guiltily I glanced down. Directly below me, the caretaker's wife was craning her head, one hand shading her eyes, the other holding a broom. Her knotted headscarf was aflame with dreadful flowers.

"*Guten Morgen, Frau Maußer,*" I called back. I made it sound casual, as casual as I could. She'd seen me gawping, hadn't she – could she read the greed in my eyes? Damn it, not good for my reputation in this gossiping village of a street, especially with her the queen of the pack.

"*Grüß Gott*, Herr Falk. Who is she, do you know?" With a poke of her broom she indicated up the street: she was pointing at the young woman, at the object of my guilt.

My bird's eye view distorted Frau Maußer's portly figure – she looked a bit like an inflated beach ball.

"No, I don't," I said. Had I said it with sufficient disinterest? Had she read my mind? The young woman was gone, had turned the corner. "I wish you a good day," I added quickly, and made to withdraw my head, wondering how she'd come to spot me and marvelling at her powers of observation...

"She was reading the names on our bells and naturally I asked what she wanted since she's a stranger and she said she's looking for a friend who lives here in Bergstraße..." A gulp for air. "So I asked..."

Her shrill voice carried remarkably; a housewife with shopping bags had paused to stare – even a scruffy youth with lips, nose and ears peppered by grapeshot who was setting himself down with beer bottle and dog near the stone steps raised a bleary eye in a shaven head.

"Ah," I said. That seemed a diplomatic thing to say before carefully ending the dialogue. Frau Maußer is basically a kindly woman, though inclined to involve herself in other people's affairs which occasionally has led to misunderstandings between us. It is not my intention to be impolite, but I possess little talent for making small talk for half an hour about what the weather might or might not do or the ailments of elderly Herr Eggenhofer in the third-floor flat beneath mine, or about Frau Schmidt opposite's drastic increase in weight; our conversations make me nervous, like having to stand in an endless queue or endure a pain which refuses to fade...

"Not at the office today, Herr Falk? Thought I didn't hear you leave this morning. Feeling poorly?"

"No, Frau Maußer, I'm..."

"Not like you getting ill and missing work."

She had propped her broom against the wall, was planting hands on hips on her shocking-pink housecoat as if this were to be the beginning of yet another of those unhappy tête-à-têtes. Briefly I closed my eyes. "Actually," I began again, "I'm taking two days holiday..." but perhaps I wasn't speaking loudly enough or does sound travel clearer upwards than down...?

"You don't look quite on top – a bit pale."

"No," I said loudly. "I said I'm..."

"Just tell me..." Her voice was obliterated by a cream Mercedes taxi roaring up the street; its tyres drummed on the uneven cobbles, its diesel fumes tinged the air about her blue.

"I beg your pardon?" I called. A window in the row of tall timber-framed town houses opposite was opening, catching the sun, catching my eye; a young mother with infant cradled on arm stood gazing out. Here and there window-openings were still shuttered from the night, in others hung featherbeds to air. And there, at the next window but one, an elderly man in shirtsleeves leaned on his sill puffing a cigarette. This was a weekday world I'd never had the time to experience – a world of mothers and pensioners, and the unemployed...

I lowered my eyes – the racket of the taxi was diminishing, Frau Maußer was shouting again "...buy you medicine or something to eat or what-not?" She was tying the cotton strings of her housecoat in a businesslike bow.

"No need," I called down quickly. But that sounded too abrupt. "Kind of you to offer," I tried again, "but I'm not..."

"No problem! I'll..."

I began to panic – wanted to be on the road to Munich, not wasting any more time. Frau Maußer is also one of those overactive persons with a rather rapid sense of direction. That her husband drinks heavily, and often isn't available for his caretaker functions so she has to fulfil his duties too, is probably the reason – though I admit there are times I have difficulty distinguishing between cause and effect.

She was patting the completed bow, reaching for her broom. "I'll pop up and make a list..." her fist round the handle had the strength of two men "...and don't forget to give me your letterbox key, you haven't collected your post yet."

Helplessly I stared down at her; already she was making for the large arched opening through our building which led to the house door and the courtyard at the back – if she got into my apartment I'd never... "Frau Maußer!" I shouted, perhaps this time much too loudly. She stopped in her tracks, scarfed head jerking, mouth open, as though she'd just been hit by a brick or a dropping from a bird.

Panic growing, I cried: "Frau Mauß er, very thoughtful, but I'm not ill – merely taking a couple of days off. Going down to Munich..."

Her free hand had risen to her headscarf, her fingers fluttered; there was frustration in her fingertips. "As you wish," she shot back curtly, and her voice had hurt at the edges.

Flustered, almost irritated, I stepped back from the window. Oh God, I thought, you've gone and done it again – now you'll have to buy her flowers or a big box of chocolates, this will be the third time this year.

I cleared away the breakfast things, washed them up at the sink as is my habit because I never bothered to buy a new dishwasher when the old one gave up the ghost, then wiped the worktops clean. Didn't take long. When finished, for an instant, I paused, gazing across the kitchen at the postcard, at the tidied table. How often I'd sat here with Judit and little Andrea. I stared at the empty chairs – and that lonely feeling flexed its claws again, clamped down on my heart like a vice.

Picking up my mobile and wallet and keys, I had opened the apartment door to the stairs when my mobile begin to ring. My breath clogged: was it Matthias? Doing the unexpected again? At the same time, intruding from four floors below, Frau Mauß er's penetrating voice echoed up the wooden stairwell; it appeared she'd found a new victim.

I pressed green.

x x x

I was on the autobahn in my old Mercedes.

My thoughts were like lead. I'd locked the apartment unhappily, walked with apprehension to my parking space. Despite the shock of the news, however, before getting into the driver's seat I'd nevertheless remembered to obediently wipe my shoes with the thoroughness that is due on the mat I hang for this purpose on the wall next to the set of winter tyres. I do it as a rite of respect for the ancient wool carpets in the Mercedes which have survived well over a generation.

Yes, I was on the road – but it wasn't shortly before ten as I'd intended, it was ten-to-twelve already. Something had happened – something dreadful. And as a result I'd had to pack an overnight bag, leave a message on Estella's answering machine to please empty my letterbox, and to try to reach my sister Eva to say I'd be staying the night. Hadn't been able to reach her, though.

I drove the old Mercedes sedately because of her age, heading south; with blocked mind I went in innocence, I went not recognising the signs. I had reached a turning point in my life and wasn't even aware of it.

Geoff, my English medical-student friend from the Munich days who changed his mind about Germany and emigrated to Australia, with whom I still share certain confidences and who is in a position to be objective, recently aired his opinion on the phone. He said that the postcard was the catalyst. I think he slyly also used the word fulcrum – meaning it could make things tip this way, or equally make them tip the other. He always was a subtle devil.

Estella's of the same opinion, however – she called it a threshold – and I suppose she ought to know.

On that long-distance call Geoff gave me a clear warning as well, which is unusual coming from him. But I can understand his reason; the person he is most deeply distrustful of apart from his own shadow is Matthias – he'd known him in those days too. For Geoff, friendships, like love, never feature larger in his life than a handful of playing cards he's loath to lay on the table, and anything less than friendship is more than cause for doubt.

Looking back now at that day early last summer makes me wonder – at fate, at the chance of life. If I'd decided not to go down to Munich, or gone a day later, the situation which was to be triggered would never have occurred. We're ships in the night, each alone – the ocean is vast; the dice are loaded against us, against encounters, and collisions. And yet somehow, sometimes, they occur when least expected, for better, for worse.

I tried to concentrate on the road, calm my nerves, think ahead. Although I'd not once needed to ask her in the last couple of years, I was sure Eva would put me up. Even if I couldn't reach her later by phone or she wasn't planning to be at home, I knew her fixed ways, knew where she hid the key – for her occasional lovers, and me. It was more personal than a hotel.

The six-lane autobahn was busy. Maybe that's why I didn't notice the Mini. Only thought about it later – it had been following me, hadn't it? Since the Wall fell, and more so since the frontiers to the East were opened, so many more cars, so many lorries in transit from abroad. But in spite of lost time I wasn't really in a hurry, I had five and a half hours till Theo, I had all the time in the world.

Thoughts of Margareth. Oh God, must see if I can help. My sadness made a lump.

I glanced down, checked the time. The round chrome clock in the walnut dashboard now said eight minutes past twelve – I waited a moment, then switched the radio on to *Bayern 5*, they give out traffic reports every quarter of an hour, and on the autobahn to Munich you never know. Apart from *Bayern 1*, it's the only station the old set can receive without too much static down here in Bavaria. A report on the latest kidnapping was coming to an end, but I caught only the tail-end of it and the topic didn't interest me greatly. The familiar warning jingle sharpened my ears... I turned up the volume for the traffic service. But no – on the A9 no jams except the usual back-up congestion north of the Munich Ring. I twiddled the knob, tried a little music...

My God. Over two years since I'd last been forced to visit Munich.

The afternoon sun blinded, shone full in my face; the asphalt shimmered and miraged, for the middle of May it was unusually hot. Perhaps the climate change was really beginning to bite. My car, to be truthful, is antiquated – has no air-conditioning. It's an old 300 SE built way back in 1967. Despite a lot of chrome, and hub caps ladies admire their legs in, it's snow-white in colour and doesn't stand out like a sore thumb. The somewhat eccentric pensioner, my neighbour Herr Eggenhofer from one floor down, from whom I had bought it a while ago for a very fair price had owned it nearly twenty-five years; he'd preened it and serviced it himself, merely taken it out at weekends and then only for short rides. With a mist in his wicked faded eye he said she had always been faithful and he was her only lover. It's a cabriolet, you have to fold back the hood by hand – a fine old lady and she at once seduced me too; now she's faithful to her second-hand man. There's no power steering, and no ABS, no GPS or any other of those modern abbreviated amenities. But it purrs like a cat on the open road, has a dashboard of walnut veneer, soft leather seats wrinkled like a ninety-nine-year-old face which you sink into, and car keys you still have to put in the lock to open the door. It reminds me of times when life was much slower and cars were hand-tooled things – costs a small fortune to keep it roadworthy; it's one of those little luxuries I allow myself in my otherwise frugal and limited life.

On this particular afternoon I drove with the soft-top closed to avoid a headache, just wound down the window; the draught of warm air dried my sweat. I went at a gentle 70 miles-an-hour although the old lady was begging for more.

Keep concentrating.

The Main-Donau canal went by. The autobahn cut through undulating forests and valleys and hills, a deadly swathe through nature for wildlife. I tried to relax, tried to suppress those thoughts; the heat was making me sleepy. But I watched out for wandering deer; a colleague of mine, and a magnificent stag, died on this stretch a few years back. The miles went by. Then there it was...

Just ahead, coming into view, what I'd been waiting for – my favourite part of the journey, at about the one-third mark. The Old Mill Valley, *Altmühltal*, the river along its floor only a vestige of the once mighty one which had carved it out of the limestone. Steep slopes, partly grassy, partly wooded, lazy in the sun – and rising up abruptly, Schellenberg, a high hill, almost vertical cliffs, commanding a spectacular view. It must've been years since I'd seen it by daylight.

Schellenberg...

Sluggishly a memory stirred. What was it? An association? Something to do with Matthias? That was all though; I couldn't put my finger on it, my brain was too distracted, too drugged by the heat.

And it was there, as the autobahn swung downhill in a long revealing curve to traverse the valley, that one of my mobiles rang. Pity, bad timing – I'd been looking forward to enjoying its scenery undisturbed as I...

I slowed down to a safer speed, reaching behind me, unzipping the side-pocket of my bag. It was the private one ringing; I pressed the button, silenced the jangle – and as I did so glanced out the window. Oh God... To my horror the peaceful valley beside the autobahn was being torn up – there were bulldozers and cranes and piles of earth high as houses, and dust particles in the air so dense they almost obscured enormous fat columns of concrete...

"Hello?" I said.

"Maggie here. You rang."

Margareth, my eldest sister. Thank God for that. Hadn't managed to reach her either, though I'd tried several times... I braked a bit more, taking another brief look, but it was too late – a wall of slow-moving lorries blocked the view...

"Hello Maggie." The floodgates were opening, couldn't stop them, the memories were forcing through. "I'm glad you called back."

"Well, what is it?" Her tone was cold and dead. How long was it since we'd last had contact – six months, eight perhaps? And that only on the phone.

"Heinrich rang me this morning..." I was looking at his anguish, I was looking at them both: at their beautiful home beside the Chiemsee lake an hour from Munich. Was looking too at their property in the city, their luxury cars and sailing boat and yacht and one or two other expensive things they possessed – I was walking for a moment in Heinrich's world gazing at all that he owned, at what would be torn apart. Schellenberg swept by, the mountain of rock rising up, the meeting of the three valleys. "...he told me the news," I said.

"Rang *you*? The stupid fool."

I could hear her agony in my ear. "He was attempting to find out where you are."

"As if you'd know."

"Precisely," I said.

"He's the last person I want pestering me at present."

"Yes."

She drew in a breath sharply, exhaled; I guessed she was smoking a cigarette. Keep calm, I ordered myself...

A confusion of images tumbled: there was Margareth falling in love in the spring filling every room she entered with her happiness; and there was Heinrich striding towards me holding out his hand saying: "*Guten Tag, sehr angenehm,*" and nearly breaking my fingers, making a healthy first impression in a powerful physical sort of way; and there was my tough little sister Eva saying bluntly as we walked in the Nymphenburg Schloß gardens on the wedding morning: "I give them three years at most before it falls apart. She's a fool, just suffering from penis worship, that's all – he's one of those chauvinist bastards who makes even T-shirt and jeans look pathetically petit bourgeois." But I'd tried to be philosophic with autumn colours bold in the trees and dead leaves rustling under my feet.

I said: "Despite everything, I'm sorry it's come to this, Maggie."

"So am I."

"I guess you tried hard enough."

"Yep."

I waited, but she didn't add anything. "He was in pretty bad shape," I said. "He really doesn't understand, does he?"

"Most men never do, not till it's too late – and afterwards they don't learn either. You're all the same."

It seemed I was receiving my dose of his medicine, so I ventured: "Generalisations are unwise."

"Well, you're no exception. Look at Judit."

I was already looking there too. I said nothing.

She exhaled again audibly. "Sorry, little brother. Didn't really mean it that way."

I swallowed. For a second I couldn't answer. From surprise, though, not hurt; I don't think Margareth had ever said sorry to me before. "That's okay," I said.

"Was under the belt."

"It's okay," I repeated, and waited. Words failed me; what can one say to someone in such a situation?

The silence lengthened. So I simply asked: "How're you feeling?"

"Like shit."

"Are you alone?"

"With a friend. You don't know her."

"And the children?"

"Little David's with me. Henri's in England with his school class. On exchange."

"Does he know?"

"Not yet. Don't want to be a spoilsport, he's having the time of his life over there."

"Well, he'll find out soon enough."

"Exactly," she said. But again nothing else.

"Are you coping okay?"

A hesitation. "Christ, Stef." Another pause.

I could feel it. It was strange – was there suddenly, and unexpectedly, a thread between us where there'd been none before? I think she could feel it too. "Can I help in any way?" I said.

"What? In Nuremberg?"

"I'm not in Nuremberg. I'm..."

"Where then?" Impatience.

"On my way to Munich. I've got a short appointment at five-thirty."

"And after?"

"Nothing planned. You in Munich too, still?"

"Yep. You staying the night down here?"

"Yes," I said quickly. "Thought I would."

"Where?"

"At Eva's. Couldn't reach her – but she hides a key."

"She's always unreachable."

"We won't argue that one," I said.

She said nothing. But she blew through her nose as if attempting a laugh. Or was she just sniffing? Or crying?

"Maggie?" I said.

"What?"

"All right?"

She sighed. It was long, drawn out. "If you want to know – no. But I'll survive."

"Would you like us to meet? To talk? Go out for a meal somewhere, if you want – if you wanted us to be alone. If you're with a girlfriend she could look after David for a couple of hours..."

"She's not here." She was deliberating. "Listen – come round after I've put David and her two to bed. Around nine."

"Okay."

"You got a pen for the address?"

"I'm driving. Just tell me."

She told me. I memorised it, and the name of her girlfriend. I noted the name but, in that instant, it didn't ring a bell.

x x x

Through paper-like leaves of plane trees the flickering white-hot sun followed me along the avenues of the residential quarter. Then Ferdinand-Maria Straße, the street where I'd been born. I still had over three hours till Theo's appointment – maybe time to find a hint of Matthias.

Big 19th and early 20th century villas stood back from the shady street, half-hidden by spreading blue firs and cedars and beech trees, each sealed into its generous secluded gardens away from prying eyes – here and there discreet blocks of luxury flats interrupted like new jacket crowns in an old mouth, giving away where the bombs had fallen.

I caught peeps of neo-Gothic and Art Nouveau, glimpses of my childhood – tall windows with ashlar surrounds, pastel shades of plaster façades, and now and again flights of steps to colonnaded porticos, or a stucco frieze with classical figures beneath overhanging eaves.

I parked in the shade near the end of the avenue, remained sitting a moment in the silence. Opposite me was number 103, my parents' old house. The copper beech, parts of the ground and first floor and the steep roof visible, recently added windows. Tobias had had the place converted over two years ago after mother at last could be persuaded to move. It was sold now: funny feeling, though – our home full of strangers. I hunched my shoulders. I didn't like the feeling.

In my car, through the wound-down windows, the hot air didn't stir. Between me and the polished cracked leather my shirt stuck to my back. In this unusual heat even the birds seemed stunned and still. There was an atmosphere of decadence, of old-fashioned elegance; in the peaceful leafy quiet the whole affluent neighbourhood seemed to be fast asleep.

Unhurriedly I got out, locked the car. Good to stretch the legs after the two-hour drive. I was walking on the small chequered red and blue squares of the pavement, stepping in patchy sunlight between our high iron railings and the plane trees; Matthias and I were rattling sticks along the rails, and Eva played hopscotch with two girlfriends on the squares...

I passed our entrance gates – in the nearest stone pillar the old bell-push and microphone and electric lock had been replaced by a modern installation. There were four bells now, and an etched glass sign for an insurance company on the ground floor. The iron gates stood open, I saw the curving driveway – I walked quickly on by.

The high brick wall of number 105 began. In the avenue of evenly-spaced plane trees one was missing, just a stump; blinding light, the sun beat on my head – I hurried on into the shade again. Reached the entranceway. On top of the red-brick pillars, stone caps with their lions – oh how often Matthias and I had ridden through on our bikes as children, hardly pausing, pushing the left-hand iron gate with a foot... there was the bent bar where we'd kicked it once too often. It seemed, here too, time stood still, nothing had changed...

The wrought-iron gates were closed now, but not locked. I went through, along the sweep of drive, round behind the big cedar tree. The Art Nouveau mansion, the stone steps up to the oak-panelled front door – just the way they'd always been. I ascended, stood in porticoed shadow. Even the old brass bell was the same. Above it there were new ones, though, with modern nameplates. I peered – none bore Matthias's family name. I'd scarcely expected that anyway; his mother was dead, I'd read the obituary in the *SZ*. At least I knew that. I glanced about, seeking a sign of him – a note, or a hint that he was there, or had been. But there was nothing...

Then why had he written what he had? Was he just fooling around? No. People like Matthias don't play games. Then where could I look? The top of the steps...

I inspected the moulded panels of the door. But they were solid, massive, there were no crevices or holes, no folded note hidden in a crack. Not round the iron knocker either. What had he meant then? I looked at the bells again, at the nameplates. Ground floor – lawyer's office. First floor, Erika and Klaus Haager-Schmidt – top floor B. Behrendt, H. Prell, N. Matski...

Prell?

I'd overlooked it. I knew that name. Heidi Prell?

There was a clock chiming – but long ago. Rows of books in galleries. And a cast-iron spiral staircase... I was peeping up her miniskirt as she descended and when she saw me looking I pretended I was waiting to climb. I'd fallen in love with Heidi there in the university library a week before but she didn't know and I couldn't find a way to break the ice, break the good news. We were students – she in law and I in economics, and the books we used for reference and the thoughts we thought were miles apart...

I pressed the bell.

Perhaps it was coincidence. Oh God, that word again. Maybe this was a different H. Prell. And even if it wasn't, as far as I knew she'd hardly had contact with Matthias, if at all – he'd been a year ahead of us. The contact she'd had was to Geoff, and what a contact – the sly devil, he'd won her without even trying because she'd done all the work...

No answer.

I pressed again. And waited. The loudspeaker grille remained silent. I thought: shall I leave a note? But I had nothing to write on. What about the lawyer's office – I could ring the bell, they'd lend me pen and paper...

There was a rattle high above me... a window was opening... someone calling: "Who's there?"

I went down the seven steps out into the sun, craned my head upwards, squinting beyond the jutting portico roof with its gargoyle shaped like a ghoul.

"Hello?" I said.

A boy leaned out of an attic window. "What d'you want?" He looked about fourteen.

"I'm looking for Heidi Prell."

"She's out."

"Ah," I said.

"What's your name?"

I told him. Then: "When will she be back?"

"Never heard of you."

"Not important. When?"

"No idea."

"Is she your mother?" I just made a guess. But his eyes could be her eyes.

"What's that to you?"

"Is she?"

"Sure. So what?"

"Will you give your mother a message?"

"Why?"

"Because she's expecting me." I was guessing again.

"Never told me."

"She doesn't tell you everything, does she. Will you?"

"No need. Come back 'bout six."

"Tell her seven," I said quickly.

But already he'd withdrawn his head, was slamming the window shut. I thought: the politeness of German youth. Even if not her character, he had inherited her abruptness. And I, at least, was maybe a step nearer Matthias.

Chapter 3

In Maximillian Straße I was lucky: three or four vacant parking slots. I took the one right next to the *Four Seasons* hotel. Convenient. As I bought a ticket, a red Austin Mini was just parking too, the other side of the street. Attractive little cars. It reminded me of Geoff in Munich in '68 – he'd brought his English Cooper out with him. "It's a hit with the birds," he'd said with a grin, and the dark rings round his eyes seemed to confirm it. Maybe that's where he won or was conquered by Heidi; I hope he got cramps in his legs.

I displayed the ticket, locked the car, crossed the busy street in the direction of Theo's *Kanzelei*. Idly I noticed that the driver still sat in the Mini. Nuremberg number-plates. I peeped as I passed, I suppose purely out of nosiness. A woman, maybe thirty-five. First glimpse: sporting type, strong shoulders – athletic almost. Then, surprised, I thought I recognised the profile of the face framed by auburn hair and tipped to an opened handbag on her lap – where had I seen it? Had I seen it somewhere? Maybe recently even? Difficult to be sure, though, because occasionally my mind has a habit of playing déjà vu, thinking a stranger is somehow familiar or I've been in a room before.

I came punctually to Theo.

And he came, almost, straight to the point. We'd shaken hands, studied each other from across the years. For mid-forties he looked older; perhaps it was the premature grey but I suspect he'd gained it in court. He's small but very stocky; he's one of the few men I've ever met who's smaller than me. After he'd offered me a cup of coffee which I refused, and asked three questions about my professional and private life, he pushed a piece of paper over a desk piled with court files tied in bows, and said: "Interesting, yes?"

I read it. And while I read I suddenly remembered: the woman in the Mini – I'd seen her that morning crossing the street below my apartment. And in that café the day before yesterday where I'd sat with Estella having coffee and having my fortunes laid bare.

Theo had marked a neat cross beside a name to save me time going through the whole list. There were dates, and sums of money involved. I looked up at Theo.

"Egon Stern?" I said.

"Egon L. Stern. Yes."

"Matthias?"

"Yes."

I shrugged. "How do you know that?"

"A little joke, just between the two of us in our wilder days."

"Are you sure?"

"The L stands for Lucifer. The avenging angel, you know?"

"Yes," I said.

"I'm sure, Stefan."

"Egon," I pondered. "An ugly name."

"Indeed."

"He disliked that name, I remember."

"Precisely."

I nodded. And asked: "Was anyone else in the know?"

"I just told you. He and I alone."

"That was a long shot, your discovering it, then. I mean, he could assume no-one knows his real identity."

"Indeed."

"But you did."

"Pure chance. I was defending a client on this list. Happened to read the name."

Slowly I shook my head. I stared at the piece of paper. "A guest of the German Democratic Republic..."

"A paid guest."

I returned him the photocopy of the transcribed, typewritten lines; I didn't ask where he'd procured it.

"So that answers one of your questions, where did he go."

"Where he eventually went," I corrected.

"Accounts for a number of years."

"Till the Wall fell."

"I'm sure he got out in time," Theo pronounced.

"And where did he go to then?" I asked.

"Well, not back to us, that's for sure."

I watched him. He watched me. "No," I said. So Theo really didn't know.

I left soon afterwards. His secretary had interrupted to say his next client had arrived. His last sentence to me was: "I only told you because you're an old friend of his – keep this strictly to yourself." And I promised.

I went out of his office in Maximillian Straße, out of his life again; something had told me it was better to leave him in the dark.

xxx

I rang the bell for Heidi Prell.

It was seven-fifteen, I didn't have long. But I'd had to drive all the way back to Ferdinand-Maria Straße again. On the way I had kept an eye on the mirror too, to check if I could see a Mini. None in sight. A dark-green Land Rover was there behind me at a distance, though, over the course of several streets. It turned off then, disappeared.

And I'd also needed to stop to talk briefly to Eva on my mobile; I was lucky – at the third attempt I'd reached her. She was in Florence, on business. She'd be away a couple of days, she said, but I was welcome to stay the night. Funny all the same, as I drove on I had the feeling of being followed. Was it simply my stupid imagination?

Heidi opened the front door herself. It really was her. She stared hard and expressionlessly at me, appraising me, before stepping aside to let me in. She'd come down two storeys especially to do it, I suppose to check I was who I said I was. She led me up with hardly a word. Side-glances now and then. She'd changed so much; her hair was short and ragged, it seemed she'd been torn by life – she looked emaciated, burnt-out and ill, dark lines beneath her small brown eyes, blank stares between her words.

The whole second floor was a communal flat now – the long wide corridor down the middle, rooms left and right with paper names on some of the old doors and placards on others. I never found out how many lived there, certainly more than listed downstairs by the bells; it must have been over seven or eight. The scene took me back to the sixties – the house occupations, the Women's Lib Movement, the communes, demonstrations and drugs.

Heidi and her son occupied the big old playroom where Matthias and I once used to play. At first glance, except for the scratched maple parquet floor there was nothing much to remind me...

"Sit down," she said. "There."

I sat. We were alone. No sign of her son. Opposite me was a television set on a stand, beneath it a deck and radio. At least she set herself beside me. She splayed her skinny, jean-clad legs, hung sinewy hands between them. Her attractive curves and neat miniskirt thighs had gone to the dogs; I don't think a starved sailor back from the seas would've looked twice.

"You came looking for me."

Was it a statement or a question? I wasn't sure.

I ignored it. "It's been a long time, Heidi."

She nodded. That was all.

"How are you?"

"Fine. You've got eyes."

Yes, I thought, I have eyes. And you look anything but fine.

"You came looking for me?" she repeated. Her voice was mechanical, dead.

"Yes," I said.

"For *me*?"

"For Matthias," I corrected.

"What's he got to do with me?"

She treated me like a stranger. "You ought to know that better than I." I didn't intend to let her antagonise.

"What gave you the idea to come here?"

"He wrote me and said." I glanced down at her body. Oh God – had she been through hell?

Slowly she nodded. "Okay."

How could she have changed so much? Remember?

"You listening?" She asked it sharply.

I raised my eyes from her lap, from the source of the pleasure of my student days in that world that was dead and gone. I looked at the grey in her skin, at the gaunt leathery lines in her face. "You know what I'm talking about," I said.

"You've come. That's sufficient." She watched me sideways, she was summing me up. Her T-shirt was grey too, hung down almost flat, her wasted breasts fallen bags, her poking nipples hard as nuts. My fingertips could have overlapped if wrapped around her wrist.

I said nothing.

No talk of yesterday, or how her life had evolved, or of what I did nowadays; no questions, no nostalgia, no inquisitiveness. A kind of sickness hung in the air, her face a mask of death. Oh God, I thought.

She sat there staring. The eyes only absorbed, took in, didn't give, gave nothing away.

So I said: "Is he here?"

Briefly she laughed – a dry cracked sound. It was totally lacking in humour. "You kidding?"

I thought: you're a wreck – this is the hell, those were the drugs, here are your scars. "No," I said.

"He's nowhere."

I thought about that. "I was under the impression he wanted..."

"No impressions."

"That he wanted to meet me."

"No idea," she blocked. Her tone was flat as her chest. "He told me to check," she added.

"Yes?"

She nodded. "Make sure."

"Well, I hope you're sure now." I stirred. This was beginning to irritate. "Listen, Heidi – simply tell me what he wants, then I'll go. I don't have much time, especially not for silly games."

"Game, Stefan? You think it's a game?"

"What is it, then?"

No reply.

"It's not the sixties any more," I said. "You forgotten we're both adults now?" But I shouldn't have said that; I'm sure she couldn't forget.

She moved her head; was she shaking it? "I've got something for you."

"From Matthias?"

She was twisting, reaching over the arm of the leather sofa. Her bony bottom had turned, touched my thigh. Did she even notice? From a bag she drew a small grey package. "It's sealed." She sat back, straightened, handed me the tape wrapped in cellophane.

Then she seemed to notice – she slid away; her wasted body was gone. "There's the player." She pointed. "Know how it works?"

I glanced away. "I expect so."

"And how to erase?"

I nodded.

"Then watch it, clean it, leave it here. Okay?" She was standing up; she did it in a jerk, hands pressed for an instant on knees. Like a jack-knife. "Go the way you came. *Tschüß.*"

She was gone, closing the door behind her. It was like yet another fantasy which had almost never been.

I sat there a moment unable to move. I stared at the door. I could hear echoes, feathered darts thudding; the dartboard was missing, so was the hook. But there were the tiny holes in the wood where we'd missed around where it had hung. At least the door was real.

Then I glanced down at the tape in my hand. Slowly I shook my head. So he knew I would come looking for him. The bastard. He was so damn certain. Kneeling, I switched on the set, slipped in the tape, pushed play. I sat back against the sofa, on the floor, watching...

A blank on the screen, just static. Then... blue sky. And sand. Nothing else. It wasn't a beach – there was no sea. And not coastal dunes – no grass, no bushes, nothing green. Just hills of sand under blinding sky. It was a desert.

"Hello, Stefan."

His voice was very quiet, relaxed.

I started. Although hardly audible, the sound was unexpected; like the gentlest caress on the skin, like a whisper in the dark – if you don't know it's coming it can be like a blow.

"How are you?"

It was uncanny; it was almost as if he were here in the room. Almost as though I could answer, and if I did he would hear.

"Look."

The picture was expanding slowly. The edges of sand fell off the screen, the slope in the middle grew. Was that a dark spot near the top?

"You can see me now..."

The spot grew too.

"...you always had good eyes. I remember. You were the observer."

There he was; a figure sitting on the sand. The image shimmered in desert heat.

"No, I'm not a mirage."

Had he read my thoughts?

The zoom stopped, he filled half the screen. Virgin sand, rippled gold in the sun, like waves, with shadows of red. I could see his sunken footsteps where he'd walked to the place. The horizon sloped, cut behind his shoulders.

"Look closely."

But I was already looking. He was a little older now. His skin was tanned, but scarcely lined, his eyes still blue. He wore sand-coloured clothes – they hung loose on his lean body. He appeared very fit. On his head his fair hair was hidden – a white headcloth wound in folds, neatly. It was white as snow.

"Yes, we're both older now."

Had he again heard my words, these thoughts in my head? In spite of myself I had to smile.

"I can see you too, you see." He returned my smile, faintly. "You've come back to our roots. Remember how we would play on the floor, flat on our bellies? There – right under your feet. You see...?"

I was glancing. There were the generals and the troops arrayed, there were the cannons we fired matchsticks with.

"...What did we play, Stefan?"

I was remembering too. "We played soldiers," I said out loud.

"That's right – soldiers. Kids' little war games."

How could I forget? And you always won, I thought.

"But we're wiser now."

Are we? I wondered.

"Yes we are. And you've learnt to win battles too, in real life."

And you? I thought. Are you still like Heidi? – still carrying your past like a scar?

"I've learnt how to lose."

His voice was so calm, his eyes hardly blinked. I could feel it coming back: that strange kind of telepathy we'd once been able to share. But I could feel something else as well. He radiated something new. He seemed so at peace, at one with himself – all that cold aggression of old had disappeared...

He lowered his eyes, for a moment his steady gaze was gone. Had he done it intentionally – did he know I also needed a brief pause to look away?

There was the first touch of spring clinging to the branches breaking through the Munich sky and the earth was still iron beneath our schoolboy feet in the English Garden where we walked deep in thought and talked. Yes, there was tenderness in the tips of the trees. And there were long hot summers close together, climbing mountains, swimming naked in the local lake, motorbikes in the South of France, sometimes with Klaus – becoming older, bolder, bent over beer-glasses in *Gasthäuser* with cigarette smoke wreathing blue, dissecting politics and life. And those brutal student seasons of unrest catching fire to the imagination and stealing him inexorably away from me... and a little later - was it only the blink of an eye? - there were leaves falling in the forest and acorns dropping like bullets through the branches where Matthias stood facing me, completely estranged, with one hand in his winter-coat pocket and hatred in his words, and we both were aware that we had reached the end of a shared road, that a door was closing...

I looked back.

There he was on his sea of sand again, sitting there so philosophically, head bowed like a recluse. Still he paused, waiting for me. Could it really be true? In those hands laid upon that lap could it be that wisdom was unfolding?

"You've noticed, then." He had raised his eyes.

I nodded. He'd almost whispered the words. It was simply a statement, a message. How could he manage it so effortlessly? Just like Eva, I was coming under his spell again.

"I've found it, Stefan." He said it quiet and clear.

What have you found?

"What you were looking for when we were young."

The purpose of life? I shook my head, wryly. Our thoughts were coming closer.

"The purpose of life."

I wanted to reach out to touch him, touch his mind. But I never found it, Matthias.

"You were far ahead of me in those days, though – you simply didn't look long enough."

"I gave up," I said aloud.

"And I got into a cul-de-sac, was tapping in the dark. You shouldn't have given up, Stefan."

"It's too late now," I said. "I've lost the incentive, lost the way." My desire to see him had turned to longing again.

"I've found the light." His eyes were clear and steady.

"Be careful with words like that."

"Yes, I'm being careful."

"What light is that, Matthias?"

"One has to learn to let go – and to differentiate between antitheses. For example between good and evil. Then the path is clear."

"What path?" I asked.

But although he was staring, he didn't seem to hear me.

"I feel close to you again, Stefan, I want you to know that. It might be our paths may soon cross. In reality. Am I right? I believe you'd like that too."

"Yes," I said.

Again he didn't hear though; he'd lowered his eyes. He was retreating.

I blinked. I'd felt the tug, I felt that old bond. I didn't want him to go. But he shrank. He faded... he was only a small figure now, only a speck on a screen.

x x x

I drove to the address Margareth had given me, parked nearby. Found a little bistro. It was after 8pm, had to get a bite to eat before calling. I sat at a small table, alone, near the window to the street. Ordered.

While waiting, I forced myself to shut Matthias out of my mind for a few minutes and concentrate on Margareth, trying to prepare myself. I didn't have much to go on but I made my brain make a brief jump all the same, back to Heinrich's anguished phone call that morning in my apartment as I had been on the point of leaving. In my head I could hear my mobile ringing in my jacket pocket. Nervousness leaping, could it be Matthias? Then another thought, maybe it's my mother. I'd shut the apartment door again, standing in my hall bracing myself, and with unsteady fingers pressed the button, said hello.

"Heinrich here." The voice was mixed up with traffic his end of the line. Could imagine him seated near his open office windows with that panorama of the city beyond.

Oh God, I thought. Then straight afterwards: there must be something wrong, Heinrich never rings. "Heinrich," I said, "this is a surprise." He'd only rung once in twelve years.

"Is she with you?" he demanded. No preliminaries. His tone was impatient and loud – it at once put my hackles up. Heinrich and I had little in common; our incompatibility had been a struggle from the start.

"She?" I said. "Who?"

"Margareth. Who the hell else?"

My God, he sounded so aggressive. My grandmother Ilse once confided loudly to me when I was a child within earshot of members of our large family: "God gave us our relatives, Stefan – thank God we can choose our friends," and I suspect she would've said the same of him too. Heinrich my brother-in-law: successful architect, the prince of materialism, emotional pauper amongst the poor rich, he who confused power with strength and generosity with love.

"No, she isn't," I said. "In fact I haven't..."

"You in Munich?" he cut in. There was such tightness in his tone, I could sense the pressure behind his words. Yes, something bad must've happened.

"No I'm not," I said.

"Were you yesterday?"

"No." Granted he never beat about the bush but this was heavy even for him. I could feel foreboding beginning to grow. Heinrich was one of those handsome muscular guys, a no-nonsense person, a leader of the pack. Born the son of a village blacksmith, he had forged a fresh path out of it all and climbed to the mountain top. He worked sixteen hours a day, with supreme dedication, building monuments of marble for big banks, and sugar-candy castles for famous actors and the Munich nouveau riche...

"Where the fuck are you then? Not at work – tried you there."

I took a breath. "Listen Heinrich," I said, "why the hell don't you tell me what's going on?"

Something broke in his throat. For a moment he seemed unable to speak. Then he was there again, harsh and cold. He said: "She's leaving me."

"Oh God." I cast about, tried to take my bearings. So what Eva had predicted right from the start was coming true...

"She's gone," he corrected. And there was desperation in his voice – like a man who's dreamed of being free then awoken to his shackles.

I remember, I didn't know what to think or say. In that first instant I didn't even know whether to be sad or glad. Images tumbled: there were summer scenes of their swimming-parties and tennis-club do's in the Munich days before their children came into the world, and before they felt forced to move out of their town house, build a place on Chiemsee lake; Margareth had been so happy, always aglow, everything she'd touched had turned to gold.

"Heinrich," I began. "I'm very sorry to hear this."

"Shit, so you didn't know," he blurted.

"No."

"Christ, thought she might be with you."

I shook my head at the very idea. "Afraid not," I said. "I'd be almost the last she'd turn to."

"Couldn't reach anyone else." Anguish now. "Only Tobias. Pompous arsehole, that brother of yours. He knew nothing either, just waffled a load of crap about the sanctity of marriage and..."

He spoke in a rush. It was like a dam bursting. He'd raised his voice, was talking about Margareth now, accusingly, tearing her apart. Bitter words broke in my ear, unpleasant things which went under the belt, things I'm sure he'd later regret. He hit out blindly, a bludgeon swinging in the dark. Oh Heinrich, I thought, this is a subject on which males like us are illiterate and you're worse off than most...

His outburst lasted a minute or so.

Yes, I remember too: it took me back, brought Judit close, our own break-up. And all that pain. I stood there in the hall, mobile to ear, and memories rose in clouds like dust disturbed on a barren road. All at once I heard the sounds of Judit coming home and her footsteps on the stair beyond the door... she was calling hello, wild kisses and drama and hugs the way she used to do each day as though we hadn't met for a month. I'd gone and got married, then I'd lost that too. Now Margareth was treading in my tracks. My little sister Eva was still single, the small cool professional; only Tobias had a stable marriage, discounting (so I'd been told) his naughty little secret beneath the weekly string-quartet skirt of that slinky second violin.

In the doorway to my large living room Heinrich was far away tearing his life in shreds, and on the open door the pinewood notches watched me like Judit's eyes had sometimes done during the silences when we failed to communicate...

"...little bitch, she's found another..."

My unhappy brain was still springing over stepping-stones in the past...

"...started a goddamn affair on the side..."

But that sentence pulled me abruptly back.

"No, Heinrich," I said quickly, interrupting. "I'm sure you're wrong there."

"What the shit else?"

"Did she tell you that?"

"Everyone lies about fucking affairs on the side."

"Not Margareth," I repeated. Should I tell him what Eva had said from the very beginning, where the problem lay, that they were too alike, couldn't give and take? But who the hell was I to give advice?

"It's not fucking fair..." he was saying. No it isn't, I thought.

"Give her a breathing space," I suggested. That's what I hadn't given Judit. "Don't put her in a cage, Heinrich. That'd be my advice."

"Load of crap. Let a bitch off the chain and it'll never come back."

"Is she on a chain, then?"

"'Course not – just a fucking metaphor."

"Well, let her get her bearings, let the grass grow over things a bit." I was talking to my own darkness, wasn't I – did I have the right to speak?

"Can't sit on my arse twiddling my thumbs."

"Do you have any other choice?"

"Sign of weakness. Got to fight for what's important. Never take things lying down. Had to fight all my life to get what I've got."

"Heinrich," I said, "I guess what you need is a truce, not another battle."

But I fear he wasn't listening, or wasn't able to. In an agonised voice he said: "She's taken the kids and just buggered off, she's destroying everything we've built."

I shook my head. "I know it looks that way." It'd looked that way to me too. "I'm very sorry about all this, Heinrich. But don't throw away your last card." I knew now for sure, Margareth hadn't been unfaithful; she'd taken the children. And I knew too – I had to end the call.

"Heinrich, listen," I said. "I'm glad you rang." I paused. "Look, I'll try to find out where Margareth is, and talk to her."

"When you do, let me know pronto." His heavy voice had taken on a tinge of hope. "Do me a favour, brother-in-law."

"That I won't promise," I said.

"Right away. I've got the bloody right to know."

"If she agrees."

"Convince her. Do your bloody best."

My thoughts were reaching out to Margareth. Although we'd become estranged, I had a duty to help, didn't I? I said to Heinrich: "In the meanwhile, should you need to talk to someone, you can reach me any time under this…"

"You ring me," he ordered.

x x x

With one hand I'd packed the overnight bag, with the other hurriedly rung telephone numbers. Tried Margareth's home one then her mobile twice – no answer, only her mailbox. I left a message to ring me back, pressed Cancel.

I tried Eva too – despite the fact that she and I were the very last to be informed of any family news. No luck there either though. I knew I was procrastinating, avoiding the obvious; but I couldn't yet bring myself to phone the only person who'd be the very first in the know. Went through my address book, found the names of friends of Margareth whom I'd met in the old days. But nobody answered. Who else, then, might know where she was?

I stood hesitating. I was down to the last straw.

Should I, shouldn't I? There was a block, an old obstacle standing in the way which made me uncomfortable even thinking about it; each of us has his shadows, and walls he can't break down. From my address book I retrieved another Munich number and rang the shop where she works part-time…

"Old English Silver and Antiques, Elisabeth Falk, *Grüß Gott.*" She answered so quickly that it tautened all my nerves.

"Hello mother."

Yes, my mother. The woman I hardly knew. The one who'd handed us on to nanny Helga as soon as we left her breast, the distant lady in the background of our childhood entertaining society friends. The same woman, too, of humble origins but noble proportions who'd married into money, fondly known as Easy Lizzy in her prime.

"Oh, Stefan! *Darling*. Hello – how wonderful!"

Yes, my mother: proud Arian matron of peroxide-blonde womanhood and denier of basic truths, still praying for the resurrection of her god Adolf, he who continues to lend meaning to the fragments of her life not pursued in bed. And the same one, my mother, behind father's weary back, who raised her insatiable faith to climax with our neighbour Hermann von B, Matthias's distinguished papa, as often as he would but far less often than she could.

"Darling, hang on a jiffy..." I heard her hand muffle the receiver, and indistinct words telling someone it was her youngest son and not to wait, till later for lunch... "There! Back again! Oh my darling, how *lovely*. However long is it since last I heard from you? I should scold you, you know..."

Here she was now, so far away, so close to my ear. I made an appropriate noise; for my mother noises were often enough.

"You really must try to keep in more regular touch. How many times have I told you...?"

Ah yes. To her credit she had tried, though alas too late, to make amends to us and over-compensate after the house of cards collapsed.

"...darling, I read about you in the papers recently. Congratulations – you're making a name for yourself! How are you?"

"Fine," I said.

I could imagine her. Could see the way she looked from the last time that we met – she's easily recognisable from the old photographs: dyed blonde hair, body well-proportioned but just a little plumper, stiff lines in her expensively lifted face. Eva reports that she still has the ability to attract men like flies. I could see her long ago, too, returning regularly from next door in a glow I mistook for sacrifice when I was in my teens; I can forgive her unfaithfulness - who am I to judge? – but I can't forgive her faith.

"So glad," she was saying, "I've been *so* worried about..."

I must be honest: my desire to communicate had evaporated the moment she'd first spoken. Obviously she hadn't heard what had happened – it would've been the second sentence that she uttered. And I couldn't bring myself to be the bearer of bad news; didn't want to hear her tears on the phone. I owed it to Margareth, as well – my sister must have her reasons for silence. So when my mother made her next brief pause to fill the lungs again, I reiterated her question: "And you?" I said. "Are you keeping well?"

"Right as rain."

"What about your heart? You had..."

"Oh, false alarm, darling. I went for a thorough check-up and my doc says I'm fit as a fiddle."

"You should do these check-ups once a year, not leave it till..."

"I promise. Oh, I'm so relieved to hear your voice, your ears must've been burning! I had a funny feeling yesterday. Meant to call you. Maggie tells me she also hears very little from you, and Eva as you know never has time to tell a soul anything. By the way, I got a letter from her last month – she'd managed to squeeze in a week's vacation in Israel. *Israel* of all places – that horrid nest of Yids!" I winced but I held my tongue; you can't turn a serpent into a swan however hard you try. "She promised to write to you. Did she?"

"Yes she did." I'd received a copy of hers to our mother with 'Mamma' deleted and my name inserted and a scribbled comment at the top saying 'to the Israeli censor: this is to save you and me time, mate'.

"Expect she told you all the things she didn't tell me. She's a wild one – I don't know where she could've got it from, certainly not from me or your father. Apparently she's in love with Jerusalem – or was it Damascus? Whenever will she settle down? But never mind, must get back to you. Are you coping all right? I know Judit's divorcing you was a dreadful shock. Such an un*usual* woman, but with her head screwed on. I realised that after only ten minutes that first time you brought her home to meet me and... and..."

"Mother, that was fifteen years ago."

"Oh I know, but darling it seems like yesterday. Well anyway, and how are things going?"

"Busy. Lot of work. Travelling a lot, too."

"I mean *private* life."

"Ah."

"All alone still?"

"Not much time to get isolated, actually..."

"Oh my darling, I know *exactly* what you mean. When your father... oh dear I nearly said... after he died, I felt the same way. You must force yourself, *find* the time. You *must* get out and about, meet more people. Go to some parties and things. There's a woman around every corner just waiting for the chance to meet a successful, intelligent man like you. Which reminds me, I spent the weekend with the von Wolkenbergs – you haven't forgotten Willi, no of course you haven't. He asked to be remembered, by the way. Well, his second daughter Charlie – Charlotta I should say – hasn't married yet. Turned thirty-four recently but rather choosy – just as well, of course, with all these *awful* new rich communists everywhere – I don't know what's happened to our Fatherland, Adolf would turn in his grave. She's a charming girl. Woman, I should say. She's matured into a more beautiful, elegant creature than Sybille even. And naturally, pure Arian stock. But, of course, you met her – how long ago was it – ten years...?"

"More like fourteen," I said.

"Oh really – my goodness, how the time flies. But never mind, what was I saying? Oh yes – you remember meeting her at that... at that, oh dear... masked ball you found so dreadful. Anyway, she'd make the most suitable wife for a man of your background – well brought-up even if a little eccentric and a mite too emancipated. And so well-educated – one could almost say *too* well-educated. And so much money. Of course Willi insists they're poor as paupers, but you know how he always talks since Adolf was betrayed and Erhard's reform. Why don't you ring up the Baron and invite her out? Take her to a slap-up dinner somewhere, you earn a good salary. Or I'll foot the bill."

"No, mother, really not."

"Oh but why? You always put obstacles in the way of every suggestion I used to make. Take that ball at the *Schloß*, for instance, darling. It was a marvellous opportunity for you to get back into our old circle after the... the scandal had died down. And see what happened? You wouldn't speak to me for a whole week afterwards, as if I were the one at fault, and that when I'd gone to so much trouble to arrange the invitation. You're too critical of everyone, darling. They *are* human beings, you know."

"That was a long time ago, mother."

"Why don't I give the Baron a tinkle and drop a word in his ear about Charlotta? He's going grey with worry about finding a suitable match."

"Mother, please don't. I'm sure Charlotta's capable of choosing her own friends. And we're quite incompatible. If she ever decided to marry, which I doubt, it'd probably be to a politician or pop-star or..."

"Nonsense! She even enquired after you last weekend. And it wasn't simply out of politeness – I'm an excellent judge of things like that. The whole family has such *char*ming manners. I must see if I can't think of some other suitable woman, too, such as – oh, I know! What's her Christian name? Goldberg the publisher's daughter, in Schrammer Straße, who Johann once..."

"No idea, mother."

"Oh but you must do. Delicious redhead. Saw her recently at a concert. On the market again since she lost her husband, so tragic, they say such a young widow..."

"I don't move in those circles..."

"Packets of money, I'm told. And absolutely *gorgeous*."

"Goldberg's Jewish, mother."

"What?"

"Jewish. I can't imagine you..."

"Oh my God, no! You're joking. Why in heaven's name didn't Gertrude warn me? They don't *look*..."

I opened my apartment door, set the overnight bag on the mat and put the key in the lock, readying myself to go...

My mother had gone off at another tangent; she was very good at doing that. "I'll hold a party," she was saying. "Oh yes, what a splendid...!"

I stood waiting to end the call.

"We'll have a dinner party, just as in the old days. And I'll see if I can't arrange for Charlotta to be there too, quite by accident of course."

"Please don't, mother."

"I'll try and get our whole family together, it's ages since I saw you and little Eva – oh what dark horses you are. If it wasn't for my Tobias, I don't know..."

"Mother, I..."

"By the way, darling, speaking of invitations, I've just received an invite for an autumn vacation in Morocco – September – from you'll never guess who..."

"Mother, I really must go."

"Yes, of *course*, darling. I'll tell you all about it soon – goodbye to you. And *do* look after yourself."

"You too. And don't forget those check-ups in future."

"No, no... bye, bye-bye," she said again as I stooped, also saying goodbye, to slip the mobile into the overnight bag.

x x x

Well, that was the memory and these were the thorns. But they didn't help. Deeply unenlightened I concentrated on the present again, on what I ought to say. The bistro was busy and my order had taken a little while. Had to eat quickly – the tagliatelle, the small side-salad. I gulped them. It was after nine already, Margareth would be waiting. I laid down the spoon and fork, laid down my thoughts too. Steeled myself for the fray.

Chapter 4

There were seven bells.
I stood in Schwabing before the town house. It was situated across the square from the bistro where I'd had the quick meal. Nice area – off Ludwig Straße, right near the heart of the city and only a few streets away from Eva's flat. The entranceway was glassed and modern and the portal reached up to the roof, but the house itself was old.

Seven bells – I scanned the names, looking for Binoche. It was the one at the top – Annabelle Binoche. Margareth had warned me on the phone, but added: "Don't worry, she won't be here." I pressed the bell. The bulging lens of a closed-circuit camera watched me like a Cyclops eye.

A crackle... Margareth's voice in the microphone said: "Come up." An electric lock buzzed. I pushed open the heavy sheet-glass door, almost double my height, and entered. An elegant, spacious and exclusive hallway: rose-coloured marble with insets of something silver, pristine white walls and a stencilled frieze, bright with hidden lighting, four floors high. In the centre, a modern sculpture with a fountain, at the far end a broad curving sweep of stairs, a glass lift in its middle. The scent of Munich affluence.

I rode up to the top fourth floor.

Slanted patent-glazing, late sun filtered through cotton screens, a panorama of plane trees in the square below, a bird's-eye view of the hall. I stepped back from the glass balustrade with its thread of stainless-steel handrail, feeling giddy; I'm not very good at heights. A gallery, a row of neat potted trees like balls on poles, a parquet floor with marble surround – a timber door with intricate inlay in another wall of purest white. Everything planned to perfection. Oh God, I thought, new rich? Does Margareth really need to have friends like this – or is it merely Heinrich's influence?

I approached.

My sister opened the door; there was no way of knowing, but she was opening another door too. "Come in," she said. She said it with a burning cigarette in her hand. "Please keep your voice down, the children are asleep, thank God." I could hear Bach, quietly, in the background.

I entered.

I'd brought a bit of Matthias along with me in my brain – but now I put him out of sight again. And once more steeled myself. She kissed me. In a tight emotionless kind of way. Cigarette smoke got in my eyes.

"Are we alone?" I asked.

"Yep."

Her clothes were crumpled, as if she didn't care; she'd lost a lot of weight. Her thick black hair, that gipsy hair, was pinned back, untidy tufts hung in disarray – there was strain in her face, and she wore far less makeup than I remembered. Her appearance was dreadful. It shocked. She used to be one of those women who always look good, well-dressed, look early thirties from twenty on and remain that way. Now she appeared careless and twenty years older.

"Been a long time, little brother." She said it flatly.

I just nodded.

"How long?"

I shrugged. "Must be nearly three years." I noticed too she'd moved her rings to different fingers, and that they were different rings. I removed my sandals, left them lying near what looked like an old church pew beside a beautiful big *Biedermeier* cupboard.

"Don't have to, brother. Not this evening."

"A habit."

"Oh those habits of yours. You never change." She stared at me for an instant over her cigarette. The ash was lengthening – didn't she care? "Pick yourself a pair, if you want." She pointed to the pew. Beneath it lay a selection of slippers. "They're for guests."

I thought: it's a good thing I've come, she's in a bad way — I'm glad I've come. I put on some purple oriental ones.

We were walking down a long, wide hall, a kind of broad corridor. Persian carpets on parquet, an antique chest, a big Chinese vase with fresh-cut flowers. A sense of generous space. While we walked I thought, too: I hope I'm going to be up to this. Past two modern chairs against a wall, then one very large avant-garde painting on its own.

I peered as I passed. My first impression: it's a good one.

"You hungry?" she asked quietly. A throw-away question half over her shoulder. She sounded matter-of-fact but very withdrawn.

"No," I said.

"You eaten, then?"

"Enough." I didn't want to trouble her.

We had reached double sliding-glass doors standing open. The music was louder. And a stronger smell of cigarette smoke. Beyond, a large drawing-room. We passed through. She was saying: "Make yourself at home — she won't be back for twenty-four hours. With a new flame." She closed the doors behind her, leaned against them for a moment. "I'll be staying here a while, has its advantages — 'mongst other things I can babysit her two."

She was walking ahead again into the room, filling me in. "This is my second home. She and her husband're old friends of mine, he died in a plane crash a couple of years back."

Plane crash. "Ah," I said, noncommittally. The penny had dropped. "You mean Goldberg's daughter?"

"The same. Know her, then?"

"No. Heard of her, that's all." Oh God, I thought — the number two on mother's Munich society list of eligibility. So Margareth moves in these circles too.

She turned off the Bach, came back, stopped in the middle of the big room, tapping ash near an island of sofas, looking at me. Her eyes were dead.

I looked away.

The light was fading — yellow late-evening light. One complete wall was made of glass, opening onto a wide roof terrace with balustrade and the tops of trees beyond. And I thought: thank God she's not here.

"Wine?"

I spread my hands. "Not important. I'm driving. Not unless you feel like drinking too."

"I do."

I nodded neutrally.

"I've got a ten-year-old Barolo red – not too heavy. Already opened."

I acquiesced. "Sounds fine." I watched her. I thought: your condition isn't exactly conducive to alcohol. But she and Heinrich used to drink a lot. So I said nothing. Maybe she could take it.

She was turning away, putting out her cigarette, saying: "And I'll make some coffee, okay? Or too late for you?"

"No," I said again. "Thanks."

I stood, one hand in pocket, observing the room while I waited. As in the hall, a feeling of space, but much more so. First impression – comfortable wealth, and tasteful. Not many objects: in the middle a low table made entirely of glass and arranged around it two padded armchairs which didn't match and two big white sofas, the kind one sinks into, on them a mass of loose cushions scattered. There were also three more large unframed canvases which took up a lot of two walls, and two antique cupboards with glass-paned doors and shelves full of books. Over by the sliding windows a stone sculpture stood on a granite block, and beyond it a black grand piano with upholstered stool turned to the sunset. A quiet air of taste and natural grace pervaded. It surprised me slightly – not what one ought to expect of the daughter of one of my mother's loud crowd of friends.

On the pale bamboo parquet-flooring between me and the first of the sofas lay an expanse of pastel coloured silk carpet. Could also be Persian, perhaps. Unhurriedly, in my slippered feet, I walked across it wondering am I leaving footprints behind giving me away?

I paused. Gazed down at the glass table. Dozens of broken bevelled sheets of glass stood pressed together, and laid upon them a single sheet rested. In its centre, a flat ceramic Zen dish full of water and floating rose-blooms, at the far end a half-empty wineglass and brass bowl serving as ashtray. Next to them, an incongruous object – it made me smile. A red-black-and-gold cosmetic bag lay on its side half unpacked, spreading female paraphernalia like the trail of an overnight snail, and a heap of used cotton buds and cotton wool pads completed the aberration.

Margareth reappeared, caught me still standing there deliberating where to sit; the aroma of roast coffee clung to her clothes.

"Not quite your lifestyle." She indicated with a matter-of-fact sweep of her arm.

"No," I agreed. "But I'm content with what I have."

"Are you?" A clack of a bottle, she set down a second glass. "Pour, will you?"

I went over, stooped and poured. Looked at the label.

"Memories of better times," she said.

I eyed her. Read the label aloud.

"Heinrich and I brought back a crate of them in the boot for Annabelle two summers ago. Still three left. She doesn't drink much."

"Two summers ago? Were they better times?"

"Better than now."

I gave her her glass, standing before her; I tapped it with mine. "To better times, then," I said.

"You're kidding."

We drank.

I was watching the black rings round her eyes. "They'll come, Maggie."

She stared at me in silence.

"They always do," I added. "Just like the bad ones."

Still she stared. No – I'd never seen her eyes so dead. She was a tall woman: she looked so washed-out, so exhausted. Nothing shone out any more.

I was about to speak again, but she said quickly: "You're too thin."

"You too."

She sighed. Hairs fell in her face. She tossed her head, drank down half the glass of wine. Sank to the sofa. Unceremoniously she kicked off her sandals, swung up her legs, stretching them along the cushions. Propped in the corner, elbow on the sofa back, she observed me over the raised rim of her glass.

"My skinny little brother."

I stood there staring down at her. "My dominant big sister."

"Not so big and dominant now."

I shook my head. On her legs were fine black hairs; I think I'd never noticed them before.

"How the mighty are fallen," she said. She said it harshly. Drank more wine.

She's drinking too quickly, I thought. I said nothing.

"Now the tables are turned, little brother."

"Not turned," I said. "I'm still in a hole. You've simply fallen from your throne."

"Throne?" She attempted a laugh, but it came out cracked. "You're kidding again."

"Forgotten? The triumphant queen parading Heinrich like a trophy?"

"Damn long time ago."

I sipped my wine. Again said nothing, didn't wish to provoke. Don't kick a man when he's down. I watched her in silence. Then seated myself at the other end of her sofa, crossed my legs, wineglass propped on one knee.

She'd followed me with her eyes. "Why're you still in a hole, then?"

I shook my head again. "Another time. You're in the hot seat today."

Emptily she returned my gaze. Drained her glass. A pause. Neither of us speaking.

Then, unhurriedly, with a neutral tone to bring her to a beginning, to get us back on track, I asked her when she'd arrived.

"Yesterday." She twisted, stretching, set down her glass with a clack. Lit another cigarette. "I rang Heinrich and told him this was it. Brought David with me." She threw the golden lighter down, leaning back.

"How did he react?"

"How d'you think?" She drew sharply on the cigarette. "Aggressive at first, then turned meek as a child." She blew smoke. It spread in a cloud above her head, hung heavy in the last of the sun. "Reason why I did it on the phone – face to face he'd've got violent."

"From what he told me this morning, I guess he'd had enough warning."

"For Heinrich nothing's inevitable – unless it's ordained by him."

I said nothing. She leaned, tapped ash, picked up the brass bowl and placed it in her lap. "What did he tell you?"

"Not a great deal," I said.

"Chucked some dirt?"

"Not really." I tried to stay neutral, taking sides wouldn't help. "Told me his side of the story."

Dumbly, she nodded. "Can imagine." She stared at me, then down at her feet.

"He was like a broken man," I said.

"Not bloody surprised."

"It got under my skin."

"It's a bloody situation." Again she stared over the raised cigarette. "He convinced you it's all my fault – man to man, keep it in the club?" She said it sarcastically, bitterly. "I know you males – your snide masculine solidarity."

"No." I shook my head.

"No?"

"I don't think he was even trying."

"Doesn't sound like Heinrich."

I watched her. "He only rang looking for you. I doubt he'd intended to talk."

"But he did," she accused.

"He needed an outlet, I suppose. He needed that."

"He chose a fine one to do it with."

"Yes," I said.

She wound the tip of the cigarette round and round inside the bowl. I wondered what she was thinking, what her thoughts were looking at. At length she said: "Emotionally, you men're all cripples. Except when it comes to aggression and sex."

I didn't answer.

She inhaled. Her dark eyes were on me. "He's one of those very masculine kinds of male. That's the problem."

"You chose him."

Her eyes fell again. She nodded at her lap.

"Remember?" I said. "Eva warned you."

"He was big, strong and determined. I loved his strength."

She'd worshipped him, in fact. I watched her lowered head; I was thinking, suddenly, of our father. She'd worshipped father too.

She took a last, jerky, puff – stubbed out the cigarette in the big brass bowl. She stabbed it like an enemy, like children kill a wasp.

"You're learning your lesson the hard way," I said.

"Yep."

The picture of our father was stronger now; it hung in my head like a film. He was walking towards me, but Margareth was there too, ten years old, coming between us yet again, taking hold of his hand, pulling him away and I hated her. I had to screw up my small fists to hide the ball of hate.

"Took you a long while, didn't it," I said.

Just for an instant she glanced up at me and I caught a glimpse of her eyes. They were beginning to swim, tears brimmed. Then she looked away again and not a single tear fell. Margareth's a tough one, she has a will of steel.

"Long while?" she echoed. "To see through Heinrich?"

"Yes," I said. "And now you've got to start seeing through you."

Her head had come up. With a brief sweep she wiped an eye with a fingertip, stared at me. "Don't get you. Explain." She reached sideways, took another cigarette, shaking it from the packet, lit it.

I hadn't planned it like this, but things were rising to the surface. "You're as much responsible for your wrecked marriage as Heinrich," I said. "Time you understood."

"Understood what?"

"Your egoism."

"Thanks for the compliment." She glared at me, she looked a wreck.

I thought: it's time to talk, Maggie – we've never broached this one before. No point in being sentimental, you're not the type; good chance for a few constructive home truths. So I waded in. Started with her selfishness, her weakness to get what she wanted, to always impose her will. "You're like Heinrich," I told her, "you're two of a kind. That was no good basis for a marriage."

"Bullshit." She glowered.

"As children we all hated you for it."

She tossed her head aggressively, blocking, turning things around. But I had her attention now. After a minute or two she pulled Judit into the conversation, accusing me of egoism too.

"Egoistic and secretive, just the reverse of her." She said it nastily. "You were closed, she was wild, you never gave her any rope. You and Judit were total opposites. Didn't help your marriage a jot either."

"I blame myself for that," I confessed.

"Not a question of blame, little brother."

"Correct, but..."

"She buggered off because of *you*. Your snidey, secretive character."

"I think with us it was a question of love," I said feebly. "Perhaps we didn't give love enough chance."

"Crap. You tried changing her, tying her down." Then she added, repeating: "Contrasts, similarities — there's no one recipe for a successful marriage, it's just a game of give and take. And don't talk to me about love."

"Why not?"

"Because that's not the name of the game. That wears off quick enough." She spoke crisply, clipped, she spoke with such conviction. "Marriage's solving the practical day-to-day details."

Oh God, I thought. I watched her watching me over her white stick of cigarette.

"Don't look at me like that," she demanded.

I shook my head slowly in silence.

"You'll be telling me next you're still in love with her." Again the sarcasm.

"Yes," I said. "Perhaps." I spread my hands. "And sometimes I think it just possible that Judit later maybe had her regrets."

"Sweet Jesus!" A laugh, brief and cracked. "Don't kid yourself." Ash fell. She brushed it brusquely aside, raising the bowl from her thighs. "You're an impossible romantic, little brother."

Yes.

Like father. The thought jumped in. And there he was again. He sat in the shadows, behind his big desk. Long straight back, gaunt worn face with those worry lines, groomed silver hair slicked straight backwards. And those graceful hands laid to rest on papers he'd been working on as I entered and interrupted him. Gentle hands, long tender hands, attentive eyes, blue-grey eyes, sunken, haunted — gazing upon me with understanding. No Margareth, no dominant big sister pushing in between. Just he and I, fifteen years old, and piles of paper on inlaid leather, an ink-blotter and fountain pen, the table lamp with its cord and milk-glass shade like half a moon, and his two black Bakelite telephones. He was so different from me, so tall and good-looking, so elegant. Why was I so small? And unhappy? But we both at least were romantics, yes we had that soft core in common. And we both, in our own ways, had learned to camouflage, I against the unforgiving gaze of conventional boys, he against the merciless world of greedy and powerful men...

"Do you really believe that, about marriage?" I asked Margareth. "About love?"

"Yes." Her tone was harsh.

I nodded. "I'm sorry to hear that."

"Sorry?"

"Yes. But it explains a lot."

"Explains?" she exploded. "What the hell does it explain?"

"Another reason why your marriage to Heinrich didn't have a chance." I gazed upon her. She was hard as nails. "You don't possess the capacity for love. Not really. If at all, you only love to think of yourself." So – now I'd gone and said it.

She watched me, in silence. A spiral of smoke from the forgotten cigarette. Those cold and angry eyes. But there was something else too – there was hurt in them now. Now I knew I had reached her.

The way my father had reached me that late afternoon, by hitting beneath the belt. I'd reticently started talking about unhappiness – my unhappiness. And he'd looked into me, dug deep down, began to speak, laid an unwavering finger on my fears; nobody had ever spoken to me like that before. I'd never forget it. Across those piles of papers he'd brutally confided: "Believe me, Stefan, I understand. Strictly between you and me, unhappiness has been my travelling companion since I was younger than you..."

His words had shocked me, shaken something frightful lose.

"...but you are different, my son. What you are feeling is frustration not unhappiness, you are puzzled because you don't yet comprehend what your life is all about. Trust me and have patience, I will let you into a secret..."

I said to my sister: "People who can't love can't give. You should've learned that a long time ago." Had I learnt it?

She drew deeply on her cigarette, the end glowed red before her face. Her eyes didn't waver, but the hurt was still there. She didn't speak.

"Father understood that, about love and giving. Mother never."

"Father?" Quickly her head came up, she exhaled a stream of smoke. "What the devil's father got to do with it?" She shot it out, a spark of anger. I'd touched her core.

"He was an unhappy man. But he never stopped giving. You should know that, you tried to grab most of it."

Margareth was so like our mother, she wanted it all, she took it all. Still I carried that seed of hate, like Eva. And Tobias carried the scar.

She inhaled again sharply, spoke through smoke coming out of her mouth: "Absolute poppycock. Father was anything but unhappy – had a wife and four healthy kids and a life of luxury." She was shaking her head. And crisply tapping ash. "Born into money, inherited grandfather's business – born with a silver spoon in his mouth."

Father sat there behind his desk disclosing his secret. "Stefan," he said, "so many people are unhappy or dissatisfied, and none of them really know why. It is because they don't comprehend what happiness is and where it is to be found. Happiness is finding harmony within oneself, it is the ability to love and give selflessly without seeking reward. In truth it lies dormant in every single one of us waiting to be discovered. It is not to be found in the world or material things – this is the secret, my son."

I remember: I perched on the edge of the leather-and-steel-tube chair, leaning forward frowning with concentration, trying to catch every word. They sounded so wise and philosophical, they were magic words, weren't they? I thought: I must pass them on to Matthias, see what he thinks, will it take all night?

"Just look into yourself and ask who you really are and what you would like to be in life. Listen to that voice within you, Stefan, not to what the world outside is telling you you ought to want..."

"That was the trouble," I said to Margareth. "That silver spoon. He didn't want it."

"How do *you* know?" Aggression again. She stubbed out the cigarette.

"He told me."

"He never told *me*." Anger. Almost accusation.

"Would you have listened?" I said. "Would you have wanted to listen?"

No reply. She bit at her lips, she was chewing on them like she'd done since a child whenever she didn't get her way.

"He never wanted to go into the business," I said. "He was pushed."

"He told you *that*?"

"He'd had a dream. To live in Italy and be a painter."

"A painter?" She watched me. Disbelief.

"In his teens he fell in love with a sculptress. In Verona. Grandfather put a stop to it."

And I could hear him saying: "You see, my son, I discovered this secret too late, and I couldn't turn back. Look at me. Am I happy? Look in my eyes, they can't lie. One says the eyes are the window to the soul..."

I had looked. Was disturbed and confused. The meaning of his words went over my head. I'd looked very hard – but I didn't know what to look for, I didn't understand.

"Remember when you were a small boy?" he'd concluded. "How we would sit together and look up at the night sky and all the stars, and how it thrilled you? Well, that was the start of your journey, Stefan. In our youth we first have to learn about the universe and the world we live in. And this you have done very well. But now it is time for you to begin searching for the secret inside yourself..."

"*When* did he tell you this?" Margareth demanded. Was that an old flash of jealousy?

"When I was fifteen," I said. "He mentioned about mother too, he knew about it – her escapades next door with Herman von B."

"Jesus Christ. I don't believe it. He shared everything with me."

"He just told you what you wanted to hear, he didn't wish to disappoint." I returned her harsh stare. "Most of his life he spent doing what was expected of him..."

I could see him hanging there, his silver slicked hair parted in the middle, broken neck, like a dangling puppet. Hanging from one of the beams in the garage behind the sports car. I was still there when the doctor and police came and cut him down.

"The bankruptcy condemned the last of the charade," I said to my sister.

He looked so peaceful, laid out on the concrete – at rest, so calm, all his cares had washed away.

"Father was a wonderful and honest man," Margareth replied. Was that a reply?

"Father was forced to live a lie."

"Load of crap."

"He was glad to go."

She held on tight to herself. "God rest his soul," she said.

The ceremony of the funeral was over, father under fresh earth: tears and hurt and retributions, the calamity of the circumstance. And during the big funeral party which followed Margareth was gone, was conspicuous by her absence. She locked herself in his study the whole of that night, surrounded by his photographs and papers and books; she locked herself in with his love. It was as if he had taken the last of hers too...

I could feel my throat constricting — I'd recalled his parting words before Ester the maid rang the gong for dinner and we'd had to go. Cryptic words, a message I couldn't comprehend: "My son, remember my words and follow your dream. When the door to happiness opens, it will open other doors of its own accord. Life is in flux, nothing stands still and no-one knows what is hidden round the next corner. Times are always changing, and change doesn't always bring good. The rich can sometimes become poor, the poor sometimes rich. There is a solace, though — the rich are often paupers inside and the paupers are often rich."

Two years later he was dead.

Margareth watched me in silence. Our thoughts were meeting, I think. Those dark, dark eyes, almost black. Dry as a bone. Don't believe I'd ever seen them cry. Then they were falling, staring downwards, sightless, turning in. She'd stopped that munching with her mouth, ceased her nervous chewing now.

I didn't move, my seed of hate was like a stone. I twisted to distract myself, picked up my wineglass and drank it empty. Must confess, in that instant, I felt like drinking some more.

x x x

"Have to clean my face," she said. "And check on the children."

I was in the way. I stood up.

She flapped at the fallen flakes of ash on her dress, swinging her legs off the sofa.

I said: "I ought to be moving."

"Don't." She stood before me, standing full height; I had to look up. "Stay a little."

I spread my hands.

"Back in a moment. Fill up my glass, will you?"

I stooped, filled it, refilled mine too. But both only half. The bottle was empty. Unhurriedly I strolled over to the floor-to-ceiling sliding windows. One was open, I suppose because of the smoke. On the roof terrace beyond, teak sun-loungers on wheels stood scattered about, and children's toys. Further away, in the dusk, I could just discern a marble table with Italian ironwork chairs, and sun umbrellas, and flowering shrubs in big terracotta pots.

Hands in pockets, I stared through the glass. The sun had set. Orange glow in silhouette trees. Above, intense turquoise.

A few minutes later I heard sounds next door. A rattle of cups. Then she reappeared, empty-handed. I watched her cross to me, determinedly.

"Stefan," she said. Again she stood before me, in the twilight. She'd removed the remains of her makeup, her face was washed clean. "Thanks." I could smell the scent of soap. Frangipani. But her hair was still in disarray. She opened her arms, stepped close and took hold of me. She hugged me very hard.

"I was wrong," I heard her say from above. "You have changed. You've matured." She said it firmly into my hair. Her words warmed. The hug, too. I hadn't expected this.

"Well, I wouldn't have put it like that," I said. I felt her strength, her solid body. "In fact, I acquired a few drops of wisdom quite a while ago." I held her briefly, thinking: her marriage is broken, her dream has gone, my God she's really tough.

I held her till she let go. Without a word she left the room again.

I was still at the windows near the grand piano when she returned. Two large cups, the aroma of coffee. And another bottle of wine wedged under one arm.

"Made fresh," she called across the room. "Forgot the first ones." She was indicating the coffee. Her voice was practical, matter-of-fact. The tension had gone, some of the hardness too. She switched on lights. A buzz outside, like a bumble-bee. I glanced. For an instant I saw myself reflected in glass; my face looked back at me like a stranger. I turned away...

"Only the insect screens," she was saying. "Automatic." She had placed the cups of latte on the big glass table. Frothy milk. And that aroma I can't resist. "Annabelle has a new machine," she added. She held out the bottle and corkscrew. "Do it, will you?"

"Well..." I hesitated. "Yes, but not for me."

"For us both."

"I have to drive."

"Don't make me drink alone."

I pulled the cork, put the bottle down.

"There's such a thing as a taxi." She picked up her wine, drained the glass in one draught. Like a thirsty dog in summer, like an addict with his shot. Then, taking the bottle, she topped up my glass, filled hers again – she filled it to the brim.

"To us," she said. She held her glass, giving me mine.

We drank. I watched her over the brim. This evening we had come a little closer – this evening I could feel it. And perhaps she sensed it too because, standing there, face to face, she suddenly said: "Glad you've come, little brother." She drank again. "On the phone, was sceptical 'bout inviting you around. No regrets now."

I let the wine roll round my tongue. It tasted very good.

x x x

We drank. Then we drank some more.

And we talked – lying stretched out on the sofa at opposite ends, our legs up side by side. Mostly it was Margareth doing the talking; I was happy to see her start to slip, start to let go. She went back, in jumps, into the past, into our childhood, reminiscing; it made us both nostalgic. She even laughed now and again. She didn't mention Heinrich once.

The wine worked its spell; she became more lucid, less careful, it loosened up her tongue. And I slid into a stupor that made me tired, and heavy as lead.

By eleven we were both comfortably boozed – so much so, I smoked half of one of her cigarettes. By midnight we were inebriated. It was high time to go.

I rolled my legs off the sofa, managed to sit upright, propped on my hands. My senses spun, the room swung in circles.

"I'll ringa... ringa taxi," I pronounced. Staggered to my feet. "Havanummer?" I surprised myself at my own lucidity.

She waved a languid arm. "You kidding?"

"No... I'll ringanummer you give me."

"Where're you staying? At Eva's, did you say?"

Where? I stood there, swaying. The room revolved. But the carpet looked safely soft if I fell. I concentrated. "With Eva."

"She's in Florence."

"Ah-haaah... yes they told me."

"She called me a few hours ago."

I squinted at her. She'd drunk twice as much as me but I could have sworn she was still clear in the head. "Florence, yes..." Time to show her I was capable, too. "Lovely city, cityofthe... of-the-arts, but nevereverbeen... neverbeenthere. Been to half the countries in the world, wanna... haveago... have-to-go-there sometime." With great effort I sought and found her last sentence. "Eva's place – haveakey. Have-a-key…"

"Sit down, little brother."

I swayed again. Planted my feet wider apart. If you're pissed you plant your feet… "Why?" I said. I was having trouble focusing. Where was she? She wasn't…

"Better stay the night. There's a spare room."

Her voice came from somewhere else. Right next to me. How did she get there? Hadn't noticed her standing up; it was as if I'd lost a few seconds, as if time had jumped, like an old re-spliced film on the screen. I turned my head, wobbled, nearly fell…

"And don't want to be alone." She was taking up cups and glasses.

I stood there, deliberating. "Okay," I said. I really didn't care.

"Stay put. I'll go and check the bed's made up."

"Lemme help." I bowed to the table, squinting at the empty wine bottles. I guided my hands towards them, but difficult, they were swinging this way and that. Success. I had hold of them. I thought: say something intelligent. To suit the gravity of the moment. Something appropriate…

I began to speak, I think about Bacchus or someone, about the wisdom in the wine – but, glancing up, bottles hung like skittles from my hands, I found I was alone.

Wasn't that a rattling next door? Far away?

Carefully, I traversed the room, arms spreadeagled, balancing, like walking a rope. The floor kept tipping, treacherously. I did my best; I made it to the opening in the wall, went through. A tap was running, a clink of glass. I managed to register: a big table, lots of chairs, on the floor over in a corner toys strewn across a rug, and everywhere else an expanse of terracotta tiles. Bright light that hurt the eyeballs, made them ache. Ah… one half of the room had an island in the middle – worktops, cupboards, a steel hood hung from the ceiling, more hanging-cupboards up there too. A playroom, a kitchen, dining-room? It was big enough to be all three.

Deftly skirting objects in the way, I staggered towards the source of the sounds. Discovered Margareth beyond the island at the far wall. Circular white ceramic sinks. Two hands rinsing things.

I set the bottles down on steel. "I'll go 'n'… I'll get my bag from the car," I said succinctly.

"Think you'll make it?" She was wiping water from her hands, turning away. She was gone... "Sure," I said... Where was she...?

"Take these." She was back again, time was jumping again – a bunch of keys on a chain materialised before my eyes. "This one's the house door." She held one key on the bunch between finger and thumb. I focused with the care that was due. Such strong, long, red-painted fingernails...

Well – I made it. Easily. Only took me fifteen minutes to find the car two minutes away; two wrong side-streets, they all looked the same, just possible I walked right past the car the first time. Back at the house door I had a little trouble finding the correct key – there were eight of them: none of them fitted. Not even the black one with the pretty Volvo sign. I fiddled, frustrated, went through them again – started laughing halfway.

When I got back upstairs I was relieved to discover Margareth had opened the apartment door I'd accidentally closed. It saved another little game with those keys. I went inside.

Darkness.

And fresh air wafting, dispelling smoke. Just a glow at the far end of the long, wide, hall-like corridor, the opposite end to the living room. I walked a little more steadily, I walked towards the light. An open door throwing rays along the parquet floor.

I knocked; Margareth met me coming in. There was white night-cream in blobs on her face. "Sshh..." She raised a finger to her lips. Beckoned. "Children sleeping."

I entered. She closed the door behind me. She had put on a black nightdress; I could smell that scent of soap again. I glanced about, bag in hand. This, obviously, was not the spare room: spacious, pastel shades, large curtained windows, an antique dressing-table and upholstered antique chairs, another very large canvas on one long wall, a very big double bed. The feel of femininity.

"Guestroom bed isn't made up," she said flatly, rubbing in the cream on forehead and cheeks. "Not in the mood for bed-making this time of night. Come in here with me." She said it matter-of-factly.

I stood there, hesitating. I felt an intruder in a woman's world – like a maggot in an apple, or a splinter in the skin. "Maggie, I could sleep on one of the sofas. Tonight I could sleep anywhere."

Her summer dress and underclothes lay discarded on the bed, and other items, perhaps not hers, hung over one of the chairs.

"Scruples, little brother?"

"Well..." I shrugged. I cast a sceptical eye to the bed. It certainly was a large one – the girlfriend, presumably, needed sufficient space to park all her playboys. I glanced at a neatly folded nightdress, too, on the side furthest from the windows. Unusual colour, the colour of autumn leaves. "Inhibitions, perhaps," I suggested. "This must be your girl-friend's..."

"Sure it is. She shares it with me." She had dropped her hands, was wringing them together, rubbing in surplus cream. "Stop dithering – I'm shagged out. It's big enough for four." She stooped. And the bag was gone from my hand. "I'll show you the ropes – follow me."

I followed, a little awkwardly – my senses still dizzy, my head still heavy as lead. Two etched glass doors, quite an expanse of wall between. She went through one. A bathroom – about twice the size of my generous one in Nuremberg. Ventilation purring, remains of steam on mirrored walls. "Mind those." She indicated toys and children's odds and ends on the floor, pushed one out of the way with a quick sweep of her foot. I negotiated, squinting, with great success.

"Here, I've put out towels. Take a shower, will you – I'm finished. Next door is the dressing room, can hang your clothes. There..." She pointed to another glass door at the far end of the bathroom, then stooped, placed my bag on the tiled floor. "Leave you to it. Goodnight." She brushed a sisterly kiss across my cheek, and was gone...

Bidet, double basins square like troughs and ultra-modern, sunken bath and separate curved-glassed shower. Tasteful handmade Italian tiles. On the broad tiled bath surround, like on the floor, toy boats and floatable objects; they reduced the picture of perfect luxury, but humanised the scene. I showered; it cleared my head to a certain degree – then brushed my teeth, pulled on a long summer shirt I use as night-clothes when I'm not at home, when I'm required to cover my sins.

Went back to the bedroom.

Margareth lay on her back beneath a thin cotton sheet, fast asleep. There were five fluffy pillows, I counted them carefully – she lay to the left, she hadn't lied, there was room for four – about four nervous strangers, about a score of good friends – there was lots of space. She'd removed the bed-drape, the folded nightdress and her discarded clothes, turned out all the lights but one. She'd opened the curtains, windows too. Her black hair spilled over pillows, she'd undone it, let it loose. She appeared tired and older in her sleep, but her slumber smoothed some lines – she still looked very attractive: I fear Heinrich was fully aware of his loss.

I walked round to the window side. Silky pile carpet, seemed deep as a snow drift, soft as down. Turned off the light, after a somewhat long search for the switch. Darkness closed in on my aching eyes, like a black smog, like a drug. I lay quietly down on the big bed, slipping beneath the broad loose sheet – left two spare pillows between Margareth and me, discreetly keeping my distance.

Lying there, submitting myself to grateful sleep, I was aware of the soft mattress beneath my body moulding itself to me. I was aware, too, of the highness of the bed compared to my low, hard futon on its frame on the floor at home. This was like floating, this was almost sensual. Perhaps I should buy me one too.

I sank like a stone enclosed in moss, slipped into deep and curative sleep. In four hours fate would be coming to call.

Chapter 5

I surfaced from a swamp.
It seemed only moments had passed. Must've been more than an hour or two, though. I was awake again; I'd just been dreaming I was in a trap, being hunted and cornered, arms pinned, unable to move, legs sucked down in a morass. My brain was drugged, my limbs still like lead, and my bladder said it needed the loo.

I opened my eyes.

It was dark. The night was warm. Deep blue in the windows, faint lights pricking through, like stars, like scars of silver. They seemed to come from the sky and the square. I peered. Thin curtains drawn back, windows open to the night.

I wasn't able to move my arm.

I lay a moment, orientating. The scent of face cream was very intense. I could feel other heat too, on my body.

I twisted my head.

I couldn't see Margareth, just feel her. She'd rolled against me in her sleep, hand on my stomach, hair at my throat, trapping my arm beneath her.

I must go to the loo.

I attempted to move again. Margareth stirred, her heavy body on my arm, a captive breast caught between us. Carefully, I pushed back her shoulder, withdrew my arm. Big breast like a rubber balloon. She stirred again, mumbled, but didn't wake.

Quickly I slid free from under the sheet, rolled over the edge of the bed... That was my first little mistake: I did it like I do at home. For an instant, still sluggish from sleep, I experienced the unpleasant sensation of falling into a dark abyss. It was a bit like in some dream or like underestimating the number of steps down a stair and treading into space. With a thump I landed flat on my back with a blow that blew out my breath. Lay disorientated. I fear I'd shouted out, but I was lucky there. Above me Margareth merely shifted, began to snore.

I let my lungs recover, feeling foolish, then got up, groping with my hands in the dark round the end of the bed. I crossed the bedroom, still groping, made it to the bathroom. In my defence I find it fair to say that I was still slightly shaken from the fall. Fumbling in the dark, I couldn't find the light switch, took a step forward on the tiled floor and trod on something on wheels. There was a flash in my brain and another extraordinary sensation – one instant my bare feet had been on solid ground, the next they were up above my head and something shot like a bullet through the open doorway towards the bed. On this second unfortunate flight through space, this time gyrating, I must have flailed my arms in desperation and grabbed for support, caught a tall stand as I flew through the air.

Margareth told me, afterwards, the noise was unbelievable.

Again I lay on my back in darkness. For an uncertain dizzy moment I wondered who had hit me. A burglar with a baseball bat – or one of the children? Then lights were switched on and I caught a glimpse of Margareth bending down on her knees beside me. The brightness was blinding, I had to screw up my eyes...

"For Christ's sake – you all right?"

Slowly I began to move, checking my body for breakages but all seemed to be okay. I opened my eyes. "Yes," I said. I blinked at the lights. I was sprawled between the second washbasin and the bidet. My shirt was twisted and up round my hips. Wriggling, I hastily drew it down. Folded towels and combs and tampons were spilled around the floor...

She started to laugh.

I sat myself upright. "I don't find it particularly funny."

She couldn't stop, not straight away. She began: "Oh Jesus..." She drew in breath. "Indescribable." Her laughter burst out again, out of control; it sounded almost hysterical.

Carefully I picked myself up, righted the stand. She was gathering towels, folding them, still laughing. My bladder was bursting.

"Listen, sister, I need a pee."

That started her off again. Holding herself, nearly choking, she nodded dumbly and went out. I sat on the loo; I could hear her laughter breaking down, was it turning into tears?

When I returned to the bedroom, she sat in the middle of that big wide bed in the soft glow of a lamp with the sheet pulled up to her waist. She was wiping her face with a tissue. At the sight of me, her shoulders started shaking again and the start of fresh laughter burst down her nose.

I climbed onto the bed, sat beside her.

"Sweet Jesus!" she said, sighing. "You really okay?"

"Apart from a broken back, expect I'll survive." I grinned. "And you?"

"Yep." She nodded. She brushed at her loose thick black hair. "My God, that was funny."

I just shook my head.

"The noise!" She sniffed and turned away, blew her nose. The sheet sagged between us like a trough.

She had started speaking again... I glanced past her. An alarm clock the other side of the bed said twenty-five-past-two. I thought: hope to God she doesn't go on all night...

"...toy shot past the bed and hit the wall with such a..."

I watched her washed-out face and sagging shoulders, the black nightdress strings, her folded arms. Then I saw them – the bruises on her skin. Yellow and brown, but some of them blue. Raised my eyes to her face.

She paused a moment, her eyes far away. I thought of Heinrich's angry hands. I said nothing.

"And you had an erection!" Her laugh burst again, it was like a bark. "That was just too much!"

Weakly I smiled.

Her hand pointed under the sheet. "Grown a bit since nanny Helga used to bath you."

"I fear not much," I said. Could feel embarrassment burn my cheeks.

"Crap." She dropped her hand to my thigh. "It's broad enough, that's what counts." She tapped it the way a housewife dabs a dead fish. "If a dick's too long, it can hurt like hell, can spoil the orgasm." Said matter-of-factly – as if discussing the fit of a shoe or the size of hotdogs. It didn't sooth me though, my inferiority went too deep. I kept my eyes averted.

A chuckle, her fingers twitched. "Piece of luck you didn't land on it, might've snapped it off." Another laugh – that ended in a cough.

She teased a minute or two longer, but in a sisterly kind of way. Pleasing to hear, different from the old days. It was cheeky and mature, not nasty, not intending to wound. Was my seed of hate being humbled? Did I have the right to hold a grudge?

I sat there in silence. I thought: this is probably doing her good, this is maybe to my gain.

She stopped. She was smoothing the sheet on her lap, distractedly. The glow from the lamp was a puddle. Then she asked in a different tone: "Found a little fanny to pop it in now and then?" and she was pointing back at my penis.

"No," I said.

"Still living alone?"

"Yes."

She was watching me blankly. "It'll happen some day."

"Will it?" I could hear the bitterness in my voice. Cold black eyes, dark circles. She must have far worse things on her mind.

"Let's get some sleep," I said.

Her eyes still on me.

Unexpectedly, she reached out, stroked my face. "Feel closer to you tonight," she said suddenly. And in her eyes, just for an instant, something flashed, cut through that cold.

"Yes," I answered.

I couldn't say more; I hoped she felt me reciprocating. I touched her face too, her creamy damp skin, touched her tiredness. And kissed her briefly beside her mouth.

She turned away, stretching, switched off the lamp. The dark wrapped round us like a skin.

x x x

There was a faint breeze like invisible fingers on my face. Slowly I opened my eyes. They were sticky from sleep.

It was day. But the light was soft, a pale lemon light. Through the open windows the early air wafted, disturbing the thin, white, drawn-aside curtains. It was fresh and cool and smelled of dawn – on my skin it was almost cold. It tickled my arms and legs. There was the first sunlight touching the tops of the trees; in the dawn the leaves were thirsty green, and the silence was full of birdsong. I thought vaguely, dreamily: how can there be so many birds in the middle of the city.

I lay on my side, unmoving, looking out of the windows, looking out at the day. My head was hollow and my eyes seemed to burn – it was bad waking up still feeling tired. Must be very early – get back to sleep.

Behind me Margareth breathed loudly, unevenly, as if she were having an unpleasant dream; she lay very close. My back was cold. I'd lost the sheet. So I twisted, fumbling behind me, found a loose edge, gave it a tug. But it went taut.

Margareth mumbled something and shifted heavily, bumped my bottom. Lethargically I rolled onto my back.

She lay stretched on her stomach, the sheet twisted round her like a corkscrew, head burrowed between our pillows, her hair so thick and spilled I couldn't tell which way her face was turned. I raised my head slightly, intending only to see if I could steal back a bit of the sheet from the other side of her... and to my horror discovered we weren't alone.

It was so unexpected, my heart contracted. All I could do was stare. This must be her girlfriend Annabelle. She lay slightly crooked, on her back, she had two thirds of the bed to herself and, like me, had lost most of the sheet to Margareth, except for her turned-up feet. Yes, I just had to stare. A lovely redhead with lots of freckles, long legs; I don't think I'd ever seen a redhead so close up before, not in the flesh, and nearly naked.

That was the problem, that was my undoing.

She wore a nightdress, admittedly – the same nightdress the colour of autumn leaves I'd seen folded on the bed, I recognised it from the night before - but it had ridden up her body in her sleep, and exposed certain secret parts of her I'm sure, under the circumstances, she wouldn't have wished to expose...

Head still lifted, I peeped over Margareth's rhythmically rising and falling back – rapidly glanced at the face in case I'd been discovered. But the eyelids were closed, she was still fast asleep. Rust-red hair strewn over one of the pillows, dangerous and wild, lashes pressed unsuspecting on cheeks. With heart bumping nervously, I allowed myself another naughty sneaky peep...

Just for a second or two.

What sacred thighs, slim but not skinny, their beauty unfolded, their secrets laid bare. And where they converged how hallowed the miniscule red patch of carefully shaved hair. How blessed the hint of what lay just below, a tiny bulge, a tabernacle, pink-shadowed fold, her holy-of-holies. I would go down on my knees and pray there all day, if she gave the word.

I swallowed. The tormenting sight at once aroused. After all, I'm simply a respectful man, just one of those dogs who religiously adores the female form. And this woman truly tested the devotions.

For God's sake look away...

So spiritual too, the way that hip was lightly uplifted, the freckled leg bent, it parted the knees – they were indeed sinful and breathtaking knees. The colonies of freckles were scarcer here and, migrating upwards, up the holy twin sisters of those heavenly thighs, they thinned progressively until there were no freckles at all, until there was only smooth white skin, confirming my worship, persecuting my faith, resurrecting my sin. My God, what gorgeous and slothful skin.

I swallowed again. Made my eyes make a tiny jump – to her tummy, to the hollow of her waist where the hem of the slipped nightdress began. Almost no freckles here either. Funny, I knew nothing at all about the distributions and tendencies of freckles, this was a new world, a paradise. There was a little mole, though, there near her hip, how very appealing – and... oh, now that was a naughty irreverent navel.

Devoutly, I watched it – on the pale rounded swell of her stomach it gently rose and fell, rose and fell. I have an endearing weakness for navels especially when they're sunken, mysterious, not just a knot.

My gaze crept upwards, such an indiscretion, folds of crumpled thin nightdress. Beneath it the bulge of breasts fallen sideways, cupped by cotton, a line of lace. Above, skin visible again – a mass of speckles, brown on pink, an inordinate concentration, interrupted only by two flimsy shoulder straps. On her throat they thinned again, over her chin and cheeks not many now, just a little sprinkling on her nose and forehead and all around her...

Oh God.

I took a sharp breath, my whole body froze. Her eyes had opened. They watched me blank and sightless for an instant. I squirmed, went hot all over. Wanted to duck, couldn't move a muscle.

They widened. Abruptly. Stared. Oh my God, what incredible eyes – intensive green, green like a witch's, green as the sea. I'd never seen eyes like these before. A sudden frown. It wrinkled her brow. A lift of the head – one of her hands was reaching to an ear, removing an earplug of wax. Long elegant fingers.

The lips parted. "Who the devil are you?" Said haughtily, in suppressed tone, a hiss, hardly more than a whisper, presumably because of Margareth. Such sensual lips, curved and wide. Generous lips. A hard and steady stare.

Helplessly I returned it, half-hypnotised, unable to speak...

She sat up. I swallowed rapidly. Her breasts fell beneath the nightdress, hung like fruit. She was propping herself on a hand, and as she did so glanced down – noticed her nakedness. The eyes flared, were there again, there was anger in them now. With the stroke of a hand, rolling her bottom this way and that, she pulled the hem down over her hips, over the start of her thighs – the whole movement was done coolly, without panic, it was almost regal.

"Have you lost your tongue?" Accusing green eyes. Oh what a voice, so rich, a voice in ten thousand. So self-assured too, with a carefully controlled touch of irony and arrogance. I liked that – I sometimes liked to employ it myself.

I gave a faint nod. Meekly. Trying to win time, trying to salve an untenable situation.

"What an impossible cheek." Her chin had raised. "You were staring at my body." She carried herself like a queen.

Yes, couldn't deny that one. Oh God. I winced. I thought: wouldn't you have too as a man, though, in my place if the tables were turned – who wouldn't feast on a sight like that?

"Sorry," I mumbled. It came out like a croak, my throat was so dry. Faintly I grinned at the awful sound. Then immediately regretted it – that created a totally wrong impression. "Unforgivable," I added humbly. That came out cracked too, sounded almost debauched. I cleared my throat. Must be all that wine we'd consumed.

"Absolutely," she retorted. Indignation.

"Yes," I agreed.

"In my sleep of all things."

I nodded. Just nodded. Wasn't that safer?

"You dirty bugger."

Bugger? Again I winced. I watched those eyes as best I could. Would a queen use such a word? Again I decided it best to say nothing.

"Absolutely unheard of behaviour."

"Well actually..." I began. Then had to stop. She was sweeping at her wild mass of hair, shaking it back from her face; it stopped me in my tracks. My God, what thick hair, what a glorious colour — it was like a bush on fire, like the sun going down.

"Well what?" Eyebrows raised. It wrinkled her forehead, gave away her age — yes, she wore no makeup to disguise, there were faint crow's-feet at the corners of her eyes and hollows of skin at her throat. She must be late thirties — forty even?

"Lost your tongue again?"

"Yes," I confessed.

"Do you make a habit of gawping at women in their sleep?" More arrogance in the tone now. The chin was higher; she regarded me down her nose — such a straight and imposing and noble nose.

"Of course," I said. "At every opportunity." I blurted it out, I shocked myself.

"Now see here. A cheeky bugger, to boot."

I stared at her. She was so unusual; she fascinated, I just couldn't take my eyes off her. Yes she fascinated — but she antagonised too. Did I have anything to lose?

Unexpectedly, Margareth snorted. Made me jump. Her breathing changed, interrupted. I dropped my eyes, afraid we'd woken her. But she was only turning heavily in her sleep again. I watched her roll over onto her back with a lurch, watched her snatch the last of the sheet from her girlfriend's feet. Allowed my eyes to linger there a moment. Such strong elegant feet, they were slightly turned in: families of freckles on their upper sides, long thin toes, manicured but unpainted nails...

"So?"

Hurriedly I turned my eyes back to the face, trying on the way to avoid glancing at those gorgeous gangly and naked legs, that nightdress hiding those hanging breasts — but not quite succeeding...

Loudly, Margareth began to snore.

There were those green, green eyes again. Steady, staring, distain in their depths. The eyes mesmerised. I couldn't have looked away now if I wanted. I gulped. Glimpsed fragments of her body floated like flakes in my mind. They thrilled me, they...

"Don't look at me like that." Said quietly but sharply.

I blinked. Panicked. Had she seen? What had she seen – were my eyes giving pieces of me away? Or was she telepathic?

But I had to keep looking. Oh God, those eyes, that face, that hair...

"I said, don't you dare." Very, very insistent now.

I wriggled with discomfort, blinked again. Forced myself; I made my eyes drop for a second. But there was her body in the way – oh that heavenly body, so mature, so full of holy curves. It wouldn't get out of my way. So I looked back to her face again, swallowing again, I couldn't help myself.

"This is my bed."

"Yes."

"Who the hell are you?" Still distain in those eyes, and aloofness.

My God, she possessed such character, she had so much poise – this couldn't be the woman my mother had meant, one of Munich's superficial society eligibles. She was too natural, too...

Between us Margareth snored on sublimely, each time she breathed out it vibrated her lips.

"I'm waiting."

"Actually..."

I shifted position awkwardly. My arm was cramped – I had to prop myself on an elbow. I gazed at that face. How could I save this situation, make amends – how could I melt her cool? Try a little humour, perhaps?

"Actually," I repeated, "would've thought that rather obvious."

"What is obvious?"

"Who I am."

"Not at all, explain yourself at once."

Oh how that face diffused, how it radiated personality. I was captured already; if I were a knight from those old-fashioned days I'd court her with the deepest of bows and the sweep of a cloak, I'd smite all her suitors and win her ribbon, carry her off on...

"I'm the lover," I said.

"Lover? What on earth do you mean, lover?"

"I believe that's what one calls it."

"Calls what?"

"When one gets picked up."

"What the devil are you drivelling about?"

"I'm not drivelling."

"Actually you are."

"This woman here – Margareth," I indicated the snorting supine form, "she invited me back." I stopped.

A brief pause. Disbelief, a shake of the head.

"For a drink – and so on," I added.

Another small frown – what a lovely frown, it wrinkled her freckled nose, furrowed her brow. Then: "Are you attempting to take the Mick out of me?"

"The Mick?" I cocked my head. "I went into this place, found her propping up the bar – she'd had more than a few, said her marriage's on the rocks."

Ah, that rich unwavering green gaze again. And those eyelashes – my God, they were red and curling like her hair. "Did she now," she said. She said it antiseptically.

"And needed company."

"Your company?" How derisive she managed to make that sound.

I shrugged. "Here I am."

A sniff. A toss of the head, of that wild and heavenly hair. No answer.

"I'm a sort of saviour of damsels in distress," I offered.

"Poppycock."

Poppycock? Hadn't Margareth used that funny word as well? Perhaps they swapped vocabulary with their intimacies, too.

"If the price is right." I twitched my eyebrows.

"I don't believe a word of it."

"No?" I said.

"No." Such certainty. Had she seen through me already?

"Ah."

"What's 'ah' meant to mean?" Her chin was raised again. How proud it made her look.

My turn to frown. "I have to confess," I said.

"What?"

"As a matter of fact, I'm her brother."

A calm drawing-in of those generous lips. "Her brother?" A tired irritated echo.

"Stefan."

"Stefan," she repeated acidly. The way she said it, it sounded like a curse.

I had difficulty returning that gaze now.

There was a brief silence between us. Only Margareth like a puffing Billy. I wished she'd stop snoring – it undermined the seriousness of the moment.

Slowly, deliberately, the elegant fingers played with the earplug, pressing it, squidging it; I saw it was soft and pink, yes it was definitely made of wax, I suspected she wished it were my nose or perhaps some other soft part.

After a few seconds she said, rather slowly I felt, and with distastefulness on her tongue: "Oh yes – I've heard of you," as though to say, Jesus look what the dog dragged in.

Then she added: "I don't wish to be disturbed again, I'm dead tired."

And I thought with chagrin, with envy: yes, I bet you are, having just returned from the sweaty arms of your new lover – no doubt you gave him what he was after quicker than expected.

"Yes," I said. "I'm sure you are." I said it with penitence, though. Oh God, why was the pack always stacked against me?

"And for the remainder of your brief time in my bed, pray keep your eyes to yourself." Again she was looking down that lovely arrogant nose.

I took an unsteady breath – this was the finale, the curtain was falling. "You're a woman who mesmerises," I managed to get out. "But I do apologise." Maybe I should don my armour after all, cast down the gauntlet and joust to the kill with that bastard of hers.

The green eyes regarded me unflinchingly. They were calm still, still cold – only the anger was gone. And the wide mouth was an earnest line.

"Accepted," she said. "For what it is worth."

For a moment that gaze remained on me. Then the face was turning away, she was fluffing her pillow and lying down. But what had that been, just for an instant, had there been something? Was it my imagination or had the corners of that mouth begun to curl, had I glimpsed the shadow of a smile?

I stared. Long body, rust-red hair spread over the pillow again, her face was out of sight. She'd twisted and turned her back on me, and her bottom was like a bell.

x x x

It was during breakfast that fate cast its fickle dice.

We were in the luxurious kitchen. Sunlight flooded. Long lines of light on terracotta floor tiles. In one corner, a children's play place, toys and animals and bright-coloured things strewn on a generous square of old rug and overflowing across the floor.

The table where we six sat was long enough for a dozen. Annabelle and Margareth had positioned the children strategically at a distance, with us the other end and me opposite them; they talked in undertones.

I'd been up two hours already: after failing to fall asleep again I'd washed, shaved and made a hasty scoot from the bedroom leaving the sleeping women alone. Had had a chat and played a bit with Margareth's younger son David when he'd appeared on the scene at about eight. He'd been surprised to see me, I think it perked him up a bit — it was from him I learned that his elder brother on school exchange in England wouldn't be back for three weeks.

Now I sat with them all, on my relative best behaviour, keeping my head low. There was something in the air.

I sat there, with little appetite, eating out of politeness and to prolong the point of departure. Dreaming of how it might have been. Yes, I kept a small appropriate profile as dictated by the rules of the game.

About half an hour went by.

The two of them were talking, I think, about Annabelle's previous evening, and Margareth's with me — personal private introspections, things which didn't concern me, so I deigned it better not to intrude. Only now and then did Margareth draw me in with a comment or a question, which I responded to neutrally. Surreptitiously, when she wasn't looking, I let my gaze linger on Annabelle, watching her, observing her. Her presence was like a magnet, it kept drawing my eyes and jerking my heart, stealing my breath away.

I only half-listened to their conversation; I was listening with my eyes.

She wore a plain blouse and rusty-brown trousers – hidden from sight now where she sat, thank God. The trousers were very tight at the top, fell in loose folds to the floor. I'd hardly dared look at them as she'd entered the kitchen to start preparing the breakfast. Yes, the way she'd walked in with a swish and proud head and a brief and distaining nod, she indeed carried herself like a queen.

She sat tall and straight-backed, concentrating on Margareth and her food. Her long, wavy, red hair was more orderly now, different now, partly pinned back and bundled high with wooden combs, partly hanging loose. I poured fresh-pressed fruit juice, sipped. Studiously she ignored me. All her movements and body language told me and the world she was merely tolerating me for the duration and after breakfast she'd ask me to go. But already I'd decided to depart before the hammer fell.

The atmosphere was strained.

Margareth looked subdued – in her situation, understandable, just a couple of days after separation. And Annabelle looked tense and tired. Two serious women, side by side with their heads together – earnest expressions, long faces; it seemed something untoward had happened on Annabelle's date.

I broke a bread roll, nibbled, cut the slice of smoked salmon.

The children were fully occupied with their breakfast and one another, and more than a little loud. I'd been perfunctorily introduced to Annabelle's pair – a chirpy four-year-old son Marcel, a precocious and cheeky six-year-old daughter Martina. Marcel was dark-haired, dressed in little blue shorts held by broad braces over the shoulders, sat perched on a battered children's highchair that had witnessed better days – and Martina, propped on a pile of cushions, wore a pretty red dress; crocheted edges, big moon daisies sewn all over. A miniature of her mother – long golden-red hair hanging, her forehead framed by a fringe. She and her brother ignored me too. Only Margareth's young David smiled a hopeful smile at me now and again – but then, he was banking on a game of football after breakfast when I left and he remembered me well despite the three years since we'd last met. Small, shy and frail for his age, he looked ill; he was getting on for eight.

I drank from my cup of coffee, watched Annabelle over the rim. Yes – she was fascinating, and beautiful in an old-fashioned kind of way. Those high cheekbones, that hair, that wide mouth, the way she held her head. Very sensual, very mature.

In the middle of a sentence she suddenly cast a brief glance at me, caught me watching. Cold eyes, blank eyes. Aloof.

"...you win some, you lose some – men're all the same," I heard Margareth saying flatly. I thought: ah now, I could contribute something to that one. But I held my tongue, I let wisdom get in the way.

Annabelle spoke, her head was half-turned away. I watched her lips moving. Those expressive lips. They were painted red-brown, like her trousers, the colour went well with her hair. Only two little lines in the corners, too. I made a correction – maybe I'd been mistaken, she could be a bit younger, maybe thirty-seven.

Oh God, how she tantalised.

Her voice was rich and clear, her words almost academic. She didn't speak for long, though. Then she ceased. Hands resting beside her plate. Margareth replying. She listened to her – and as she did the tip of her tongue peeped out, sliding along her lips.

The minutes ticked by.

I continued eating, a minimum of butter, and English marmalade. Tried to indulge in the flavour, but I was so nervous, so on edge.

A burst of giggles at the other end of the table.

She leaned back in her chair, head turned briefly, checking the children. How long her neck was, and how elegant. She breathed in, deeply. And her breasts swelled making round hanging mounds in her blouse; she wore no bra, did she? The sight...

Her head had turned back unexpectedly – she was gazing directly at me again. Our eyes met. Oh those startling cold green eyes. I felt a wave of hotness swamp me, like I'd felt the first time in her bed. I tried – but I couldn't look away. Her gaze was steady, unblinking. It thrilled, it made me sweat again.

Margareth was glancing at her, then at me. A brief pause.

Margareth twisted her head, said something to the children, sharply, but I didn't hear the words. There was silence. A stretching silence between her and Annabelle and me. Oblivious, the children chattered on, a pitter-patter of childish talk. Seconds ticking. I looked at my sister; met her dark eyes. They watched me over her raised coffee cup. Guarded, blocking, giving nothing away. But they were frowning.

"What're your plans for today?" She asked it suddenly, unexpectedly.

I shook my head. Had to adjust.

"Staying in Munich?"

"No," I said. Then I thought: you fool, don't say that. "At least, not necessarily another night..." I began.

"Have to get back to the firm?"

"No." I shook my head again. "Taken a couple of days off."

She nodded. Just nodded.

Beside her, Annabelle slid a slice of fresh fruit between those red-brown lips, following it in with a finger. She sucked on it, deliberately, was she savouring the flavour? Eyes closed, red curving lashes, freckled face; I longed to be that fruit.

Again a silence.

My plate was empty, my glass of juice too. I could hear the minutes ticking away; my time was running out. Were they waiting for me to say something? Were they waiting for me to stand up, excuse myself and say goodbye? They'd planned it together, hadn't they? To give me the push if I tried to overstay, they'd been long enough alone together in the bedroom and bathroom to plan that.

"More coffee?" said Margareth, matter-of-factly.

"Well..." I grasped at the straw. "Please."

She poured. Put the stainless steel thermos jug down again. Was looking at Annabelle, Annabelle at her. Exchanging glances. Something passing between them. Unreadable. Was that reproach in Annabelle's eyes? Were they saying – you shouldn't have done that? Were they hinting – offer him an inch and a bastard like this will take a mile?

I stirred in a little milk.

When this cup's empty, this'll be the *coup de grâce*. Then I'll stand up, say cheerio, take David down to the square outside for that promised football game, and then that's it, drive back to Nuremberg...

For God's sake say something, I ordered myself – take the initiative, try to save the situation, this'll be your last chance. I took a breath, I said: "And what are your plans for today?" I said it without looking up, tried to say it casually.

"Nothing special." It was Margareth answering. "You, Annie?"

A pause. Then: "No."

I raised my eyes. Annabelle's chin rested on hand, elbow on the table, her gaze still on Margareth. "I would suggest we take the children to the English Garden," she said. A very slight pause. "The two of us." Said pointedly.

"It's school holidays," Margareth explained. "Whitsun break – in the kindergarten too."

More exchanged glances.

"Ah," I said. And then I added: "I presumed, Annabelle, you were a career woman and would be rather occupied with work."

Her face turned to me unhurriedly. Chin still rested on the back of her hand, on those beautiful slender long fingers – on fingers with two rings. "And what made you presume that?" Distant eyes. Distant, and guarded.

Oh God, that face, the chin slightly raised and inclined at an angle – and that body, that deportment... she had a glow, had an aura about her. I thought: you're one in a million.

"An instinct, I suppose," I said.

The way she sat there, and responded, that unapproachability – she seemed wrapped in a cloud of calm, in a cloak of comfortable wealth. She seemed to say: what you see and hear is only the tip of the iceberg, don't come too near or I'll sink you.

"Instinct?" A hint of lifted brow.

"Yes," I said. "That indefinable something. And your hands."

She blinked. But didn't take away her eyes, or her guard. Eyebrows high and arched. "My hands?" Had I managed, at last, to surprise her?

It lent me strength, it emboldened me. "You have interesting hands," I said. "Artistic hands." And unforgettable face, I thought. And haunting body. Everything about you is haunting.

She watched me in silence.

Margareth had stood up, was walking round behind the island in the middle of the room. Her head was hidden by the stainless-steel extract hood and hanging cupboards.

"I guessed you might have something to do with the theatre," I said. "Or perhaps are a concert pianist?" I felt better now, being able to talk, felt my confidence slowly returning.

Still she regarded me, blankly, sitting erect; I risked a rapid glance downward, couldn't help myself. Was thinking of her body again, found it hard to hide the thought.

"Not a bad guess," called Margareth in the background. The clack of a saucepan, a cloud of steam, a wire basket being lifted. She came back with a nest of boiled eggs. I watched them watching each other. Communicating. Solidarity between them, a symbiosis – such easy intimacy.

"I studied interior and graphic design," Annabelle said. Neutral voice, under perfect control. "The piano is a hobby."

There were those clear green eyes again. My desire was welling, it thickened my throat. She was staring into me. What could she see this time? Lasciviousness, lust – did my mouth look lecherous too? Should I shut my eyes?

I returned her stare. What could I say now, then? With words I was failing to reach her. Could nothing draw her out of her shell? Oh God, those eyes...

There was something creeping into them, into the green, something changing. They'd noticed, hadn't they? They knew what I was thinking. Was that anger? Were they filling with disgust again as they'd done in her bed?

I opened my mouth to speak. But nothing came. I wanted to mention her piano, her grand piano at the living room windows, say something intelligent, maybe a bit philosophic – but in my belly was only desire, in my head only hunger to be touched...

And then it happened. Just for an instant, deep in that green – it was like a veil drawing aside... a sudden glimpse of something bright, a flash of something wild, or was my hunger playing tricks?. Had for an instant in those depths sparked the colour of my desire?

My heart bumped. I felt dizzy...

"Like a boiled egg?" Margareth asked, prosaically.

I glanced. Her expression quizzical – almost guileless.

"Actually..." How could I think about eggs? Hurriedly I glanced back at Annabelle. The stare was still there but the veil was closing... Another flash – but this time a flash of fury, yes almost of hate... So I'd read the message wrongly.

"No? As a kid you used to love them." Margareth's voice, half-taunting.

Take one, I ordered myself. Take advantage, help prolong your stay. My fingers were reaching. "Thanks," I said. I grabbed at an egg, I grasped at the straw.

"There's an eggcup."

"Ah." The brown speckled egg had burnt my fingers.

"Fresh toast."

"Yes." I removed a piece. And said to Annabelle: "Thanks for your hospitality."

"Accepted." Blank stare like a concrete wall.

Hadn't she said that once before? And then added something nasty? Yes, I'd read her wrong. Nothing to lose now. "The condemned ate a hearty breakfast," I said. I managed a cracked grimace.

And Margareth shot back: "What's that meant to mean?"

"I suspect I'm in the way."

"Suspect?" echoed Annabelle. She had risen, her eyes were elsewhere.

"You reckon you're over-extending, then?" That was from Margareth. Said with such exquisite sarcasm.

Annabelle stooped at the other end of the table, distributing eggs to the children. Her whole body was now in view; the tightness of her trousered bottom made tautness in my brain.

"No thank you, Auntie Annabelle," I heard Margareth's little David say in his quiet polite way.

Auntie? I thought. Annabelle tapped her small son Marcel's egg, sliced off the top with a spoon.

I said to Margareth: "I imagine it isn't every day your girlfriend Annabelle wakes up to find a stranger in her bed."

"Don't bank on it."

Annabelle had returned to her place. They smiled faintly at one another – reciprocating knowing smiles. It irritated. They had me out in the cold.

I broke open my egg, cut toast. Looking up, I said to Annabelle: "You work as an interior designer then, or in graphics? Or both perhaps?"

She was sweeping back her hair with both hands. She shouldn't have done that; it exposed the delicious nape of neck. "Both," she said flatly. A pause, then: "Freelance."

"Respect."

"Thank you." Said expressionlessly.

I nodded. Glanced away for a second. By chance my eye fell on Martina. Methodically and with a marvellous precision, she was picking off pieces of shell from her egg.

I looked back, took a breath. "And you manage it in spite of your two children?"

"Correct." She was pouring more coffee now, for Margareth and herself.

I searched about in my head. Her answers were cut so short there was nothing to hang a new thought on. Try something less banal, I ordered myself.

"I can well imagine that the children are very fulfilling..." I began. I was struggling... I dipped another finger of toast into the soft liquid yoke the way I'd always done as a child... "But no doubt you need food for your intellect too – a fact that presumably many mothers fail to recognise."

I leaned forward, toast and egg-yoke poised, opening my mouth, and as I did so caught a glimpse of young Marcel's face watching me. His round eyes were wide as saucers, were so wondrous I missed her reply...

"I'm sorry," I said, munching. "I didn't catch..."

"You ought to know," Margareth translated flatly. "You've got a daughter of your own."

My eyes glanced between the two of them. "I lacked any talent to combine," I said to Annabelle. "I fear I buried myself too much in my job."

"In your wife, too," Margareth said tartly.

"Yes," I agreed. "In a manner of speaking."

More exchanging glances, more subtle smiles. Annabelle sipped coffee; I saw she drank it black.

I thought: my God, why the hell did Margareth say that? Does she smell a rat, can she smell my lust – is she throwing another spanner in the works just to make doubly sure?

"My ex-wife," I explained. "She..."

"Sensibly, she ran out on him and took their daughter with her." Margareth, elucidating – with more of her smooth sarcasm.

I thought: what are you doing to me, Maggie? I cast her one of my best and meanest of looks. "That's rather unsisterly," I said.

"Truth always hurts," came the ricochet. She pouted strong red lips. And to Annabelle: "My younger brother's a bloody-minded little devil – nobody can stand living with him for long."

What should I say? Her bitterness was apparent, her intention very clear. "You're being unjust." I spread my hands...

"Uncle Stefan?" A whisper. Fingers touched my arm. I looked round. David stood beside me; large sad eyes. He pulled gently on my shirt. Beyond him I glanced Martina, her near-naked egg gripped in both hands, angelically peeling off the last bit of shell, dropping it on a strewn pile on the timber tabletop.

Another gentle pull of the fingers.

"Yes David?" I tried a smile; I was very fond of David. Although we seldom met, I never forgot his birthday and Christmas presents...

"Uncle Stefan, when can we... when can we go and play football?" Still in a whisper, his serious pale face almost on a level with mine...

"Not now, David." Margareth's interrupting command. "Go and sit down again, finish your breakfast."

Martina's head tipped on one side, her small mouth trying to bite at the egg.

"Uncle Stefan, can we go afterwards, when..."

"David, I said go and sit down," repeated Margareth louder.

"Martina!" Annabelle's voice now. Insistent. "Little snail, please put it back in the eggcup and use your spoon."

Engrossed, oblivious, she ignored. I watched, fascinated. Children's hands, like chopsticks, are nature's natural tools – just a little clumsier. I started to stand, I could see what was coming...

"Martina, *no*!"

Too late. Martina gleefully squeezed the egg. It burst.

"Hang on, David," I said, patting his shoulder as I passed. Yellow yoke dripped down Martina's fingers and hands onto the pile of shell, made a snaking trail across the table as she twisted, innocently licking her hands.

"Martina!" Annabelle called. "You silly goose – I warned you." She had arisen, but I was already there. Firmly I guided Martina's dripping hands and the egg to the plate, and with my napkin began wiping her fingers, wiping the worst of the mess. Small perfect fingers, they reminded me of Andrea's...

"I'll take over, thank you."

Annabelle was there, she stooped with a sponge. She was suddenly so close she made me draw a sharp breath, her fingertips almost brushed mine. I stepped aside. Brusquely she began cleaning Martina's wrists and hands. Her body bent like the bough of a tree, her blouse had fallen open. I glimpsed the start of freckled breasts.

Martina struggled, complaining.

"Sit still, silly goose."

"I'm not a goose." Martina struggled again, cocked her head, peering up at me. Hurriedly I raised my eyes.

"And stop looking away when I'm speaking to you." Deftly Annabelle wiped cheeks and chin. "You're too old for this nonsense."

I could smell her perfume. It was faint and discreet...

Small hands scrabbling ineffectively. "Mamma, I'm not..."

"Behave yourself."

The scent intoxicated, I breathed it in. My desire was so strong my legs went weak.

"And stop making an exhibition of yourself."

Close up, her red hair was wispy and fine, loose strands fell on her naked neck. My God, how I'd love to kiss that nape. Still she leaned, concentrating. Oh that holy body... it stood barely two feet away; if I were to reach out I would be able to stroke that neat bottom, stroke that hair. I swallowed rapidly; my hunger overwhelmed, my feelings had come undone. Again my eyes slipped, glanced for an instant at her peeping freckled breasts — they were elongated, firm, they...

They were gone — suddenly. Had risen with a jerk, the cotton tautening, closing upon them. Hastily I looked up, discovered her eyes. They held mine. Oh God. I panicked. They'd caught me again, now they'd caught me staring down her blouse. Awkwardly, guiltily, I gulped. Tried to block my mind, but the hunger in my body kept on breaking through. Helplessly I gazed back at those unforgiving eyes.

"How dare you." Said suppressed beneath her breath.

A small movement at the edge of my vision. Martina's fidgety arm caught the jug of juice — it wobbled, slopped. I shot out my hand to catch it. I guess I was nervous, I guess any man worth his salt would've been in the circumstance... Accidentally I struck a mug of cocoa with my elbow, knocking it over as I grabbed the jug; a vulgar brown liquid tongue stuck out across the beautiful timber table.

Martina giggled again, clapping her hands. I heard Marcel beyond her squeal with delight.

"Annabelle..." I began. "I'm sorry..." But I had to stop — there were those arctic eyes, unchanged, like before; I had to stop because of that stare. It ignored the jug and the mug, it was turned full on me still, like a searchlight, like a sword. Words choked in my throat, I could hear my heart, my body impaled. Could only stare back. I wanted her so badly, I wasn't in control. Oh God, the red flag was up... something exploding, I suddenly sensed it, a lid about to blow off...

She took me by the chin – fingernails squeezed. It was short and sharp. My skin contracted. Only lasted a second then they were gone – but they took me completely by surprise like the crack of a whip or a cat stroked too long digging its claws. No-one's ever done something like that to me before.

I tipped my head on one side; I still disobeyed, I was impotent. She stood unmoving, quite stiff, she'd drawn herself up to full height. Her chin was high, she looked like a goddess. Yes, she stood there before me, half a head taller, I had to look up to look at her face. Her lips parted, her wide mouth was a slit I would have sold my soul to slide my tongue inside. I simply kept on beholding her; her body was a beacon, her proximity a drug. Oh my God how I craved for her touch.

Then her hand came at me again. It took me by the upper arm, firmly, crushing; her head swooped close – yes, there was her perfume again, bewitching, and the brush of her hair on my cheek. I was a drowning man... A whispered hiss in my ear: "I warned you. Don't you ever look at me that way again." The manicured fingernails once more in my flesh – I prayed they'd stay for ever.

But they didn't. Again they were gone – and so was her perfume, so was her hair. I was left standing, deserted, with only a sensation of where she had been, and the last sacred particles of that scent...

"You cheeky bugger," Margareth pronounced, from the other end of the table. She'd lit a cigarette, was watching me. She tossed her head, blowing smoke in the opposite direction to the children...

"What's a bugger?" little Martina demanded. Inquisitive eyes.

"An adult word," came Annabelle's prompt reply. She was mopping the mess with the sponge. "In this case it means clumsy idiot." She turned away, walking back over to the enamelled sinks.

"Idiot, idiot," sang little Marcel, banging his egg-spoon clutched in his fist.

"But Mamma, he only spilt cocoa," Martina called, sensibly pointing out. She was twisted in her chair, the cushions beneath her dress twisting too, peering queryingly after her mother...

"Uncle Stefan?" A careful tug, it was David again. He pulled more firmly, saying in his small subdued voice: "I've finished my toast, can we go soon?" And when I looked there was butter on my shirtsleeve where his fingers had been. I smiled at him again – I really did my best. "Please." He gazed up at me with eyes so big and innocent they could have softened stone.

I glanced across to Margareth to check but all I saw was clouding smoke – she'd followed Annabelle round behind the kitchen island.

"I'll fetch my football, it's in the bedroom."

"Fine by me," I said, defeated. "I ought to be moving anyway." The hour had come, I had no aces up my sleeve – it was time to beat a retreat. "We'll have to ask your mother first if it's okay, though."

"Mummy, Mummy..." loud now, excited "...can I get down now? Uncle Stefan says..."

"Pipe down, David. I heard." Margareth was returning, cigarette still in hand. "You're not the only grain of sand on the beach." Impatience in her voice, and irritation. Annabelle was coming with her, they were side by side.

"But Mummy," more subdued, "Uncle Stefan promised..."

"What Uncle Stefan said'll have to be saved for another day." She leaned, tapped ash. "Change of plan, kids..." She inhaled, blew smoke up in the air, glanced at Annabelle walking to the windows. "You're all coming out with me." Then to David, again: "Uncle Stefan and Auntie Annabelle are going to stay and do the breakfast things."

My heart lurched. I watched Margareth. Studiously she avoided my eyes. Were my ears playing tricks? I looked over at Annabelle. The clack of windows being opened. Her arms were stretching, her back was turned, her bottom pert and provocative... she stood there luscious against the light.

"I'll help them, Mummy," David said stoutly, stubbornly. "Then we can all go out together."

"They also have things to discuss." Margareth roughly tapped ash again. I thought: she's angry, isn't she?

"*What* do they have to discuss?" It was Martina. Her tone was emphatic. She flipped back her long red hair. Her stare was indignant.

"Adult things," said Annabelle. She was passing us at the table, ignoring me, returning to the sinks.

"What adult things?"

Clack of a bin, a rustle. Annabelle stooping down, half out of sight. "Don't be nosey, little snail," she called. She straightened again, visible again. The sound of water. She was rinsing, leaning.

Beyond the hanging cupboards I could clearly see her; I followed the bow of her body.

"We're going to the English Garden," Margareth said.

"But Mummy, I want to play football."

"Well no-one's intending stopping you," she snapped. "Lots of other kids there to play with." Aggressively she stubbed out her cigarette.

"But Mummy..."

"And we're calling at *Panelli's* for ice cream on the way. You've earned a double portion."

"Yes?" Hesitance, but eyes brighter.

"Ice cream, ice cream," little Marcel echoed happily, banging with his spoon again like a drummer with a drum.

"Off with you," Margareth ordered. She was rising, gathering cigarettes and lighter. And then she said it... the last words I wished to hear: "Say goodbye to Stefan, all three of you, then off to the bathroom."

My heart contracted, I sank like a stone. That's it, I thought. That's what they've planned. Not my reprieve – just a brief brutal lecture from Annabelle on male manners, then I get chucked out on my ear.

Margareth was helping Marcel clamber out of his high chair. He scampered over to me, said goodbye, followed more slowly by Martina. She cast me a last suspicious glance, said goodbye grudgingly. She had her mother's hair and that lift of the chin, but she didn't have her eyes. I was glad about that. She followed her brother out. Margareth and Annabelle were exiting too.

Like a miniature gentleman David offered me his hand, stiffly and formally. "Goodbye Uncle Stefan," he said.

I stooped, gave him my customary hug; he hung onto me longer than usual. I planted a kiss on the top of his head. "Next time, we'll get that game of football, David," I promised. I tried to say it gallantly, which is not easy from a sinking man. In the background stamping feet, a small voice calling: "I want strawb'ry and choctlit and..." and Margareth shouting, "*First* the toilet, *then* wash your hands, afterwards brush your teeth *tho-rough-ly*." David smiled too, suddenly, but it was weak and fleeting, it was very like mine. His eyes fell elsewhere, he was letting go my hand; I guess he'd already forgotten me before he reached the door...

I was alone.

Slowly I seated myself at my place at the table again. Nervously waiting for the storm. Stared at my cold abandoned egg and half-eaten toast. I'd lost my appetite completely now; I felt a bit like that egg.

I thought: if only my friend George were here, that master of the passions, that maestro of the bed. Yes, my God, I needed him now, to lead me beyond my limits and show me where to go. I smiled wryly at the egg. Ah yes, George would know, he'd had the best of teachers – German mother, a pretty little stripper back in nineteen-forty-six, father a jaunty British Army de-Nazification officer so impressed by her credentials he made them his permanent home. Maybe I should give George a quick call – lock myself in the loo with my mobile and whisper my predicament, beg for crumbs of his priceless advice. But my two mobile phones were in my overnight bag in Annabelle's dressing room a hundred miles away, and the hourglass had already run dry.

Chapter 6

The apartment door shut; it shut with a solid slam, cutting off the chatter of children's high voices and the scurry of their feet.

There was silence.

And into the silence quiet footsteps coming along the hall outside. I rose. Annabelle entered. Without a word she turned, walked behind the island.

We were alone together.

I stood there near the long table, she was over by the pristine white enamel sinks. I didn't know what to say, what to do. All my bluster and bluff had forsaken me, I was an empty puff of wind. I ventured a glance. She was washing her hands; her red head of hair dipped forward. I watched the water fall.

Waiting for the onslaught.

I felt helpless as a lamb. I thought: what would George do? Sidle up to her, slinky and cool as Casanova, tear off her trousers with a flick of the hand and take her on the worktop, or do it grinning standing up? She'd go willingly, greedily, wouldn't she? He had a way about him, women never said no to George...

And me? What did I do? I simply stood there shaking, nervous as a teeny. Help me, George, for God's sake – send me inspiration...

She turned off the mixer tap; she just pushed its silver stick. Her freckled arm reached for a towel; I followed her effortless movements as she began to dry her hands. For God's sake at least say something, I said to myself. Isn't attack the best form of defence?

My eyes wandered, I was reduced to seeking inspiration on my own: the beautiful kitchen with its island in the middle, expensive fittings, the stretching timber table before me still covered by abandoned breakfast things – the luxury of space. Should I say that, perhaps? You possess a very tasteful apartment, did you design it all yourself? Or... I glanced wildly about – was she watching me, it was suddenly so still, did I look like a hunted animal, like a cornered beast?

She was hanging up the handtowel in a row of other towels; she wasn't even looking at me. But in a moment she'd be coming. My eyes alighted in panic on the untidy table – yes, of course, I could ask her that... Annabelle, can I help you clear this stuff away? Or shall I...? Oh God...

She was emerging from behind the island, coming towards me...

The sentence shrivelled as soon as conceived, like a stillborn baby in my brain...

Ah, my God, this is it.

But she had stopped; she was ten feet away. She leaned her bottom on one of the tall ebony cupboards this side of the island where the cupboards went up to the ceiling, went down to the floor. Yes, she had stopped, she was considering me; she was still so far away.

"Well?"

That was all she said. The expanse of terracotta floor tiles stretched between us like a no-man's-land not to be crossed. I had to say something now. I spread my hands... I dug about, desperately, my mind was in a whirl. I was still digging – but all I found was: "Can I offer any assistance?"

I discovered one of my hands, nonchalant, indicating the tabletop. It surprised me – how could I do something so casual, inside I was a bundle of nerves.

She folded slender freckled arms, leaning back her head on the cupboard, looking at me; she was looking down her nose.

"Do you think you could?" she said. She said it flatly. A total lack of expression.

Could? I thought. "Well..." I spread my hands again. "Yes, I suppose I could. I'm used to doing..."

She sniffed. It froze me in my tracks.

She raised her eyebrows – it wrinkled that freckled brow. "Do you think that is really what you want to do?"

I swallowed, loudly – clearly I heard the gulp, had she heard it too? My thoughts were clogged.

"No," I confessed. I muttered it.

She made me so small; like a worm, squirming on her hook. What the hell was I doing – what had I done, or tried to start? A woman like this could eat me for breakfast.

"Well?" she repeated.

She was just staring at me. So refined, so calm, so cool.

"Look," I said, "Annabelle..." I stopped. "I really do apologise."

"For what?"

"For the greed in my eyes."

"You are becoming repetitive."

"I felt..." I began, "...felt perhaps a double dose of repentance might be appropriate."

Minimally she nodded. "That's better."

"Is it?" I blurted. At least I imagine I blurted. It emerged quite quietly, though.

And she said: "No doubt repentance is a possible first step, regardless of whether uttered in bed or without." Said with distain.

Oh God, I thought, she's back to that again.

I didn't speak. I couldn't. Haplessly I stood there.

"On the condition, of course, that it is meant sincerely."

"Of course."

"Of course?"

"I have great regret."

"In my bed you said you were sorry too, then over breakfast you did it again. In fact you do not regret it at all."

Did I? No, of course I didn't. I frowned. Lowered my eyes for a moment.

"I meant, I regretted hurting your feelings."

Slowly she turned her head this way and that, rubbing the back of it on the cupboard – not taking her eyes from me.

I don't know where I found the courage – perhaps it was that silence causing me discomfort, or because I had little to lose; the thought just popped into my head.

"Did I hurt your feelings?" I asked.

She stared at me. She stilled her head. Her eyes didn't blink. Had I touched something at last, had I managed to get under her guard? She began rubbing her head slowly to and fro again. Then she said: "Do you make a habit of staring at women in this way?" and her voice had a brittleness to it.

A habit? I swallowed again...

"Undressing them with your eyes?"

Had to wince at that one, inwardly at least. And I thought: well, not a habit, no. Just occasionally – if I'm sexually starved or feeling depraved. But I'm normally unlucky, normally there's nobody deserving around I fancy to feast on with my eyes.

So I said so. "No, very seldom," I said, and added: "I hope as seldom as you."

A flare in her eyes. Then: "You are a good liar." She watched me.

I shook my head. "I'm many negative things, but that I'm not."

"No?"

"No."

"And pray, why should I believe you?" Still she leant there against that high cupboard, still her arms were crossed; her breasts lolled, resting upon them.

Don't look at them, for God's sake – or maybe this time around she'll grab for a kitchen knife, go berserk.

"Do you want to believe me?" I ventured. Was the old me starting to march through again?

She blinked. She stirred. But she didn't push away from her prop. "Admit it," she said down her nose. "You are one of those men who makes a hobby of gawping at women."

"Well I always turn around for beauty."

"You must have a pretty stiff neck then."

"Sadly not – beauty is a rather rare creature." I thought quickly. Added: "In Warsaw or Dresden one can spy it perhaps twice a day if one's lucky, in Munich once a month."

"It is not beauty you are after, your goal is purely seduction and sex."

A single-minded woman; how could I wean her away from this subject? "I imagine a lot of males would take that as a compliment," I tried.

"And you are a typical male."

"I'm afraid you're reading me through the wrong glasses."

"So?"

"Yes."

Eyes considering me, carefully. "What kind of man are you, then?"

"Well, I have my little vices," I suggested, "but..."

"I am certain that you do."

"But women wouldn't be one of them."

"You mean to pretend you are not the..."

"Yes, I guess I'm not the perfect man – I pick my nose in public, and when no-one's looking eat all the crumbs from the floor."

"Do have a shot at being serious."

"Aren't I being?"

"I know better." Green eyes gazing. Steady eyes, beautiful eyes. For her I'd look over my shoulder all my life.

I said earnestly: "It seems to be my fate to be a misunderstood man."

"That is not what your sister told me."

"Ah." I spread my hands. Oh God, I thought, what the hell has Margareth given away? "I fear she's not the perfect sister, just like I'm not exactly the perfect man."

"If not misunderstood, at the very least you are a slippery one."

"Slippery? Did she tell you that too?"

"She told me you were doomed to divorce."

I tried to take the jump in my stride. "Well that's probably true," I said. "Though I believe she was also making due reference to her own marriage."

She stirred her folded arms slightly again, it stirred her breasts. Oh God, how those breasts aroused, and that tilt of her hips, the sensual way she leaned there regarding me – yes, the curve of her body was like a bow. In spite of her distance and her game of cat-and-mouse she was once more inexorably winding me into her web...

I stiffened, got on my guard... the tip of her toe had traced a small arc on the tiles. She lowered her eyes, looking at it. "How long ago?" she said.

"The divorce?"

"Naturally."

"Six years."

"Haven't you found someone new?" Neutral voice. "With all those vices and tricks of yours?" Her eyes were there again.

"No." I hesitated. Inside, I thought: why did she ask that? Is she offering a crumb? Quickly I said: "Though not for lack of trying." I managed to return her gaze. And added: "Despite the wisdom of the scriptures regarding search and find, it unfortunately didn't work for me. In fact I've more or less given up the good fight." Good, I thought, we're on a new track. Sounds more constructive, sounds...

"Have you now." Said dryly. "That depends on what you are searching for. I should have imagined what you have in mind is as plentiful as pebbles on the beach."

Ignore that one, I decided. "In reality I've been looking out for perfection for the best part of twenty years."

"Perfection?"

"Yes."

"That is a fool's game."

"That could be at the root of my problem."

"And your first wife? Didn't you find perfection in her?"

"It might be a greater accuracy to say she found me."

A lift of a freckle-infested eyebrow. "Then she herself most certainly was not searching for perfection."

Another barb. I winced. "You are too generous." My fingers wriggled. Quickly I stilled them, though – they might give me away. As innocently as I could, I slipped one of my hands in a trouser pocket. Was she playing the same game still, or was it deadly serious?

"You do me an injustice," I said.

No answer. She continued observing me down her long and noble nose, this jewel of a Jewess in gorgeous witch's disguise.

Her foot traced another small arc. Then she said: "You are one of those lone wolves who hang out in bars lasciviously leering at women."

Ah, such delightful sarcasm. She was enjoying this, wasn't she – making me small, putting me down?

"You're wearing those glasses again," I said.

"On the contrary. I know your type: pick them up, seduce them, leave them in the lurch then go roaming again." She pursed her lips.

"You're a hard woman."

"Your sort is not difficult to recognise."

"Your opinion of men is about as tender as a bull in a teashop."

"China shop."

"Yes. Of course."

"I have my reasons."

I was losing the struggle. I stood there, one hand still in my pocket, the other beginning to squirm. Quickly I considered: should I hide it too, in the other pocket? Decided against it. Too casual, too laissez-faire. That would probably create an even worse impression. I summoned up the courage again, I tried a confession: "Actually I don't often hang out in bars, but were I able to make the acquaintance of such an interesting woman as you there, I'd change my habits like a shot. I'd..."

"Oh would you just?"

I cocked my head a bit on one side – could it maybe help melt some of that ice? "As a matter of fact, in the hope of finding you I'd frequent those bars every night and all the other bars in town."

"And no doubt other unsavoury establishments, too. Aren't they all grist to your mill?"

She wasn't taking me seriously, was she?

"Ah," I said. "You mean like strip clubs and peepshows and what not?" Against all the odds I cocked my head again. "You display deep knowledge in this area, perhaps you might like to enlighten me – my naïvety thirsts to..."

"Pray, don't let me cramp your style. You have made such an erudite beginning."

No, I wasn't coming on.

"Would you divulge something?" I asked.

"That is highly unlikely." Piercing eyes.

"Indulge your secret and tell me, where do precious exceptions to the rule like you go if not to bars and peepshows and...?" I paused, and squinted, produced a pained expression, "...I've been scouring concert halls in the intermissions, and prowling museums and art exhibitions till my shoes wore out and my hair went grey. Where do the special ones like you go?"

"I would have thought that perfectly obvious. They deliberately go where you are not." Cool, cool gaze. Not one melted drop from the ice.

I thought: my God, she always has an answer, can't she give me a break?

"I'm sorry to hear that," I said. "I'd imagined, with your indomitable intelligence and natural grace, you would've been endowed with better judgement – I mean of my true character." Unconsciously I flapped my free hand. Caught it on the outward swing, got it under control again. It hung there awkwardly, flaccid as a flag yearning for a puff of wind, it hung as if someone had shot it.

"Stop blustering."

"Yes," I said. Better not contradict.

"You don't fool me for an instant," she repeated.

We were going round in circles...

"It is my body you were after." She said it antiseptically.

Oh God. Yes, I thought. "No," I began. Then straight afterwards I thought: you're lying, you told her you don't lie – but doesn't everybody lie about these things...?

"Yes, but only partially," I corrected. "Agreed, your body awakes – no, radiates, sorry – an insatiable and unholy reverence..." I stumbled, stopped, had got a bit in knots there. "I mean irresistible, of course," I corrected again. Had tried to say it humbly though. But all the time, her eyes were there. So I started to add: "But it's not only..."

"You are in for a whopping disappointment," she interrupted calmly.

Damn it, I thought – I walked into that one.

"You're an unforgiving woman," I said aloud.

"And you are a roaming cowboy of the very worst sort."

No I'm not. Just set off on the wrong damn foot. I said: "Is there nothing I can do to show you how uncharitably you're treating me?"

"Given your one-track mind and clumsy limitations, out of the question."

I thought: I'm a knight of old, I'm fighting against the odds. "Allow me..." I began. Feebly I lifted my broken sword: "Allow me nevertheless to present a small offering..."

"Offering?"

"Yes."

"If you must. If you can."

"If I may." My God, she's so fast. "Well yes, I confess to my original sin of putting my wrong foot forward..."

"Is that what you call it?"

"For lack of a more poetic expression, yes."

"Uh-huh."

"But you carry the blame for irresistibility, for tantalising. You dangled your apple under my nose, and I'm only a mortal man."

That red head of hair rubbed to and fro slowly on the ebony wood. Steady neutral pondering gaze. I thought: have I managed to reach her with this final thrust, have I managed to pierce her perfect skin?

But all she said was: "Oh come on Casanova, don't play Adam and Eve with me. Can't you do better than that?"

No I couldn't. "Well I imagined..." I began. "I suppose..." But again words failed. Ah yes, I'd supposed so many things, I belong to that breed of men who can't communicate this kind of stuff.

So I gave up the fight.

I dropped my sword with a tinny rattle – closed my eyes, balled my hidden hand. I'd been after so much more, hadn't I? Her quick intelligence, her character which radiated, her cheekiness which sometimes broke through. And other things too: the furnace of red hair, the depth in those bewitching green eyes, the way she held her head – those indefinable unexplainable things one just can't put one's finger on. Couldn't she see that, couldn't she feel it? Hadn't I had a sense of destiny, an indelible print that this one was written down for me?

Explain to her, for Christ's sake.

I can't. One can't put things like that in words, I'd sound like a soap opera, like a stilted cliché. I stood there uselessly, was I starting to sway? My God, open your eyes, else she'll think you've gone into a trance or something, or fallen asleep on your feet.

I opened them. The green gaze was still there. Nothing had changed. Still she leaned there on her tall cupboard.

I was paralysed. I couldn't touch, she'd have murdered me. I couldn't speak, so I tried to show – I did it the only way I knew: tried to tell her with my eyes...

She stared at me. Into me. Didn't say a word. She was absolutely still. With penitent heart and head tipped on one side, I gazed at her face, at that furnace of hair – I told her how I felt inside, I concentrated very hard.

Was anything changing? No, nothing. She wasn't answering.

Or...

Or was I wrong? Wasn't there perhaps a little something, wasn't there a subtle difference – in the air about her, in the atmosphere? Was it my instinct? Or was it merely hope playing tricks, wishful thinking? A voice in my brain said look more carefully. So I looked.

Yes. There was a change in her eyes. Something was melting – the enmity, the sarcasm? That coldness? Wasn't that a slight softness coming through? And her mouth, her lips? Was that a faint fold in the corners?

The lips slowly parted... the tip of her tongue appeared. Small and pink. A tiny point – it slipped, it moistened. Just for a moment. Then it was gone.

The eyes blinked. Oh God, that gaze. So deep and green. The eyes were widening, they were very intense, were they telling me something, letting me in? Was that veil once more being drawn aside?

A movement. Distracting. Again I stiffened, steeled myself. A toe began stroking the floor again. I could hear my heart. It pumped, it bumped, I could clearly hear it in my ears. And my senses were sharp as a razor blade. Her gaze consumed – I could hardly keep watching. I thought: say something, anything – break this silence before it bursts...

"Sssh..." she said. That's all she said. Had she known I was going to speak?

Slowly, very slowly, she unfolded her arms. They freed her breasts. I had to look – only for a second. Her gaze didn't wander. Something glowed, burned, then flared in her eyes. Her hands were lowering. She placed them behind her, they were out of sight, her bottom pressed upon them. Her head was back – her hips were tipped, her stomach was curved like a crescent moon. She looked so desirable she made me sick.

She spoke. Again. Her voice was low and controlled, intense as her stare.

"You are looking at me like that again."

I couldn't stop. Her eyes mesmerised.

"Don't look at me like that."

I lowered my eyes. I had to obey. But then I had to look again.

Her lips were parted.

"You're doing it again," they said.

I couldn't speak. They were lovely lips, expressive lips. They were well-formed but they didn't pout – weren't pumped up from doctors' needles, not swollen, not silly or artificial like those from the superficial set... they were her lips...

"You have dangerous eyes."

Her sentence hung in the air. I swallowed. Do I? I thought. That I doubt. Still I couldn't speak. Nobody had told me that before; it must be the way she looked.

Again I glanced down – as far as I could. I suppose further than I should have. And started, startled...

Was that another movement? My eyes dropped from her thighs to her feet. Yes. One leg was bending, a foot sliding back, a heel had raised. Then the top half of her body was in motion, pushing away from the ebony cupboard. She looked like a cat about to spring...

She was coming towards me.

Yes, my brain was dizzy, I was shaking inside. I held my breath, watching. I remember: her trousers swished. Oh the tautness at the top, how it showed off the bulge, the little creases of her holy place...

"Sit down."

She came round the table, she was coming close.

I sat. Like a dog. I would've begged if she'd said it. I would've done almost anything.

She stopped beside me, but she didn't touch. She stood motionless, stood so near I couldn't see her face. I began to tilt my head back, following her body – from her slightly rounded stomach, up her blouse to her breasts slowly rising and falling... her proximity overwhelmed. I perspired. Could feel her gaze, had to stop my eyes before they reached hers. Didn't know what to do with my hands – wanted to run them round her waist, bury my face in her body. Wanted to feel her warmth, hold her; I hungered for her warmth. Unsteadily I laid them on the table.

She stood there. Not speaking.

I glanced up to her eyes. They were different eyes, their gaze shredded my stomach, they sucked me in. Again I had to look away. Stared at my hands lying near the breakfast things, I hardly dared to breath.

Then she was turning... something brushed me...

I blinked. I nearly panicked. That faint smell of her perfume again. And a fleeting sense of contact – just for an instant. It burnt a hole in my brain. A sound of plates or cups on wood being swept gently aside.

She'd brushed me. With her hand – or her arm. Or her leg? Accidental? Or had it been her purpose...

She'd sat down on the table right next to me. One thigh rested an inch from my hand. If I splayed my little finger, its tip could touch the trouser cloth. The thigh was flattened, spread on wood. My hand lay paralysed. There was sweat prickling my forearm, perspiration in my palm.

I wanted to touch, I dared not move. Didn't even dare move my head. I was the dog who'd disgraced himself, she was the one who could call the tune, she had all the cards in her hand. I could see her body from her hips to her feet. Her legs hung down, her knees apart – her hands together in between. The way they were placed they seemed to be praying, in the temple before her holiest of holies.

Gently her legs began to swing to and fro – slowly, almost imperceptibly, a mesmerising pendulum. With each small movement her thighs moved too. It was so sensual I feared I'd lose my mind. I thought: I have to look up now, no other choice. Can't just sit here like a pimpled adolescent staring at her thigh; I'd left it too long as it was. Everything I'd done since the first moment I set eyes on her, I'd managed to go and do wrong.

I lifted my eyes. And as I did, I noticed... her hands changed position, seemed to cease their prayer. My heart was lurching, I felt tense as a spring. I was so aware, so over-sensitised, I noticed every detail; I could have picked out a crack at a hundred yards, I would have jumped at the touch of a fly...

Had to tip back my head; my neck was like rust. My eyes reached hers. They stared down upon me. They were opened like windows, the veil was gone. This time I knew it, they were letting me in. The pupils were large, dilated; I was passing through – my heart leaped at what I saw, I couldn't breathe, I could hardly believe what I'd seen. I thought: this kind of thing one only sees on the screen. I stared, I sweated; those eyes were a mirror, I was looking at me.

Her hands separated from each other... I sensed it – did I only sense it? I couldn't see anything outside her eyes. Yes. There was a movement, something below. Still I was helpless, still I couldn't move. My arms were cast-concrete, just lumps on the table...

One of her hands was raising; I felt it rising into view. It was coming very close... fingertips touched me, they brushed my cheek. I jumped. They were light as a leaf, they cut like a blade. Closed my eyes again. Couldn't help it. The fingertips traced a faint trail on my face...

Don't let them go away...

Before I was aware, I had raised my own hand, my fingers closed over hers. Stiffly, clutching, I pressed them clumsily to my cheek... felt their warmth, their slender form. Their tenderness. My eyes were tight shut – my world was reduced to the feel of her touch. My heart seemed to stop beating. Everything stopped. Just for a moment time stopped still. I was in space, in limbo, the pace of life had ceased. I thought... I thought nothing. Nothing at all. All my senses were concentrated on that spot, on that contact between her world and mine. I wanted to hold those fingers for ever...

I opened my eyes. Looked at her.

Felt guilty, couldn't move a muscle, felt such a fool. She didn't speak, didn't smile, didn't move. Even her trousered legs hanging down were stilled. She simply didn't do anything. Just those eyes communicating.

Seconds passing...

Her eyes absorbed. They sucked me in, swallowed me whole. I began... I cleared my throat, about to speak...

"Sssh."

The sound was soft; it shocked my senses like a gun, like her touch had done, penetrated my brain. It...

It thrilled.

Hadn't she said that once before – a minute ago, or was it an hour? Somehow, though, it hadn't hit me – not like now. Now it dug into my depths, awoke this thrill, this longing, stole this hunger from my tongue, spoke to me, across that wide, that lonely gulf: it said take it easy, said there's no hurry. It said everything.

She was bending slightly, stooping to me, lifting her other arm. It came into sight, reached to me. She held my face in both her hands.

I wanted to stand. Reduce the distance, bridge the gulf – draw her close, close the bond to her body, feel her warmth in every pore...

But still I sat there turned to stone.

She was leaning forward, her thighs sliding from the table. Why was I unable to move? Her feet touched the floor tiles – was that really her face coming near? Were those real lips starting to part, their moist gloss reflected the light from the windows, did they really intend to kiss? Or was this only that cruel dream again, and in an instant I'd be awake like so often before, reality taking me by the throat, gloating at my loss?

I watched that face, followed those eyes. They came nearer – they were still not smiling, was something wrong? They were open wide, they looked so serious. Were they asking questions, were they querying me? Or was what I could see only a reflection of my fear?

A slight pressure on my cheeks, a light press of her fingertips, as if talking to me. She was drawing me up. Had the impossible happened and it wasn't a dream? I felt so pathetic, I couldn't believe, it wasn't real. I was still cramped and incapacitated. I had to be led; I couldn't take the initiative. She drew me with an elegance. I had to obey, I prayed to obey; she had me eating out of her hand.

I rose slowly. I stood before her, stood there trying to be a man. Inside was more like a lamb going to the slaughter. She was at least six inches taller than me, it was history repeating itself – even standing quite straight, again I had to look up. I felt ashamed, I felt so small in every way. Except for my feelings.

She gazed down at me. I gazed back. I was staring at my inhibitions, staring at my passion. Would this fantasy dissolve? I touched her. I touched one shoulder with my hand. Tentatively. Touched this dream, still half-expecting it to perish. Oh, that freckled face, it fascinated. A private beauty radiating. My fingers lingered on her shoulder, trembling. The blouse was thin – the feel of her skin through silk excited. I breathed in that scent. I breathed in the colour of her rust-red hair, breathed her breath in her hovering face. Glimpsed impressions: lilac blouse, tiny buttons, a line of lace – I was aware of the creases on her brow and near her eyes, the length of red lashes, aware of strands of loose untidy hair, the swell of her breast as she breathed; I was aware of everything...

But still I stood there, hesitating – savouring the moment, flavouring each sensual glance. Neither of us had spoken a word – words seemed so superfluous.

Yes. She was waiting, wasn't she?

The thought made my stomach churn. Feelings bumping, expanding. My God, I was nervous. So tense. Could she feel it too? See it too? I'd plastered a feeble grimace like a mask on my face to disguise. Feelings starting to explode – couldn't keep them under control any more; I was a dog on heat. The dizziness grew, a heady dose like being drunk. I looked at her lips: her mouth was opening but somehow I knew she wouldn't speak. How I'd love to kiss those lips, that mouth. I looked at her eyes as best I could. It was my move now – my move in this critical game of chess.

I touched her other shoulder...

And the dream continued. Still her face hung there, her body didn't disintegrate. I felt her flesh, real flesh, could almost feel the blood pumping through her veins. At last I was touching her world. It was warm, soft. I was bridging the gulf. My God, this sensation... my loneliness was dissipating, had turned to longing – it wasn't a dream. Yet still I was scared, still I scarcely dared to believe. Carefully, as carefully as I could, I stroked her skin with a finger. Felt it through the silk as though the blouse wasn't there. The voice in my head was there again – said: slowly, slowly. So I did it very slowly: I tried to touch her like I guessed she loved to touch herself...

My feelings were overflowing...

Carefully, ever so carefully, I let my finger wander, over her shoulder, over the small roundness and down to her arm, inch by inch I followed it with my eyes...

She stirred... Careful. My hand had come dangerously close to her breast...

Unexpectedly she drew in her breath. Her body swelled... the tip of my thumb brushed the side of the breast, accidentally. It was only accidental – I wouldn't have dared if I try. I panicked. Quickly I withdrew my finger from her arm.

She breathed out. Rapidly. Her breasts dipped. She stirred again. Her breath was coming quicker. It came through her mouth, not her nose. I deliberated. My heart bumped unsteadily, then jumped with joy, with anticipation...

I touched her breast again. Glanced. Her mouth was open like a hole. Yes, I touched that fascinating breast on the side where it rested near her arm – furtively, lightly, as lightly as a raindrop landing on a leaf, just for a few seconds, just as though it were my own I stroked it through the silk. It was resilient as rubber, soft as a peach, hung like ripe fruit from a forbidden tree.

She sighed. It was almost a moan.

My breath accelerated to a rasp. Her shoulders sagged. Her chin came up, her eyes were staring, oh that open mouth. She raised her hands to my throat, they were tender as down. I'd never been touched this way before. Judit had been so... for God's sake don't think about... she let them glide, let them slip. Then pressed her palms upon my chest as if to push me away...

My God, had I already gone too far? I dithered. Let my arms fall hurriedly. I just stood there. Afraid to do something else wrong, or too soon, something which might offend. The prize was too great to put at risk. My brain cried out, my thoughts in a whirl; my body was a knotted bundle of nerves.

I braced myself, waiting to be rejected, waiting to be shoved away. But her fingers were moving again, away from my chest – they crawled like soft spiders under my arms, reaching behind me. She was leaning forward, just a little, was drawing us close, very close, very slowly – and her cheek was turning away. And as it turned, looking up, I glimpsed closed eyelids, dark red lashes on tired skin, those crow's-feet at the corners. Then they were gone... and her hair was there brushing my face, tickling; my heart missed another beat, I was struggling for air, did I dare breathe? Her perfume filled my nose, killed my brain, it was stronger now, more intense now, it smelled of my longing... I breathed it in. Then gulped for air again... her fingers were creeping up my shoulder blades... she was straightening, stepping to me... her hands drew me from behind, fine strong fingers, certain hands – I felt her breasts press into my chest then her stomach was there soft on mine, and her hips, her thighs...

Our bodies had met, they could hardly come closer... our two bodies were almost one. She stood quite still. Not a sound in the world. I couldn't hear a thing.

I stood there too. Arms helplessly dangling. My face was buried in her hair, my cheek upon her neck. And I knew for sure... I'm not fantasising, this is not a nasty trick. I felt myself sway – I moved my feet, a tiny shuffle, I didn't dare to lose my balance... raised my arms, so far away they scarcely seemed to belong to me – placed them round her timidly, enclosing this wonderful body, embracing it.

I shut my eyes.

I was in paradise, I'd entered heaven. The gates had opened, I was walking through – the disbeliever, that lost religion I'd thought was gone for good, I was a believer again.

Yes, I stood there, as frozen as she.

Felt her fingers high on my back, on my bones – I could count every fingertip digging in my skin. Oh that body, that heat, that press of this female body moulding onto me... was I ready, was I worthy to receive?

There was something starting to flow...

I could distinctly feel it, seeping through my body, flowing through my mind, loosening and relaxing – it was like a thousand rivulets running into one, smoothing, soothing me, washing me clean, melting all my tension, untangling each knot.

Yes, standing there, a broken doll, all through my being everything was beginning to flow – like thick stiff tar made molten by the flame, like liquid honey tipped from the lip of the crystalline jar. I could even start to sense, somewhere down in my depths, a hint of my old self stirring. Hello my unfaithful friend, it's grand you're revealing yourself once more; I thought you'd got the blocks for ever. I could perceive, too, those ghosts departing – the loneliness and isolation, all the depressions and hang-ups and dirt, it was like a sink of washing-up water when someone's pulled out the plug.

I began to breathe more freely. I was crawling out of weary winter where all is dead and cold; I was sprouting like the first bud, I was sailing into spring. And saying goodbye to it all.

My legs went weak, my muscles sagged; I feared maybe I'd fall. I hugged onto that body, sucking up its warmth and drawing on its strength – I held onto that softness very tightly, I leaned on this mighty prop.

But all at once I was caving in, my throat was thickening... A tiny panic grabbed me. What was this in the midst of my joy? What was happening? Could these be tears trying to get out, or an inward scream? My panic grew. My God, I thought, am I about to cry? For God's sake get a grip on yourself. Where's all your cool and control – where's that secret macho man? Has it all gone down the drain?

I suppressed it. Drew in a sharp breath, it shook my chest; hastily I let it out again – it emerged in a long and drawn out sigh.

Her fingertips released their pressure, still I held on tight. They pressed again, lightly, let go. I sensed her body retreat. Her hair brushed my face, caressed my skin; she was leaning back... Impotently I relaxed my grip – I wanted to do anything but that. With desperation I left my arms loosely behind her back, opened my eyes. Blinked at the brightness.

She had my face between her hands, looking down upon me. I was afraid of what she might see.

"Annabelle," I said. My throat was croaked, I had difficulty looking her in the eye. A catastrophe. I felt so ashamed, only half the man, showing weakness not strength, not taking her hand and leading the way. My God, what must she think of me?

She smiled. Faintly. It lightened her lips, creased the corners of her eyes; she had smiled for the very first time. Was this a positive omen? Fingers. Those fingers like feathers were stroking my cheek again...

"It's all right," she said. Nothing more.

All right? I thought. Isn't it anything but all right? I couldn't speak. Had she sensed it even before she let me go – could she see it now? My eyes were dry but wasn't my face giving me away?

Her smile was soft, secretive. It was like a smile reserved for lovers – but we weren't lovers, we'd only just touched.

A sudden memory. I froze. Estella was speaking; hurriedly I plastered another mask on my face, tried to hide behind it. Her words echoed in my brain, haunting, the ones she'd stabbed me with: "Men're often the opposite of what they appear, the tougher the shell the more vulnerable and insecure inside – you'll never fool a woman worth her salt."

I lowered my gaze.

Hands cupping the lines of my jaw now, raising my face to hers. I felt so bad, and yet so good. Still I couldn't speak. She was stooping her head, her lips were pursed, they were almost there... she kissed me gently on my cheek; she kissed me the way one kisses a child. I thought pathetically: she did it in pity not passion. I stood there helpless as my hands. Tried to smile too.

"Hold me," she said. A whisper.

I held her. I held my breath.

Her breasts flattened against my chest again, her stomach and hips too. Could this be a contradiction? Wanted to read her eyes – but her face had disappeared, it was over my shoulder. I buried my face back in her hair, I held her like a drowning man.

"Annabelle," I murmured. I murmured it to myself – I couldn't help it, no I could hardly believe. I muttered it to help confirm, hanging a name on this dream. Could she really feel attracted to a weak man like me?

Her fingers were travelling upwards, their tips were light, the way they touched was totally erotic. They tingled my shoulders, they tangled my hair. Yes, my God, I felt so weak. Began to stroke her the way she stroked me. Oh God, Annabelle, I thought, be my mentor be my teacher, teach me how, it seems I still have so much to learn. Her body absorbed me from top to toe, the touch of her fingers inflamed. I stroked her skin through the blouse, through the slippery silk, slowly, slowly – down her back, down each side of her long slender spine. Her body rubbed upon me. I gasped. My tool grew out of its small flaccid stump. I thought I would choke, I could hardly breathe my heart beat so loud; it broke the last bonds restraining me. I felt her hands on my nape, in my hair, tearing it softly. She was breathing more quickly, I was suffocating, I was gasping for air; every time she breathed it was hot in my ear.

I reached the hollow above her hips, reached her trousers, there where the rise of her bottom began. My nervous hands, I sensed them shake, I made them pause. Then spread them outwards towards her flank, made them pause again, hanging there, hovering, paralysed. My tool was stiff. It pushed through my trousers trying to get erect, poked her leg, got caught in a fold of my underpants.

I let my hands have their way; my hungry hands...

Let them creep. Could feel the curve of her bottom through taut thin cotton – let them reach its rise, caressing, it was firm and rounded; I let them slip down over the mound, felt the faint edge of her pants beneath, held each neat cheek in my palms, felt their beauty, felt their heat, kneaded them very gently – the only signal I could muster to indicate maybe I was still a man.

Her breath was louder in my ear, long drawn-out sounds. She teased my hair, squeezed my neck, those fine freckled hands full of strength – they clasped my skull, tipped it back. I sensed her muscles in her backside tensing...

"Look at me..." she whispered – or was it a shout, was it a hiss? Her thumbs were pressing under my jaw. I opened my eyes hurriedly, again I had to obey...

Her eyes gazed down, they were open wide, they were staring and glazed... "Look at me the way you did..." Her mouth was a hole again, I could see the tops of strong white teeth... "I want to be looked at like that again..."

...but I had no choice – couldn't help myself, couldn't have stopped if I tried. I returned those aroused and excited eyes, they matched my own. She watched me for an instant, she let out a sharp and strangled sigh, held me fast with her fingertips, my face, my cheeks; beheld me as if she'd seen a ghost. She was sweating; I felt it through my shirt, through her blouse on my chest, I saw it on her brow – she exuded heat like glowing embers, like an open fire.

In my groin, between my legs, there grew an ache. She swooped her head, pressed her mouth upon my lips – it was damp, it was hot, it didn't go away, wasn't a peck like the one before, it pushed and nuzzled...

She's kissing me...

My heart had sunk into my stomach, the ache increased. I think I moaned on her mouth. Shut my eyes tight; didn't trust myself to use my tongue, afraid again I might do something wrong. My feelings were exploding but all I thought was: sit on your greed, don't go too fast, don't wreck your chances...

"I abhorred you for staring."

She spoke on my mouth, it vibrated my lips. I heard the words, they turned me inside out. Yes, I thought – but how could I have stopped myself?

"Yes," I said. I tried to say it with penitence. I nodded my head; it rubbed our lips. "And I adored me for daring." My throat was thick. "But I feared I'd..."

Her mouth had brushed away, was gone – her hand was there instead. She pressed my words with her palm. It smelled so intensely of her scent, it drove me mad. I opened my eyes, had to; I know I looked with hunger, I looked with greed.

"I don't make casual sex," she said. "And I don't intend to start."

I shook my head. There was a hollowness in her voice; was that my longing on her tongue? I watched that fire, I was burning too – I nibbled her enclosing hand, gently bit it, kissed it.

"I never make casual anything," I said, "and I wouldn't know how to start." My breath was hot on her hand. I felt sick with desire; my tool ached in its trap, tangled sideways in my trousers, straining like a dog; it caused me pain. As unobtrusively as I possibly could, I stuck out my bottom, wriggled my hips... only made it worse. My God, how could I free it without appearing an idiot, without having to take my hands away from this beautiful behind?

She was breathing more loudly, unevenly. It tickled my cheek, I almost choked. I stroked her bottom again, nervously, those cheeky mounds in my perspiring palms, indulging in their dangerous curves; she breathed more quickly, through mouth and nose, moving herself beneath my hands. I groaned again. Let my fingers inch on down, exploring, shaking with anticipation... reached the meeting of those mounds. I hovered, I held my breath – touched the deep and secret indentation, that hallowed valley between her cheeks, visualising how she might feel if she were naked.

We stood there, embraced, fixed to the spot. I could feel her heartbeat – or was it mine? I ached in the places I'd long forgotten, gently fondled that holy fold...

She stiffened.

No...

I stiffened too, my fingers froze. No? Had she spoken the dreaded word – or was it embedded in my own brain? My tool had reached the breaking-point, the pain excruciating. She struggled. Was shaking herself. Or was she shaking me? The top half of her body broke away, arching back, trying to free her arms imprisoned under mine. I glimpsed her face above me. It was now or never... bending like a boxer half-felled by a belly-blow, I released the prize with an unhappy hand, whipped it round, scrabbling, freed the offending devil, hurriedly jerked upright again. Oh, the relief. The lid was off the jack-in-the-box. I think I moaned. My tool had sprung up, squashed itself between us.

But she'd extricated her arms now, her elbows broken free. Still leaned back, she was holding my shoulders, staring down at me. Her face was flushed, her fingers a vice, her breast swelled and fell, her breath came in fits and starts as if she'd just reached the end of a race. Please no, I pleaded in my brain. I was clutching her bottom with both hands once more, pressing her beguiling soft stomach to mine; I hugged her like a long lost trophy I didn't dare to lose again.

She tipped back her head and tossed her hair, her eyes were wide, her mouth still a hole. I could smell her, could feel her heat, feel my own, her whole body seemed to be swelling – her thin trousers were damp beneath my palms, her armpits wet through the blouse. Oh how lovely she looked, so abandoned and wild – her cool was all in tatters, her elegance undone.

I stood stock-still. Like a mouse. This was it, wasn't it? The border crossing, the moment of truth, the turning between the tides.

My God, that gaze.

She released her grip on my shoulders. Hands laid upon my chest, pushing, kneading – was she on the point of pushing me away? I hung there at the precipice, toes on the edge. My throat was dry, I tried to clear it. I parted my lips, about to beg. "I think..." I began...

"Don't think."

Again the tips of fingers touched on my mouth, fell back to my chest. Her hips stirred. Her whole body was beginning to sway, to move against me – as if to music I couldn't hear. She hadn't retreated. Was this another reprieve? She was still so close, had she made up her mind – to let me off the hook? I felt so good I could've flown away on a hundred heavenly wings...

She was pressing herself on my private parts, her tummy sliding from side to side – a rolling rhythm that swamped my mind, like the magical beat of a tune. I gasped. A rapid intake of her breath, her eyes were half-closed, her mouth opening very wide. I could feel her tummy hot on mine, my legs were shaking she aroused me so. I began to stroke her where I'd stroked her before, along that fold, that secret place, I allowed my fingers to follow it further down...

A quiver. She was suddenly still. The music had stopped. She shook herself, tipped the top half of her body back – she looked at me very hard.

I swallowed. Oh god...

She pushed me away. That's that, I thought. I've done it too fast, I've gone too far. I dropped my eyes. Felt like someone caught in the open with his trousers down.

"Annabelle..." I muttered. It emerged like a growl. Had to clear my throat again. "I'm sorry. I..."

She only smiled, though. No reproof, no flash or angry rebuke – no rejecting shove. She was taking my hand, and turning... she was squeezing it, telling it things... could this really be? My ears were ringing and my brain was blocked so I tried to listen with my body... yes, she was turning away. Firm fingers, certain fingers, fingers which said what they wanted to do. I thrilled... I wanted to too – wanted anything going, I would take any offering she might bestow, be it great or small, anything was better than nothing at all... My senses rang, my stomach lurched...

She was glancing at the table, her face suddenly out of sight, a twisting mass of rust-red hair... No, not that, I prayed – oh God no...

I was being swept round, she was drawing me... please no... Judit had loved tabletops too – and wooden chairs from behind, and dressing tables, anywhere bruising and hard that disabled my good intentions, cramped my inhibited style... No, not like this... this was Judit's game with fingernails tearing flesh, wet bush of black hair presented in absurd positions better reserved for acrobats, my kneecaps in ruins and my chin caved in. All her joyous and carefree perversions inflated by pain, dedicated to places presented in her amazing and ample well-padded behind...

But no... thank God...

Blinding sunlight...

She was towing me towards the windows and the children's corner of the room, she was leading the way: I went with relief, a nervous beggar in rags, with pumping heart and pounding blood, in a daze, in a whirl. I went obediently, unversed Gentile with experienced Jew going to the initiation...

She stooped to the rug and still holding my hand swept building bricks and dolls and toys aside. I glimpsed a pretty picture book and a brutalised one-eyed bear, a dented tank-engine pushed out of harm's way.

She was bending, she was undoing her sandal-straps, casting the sandals aside. She sank to that rug of many colours, pulling me to her; one of her hands was plucking out combs, her hair spilled, a cloud of burning red. I thought very briefly: the bets are on she's not doing this here for the very first time, let's pray she'll be gentle with me...

My legs gave way, I stumbled, fell to her on the floor.

The pile of the rug had seen better days – I landed on it on all fours; it leant my knees scant protection but I didn't care, I didn't care about anything now. She lay on her back, one leg stretched out, the other bent; her arms were like an invitation, her body like a calling bell. I thought wildly: does she wish me to lie upon her like this or should I begin to undress her?

She shook her head, that cloud of hair. Had she heard my thoughts? She smiled a slow smile, beckoning. Sultry eyes and freckled face, lined face, mature, aglow, her breath was like a rising breeze. So I came closer, on hands and knees, grovelling to this queen. Her lips were parting again, opening, her mouth a cave I ached to slide my tongue inside. I knelt beside her, I was her knave, about to stoop to kiss, her sea of hair spread out in waves like fire on the floor. But her hands were reaching up, she started slowly undoing my shirt. Thin deft fingers, steady regal fingers. With shaking arms I bowed to her blouse... glimpsed Judit leaping at me, ripping at my clothes and bursting off buttons, then wriggling, wrenching up her skirt. Panicking, I fought the image back. Nervously, clumsily, bungling, I began to open those tiny buttons, that slippery silk; I did it with far less grace than she. There was the beginning of those bare speckled breasts, the top of a low-cut slip revealed... Wasn't even halfway through when she drew my shirt out of my trousers, stroking it open, and there was tenderness in her touch. Her movements were minimal and stealthy and practised, like a magician, like a cat...

Judit's teeth bit my nipples, they bit my lips, her mouth nearly swallowed mine; she got herself going at the rocking chair, she had me by the balls...

I winced. My hands an interrupted fumble abandoned on the blouse.

...Judit's skirt was high, her pants were gone, she bent herself over her favourite chair – her fruits on display for the man to desire, yes her beauty was open wide...

"Sssh..." Half-closed green eyes, that smile touching the lips: I was back with Annabelle.

She began on the belt to my denim trousers. As she pulled out its tongue in a long eked-out, slow-motion loop, light fingertips brushed my navel, stroked across my skin. Like the cut of a knife. I jumped – drew in a sharp breath, all the muscles of my stomach had gone into spasm. I bowed over my knees, I was gasping again – or was I panting? All thoughts of Judit flew out the window.

A slender hand slipped round my neck, drawing me to her, another hand laid down on my thigh, tickling, fondling, stealing my breath away, stretching me out beside her. A pressure on my nape; she turned me on my side. Freckled arms on my naked chest, now, freckled hands in my hair.

"Look at me."

I was stiff as a poker, I was hot as hell. Heard her voice from far away; again I had to obey. I looked at her. Felt one of her legs creeping over mine. It began to bend, it lay itself cosily in my lap. My world was exploding, we were so close. I looked in her face: glowing and freckled, her face was flushed, her eyes sparkled like the sea, was that special smile really reserved for me?

Fingers gently pushing my skull, guiding my mouth towards her. I was moaning. Had to kiss that mouth. Her lips were near, had faint little lines, they were moist, they were full – they were coming closer, meeting mine, oh my God... they were letting me in. But as I entered, her tongue met mine, licking it aside, slipped stiff and liquid and ever so slowly inside me; she kissed me like no-one's kissed me before. Her tongue expanded, contracted, as if it could breathe, as if it had a life of its own – my lips received it greedily, my mouth enclosed it like a womb. Oh that kiss, so certain and longing, I wallowed in it, it told me what I'd missed for so long.

I felt her leg along my thigh, her slender knee was nuzzling into me, it pressed my penis, caressing. That touch inflamed me, it shot up my legs, like a punch, like a glorious pain. I thought: my God, I'm going to...

I was groaning now. I shut my eyes tight; in my body bells were pealing, the mountains moved and the hills rejoiced, resounded, choirs were singing songs of praise, my whole body was glowing, expanding, my mind caving in, my brain was a tomb empty and dry – all those useless things my thoughts had spun through the cobwebs of time disintegrated into dust. I tried to sigh, cry out in relief, call her name. But no words remained. There was only space for jubilation, only room for revelation, for pure unadulterated joy. My senses were all in disarray, my control was broken down.

I felt myself coming...

For God's sake, no – not now, not yet...

Panicking again, I tried to stop. But my feelings were king, they'd donned the crown, my stomach rising and falling calling the tune – this queen of hearts was gathering me in, into her gown of blinding gold. My breath broke in gasps, my throat was rasping; I was fighting for air, must've looked absurd like a fish out of water. I held onto her, quivering. It seemed I'd stopped expanding now, had reached my limit, was starting to implode, the whole of my body was drawing together, all my fibres pulling in, the fluids rising like sap in spring, everything funnelling, tunnelling, concentrating – squeezing me into the source of myself, and building up to burst...

I came... in a rush, in a roar, in a furnace of flame, the Earth fell away – in a flight to the stars without a name I soared into the universe. I'm sure I was choking, crying out. It burned up my body, consumed my soul, a fiery flushing ache, sucking my being out of its core, an ecstatic arcing race through space with no beginning or end...

Seconds stretching – or minutes like hours – time was in limbo, time ceased to exist. And on that long flight, gradually, grew a grateful feeling of emptying out, of a load discarded, of complete and utter relief... Then somewhere, at some point, I was slowing down... braking, abandoned and spreadeagled, a sense of lightness taking the rein, of turning to a leaf that time had torn off – floating gently back downwards...

I came drifting, sinking, in slow motion, content and fulfilled, happy even... down towards the Earth again. Far too soon, it seemed – I wanted to fly on for ever. I was cleaned out, a vacuum, my desires drowned and dissipated, washed away on the wind like a hunger stilled or a thirst that's been quenched. Slowly I settled. Level by level, dream by dream, that journey through space came to an end.

Awareness was creeping – I was back in a room.

I flailed, I struggled, I tried to recapture those feelings anew, tried to fly up once more. Impotently, I flapped my worn feathers on exhausted wings – I wanted to walk on water again, take another trip to the moon.

Chapter 7

I lay there. Exhausted and satisfied.

Lay wallowing in a hot stagnant puddle of mud, a foetus in the womb, a shrimp on the shore. But I wasn't allowed to wallow for long – awareness was creeping. It crawled through the crevices, through cracks in my skull. With horror I realised what I'd done. Guilt came grovelling, my bad conscience grew legs, rose like an ogre, filling my brain. Thoughts were coming, too, words beginning to form: oh God, how could I have? I'd come far too soon. Like a hapless adolescent doing it for the very first time, like a dog on heat behind the dustbins...

I shifted in discomfort.

Sensed myself still spreadeagled on my back on the rug. Sensed the long leg still upon mine, knee still lying in my lap.

I opened my eyes.

Brightness. Hovering face looking down at me, a curtain of hair.

Discovered my head was raised, not on the floor, it lay on her arm, had she placed it there? The crook of her arm was like a cushion. For Christ's sake, I thought, why didn't you exercise self-control? Stupid bugger – now you've burnt your boats. I felt so embarrassed... secretly I squirmed, my embarrassment burned all over my skin.

I blinked. I had to speak.

"Condemn me," I said. It came out in a strangled croak, like the broken man I felt.

Fingers stroked my face, an arm resting on my chest. No criticism, no abuse. All she said quietly was: "My poor starved one."

I thought about that. Yes – that described me to a tee.

Her head had lifted slightly. I sought her eyes, I found a smile. In shame I said: "My embarrassment is a bottomless pit." I said it with true humility.

The fingers combed through my hair, tousling it, entwining, tingled my scalp. Came to rest near my ear.

"Sssh." Her gaze poured down like honey.

But still I felt so ashamed, felt such a fool. I shifted again – then felt something else too. A wetness, a stickiness, on my belly beneath her knee. Made me feel even worse. I squirmed again like a worm. And silently cursed.

Till I saw her eyes. They were speaking to me. I watched them helplessly. They were starting to tell me things – they did it like her hand had done the other side of heaven, how long ago was that? But the eyes were talking about different things, about hunger and greed, now, and wants and needs – they seemed to speak right through me. Her pupils were dilated – they were big and black as holes despite the light, and her face was flushed more than before, her long neck too – the flush flowed down her throat into her half-undone blouse, down to her breasts, down till the slip concealed...

Fingers... fingers running round my ear. She clasped the lobe, fondling it, swooped her head and kissed me on the mouth. It was a long kiss, wet and firm and strong, a longing kiss I didn't care to reciprocate – it tasted of lipstick and saliva and salt, it tasted of...

Suddenly, her lips were gone. Her knee, too – her leg was sliding off mine. She slipped her arm from under my head, was rolling over – she was on her knees beside me, hands sweeping my open shirt apart and laying themselves flat on my puny chest; it was like the laying on of hands, she knelt as if in prayer.

Oh horror of horrors; I watched those hands, glanced at the ends of my unbuckled belt – she's about to go for my trousers. I lay there. I was a drowning man, I didn't dare respond. Inch by inch, inexorably, inside the denim in warm liquefying slime I felt my private one shrink. Don't panic, I ordered myself...

Her hands were lifting... but to her blouse.

I panicked.

She undid the last little lilac buttons, the edges opened like curtains drawn aside, exposed the rose-coloured slip. It was very short, didn't reach her trouser band, I glimpsed a line of pale skin; her navel watched me like an eye.

Oh God, I can't, I told myself.

On the front of the trousers were three very large red buttons about as big as dinner plates, her fingers undid them one by one. Like a flap the cotton fell away, a zip and a clasp came into view. Kneeling upright, she took my hands, leading them there...

The panic took me by the throat; my private parts had shrivelled to the size of dried-up prunes. I thought wildly: she wants me to do it again, do it properly this time round – can't she see I'm all bluster, I'm not the man?

She'd placed my fingers at the top, right beside that clasp. I stared aghast, I couldn't run now could I, she'd put me on the spot. Her pale tummy rose and fell, it pressed against the trouser band, even a fool could see it wanted to get out. With harassed hands, unsteady hands, and fingers stuck inside the band against bare flesh, I unclasped the clip from its hook, began to open the golden zip. My fingers fumbled as I pulled, and as I pulled her body peeled out like fruit from a skin.

Pure white flesh – from where I lay I could see it all... the zip was long, it went on down. Quicker – in a second she'll be going for mine... Holy flesh, white as a lily, so smooth and soft, the peep of brief lace underpants...

God, look, her hands are coming at me – let go the catch, be a man, better do it yourself... With eyeballs rolling beneath tight-shut eyes, flat on my back, desperately, I reached to my trousers, to the row of buttons I knew too well. Could visualise my perished state, imagine the mess – arise old thing, for God's sake rise, do your duty, can't turn back now... first button open, going for number two...

Fingers... again those fingers, strong and sure – they were taking hold of my hands, they had them fast, pulling them away.

I opened my eyes.

She knelt there like an invitation, trousers open, tummy protruding, that little pale triangle, that hint of lace. Her hands released me, thumbs moving to her sides and hooking in the band, wriggling her trousers down – down over her hips, over her bottom... they fell to her knees like a concertina. White lace pants, oh yes so very brief, so much pale skin. No freckles there. I stared a second, swallowing. Then she was dropping, sitting down beside me and taking my hands, drawing them to the legs of her trousers.

"Pull, please pull."

She was turning onto her back, her head was gone, she was facing my feet, was sliding her bottom towards me on the rug. I pulled...

Her knees were raised, her legs were high; I drew those loose trousers slowly down, over freckled calves, over naked feet, till they fell free. The material was warm, it smelled of her; I buried my face in it, breathing it in, before casting it away. A glance. A golden glimpse. Long legs lowering, parting – and where they met, forbidden fruit, a wisp of waiting lace.

"Come..."

Arms snaking, hands gently twisting my shoulder, fingers taking me by a wrist; they picked it up like the delicate beak of a bird, they took it and showed it the way. I had to look.

I lay turned on my side, her face at my thighs the other way round, my head near her hips. Her body was hot. The tips of my fingers alighted, they touched the dew on her leg. My wrist was alone now, it was all on its own; no, I couldn't help it, I just had to look. My fingers were tracing a line on her leg, a path through the warm dew on her skin, they came to the place between her thighs, the holiest of all the places. I could see the small bulge, feel the soft rise beneath the cotton and the lace, feel its wetness, hear her breath. I let my fingers linger a moment; to touch her there was such a joy. I heard her breath come more deeply. Then carefully I began to stroke that bulge; I stroked it the way one strokes a child – along its rise and further down, until my fingers were out of sight.

She sighed, she stirred.

I pressed. Ever so lightly. It was like a cushion.

She moaned. I thrilled; I loved the sound.

I pressed again, just with the side of one finger. It sank a little, into the cotton, into the wetness.

She moaned once more. She moved.

I could feel her heat, feel the stickiness on my hand, upon her skin, along her thigh. I touched her with a fingertip, just like I touch my eye, then traced it in a languid line along the small fluid fold. It was hotter here.

She tipped her hips, rolling them slowly, a light rhythm right and left. She groaned – a slow and deep, an eked-out sound. A wonderful, a very sacred sound. The dividing mound was getting wetter. I nestled a knuckle into the softness, it was soft as moss. She moaned again.

I nuzzled it a little deeper.

"Mmm..." A murmured groan, another moan.

I could smell her smell; it intoxicated. I couldn't resist. I dipped my lips to the lily and suckled its nectar, I licked at the cotton, her milk was flowing; it was honey to my tongue. Beneath my nose the lily began lifting, weaving – I heard a small cry... I kissed her again where it pleased her... another cry... I supped her excitement, it sweetened my joy...

Then sudden unexpected stillness. No more movement. I lay quiet as a mouse.

A drawn-out sigh. But still no movement, none at all. Had she reached her climax – had she come already? I kissed the cotton one last time, bade it farewell with the tip of my tongue.

A quiver, a shiver. Then a little shake. Her bottom stirred, a leg lifted slightly, her thighs opened wider. It tautened the tiny white strip of wet cotton, smoothed the furrow my fingers had travelled, that my lips had feasted upon. For seconds my eyes savoured her sacred place, the flower in the heart of her secret garden she'd allowed me to visit; I could scarcely credit where I had been.

Slowly I raised my head; the hidden flower fell away. I bent, propped on an elbow, lifted my eyes to behold her. Above the border of her shaved-off hair an expanse of bare skin, and her navel, and beyond, the silky slip pulled up, the carefree wings of the blouse unfolded, all I could see was her head tipped back abandoned beside my hips – a chin, a nose, wild red hair in a tangle tipped over my leg and spilled on the rug...

"Don't go away..." A hollow whisper, like a poem, like a prayer.

The head turned sideways towards my waist, with her nose she touched my trousers, touched my tool, stroked the stiffness like a feather, made it tingle – I hadn't believed in a resurrection, hadn't realised I'd risen again...

Her arms were lifting, hands groping blind, finding my face, guiding it again... Stolen glimpses... last outposts of freckles on pale bleached skin, that navel coming near – was its eye watching me, was its pink and cheeky hollow smiling at me now? Certain hands, knowledgeable hands, they held the back of my skull, they pressed upon it, steering, pressed it to her...

"Aaahh..." she sighed...

She buried my face in her belly... soft and hot and rubbery, scent of perfume. Her body here, too, was covered in dew, rivulets running, I bathed my eyelids in her skin, kissed the droplets one by one, and ran my hand between her legs towards the flower, the imperfect gardener come back to do her bidding, if it be her will...

With bated breath I touched that feminine bulge once more, started to fondle the precious fold; I bowed to my grateful task, attending to each little detail...

"Mmmm..." Another long sigh.

She caressed my head, rolling it gently, sinking it into her lovely flesh; I drank more droplets from her skin. Beneath the tips of my fingers I felt the swell, I couldn't see – but beneath the flimsy cotton were the petals opening, had the flower begun to bloom again?

I kissed that flesh, had to look again; withdrew my head from her belly, felt her fingers let me go. I wriggled down, like the serpent, and laid my cheek upon her thigh. My heart was bumping, I watched that place where my hand was playing, I never wanted to look away. Her legs were open in all their glory – the sight nearly made me sick. The mound filled and rounded the flimsy cloth, gave off heat like an oven, and each side of that slender concealing strip the glow had spread, her thighs flushed a fiery pink. It roused me more, it tantalised. I wanted to sink my mouth to this sacred mound, to kiss it, to lick, to bite, to swallow her whole... the desire began to overpower... I would give the world in exchange for a promise, I'd go to the temple on bended knee, I would worship here all my life – if she allowed, if she gave the word.

With very careful fingertips I prised at the edge of the cotton, trying a sneaky sideways approach, squeezing to get inside. Too tight, my bad luck, foiled by the maker – there wasn't room to move. As delicately as I could I retrieved my fingers from the trap...

"Mmmm..." A heavenly murmur.

Another movement. Her bottom rose, her hands were peeling the top of the lace away... A brief glimpse, a gorgeous glimpse, it made my heart and stomach leap: that little wisp, that tiny tuft of red hair peeping fine as down – she had left there hardly any hair. I held my breath, went very hot... she was picking up my wrist again; she lifted it like before, as if I wasn't there. She slipped my hand inside the lace, the little triangle, all that was left, oh this queen of queens. My heart was racing... she placed my fingers on her throne.

Soft and liquid, oh that heat, soft as silk, it almost made me sick again. I felt her thrill. I gasped, she moaned...

My fingers fumbling, nervous, touching – her nakedness was ecstasy. My fingertips hovered, lingered, I was at the threshold, I stood on the holy temple steps. Would she let me enter, did I dare?

"Come..." A far-off whisper, faint as the breeze, clear as a bell.

I was losing my mind. I dipped a finger inside, just for a second was my intention, held my breath, the gates were open, I was slipping in – lips enclosing, tantalising, I slid in deeper, hot and milky tunnel squeezing, sucking...

A hand closing over my hand, stroking, guiding, she was the queen, I her knave bowing to her every command. She led me in, down the corridor, down liquid pulsing narrow darkness... leading me into her holiest of holies, into the cave...

Something expanding inside me, taking over, taking the reins, beginning to obliterate, my breath constricting...

Stop.

I stopped. A pressure. My hand was being held back... being slowly withdrawn. A sudden sense of disappointment, separation. Gone was the cave, its innermost secret still concealed, gone the slippery tunnel I craved to continue to slide along; the taste of temptation still overwhelmed. My body was burning, but I had to leave – my queen was leading the way.

"...Mmmm..."

She laid my fingers back upon the fold again, led me higher between the petals, between the lips, the cotton pressed my hand to her. A little higher – she was panting, moaning...

"...oh yes..."

She was inside the cotton, she was with me there... small firm slippery knot, my finger placed, she was rubbing me on it, holding me fast. Deep inside me something imploding... I could hear her noises, they were music to me...

I peeped out from under half-closed eyes, hungered eyes going blind... glimpsed her rolling the lace further down, it peeled away, she was naked there now, she was open and liquid, her secrets revealed, she was fiery red – and just above, my hand like a beast, her fingers a fan.

Something drawing in again, through all my being – different though, not like before, not concentrating to a spot but swamping... felt her clasping, heard her gasp, had to squeeze my eyes tight shut, couldn't call out, didn't want to, it was all within. I was overcome by a heat, a wave, it bowled me over, all of me, wrapping me, enclosing me in a cocoon – a falling feeling, almost fainting, a dizziness without compare... I thought – did I think? – could I, can one come, too, in this way?

She was squirming, twisting, crying out, she clutched my fingers to the flower holding it hard, milk was flowing, seconds flowing, over her and over me... I was slipping, sliding, gliding away, swimming in an endless sea...

All was nothing, nothing all. Then all was still.

Senses slowing.

A sigh. Her fingers relaxing. A tiny squeeze, a gentle caress across my hand, upon my skin. Then the fingers calmed, settled, they fell asleep.

We lay there. There was only her, there was only me.

x x x

I don't know how long we lay like that. Could've been quite a while.

I opened my eyes – blinked at the brightness. Awareness gradually creeping in again, of things around me, outside of me: her fingers sticky on my hand, sunlight falling on her skin, her thigh beneath my cheek. No dizziness now, just a wonderful calm...

She stirred; her fingers were gone. Then they came back, trailed through my hair, touched my cheek. I could smell her on them, oh what a smell. Again the scent of her intoxicated. I lifted my head; it had stuck to her thigh. Took her hand, pressed it to me, kissed those fingers. Now I could taste her too.

Craned my neck, searched with my eyes. Found her face, her head had risen. Wild hair abandoned, green eyes watching. She wiped at strands of fallen red, the damp hair darker now and stringy – an arm crossing her face, retreating; a look intense, a smile revealed.

Hands stretching to me again. They lifted my head, laid it aside, laid it gently on the rug. Her back arched, hips rolling, tipping – with practised grace she drew the lace up, hiding her heavenly place, and covering the tiny fluff of hair. All I could see was the little white triangle on lily-like skin, and the flank of a freckled leg.

She was sitting up; I twisted my head, watching her – she was watching me. Slowly, neatly, she shed her blouse, swept it away, let it drop; all she wore now was that slip, long hanging breasts beneath lilac silk.

"Lie on me. Want to feel you..."

Feel?

Oh God yes, I thought, I want to feel you too. Why the hell didn't I think of that myself? I rolled, scrabbling, onto my knees, happy as a dog that's been let off the leash, eager to fulfil her latest command. I knelt beside her, I prayed to please. Looked down on her, just for a moment, to behold her beauty, just to take her all in. Burning hair, string-like straps of the slip, lots of freckles on pale mottled skin. The flush at her throat had faded now as though it had never been...

"Don't look like that..."

I shook my head, I dropped my eyes.

"My sad and serious one..."

Sad? Serious? How could she think that? Is that what my face was communicating?

Arms reaching. She stroked my shirt from my shoulders – it fell away. Fingers on my skinny naked chest, those fingers like feathers, the touch of silk.

"Come..."

She had splayed her legs, I came between, still in my trousers – and as I came she took hold of the buckle of my hanging belt and pulled it out, cast it off out of harm's way. Again I felt such a naïve fool. I lay down upon her, my body on hers, skin on skin; I lay like a child. Felt her softness, felt her warmth – felt each roundness moulded to me. Her breasts had lolled sideways, they'd fallen apart, they formed a soft cushion between my chest and my arms. I kissed her neck in the fold of her shoulder, I couldn't reach up higher, was too short. Her hands encircled, her arms entwined; she lay unmoving, holding me.

I clung to her body, a babe at the breast...

Long stretching neck, soft throat swooping down, a world of hair – the scent of her perfume, the smell of dried dew. I thrilled to it all: comforting mother, the joy of just being, the jewel of this queen; I wanted to be here for ever... I was in paradise, all was perfect, I drank it in. This queen of queens I'd only met a few hours ago I felt in my bones I knew already, I knew I'd known her since my birth. If she stands up now, I'll lay my body at her feet, I'll be her pauper, I'll be her prince, I'll beg her all day to say please.

I touched my lips to the side of her throat, I supped some more, I drank my fill. And as I drank, I thought: am I really the man after all, can it be I'm worthy of this prize? After half a life, has all the waiting been leading to this, was it written down somewhere in the book of life, has it been ordained? What does she think – is she thinking this too?

A movement. Infinitesimal. I could sense every silence, every change, I could hear every sound.

Her arms slackened. Slowly they slipped down my bony naked back. A wondrous sensation. Then they slid further down – I felt her hands reach to my trousers, to my bottom through the cloth, strong elegant fingers, pianist's fingers, spread out over my buttocks, squeezing; she pressed me into her thighs and belly and her grasp was a vice...

"Mmmmm..."

The sound was drawn out. Like a satisfied smile, like a longing relieved, like the humming of bees in the summer sun. It buzzed in my hair, it vibrated my skull. Such pleasure in the sound, almost ecstasy, it seemed to go through and through her – why couldn't I enjoy as much as she?

It was my trousers, wasn't it – they were to blame? They irritated. Damn it, why hadn't I taken them off like she did? They lay between us, they got in the way, down there I couldn't feel the touch of her skin. Yes they got between us like an unwanted rag, like the prude not undressed at an orgy. The crutch was tight too, and my tool was crushed flat, squashed on the bone at the base of her triangle of lace – why did I do everything wrong? Can't take them off now, though. Far too late.

I shifted, wriggled a little bit lower – my penis popped down over the ridge to her throne and my chin towards her slip. Her hands went with me, but her palms stopped pressing. Then her fingertips started kneading, they were kneading the seat of my trousers – oh God, how thick the denim seemed. Were they laughing at me?

Yes, she'd stopped pressing...

The thought undermined. Had I made too many mistakes, maybe, made a fool of myself once too often? Was her mind clearing and she could see through me now, had she started to have serious regrets, was she about to push me off? I'd gone too fast, that was the problem. If one's not simply after sex, is after something deeper, one shouldn't jump into bed so quickly – should one? Even with Judit we'd waited five weeks. It was my impatience, goddamn it, and my greed. Had I played it cool I could have planned each step stealthily like the master at chess, I'd have known when to take off my trousers...

My cheek lay on her slip. Freckled skin above, the rise of a breast below. I nuzzled my nose into the swell... soft, warm, rubbery. Faint footprints of perfume; I breathed them in. Yes, all this was paradise. But for her – was it paradise for her too, or was I just one of many? She'd been initiated in the mysteries, knew exactly what to do – she must've had so many men. Was I only a plaything for an hour or two and then I'd get the boot?

I fondled the breast, uncertainty grew. I followed its curve, touched its tip. The nipple was flaccid, not erect and hard, it wasn't aroused, it was fast asleep. Was this the end of the road?

Had I read the book wrongly? Wasn't I really written down there for her, had there been a nasty mix-up? Had the Master of the Fates just discovered the blunder and whispered it in her ear: apologies for the misprint... or, sorry two pages got turned by mistake, this little runt isn't destined for you, the right guy's not due to turn up till next week?

I teased the tip desperately. It didn't react. So I laid my lips there instead.

She was about to laugh in my face, wasn't she? In a moment I'd hear her say: "That was just a bit of sex on the side, boy, don't let it go to your head."

Her hands were still, they abandoned my trousers. They lifted my head from her breast, turning it, making me look up at her. She didn't make it easy looking. Distant green gaze. It seemed to say: you're the case of mistaken identity, you're just a second-class substitute man.

Didn't it?

She parted her lips as if about to speak; I didn't want to hear. Quickly I lowered my eyes, lowered my head to her breast again. Had to take one last nibble, one last nip. I hung onto her body, I clung there like a leech.

x x x

She said: "Want your shoulder, want to see your face close up." Her words came from above.

I swallowed. Buried in the warm cushion of breast, once more I couldn't believe. I thought to myself: these are not words of rejection. I stared. Could see the rug stretching away. Could see toys, too, and a cast-off hair comb, big and rust-brown. This is like torture, I told myself – this terrible guessing game...

With courage resuscitated, with rescued hope, I began to clamber off her. And as I did she raised a knee, slipped a leg between my thighs, neatly rolled me onto my back. The carpet was gone, and the toys and the comb – all I could see was her. She knelt there on all fours, propped on her arms gazing down upon me. Tangled broken hair like a burning bush, lined and freckled face. It was a very long stare, it went right through me.

And suddenly... I knew for sure: despite the insecurity, I loved it all, despite the doubt I loved everything I felt and saw. She was nodding, very seriously, very slowly. Her eyes didn't go away. Why was she nodding? Could she read my face, could she read my thoughts?

"Don't look so sad," she said. "You are looking sad again."

Again I swallowed. I closed my eyes.

"Look at me."

But I couldn't look, I didn't dare. "I'm one of these guys who grins when he's angry," I said into my dark. "I apologise for this frailty." I could find no other offer of explanation.

I felt her turning; my legs were being turned too. Her thighs squeezed one of mine, she was lying down beside me. Hair brushing my face and my chest – found my arm stretching out, the nape of a neck coming to rest. A head laid itself down on my shoulder.

We were on our sides, facing, legs entwined, that I could sense; was that a knee resting in my groin? Kept my eyes tight shut though, still I chose the dark.

"Look at me now, my apologetic one."

Warm breath on my skin, that hint of perfume again, the slight pressure of the knee. This time I had to obey. I opened my eyes. Could scarcely focus: freckled face close, green eyes close, parted lips. I felt so nervous, what was she about to convey? I stood in the arena, I'd fought the fight, the verdict was near – thumbs up, thumbs down? My heart lurched, I held my breath, this was the moment –

everything depended upon what those lips uttered, and the position of that knee.

"That is better," she said.

Was that a hint of a smile?

I tried to nod sagely. Strands of hair tickled my cheek.

"Was it so difficult?"

"Immeasurably," I said.

How mature that voice, how penetrating that gaze.

"To let me read your eyes?"

"Ah my eyes," I agreed. "I feared to create more confusion." You're lying, I thought, you're breaking the rule – you were scared to divulge your fear.

"No confusion, my worried one."

Worried? Could she see that too?

A hand appeared before my face. Fingers walked a path down my nose. "On the surface, almost all men show the opposite of what they are like inside. It makes reading rather easy."

I swallowed. Was that Estella speaking?

"Ah," I said, "is that a fact?"

"Mmm. One of your gender's many little games. Rather sad, really."

So I confessed: "Then I am like almost all men." I wasn't lying now.

The eyes watched me. "Are you?" How clear they were, how they suddenly sparkled. Did they say they disagreed?

"Well?" she demanded quietly.

This was one of those questions I felt it best not to answer, so I lay there saying nothing.

"And what are you feeling inside now?" she asked.

I considered that one with undue care. Knew I had to reply this time.

Watching eyes. They calmly blinked. The lashes were red like her hair.

"Like a rat in a cage," I said.

"In a cage?"

"Like a rat that longs to be free."

A smile. It laid lines round her eyes. Yes, this time it was a real smile.

The knee gave a light press.

It thrilled, it gave me hope. I closed my eyes for a moment. That was very important what she'd just done. I opened them again, secretly I prayed she'd help me get free.

I said to her eyes: "I love the way you do that."

She did it again. Just as gently. Her smile was still there, lingering – but the lines had changed place; it wasn't the same smile as before.

I dared me, I had to summon up all my courage. "I love everything you do," I said. Had to drop my gaze for this confession.

"You remind me of my poverty," I explained. "It's like heaven for a rat in a trap." Still I kept my eyes lowered; I was looking at her body. Beneath the slip her breasts hung sideways now; I just couldn't lift my gaze.

Her knee didn't move, but it didn't go away either. Slowly, I stroked a breast through the silk... and heard her say: "I have not met one quite like you before."

It froze my hand; again I held my breath. Then I said: "I suspect you never wish to again."

"Actually, no." She paused, then added: "No, I would not say that."

I raised my eyes and looked at her lips; still everything depended on what they said, and how – now that her knee had spoken. "The one who does everything wrong?" I queried. I couldn't look her in the eye.

"Oh, you would be surprised."

The words gave me strength – was I deserving, or was she just being kind?

"I would?"

"Mmm." Another pause, a stirring. "I have met all sorts..."

I could just imagine – the Munich machos, the smooth sons of the rich, the professional lovers with carefully bronzed bodies and one hundred positions... I'll bet they've all been in her bed...

"...it is not a question of doing it wrong or right, it is simply a matter of feeling. And natural imperfection is rather refreshing."

It was only a small swat, didn't hurt too much. I dared to look further up now. "You are too charitable," I said.

Were those eyes laughing? "Charitable, my ironical one? You believe so?" Her fingers slid away, slid out of sight. Then they dug me in the ribs. "You should see me in one of my generous moods." A cheeky flash of the eyes.

"I pray I may get the opportunity," I said, humbly.

"Do not count on it."

Don't count on it? What did she mean? That stopped me in my tracks. A small panic again, a queasy feeling. Did she mean I wouldn't get another chance...?

"No?" I said.

"No."

"May I ask why?" Could she hear the panic in my voice?

"They are reserved for those in need."

She was teasing. She'd mimicked me. I sighed, and settled again. Thank God she'd said that. It let me off the hook. It did, didn't it? I answered, tongue in cheek: "But I'm a needy one."

"Oh yes?"

"Yes." With her one walked a tightrope. "In fact my needs are very great."

"You are kidding." A little laugh. And that intense stare going through me again.

"Kidding? Actually no – I just don't always let it show."

"Oh, you poor one. A typical man after all?"

"It's a dog's life, yes." I tried a smile. "It seems we men are doomed to a life of lack and loss and sacrifice. And the non-fulfilment of those little needs."

I got another dig in the ribs for that one.

"Your pathos drives me to the verge of tears," she pronounced. Her voice was soft and low.

I took my hand from her breast, and put it to her face. I touched her mouth, I touched those lips; oh how I loved that voice.

"Yes," she agreed. "Sssh," she added. "Enough of this." She settled her head on my skinny shoulder again.

I lay there close, I closed my eyes.

x x x

I had the sensation of waking; had I dozed off for a moment?

The faint rise and fall of her breathing, of her breast, mesmerising. And her neck upon my body like a sleepy graceful swan. Still the heat off her skin, and the scent from her mass of hair spilled over my shoulder and chest – still that cosiness like in a cocoon. I'd lost my touch on time.

Lazy sounds of traffic through the tipped-open windows, distant, lulling. Faint music filtering, too. I think it was REM, but I might've been mistaken.

My arm had gone to sleep, the one beneath her head.

I shifted it slightly, flexed my fingers. Pins and needles. How long had we been lying here? I'd disturbed her nape; she raised her head. No words. Expressionless eyes, penetrating eyes. What were they thinking? They gave nothing away.

I managed a crack of a smile.

She didn't try returning it. Just strain-lines and freckles; her face was neutral, its feelings asleep. Then her eyes were gone. With a slender hand she scooped her hair back; it spread across the carpet like a fiery opened fan. Her head laid itself down to rest again.

Something was intruding. I became aware of a pressure. My bladder was full. But it could wait, didn't want to break the spell – I guess it would hold out at least another...

A bell....

Was that a bell? Or was it something still fastened to my brain – from the music through the window just now, or a vestige of the song that had sung when she offered me her throne?

But already Annabelle had stiffened – so she must've heard it too. I felt her body tensing; her head was coming up.

The bell rang again. Shriller, demanding.

Well it won't be Margareth or the children, I thought, because Maggie has a key – probably a travelling salesman, or Jehovah Witnesses peddling their version of the Lord.

Don't answer it, I prayed.

It rang again, stubbornly. And this time several peels, like a tune being played. Annabelle sat up, propped on a hand, looking down at me. "Martina," she said. She said it with perfect calm. "We have two or three minutes." Her body was retreating, strands of hair across my skin; her knee had gone, my legs were all alone. She was standing up. Added matter-of-factly: "I always make them use the stairs."

Just for a moment I couldn't move, lay there on my side, watching. Freckled legs and arms, the short slip with its threads of shoulder straps, the tiny white triangle of cotton and lace; her nakedness shone like a beacon as she stooped to gather her clothes.

I got to my knees, reached for my shirt. She was stepping into her trousers and pulling them up those long and hallowed legs, hiding what I adored. Thin fingers drew on the clasp of the zip, the lace was disappearing too. Goodbye sweet throne, I thought, goodbye. One by one the three big red buttons were closing; her secrets were safe again.

I had to look away to put on my shirt, but I saw her slip into her blouse – she didn't bother buttoning it, still those curtains drawn aside. I stared like a naughty boy. Her hands were high, her head tossed, she lifted her red hair and swept it backwards outside the blouse. I still have that pose printed like a photograph in my brain; I peep at it now and then if I can as if it were yesterday.

She bent, hooking a finger through her sandal-straps and picked them off the rug; she bent with so much grace. And still bending, she quickly gathered toys and things in, scattering them on the space where we had been; how good she looked from the back.

"Come," she said. She'd glanced round, straightening. "Don't dawdle now." She was making for the doorway.

I picked up my belt, threading it, peering, pulling it through the thongs – buckled the ends. Started to do up my shirt...

"Come with me," she called – she was near the door. "Come to..." She was round the corner out of sight, I didn't catch the rest.

Slipped into the slippers, those oriental ones of purple and gold with bobbles on the upturned toes, and began to follow – glimpsed a big hair-comb near a ball, stopped to rescue it. Then hurried into the hall. Small stamping footsteps audible beyond the apartment door, tiny fists hammered on wood. I glimpsed Annabelle at the far end of the corridor entering her bedroom. Squeaky voices screeching: "Mamma, Mamma, we're back!"

I stopped. I dithered, thought: tuck in your shirt. Lifted it, looking down, peering – damp dark patch on the front of my trousers. The tune on the bell chimed again like it had done before. Better leave my shirt hanging out...

I opened the heavy door.

Chapter 8

Two small bodies like bullets shot past, calling: "Auntie Margareth forgot the key, forgot the key..." leaping and singing, followed by Margareth's more distant out-of-breath orders: "...shoes off in the hall *first*, into Martina's bedroom *second*. Then I'm going to finish the story of the magician in Bear Mountain, *okay*?"

Squeals of delight.

"*Okay*?" A firm repeat.

"Thanks, Auntie Margareth," called little Martina. She plonked herself down on the pew opposite, making Marcel do the same. A brief stare at me – it was almost a glare. Then she was bending to her feet...

A small hand stroked my arm.

"Hello, Uncle Stefan." David greeting me in his shy earnest way. "You're still here."

"I'm still here."

Such serious eyes. But a spark of pleasure in them too. "You said you had to go."

"Another change of plan. Have to soon, though."

He stood in the doorway, one arm round his football, the other still touching me. "Your shirt's hanging out," he pointed out. "You had it tucked in when we left."

"Yes," I said. I ruffled his hair, drew him close, pressed his cheek into my side. What else could I say? David was a true observer.

Margareth walked in. I stood there in the slippers: too late I noticed I'd confused the left one with the right. "You forgot the key?" I said. I tried a weak smile.

"No. Left it on the park bench, had to go back. Was still there – bit of luck." Her eyes appraised me rapidly, skinning me with her gaze, weighing up the situation.

"Did you do all the washing-up?" David asked.

"Well…" I began. I had totally forgotten. "Actually no, not yet…"

"Why not?" He let go my arm. "You could have come with us, then." His serious face looked up at me – disappointment drained it dry.

"Adults sometimes have more important things to do first," Margareth told him tartly.

"What was more important, Uncle Stefan?"

"David, go and help the other two with their shoes please – you're the eldest, don't forget."

She waited. He hung his head, turned on his heel, obediently crossed the hall. Martina was unbuckling shoes. Marcel squatted now, fiddling on the floor.

Still she waited, watching the children – waited till they were finished and had started to scamper away. And while she did, surreptitiously, I swapped the slippers and got it right.

"Well, little brother?" She was staring at me. Tired dark eyes, cool eyes.

"Well, sister?" I answered. I suppose my gaze was giving my guilt away.

She pursed her lips. "So your shirt's hanging out and you haven't washed up. Is anything else hanging out?" She raised my shirt-front mockingly but, gratefully, didn't glance down.

She stooped her head, brushed her cheek on mine, let it linger a moment. "You smell interestingly female in a French sort of way." She retreated her head. Despite her drawn face, a trace of faint humour.

"Don't be vulgar, sister."

"Hope you treated her like a lady."

"It might be more accurate to say she treated me."

"Can well imagine." Her gaze was cold again. "Reckon you owe me a bottle or two of the best Toscana."

"Agreed."

"Don't let it go to your head." She watched me. There was a touch of bitterness now. Then she said: "I want a word with you later – alone." And without a pause, but with a shade of sarcasm: "Can I assume she's in the bathroom?"

"I guess so."

She was turning away. "I'll keep the kids at bay."

I laid my hand on her arm. "Thanks, Maggie."

She tossed her hair. "Did it ninety percent for her."

"Only ninety percent?"

"Anyone could see you were a starved little bastard – Mr Ten Percent."

I let that one go with a shrug.

"Annabelle too." She turned away again. "Now you've both had your fill, *basta*. End of the story. I suggest you go and wash her off you." Her back was turned. Then over her shoulder she added: "Children notice everything so for God's sake change your trousers."

She was gone... striding off determinedly. I stood there unhappily. What had she meant? It was only about sex? Had she and Annabelle planned this together? My heart began to sink again. I tried to cast away the thought, but Margareth had sown the seed...

x x x

I was in her bathroom, alone. I stepped into her shower; I stood there behind curved glass where she had stood, I stood in the water she had left behind. With everything I touched I was touching her: the shampoo, the loofah glove, the still-wet soap. And when I opened a glass flagon with an expensive name in the wall niche I could smell her too.

Then I was in her dressing-room. Built-in, wall-to-wall cupboards of sliding glass, hidden lighting, a shimmer of green, a lacquered Chinese chair. Everything exclusive, quality priced beyond my reach.

I didn't belong.

What was I doing here? I felt like the devil on the prowl who'd forgotten his place, lost his way, I was trespassing in paradise. Had I had my run, that was it, was the fun over as Margareth said?

I stood now in clean underclothes from my overnight bag and the blue jeans she'd laid out for me. Her blue jeans. I'd wriggled them on very carefully, not much space in there to breathe. Was about to remove my folded fresh shirt from the bag too.

Annabelle scratched on etched glass, entered. She paused, appraising, at the other end of the room; she wore a fluffy dressing-gown. I looked for the signs. There was a glint in her eye, did I have a chance? Try a little humour, I thought.

"I did your bidding," I said. "Popping in a prayer that your washing machine is old and slow and your iron has blown its fuse." Pointed to the tall wicker container like an oversized snake-charmer's basket for used washing out of which my soiled trousers peeped.

"You will have to pray harder than that."

Was that a twinkle even? Could I risk a little more? Unrepentant I ventured: "I'm sure I shouldn't bother you." Cocked my head on one side.

"No, I am sure you shouldn't."

She approached. I could see the dark rings, the tell-tale lines in her face. I was thinking seriously: how long would it take – washing my trousers, drying them? How long could I prolong the pleasure, postpone my going?

"Were you to go down on your knees, we might manage to extend the process for all of three hours." She was looking me in the eyes guilelessly.

Had she read my thoughts?

"So you can stay to lunch." The eyes didn't blink. "You'd like to stay for lunch, wouldn't you?"

I wilted beneath that gaze. "Yes," I said. And secretly I thought: and for dinner too. In fact I'd love to stay all night and all next day – I'd love to stay on for ever...

I gasped. She had touched me. A finger hooked itself in the top of the jeans. They really were rather tight.

"Yes?" she murmured.

"Yes," I repeated, not trusting my tongue. "That was part of the heavenly plan."

"Uh-huh."

I took another sharp breath. Felt something stirring.

"Only a part of the plan?"

I couldn't answer.

Her eyes were wandering down.

"You are distorting the form of my jeans," she said.

"I am?"

"Mmm."

"Ah."

"Making a bulge where there shouldn't be a bulge."

"Ah."

"Over my private spot."

"You have a private spot?"

"I do."

"Well I'm glad it's private, I'm glad about that."

"They are my favourite blue jeans."

"Yes."

"Yes what?" she demanded.

"I appreciate the sacrifice."

"Indeed it is. I do not do things like this every day for my lovers, you know."

"Glad to hear that too," I said.

Her finger tightened its hold, rocked me gently to and fro. "Pray let us return to the other part of this plan of yours," she breathed – it was hot in my face.

"Well..." I began.

"Well?"

"It was just an idle thought."

"Idle thought?"

"Yes. That we ought to win ourselves a little time."

"We?"

"Yes."

"Time?"

"Yes."

The tip of the finger had stilled. "This is a most elucidating conversation," she said.

"Yes."

"Stop saying yes."

I nodded. Her eyes held mine. In front of my stomach she fingered the band thoughtfully, I could feel her slender knuckle pressed on my flesh.

"Time for what?" she said very quietly.

I took another breath. Had to tread carefully: was she egging me on, was I making a fool of myself? "Well," I said seriously, "I thought so we could..."

"You have been thinking again?"

"I have."

"You do too much thinking."

"I do?" I frowned. I continued: "Actually I was just mulling over the idea that this way we could find opportunity for getting to know each other better."

"Mulling?"

"Well, yes..."

"I shudder at the thought."

"Oh you do? But – nevertheless, speaking as one intellectual soul to another I feel sure a little additional time would bring our brilliant minds together and..."

"You do?"

"Yes."

"Might it?"

"Yes."

"In what way, pray?"

"Well..." How close her eyes were, how close her face, how firm that finger just inches from my navel. "For example, through delving into aspects of our characters and our opinions about the world, we would surely discover great compatibility..."

"Do you seriously suppose I am interested in delving into your character?"

"...we would surely discover we share certain fundamentals in common..."

"God forbid. I perceive with horror the dregs your character must conceal."

"I assure you there may well be a few pearls in the midst of the mud."

"Do put my mind at rest."

"Well, it would be hard to put it in a nutshell, you see – it would take a little time."

"How long, pray? Half an hour or so? Five minutes?"

"I fear at least till teatime, if I were just to pick out the plums. And in addition let us say till dinner for more marginal things like hobbies and..."

"Hobbies? You actually pursue hobbies?" Her voice was a purr. "How fascinating."

"Yes," I said. "So character-forming, you know."

"You mean like stamp collecting, or playing with model trains...?" Her finger began its rhythmic rocking of my body again.

"Or twenty-two grown men scooting backwards and forwards after a big leather ball for an hour and a half and trying to boot it into a net?"

"Well I haven't quite progressed to those heights as yet." I paused. "Then of course there are my interests. One shouldn't forget..."

"You have interests?" Now there was almost honey in the purr. "I am absolutely on tenterhooks."

"Well one does ones best." I paused again, added: "And after that, over an after-dinner brandy or two, I could round things off with the list of my commitments."

"You don't say. You have *commitments* too?"

"Well... yes – one's expected to, isn't one?" I closed my eyes for a moment, that finger was doing things. "I mean, when one gets to know someone new, one has to create the right impression. I'm thinking here of the environment, that always goes down well with involved ones like yourself – for example, like every week my obediently carting those crates of empty whisky bottles half a mile to the glass containers instead of sneaking them into the dustbin along with the dead batteries, and like the unfortunate necessity of plastic in the yellow sack..."

The fingertip had released the band of the jeans, reached my navel, gently circling.

"What about carbon emissions, my conscientious one?"

I concentrated again. "What about them?"

"Ever heard of them?"

"I'm constantly on my guard for anything new, you know. Here my commitment goes..."

"Mmm, that dangerous word again."

"...goes deeper than..."

"You drive an old Mercedes, I hear."

"Well, yes. A tiny exception to the rule."

The finger was in my navel now, doing a little exploring. It set my muscles quivering, I almost lost control.

I managed a small dirty chuckle; it helped to disguise. "But I assure you I stick a cork up its blackened exhaust if there are any activists sniffing around."

"How low can a man stoop?"

"Oh you'd be surprised..." I had to stop suddenly again. This time I was forced to blow more heftily through my lips; her finger had done its job. I laid my hand on her hand, I had to bend a bit.

"And you'd be surprised, as well, how long all this can take," I said to the lovely freckled hollow in her throat, "this list of commitments and hobbies, these pearls of wisdom and my candid opinions about the world..."

I straightened again; her face rose into view, her eyes were there again.

"In order to place you in the picture there's enough to fill a book, you see – all in all it would easily bring us up to midnight..."

How warm her hand was under mine...

"Midnight?" Oh those clear, clear eyes, that expressive mouth.

"Yes," I said, nervously. "And then we could relax."

"Relax?"

"Yes." Her finger was quite still now, I could feel it lying there. "Perhaps a little Chopin on your piano, and another glass of wine. And through the windows the moon coming up and..."

"Chopin?" The corners of the mouth curled up, but then they fell again.

"Yes. Or *Chopsticks*, if you prefer."

"I am certain I would not."

"Ah. But... but I'll make a contribution too, of course – I shall turn the pages of the music for you, you only have to give the word."

"How about a little whistle?"

"I guess that would do. And in between the pages I will light a thin green candle and set it on the grand, it would go so well with your eyes."

"How very thoughtful."

"And when the music's done and the candle's burnt down low, then... then we can relax a little more."

"In what way, pray?"

"Ah – all the options are open, I feel."

"May one presume this brings you round to the rug again?" A tiny twitch of the finger beneath my hand, then it lay down again.

"I was thinking one shouldn't quite rule it out."

"You are starting to think again."

"Yes."

"Do not."

We stood there face to face a moment in silence. Slowly, gracefully, she withdrew her hand from beneath mine, stepped back.

I nodded.

"Enough of this nonsense," she said.

"Yes," I agreed.

"I would suggest you finish dressing for lunch." She was back to being a queen again.

x x x

She sat against the light from the window.

Her back was turned, her naked legs were crossed, her dressing-gown was gone; she sat on the padded embroidered stool before her antique dressing table, in her underwear. In one hand a cosmetic pencil was poised, in the other she held a small mirror.

I paused near the table. She was concentrating, she didn't look up. I had dressed. I stood there in the oriental slippers and felt like an intruder again.

"May I?" I said.

She glanced sideways, back to what she was doing. "My polite one." A trace of smile. "Naturally."

I drew up a chair. It was carved and old with upholstered seat. Straddling it, I sat down on it the wrong way round, arms on its curving back. I had to do it delicately, her blue jeans had reached their limit.

A silence. A relaxing recuperative silence. Then, after a minute or so: "Are you often like this?" she asked. I supposed she was speaking of my childishness from just now.

"No, I'm afraid not."

"Afraid?"

"I'm more often accused of too much seriousness, I believe ninety-nine percent of the time."

I watched her a moment, then glanced out of the windows. I could see the tops of the trees in the square. "I like to think they're exaggerating," I said. "But I suspect they're onto something."

"I suspect so too."

I followed her movements. Her face was tipped to the light, she was pencilling. I didn't speak. But I was thinking: this is the last chance alone with her – when we leave the bedroom it'll be too late.

Briefly she leant forward, exchanged the pencil in her hand for another. I tried not to look at her body. As she straightened she side-glanced for an instant, concentrated again.

"Am I making you nervous?" I said. I said it as neutrally as I could.

"Nervous?"

"I mean my sitting here watching you."

Her eyes turned. Expressionlessly she gazed at me. "You make me nervous since I first set eyes on you."

I swallowed. Again didn't know what to say. I glanced away, glanced at the trees, then back to her.

"I'm glad about that," I said.

Her pencil hung motionless in the air. Just for a second her eyes were still there and I could see it again – that intense and glowing burn. Then her face turned away and the pencil moved; she continued lining her eyes.

I changed position on the chair. Just slightly. Had to be careful moving about. Neither of us spoke. I watched her profile, I watched her hands. My elbows rested on the carved timber chair back, my chin was in my palms. Then my eyes slipped down her body to her lap, to her thighs, to the line of her legs...

"You have a daughter, I hear."

I concentrated.

"Yes," I said.

"What is her name?"

"Andrea."

"And how old?"

"Twelve." I thought: my God, she'll be turning thirteen in a couple of weeks. I must send another present and card for Judit to secretly intercept and destroy.

"In the States," she said. "Is that correct?"

"Yes."

"Do you have regular contact?"

"Sadly, I have no contact at all. Or perhaps I should say, I write and send things which fail to reach her. My divorced wife wishes it that way."

"Why?"

"Perhaps she's afraid of my influence, she was always afraid of that. And she's a woman who almost invariably gets her way."

"That is sad for you."

I nodded, emptily.

"Is it sad for Andrea too, do you think?"

"I would like to think so," I agreed. "We were once rather close."

"It would seem jealousy is at work here." She paused her pencilling. "One should never pressure children into choosing sides."

"Well," I said, "my ex-wife is an impressing woman."

I stopped there. I thought: better not venture into the jealousy bit.

"Does your ex-wife have a name?"

"Judit."

Annabelle didn't reply. She stretched, put down the pencil, took up a stumpy blusher brush.

So I added: "And Andrea lives in the land of instant gratification now. She no doubt has plenty to distract her mind."

"Is it better here in Europe?"

"Hardly," I agreed.

She was brushing highlights onto her cheekbones; she had such a fine bone structure, she didn't do it for long. Laying the brush aside, she drew the stool closer, leaning forward, inspecting herself in the wings of the long bevelled mirrors.

"Did you in fact leave Judit, not the reverse?"

"She left me."

She nodded. Fingertips lightly wiping. "Do you still love her?"

"I miss her sometimes."

"Do you think of her often?"

"Sometimes."

She watched me in one of the mirrors. Her reflection hung there like a film, like in a parallel world.

"And you?" I said. "Do you still think of him – of your husband?"

"He is dead. He crashed his plane."

"I heard."

"I think of the bad times," she said. "It helped me forget."

"Helped?"

"Mmm."

"What about the good times?"

"They are what I used to love. Aren't they what we all like to love?"

"Yes," I said. I hesitated. "I'm a specialist there."

"You are not alone."

I watched her, chin in palms. I dropped my eyes; she was looking through me again.

"You live in Nuremberg, don't you?"

"Yes," I said. "For over fifteen years."

"Why did you leave Munich?"

I looked back at her reflection in the mirror. But her face was turned – it was looking at me. "That's a long story," I said.

"Is it?"

"Perhaps another day."

"Another day?" She watched my eyes. Her expression was blank like closed curtains again, no smile in it now.

Slowly, uncertainly, I raised my head and steepled my hands, propped my chin up on them. I took a breath, took the plunge. "Is there going to be another day, Annabelle?"

She sat there on her embroidered stool, hands laid in her lap. Her head was still turned to me; her back was so straight. I could see her considering, weighing things up.

"Yes," she said. She said it flatly, quietly, said it very simply.

My heart staggered and stopped for an instant, then began to beat again. But rapidly, irregularly. I wanted to jump up, do a little somersault and dance a jig, I wanted to shout out loud.

But I couldn't move, couldn't speak.

We were watching each other. Something was flowing. She parted her lips, I watched them open – I waited on tenterhooks; I wondered nervously what she would say.

"We will just see," she said.

"Just see?" I managed to get out.

"We have to take it slowly."

I heard the words, they entered my brain, they nearly overwhelmed me. She really was, she was holding open the door. But what did she mean... slowly?

"Yes?" I queried. "Do we?"

That was my voice. It sounded so far away. Had I said it coolly, maturely, had I blurted it out?

"Mmm."

Not just her mouth and her face, her eyes were so serious too.

How slowly? I thought. How long does one wait to do it slowly? A week, a month?

"How slowly?" I asked.

Her head moved perceptibly from side to side. "There is simply no hurry."

"I beg to disagree."

"You do?" Watchful eyes. "But that is not allowed."

"I'm caught in your web already."

"Don't say that." Eyes creasing at the corners.

"Can't you see my body? It's bound to all your strands." I tipped my head on one side.

"And don't do that. Don't look at me like that."

So I lifted my chin from my fingertips, laid my arms flat on the back of the chair again.

"We have only just met," she said, practically.

I shook my head. "I feel I've known you years and years."

"Don't make it so difficult."

How lovely were her eyes. And her makeup so tasteful one could hardly tell it was there.

"You really are an impossible one," she said. "I have two children, two very demanding and inquisitive children with eyes in the back of their heads."

"Even ten would be no deterrent," I said, and I knew it wasn't a lie.

"I have to be careful. Even assuming I find time to get to know you at all, you must understand that my hands are tied."

"I'm full of understanding for things like that."

"You are?"

"For me human bonds should be like elastic bands, though, not chains."

I think that touched her. She frowned – but it was such a lovely frown. "Listen, we are adults," she said. "I don't intend behaving like a teenager." And then her chin arose; it turned her into a queen again, she was fully in control. "I have commitments to others, and you no doubt too."

"Ah... these interesting commitments," I said earnestly. I began to tip my head sideways again – corrected myself just in time. "Are you speaking, for example, of my serious commitment to you?"

Lips pursing. "You are trying to make it harder and harder."

"This was part of my good intention."

Another frown. "There is Margareth, too. She is in a bad state. You must appreciate that she also needs a lot of my attention."

"Yes," I said. "I realise that." I thought: her voice is so calm, so rational – how can she be so calm? I shook my head again, dropped my eyes. Did I have to stop – was it time to give up the good fight? My God, there was so much at stake.

"I bow to your better judgement. But..." I hesitated.

"But what, my impatient one?"

"There's a problem," I said, looking back at her.

"A problem?" Red eyebrows raised, small wrinkles showing. "What sort of problem?" She asked it with so much composure – could nothing undermine that calm?

I put on a pained expression. "I don't have your telephone number."

She smiled. She actually smiled. And she uncrossed her legs – she really shouldn't have done that. I forced myself to concentrate, to keep focusing on her eyes.

"I might just be capable of jotting it down for you, don't you think?" she said. She said it so sweetly. "You know – on a little piece of scrap paper?"

I leant back again, hung my arms over the chair.

"Would that solve the problem?"

"Well... perhaps..." I began. I had to spread my hands again...

"Then you will have my number so you can ring me on the telephone. And you already have my address here, so you know where to call by in the future without losing your way."

"Ah," I said. "I may call by? In spite of my unhappy sister, and two strenuous kids with X-ray eyes? I don't have to wait till your two are grown up?"

"I believe we might allow one or two exceptions to the rule." Her smile lingered. "Shall we say the first one in early autumn when Margareth, hopefully, is back on her feet?"

"Ah – so soon? Isn't that rather rushing things? I mean, I was reckoning with the end of next year."

Her smile had spread, it crept over her freckles, over her cheekbones, it mellowed the lines of her made-up eyes.

"Cheeky one."

I watched her. How expressive her face was, how much it radiated – it made queasy holes in my stomach the size of big stones. I would die, wouldn't I, if I lost her?

"Well I'm glad to hear this," I said to the face. "This puts a different complexion on things."

"Does it now?"

"Yes, I'd been worrying at something, it was nagging me, I couldn't get it off my mind." Oh how those eyes watched me, they didn't let go. "Now there's no danger of my forgetting the details of your freckles till I meet them again."

A flash of the eyes. Had I hit a soft spot this time? "Do not mention those," she said. Her chin was up again.

"No?"

"Definitely not."

"I find them rather..."

"I detest them," she retorted. "I have since I was a child. So don't you..."

"I've always found freckles rather sexy," I said seriously. "In an adolescent sort of way."

"Don't you dare bring them up again."

"They go so well with your hair."

"Stop pulling my leg."

"Ah..." I stopped. Gave a dirty little chuckle. "I'm glad you mentioned that."

"What?"

"Your leg. Or rather, your legs. I've been wanting to get it off my chest since they first confronted me, I've been wanting to pay you the compliment. These armies of freckles swarming over them lend them a certain maturity – they give you an edge over younger women."

"Cheeky bugger." She stirred on her stool, her chin was still high, there was doubt in her eye.

"Yes, I shall remember them well through the winter months while I'm sitting waiting alone in the cold," I said stoutly. "I shall visualise each individually and worship them one by one."

"Don't be silly."

"And at the same time I shall visualise, too, those private little places they've failed to colonise."

"Stop now, please."

"Your kneecaps, for instance – and a bit further north beginning near that tiny tuft where a razor naughtily shaves, and spreading down..."

"Don't." She stirred again.

"It will bring me consolation."

Slowly she shook her head, raised it, watched me down her nose. "In a moment I shall be forced to get my handkerchief out." She was on her high-horse again.

She closed her legs, hands smoothing her thighs – she rose unhurriedly to her feet... she was walking past me, expression neutral, she was out of sight. I thought: I've irritated her, I must stop being childish. I stared ahead – at her dressing table, at the empty stool...

Then... unexpectedly, arms were reaching from behind me, she was suddenly bending, body pressing into my back... and my heart began to bang again. Her voice breathed in my ear: "Of course, any postponements of such a nature are entirely up to you."

Her arms were clamped around my chest, her chin rested on my shoulder, her cheek was at my hair.

"Oh my poor one," she said. "So impatient, so greedy." I could smell her perfume, smell her skin, I was back in heaven again. Her breasts pressed on my shoulder blades; I closed my eyes, contentedly, I smiled into space.

Sweet silence. Seconds stretching. She hung there, didn't move.

Then I heard her voice, quietly: "A penny for your thoughts," she said. Her arms were like a vice.

I struggled to take a breath; I felt so good I didn't want to speak – all the joking inside me was gone now, my laughter had died a natural death.

I said: "I was thinking of the autumn."

"Uh-huh."

"And the colour of your hair."

"Mmm?"

"Yes."

"And that is all?"

"And your eyes," I said.

"Uh-huh."

"Taken all together I find that quite a lot."

The gentle breathing through her nose was warm upon my ear.

"Those are rather lovely thoughts to think," she said. She reduced the tightness of her arms. They enfolded me still, though, they didn't go away. Her body hugged closer, she was crouching; I heard the old chair creak.

Fingertips. I could feel them through my shirt on my skinny chest, on my ribs, slowly moving, as if they were lost in thought.

I said: "There was one other thing I was also thinking, though..." I swam in my sea of happiness, I floated on and on...

"Mmm? You were thinking so many thoughts?"

"Well, just a little one. That I'd wait for you for ever."

The fingertips stilled a moment. The breath on my ear was like a soft breeze; I could almost hear it speak. Then the fingers were playing over my ribs once more, they were gentle as gentle could be – and the way she sat behind me our bodies had become one again...

"And what're you thinking?" I asked. I had to hold my breath.

"Mmm, that would be telling." Her head rested against mine, her lips were so near to my ear.

I said: "I'll give you two pennies for yours." I didn't know what else to say, I was hardly able to think. How wonderful those arms around me were, enveloping me, how wonderful her thoughts surrounding me, I wished they'd swallow me whole.

"I was thinking of tomorrow," she said.

"I don't think that's very wise, do you?" I could think only of here and now. I took a long breath. And when I let it out again it shook my shoulders, shuddered my breast. Then I heard her say, unemotionally: "I would like you to stay the night."

Chapter 9

I went into the long wide hall, carrying my overnight bag.
Margareth was standing leaned on the door jamb to the children's bedroom, arms folded, her back to me. The door was open wide. Not a sound from the children. As I approached she heard me, turned her head, looked at the bag.

"Uh-huh. Just leaving?"

I stopped beside her. "Actually, no," I said. I glanced through the open doorway. Two used bunk beds and a portable camp-bed with strewn bedding, a chaos of clothes. All three children lay flat on their stomachs on the wooden floor drawing and colouring. They lay like the spokes of a wheel.

"Annabelle asked me to stay the night."

Her eyes said: I'll bet she didn't, I'll bet you twisted her arm. There were dark rings under her eyes. She just nodded, didn't reply.

"Is that a problem for you?"

Slowly she shook her head. "Not for me," she said. Her voice was dead.

I glanced back at the children. All three had their heads down still, buried in concentration, lost in their private world. The only sound was the clack of a crayon dropped in the pool of pencils and the scrabble to pick up the next.

She inspected me from top to toe, coming back to the top of the jeans. "You appear to've grown a bit."

"That would be one way of putting it."

"You in a habit of wearing women's size thirty-six?"

"And that would be another." I returned her gaze.

"The next door," she said.

"Sorry?"

"The spare room. Next door." Still she leaned there with folded arms.

"Ah."

A mobile phone, muffled, began to ring...

Her dark eyes didn't leave me. They were hard. And dead, too, like her voice. Again I guessed what they were saying.

"We'll talk later," I said.

"Your bag of tricks is ringing." Abruptly she turned on her heel.

Hunkering, I put down the bag on the Persian rug on the floor and, as quickly as I could, unzipped the side-pocket. Took out the two mobiles to check which was ringing, raised the private one, pressed green. I'd forgotten they existed; they and I were in two different worlds.

"Hello?"

No answer. I checked the display; it was receiving but no number appeared. I thought: maybe it's Eva phoning from Florence with bad reception.

"Hello?" I repeated, louder. Still nothing. Sometimes, too, I experienced this problem with calls from Geoffrey in Australia...

"Third time lucky." A chuckle. A man's voice, quietly, as if far away. A voice in a void. Despite the years I recognised it at once. But the chuckle had changed; it was far lighter, more relaxed than it used to be. How curious.

I couldn't speak. My throat constricted.

"I'm allergic to mailboxes." The tone was lazy; was that a twang? A faint accent? Coming down through the years though, essentially the voice was the same.

"Ah," I managed to get out. I took a deep breath. "Mailboxes." Took another gulp of air. My breath came in chunks, my heart was to blame – my heart had almost turned to stone. "Sorry about that."

He didn't reply.

I was frozen in time. It was like a film that's ground to a stop. I was thinking: is this really happening – or am I fantasising again? Am I really hearing his voice? I felt the jab in my breast like a dart of joy. Mixed with nervousness, shot with doubt. I heard myself say: "Glad you tried though. Despite ones allergies one should always persevere."

And Matthias replied: "You once said you're allergic to life, remember?" and he said it so quickly, so spontaneously, it overtook my tongue.

I'd forgotten that. I cast about; I was a man who'd lost his script.

"Not sure that was true at that point in time," I said. "But maybe there was a spark of clairvoyance."

And I thought: that's slightly better – you're improving. My heart was improving too. It was slowly steadying.

A quiet laugh in my ear. That was all. The laugh was so laid-back. I waited – but nothing else came. Except memories. I tried treading on them, tried muddling them about in my mind, for inspiration. But nothing came there either. Just that tangle of memories, like a Gordian knot.

After a few moments, only one thing of any use had appeared. I decided to risk it.

"Good to hear your voice." I said it carefully. But I meant it.

"Yours too."

This time he hadn't overlapped my words, he'd made a deliberate pause like me.

Another silence. But not awkward.

Absurd. In spite of all my waiting for his call in Nuremberg and the inquisitiveness the video had awoken, I still didn't know what to say. I thought: shall I mention I'd viewed the video? No. He'd know I'd seen it, presumably, otherwise he wouldn't be ringing. Or I suppose I could ask where he is now, is he back in Germany – or how's life treating him. But that'd be too mundane.

I cleared my throat. "How are you?" I said. My throat was easier now.

"You don't mean my health." A calm statement.

"No." I meant just about anything else.

"Fine," he said. "Busy."

"Busy with what?"

"This and that. Serious stuff."

"Stuff?"

"Stuff that will interest you."

"Ah."

"A new direction."

He was blocking. Why? Didn't he want to say it on the phone? "Here in Germany?" I asked.

"Mostly."

Brief pause.

Keep the ball rolling, I thought. So I said: "Thanks for the video."

"A pleasure."

"You haven't lost your touch."

"Nor you."

"Made me curious," I said. Said it as a confession, another small concession.

"Was the idea."

"And the postcard."

"Glad you indicated interest." He stopped. Then he added: "Shall we meet?"

"Yes."

"Good."

I could hear his faint breath through the mobile, could almost hear him thinking.

"We'll make this short, then." His breath emerged in a long slow sigh; he seemed in no hurry. His breath in my ear nearly touched.

"When?" he asked.

Soon, I thought. As soon as possible. But not today. Because of Annabelle; I wouldn't miss this day with her for anybody in the world.

"Make a suggestion," I said.

"I'll call you. Okay?"

"Okay."

"Till then." The line went dead.

I could've kicked myself, I hadn't asked for his number. I shook my head, irritatedly; I was hanging from his thread again.

I stood there, mobile in hand. He was gone almost before he'd come. Then there it was – I felt a slight pang. He'd sounded so natural. Like the old Matthias, but with all the pressure dissipated. He was the same as in the video, so maybe it hadn't been just play-acting where he'd sat there on the sand. Yes, the pang was for something precious I'd lost when he went, what I'd missed. I knew now for certain I yearned to be close again.

I glanced at the mobile, paged to incoming calls to see if the number by any chance had registered there. But all that appeared was 'no number' three times at the top of the list; so he'd been telling the truth here as well. My eyes slid to the previous calls listed beneath – to see if Eva had tried to reach me, too. She hadn't. I clicked a key to block the buttons, left the phone on, slipped it in my jeans pocket. Picked up the bag. I walked the three or four paces and opened the spare room door. As I entered I heard my sister in the background saying: "Okay kids, still another twenty minutes so no panic..."

I was standing in a busy functional room warm with Toscana colours. It apparently doubled as a workroom, too: along the window-wall big tables with computer, printer, telephone and loads of stuff for graphic design. Apart from that, cupboards, a complete wall of bookshelves full of books, a single convertible sofa-bed, an antique chest of drawers. The pulled-out bed had been stripped, the mattress bare except for a folded coverlet. On the parquet floor near a crumpled loose rug and an opened suitcase, a fat green school satchel sat like an overfed frog.

"David's."

At her voice I turned. My sister stood there in the doorway.

"We put him in here the first night but he doesn't like being alone, so yesterday he was permitted to move in with the other two." She was coming in, closing the door. "Lucky you."

I watched her. "In a manner of speaking, yes," I said.

"Otherwise you'd've got a *Lilo* on the kitchen floor." She took a few steps towards me; they were determined steps. "Or the boot."

I didn't reply.

She was observing me coolly. "In my opinion the boot'd be better."

She leant her bottom against the old inlaid chest of drawers, propping her elbows up behind her. I'm sure it would have caused the cabinetmaker of two or three hundred years ago to wince.

"Your charity was always immaculate," I said as equably as I could.

"Don't start those clever little word games with me."

"I considered it more civilised than 'fuck you'."

She didn't blink. "Give me blunt but honest expletives any day."

I shook my head. "Well, you're going to miss those now, aren't you." I was speaking of Heinrich.

"At least I knew where I stood." Without a pause she made the jump: "Annabelle looks like a cat on heat." She was back where she'd begun.

"I think she looks the picture of grace," I said carefully.

"Not my impression."

I stooped, put down my bag. "And when did she manage to make this impression?"

"You were under the shower."

"Ah."

"You find her attractive?"

"Since you ask, sister – yes."

She watched me with her dark eyes. I waited.

"Sexually," she said. She said it with emphasis. "Only sexually." It was a statement.

"Also sexually."

"Crap. At breakfast you were acting like a starved sailor just back from submarine duty. Sex is all you're after."

"Then I have to disappoint you."

"You've had your screw, now bugger off."

I shrugged faintly, returned her hard stare. I didn't bother answering.

"You've both had your screw, that's what she needed too. Lucky for you. Now call it a day."

"You believe that's all she wanted?"

"Sure."

"You can't be so sure."

"She told me."

"She told you that?"

"Before breakfast. That much I can tell you."

"There's more?"

"No." She bent a leg, shifting her prop on her elbows, hooked a naked foot on one of the drawer handles. "Yank your brain back out of your randy trousers and apply a bit of intelligence. She's had some bad luck with one or two suitors recently, that's all. She was simply a bit starved physically, needed some sex. *Basta*. Same goes for you."

Slowly I shook my head again. "Why, Maggie?"

"Why what?"

"You're bent on getting me out of the way."

"I know her, we're very close. You're not what she's after. Matter of fact you're 'bout the opposite of what she's searching for."

"She's searching, then?"

"You ain't in her league, buddy boy."

"League? I don't think in terms of leagues. I'm..."

"Everyone else around here does, so you'd better start too. 'Cos that's what her crowd is like."

"I'm talking about an intelligent and mature woman, not..."

"She's that for sure. And you can bet your last dollar you're not the only one angling for her. You wouldn't've stood a chance anyway."

"A woman like her can decide for herself if she likes what she sees..."

"Uh-huh? And what d'you think she sees in you?"

"Why don't you ask her?"

"Don't need to. People in her class tick differently. Don't kid yourself, sonny boy. Ever heard of money? Ever heard of the right match?"

"A lot of good it appears to have done her up to now."

"Oh come on, brother, don't be naïve – she's got to choose from one of her own. Two're already tagging along and she'll decide the right one any day now, you can bet your boots. She's matured so much – she's a different woman than the one who met Pete."

She stopped. Her heel was still hooked on the handle, she rocked her knee to and fro. "You'd only get used for a while 'cos you're a novelty, then get chucked away. You'd only get hurt."

I swallowed. But I made myself keep watching her eyes.

"So much concern for me suddenly?" I said. "Thought you only had your best girlfriend's interests at heart."

"I do. It might've hurt her too. And might hurt her reputation."

"Reputation?" I had to smile. But I suppose my sarcasm turned it sour.

"You heard." She tossed her head, dropped her foot to the floor, drew her elbows off the chest of drawers. "You're infringing on the big league, brother. You haven't a clue 'bout how they live and think. They've got a codex – they keep their skeletons in the cupboard but soiled goods go down in price. Go talk to Heinrich, he has lots of them as clients, he knows his way around."

"Codex?" I said. "Are you suffering the delusion they think more nobly than you or I?"

"'Course not. But they're birds of a feather, have their own rules. And they've got the cash and they've got the power. You're an outsider, not in the club."

I shrugged again.

"And you're a ditherer too – she's used to bastards who know what they want. Least she knows where she stands." She stared in distain. "You never tie yourself down, you're the hurting kind." Said harshly.

"You exaggerate, sister. I simply was never able…"

"And if you ever tried messing around and harming Annabelle, you'd have papa to contend with – you'd never know what hit you. He could wreck you and your career at the snap of a finger."

"I've never met papa, and I'm not interested in…"

"Don't try – he's a bastard."

"Well, I'm sure you're right there."

"You heard of him? The publisher?"

"Heard of him." I shrugged once more, dismissively. "It's not papa I'm…"

"You've no idea. He brought down a politician once, and Heinrich could tell you a thing or two about colleagues who got in his crossfire." She stared at me down her nose. "You've no conception what you've stumbled into here – so just you take your mitts off her, she's out of bounds." She pushed away from the chest, stood before me, crossing her arms again. "You're not her type, you're not her world."

"No?"

"Nope – she's one of the eligibles, not for the likes of you."

"Well, you're part of her inner circle and you seem to be doing just fine."

"I'm not a nasty sarcastic little shit like you, and I learnt to play by the rules."

"Ah, the rules. I'd say that's for her to…"

Her hand tapped my chest; she'd uncrossed her arms, her fingers had turned to a fist. "My God, and she has two small kids. Stop buggering about, that's not your cup of tea, brother – never open a bloody book you don't intend reading to the end." She took away her hand, let it fall.

I watched her. "With every page you arouse my inquisitiveness."

"Don't be a damn fool." She was swinging roughly away, her arms were stiff at her sides. "And don't come crying to me later that I didn't warn you." She was walking to the door. "I intend warning Annabelle too." She had turned, her hand was on the door knob.

"Ah," I said.

"She's a realist, though – she won't take much persuading."

"How loyal of you, sister – I'm sure you'll do your very best."

She exited, not closing the door. I left the bag on the floor near the sofa-bed, went out too. I thought I'd make myself useful so I walked along the hall to the kitchen.

x x x

Everything was as I'd last seen it, except that from the table someone had removed the butter, salmon, ham and cheese, I suppose because they'd otherwise have spoiled in the heat. I cleared the breakfast things onto the side, wiped the table-top clean; I tried not to look at the children's rug.

While opening wall cupboards and the fridge to find homes for jams and juices and stuff, young Martina marched in with a businesslike air and caught me with packets of cornflakes and *Weetabix* in my hands and a helpless expression on my face. Little Marcel pottered close behind.

"Mamma has jeans just like yours," was her first comment. She stood there with hands on small hips and looked me straight in the eye.

I made a noncommittal sound; I didn't wish to offer rope.

"With a zip at the side too. Men have zips at the front."

"Women too, Martina. It's just a matter of taste." I peered at her over the packet of cornflakes. She had a cute little concentration of freckles on cheeks and nose. It seemed she was satisfied.

"I'll do that," she told me practically. She took the cereals from me.

I began rinsing off the crumbs and food remains from the plates.

"I heard you in the kitchen," she announced. She had clambered up on a worktop, was kneeling, closing a wall cupboard door. "I've come to help you."

"Thank you, Martina – I could do with some assistance."

"And Auntie Maggie told me I could."

I began filling one of the pristine circular enamelled sinks with water, squirted in some liquid soap, started with the washing-up.

"What're you doing?" she demanded. She jumped down, looking up at me. "Here's the dishwasher." She indicated with a small index finger, and opened the flap beside me with a snap. It was empty and sparkling clean.

"Ah," I said. "I don't possess one any more so I never thought to look." She was watching me and storing away that titbit of information, probably saving it for a rainy day. "Well," I told her, "today we'll be old-fashioned and do it by hand."

She nodded. "Mamma sometimes does it this way too when there isn't very much."

"Great minds think alike."

She didn't understand, asked what I meant. I explained; watched her silently mouthing words. Her lashes were long and red and curved, her freckled little nose noble and straight. But her mouth was round like a cherub's, and although the eyes were big and intense they were brown with flecks of grey. I thought of her father who I'd never met. Her hair and freckles were her mother's; perhaps the rest she'd received from him.

She was shaking open a fresh drying-up cloth she'd withdrawn from a drawer. "Is Auntie Maggie your friend," she asked. She said it so directly, it sounded prepared in advance. She stared inquisitively at me.

"She's my sister."

"Are you here because of her, then?"

"Yes."

"Why?"

I glanced at her sideways while I washed. Her directness was refreshing. "She invited me over yesterday evening to talk. It got a bit late so I stayed the night."

"You didn't sleep in the spare room. Why did you sleep in mamma's bed?" She was watching me critically now. Suspiciously.

"Your mamma wasn't there. Brothers and sisters do that sometimes." I continued rinsing plates. Then I added: "And the spare room bed wasn't made up." I smiled at myself; why did I need to justify?

"That's wrong," she informed me.

"What's wrong?" I said it neutrally.

"Mamma says, always start with the glasses."

"Ah."

So again my answer had satisfied. The subject, it seemed, was already dropped and forgotten. I nodded at her changing expression – it was going back to practical and matter-of-fact. How quickly most children forgive and forget.

"It'd be better if I wash up but you don't know where anything belongs. So I'll dry up," she told me.

"Me too," echoed little Marcel. I leaned. He was standing the other side of her.

"You're too young," she retorted. "You'll break things. Go and sit at the table." She laid down the cloth, a world-weary look hung with importance on her innocent face. I saw her at a sideboard by one of the windows. She gave him paper and crayons, adding: "Now you can do another drawing, and try to do better this time."

Quite the little boss. I began obediently on the glasses.

"That's not right for glasses." She tapped my knee, opened the cupboard under the sinks, handed me a yellow mop with wire handle. For six years old she was a real little housewife.

As I continued I side-glanced at her now and then, her arms raised high and stretching to reach the back of the built-in draining board, precisely drying each glass, polishing, placing them in neat order on the snow-white worktop. There was intense concentration in every move, each object handled like a precious egg...

"What did you talk to Auntie Maggie about yesterday evening that took so long?" She was looking at me with those large clear child's eyes; the question caught me unawares. So I'd been mistaken – she was back on her subject of interest again.

"Your auntie has a lot on her mind at present."

"Oh I know all about *that*. She's going to divorce Uncle Heinrich. Is that what you talked about?"

"Yes."

Coming from a child, the bluntness almost unnerved me. I wondered: is she merely repeating the words from Margareth or her mother? She reminded me of my daughter. Andrea had been not much older when Judit took her away. Although repeated like a parrot, there was awareness behind the words; did the innocence deceive?

Martina seemed, once more, satisfied with my reply. Again the subject was abruptly dropped.

"They're not my real auntie and uncle, you know – I just call them that. I don't have proper aunties and uncles mamma's age because mamma's an only child, and papa's sister lives far away and never comes to visit. She doesn't send me presents either since papa died, so she doesn't count."

She stopped, took a quick breath, looking serious. "Grandpapa Elijah's brother and sisters and mamma and papa are dead too. They all died in the War. But his papa had a brother Albert who survived because he wasn't here, he was in South America. He's called Great-grand-uncle Albert and he has an English wife called Mimi, but they live down on the Tegernsee lake and they're very, very old, so they don't really count either, you see."

"Ah."

She looked pleased with her long monologue. My God, I thought – so many in the family lost. I wondered: does she have an inkling of the implications of what she just said? Importantly she picked up the next glass. I thought the danger was past, but she swooped in again. She was like a fencer, darting in and out, always on tiptoe, always on the move.

"If you're Auntie Maggie's brother, then I s'pose I could call you uncle too." She peeped suddenly shyly sideways beneath those magnificent long lashes, looked quickly away again.

"Well, I'd have nothing against it," I said. I was thinking of Margareth's warning words, so I added: "But you must ask your mamma and Auntie Maggie first."

"Why?"

"Because that's the right thing to do, Martina."

She polished the glass, round and round. It was obvious, in her eyes, this was no answer; there was frustration in her fingers. Then she came at me again: "Are you a friend of mamma's?"

Ah, those big penetrating eyes.

"Yes," I said. It seemed the most neutral thing to say.

"How long have you known each other? You've never visited us here before."

"No," I said, stalling. The answer to this had to be carefully considered. "Your mamma has known my sister a long time," I explained. "But I only had the opportunity to get to know her properly this morning."

"Do you like her?"

"Yes."

"You're not the only one."

Such a simple sentence, but it struck me like a careless stick. "Why do you say that?" I said. There was a sudden heaviness in my heart, there was a deadness on my tongue.

"She has lots of men friends."

I was recalling Margareth's words again; now I was sinking like a stone. "Lots?" I repeated dully. I paused, leaned on my hands in the water.

"Three – well two, at least. The one from yesterday evening doesn't count any more."

"She told you that?"

"I heard mamma telling Auntie Maggie all about it before breakfast."

"I see," I said. "And the other two?" I'd tried to make it sound offhand – it came out like a cannon shot.

She glanced at me. "She's known them much longer than a year."

Oh God, I thought.

"They're admirers, she says."

"Ah," I managed. "Really."

"What's an admirer?"

I stared down at her demanding little face. "When one looks up to someone. Thinks a lot of him or her." I had to clutch at a straw; I had to somehow find out more. Rapidly I sought a follow-up question before Martina made another impulsive jump. "And do you like them?" I asked quickly.

"Oh I've never met them. They phone her here though, then she goes out. She never brings them home. Auntie says she shouldn't till she's sure. You've stopped washing up."

I glanced down at my hands – as if I wasn't responsible for them, as if they didn't belong. Till she's sure? I thought. After a year or more? That's a hell of a long time. And I also thought: then perhaps she hasn't decided yet. I felt a small cold comfort that slightly slowed my rate of descent...

"Why have you stopped washing up?" Impatience now.

"Just a short pause for thought," I told her. And carefully I asked: "And do you understand why she has to wait till she's sure?"

"Oh yes. Mamma's looking for another papa for us, you see. Not a proper one of course, because you can only have one real papa."

"I see," I said again.

"You're the first man friend of mamma's I've met. But you don't count because Auntie Maggie invited you. You said so."

I nodded, unhappily. Tried steering her back to the apex of my pain again, in search of possible further solace. "And does your mamma like her two admirers?"

"She told auntie both would be suitable. What's suitable?"

Again I had to explain. In the middle I was interrupted by: "How long are you staying? You're not leaving today."

In spite of myself I managed a fractured smile. "Did you overhear that one as well?"

"No, Auntie Maggie left us while we were drawing pictures and went into the spare room with you, but she shut the door. And now your bag's there."

I shook my head. Annabelle had been right. I too never cease to be amazed at children's powers of observation. "I expect only till tomorrow," I said.

"You only wanted to come for yesterday evening," she pronounced. "Are you staying because of mamma?"

"Yes," I told her truthfully. "She's invited me."

"Thought so. She had a look."

"A look? What do you mean?"

"You were in her bedroom all the time auntie was telling us a story. Afterwards she popped in while we were still drawing and she had a funny look."

Ah, that kind of look, I thought. "I was only taking a shower," I explained.

"Why didn't you use the shower in the spare room then?"

She'd got me there – I hadn't noticed it contained one; I guess Margareth must have distracted me. For a moment I was at a loss – I was being interrogated by a six-year-old, she had neatly caught me out. Then I said: "Perhaps your mamma thought it more practical – my bag and clothes were still in the dressing room from last night, you see."

"Was mamma in her bathroom with you?"

"No, Martina." Now it was I wanting to change the subject. Before I could, she said: "Why are you wearing different trousers and shirt? You had others on for breakfast."

"After a shower one normally does, you know."

"Didn't you have a shower when you got up, then?"

"You're an inquisitive young lady."

"What's inquisitive?"

"A girl called Martina asking so many questions. Now – let's concentrate on the washing-up, shall we?" I busied my hands again.

"Mamma never had that look before. Is that because she likes you?"

That stopped me in my tracks again. A look because she liked me? I thought about that one. The sinking stopped too, hope rose again.

"I don't know, Martina. Why don't you ask her yourself?"

"I did. She told me it was a grown-up's secret."

"Then it's a secret," I confirmed. I confirmed it very gratefully; the load on my heart began to lift.

"That's not fair."

"I thought you wanted to help dry up."

"There are still bubbles on that one." She flashed me a look that said she was sick of adult avoidances. "You're not rinsing properly." I had to admit she was quick with revenge.

"Is that so," I said. "Well nobody's perfect."

"What's perfect?" Her chin raised as she asked. She did it like a miniature of her mother.

So I explained this word too. And as I finished the sentence another voice extended it saying quietly: "But some are less perfect than others," and when I turned hurriedly to glance, Annabelle stood over at the table beside Marcel running her fingers fondly through his hair.

She had put on a dress. And what a dress; I found it wonderfully fit to provoke. It clung more than hung to her body, but without being tight; silky sea-green and sensual, the colour of her eyes. And she hadn't left her hair pinned up with clips; it was still high but all billowing loose now, it billowed like a big fluffy ball...

Sharply little Martina told me: "You've stopped washing up again." Even at that tender age she made it sound petulant and sarcastic.

"Yes," I said. Still I couldn't look away from Annabelle. Nervously I thought: has Margareth been talking to her already – has Margareth got at her now?

She crossed towards us. My breathing came quicker; I watched the way she moved.

"Thanks." She'd stopped beside me. "You don't have to, you know. You are meant to be a guest."

Those green eyes regarded me, they made me jumpy. Is that a warning glint in them, has Margareth managed to persuade – is that why she took so long?

"Guests can help too," said Martina bluntly.

But I hardly heard. I was gazing back at those eyes: I sought in their depths for any sign of cool, any reversal, for any hint of change of heart.

I said: "Actually, Martina's doing most of the doing – without her help I'd surely hardly have started."

Martina cast me a gratifying glance.

And Annabelle said: "How unexpectedly diplomatic." Was that a frown, or just a quizzical crease? "I hope I am not disturbing you then."

"Yes you are," Martina said. It was sharp as a knife again.

Sovereignly her mother leaned the slender rise of her bottom against the worktop next to me; she looked so immaculately unperturbed. I peeped for a second at the dent in her body that the worktop made. A thrill pierced my stomach and shot upwards. I thought: will my hand ever be allowed to touch her there again?

I concentrated. Began on the plates to keep Martina occupied, and to disguise the nervousness in my hands. I steeled myself, took a quick breath, I had to know. I said as casually as I could: "My caring sister cornered me just now and held a brief bruising lecture – did she do a repeat performance with you by any chance?" and I hoped the formulation would pass over Martina's head.

"What's a lecture?" Martina shot out.

I winced. This child possessed the reactions of a sniper whenever someone popped up their head. Annabelle's eyes said serves you right, were vaguely reprimanding. She hadn't answered, had she?

"Well, what is it then?"

I turned my head. Martina stood with hands on indignant hips, glaring up at me. Traitor, her face told me. "A talk on a particular subject," I said to her. "With lots of factual information."

"Which subject?"

"Little girls should not be nosey," her mother intoned calmly, leaning round me. "Curiosity killed the cat." Her slender arms were folded, her breasts rested on them like they'd done that time once before, that time about a thousand years ago. Again I had to catch my breath, I had to close my mind.

"I'm *not* a little girl. I'm six years and eight months. That's almost *seven*." Her small hands had turned to tight fists.

I rinsed several plates, laid them on the fluted steel drainer. "That's a grand age," I said to her seriously. "At six years and eight months I didn't even know what washing-up was."

"Do you speak French?" Annabelle asked me in French.

"No." I side-glanced. A wistful smile on those expressive lips. Was that a good omen? I thought: risk it. I gave her a deadpan stare with half-closed eyes. "Just a smattering of Swahili," I said in my best stilted business English, "and Urdu of course, but..."

"That's not *fair* – you're to talk *German*," little Martina ordered petulantly. She shook my arm. "If you put the plates like this they drain better," she continued, showing me, leaning them against a bowl. "And the top one's got to be rinsed again. Look at all the soap bubbles." She handed it pertly to me.

Annabelle said in perfect English: "I have a very sweet but precocious daughter who understands far more than she should. What did Margareth lecture you about that was so bruising?"

I think I blinked. I didn't know what English 'precocious' meant, just had to guess. I took a brief breath, frowning, searching for suitable words. "About you and me," I answered in English. "She is afraid something could grow, could - how does one say? – develop between us. She gave me a nasty warning."

I rinsed the plate, distractedly, searching for other words; I floundered beneath her fluency like a drowning man. "She... she was very sharp – no... blunt..."

"What're you *saying*?" Martina stamped her foot. "I want to *know*."

"Martina behave, or you go to your room," Annabelle said firmly. "And you know the rules. One is not to interrupt when someone is speaking."

I winked at Martina to show a speck of solidarity, but was brutally rebuffed – oh what a face, a picture of six-year-old fury. To Annabelle I added, blundering on in my primitive working English: "She told me we are like oil and water, said to me that I and my rusty thirty-year-old Mercedes are not part of your world. She described to me your life. You know – millionaire parties every night and holidays on private yachts, and a new Porsche from papa every year..." I tried another squint.

"Well, she is right, of course."

"Yes," I said. "Of course."

Annabelle's face gave nothing away. I wondered what my own eyes were telling her – were they casual and calm with a subtle sparkle of intelligent twinkling humour – or more the glazed petrified gaze of the hunted? Hurriedly I explained: "Naturally I disagree. I prefer to find... no, to... discover truth of who you really are for myself. I prefer to paint my own picture, if one can say that in English."

"Yes, one can."

"Ah."

"How very graphic."

"Ah yes. I was thinking of a modernistic picture perhaps, like Sidney Pollack and painters who throw things – the way I see you when I close my eyes – lots of red speckles and gorgeous green blobs and rusty streaks and... and angry squiggles of... might one say - antithesis"

"Antipathy."

"Ah..." I stopped, gave up. I said: "Did she warn you too?"

"Yes."

"I see."

Her lips parted. "She recommended that I chuck you out. She insists you will never commit yourself, you are only the hurting kind."

I managed to shrug. "Well," I said, "that, of course, is one of my strengths."

"Mmm."

Had to look down, could feel her gaze. Wanted to revert to German, wished her daughter were not there. My hands remained sunk in washing-up water.

She stirred. Arms still folded she leant towards me, her shoulder unexpectedly brushed mine. She even produced a little laugh.

"What're you *doing*?" came Martina's small demanding voice. "What're you *saying*?"

"I'm telling Stefan some things in English," Annabelle said. Her shoulder was gone.

Stefan? I thought. She said Stefan. I looked up again.

"What things?" More petulance.

"Amusing things, but not for your ears, little snail."

"That's not *fair*." And to me: "You're not to keep stopping washing up."

"Okay." I started busying my hands again.

A small fist tapped my arm. "I started kindergarten when I was only four-and-a-half," Martina informed me steadfastly, stubbornly picking up her subject where she'd been interrupted. "In September I'll be going to first-year school already."

"Well that's grand," I said. My gaze was back on Annabelle. A saucer slipped out of my hand, clacked on cups in the water...

"You're not looking what you're *doing*," I was reprimanded.

"Martina, cut that out, please." Expressionlessly, in slow motion, Annabelle freed her arms, let them fall. She turned to me, she was close again. She touched my cheek.

Oh God. Couldn't move, couldn't speak. I could smell the scent on her skin.

Martina had stopped drying-up – her small head was held high and cocked, peering round me inquisitively.

"What're you doing *now*, Mamma?" she demanded. Her voice was indignant.

"I am touching Stefan. I am stroking his cheek the way I sometimes stroke yours, little snail."

I marvelled at her cool.

"One only does that if one's very, *very* good friends," Martina announced determinedly.

"We are good friends."

Good friends? Her words were balm. I lurked like a thief behind each one. A warmth like soft down wrapped round my brain.

"You only met this morning."

"If one meets someone nice, one sometimes feels it straight away. You remember how it was with you and Sabina on your first day in kindergarten?"

No answer.

"Well?"

Grudgingly: "With Sabina it was different." A small glowering glance.

"How different?"

Again no reply.

Annabelle was turning. She leaned round me; her body touched, one of her breasts brushed my arm. Behind my back she was offering an outstretched arm to Martina. "Come here, little snail."

A stubborn shaking of the head.

"Come here." Again her body retreated from mine. She hugged Martina to her, swaying her gently to and fro, before letting go.

"Now how about helping Stefan get this job done..." She ruffled Martina's golden-red hair, her voice was matter-of-fact. "Then you can help me prepare the lunch."

Martina looked at us sceptically. Her small arms hung at her sides, the forgotten cloth trailing a tail on the floor.

"And while we do lunch Stefan can make up his bed."

She was turning away, she glanced at me. "I have put fresh sheets and stuff in your room," she said. She gazed at me with guileless eyes. "You do know how to make up a bed, do you?"

Chapter 10

The six of us sat on long benches in chestnut-tree shade. Mottled light above us, gravel beneath our feet, the trestle table of scrubbed yellow pine; a typical Bavarian *Biergarten*. It lay in the heart of Schwabing only three streets away, so we had gone there on foot – I'd invited them out to lunch; after all her hospitality I felt that the least I could do.

Two pleasant hours, a lull in the struggle to prove my mettle, show my best side. How dishonest we can be when we meet someone new.

We ordered, we ate; Annabelle, Margareth and I drank wine. I allowed myself only half a glass, and I noticed Annabelle did the same. I had little appetite, too: I was being fed by better things, I was feasting on that face.

I sat there in the pleasant early summer shade, I the outsider. Yes, I sat there indulging in this congregation of the families, and the familiarity they conferred – they were bonded by time and habit, had all been so close for years.

Or was I, perhaps, mistaken?

Even Margareth had ceased to cold-shoulder me now, even she was doing her best. Her eyes were steady and careful, though: my sister wasn't the forgiving kind. Could it be they were, in fact, drawing me in and I was becoming a part of it all?

I kept in the background, saying little, indulging in peeps at Annabelle: speckled light on her freckled skin, patches of sun in her hair. A feeling of belonging began to grow, a feeling I'd missed for so many years. And there opposite me, sustaining me, the catalyst, my trophy, the door to this other world.

I jumped...

My mobile was ringing – it vibrated on my thigh.

"Hello?" I said.

"Hello," said Matthias quietly.

My heart staggered. Hadn't expected he'd ring back so soon. I stood up quickly, started walking away.

"Where are you?"

"In Munich," I told him.

"Yes." He said it neutrally. But curious, I had that sudden sensation he said it as if he knew.

"For how long?"

"Well..." I began. I was glancing about. Occupied benches and tables in the tree-shade, people drinking, conversing. Beer mugs, cigarette smoke. Was he hovering somewhere – was he watching me?

"Probably only till tomorrow," I said.

"Let's meet."

My heart jumped again, a little leap of anticipation. "Yes." I glanced back at our table. Margareth had her eyes on me. But only Margareth. "When?" I asked.

"This evening."

This evening? So suddenly – after all these years, suddenly at such short notice? Damn it, I thought. "Damn," I said. "This evening I can't. Not today."

"Pity." Again said neutrally. But did I detect a slight pressure there behind the word?

A brief silence between us.

I so wanted to meet, it seemed he did too. "And tomorrow?" I said. "How about tomorrow?" I could stay at Eva's if I had to.

"Can't say. Maybe."

"Or Sunday? Would that be better?" Wouldn't have to be back in Nuremberg till Sunday night.

"Possibility."

Again a silence. Was he deliberating, was he waiting? Could I persuade him? How much did he want to see me again?

I said into the phone: "It's been so long. I'd really like to meet."

"Yes."

I missed him still, didn't I? And I was inquisitive. I closed my eyes a moment. All those questions were leaping into my brain again. How would he be now, had he really changed? What had made him get in touch, what was he doing nowadays, what was he involved in? Why had he apparently only wanted to renew contact with me...

Matthias's voice was there again. "I'll call you back."

This time I didn't forget. "Give me your number, Matthias, I'll call you."

"Nothing doing."

"Why not?"

"Not easy to reach me. Not at present."

"I see."

"Till then."

He was gone.

Did I see? Not really. But I didn't think about it, I was simply glad he'd called. And ought to go back to the others, not polite just walking away.

I returned to the table.

"An old flame?" said Margareth. She said it with humour though, not nastily.

"An old friend," I replied.

I sat there relaxing again, indulging again. Time passing...

Before me my bare arms lay flaccid on the table – had that feeling they weren't really a part of me. I'd hardly drunk any wine, but there was a heaviness, a hotness, flowing over me. Felt lazy, languid; I'd reached the dead point of the day. I saw that Annabelle's glass was nearly empty, Margareth's as well. Maybe they'd like some more. Sluggishly I picked up the bottle but it was empty too.

I waved to the waiter.

Annabelle leant forward. Mottled shade on her shoulders. How green were her eyes and her dress. She laid a finger on my arm. I felt her touch, felt a flame – so those arms were really mine.

"Not for me," she said.

But Margareth contradicted: "Oh come on, celebrate with me, this is my first real day of freedom – don't leave me in the lurch."

The waiter approached...

I was in a dream, was whispering in his ear, I was losing my touch on time... A glimpse of greased-down hair, a glimpse of occupied neighbouring tables... Was he gone – was he still there...?

Fresh cola came for the children. Or was it only something someone had said? Ice and lemon slices floating. I was being gently criticised. A label held before me... "Yes"... A cork being drawn, the gurgle of wine. Then strawberries and cream arrived too... cries of spontaneous children's delight...

"Oh, Uncle Stefan!" That was Martina, proudly testing her new acquisition; she'd wangled permission from the ladies between the first and second course.

The three of us adults raised our glasses, they rang together like a bell.

"To freedom, sister," I said.

x x x

We were back in the apartment, the children were changing their clothes.

"Birthday party," Margareth said by way of expansive explanation. She sounded a little tipsy, I wasn't surprised at all. "D'you want a cup of tea?"

I stood there in the living room, I was peering across at one of the two works of art on the wall. In the background coming nearer I could hear Annabelle's footsteps on the parquet floor down the hall.

"No thanks."

I stepped back to get it in better focus and accidentally knocked against the grand piano – the open lid crashed down with a bang.

"Sweet Jesus!" That was Margareth.

"Sorry," I said. My voice was feeble, there was a pain at my hip like the blow from a hammer. As I raised the heavy ebony lid to set it back on its prop, the taut strings were still rumbling like thunder.

"Everything all right?" said Annabelle, calmly entering through the open sliding doors.

"Just my little brother smashing up the furniture."

"Oh, that prop again. I really must have it seen to."

I shook my head. "I apologise," I said. I was rubbing the hurt on my hipbone.

"Wouldn't leave him alone here too long, if I were you," added my sister. She swung away, crossed the room, went out to the kitchen without a smile.

"Any damage done?"

Beside me the reverberating tones had just died. I peered at the piano, at the offending prop. "No, I don't think so," I said, pointedly bending and inspecting.

"I meant you, you humorous one."

"Ah," I said, "I'm glad you asked that." I rubbed my hip again. "Now that's an entirely different kettle of fish."

"Is it now." She gave me such a sweet, weakly smile. She was coming over towards me.

"Oh yes. I think a thorough inspection would be most appropriate, in case something's broken." I twisted, peeping at myself. "If I unzip the top here perhaps you would help me extricate myself from your jeans – so you can..." Coyly I cast her a twisted squint.

"Get at what?" she breathed. She stood before me, she stood rather close – laid her hand gently between my legs.

"Get to the heart of the matter..."

She squeezed. I groaned, began to gasp and bend down.

"Would stroking here help, do you think? A little massage to ease the pain?" Her grasp had grown stronger. "Did you say it might be broken?"

I was laughing, half-choking, I was bending down double almost butting her tummy, trying to fend off her hands. She had it in a vice-like grip...

"Can I be of any assistance, kids?" Margareth called, walking in with a tray.

We stopped. I straightened, I was still laughing. I stood there like a naughty boy.

"Just inspecting the damage to the *Steinway*," Annabelle answered sovereignly. "Then we got distracted by his kettle of fish."

"Sorry to hear that." Margareth managed a sickly smile; she put down the tray with a clack.

Annabelle looked at her wristwatch. "Must check the children, time we were leaving." Turning away she said: "I'll be back in about an hour, you two." And then over her shoulder directly at me: "Do you think you will be safe here alone with your sister?"

I was just pecking at the jeans to restore some order; I hurriedly spread my hands. "Well..."

"What are you doing there? Leave it alone." She smiled another sweet smile, walked out and began calling the children.

I followed unhurriedly, went down the hall to the spare room, fetched my bunch of keys from my bag; I'd decided to offer my services. Voices, squeaky voices, excited noises, coming from the children's bedroom next door. While waiting for them in the hall I discarded the slippers, put on my sandals.

They emerged, washed and preened. All three looked grand in party best.

"My," I told them as they approached, "you're all looking so fine." And to Annabelle I said: "And you're looking tired."

"Oh no."

"Tell me the address and I'll drive them over." She couldn't have had more than three or four hours sleep; it seemed the right thing to do.

"Are you serious?"

"Yes."

She paused, considering, watching me. Then: "Well, thank you. I won't say no." And to the children sitting in a row on the pew putting on their shoes: "Did you hear that, children? Another change of plan. Stefan is going to take you." She stooped to help Marcel with buckles. Over her shoulder to me again she added: "Take my Volvo."

I held up my keys.

"Is it safe for the children?"

"It's safe," I said.

"But it is so old. Do you have seatbelts at the back?"

"I do."

"You will be sure they keep those belts firmly closed..." She gave me one or two little instructions, then told me where the party was and the easiest way to get there. It was in a fashionable suburb in the best part of town. "Cleo is the daughter and her mother's name is Stammberg, the senator's wife. Here are the presents." She handed me a carrier bag, and also door keys.

The children trooped out. At the apartment door she stopped me; she stopped me dead in my tracks with the touch of a fingertip. "Thanks," she said simply. Fingers on my cheek, searching eyes.

"Get some rest."

"Mmm."

"I'll be careful," I said.

"I know you will. And be careful of the senator's property, too. She is a rather dangerous one." She paused, as if hesitating. Then just blinked, turned away.

x x x

So we drove to Cleo's party.

I'd folded back the hood, the children were thrilled. I only do it sometimes in cities, or for short drives on country roads. I drove sedately. Little David sat beside me, Annabelle's two behind. I kept an eye open for the law because of David on the front seat, and I let him steer for short stretches in streets with hardly any traffic: he loved that.

It was while regularly checking in the mirrors that I happened to notice a Mini following us at some distance for more than a quarter of an hour. But it disappeared eventually so I guessed it was just coincidence.

The drive was otherwise uneventful; just children's chatter and giggles, the occasional cries or claps of hands. When the novelty of the open car wore thin I gave them a game to occupy – counting all the pedestrians on the pavements who wore a hat to see who had the quickest eyes. Yes the journey was uneventful, it was upon arrival that things came undone.

x x x

"Did everything go smoothly?"

Annabelle lay relaxing on one of the sofas; I'd just walked in. She had twisted her head, she wore an especially glib and worldly expression – I could particularly well understand why.

You wicked one, I thought. Casually I spread my hands. "Naturally." I crossed over, laid down her door keys with a rattle on the amazing table of glass.

"Sit yourself down." An open hand offering.

On the other sofa Margareth was propped with legs up along the cushions too, a newspaper held high. Briefly she tipped it, acknowledged me with a nod, peering over half-moon glasses, then continued reading the *Süddeutsche*. I chose the armchair at right-angles next to Annabelle.

"Do tell me all about it."

I leaned back, steepled my fingers. In the background an oldie played – indistinctly a male voice was singing, "...*believe I can fly, I believe I can touch the sky...*"

"All about what?" I put on my blankest and most innocent face. The memory of the encounter half an hour back still smarted in my brain.

"About how it went with Simone."

"Ah, Simone."

So that was her name. That Munich snob of the unpleasantly superlative class. I could still picture her there on the steps of the villa, distastefully inspecting the four of us down her provocative turned-up snub nose – attractive brunette dolled up in short, low-cut, red dress with pert little backside and stiletto heels to accentuate, breasts sharp and pointed as her tongue.

"Well, actually there's not much to tell," I said. "I drove over, delivered the children, drove back."

The big armchair was extremely comfortable, the kind one sinks into. Cushioned seat and back, padded arms. My body soaked up the luxurious softness.

"Oh really? Nothing else?" She smiled that slow and guileless smile which had already made good acquaintance with me.

"Were you expecting something else?" I squinted with apathetic, half-closed eyes.

"Don't look like that. That looks so horrible."

So I drooped my mouth instead.

She pulled a face. It distorted her beautiful freckles. "I am waiting." Imperceptibly she raised an eyebrow.

"Ah... Yes..." I eked it out. "There was perhaps one small thing." Unhurriedly I crossed one foot over another beneath the fractured sheets of glass. "You omitted one tiny detail," I murmured.

"I did?"

"It appeared the invitation was only for Martina – a girls-only party."

"You don't say."

"Yes, at the sight of the boys, the apple of the senator's eye became unduly unaccommodating."

"What a delightful way of putting it."

I nodded. I paused. Behind us Lou Reed had begun to sing a song. I concentrated. "She even made a little speech. It went rather well with all the balloons and the streamers festooning the portico around her." I paused again, listening – I do rather like Lou Reed. "She gave me clearly to understand that I was placing her in an absurdly awkward position which was rather a silly thing for her to have said, coming from one who is surely deeply familiar with all the positions." I cast her another apathetic and drooping glance. "It rather raised my hackles, actually."

"How frightfully upsetting. I do hope your response was appropriate to a senator's wife."

"Impeccable."

"How could I have thought otherwise." She stirred, she raised a knee. Her dress slipped up her thigh.

I did my best, I didn't look. I said: "I did observe though when I offered my hand that she touched it as if it might bite."

"Excellent." A sparkle of pleasure in Annabelle's eye. "You must have made an admirable impression."

"Well I wouldn't say that. In fact I feel it was she doing most of the impressing."

"How intriguing." Another sparkle, another movement. Her foot was rising, it came towards me. She just opened her legs and delicately laid the foot on my knee. "Do tell me."

"Tell you what?" How beguiling were those legs.

"Your opinion of her."

I focused hard on her face. Be careful here, I told myself. "An intelligent woman," I said.

"Uh-huh." Her foot began gently rocking my leg.

I had to take a breath. "Quick mind. Fast on her feet too... and..."

"Faster than you?"

"Oh yes. And sharper." I couldn't help it, it was such fun to tease – and I could see the teasing mirrored in her eyes. "Attractive too, from what I could see. Of course, she wore a dress over it – a dazzling red dress which almost managed to cover her modesty."

To the left, to the right then back again – her foot imbued my leg with a gentle rhythm all of its own.

"Her what?" she said. A spreading smile now.

"Her Munich modesty. Very sexy... very sexy hands, I find."

"You found time to look at those as well?"

"I always attend to the little details."

I watched her. I made myself stop: I told myself I had to stop this nonsense. But it wasn't easy. Somehow she killed my earnestness, she brought out the mischief in me – all I wanted to do was laugh with her, be close to her, and touch. So I said: "All in all I was very moved by the grace with which she puts people down and the arrogance of her tongue."

She stilled her foot.

I thought: Oh God, have I offended her – have I gone too far? She pursed her lips but didn't speak.

"Have I trodden on your toes?" I asked.

A slow shake of the head, that was all.

"Are you close friends?"

"Not close. We have simply known one another since our schooldays."

"I'm glad about that." I nodded. "You've just risen again in my estimation." I waggled my eyebrows. "I confess you'd slipped a notch or two."

A small pause. Her foot began tipping my leg again.

"I'm a little allergic to this breed," I confessed.

"Mmm. She is a dreadful snob, I agree, and rather calculating. An only child, very spoilt, and tough as steel."

"She bruised me badly with every blow."

"I do apologise. It was naughty of me."

I shook my head.

She stirred, changing position, wriggling a bit closer, stuffing loose cushions behind shoulders and head. Both her knees were in the air, bent now; she laid her other foot on my lap.

I closed my eyes, closed my brain, she was showing quite a lot of thigh.

"Is that too heavy?" Said softly.

"No," I managed to reply. Opened my eyes again. Tried to return her gaze.

"It was time to pull her leg, you see."

"Are we back to the boys?" I asked.

"Mmm."

I cleared my throat, it was getting thick; I could feel the heat of her feet high on my leg. "She doesn't like little boys? Only the bigger variety?"

"Mmm. She has three daughters and only invites girls to parties."

"Ah," I said. "How singularly one-sided, how frustrating for us of the weaker sex."

I got another twinkle for that. She said: "It has been causing bad blood for some time amongst the mums with sons. We had got a little fed-up."

I chuckled. "Well, I'm glad we won the battle of the boys, even though she most certainly won the war."

"Please forgive me."

"I enjoyed it," I admitted. "I sometimes rather like war games."

"Mmm." Another twinkle. "I heard." Like a feather, one of her feet began sliding softly along my thigh. Her knees parted: they allowed a peep of more than a lot of leg now.

I took another heavy little breath to steady myself; stoutly I raised my eyes. "You did?" I said. "You have spies in the bushes?"

"Simone rang me."

Oh God, I thought – so the cat's out of the bag. I raised my eyebrows as reply.

"She was livid."

"She was? About the boys, I imagine."

"About you, too."

"Ah."

"You really are a devil." Now her smile had turned to smug.

I spread my hands. And popped on my innocent expression again.

"She wished to know where I had dredged up Graf von Falk, such an inflexible Prussian officer."

"Ah."

"I hear you were rather a bully."

"Well..." I puckered my lips. "Perhaps I did click my heels once or twice."

She laughed. It came out like a gurgle. A silence. Neither of us spoke. "...*Angie, Angie...*" sang Mick Jagger resignedly, far away.

"You have an attractive laugh," I said. I said it seriously, I meant it.

She watched me with those green, green eyes. Didn't reply. Her sacred little row of toes stroked gently back and forth along my thigh, the secret space between her legs opened and closed. I had to glance – then quickly glance away. Back to her eyes.

They blinked. They blinked as contentedly as a cat. "Shall we change the subject?" she said.

"Yes."

"Before we start being childish again?"

"Yes." I had to swallow, she was arousing me so. I closed my eyes...

"*...not a penny in our pockets...*" sang Mick.

"Shall we even be serious?"

"I'd be deeply grateful if we could try," I said.

Her toes had stopped sliding. Tenderly they dipped into my skin, clawing softly like a kitten. "Is that nice?"

I could hardly breathe. "Yes," I gasped.

"Look at me."

I looked. Oh God, those eyes again. Clear and steady, sucking me in. And the lashes above and below, they really were red – I could see them curling, and see the dark little dips beneath where the skin of her cheeks met her nose, and I could see the freckles, too, like mottled shade all around. I just had to look, now, I could have looked for the rest of the day. I looked so hard and helplessly and so long I knew I was giving myself away...

She spoke. I dropped my stare, just for a second, I saw her lips move. How I loved those lips too... was I falling in love, or had it happened already – had it happened the first second I was allowed to behold her?

She said: "Would you touch me." It wasn't a question, it wasn't a command, it simply flowed out of her mouth and across the gulf, flowed into my hands. I touched her. I touched her toes, her holy feet. I would have kissed them if she'd wished, I would have washed them with my tears – I knew I'd worship the ground they walked on till the end of my days. I felt their smoothness, could feel their grace. They slid across me, she was lowering her knees...

A rustle. I looked up. Margareth had lowered the newspaper, was glancing disinterestedly. Her half-rimmed spectacles glinted gold; each side of the frames a black band hung, running behind her neck. She reminded me of a stern if elegant university professor. I'd never seen her with reading glasses before; she always was a far-sighted woman. With another rustle she turned a page, went back to reading.

My fingers were around Annabelle's foot. Carefully I stroked. There were tiny freckles on its upper surface, but none on her long pale toes. I stroked the freckles, smoothed the skin.

"Mmmm..."

Raised my eyes. Her head was rested back on cushions, her eyes were closed, red hair billowed all about. Her body lay there, long and abandoned, lovely in that slinky dress. I looked down at my hands again, to see what they were doing...

"Why did you leave Munich?" I heard her say.

My thumbs had travelled to the sole of her foot, had begun to carefully knead it.

"I wasn't happy," I said.

"Why was that?"

"There were roots there but they didn't go deep." I watched my hands; they seemed to have taken on a life of their own. They stroked and kneaded; I smiled upon them. They were off the leash, I'd let them go.

"Weren't they the only roots you had?"

"Yes. But I was always searching for that something. I didn't find it here."

"And in Nuremberg?"

"It wasn't there either."

"Not even with your wife Judit?"

I stared at my hands, I stared at her foot. Such an elegant foot. "Yes," I said. "I thought I'd found it in her till I lost her. Then I knew I'd lost it for good." My fingers had crept up to her toes. Gently, I thought. I massaged them lightly between fingers and thumb.

A silence between us. Jagger was gone now, there was a different song...

"And now?" she said.

The toenails were small and manicured. They were varnished too – a colourless varnish. Yes, I wanted to stoop my head and kiss them. I said: "Now it's one step worse, now I'm disillusioned too."

I glanced up again. How high the hem had ridden up those thighs. Then I discovered her eyes had opened. So I added: "I must have looked in the wrong places."

"Mmm."

I nodded. "My father once confided in me – he told me the secret. He said happiness is to be found inside of us, not in the world. So I looked there too. I looked a long time and found nothing. Was he right, do you think?"

"Yes he was."

"I found only emptiness." I stopped. Considered. "And a hunger I couldn't still," I added.

Another silence. And in the background a man's voice, deep and mature and melancholy. I cocked my head...

"...you're living for nothing now, I hope you're keeping some kind of record..."

"Who's that?" I asked. I watched her watching me.

"Cohen," she said.

"Ah yes." I nodded vaguely. "I think I've heard of him." I nodded again, slowly. "I like Jacques Brel, too. Do you?"

"I do."

"You must understand him much better."

"Mmm."

How soft her eyes were. They really could get very soft.

"Tell me a little about your father," she said quietly.

I readjusted. "I loved him," I offered. Then I chose some more words more carefully: "But he hanged himself when he was nearly young and I was too old to forget. I think he found his happiness, though. He took it with him."

"Margareth told me." It was just a murmur.

"He was a man full of wisdom," I added. "In deep contrast to my mother. I miss him. He left a big hole in me."

A pause. She didn't speak. The pause lengthened. There was that melancholy voice coming through again — it must've been rather a long song...

"...thanks, for the trouble you took... from her eyes..."

Then she said something very nice. She said: "He left you his wisdom, didn't he, so that didn't die. You have his wisdom too, my philosopher."

I shook my head. "I'm anything but that," I let my eyes fall. "But thanks for your generosity, and your kindness." I dropped my eyes right down to her feet this time, I couldn't speak of my father any more. Instead I tried to listen to the rest of the song being sung, but it was in English and complicated and I couldn't really follow the text too well; the poetry went over my head. I liked that voice, though; I liked its mellowness and gold, I liked its pain.

My hands were exploring. I watched them. They pressed the skin between the sole of her foot and her toes — it was like a little pad...

"Mmmm..." She murmured. She stirred.

"Is that nice?" I said.

She was rubbing her head slowly over the cushions, turning it pleasurably this way and that. "That is very nice."

"Judit taught me. Something from her more exotic eastern bag of tricks."

She watched me with half-closed eyes. So I did it again.

A flapping of newspaper, then it was being impatiently tapped. "Children, I'm going to leave you to it." Margareth's voice, but amusement in it.

Immediately Annabelle turned her attention, turned her eyes. She raised a hand, fluttering her fingers, sending a smile. "Stay," she said.

"Want some sun."

I raised my head, glancing between them. They were exchanging glances of their own again; close, familiar, no words needed. Like at breakfast. Then Margareth was folding the *Süddeutsche*, laying it aside, her glasses rode on the end of her nose. With the flick of a hand she picked them free, let them fall; they dangled from the band. Standing there, she simply said: "I'll be out on the terrace – scream if you need any help." I had a sneaky feeling she hadn't been speaking to me. She took up a book and spectacle case from the table, wedged them under her arm; she was walking away, unbuttoning her blouse as she went.

Annabelle settled her head back on the cushions, but was following Margareth with her eyes. I had stilled my hands, couldn't read her thoughts. Wondered if I was in the way.

"You have stopped massaging." A low and sultry, a golden voice. Her gaze had returned, it swallowed me up.

I bowed my head; I was very glad, she'd made it good again. I replaced my fingers on the little pad. Through the open terrace doors a scraping sound, a sun chair being pulled.

Annabelle stirred again, she moved her legs this time. I allowed a sneaky glance – over her ankles and up her calves, on over her knees, right up to where her dress began, then quickly back again. Her freckled legs had opened again, taunting again.

"Those are my shoulders," I heard her murmur.

I slid my fingertips, pressed some more.

"And that is the nape of my neck."

"Ah," I said. Now I understood.

Another silence. A pleasant silence...

"*...I'll cross the stream... I have a dream...*" A woman's voice, faintly. It was happy, though, it was full of hope.

That's Abba, I thought. It reminded me of Judit, of the early days – it reminded me of many things. I forced them away – I surprised myself, I found it wasn't hard. I deserted the toes and massaged on, along the length of her foot, very slowly. Glanced to the windows. Margareth sat out in the sun on one of the teak sunbeds, legs stretched; she'd shed her blouse and drawn up her skirt, her bra was black, she had heavy breasts.

"*...I believe in angels...*"

I reached the ankle, reached her heel. Angels, I thought. I could believe in them too – I could believe in almost anything now, and I hardly have to try. There were hollows at the heel, just below the ankles. I lingered there.

"Aahhh..."

Such a drawn out sigh. I stroked with the tips of my fingers in ever smaller circles, it seemed not a bad idea; I'd got that bit from Judit too – that was one of her arousing ones. I made a little pause.

"Mmm. Do that some more."

I did it some more. The skin was smooth, almost creamy – yes, her skin was soft as silk. I lost myself in the movements, I lost myself in thought...

"My poor one."

My senses jumped at the unexpected sound although her voice wasn't more than a purr, they drew together like a tautened string. My poor one? What did she mean?

"How could you never have found happiness. You possess all the ingredients to understand."

I looked up at her. I watched her watching me. She lay there in all her beauty, her body was like the song. Should I tell her? That I was happy now – but that it all depended on her?

"Isn't happiness so elusive?" I said carefully to those watching eyes. "Even if one stumbles upon it – isn't it something that's bound to get lost like the innocence of a child?"

Slowly she shook her head. She was shaking it to show she'd found the secret, wasn't she? She was surely one of the lucky ones – like Estella. Estella had discovered it too, she'd sometimes tried to explain it to me, tried to lead me onto the path.

I gazed at Annabelle – at the calm within her, at that indefinable certainty she radiated which I wasn't able to touch. But did I really care? I gazed at that lovely head, surrounded by all that wild and abandoned hair. Oh God, yes, I loved her already – wasn't that all that counted? Or would I lose this too, like I'd lost everything else of worth up to now because I didn't belong to the initiated? Was she, too, bound to walk away, in one year or a week – or even one day? Had the Master of Fate marked me down as ineligible to be ordained in this the greatest mystery of life?

"There must be some things which make you happy," she said quietly.

I shrugged. "Well..." I paused a moment to rest my hands. "Little things, perhaps. Like a good book or conversation. Or a concert or a film." I nodded to myself. "You know, like an Ingmar Bergman, *Face to Face* or *The Silence* and so on. Or any film with Jeanne Moreau." That last one I popped in as a plum.

She smiled a little smile. Such a very private smile.

"You like those too?" I asked quickly.

"Mmm."

"They found the secret, somehow."

"The secret?" she said.

"What you're on about. This business of happiness."

She smiled again, that very personal smile. "I am not certain they did. But Fromm did, and I believe even Cohen too."

"The one singing that song just now?"

"Mmm, that one. The Canadian Jew." She twinkled. "But don't let us..."

"Ah, another Jew," I interrupted. "We've come round to your chosen people at last, have we?" I attempted a small significant grin.

"Spare your irony, please."

"I'm sorry."

"You are trying to distract again."

"I'd do anything to do that," I said.

She allowed herself a little laugh, lying there on her cushions. She looked so good. "So you see," she said, "there are in fact some things which bring you happiness. That is a good beginning."

You're a stubborn woman, I thought. "The feeling quickly wears thin, though," I said aloud.

"I wonder why that is."

I shrugged again and shook my head. I was impotent to reply.

"Think of your father's words."

"Yes." I was already thinking. But I'd thought of that so often, and always hit a wall.

"Wouldn't you agree with him that happiness lies within?"

I was back in the study, that sunny late afternoon. "He spoke to me of motivation," I said. "That motivation is a path which can lead there, he said it's the magical force within. But he went way over my head." I could see them again: those particles like dust caught in the sunbeam above his desk. "He said if he could start over again, he'd find his on an island, he'd go and be a painter. Just paint and exist and watch the sun come up and the stars at night in the firmament."

I stopped. Suddenly I felt so close to him. Just for a tiny moment it was almost as if he were there. Yes, I stopped and spread my hands.

And Annabelle said: "What motivates you then, my uncertain one?"

I thought about that for a second. "Well..." I began. "I couldn't be a painter – or compose music or poems, or any of those creative things. And to sit and stare at my navel all day would surely bore me stiff."

"And your work? Doesn't that motivate you?"

"No."

"No? Not at all?"

"Did at the start, perhaps," I said. "But there's too much power and money involved – if you lift up the stones and peep, you only find a load of corruption and greed and dirt underneath."

"How dreadful." She gazed at me thoughtfully, as if her mind was on the move. "What is your work, then?"

I shook my head. Glanced to the windows: Margareth was reading her book, she wore big sunglasses now. "Didn't my sister tell you?"

"No."

"She told you all my other nasty little habits." I tried a smile; it didn't work. She just lay there peaceably, waiting.

"I give you three guesses," I said.

"I don't like guessing games."

"I'd love you to try."

Unhurriedly she rubbed the back of her head on her cushions again. "Something to do with politics, perhaps?"

"Not a bad guess, naturally." I shook my head. "But God forbid."

"A corrupt industrialist." A mischievous smirk.

"Getting warmer."

She sighed. It was such a lovely sigh. "I have no idea. Tell me, please."

"Just one more try."

She wrinkled her nose, pursed those expressive lips. "I know," she said, "a spy!"

I managed a real grin this time. I chuckled my dirtiest chuckle. "How did you guess?"

"You are pulling my leg." She stared at me down that elegant nose. "But you would make an excellent spy."

"I would?"

"Small and inconspicuous. And that poker face."

"I don't like the small bit."

"I am certain that all successful spies are small." She stirred again, wriggled her foot. "You have stopped massaging again."

I bowed to her will. I began on her sole. And told her what my profession was.

She was silent a moment. Then she said: "When I first saw you this morning, I thought you were a doctor." She said it seriously.

"I fear my dedication wouldn't go that deep."

"I believe it could."

I dipped my head, in gratitude. Said nothing. I was thinking of Geoffrey, my doctor friend in Australia; he had motivation, didn't he, yet he was lost in the dark like me. My fingers moved along the side of her sole.

"Why did you choose this as career?"

"I thought I could make a difference," I said. "I fooled myself I could play a part."

"Tell me."

So I told her. But briefly. About my initial hopes and naïve dreams of bringing some morals back into business even if in a very small way. About the powers that finally killed my father and were slowly strangling others too. And I told her about my growing disillusionment and impotence, that swimming against the tide, about the politics and lobbies and industry, the networks of the establishment with their garbage and their greed. Then I stopped again. Stroking her slender foot was so calming, so relaxing; it brought me consolation and balm...

Annabelle was speaking now. I just gladly listened. And while I did I raised my hands, laid them on her other foot, began to stroke that instead. She had steered away from the topic of my work, I was very glad about that; whenever I was forced to talk about it I felt like a broken man. Yes, she'd returned to the subject of happiness, was speaking of other things now, deeper things, more esoteric – I tried my best to follow her, didn't wish to disappoint. In truth, though, I would have preferred the silence, and her body, would've simply liked to ask her if she was of the same opinion as I and could I just lie beside her.

I think about a minute went by...

I let her words pour over me like honey running in the sun. My hands moved automatically, curling round her foot, pressing and stroking; I let them go whichever way they wished.

She was talking about the meaning of life and the role that happiness played, she was getting perilously close to the core – well I'm the master of failure of this one, I thought, I've been wrestling with it since my teens. I squeezed myself further together, I listened with only half an ear. Then hung my head so she couldn't see and slowly closed my eyes...

"...and the secret of life is life itself and simply accepting..."

Yes, I thought, that's the beautiful one. I stumbled on that when I was twenty-six and I've been stumbling ever since. I mumbled something appropriate and fell into my abyss again.

The seconds ticked by.

"One shouldn't worry over it, Stefan. Or try to analyse it."

"No," I said, obediently. I'd been busy analysing most of my life.

"Life and your potential for happiness are both inside you."

"Ah." There it was again - that something so unhappily familiar...

"Simply relax and go into yourself now and then, and meditate. Try not to think any thoughts..."

Oh God, I thought. Meditation. That's it, that's what Judit tried on me once – in her esoteric yoga group; it had ended only just this side of catastrophe. We'd been doing the Tree of Life one, balanced on one foot: I'd tipped sideways and flayed my hands, knocking my neighbour, bowled him over and the shockwave went down the whole row. I frowned into my lap; I still got cramps and dizziness just thinking about it...

I was on her toes now, I noticed, working my way along the row. I felt like the last of a puddle in hot sunlight that's starting to go dry. I decided it better not to answer, decided to hold my peace.

She was speaking again. What a wonderful voice she had. And what pearls of wisdom were issuing forth; they reminded me of

Estella at her best. I crouched there receiving them, I sat there like the swine.

"...and you will notice the changes, you will begin to see the signs."

"Signs?" I said. I raised my eyes, I risked a glance.

She lay there looking at me, so casual and calm. "One becomes more aware," she said simply.

"Of what?" I knew it – I knew what she was going to say. And then she went and said it.

"Of oneself, for example, and things happening around one. Things you used to think were only coincidence."

I blinked. There was Estella back again. I smiled. Then I tried a laugh – it came out like a choke. "You remind me of my good friend Estella," I said. "A platonic friend." I cleared my throat, and added: "Despite the best of my efforts." I gave another little chuckle. "She talks about the same sort of stuff. She's been working on me too."

"Uh-huh." Green eyes watching, expressionlessly. "That is good to hear." The eyes had me very tight, they held me in a vice...

Scraping sounds out on the terrace again.

I had to tear my eyes away, her look was so intense. And as I did, in the background of the room, an old Ray Charles record had just begun. I recognised that one. That was *Georgia on My Mind* – of all the oldies which had been playing that was the one I knew the best. I allowed myself a moment of indulgence.

I turned my eyes to the windows. It was only my sister changing her position. I saw she'd put her book aside, she was lying down on her stomach; I thought her breasts far too large for comfort.

"*...through peaceful dreams I see, the road leads back to you...*"

And Annabelle said hauntingly: "You have Georgia on yours too."

I didn't dare reply. Nostalgically, I sat there looking across the room towards the late afternoon, and the light from the terrace was turning to the colour of her hair.

Chapter 11

The evening was not just a surprise, it was a jewel.

It was like something out of nineteenth century literature, or a set-piece historical film. Personally, I had never experienced anything like it, hadn't even considered such a thing possible nowadays. It merely went to confirm Margareth's words once more that I wasn't in Annabelle's class.

She had invited a concert pianist to play, I gather she'd planned it weeks before. She introduced him as a friend of her family. Cohen – Benjamin Cohen. They were on Christian name terms; he embraced her in cloak and silk scarf at the door as if they were long lost friends, and in the hall stripped down to open shirt and check trousers when I was expecting white tie and tails. His wiry wild hair was dark and wavy with eccentricity at the tips of the curls. He had the air of a master magician, the presence of a foreign prince.

The children were enchanted, they each got a special kiss. Even I who didn't frequent concerts so often recognised his face and had heard of his name. He was famous, I'd read, a colleague of Simon Rattle and Barenboim, he came direct from orchestral rehearsals for a Beethoven concert in Munich the following evening.

Annabelle did it in restrained and tasteful style; canapés with wine by candlelight and easy intimate conversation before he began to play. She and Margareth allowed the children to stay up, dressed appropriately for the occasion still in their party best – and they themselves attired like the good old days. I had nothing else to wear except the freshly washed denims and slightly soiled shirt; I looked like a tramp. Annabelle said what did it matter? She also said, cheekily: "If you really persevere, you might allow your inner qualities to shine through." Squatting in the background I remained in deep doubt.

There were only two other guests, apart from me: a delightful old lady from the house next door, and a certain Detlef Fuchs. He was introduced as her dear cultivated neighbour from the first floor. A self-possessed and perfumed dapper little man, my age, in expensive jewellery and handmade shoes – he walked with a hint of a wiggle in his hands and hips, exuded homosexuality from every pore. It appeared he was already acquainted with the pianist. I rather liked him; I like people who don't fit, don't conform.

The maestro came at eight, supped with us, then took little Martina beside him on the piano stool and guided her through three popular pieces – I hadn't known Martina was musically minded, she had a remarkable gift.

We'd rearranged the furniture and turned the grand so we could all watch his movements, see his hands. I was separated from Annabelle by Detlef; we sat in the second row and her arm languidly lying on the sofa back lay behind Detlef not behind me.

When finished, he lifted Martina lightly down offering words of praise and gently stroking her glossy red hair. He had fine long fingers, and an aquiline nose. As she trotted back proudly to join the children on their cushions on the floor he gave Annabelle a knowing nod and his gaze was intimate, too; I wondered if they'd ever made love.

Then he settled himself, bowing slightly forward and closing his eyes; he appeared to be withdrawing into another world. Almost tenderly he touched his fingers to the keys.

He played, it seemed, for hours.

The twilight faded and the night came on; he had a wonderful touch. Between each piece, in the pauses, he gave explanations for the children and although I tried to disguise it he did it for me too. He played Beethoven and Schumann, and Chopin and Liszt; he held all eight of us in raptures. In his proximity flickered a personal flame which a concert hall cannot provide.

Near the close, diffidently, at his beckoning invitation, Annabelle joined him. They sat side by side and played a duet; she had no music sheets, they did it as if they'd done it often before, they played almost as one. Watching her talent from those hidden genes and her natural grace, fascinated, I felt so proud of her, I felt so small. More than once during that long piece I thought: Margareth's right isn't she, I don't belong, what the hell am I doing here? And I know it was in these moments, with that sinking feeling in my gut, I realised it was only a dream and dreams don't last that long.

When he departed it was nearly midnight; he exited with a rich Baroque laugh and a swirl of his cloak wrapping Annabelle inside. Then he was gone. The old lady and Detlef Fuchs left soon after – I remember Detlef's delightful manners, and his tears which the music induced. I offered Annabelle my special thanks for extending my stay and the grand surprise, for including me in the soirée.

We were all tired but exhilarated, went straight to bed with classical strains in our heads. I remember too, as Annabelle said her goodnight, the dark rings beneath her eyes and the finality of her words. "I'll wake you in good time in the morning," she said. "I have my first appointment at ten."

I knew my time had run out.

x x x

I lay alone on the sofa-bed near her worktables, beneath a thin summer sheet; I was naked because of the heat. Perfunctorily I had washed in the small connecting bathroom that doubled as utility room. I wished I could've shared hers.

Despite the joy of the evening I had begun to feel depressed. The thought of having to go hung in a lump in my head. I felt a bit like a boy with his toy taken away. How immature, feeling that way at mid-forties.

I struggled with the thought, trying to suppress it, I needed to sleep. A fragment of a Chopin prelude came and went. The truth was plain: I didn't want to leave next morning – how soon could I attempt to see her again? Would I ever see her again? Nothing was clear, nothing defined – barbed wire in my brain. But I had to try. This required delicate planning.

The minutes ticked by.

I lay there in the dark. What could I do to make the difference, tip the scales? Faint hints of her books in the bookshelves – vague silhouette of her computer against the window, against the black of the night. I stared despondently. In four or five hours the sun would come up, flood all the details in light. Then it would be too late. I could see me... I was sitting at breakfast, the clock on the wall said quarter to ten – she was standing up, time to go. I thought: this isn't the way to say goodbye – why hadn't we taken a little time together before retiring to bed? I was a fool, why hadn't I taken the initiative? She was gathering her bags, she was in a hurry, her mind was jumping ahead. She'd forgotten me already, hadn't she? What to say? It was too late to talk... in front of the children and Margareth, over abandoned breakfast things – what can one say in a situation like that?

The minutes ticked on. I could hear the alarm clock in the darkness tapping them out, second by second...

No inspiration. Brain totally tangled. Get some sleep, then. Maybe inspiration will come in a dream. I concentrated, tried to think of nothing. But thoughts kept on crawling. I turned on my back, stared in the dark at the ceiling that I couldn't see. Didn't help either...

Finally though – had a whole hour gone by altogether, or only a half? – finally I made it, I think, because images I'd been looking at broke into fragments, smoothed into strange forms, and bits of music came creeping through... I drifted away on flakes of Liszt – slowly I suppose I sank into the gooey sucking mud of sleep, but I can't remember, I was no longer there...

Sounds. A scratching on wood. Disturbing the sequence of thoughts and things. I floundered. A scratch at a door I presumed was a dream or a figment of my imagination. I was surfacing, groaning, gaining awareness, was rising up out of my muddy warm and cosy womb...

For a moment there was a light in my eyelids and I was half-awake, then a door was shutting again and a sudden thrill threw my thoughts to the wind and the scent of Annabelle was in the air... was it only an extension of the dream I'd been in?

My eyes were wide open now, and my senses alert, my heart jumping and jolting – my lungs tried to keep pace. The last thing I saw was a line of light below the closed door from the hall outside, and a pinprick from the keyhole like a star far away. Then a silhouette had erased the line, extinguished the star; Annabelle was lifting the sheet, slipping in beside me, whispering in the dark. I felt her tummy press on my arm. There was a wisp of silk touching my skin, and the stroke of her hair, the scent of her perfume overpowering; I closed my eyes tight, I held onto her body like a drowning man.

"Mmmm..." she breathed. It was close to my ear. Again that thrill almost killed me. Fingertips... touching me, exploring my skin. I mumbled into the dark. Her body was warm, was soft through the silk.

"Mmmm..." she breathed again. Her fingers, light as down, had reached my groin. I groaned.

"Sshhh..."

I felt her stretch up; a breast caressed my shoulder then my face. She pressed switches beside the bed I hadn't yet learned were there. Reading lights and a standing lamp bathed the room in white.

She wore her nightdress from the night before. She was turning, kneeling, peeling it over her head, drawing it clear, casting it off like the skin of a snake – dropping it in the abyss in the faraway world outside the small bed. For a moment she was crouching naked next to me – slim back straight, breasts hanging and elbows raised, hands up high undoing her hair. I glimpsed armpits unshaved and stiff brown nipples, the lines in her face as she stooped to me swooping her head. Then her mass of hair fell over me and all I could see were green eyes very close and all I could smell was that scent. She kissed my mouth, it was wet and soft, I felt the tip of her tongue. Her body was there too, it sank down beside me, her arms snaking, turning me.

"Come on me," she whispered.

She was drawing me onto her. Long strong fingers. I was between her legs, her tiny tuft tickled my skin, sickened my senses, swamped my brain. My tool was stiff; it was so taut, so tight it almost hurt, I thought it would burst. Her legs were open, she was raising her knees.

"Come..."

I thought: I must arouse her first, this isn't fair, I should...

Fingers slipping between my hip and her thigh, they stroked my penis, guiding it. I moaned, I sighed. They had taken the tip, they touched it to her holy place, the lips of that thrilling lily, they were hot and wet like her mouth had been. She rubbed it gently to and fro and I began to lose my mind...

"Come in me."

Carefully she drew the tip and dipped it in, wriggled closer and I was sliding inside. I gasped, I panted, I caught my breath, the burning ache spreading down my legs. Her hand was gone, her arm withdrawing, I sensed her fingers creeping, they pressed my behind.

Slowly I slid deeper inside. She was hot and slippery; her body enclosed me, sucking me in. Felt dizzy. My heart beat faster, my stomach turned over, I was so aroused. I was in the tunnel my finger had explored half a day, half a lifetime ago. Like a small sticky tube it gripped me, squeezed me softly, wouldn't let me go. I moaned again, I know I groaned again from the depths of my soul...

"Sshhh, my aroused one – have to do it quietly, must not wake the sleeping ones..."

Her words were so collected, I marvelled at her calm; they were warm on my forehead, though. Spreadeagled, I sank deep, deep within her till I could go no more. She enclosed me like a tight and pulsing fist, full of milk and honey, full of anointing oil – this queen of queens was swallowing me up, squeezing, teasing me, nearly driving me mad.

Ever so slowly I withdrew a little, back down that slippery tunnel – just to repeat the gorgeous sensation. Must've retreated too far. I felt her fingers tauten, stop me, pressing me firmly – I felt each finger, each fingernail... again her lily received me with opened petals, surrounding me with that wonderful slime, welcoming me. Willingly, obediently I slid inside once more, greedy to be taken, to be sucked back in. I was so sensitised, just like I'd been before the very first touch, I could feel every cell as I slipped, each inch of this paradise, each tightening of that heavenly tube... then the whole of her was taking hold of the whole of me.

A tremor... it went right through me. I was exploding, I was coming. Yet I wasn't. Ecstatic. It shook me to my bones. It subsided a little. Had been like a climax. I floated. Moving inside her. Hot and soft and milky. Silky almost, all around me, squeezing me tight; her body was like a glove. Oh God, what a wonderful world, these were truly the gates to paradise. She was moaning. I was moving some more. Withdrawing slightly. Pressing again. She had me in her holy grip. Another tremor... it touched my substance, turned me inside out, lifted me up, I was surely coming now... a burning ecstasy. Exploding again. Hovering. Fading again. I floated in it like before, it carried me along on ever gentler wings but seemed to refuse to set me down. Moaning. Was that her, was that me? Hands on the sides of my hips, holding me a moment, so certain, so sure, her body rolling gently, arching – her hands on my chest now pushing me away. Did I have to stop? I was still in her sweet tunnel, though, trapped fast in this dream, I was in her hot cave where I wanted to be, in her holiest of holies where I prayed to stay. I stretched up on my arms, her face and her shoulders had fallen away and her cave was tipping, guiding, my tool turning within it stiff as a rod. I could hear me panting, I bit my tongue. Another tremor shook me through and through. Came and went, in a climax, in a flash. Her tummy and hips were undulating, they held my tip on a swollen spot, it aroused me so much I feared I'd cry out. She was gasping, head back, her hair everywhere – she closed her lips tight, breathing in and out wildly through that beautiful nose, her head was tossing from side to side; I had to stare, just for a second...

My penis ached, I ached all through, in every pore, my welling greed demanded more and more. Shut my eyes... hands clutched my bottom, nails dug in my flesh, her body beneath me shook like a leaf, impaled upon me, her pauper and prince. She was breathing so loud and so long, I wanted to swallow every single breath – her nails dug deeper, oh what wonderful pain, go deeper and deeper...

But they were gone already. Arms reaching, pulling me down. My chest slipping on hot wet breasts, my face in her perfumed hair. Her mouth pressed to my ear, her tongue was licking, her teeth bit my lobe.

"Come..."

Her legs were lifting. Like snaking scissors they wrapped around me, I felt her feet, those naked feet, those heels, those squirming toes, felt her thighs squeeze me in a fleshy vice.

"Come..."

That golden voice, that royal command close in my ear. Her teeth were nibbling, biting, how I needed that pain, how did she know? She was wriggling beneath me, a wonderful rhythm, I couldn't stop – she was a sucking sheath drawn around me slipping and sliding, making me burn, making me come, making my body obey. I was coming. An ache, an all-consuming ache from top to toe... couldn't stop now even if I wanted... aaaahh... there were those tremors building up, but not quite like just now. The ache reached a pitch, began concentrating. All my fibres were drawing in again like they had on the rug those countless hours before, picking me up in a mighty wave that swelled and swamped and stole my soul... I held onto her, I don't know where, to her hair or her arms – I held on so hard, wanted to hold her till the end of time...

I came...

...I her prince, her knave, once more on an endless flight through eternal space, a consuming flame, leaping higher, a burning rush flushed out my body – deep inside her, deep within her secret cave the whole essence of me exploded, shot forth.

x x x

We might have lain there quite a while, for when she stirred it woke me. Drying sweat, the heat of skin; two bodies one. She was moving under me, stretching, shaking me gently. My shrunken stump had stuck to the lip of the lily. I raised myself, made to roll away. But she simply turned me on my side, turning too, tucked my leg between her thighs, closing them like a book.

I slept again; I slept with my arm around her, my face lost in her perfume, buried in hair.

x x x

It was four-forty-five according to the alarm clock.

And already it was getting light. A soft May glow in the Munich sky, and the tops of roofs beyond the tipped-open windows crisp clean silhouettes. The promise of another of those nearly perfect early summer days.

But my heart was heavy. And my eyes burned with tiredness, my head was hollow as a drum. Annabelle had propped her cheek on her palm, was tracing a line with her fingertip along the wrinkles in my face. I knew, in a moment or so, she'd be pulling on her nightdress and walking out the door.

We lay there face to face.

Dawn chorus of birds, the clack of the clock, otherwise no other sounds. I thought: there are so many things I want to say – isn't there anything she wants to, too? So I decided: wait for her to speak first. I watched her eyes and played with a strand of red hair.

But she said nothing. Was she too tired to talk? Dark beneath her eyes, a furrow on her brow; they showed her age. We were two ships on the ocean, a bit battered, not quite young. I was glad about that.

Still she didn't speak.

Her fingertip was travelling still, it reached my upper lip. And paused. Her silence forced my hand.

"Annabelle..." I began. I didn't want to leave with ends still open, didn't wish to leave like this.

Her finger moved again; I felt it scratch on my unshaven face. It pressed upon my mouth as if to say no.

"When will we meet again?" I said. I said it as casually as I could.

The green eyes gazed expressionlessly. She made no reply.

I thought: what do I say now? I cast about in my empty brain, was sure that gaze was following my every single thought. But no words came, they'd abandoned me again; I didn't trust myself to speak.

She blinked. Was stroking my lips – back and forth. Then her fingers wandered to my rough stubbled chin. She said simply: "Will we?" and left that deadly mighty question mark suspended in the air.

"Won't we?" Chaos inside. Everything crumbling. My exhaustion hadn't even blunted the blow. I made my eyes fall – feared what they would show. They came to rest on her body. On freckled skin, on breasts hanging down. The nipples weren't swollen, not stiff any more, and the exciting redness of that flush was gone. Emptily I thought: will I never see her naked again – won't we even manage to meet? Foreboding crept up out of the rubble inside me where ecstasy had briefly been king. It clutched me like claws, it tore at my gut, and wouldn't let me go. I stared down at what I worshipped but my brain was crawling beyond. I was thinking of all the other men to whom she'd exposed this body and mind – those other knaves who'd been allowed to sip her once, had they all craved to win her crown like I was doing now?

"I want to see you again," I said. "Want to see you very soon." I looked back up to meet that gaze; my heart was heavy as lead. "In fact, about one second after I walk out your door," I added, before I lost my nerve.

"You do?"

The fingers were on the move again, they'd fallen away from my face. Oh those unreadable, unconquerable, those green and queenly eyes. I took a breath, unsteadily, a heavy and broken breath – my lungs were like lead too. I took a breath in preparation to reply. But again I couldn't find the words, I didn't dare to speak.

Chapter 12

I came out of an unpleasant dream.

But the dream continued, the scene was the same. Everywhere was pain – in my arms and legs, in my ribs and hips and my head. I didn't trust things enough to open my eyes.

It was night-time. I could see a dark street; there were looming shadows – of houses. Windows shuttered, unlit. All about was black and grey – there was no colour. There were reflections, though. It must have rained; perhaps a sudden summer shower that came in a downpour and left a few puddles. But where there are reflections there must be light – and where there's light there's colour. I had a desperate yearning for colour to cheer me, dispel the dreariness, distract the pain. I peered about without moving my head. There... a street lamp, cold and white – and on a wall a street sign in Gothic script. What did it say, what was the street name? I couldn't read it – it was too dark.

I lay on my back.

Yes, that I could ascertain. But where were my hands? I moved my fingers to give me a guide. One was there, at my side – it was fine, I could open and close it. But the right one had gone.

I panicked.

Fear rushed in again. Again? Why again? My heart beat faster, irregularly – it bumped and staggered. But at least it beat. That must be a good sign. What had happened? Why was I afraid? I felt cold, undiluted, panicking fear, like a fist, like a fog, like dizzy vertigo on the edge of a cliff. One of my hands had disappeared.

I was perspiring.

On my forehead drops of sweat prickled, tickled my skin. But my skin was cold. Drops of blood on cobblestones, pearls of dawn dew on concrete, in chains on cobwebs, before the sun came up. I shivered. The movement hurt. Blood? Dew? Was I fantasising, delirious?

My panic was complete.

Don't open your eyes. Don't let them see.

My breathing seemed shallow so I took a deep breath. And gasped. Was that a knife in my lungs? Or a lump of steel? Or maybe a weight was compressing my chest. Don't make a sound. And don't let them see you move.

But I needed air, oxygen. Breathing is life like the beat of the heart. Slowly, very carefully, I opened my mouth a crack and filled my lungs. The knife jabbed several times, but it was blunt now, it was less severe.

I tried listening.

There were bells. No, not bells. There was something ringing though, far away, indistinct, but not quite like a bell. A mobile phone? Or a digital clock? And there were murmurs, indecipherable – oh God, were they still there? My fear frothed up again, like foam on the crest of a wave. Was who still there?

I cowered motionless...

Waiting for more pain again. With eyes still closed I strained to hear the voices. The shadows were solidifying. Something was coming back... a memory. Were those their voices outside my head? There were figures, five of them. Black against silver grey. I tried to look away but my feet kept walking, it was like in a nightmare, it was drawing me on, sucking me in... And there was a lump on the pavement that might have been human, or a dog or a sack humped and bent. The five were dancing – then one went down, or was he kneeling? Another lump...

Don't go near, I warned myself, that's no ordinary fight...

I hung back, hesitating. Another figure went down on top, with a tiny flash – was it a light or a knife? There was grunting like pigs – could hear the thud of wood on bone...

I was scared – I could feel my fear in the hairs on my skin... I was casting about hoping to see others who'd help... I could hear my voice shouting... I stared mesmerised at silhouette men just yards away with heavy boots and baseball bats, slugging the lumps like butchers beat meat, hammering flat their entrecôte steaks. I felt sick – I knew I ought to help, I was sure I wanted to run. I bawled at the dark in frustration and fear...

One – no, two figures were coming at me. I stood there helpless, couldn't move – I was paralysed. Could no-one hear? No lights in the buildings going on. I smelled sour sweat, I could smell my fear – I raised my arms to protect my head and a club hit my body, I went down like a skittle... there was horrible pain, had they shattered my spine? There were blows bludgeoning down from all sides...

My ears were exploding – but from far away I could hear the chant, hear the words: "Kill the bastards."... I tasted blood, I rolled up in a ball – and hatred blew up in my head. Does it take seconds, or a minute or two? How long does it endure till one's dead? I heard someone screaming, I knew it was me – I knew I had nothing to lose – my brain was on fire spitting fury and fear, I was bawling at myself to try to crawl, try to get away from this horrendous pain... and that was when it happened. A baseball bat cracked on the cobbles near my head and clattered free – I tried to kick out, couldn't move a muscle, just searing pains... then something heavy fell on me like a sack of coal, must've broken my back, it knocked out the last of my breath. The stench of sweat was strong as a curse, I started to wretch. There was ringing, singing, in my ears, drowning out coherent thought, but I sensed a sound which didn't seem to fit and felt a change in the bruising air outside my brain...

The weight was dragging away, taking away too the suffocation and stink – and as it did, for an instant there was a different smell, a kind of odour I couldn't place yet was somehow familiar, it chilled my body to the core. I think I thought I'm about to die... I heard footsteps, noises, something rattled, more footsteps, hurried, fading. Then all the sounds and smells were gone.

I lay, afraid, alone, a broken foetus on the cobbles. I listened. My eyes were still closed, I kept them tight shut. Only pain was all around.

Were they lurking – waiting?

Nausea. A sickening sensation in nose and throat. Like a knock-out, long ago, in the school ring. Someone moaning – was that coming from me? I tasted blood. Could smell blood too. And there was a wetness over my trousers, between my legs – had I peed in my pants?

A siren wailed, coming closer.

x x x

I was lying, still, on my back.

I wasn't on cobbles, though, I was on cushions, or on a bed. So they weren't waiting for me. I could move, I told myself. I could open my eyes if I wanted. Still I lay there.

Relief coming pouring in. I started to cry.

Water welling behind my eyelids – I wept without making a sound. After a while I tipped my face sideways, blinking to clear the brimming puddles of tears; I wanted to wipe my face – but, still, my right hand wasn't there. Quickly I wriggled the fingers of the left one; a small sense of relief that they were still there. I lifted the arm, carefully. It rose to my face at my bidding. Only at the shoulder was a lump of pain like an embedded boulder. I let the arm lie down again. But it missed its mark and struck a frame over my hip knocking it sideways. Something hit my heart like a hammer – waves of pain swamped my breathing, broke over my brain; I wanted to scream. I bit my lips... sshh... they mustn't hear.

But, no – you can. If you want. I thought you'd established that they'd gone. You remember?

I remembered.

I remembered, too, the blue flashing light – and the siren driving me mad, tearing my nerves before they switched it off. Blue. So I could see one colour at least. And I recalled peeping – out of the corner of one eye, across the black cobbles as a big limousine and a police car braked, screeching to a stop. The colour blue was still swinging. There was an instant of silence before car doors opened, a stillness when nothing moved and no-one was there; I took it all in. There were two shapeless heaps not far away, motionless, and two baseball clubs on the cobblestones near my face. Otherwise I was completely alone.

I remember – I thought: funny they didn't take them with them. Then there were window shutters rattling, lights in houses going on. And there were two figures walking briskly, flashing lights bobbing, the green of uniforms in the beams of cars. And beyond, blackness, pricked by distant lit windows. One of the police officers held a gun.

And over us all the swinging sweep of the blue light they hadn't turned off – round and round... and round...

The tears on my face had dried; they were sticky like glue. My lashes were stuck too, and tickled. It was time to open my eyes.

I did. Furtively...

Sunlight. It was no longer night. Reflections of sunlight off glass in high-up windows behind me, hints of trees of leafy green, and white metal shutters with lots of grey lines and light in between – and, visible out of the corner of my eye, a row of glass-screen cubicles each containing a bed. There were hanging gondolas on ceiling-mounted rails full of electrical connections and gadgets with spiral flex cables, there were batteries of electronics and screens and machines behind each of the beds. Digital displays showed numbers and lines that quivered or waved. And all almost without a sound.

These images I'd managed to take in without moving my head. Now I began on myself. I lay almost flat, my head tipped a bit on pillows. They were big and soft, curled round my ears. I gazed down at myself. On my chest and shoulders a smock was draped, with no buttons. I thought of straight-jackets. The arms were very short, hung empty and loose. Over my pelvis and hips was a raised construction covered with the bed sheet. It looked like a small trolley without afternoon tea. And I had two hands on two arms. The right one that hadn't been there hovered before me, the arm stretched in the air hung from a gallows-like frame. Between shoulder and elbow it was stiff as a board in a plaster cast, the rest of it fat with bandages down to the wrist. The back of the hand looked puffed and yellow. I ordered the fingers to move, and they moved. I could even feel something too, now – like pins and needles.

Slowly I turned my eyes. The other hand was attached to a tube from a plastic-bag drip, an intravenous connector on its back; it seemed so far away.

I couldn't see my feet. Very carefully I wriggled my toes. Steel nails of pain stuck into a leg and struck my thigh in a burning jab as if it'd been branded in fire. Again I raised my left hand – to check my chest. The infusion bottle wobbled like a sack at the top of the tube. Gingerly I lifted a fold of smock: a taut beige covering, bandages peeping above and below. I looked a bit like a Victorian lady squeezed into a corset.

My bottom was sore, seemed flat as a pancake. But I told myself: don't shift position or move those hips. So I went up to my head. Flexed my jaw gently to and fro, ran my tongue round my teeth. Nothing broken there. I made a grimace, then forced my brows to rise and fall, tensing the skin on my skull. Quickly desisted. One cheek had caught fire, something was stretched tight in my hair and two fists took hold of my head, squeezing my brain in a vice. A sharp headache began as though switched on like a light; it banged between my temples and down the nape of my neck, set my teeth on edge.

I lay absolutely still, as if my life depended on it. Only allowed my eyes to continue to roam. Above my left hand hung a white switch from a flex, a red button in its middle like a Pekinese's penis. It was there to press so I didn't – wanted to be alone.

Over the end of my bed, opposite, was a white wall with large glass windows and wide sliding door, also glazed. It had been left open. Beyond lay a corridor white with bits of blue and full of light, and the other side of it a nurses' station like a glass box with consoles flickering. There sat two nurses in pale green with caps on their heads, one turned away, the other in spectacles telephoning.

I rotated my eyes left and right nearly ninety degrees – just similar glass walls, those rows of rooms like my own, patients in various poses. Lots of tubes and machines and more blinking screens. I looked back at myself, at my supine body, let my gaze go out of focus. Turned my thoughts inwards. What time was it? Tried to take my bearings. It had been Sunday night when I left the cinema after the late-night film. My seminars had finished that afternoon – I'd driven back exhausted, given myself the evening off, had wanted to let my hair down. Now the sun was high. High? Yes. Bright light streamed in through slats coming from behind me above my head.

Must be after midday. Monday then.

Monday? My day of rest, after seminar weekends – so no problem there. Usually rang the office, though. Just in case. Monday... it'd been on a Monday I'd rung Annabelle, too. But that was two weeks ago. I'd never forget that Monday. We'd talked for two hours, about this and that; my heart had been nervous choking my throat, but without a word of it able to get out. No result, no conclusion – no real indication how she felt, no hint of us meeting again. Then the following Friday she'd called me back: yes, maybe we could meet some time. Maybe. How the thread of my life hung from that word. Since then, though, I'd heard nothing more and didn't dare call again, had forced myself to play it cool. So...

So it was Monday. Sixteen long days since Munich...

I had to move. My bottom ached as if all the blood had been pressed out, as if I were lying on a block of wood. Very, very carefully I rolled my upper body a bit to one side, tipping my hips to relieve the load on one buttock. The expected pain was still brutal. I jumped – it tensed all my muscles into a knot and I might have cried out, or just thought I had. Shock waves shook me from head to toe, nausea tried to overwhelm me. I felt sweat break through my brow. A yellow light began blinking on a screen behind me – I could see it reflected in the corridor glass. Beyond, the nurse in glasses was glancing at me.

Quickly I shut my eyes, feigned sleep...

And there was Matthias. He hung suddenly in my head. Matthias, Matthias... his image was clear. But why him – why had he appeared?

Cracks of light between my eyelids...

Monday... Yes. That was it – Monday. The penny dropped... it was this evening Matthias was coming. "On Karl's Bridge in Nuremberg, 6pm," he'd said. Our meeting up hadn't worked out in Munich those two long weeks ago. And now? Now this. Couldn't meet him now. Couldn't ring him to warn him either, no number, could hardly...

Slits of light still. I squeezed my eyes tight shut this time.

The headache throbbed, keeping pace with my pulse. I was in the dark again – the night closed in, I was back on hard cobbles. The blue beam sweeping steadily in circles had been joined by two others; they silently criss-crossed the dark. Ambulances. Rear doors opening letting out light. Men in orange and white pulling out stretchers. One man with a box came stumbling at me. When he reached me I could see only wrinkled orange trouser-legs, till he crouched. "Can you understand me?" he asked.

"Yes," I said. He asked if I could move, he sounded so calm – I didn't know, I hadn't tried. I shut my eyes. Now I knew what it must feel like being run over, guess my body consisted only of pain. Professional fingers checked me over, starting with my head. Thankfully no further questions – he seemed to know well what he was doing, I was very, very glad about that. I slid in and out on the edge of consciousness, my awareness came and went. He called out something, it must've been over his shoulder – it wasn't for me, didn't interest me, it went way over my head. I was floundering here and there. The steady hands injected me... other sirens destroying the silence... they jerked me awake, I stared – more green uniforms, bright lights on stands, the big black BMW still standing there... a hot feeling spreading, in my mouth a sickly sweet taste... silhouette figures, white and red plastic tape being stretched... the heat consumed me, a sense of swimming, of peace, of pain draining away – I sank into a swamp...

"Herr Falk...?"

Something touching my left hand.

I opened my eyes slowly. Blinked at the bright light. It was one of the nurses in pastel green. Very plump. She leaned close, peering. Glasses. Speckled rims of pink and red. "I'm Nurse Susanne, how are we feeling?" said her rosy lips. She had a mass of brunette hair bundled up tight behind her cap, and a mole above her mouth.

I didn't know what to say, so I said nothing – was I in a position to judge? Her glasses had wings, were like bright butterflies, her body an inflated balloon.

"We got into a fight, didn't we?" she remarked motherly. Her dialect was so thick one would've needed subtitles for those from Düsseldorf or further north. "But don't worry," she added as if to calm. "We're in the intensive care unit in Klinikum Süd now."

Klinikum Süd? Klinikum... where was that? "Munich," I mouthed stupidly. I shocked myself – the word came out like a vulgar croak.

"In Nuremberg, sweetie."

"Ah yes," I said. That didn't sound better either. I tried clearing my dried-up throat. "Of course."

Her peering face retreated in a long high arc; it made me giddy. I struggled to keep my gaze focused on it. She was straightening up. Then coming closer again. Arms stretched over me, past me, out of sight, and her uniformed body hung in front of my nose. Sounds of her pressing switches or buttons; her massive breasts swung unsupported, wobbling the green of her gown. I rolled my eyes away, I think my mouth had sagged open. I thought: obviously she finds me irresistible, she's out to test my reflexes – this cuddly and fearsome wench from the Franconian forest...

Her face dropped back down into view. I got it in focus again. A pretty face, angelic almost and surprisingly well-proportioned compared to the fertile Aphrodite rest.

"We must try not to move, Herr Falk," she said brightly.

The remarkable bosom filled my visual world again – she was patting pillows behind my head. She did it quickly and carefully, supporting but not tipping the back of my skull; it caused little pain.

"Do we need to pass water again?"

Again? I had no recollection. Oh God, had she had to do it for me – or had I piddled in the bed?

"No," I said hurriedly. Oh God, I thought again – how do I do that if I must? I transferred my concentration to my faraway bladder, praying the drop wasn't dripping too fast.

"No," I repeated. Was that petulance I could hear in my voice?

"Buzz when we do."

Buzz, I thought unhappily.

"We don't have to fret. We're on a liquid diet for a while."

Are we? Thank God for small mercies; I could almost hear my bowels sigh in relief.

"How's our throat?"

"Throat?"

"Mineral water? Tea?" she asked. "Something to drink?"

She's trying to provoke me. I think I frowned. "A little shot of brandy would be fine," I croaked.

She'd stepped back, stood there brazen, with her broad child-bearing hips and hairy naked legs, with folded arms on buxom chest; she'd managed to hook them underneath, they served as a platform for her breasts. For a vague instant I wondered what she'd look like in a dirndl bending down – but then again, I fuzzily thought, perhaps better not. She'd knock the boys clean off their feet and drive them all to drink.

Beneath her golden-eyed stare I wilted. "And a nice cup of tea," I added weakly.

"Herbal or fruit?"

The way she said it, with that fulsome mouth, with those cupid lips, I'm sure the man in her life would stand on his head whenever she whistled, wherever she wished. She wasn't my type of lady, but ones like her are the salt of the earth. I thought: when I'm feeling better later, I'd love to pull her leg, and I bet she'll pull mine harder.

"I always prefer it herbal," I said.

Unfolding those arms and releasing the load, she went out with rolling gait and friendly grin. Only to be replaced, a few seconds after, by her colleague. How life is rich in contrast.

"I'm Nurse Barbara." The cold voice cut like a sterilised knife. High German. Just the sound of it raised my hackles. She didn't approach. I appraised her as best I could. Short, starched, blonde hair, tiny tight breasts, a thin mean mouth to match. Maybe thirty or more. A no-nonsense lady. This must be the Boss.

"A Kommissar Schumann is waiting outside." Each clipped word came out staccato. Everything about her was sharp and thin – from her nose to her shoulders to those fresh-razored legs. Very attractive, though, in a Nordic way.

I winced. I thought: she's not one of the forgiving kind.

"He wishes to take a statement as soon as you're able."

"Ah," I said. My own voice was still hard and cracked. I watched her. As carefully as I could. She still stood in the doorway so stiff and erect. Are we able? I asked myself. My eyes blurred. I had no idea. Everything was shimmering. Where she stood was like a mirage – her skinny form melted to a wavering line.

"How long's he been waiting?" I asked.

"About an hour."

I screwed up my eyes. That was better; I could focus again. I squinted at her, I mustered myself. "Then I suppose we should let him in." I tried to mimic her junior colleague, but it didn't come off at all. The lop-sided grin also not. At least, though, I succeeded in getting the sag in my mouth under some control.

She was turning on her heel. To that gaunt profile I said: "By the way, I have to phone my office. I..."

"You are not in a fit state to ring anyone." She'd half-turned back to me. Her cap was correct, her skinny spine straight.

"Then can I give you..."

"We already have."

"You have?" I mumbled.

"Nurse Susanne found your mobile in your clothes. It was still switched on. She rang your two listed emergency numbers to inform."

"Well... I appreciate that..." I let my voice trail off. The nurse had gone – there was no-one there.

I let my eyes fall shut. The dark closed in again. Night and shadows. But also a brightness. The floodlights were blinding; I could clearly see green and cream police cars and three ambulances, but I couldn't distinguish the faces...

A sharp voice with a cutting edge speaking briefly in the distance... hadn't I heard that voice just a moment...

Fingers touched lightly on my left hand. They made me jump; I'd not been expecting a Kommissar to touch. Pricks of pain. I opened my eyes again.

"Hello," she said. A different voice, not sharp at all. This one was soft and low and mature, I knew this voice too...

Oh no – it couldn't be. I must be fantasising.

She stroked the back of my hand, tenderly. And, stooping, brushed her lips to my cheek. I could see them coming, but I couldn't feel. So it was just a dream.

I gazed at her. Amazing: even her perfume was tangible. She wore a smock the same green the nurses wore. Crafty of me, I'd managed the swap. Dream or not, though, it was good to see her again – it was a thousand times better than good...

"You must leave at once."

No-nonsense Nurse Barbara came stiffly into view, casting a brief glance at Annabelle – the glance she cast was fit to kill. Well, at least she looked like the real thing. Jerkily she reached me a small plastic container without a smile, without a word, but Annabelle took it from her. It was rising to meet me; its lid was closed, it had a short spout and a hole. Long artistic fingers held it to my mouth – I'd know those fingers anywhere... they were helping me drink, supporting the back of my head with such care. The headache increased in leaps and bounds. Peppermint tea. It was warm, not hot, without sugar. I swallowed, cleared my throat, watching her in silence.

She smiled a smile – ah, that enigmatic smile. Knew that smile too.

The tea tasted good; it wet my mouth, loosened my tongue. For a dream it was convincingly real. I took another sip, just to feel the fingers close again, just to smell that scent on those hands.

Green eyes gazing.

"Pinch me," I said to them.

That's good, I thought. I felt pleased – the voice sounded more like me. The lips smiled again. This time there was something else in the smile. Was that relief I could see? She squeezed my hand, gently. She was turning her head and nodding.

"Thank you." That was her voice again. So mature, so calm.

A man appeared beside her. Blurred, out of focus. "Take your time, my dear," he said. A stranger's voice. But quiet, paternalistic almost – a rather pleasant voice.

"Not more than ten minutes, please." That was Nurse Barbara, staccato.

Annabelle was withdrawing her hands. They were really her hands, weren't they? "Till later," she whispered. I tried to hold onto them but already they seemed to have disappeared. And her face was retreating, too.

The man reappeared. Clacking sound. He was sitting down. I suppose he must have pulled up a chair. So they even had chairs here...

"Kommissar Schumann, *Mordkommission*..." I heard him say... but I was looking away, my eyes were following Annabelle, dizzily, I think they watched her a long time after she'd gone...

Then all was blank...

"Herr Falk, I have to ask you a few questions."

There was that pleasant voice again. I focused. A few questions. From the *Mordkommission* - my God, had someone died then?

"Yes," I said.

"I'll be as brief as possible."

I wanted to nod. But I shouldn't do that – so I didn't. "Fire away," I said. How good it was to see her again. How lovely she looked, how exciting the touch of her hands...

He began his questioning.

At first I answered automatically; I wasn't there behind the words. I was still looking at the picture I'd made of Annabelle passing out through that big open door. I could hear my voice but perhaps it wasn't really mine. Her red hair was wound up in complications, and her borrowed green gown bound by bows down the back. On her feet she wore elegant high-heeled shoes each wrapped in plastic covers with elastic tops they surely weren't designed for; under the circumstances I thought she moved with amazing grace...

"How many assailants were there?"

I floundered. "Four." Forced myself to focus again.

"Are you certain? Only four?"

"Yes," my voice said. And my brain said slowly: Only? Wasn't that enough? Then I went back to more important things...

I could still see her...

Those freckled bare legs beneath the gown, and the way her head of hair turned to fire in the bright spotlights in the corridor – and then there was a jump and I was sitting with her in her drawing room and Ray Charles had gone ten minutes ago and she was removing her feet from my lap, standing up, and behind her in the shadows that Canadian Jew with the golden voice was singing "...*touch me with your naked hand or touch me with your glove*..." and I knew my mind was playing tricks with me...

"Could it conceivably have been five or more?"

I think it was after this last question that Annabelle finally faded into darkness and I was on the cobbles again...

I was counting...

No, there were four – and two others on the ground.

"No," I said

And straight after that, like a jump in my brain, I thought: can that even mean both of them are dead? I stared at them lying there in the night, crumpled like black fallen sacks. That was the only question I asked the Kommissar.

"Regrettably, one's dead," he said. "The other in critical condition. In case it's any consolation, you probably saved his life."

I shook my head – but very minimally, because of the hammer inside my skull. "I didn't save anyone," I said. "I just got in the way and tried to run."

He continued his questioning. In chronological order, building a picture; he was very methodical. I'd seen so little – but he seemed satisfied. Then he came to the final bit where they'd broken off and disappeared, and here I was able to give him a few details – the cold touch of the knife, the smells, the weight that crushed me.

"Did he stumble, do you think?"

"Possibly."

"Or trip? While he was hitting you?"

"No idea."

"Was it he holding the knife?"

"I suppose so."

"But you said he'd dropped the baseball bat and then he fell."

"Yes."

"Could it have been the second assailant with the knife, then? You say two attacked you."

"Yes. Possibly."

"Possibly?"

"I only saw the one up close, the other was mostly behind me."

"They didn't use the knife on you – the doctors have confirmed that. They didn't use knives on the other two victims either."

"I suppose I was lucky there."

"You were very lucky. Now let's come back to the one who fell on you who you saw closer up. Did you see his face?"

"No."

"You're the only witness. Do your best, please. Are you certain you didn't get a glimpse of any part of his face?"

"Yes."

"What about his hair? Long? Short?"

"I didn't see any, so it must've been very short."

"Colour?"

"Just a silhouette. Too dark."

"Describe his clothes, please."

I described the little I could.

"Anything else?"

"As I said, he stank of sweat. A particular smell. That I would recognise again."

"Did he say anything? Or did the other?"

I told him of the grunt and curse one of them had uttered. Then I heard a voice in my head I hadn't remembered till now. "Someone said – 'Get up Franzi, get the fuck out of here'. And then they were gone."

"A man's voice?"

"Yes."

"He spoke German?"

"Yes."

"Any accent?"

"No."

"Dialect?"

"Too quick to tell."

"Can you describe his voice exactly? Rough, smooth? Deep...?"

I briefly closed my eyes. I was sweating, my head hammering again. It seemed even thinking caused strain...

The questions continued...

To aid my concentration, I studied him from top to toe – his hair, his face, his little bowtie and crumpled clothes, one polished brown shoe just visible over the edge of the bed when he crossed his legs from right to left. He was small, about sixty, beginning to go bald. His manner was quiet and polite – the kind of man one would least notice even were he in the front row.

After a short while he closed the notebook in which he'd been making notes.

"Well, Herr Falk," he said, "that will be all for the time being. I'm grateful for your assistance." He was rising...

He added: "We've taken your clothes for analysis, I hope you'll understand."

"Analysis?" I queried. But I really couldn't care.

"For the forensic boys, you know – traces of blood, hairs, fabric fibres, that sort of stuff. DNA, you see. They will, of course, be returned to you in due course."

He set the chair against the glass wall. That clacking again. Metal and plastic. "We'll need you to sign a written statement in a few days. For the inquest that will be sufficient." He nodded at me, politely dipping his head. "Should it come to arrests and a court case later, you may be called as witness. In the meantime we'll do our best to disturb you as little we can. I wish you a speedy recovery, Herr Falk."

He was turning away. He moved deliberately, not quickly. As he opened the sliding door he paused and said: "By the way, the press boys were here. Our blonde young dragon Nurse Barbara sent them packing, but should they manage to slip through her talons next time please tell them as little as possible." He didn't smile at his humour.

I watched the upper half of his body beyond the observation windows move along the corridor, but I didn't look for long, I was looking for Annabelle. No sign now. Other figures...

A doctor in white with open coat came in, followed by Nurse Barbara. He greeted me perfunctorily, didn't introduce himself; got to work without a further word. He was young and stressed yet self-assured. Nurse B and he appeared to be a practised team. I watched her movements helping him, efficient and professional – watched the doctor methodically checking various parts of my body. His fingers were pink and scrubbed, the nails perfectly manicured – they glided about hardly contacting me, as if they were afraid of touch. Wherever his hands paused, he explained the condition – bruising, dislocation of the shoulder, broken arm, broken ribs, concussion, haemorrhage, suspected pelvic fracture... his voice wasted no words, was almost monotone. I suspect the list sounded worse than it really was. Briefly he returned to two parts of my torso; of my hip he said. "We'll X-ray that again tomorrow – if a fracture's confirmed, you'll only be on crutches till six weeks from now." And pointing at the plaster cast he added: "We'll get that off as soon as the shoulder's satisfactory and put the arm in a sleeve... so..." He bent his forearm across his stomach as if to illustrate.

Then he was gone. I hadn't been able to read the tag on the open coat, hadn't bothered to ask his name.

Nurse Barbara was covering me up, draping the smock over shoulders and front again – it hid the corset, disguised the worst; it wasn't possible to put the thing on. She set the light frame across my pelvis and thighs, drew the sheet back over me. My right arm still hung extended from the gibbet in a rigid Hitler salute. Stretching my fingers straight, I found, added to the effect – but I only dared do it that once. Should Neo-Nazis come visiting, they surely would be impressed.

Her arms were reached up adjusting the drip.

"Sit or lie?" she said. She uttered it a bit like a clipped Prussian command, thin hands now hooked on narrow hips. Her eyes met mine just for a moment – they were cold and impartial and steel-grey.

"Sit," I said. "Kind of you to ask."

The hydraulic hummed, lifting my upper half – she had the remote in her hand.

"Thanks," I added. She was tipping me forward and it hardly hurt, except in the lungs and over my scalp. Her fingers were surprisingly strong, they wedged the first pillow against my back. I breathed several times, shallowly, to alleviate the pain, tried not to think of the three broken ribs. With bandaged chest and bandaged head and arms I must've looked laughably like an Egyptian mummy. But at least a mummy that moved. She was leaning next to me, her head was near, her body had bent like a willow. Her little green cap was clipped with kirby grips to her short blonde hair, and her skin was very close. I could smell her. She smelt fresh and clean, efficient and thoroughly scrubbed – she smelled of scented soap. Actually, she looked rather sexy from the side.

Professionally, she puffed the last pillow. "Okay?" she said near my ear, wedging the pillow.

I'd twisted very slightly, trying to help, I'm not used to others doing things for me – accidentally my elbow bumped a small breast. With a jerk she straightened, glanced sharply down on me; she looked down with a look that could kill.

"Okay," I said apathetically. I really wasn't in a state to care what I bumped, so long it didn't cause pain.

She was stepping back. Pointed abruptly where she'd hung the remote. "Don't touch it," she ordered tartly. "If you need to move, just press the buzzer."

I nodded helplessly: she'd touched a short-circuit in my fuddled brain. "If you want me you just have to whistle," I croaked. "You know how to whistle, don't you?" I attempted a crack of a humourless smile. But my little joke, it seemed, fell flat on its face.

She shot me that look again, the kind she might reserve for rapists. Poor lady, I thought fuzzily, I suppose she's too young or doesn't watch the old movies, I suppose she's never heard of Bogie. Again, I wasn't in a state to explain. Guilelessly I tried to return that glance.

Oh those cold, cold eyes. Already, though, they were blinking, switching away.

"Thanks," I said again. And I thought: perhaps she had a bad childhood, perhaps she's been hurt too much. I watched her stiff retreating rear; yes, I guessed she was the wrong side of thirty-five.

"I have a question," I said.

She stopped. "What?" A twist of head over small shoulder. "Make it quick. I haven't got all day." Tight body tense.

No, I thought. But in the night perhaps you do, to brood about nasty men like me and how unfair the cards have been cut. Aloud I said: "Is Frau Binoche still there?"

"Binoche?" A hesitation. A small pinched frown. "Oh her. No – I sent her away. Nurse Susanne had no business allowing her to sneak in."

"I should like to make a little correction there. She's not one to sneak in anywhere."

"Nevertheless – at present not permitted."

Well at least she'd turned to face me now. She added starchly:

"The Kommissar was the only exception. No visitors, Herr Falk."

"That's no visitor, Nurse Barbara." I tried fixing her with a beady eye. "That's my life blood."

"No arguments."

"She came a long way." I was having difficulty focusing.

"I told her to come back in two days, then we'll see."

"Two days?" I rolled my eyes – didn't have much problem doing that. "This is the request of a dying man. In two days…"

"Now don't be silly, Herr Falk." She'd stuck her little hands in the pockets of her gown, I could see them pressing on her thin thighs.

"She's a stubborn one," I said, daring to share this small confidence. "As a matter of fact you've got that little characteristic in common so I'm certain that you'll appreciate. Couldn't you take a quick peep just in case… perhaps…"

"The answer is no." She blinked, though. Was that a slight weakening, a small concession to the one about to kick the bucket?

"Not even for a box of chocolates?" I squinted, I let my mouth sag. That wasn't hard either.

"No." A twitch of the lips. They were painted pale pink – was that a crack at the corners?

"Wouldn't a big box of chocolates with a special golden bow to go with your Hanoverian hair melt that…"

"She left, Herr Falk." She was withdrawing those tiny strong useful hands again. She was about to go…

"Could we meet in the middle – one day instead of two? Just to prove that you did your best and nearly stood your ground?"

"I have to go, Herr Falk."

"Her number is in my mobile if Nurse Susanne were just to look under the letter B."

"We have our rules."

"I only met her sixteen days ago…" was struggling now to keep her in view, "…give or take an hour or two." I tried to put some desperation in my lopsided mouth. "Can't you share my horror at departing this life having failed to see her one last time? Grant this last wish from a fading man and I'll put in a good word for you when I pass through the Gates."

"I see you are going to be one of our more trying patients, Herr Falk."

The headache had grown to the beat of a drum, and exhaustion clamped down like a lid. "Just smuggle in a bottle of whisky each day and I promise I'll be meek as a lamb." I sat there, leaned back, she was fading now…

"You're unnecessarily tiring yourself out. You have to rest." She was turning away, touching a skinny hand to the edge of the door.

"Yes," I said. "You're right. I think I will."

She cast a brief glance at me over her shoulder again, and I thought I heard her say coolly: "I'll see what I can do," but I might have been mistaken.

Chapter 13

I think I fell asleep without knowing. There is a gap, the real world around me was gone; I dreamed. I think I dreamed of green fields from my childhood...

Something touching me. Stroking me.

But I was alone in the sun, the meadows rolled down the slope of a hill – I lay curled, close to nature, close to the earth. The sky was blue through stalks and sorrel, there were flowers on long stems; moon daisies and buttercups and campions, and poppies and cornflowers. I could smell natural scents and the juice of the grasses...

The touch was intruding – the fingers were drawing me out of the dream. I awoke with closed eyes; it could only be her. Without opening them I turned my hand over, felt the pull of the drip, knew where I was. I enclosed those fingers.

"Annabelle," I said into the dark.

They pressed lightly on my palm, like a kiss brushed on lips. "Hello, my Michelin Man."

The feeling was good, the sound of her voice too. I digested them luxuriously. Then opened my eyes. She sat on the edge of the bed, carefully perched between me and the frame. For a long minute we just watched one another. She smiled; I smiled back.

"What have you been doing?" she said quietly. She stroked my hand again.

I shrugged my shoulders but it hurt my chest, so I desisted. I still felt drugged. Only slowly did it start to occur to me that I was hallucinating and it wasn't really her, and it hadn't been her for those moments before the Kommissar came in – there was no way she could've found out what had happened and come up from Munich so soon. Had the staff nurse been pulling my leg, then? Or was Nurse Barbara a fantasy too? How often the wish is the mother of hope.

"My local hero."

I shook my head at the apparition. "I got in the way, that's all."

But still her touch was there. Could one come out of one dream and straight into another? Of course one could.

"...reporters and photographers outside. Should they be sent away?"

"Please."

She went out, but seemed to return before she'd gone because her sentence continued as though uninterrupted: "One was rather pleasant, actually, and wished you a speedy recovery. He wanted me to take a picture of you."

"God forbid." I lay there helpless – was I floating away?

There. Her hand was there again. Seemed almost real.

"This is not really you," I said. I said it through fog. And right afterwards I thought: oh God, that sounds clichéd.

"Yes it is."

"It's a nasty little dream, you know."

Fingers in mine. And her voice: "Nasty, yes. But not a dream."

"Pinch me again, then."

A gentle pinch.

"Not convincing. Do it again."

A tickle in my palm.

"I should like to believe you." I said, disbelieving.

"I should like that too."

"But there's something standing in the way, you see." I mustered myself, I sought the words though the fog. "No-one knew your name till I told them." I'd got her now. I knew the little tricks my brain was playing. "No-one could've rung and told you."

Another tickle. Gentler this time. "Nobody did."

"No?" I queried.

"I drove up early this morning..."

She was disappearing. Or was I slipping away? I could hardly see her – was I going blind? I tried to hold onto her voice...

"...thought I would give you a surprise."

Surprise?

"You mentioned on the phone that after seminars you take Mondays off..."

Ah. Yes. Monday – today's still Monday... Was that my voice – or had I only thought it? I could hardly hear me either.

"...invite you out for breakfast before continuing on to Erlangen..."

Erlangen? That's...

"I had an appointment..."

Where? At one of the clinics? The university?

"...caretaker's wife saw me when you didn't answer your bell..."

"Ah," I said. I think I said it too loudly – it echoed in my head. I was suddenly desperate to hear my own voice again. "Frau Maußer," I called. There was something still wrong. Although Frau Maußer knew everything and more, even she couldn't have known that. "No," I said. "Not possible." But my voice had faded too. In panic I moved; I think I wrenched my body. The sudden pain was like a thousand pincers squeezing all my nerves...

"...Stefan...?"

Had I shouted something? I was sitting up; the pain had shaken me awake.

"...call the nurse...?"

I gasped. I blinked several times, and focused.

No, oh God no. It was okay now. I could see her. All was clear again – her hair and her face and green gown. In fact the gown went exceptionally well with her eyes. I was aware of staring at her. The pain went on in waves – but like the tide gradually going out. I breathed through my mouth, till my breath slowed down too. The pain receded. I floundered... what a heavenly feeling... I was high and dry now; I was stranded on the rocks.

"I'm fine," I said.

There – Her fingers were stroking again – the feel was firm and clear on my hand, and on my arm. My skin tingled at her touch.

"I think you are not telling the truth."

"I'm fine," I confirmed.

"Don't be stubborn."

Stubborn? I nodded – I did it very carefully because of my skull; I cast her an anaemic grin.

"Silly to be unnecessarily brave – I can get help, you know?"

"Annabelle, I've never been unnecessarily brave the whole of my life – I'm anything but that." Yes it's true, I'm fine, I told myself. And I was. I was back there in reality and feeling good. The fog was gone and so was the dream. All my senses were functioning normally now and my brain was working again.

I stared at her, it really was her. I could hardly believe. A feeling of joy welled within me: I was sitting there in bed in a clinic and Annabelle had come to visit.

"What was that about Frau Maußer?" I said, just to prove I was back again. Frau Maußer... with a jump I thought of my firm. Oh God, I must ring them soon, they ought to hear it in my own words – it appeared this business here was going to take longer than a day or two.

Annabelle's eyes were on me, they gazed at me, they looked concerned. And her mouth – that wide and generous mouth, was deliberating. Then the lips parted – they said: "Frau Maußer told me what had happened, Stefan. And that you were here."

I shuddered at the thought – and the firm flew out of my head. How the hell had she found out – did she have informers on every street corner, or had she simply bugged my phone?

"She was so helpful."

I rolled my eyes. "Frau Maußer is a remarkable woman."

"She sends you a big hug and said she will come and visit you soon. She was almost motherly."

I shuddered again. "Well," I said, "I suppose at a great stretch that's one way of describing her." I managed an unhappy smile. "If one's drunk, or in an absurdly charitable mood."

"Don't be undeserving."

"I'm an undeserving person. How the devil did she find out?"

"From the police."

"Ah." I nodded. And I thought: well, of course – she's got spies planted there too. She's got them planted everywhere. I cast Annabelle another feeble grimace. "Ah," I repeated. And held my tongue.

"You are thinking nasty thoughts again."

"I confess they tend in that direction."

"Don't. She was so sweet." She pressed my hand. "She told me that the police only called round to check where they could contact next-of-kin."

"Next-of-kin? I'm not dead yet, you know."

"Now stop it." She smiled.

"If you need a list of undertakers you just have to say the word." Another squeeze. Another smile.

I returned her gaze. I'd stopped. Wanted to, anyway – seriousness was seeping through. I sat there propped, taking her in. Yes, incredibly, it was really her. What had she said? She'd intended to surprise me, go out for breakfast. So she'd wanted to see me again. A miracle had occurred.

The silence stretched. It was a pleasure simply beholding her. My heart began to stir, beat faster: in spite of my state, in spite of it all, I felt the fingers of thrill creeping up, permeating every pore. I watched those green eyes watching me. Then I decided to take the risk, take the plunge. I said: "I've missed you."

Her hand on mine gave another small squeeze. Otherwise she didn't respond. Her eyes were reading into me.

"Have you missed me too? Just a tiny fragment?" I twitched my eyebrows. Then winced, I'd forgotten: it hurt like hell. "Somewhere in that careful heart, that beautiful unforgettable brain?" My headache was banging again.

Steady gaze. I knew that gaze.

Oh God, I thought right afterwards, I shouldn't have said that. These are things one isn't allowed to say. But having said it, I felt what the hell, so I added: "Missed my charm, I mean – my indomitable humour, my insidious allure?"

Softening gaze. A trace of faraway smile. The fingers were quite still now.

"Mmm."

It was just a murmur. It moved a mountain in my gut.

"I do so love the eloquence of these long explanatory speeches of yours," I said.

"I was certain you would."

Oh God, those eyes. I loved those eyes, the way they looked. My gut was churning deep down and hidden beneath the bandages. I swallowed – it made a clacking sound. My throat was very dry.

I cleared it. "Just to think of all these lengths I've gone to," I said. "Getting beaten up and landing here." I said it very seriously, my humour was completely on hold. "To awake your pity and entice you over – it was all to no avail?"

"Mmm."

Her fingers stirred again, they traced a line on mine. Then went away. They were rising, stretching, they picked up the plastic container with the tea, held it to my lips. Her other hand snaked round my skull, tipping it to help me. Gratefully I drank. Leaned back again.

"I thought you might like the surprise," she said quietly.

"I'm sorry I missed the breakfast."

"I enjoyed it on my own."

"Glad to hear about that. But I do appreciate your surprise."

She smiled down upon me; her hand was there again. I said: "Perhaps we could repeat that one day. The breakfast, I mean."

"I suppose we might."

"We could do it at my place. And take it very slowly. You'd be welcome to stay the night."

A languid look. A guileless smile. "At a stretch we might have considered the latter, but I am afraid it is out of the question now."

"It is?"

"Mmm." Her second hand was indicating the bandages over my body and pointing to the frame. "I spoke to the doctors this morning because I knew this would be the first thing on your mind. They assured me that in the heat of the fray some little things got broken off."

"They did?"

"Mmm. Irrevocably broken off."

"I don't like that smug look in your eye."

She laughed. It was so carefree. How I loved that laugh – it was like a happy gurgle.

"But don't worry your little head about it," she said. "I am certain we will find something else more fulfilling to occupy us." And she was suddenly serious again. "For example, a new exhibition has just opened last Saturday in the New Museum here which I should very much like to see."

"Manet."

"Mmm. And Turner" She laid her free hand back in her lap.

"And afterwards I'll invite you to lunch," I said. "At a small place I believe you'd like not far away."

"Please let it be the one the other side of the courtyard."

"Of course," I said. And I thought: my God, she knows her way around.

"I shall introduce you to the new curator, he has just moved here from Berlin. You would both get on like a house on fire."

"Anything to keep me distracted." I gave her my nastiest sneering gaze.

"Naturally." More of that secret smile.

And again I thought: isn't there anyone worth his salt she doesn't know? I dropped my eyes, looked at her lap; her hand lay there curled on the green of the gown. The sleeve had slipped up; on an elegant wrist a slender golden wristwatch peeped...

She was speaking again, talking about art. I listened, now and then contributing comments — I think it was about the Neue Pinakothek gallery in Munich. But mostly my eyes were fixed in her lap, my thoughts were on her thighs...

A few minutes later I heard her say: "I must go soon, I promised the staff nurse," and I saw the wristwatch rise, being delicately turned.

"Stay," I said. "You do me good."

"We have to be realistic." Gently she stroked my hand. "And practical. I have brought you a few things from your bathroom and a book from beside your bed. I do hope you didn't mind. Frau Maußer let me into your apartment."

I squinted. "With what?" I said weakly. "Her personal battering ram?"

"She knew where you put your spare key."

"She did?" I had to wince once more. I'd thought no-one knew except Estella — it was so dark up there in the ill-lit stairwell, so many hidden crevices. "Ah," I said, unhappily. And I thought: I'll have to change that little habit — how often has she sneaked in there to take a snoop when I'm at work? I closed my eyes momentarily; I felt completely naked.

"My frowning one — you didn't mind, did you?"

"Oh no," I said bravely. "I'm just trying to suppress the image, you see. Two women poking through all my porno magazines and touching my teddy bear."

"How silly of me..." She smiled a quiet and cheeky smile. "If only I had known I would have brought them too." She laughed again, that gurgling laugh. She leaned forward, a change of tone: "I brought you some flowers, but the nurse confiscated them. It appears that no flowers are permitted in here."

"How very sweet of you." I mustered my sweetest grimace. "But what about that crate of whisky, did you at least succeed in smuggling...?"

"Confiscated too. She is keeping your book and post safe as well. You are not allowed to read at present."

"My post?" I said in a strangled voice.

"Mmm."

"But..."

"We found your letterbox so full, Frau Maußer rightly thought it best to empty it."

"But it was locked." I paused, I cleared my throat carefully. "And I'm the only one who has a key."

"Frau Maußer's fits yours too, it seems." The smile was calm, was so sublime. "She had to jiggle it in the lock a bit, but it worked."

I stared. Aghast. Instinctively I jerked my hand...

But she held it fast, then shook it softly. "Now don't start getting uppity again, my choleric one." The drip tube swayed to and fro, the bag wobbled haphazardly on its hook. "It was good she could. I begged her to do the same each day until you are better. She made a very reliable impression."

Thorough too. She'd scrutinise every letter, every address... oh God, not only had she stripped me naked, now she'd got me by the balls. I took a sharp frustrated breath. But I'd forgotten. In my chest a dozen knives stabbed their steely points again. I gasped, and coughed – a pain pierced through my lungs, shot up my spine, split my skull in two. I sat there, mouth gaping wide open, taking lots of tiny shallow breaths.

She was stroking my hand slowly, soothingly; concern in the touch. I looked back at her, shook my head.

"My poor one," she said.

I shook my head again. "You just ruined my reputation," I said. "My good name is all in shreds."

"Silly one."

"You fail to understand. That incorrigible lady has X-ray eyes. And a copper kettle too." I tried a sly and sheepish smile; the waves of pain were fading now. "She'll steam open each piece of my correspondence with inquisitive talons and cackling laugh –

especially the anonymous packets of my eagerly-awaited pornographic latest editions. It'll be all over town by tonight."

"I really must leave you now."

"Yes," I said.

"I am not allowed to tire you out."

"I appreciate the thought."

"You are looking very groggy." A soft, a sympathetic smile. "My Michelin Man."

"Well thanks for doing your very best not to over-stress me."

She was withdrawing her hand and standing up. Such a cute twinkle in her eye. "Is there anything you need I should bring?"

"You were thinking of next year?"

"Mmm."

"Thanks," I said. "For the next few months it seems my needs will remain reduced to the present level of an infant. You know — a potty, disposable blow-up diapers and a substitute plastic breast of tea."

She was stooping close. Stay, I prayed. The particles of her perfume were there again. "I have arranged for you to be brought a telephone," she breathed. "A left-handed telephone." She breathed it in my ear.

"This is an intensive care unit," I whispered back. "I'm sure things like that are against the rules."

"It cost a little donation in the coffee collection tin." The breath through her nose was a breeze on my face and her perfume burnt a hole in my brain. "Then I can call you, or you me, and if you are feeling up to it I can pop by."

I looked in her eyes. My heart made another lurch surely hard enough to light up all the lamps on the monitoring screens.

"From Munich popping by is perhaps a slight understatement," I suggested.

"Not from Munich."

How I loved her face hovering there; I dared not say a word.

"I am staying here."

"Here?" I savoured the thought, it stuck to my tongue.

"For a few days, anyway. I have found a room in a little hotel. Not far from your apartment."

"But the children...?" I let the sentence taper off — my life is full of unfinished words.

"Margareth is holding the fort."

Strands of her hair caressed my world. "You can't do that," I said.

She touched my face, placed a finger upon my lips. Her eyes were there before me.

"Then at least stay in my apartment," I said.

A shake of her head. That was all.

"Hotels are so impersonal," I tried. "In the chest of drawers in the bedroom you'll find fresh sheets and towels. And before you leave in a year or two, if you have to, please leave your prints on the cushions, and everywhere."

Faint smile. Again no reply.

"My cleaning lady comes Wednesdays. If you can put up with the chaos till then."

"Actually, everything was very tidy."

I managed a smile. "I like the surprise in your voice."

I wanted to touch her, to stroke her face. I lifted my left arm, but the muscles shook. It seemed my energy was evaporating as though someone had pulled out the plug.

Then it occurred to me, and I said: "No you really can't do this. Anyway, you have no clothes and things."

"That is no problem."

"Yes it is a problem."

"I shall drive down now and pick them up."

"Oh God, no." I tried raising my arm again. "Annabelle listen, I've got colleagues and friends who can visit..."

"I am certain they are busy working people."

"Most, not all – two are freelance." I looked at her guiltily; I was fighting against myself now. "And you've got your hands full too. They'd be ..."

"You would prefer them to me?" Said slowly.

I thought: I'm craving for you to stay. "I'm very glad you asked that," I said.

"So this is settled?"

I nodded.

"It is not too late. And while I am there I shall put the children to bed and explain to them what has happened."

"Not too late?" I frowned.

"Mmm."

"What time is it then?"

"Nearly five."

I thought about that. It seemed more like midday. "There's a hole," I said.

"I am certain that is normal."

I frowned again. Concentrated. Was thinking of the children. "Please give each of them a small kiss from Uncle Stefan – just to help me re-establish a foothold on paradise lost."

She watched me. Pensively. Put her head on one side. "Yes, I will," she said and her eyes were far away. "My philosopher," she added quietly, and gently stroked my skin.

My heart stirred again. Although it wasn't true, I loved the way she said that.

Then she blinked and made a jump: "Before I leave, something practical," she said, and I could see she was gathering herself. "I noticed your fridge is very full. I will empty it of perishables, and air the rooms."

"No, really not." I felt bad about that one. "Estella can do that. She lives only a few corners away."

"Ah, your Estella." Another distant smile. "The one who lights your dark."

I chuckled. So she remembered – was there nothing she forgot? "Only on winter days," I said, and decided to leave it at that. I was looking at Estella, looking at my fridge, too. Yes, it was packed full, as always, I'd done the week's shopping on the Friday morning before driving off to the seminars.

"She's used to doing it," I said. "I do the same for her and Lars – it's our little symbiotic trait."

"Well just this once I shall be her substitute."

"I don't wish to impose."

"You are not imposing."

"Thanks," I said. I put on a pained expression. "And should Estella find out, at least she's one of the forgiving kind." My eyes were in the fridge again; someone else had popped into my mind. But before I could speak, Annabelle asked: "To avoid troubling your remarkable Frau Maußer, would it be sensible for me to take along your bunch of keys?"

"Ah yes," I said, "indeed it would." I was slipping, wasn't I? "They must be with my belongings here somewhere."

"I imagine together with your other little knick-knacks – your knuckleduster and bludgeon and so forth, don't you think?" Another stroke of fingers on my face. I noticed she carefully avoided my forehead.

"How well you know the fighting trade." I chuckled again. Herr Eggenhofer hung in my head. "Could you do me a small favour when you get around to sniffing about in my fridge?"

"You need your teddy bear?"

"Desperately." I grinned. "No, actually – I should be very grateful if you could give everything to my neighbour Herr Eggenhofer. Also the imperishables – the beer and the tins and the bottles of wine. He lives on the floor below me."

"Herr Eggenhofer."

"He's a needy person."

"He is?" Her gaze lit up. "Don't I know another poor one who insists he is needy, too?"

"I'm trying to be serious," I said seriously.

"I believe my services might stretch to that."

I watched the mischievousness in her eyes. "There is one little condition, though – you..."

"I do not like conditions."

"With a woman of your loose character I'm afraid it's a necessity. You're not to flirt with him. He's a very attractive male."

"Uh-huh. In that case, definitively no conditions."

"He's eighty-four and still not past it. He's the terror of the town."

"He sounds delightful."

"He is. It was he from whom I acquired the old Mercedes Benz – you know, the one with the undue sag in the back seat..."

"Ah-hah..."

"I have it on his best authority that during his prime this particular place was second home to him and not to him alone, which would go a long way to explain its unhappy state and why you must promise not to let him get his knobbly hands on that car key, not let him take you for even the shortest of..."

"Martina did mention some broken springs on the way to her party." She laughed. Her lovely chuckling laugh. "Naturally I imagined it must be your second home too."

I summoned my left hand to rise and give her a hearty poke – but my fingers and arm still shook, were weak as water. I was forced to let them fall again.

She was starting to stand. "Well, my charitable one..."

I watched her face retreating. Now I could see all of her hair. Say something else to keep her... for God's sake stay a little, I thought, don't leave me alone with myself.

"I'm fond of him, you know," I said. "He spends most of his small pension on the rent, and the rest on cigarettes and contraceptives."

But it seemed that wasn't food for her for further intellectual thought. She was stooping her head to me briefly; her face and her perfume were close again.

"Give him my regards," I told her.

She touched me. She did it very carefully. For several seconds the skin of her cheek was laid on mine, silk on sandpaper. I closed my eyes; I realised I hadn't shaved for more than a day.

She turned away. I watched her. Stilettos in their plastic covers, the green gown at the back had come undone, little strings hanging down. I watched her go.

Later they injected me with something through the connector on the back of my hand. I can't recall the rest of the day.

x x x

I was brought a telephone next day. It came in between two short visits from Annabelle.

I watched them, I lay there motionless; I just watched their movements with my eyes. I was beginning to get used to this. They plugged it in between other plugs and put it on a small trolley – they said the chip-card had already been paid for, but I wasn't really listening. They activated the phone.

I remember: that was the afternoon there were sudden flashes of light from the corridor in my eyes followed by a scuffle and slightly sharp words. I later learned that a small pitched battle between the Boss and the Press had been the cause. It was also the afternoon, during one of those precious moments when one thinks one's completely alone, that I let out a long, satisfying and necessary fart which reverberated round the room; I hadn't heard her, my eyes were closed in pleasure, I hadn't known that the staff nurse had just walked in. But being where she was, and who she was, I guess she'd learned to live with these things. Actually it was one of my little highlights of the day.

Somewhere deep in my foggy brain, and surreptitiously, I planned a second box of chocolates for that one, with an extra big golden bow.

After two days I was able to use the telephone – as long as it was left in reach and I didn't have to tip my hips, and as long as I got someone to discreetly close the sliding door. Apart, of course, from Estella one of the first calls was to my office; I spoke to Benny and afterwards Cornelia, and begged them to keep the rest at bay. But the very first of all I made to Annabelle, on her mobile. "Checking up on me, my jealous one?" came her calm and sultry voice. I really was acting like a child.

I tried to do better with Estella, but had to persevere. At the first attempt came Lars' clipped and efficient recorded voice saying with a disgustingly attractive Danish accent: "Please leave name and number, we'll call back." At the second attempt the line was engaged, at the third I was luckier. The ringing tone burred. I lay there in bed gazing into space, waiting. Could imagine her telephone on the floor, the cable snaking. Could see me sitting there too, from my last visit – a half-empty wine bottle, canvases leaning, her cluttered studio flooded with northern light...

Lars answered. Damn. Briefly we exchanged pleasantries. No, Estella had been in Italy since Saturday, wouldn't be back till tonight. Each time Lars and I talked or met I felt like the second-hand knight who's just lost the joust, had his ribbons spurned, lost his damsel to the better man. I left a message, left my new number.

But Estella didn't ring back. The very next day she came to visit. She arrived just after Annabelle had departed; did I detect a little telepathy there?

She floated in, as was her way. She floated in like a cloud.

"Estella," I said.

She stooped, she kissed me full on my mouth. Estella the successful poetess and artist, the keeper of the mysteries, Estella the one whose body had always been out-of-bounds.

"You were in my thoughts all Sunday night," she said, hovering before my face.

"Ah," I said. I tried a sceptical squint. "And I thought I was there for good."

Intense blue-grey, wide-set eyes looking into me, looking through me. And thick hair puffy and fair, eccentricity in its waves. A knowing nod. Then, a bit hauntingly: "You popped into my head and wouldn't leave."

"Ah," I repeated. "That's my special talent, you see. Popping in under your guard."

She gazed earnestly. "And now I know why." She indicated my body with a heavy-ringed hand.

"Coincidence," I said. Just to provoke.

"Not coincidence," she countered.

"Admittedly strange," I said seriously.

"You consider so, Stefan?"

"That's your special talent."

She drew the chair close, seated herself, bundling the bottom of the obligatory green gown up onto her lap exposing old denim working trousers. Smears of oil paint on thighs and legs. "Lars told me what happened to you – it was in the papers."

Oh God, I thought. "At least that saves us explanations." But with Estella things like this, anyway, required no explanation.

"Pain?" she said, intensively, frowning.

"A little."

Another nod, watching. "Never mind." And with lighter tone as if reciting: "Bad wounds heal but bad words don't."

I liked that. "That's nice," I said.

"Persian proverb."

"You always find appropriate words."

We exchanged glances.

"Subject change?" she suggested.

"Please."

She spread out her legs, feet stretched. She had long toes; I could see them through the plastic covers, they stuck out of her sandals. "Fill me in," she said. "Munich. Your friend. Did he phone, did you meet?"

I filled her in – about Matthias and the steps and video, and Theo, and about Heinrich's call just before I left and Margareth's separation, my staying on in Munich. Then I stalled.

She sat there watching me. Then she said: "Well, well, well! So many interesting things happening to you all of a sudden. D'you believe me now?" An enigmatic smile.

"Believe?"

"The postcard, the threshold. What I told you on the phone."

She'd told me when I rang her seeking her advice that the card hadn't come out of the blue, that the timing wasn't coincidence, was a sign to be acted upon. She told me an event like this could also lead to other changes – she told me lots of absurd stuff...

I returned her gaze. "No," I said, and shook my head. "Of course not." Couldn't help thinking of Annabelle, though.

"Consider with more care," she said unperturbed. "The postcard, the phone calls. Just look where the signs led you – to where you never intended to go again, to Munich of all places!"

"They're not signs, Estella." I laughed a cracked laugh. "Don't be silly."

Quietly she smiled. It was another of those smiles reserved for the initiated. She didn't speak.

"Life's simply full of coincidence, full of chance," I said. "Over which we've got no control." I meant it; I said it with conviction. But was I defending myself?

Ah that gaze. It was so intense. "A singularly male point of view." Her tangled hair shone – in the bright lights of the room it was silver-gold.

"I fear I'm a typical male."

"It's full of opportunity, not chance, Stefan. Coincidences are signs of opportunity sent to benefit us. Remember?"

Oh God, there she goes again, I thought. "Then we agree to disagree," I said.

But Estella was a stubborn one, she just kept going: "When one acts upon them one's life starts flowing in a new direction. And that's precisely what you did. Haven't you noticed something's begun to flow?"

I shook my head again. "Ah Estella, you always had mystical tendencies."

That gaze, that smile, still upon me – she smiled like a wise teacher on her pupil, like a mother on her child. She said:

"Remember when we first talked of coincidence?" and her voice was light as air.

"Yes," I said flatly. I remembered.

"Down by the river."

"Yes." I could see the reeds, and the dragonflies, the ripples reflecting the sky. That lazy summer afternoon.

"And you were unreceptive." Her voice was dreamy, misty.

"Yes." I remembered it well.

"But you're more receptive now. I sense it."

Was I? Could that be possible? No — a load of nonsense. Annabelle floated in again... Well yes, one thing had led to another, a bit like Estella had foreseen. Admittedly a curious coincidence. But nothing more, though.

How mesmerising was that voice, how lulling like a breeze. I could see the water, the river flowed...

I stared down at the bedclothes, at my body beneath the sheet. And ordered myself to be careful, let realism in again. Don't give her any rope, I thought. Yes, I could see the river flow by carrying bits of the sky. But I could see that gathered-up dress of hers, too, those unguarded thighs amongst the daisies and the grass. They brought me down to earth. I shook my head; Estella was a bewitching one, I had to be on my guard.

"Have you always believed this stuff?" I asked.

"Stuff, Stefan?"

"Well, whatever one calls it."

"Since I was a child."

"Ah."

"It's part of life."

"It is?" I turned my eyes back to her, said tongue-in-cheek: "Did it just come to you, then? In a blinding flash, or something?"

"You're being trite."

"Sorry."

"My grandmother taught me."

"Taught you?"

"She used to tell me stories in bed before I went to sleep."

I gave her a little twinkle. "So they were just stories."

"Not at all. She simply wove pictures around phenomena she was familiar with. She showed me lots of things."

"No," I said. "Like what?"

"She introduced me." Her eyes were steady, they searched mine carefully, introspectively — they were much more blue than grey. "To apparitions, for example. And auras. For her they were visible."

"I'm sure she was pulling your leg."

"Naturally not. I can sometimes see them too."

That startled me. She's kidding, I thought. Estella's lots of esoteric things but she's surely not that far out. "You're joking," I said. Unhappily I twitched the fingers of my healthy hand. "You never let on about that before."

"Don't treat these things lightly, Stefan."

"Ghosts?" I echoed. "Auras?" Oh, come on... I was trying to be serious, trying to imagine – could she see mine too?

"It is merely a question of perception," she said.

"Oh yes?"

"It starts with awareness of the messages, and listening to them. What you keep calling coincidences."

"Messages?" I gave my fingers another little twitch.

"The signs."

"Ah," I said. "You're back to signs again." I shook my head, watching her disbelievingly. I'd never met anyone who claimed this ability, I was sure even Estella couldn't. I said half-heartedly: "Can you see my aura too?"

She didn't answer.

Ah, those crystal eyes. I shook my head, I felt like glass. "Not lots of colour, I imagine," I ventured. "Suppose mostly black and shades of grey."

Still no answer. She just gazed at me with that cloud-like faraway look.

"You never cease to amaze," I said.

She blinked. It was so sublime.

Seconds passing... She stirred. She brushed at the gown, exposed a wrist, glancing at her watch.

No, don't go, I thought. Not now – things are just warming up. Quickly I cast about for something to nail her. How about poltergeists and haunted houses... or how many ghosts have you bumped into this year? But I was too slow...

"You have to learn to walk before you can run," she said, a bit sternly.

Ah, a succinct remark. Did she mean I'd need more than a month or so before making the grade to ghost-encounters and aura-analyses? I gave a little chuckle. "I'm afraid I'm a cripple," I confessed.

"No more than many. Your realism merely gets in the way."

"My realism and common sense are my faithful crutches, don't you see?" I stopped. Felt pleased at that little allusion. "I could never attain your lofty heights – in fact I'd stumble at the first step up that mountain."

"It isn't a mountain, Stefan. It's a path."

"Must be stony and narrow, then." I frowned. Made me wince, though. I took a recuperating breath. "Haven't even had a glimpse of it yet."

"Oh yes you have. You've just forgotten."

"Forgotten?"

"Think back."

Shook my head, but carefully. "How do you mean?"

"Anyone with your level of awareness passed the threshold in his childhood."

There was that word again – that exotic word of hers. My God, she was too way out for a guy like me. I wanted to frown again but didn't dare.

"Think back," she repeated.

I was. My childhood... I searched around for thresholds and paths, looking for anything weird, anything in her line of esoteric stuff. I floundered about; I was seeing nothing.

"No," I said, "can't find anything." Then added, by way of explanation: "I didn't have a granny like yours – my life was very lacking."

She didn't reply.

I was still thinking back, though, but I suppose I was only playing games with myself, I wasn't treating her subject with the sobriety that was due. I let my mind wander. Grandmother. I'd only known one of mine, my father's mother, that stiff abrupt old lady who used to quote Confucius and Goethe at dinner – I'd never received stories about auras and things.

I felt Estella's stare. Continued to try to concentrate...

Yes, grandmother died when I was only eight. I could see her lying there on her bed in the room that smelled of death – the priest, the nurse, all the family gathered around...

"No," I repeated into space, "there's really nothing, you know." Then why was my mind fixed on grandma, why had Estella mentioned hers?

Grandmother had been in agony for half a year; but she looked so peaceful now, the pain was slipping from her face – then she was going, she'd stopped breathing, there were people saying last goodbyes and people trooping out...

And then, suddenly, there it was – that memory I'd suppressed so long because I didn't understand. I was gazing at grandma's body and Eva stood beside me, slipping her hand into mine and squeezing it to tell me something. The priest had turned away, and the nurse was opening the window to let out the soul the silly way they did in those days. Eva's eyes were wide, her little face was lifting up as if following a movement. She was staring at the ceiling...

Is that the sort of thing Estella was looking for? Involuntarily my fingers twitched again. "Well – maybe there is something," I said slowly. "Not what I experienced personally, but what Eva maintained she did in my presence." I clenched my fingers, made a fist. Then I recounted to Estella what had happened, and at the end: "She said it was a vibrating light, that it was grandma." I shrugged my shoulders dismissively. "Eva was only six, though – presumably the emotions surrounding the death fired her fantasy."

"That was your grandmother's soul," Estella said. Was it necessary for her to say it with such certitude?

I watched her eyes as best I could. "Her soul?" I fear my smile was more a smirk.

"Undoubtedly."

Couldn't look any longer. I tipped my gaze, to her eccentric hair, to the band tying back its untidiness. Were those smears I could detect in the pale blonde waves? "She couldn't have seen it," I said. "I couldn't."

No answer. Just a lift of eyebrows. Yes, I think those were traces of paint in her hair.

"You believe in the soul, too?" I cleared my throat, it was getting croaky. "Departing the body at death, flapping its wings and flying up to heaven? Stuff like that?"

That tore a bit of a hole in the gravity of the conversation.

A silence.

It must be getting pretty crowded up there, I thought. I only thought it though. And decided against asking her, tongue in cheek, if she'd happened to observe any souls recently too.

She gave me another of her special knowing looks, one of those which took in the male world with a weary distain – and raised both hands, combing them through that hair.

"Sorry Estella," I apologised. "It seems I belong to those unhappy legions of the unenlightenable."

A warm laugh, a flap of her hand. With a wave of an invisible wand she changed the subject, began telling me about an idea she was developing for an oil painting series in her summer collection and what did I think?

It wasn't until just before she left that I let the cat out of the bag and shared the little additional detail I'd failed to confess: I told her about Annabelle.

x x x

With the arrival of the telephone came one or two calls from other people – from Margareth in Munich, and my mother on a trip with her so-called boss in South America, collecting items of art she said. I hadn't realised English antiques were so common there, but I was happy she was so far away. And there was a brief stiff one from my brother Tobias in between meetings of the board. The one who remained silent was my younger sister Eva. Unexpectedly she came to call instead.

She marched in one evening draped impatiently in protective clothing put on the wrong way round and almost hidden behind a cloud of flowers. Nurse Barbara was off duty, and Susanne had a big broad grin.

Eva came in stripping off the obligatory gown with her free hand, swapping the big bouquet from right to left, casting the gown on the chair. Annabelle had left three hours ago, had to return to Munich. It was my fifth day in the clinic.

"Eva," I said.

Behind her, reflections of late evening sun off the corridor glass. I now could twist my head nearly a quarter circle.

"Hello, Stef."

She looked chic and slim and efficient in her tight-fitting working clothes – a bit like one of those television anchor women, I suppose. She was much smaller than Margareth, even shorter than me, and had the compact kind of figure Maggie later told me she sometimes still dreams of for herself.

"You're looking good," I told her, looking at her clothes. "But it seems to stop at your eyes."

Her small face was drawn and grey with dark rings. And her greeting smile switched on and off like a light.

"You're damn right there."

She lowered the flowers briefly over my chest like a peacock display, then laid them at my feet on the frame. "An unburnt offering," she said flatly. Then unhooked the strap of an elegant leather shoulder bag and dumped it on the bed too.

"Thanks," I smiled. "Strictly forbidden, I'm afraid."

"What isn't here? What the hell."

"Thanks all the same. They look a bit like the way I'd like to feel."

She nodded briefly. "I presume I can't touch you."

"A kiss is not a touch."

She stooped. Her cropped dark hair grazed my face – she gave me a firm peck on each cheek. Already her head was hurrying to retreat but I managed to hang my left hand on her shoulder which impressed her and she stopped in unhappy surprise. Her face was before me, and frozen, her eyes haunted. I could see her stress, almost touch the tension.

"What's the matter?" I asked.

"Not your problem," she said. "By that I mean, we'll talk about it when you're recovered."

"I'm recovered enough to feel concern."

"Let's talk about *you*."

"Don't let's do that," I suggested.

She ignored me. "What the devil happened?" Eva's not one to be deflected from goals. "Found a message from the clinic on my answering machine when I got back this afternoon. Was in Rome and Barcelona on business."

"Sorry about that. A silly idea of my mobile phone company with emergency numbers."

"Don't mean that – rang here at once but they wouldn't tell me a thing 'part from the fact you were admitted last Sunday night. And couldn't get Margareth on the phone. You've had a car accident?"

"I simply got into a fight I wasn't meant to."

"A *fight*? You're kidding."

"Actually no." I shifted my shoulders uncomfortably. "I do it every now and then, you know. Just to keep my hand in, and let off a bit of steam."

"Don't be silly – be serious. With whom?"

I shook my head. Took a breath, but not too deep. Briefly described what had happened – and, because she demanded it, the extent of my bodily damage. After I'd finished she still wasn't satisfied, began to ask questions again.

"Oh God, Eva, let's call it a day, can we? Let's talk about anything else. I'm just about all I've heard of since Monday." I cleared my throat; it was still dry from the clinical air. "Excuse the bad sentence construction."

She retreated; left my hand in the air. She drew up the chair in silence and sat down on the discarded gown.

I was explaining: "I need to sink my teeth into the real world of healthy flesh again."

"Flesh? Uh-huh."

"I mean, offer me distraction. I'm not good being constantly surrounded by my petty suffering."

She nodded. A curt jerk. She watched me. Her lips were pursed; I'd always liked her lips. Full, firm and determined. "Long time, no see," she said. It was a statement. No emotion attached. Oh those haunted eyes.

"Yes," I said.

"Must be two years or more."

"Yes." What else could I say?

"You phoned me recently, though. Out of the blue. 'Bout a couple of weeks ago, at work. I got the message, but too late. Was on another trip."

"Yes."

"Yes what?"

She was demanding so many answers. "I was going down to Munich," I said. "Wanted to see if we could meet, and if I could stay the night." Yes, I thought – that fateful Thursday. The day I saw Matthias on video – the day before Annabelle. The day my life turned around.

"Yes," I reiterated. Oh God, it seemed so long ago.

"I called back. Your mobile was dead."

"At least thanks for trying." I remembered. I hadn't touched it for two days, and when I did, discovered the battery was dead.

"To what did I owe the honour, then?"

I smiled, discreetly. Watched her haunted eyes. "To talk about Margareth." And Matthias, I thought. But don't mention him now.

"I see."

Eva was a resilient one. She'd developed a shell like a shield as a child – like me. Because of Margareth, and our mother, and also because of the scandal and prying reporters and having to hide the shame. But like most hard people she was soft inside, and vulnerable. Knowing her from our childhood, I could see her through the cracks.

"She told me you came down to Munich because of her," she said.

"Yes."

"You. In Munich! Could hardly b'lieve it."

"No."

"That was thoughtful, brother."

"I'm a thoughtful guy." I shook my head, dismissing. "That was the least I could do."

She pressed her lips together, deliberating. I saw the pain behind her eyes, her mind wasn't on the subject. She was hiding herself, keeping me out. I could feel the pressure, too.

"Heinrich's a bastard," she said.

"Is he?" I attempted a shrug – could only do it lopsided. "He's a typical male."

"You're almost all bastards."

"Yes," I said. "I suppose we are. One way or another." And I thought: isn't that why you women were created – to save us crippled men from ourselves?

"She's well rid of him. I warned her from the start."

"I recall."

"She'll get over him."

"Yes," I said. "Don't we all, sooner or later? Just a question how jagged the scar." I watched her. She was doing her best, her armour thick, her head held high – like a wounded knight holding me off on the tip of her lance.

Then she shot it out: "Fucking men." Her eyes were hard, her hate was hot. It shocked me. But it broke her lance, I was glad of that, her defence was down at last; and I knew she was no longer thinking of Heinrich...

"Their brains in their balls and their pricks where their emotions ought to be." She crossed her neat legs; her short skirt wrapped them tight. "Trouble with most men is they know far more 'bout greed and power than love – they need to dominate. And when they don't get what they want, they destroy."

"That's a harsh judgement," I said. But it was the old, old story, wasn't it? My younger sister – small, tough and attractive, a tomboy in her teens, queen of emancipation now. I lay there propped on the pillows unmoving.

"It's a fact of life – of a woman's life. In marriage, in affairs, at the workplace. Emphasis on the latter."

Ah. I watched her, carefully. Waiting. The dam had broken but the wall of water hadn't yet burst through. I watched and remembered – I was glancing backwards. She carried an old and heavy load, like a cross to bear, like a burden on her back. Yes, I remembered: the female frustration and hate, the breaking of the chains. She'd even done her turn in the lesbian fold after Matthias disappeared and her passion for him ran onto the rocks. And I remembered too, from the moment she stepped into her first job, the way she expressed it, the constant source of her frustration which accompanied: being born an ambitious woman in an incompetent male world. Eva was still the wild one, the bitter one – small of stature but a lioness, not one to waste energy or words.

"I'm being bullied at the company," she said. "Discriminated against."

She said it icily. Her voice was suppressed, like a hiss, still half under control.

"By whom?"

"The executive level. They're bent on destroying me." She stared coldly.

Oh God, I thought. I just lay there.

"Been going on over half a year. Can you imagine?"

I nodded slowly. "Why didn't you ring me when it first started?"

"Thought it'd blow over."

"This kind of thing seldom does."

"You familiar with this phenomenon, then? This shit?"

"Yes." I'd been approached twice by victims between seminars, I'd had to read up on it. "It's fairly widespread. And it comes in different forms."

"Yep..." She tossed her head. "It happens too fucking often. Practised by women too, I hear."

"Not an exclusively male domain."

"But at my level it's always a male game and it's pure fucking hell." She sat straight-backed, her neat, naked legs were still crossed – they were slim, brown, made a healthy impression as if she played sport a lot or was much involved with fitness machines.

"They're trying to get rid of me."

That surprised me, after all she'd achieved. "Why?" I said.

She didn't answer.

"Do you have a new boss?"

Still she didn't answer, perhaps she hadn't heard. She gazed bitterly into space.

I didn't know much – but I did know she'd gone to the company more or less straight from business school when it was just a small, old-fashioned family firm hand-making saddles and shoes and stuff. Right from the start she'd persuaded the senior partner Alex to modernise and diversify. A new range of articles for the big names.

"You must've been in this company nearly twenty years," I said.

"Twenty-one." She paused, staring, as if she were staring down the tunnel of time. "Built the damn thing up from scratch. When I came in – profit margin less than half a million and faltering. Worked my guts out and we didn't look back." She stopped.

"Tell me." I meant the recent bit. She was always a dark horse, never let on much.

"Nothing to tell. Turnover last year fifty-three million before tax. I was department head sixteen of those years. Now they're after my blood."

"Not Alex."

"No."

She stopped again. Deliberating. Was the circle complete? I waited. Nothing came. So I said: "They can't touch you. Can't fire you."

"They'll try."

"I doubt it. Would cost them a bomb in compensation. Discrimination is doing it the cheap way."

"Hoping I'll sack myself."

"Yes," I said.

"Fucked if I will."

Still she was staring ahead, eyes far away. She sat so straight. Her lips were pressed together, I could see she was shutting herself in again.

To help, I said: "Who's they, Eva?"

Dumbly she shook her head.

"Fill me in."

"What's the point?"

"Before it strangles. Before you get ill."

She dropped her head. "Alex has left." She gathered her arms, hugged herself. "Couple of years ago." She stopped.

I waited. Said nothing.

"It's a family business – you knew that. He had a stroke, but survived. Sold out his share to his brother Max, and emigrated. Max is weak, not into things, not dedicated. And can't stand strong women." She was staring at my bed, she wasn't staring at me.

"Shit," I said. And left it at that.

"Shit's not the word for it. Brother Max brought in a CEO to run things – a Herr Reubel. Ice-cold bastard, highly intelligent. Knows nothing 'bout sales or client working relationships, but brilliant on the technical side."

She nodded her head, grimly. As though to confirm her own words.

"For a while we got on okay, I reported direct to him, he cleaned up and computerised the manufacturing side, left me in charge of product development and sales..." Her voice was dead, a monotone. "Then the axe fell," she added. It sounded so final. Again she stopped. I don't think she wanted to start up again.

"In what form?" I said.

"Another new male fucker."

"Explain please."

"Can't you guess?" Her head came up. "You know all these fucking managerial tricks – it's sods like you who teach them."

"Guessing isn't constructive here, Eva. And you know me well enough – you know I don't subscribe to dirt."

No answer. A hard stare.

"Accepted?" I said.

Curt nod. Nothing more.

"I'm good at listening. So tell me."

She sat stiff and hurt, watching me. "Reubel created a new position between himself and me. 'Bout a year ago." Her arms were still hugging. "Even had the nerve to invite me to apply for the post which he promptly filled with a new man – a slimy little Austrian named Schultz. Has old connections with Max's family estate. Ingratiating yes-man, ideal for what'd been planned." She paused again.

"Nasty," I said.

"Yeah, but at first I was too dumb to see. For starters Schultz wormed his way into my confidence and picked my brain to learn the ropes. In my naïvety I even helped. Pretty incompetent bugger but can charm the pants off female clients..."

She continued for a minute: details and company structure. Abbreviated, chopped-up sentences. I listened; I could half-visualise what might come. Then she said: "Just before last Christmas while I was on a business trip, Schultz changed the chain of command and pounced. Sly little bugger. Increased the salaries of my four heads of sales, passed the word he was the new boss, not me, and got them to report direct to him. Buttered them up, made them feel important. Can you imagine, brother? I get back and the world's turned on its head. Fait accompli."

"I'm afraid I can."

"And my faithful well-trained staff – knives in the back. I ask you, in our bloody trade who's got backbone?"

"In what trade is it better?" I shook my head. "And they fell for the bait?"

"Yep. 'Cept for one, my best. She warned me soon as I got back."

"Well, I guess you didn't take it lying down."

"Straight to Schultz. Confronted him. He said talk to Reubel. Reubel blocked me, told me all communications to come via Schultz. That was it. I was ignored and bypassed."

"I'm in the picture."

"Worse to come. Shortly after, Schultz did a restructure – broke up my teams, shuffled everyone around. Reubel was behind it though, Schultz's just the bumboy. People got tasks and markets they hadn't been trained for, efficiency and harmony went down the drain. Not to mention motivation."

"We know that one – that's the Pol Pot one. Everyone with brains or spectacles gets killed. That's a nasty one."

"That's divide and rule. Reubel's a fucking stupid fool, he's wrecking..."

"Not stupid, sister. It's the total control thing. It's Hitler and Stalin rolled into one. That's the strategy for the insecure little guys, the ones scared of the strengths and prowess of others. But let me offer consolation – like any..."

"He's wrecking the company, reducing the profits."

"Go and prove that one to Father Christmas – as long as profit is there who's to tell? But like any dictatorship it's based on fear, it's self-destructive in the end."

"What the hell's the use of in the end – five years, ten years?" She'd opened her arms, was wringing her hands. "The work climate's reached rock bottom. He's destroying everything I built." Fury in her fingers. "My best people came to me complaining. One of my sales heads, Martha, had a breakdown, another got ill. And a third threw in the towel, found himself another job."

"Sure," I said. "That's the dictatorship syndrome. The people get sick. But what about you? What's...?"

"Now there's a second reorganisation – Martha's been sacked, just like that. She's too ill, won't go to arbitration. And one of the least able men's been promoted by Schultz to a position directly beneath him – another of these bastards who gets a thrill kicking other's arses." She stopped for breath. Hands shaking in anger.

"Unhappy details," I said. "Tell me about you though, Eva. Where does all this leave you?"

"High and dry. But I'm fighting them."

"How precisely?"

"Do the rounds of my customers to get new orders like always, refuse to give in – putting a good face on it. Block the bastards at every turn. They hate my guts."

"Sure they do. But inside the company they've totally isolated you?"

"A figurehead. No power. Essentially I sit and twiddle my goddamn thumbs. Reason I'm on the road so much." A bitter stare. "And no information – have to get that from one of my old subordinates behind their backs. Need it for customer contact."

I spread my one good hand. "They cut off your head."

"Yep."

"But they know they can't sack you. As I said."

"Want to break me. War of attrition? That's how it feels."

"Yes," I said.

"Recently they've done something perverse, though – given me the glorious title of Vice President, plus a small rise."

I shook my head. "Just a little trick – in case you go for arbitration on grounds of discrimination. They know all the tricks, sister."

"Want to pull the mat out from under my feet. What my lawyer said."

"Ah." I watched her. Her hollow eyes, her dark rings. "You have a lawyer. I'm glad to hear that."

"Found one a couple of months ago. Needed advice how to go about things."

"Is he good?"

"Best there is. Specialist in employment arbitration."

"What does he say?"

"Said he'll take on the case."

"And?"

"Working on it. Said I needed proof, something black on white."

"There's never that, Eva. They're not fools, you know."

"Tried to get some of my old staff to bear witness." She stopped again, shook her head.

"And?" I repeated.

"One finally agreed. Then backed out. Scared 'bout her job. They must've got wind of it – that's when they gave me the title and rise."

She gazed at me. How bad she looked. I thought: there's no cure here, she's got no choice, she'll have to quit before she gets ill. Carefully I said: "So how does your lawyer judge your chances of suing now?"

"Advises against it. But says if I really want, could have a try Shrugs his shoulders."

"Have a try? The man's a fool. What's his name?"

"Schmidt-Rednitz."

"Heard of him. Big fish," I said. "He'd cost you a packet, that's all." I shook my head, slowly. I was looking at her hollow eyes again. Then I said: "Can I give you a bit of advice, Eva?"

She returned my gaze, didn't reply. She'd clenched her hands again.

"You've got to go about this the right way."

She jerked her chin curtly, still didn't reply.

"You're burnt out. At present you're not in a..."

"'Course I am – this business's killing me. But I won't give up."

"I can give you an address," I said.

"Address?"

"A therapist in Munich. A specialist for discrimination victims."

"Don't be absurd – don't need a bloody quack."

"She'll work you through the trauma, help you get back on your feet. Help you cope at the workplace and prepare you should you wish to go to court."

She eyed me, sceptically. "You know her?"

"Of her. Had to help someone once. I'm told Karla's very good. And she works with a lawyer who's got experience in discrimination cases – also a woman. A Dr Heike Meier."

She nodded. Said nothing.

"With their guidance you can make decisions, decide on a strategy."

"Okay."

We watched one another. "It is traumatic, isn't it?" I said.

"It's a horror."

"You must avoid getting ill."

"I'm on the way."

She stood up. Abruptly, jerkily. Pushed aside the chair; the crumpled green gown draped on its back fell to the floor. She ignored it. Crossed her arms tight, hugging herself again, cast a rapid nervous glance at her handbag.

"Jesus," she said sharply, "why can't one smoke in this goddamn place?"

"Go out and smoke then." Doesn't one have to show consideration for the vices under circumstances like this?

She concentrated her gaze and frowned, shook her head quickly as if reprimanding herself, strengthening resolve. And turned – stared out of the windows above me.

She began speaking again – in a rapid frustrated tone. I just listened in silence; she wasn't looking for replies. Her sentences were hard and bitter like they had been at the start. She stood there hugging her pain, squeezing it out like goo through the cracks. I was glad for her, she was starting to let things out. She reminded me a bit of Heinrich that morning on the phone – how many of us need a safety-valve for stuff we've stowed away too long.

She was talking about emancipation, the lot of women like herself, and the mentality of German industry bosses seen through her critical experienced eyes. I recall one venomous tirade in particular: "I'll tell you how these fossilised macho arseholes view us women," she spat. "Over-emotional, suffer the curse, liable to get pregnant any time – flirt with them, screw them, but for Christ's sake keep 'em away from the top. Male domain – always was, always will be, *jawohl*. Can't afford their hysterics up here, and anyway can't sing dirty ditties and tell 'em dirty jokes propping up the bar or standing pissing in the Gents. Never forget this rule number one, ol' boy."

She said a number of other things too; sometimes in between them she'd sniff, and her sniff was like a sneer.

I lay there, leaned back, resting my head, watching her prise open the cracks. After about five minutes she began focusing, though, and I concentrated a little more carefully because she was back to her present source of pain again.

"Alex was a rare exception," she said. "Ebullient egoist as he was, he wasn't scared of a skirt and always said fuck to the rules."

She stared at the sun.

"Thank your lucky stars," I suggested.

"He just wanted the best people around him – *basta*. So that's what we did, built a great team, female and male where talent was the major currency." She glared, brown eyes flaring. "And now it's all being destroyed by more of this incompetent male crap. Makes you want to puke."

"No argument," I agreed.

Fists clenching. "Makes you want to grab a gun and shoot this pair in their balls."

"Get out," I said.

"What?"

"There's no cure for this kind of affliction. One just has to cut ones losses and go."

"Never. I'm fighting this to the end."

"Gather your strength and go for compensation," I said. "A lot of compensation."

Arms dropping; she stuck her hands on her hips. "I want reinstatement, brother, not buggering off with a sack of gold." Ah, that undying fighting spirit. She suddenly looked so good: tiny and determined and sexy in those tight-fitting working clothes. I could imagine how she worked her magic on her clients, whichever sex.

I said to her, firmly: "My advice would be, get out and set up a company of your own. A woman of your calibre shouldn't…"

"*This* is my company – put eighteen years of my life into it. Me and Alex built it into what it is today."

I watched her fury, I watched her hurt. The setting sun was red in her face. "Okay," I said. "Then promise me one thing, sister – get in touch with Karla and Dr Meier and let them show you the ropes."

"Will do." She released her grip on her hips. "Least I'll promise that." She let her hands fall.

I nodded. I thought: thank God for this small mercy.

She was letting go; I could see it, she was turning into herself. Perhaps a private moment reserved for her alone. I lowered my eyes – back to my bed, back to my body lying there, I stared at the flowers at my feet.

Maybe half a minute passed; it was like a punctuation mark, like the pause between changing trains. I thought: maybe I should add a word to what we've just said when she comes back from wherever she's been, a word of consolation, a little ray of hope, a tiny pearl for her to take with her to look at in the dark. But something distracted me, made me raise my head. I'd heard no sound, she hadn't moved, yet I somehow sensed a change.

I looked back at her face.

Tears ran silently. They glistened in the evening light. She stood stock still as if turned to stone.

"Eva," I said. I said it quietly, knew I should say no more. Wished I could stand up and lend her a shoulder.

She shook her head, said nothing. Glanced at me for an instant then away again. But the glance was enough – like a wounded animal, like a hunted beast. That glance went right through me. I tugged myself more upright by the hanging triangular grip. I knew though for now there was nothing I could do. Still, my cold heart went out to her, I knew her so well, we were two peas in a pod.

A faint rumble.

The large glassed door to my room was sliding open...

Eva swung her head. Turned rapidly towards the chair, wiping discreetly at her face, then changed her mind – sat down on the bed beside me instead, back half-turned to the door.

A nurse from the evening shift stood in the doorway. Her hand was raised and leaned on the frame. She seemed to be hesitating, looking at us, glancing at the big bundle of flowers, taking in the scene. Eva twisted, stretching her arm behind her, groping near my feet. She pulled her shoulder bag onto her lap.

"Sorry..." the nurse said. "But..."

Eva ignored her, had snapped open the bag and was fumbling in it, sniffing carefully, quietly. She shook out a tissue – she wiped at her cheeks, her face towards me, blew her nose.

"It's past visiting time, I'm afraid," said the nurse. A tiny pause. "You ought to go at once, but... well, stay another five minutes if you wish. Okay?"

Eva was shaking her head. I glanced between her and the nurse. "Okay," I said.

Still she hovered there. She had curly dark hair and round brown eyes – her green cap sat askew.

Eva held a small mirror and pencil to her face.

"How're you doing?" the nurse asked me. She was peering alertly.

"Fine," I confirmed.

"Sure?" Scepsis in her face.

"I could keep on going all night," I said.

She nodded. Glanced at the flowers again, then down at the floor, saw the discarded gown near the chair. She pushed away from the door, came over, scooped up the bouquet and, stooping, retrieved the gown. Turning away, she added: "You had another visitor just now, by the way – 'fraid I had to send him away."

"Ah," I said. And thought, thank God: someone from work had wanted to call by. Not in the mood for that. I was watching Eva repairing her face. Then I thought: maybe I ought to ask.

"Did he leave a name?"

"No."

Eva's hands were held high, the mirror close, pencilling along her eye.

And the nurse said: "Didn't seem important, though – didn't try persuading us."

"Ah," I said again. That'd be Benny, for sure.

With a neat jerk she flicked the gown from her hand over one arm, hugged the flowers with the other. "Sorry, but rules are rules and only two of us on duty tonight. Got our hands full."

I'd only seen her once before; she was a nice kind of nurse. So I just smiled.

An alarm began ringing.

It was penetrating. I glanced away in the direction it was coming from. Through the open doorway a light was flashing on the wall. Then behind one of the observation windows to the corridor I caught sight of a face – it was indistinct.

"I'll bring you your toothbrush and things later – say if you need any help."

I looked back at the nurse. Watched her hurrying out. My eyes wandered again, past Eva, past her cropped hair, back to where the face had been, expecting it would be gone. But it wasn't.

It hung behind the glass, behind the middle window. The face seemed to float, its body almost lost, buried in reflections of the dying summer sky. It was motionless, it was like a ghost. It was looking directly at me.

Chapter 14

My skin contracted, my heart bumped like someone kicking a bag.
    Another alarm went off, much closer, but it wasn't as loud as the first. The nurse was in the corridor outside – had stopped, startled. The face moved. "...asked you to leave." I could hear her quick voice – she was peering over the bouquet of blooms. The face had a body now. It stood in the doorway, said nothing. "I must insist. At once. We have an emergency."

I watched him watching her.

He stood there quietly. He was dressed like a doctor, except that he was also in green – or like a surgeon perhaps, all he lacked was mask and gloves. He didn't say a word. I could imagine the look she might see in his eyes. His head made a slight movement, a simple gesture. The alarm was still ringing, the nurse was nodding briefly; she hurried away.

And he was looking round at me.

I stared at his face. There was calm in it, there was a kind of peace I know I'd never seen there before.

Suddenly Eva turned her head. She must have caught sight of him in her mirror, or out of the corner of an eye. Her bottom through the bedding was firm against my side; I felt it go stiff as if she'd been struck. With a start she sat up straight, dropped her cosmetic pencil. And Matthias was coming in.

"No," she said. She said it beneath her breath.

She let her mirror fall forgotten on the bed. Her pencil rolled across the floor. He stooped, in slow motion, agilely; his long thin fingers picked it up.

"No," she repeated. She sat there still stiffened, completely erect, her arms hung down, her hands each side of her tight neat bottom, her small fists pressed on the bed.

He put down the pencil, paused before her, like a panther, like a cat, deliberately. Yes, he'd always done everything with deliberation. His smile was slow and faint, a shadow on a wall.

He was peeling off the protective clothing and the plastic from his feet; unhurriedly he draped them over the end of the bed.

I remembered him as taller; he was still so thin. The stubble of fair hair on his skull was close-cropped, it was almost shaved – he looked very fit; he looked like in the video except now without the hair. But... here in reality one could see more – there was a gauntness in his cheeks like the hint of self-denial, there was a tiny white scar at one temple, and his sunburnt skin was olive not brown. He wore neutral clothes of beige and grey – old safari trousers with large flapped pockets, a thin linen jacket hung loose and unbuttoned from the shoulders of his shirt. And there were canvas espadrilles on his sinewy feet and the soles were made of string.

He stooped over her.

She looked so small, sitting there unmoving. And then I saw her face. Like a schoolgirl again, in love with him again, under his spell. Had the years washed nothing away? She began rising to her feet but he stopped her with hardly a touch, hands lightly on her arms.

Her head was lifted; they kissed on the lips, they kissed like lovers – slowly, intensely, as if they'd only been parted since yesterday.

Their faces were in profile, I couldn't see her expression now. But I could sense her body, sense a strength flowing in, feel the glow – her aura lit and filled the room. Yes, she was still in love, wasn't she? Her whole being cried out without a sound that, mature as she was, she'd give herself with no condition, with no strings attached again.

Matthias kissed with his eyes not quite closed. He was in charge, he was in control. Just the way he used to be. At least that hadn't changed. I watched him; I couldn't explain, I felt a sudden wisp of foreboding like I'd felt on receiving his card.

Then it was my turn.

He bent his thin body, coming nearer. Touched me carefully, with both hands – he knew exactly where to touch. His sinewy fingers were spiders on my arms, on my shoulders; no-one else had dared to touch me there except the doctors since my admission Sunday night. I could feel their power, feel their certainty, though they scarcely squeezed me hard. I thought: I wonder what they've been doing down the years, I wonder what these hands have done?

His sunburnt face came down close. He smelled of soap, simple, efficient, like Barbara the nurse. His cheeks grazed mine, first right then left, dry lips on my skin. Was this a fresh blessing from a new Matthias – or the old kiss of death?

In the glimpse of an instant, as he drew back his head, I caught his eyes shut. He looked so at peace, almost like a corpse. And a sentence sprang up suddenly in my head, a quotation I couldn't quite place: '...*deaf ears which can hear and closed eyes that can see...*' I concentrated. No – not a quote, it was from a poem. A line Matthias had composed, long ago when we were still at school...

His face was withdrawing. Then it paused. He leaned before me, his hands feathery light, they hadn't left my arms.

"Stefan," he said quietly. Nothing more.

This old friend, this man of many talents, this other part of me. There were faint wrinkles round his eyes now, they mellowed him, otherwise physically he seemed to have hardly aged. And that calmness, that tranquillity he'd emanated a few minutes ago hadn't departed. It gave off a glow like a lighted lamp; it was as if he'd found an inner peace or something precious no-one could steal which warmed him from within. Could it be it was there for good?

We gazed at each other.

His face was inscrutable, gave nothing away. I couldn't control the cascade of my thoughts. Is he an extremist still? Or has a miracle happened, has he metamorphosed? Has he converted to a teacher perhaps, or a preacher – a prophet? A man of extremes; he could be a disciple of God, or the Devil. Is that a new halo round his head and a crown of thorns, or the old ring of barbed wire enmeshing his brain still tangled in Satan's tail? This guy was capable of going either way; I could feel the warning prick.

"Matthias," I said. I was a hollow echo, it was the way I'd always been. I began to raise my good left arm then changed my mind; I found I couldn't touch him.

So I tried again. "Been a long time," I said. But it sounded so clichéd. I knew I was still afraid.

"Too long."

His answer came pat. Quiet and quick. It somewhat surprised me.

"Too long?" I said. One had to query statements like that.

A trace of a smile. It came and went. He retreated. Pulled up the chair, calmly seated himself. I watched his body. No superfluous motion, no waste of breath; he still moved like a cat.

"Yes," he said simply. Then his eyes were gone.

He was looking at Eva. And she at him. Exchanging glances. She sat frozen, a block of stone. She didn't speak, didn't move a muscle. She looked like a small mesmerised creature. Tough, independent, fighting Eva – reduced to the size of a mouse.

I waited. Watching. Unspoken things passing between them. I sat there, propped against the pillows. Fragments of so many memories fluttered through my mind – like pages leafed in a scrapbook, like the shorts for yesterday's films.

Matthias's eyes had returned to me. Was that a speck of sadness in them – a tiny flake of regret? Was he capable of harbouring such feelings or was I fooling myself? Then he blinked, and the eyes went blank.

Eva moved her hands. She was putting the pencils and mirror in a cosmetic étui back in her shoulder bag. She snapped it shut, laid it behind her near my knee. I thought: what should I say? It was really true, I could say a thousand things.

All I found was: "Too long requires explanation."

He returned my gaze. Oh God, that calm, that cool. Could nothing faze him?

"You've been in my thoughts," he said. "Regularly."

"I find that hard to believe." I considered his sentence. Should I say it? "You've been in mine too," I said.

"Since the postcard?"

"Not exclusively."

"And before?"

"And sometimes before." I swallowed. Tit for tat. Parry and lunge. Would this dialogue with Matthias only be a fencing match?

Slowly he nodded. "We were close friends, Stefan. Very close. Essentially one never forgets good friends."

"One bond, one blood?" I was quoting from his postcard.

"Yes. It always remains. One never forgets."

"Doesn't one?"

"No."

"You haven't put in a great deal of practice, it appears."

"No," he agreed. "That's true."

I could feel it; my nervousness. "And in fact..." I said – it had to be said, "...I was the only close male friend in your life."

He regarded me steadily. Those pale blue eyes, those small hard black pupils missing nothing, taking everything in. They didn't wander, didn't blink; their colour hadn't faded with time. His hands were unmoving, too. Didn't fumble or fidget. They lay on his lap as if asleep.

"Correct," he said. No argument, no resistance. "Good friends are hard to find."

I wanted to tell him: not that hard – not if one has the capacity, not if one has the need to share. But here I held my tongue, hadn't I been reproachful enough?

"You couldn't reach me," he said. "I know. Not even if you'd wanted."

No, I thought. And how I'd wanted to – I'd wanted to like hell at the start.

"I considered contacting you some while ago. One day I simply had the need."

Ah. There was that word out of my thoughts; was he able to read my mind? Still I said nothing. Good to hear it, though. It sounded almost human.

"Curious that I postponed." No sign of sentimentality. But was there a touch of self-reproach?

"Had the need been strong enough no doubt you would've tried," I said.

"No doubt."

I shrugged. "Anyway – now you have, so it was meant to be now not then. One says there's a reason for everything."

His eyes watched; like a hawk. They were coming alive though. "I like the way you say that." They were penetrating.

Oh God, it was good to see them again. In spite of everything.

"That's the way life is, Matthias."

"Moslems say, 'It is Written'."

"Yes," I said. "And what do you say?"

"I believe so, too." He nodded briefly. He paused. "You know, it's things like this that I've missed."

I waited. But I could feel it; the ice was beginning to break.

He elaborated: "Our conversations, our philosophising, the way you think." He smiled again. Fleetingly. It was almost tinged with warmth. "Yes, sometimes I've missed your company."

Again he surprised me. In the old days, in the final days, he would never have made such an admission. Maybe, like the skin around his eyes, his character had started to mellow too.

"Yes," I said. "I've missed you too, Matthias."

I think we regarded each other for several seconds; I could sense me relaxing my grip on my rapier, I could see me lowering my guard.

It was my turn now.

"You've matured," I said. I corrected myself: "You give the impression you've matured."

The eyes considered me, in silence.

"As if you've found something. There's a calm coming out."

"Yes?"

"Yes." I watched those eyes. "It used to be conspicuous by its absence."

I saw it. I'd touched a nerve. He was closing up. He was closing the door he'd just begun to open. Had I pried too soon, had I hit him on the nose? I said rapidly: "Or are you just playing games again? You used to be good at that." I knew the old Matthias too well. If he started clamming up you didn't show regret or turn soft, you just hit him hard again.

He didn't blink.

"Remember...?" he said. Slowly he tipped back his head, regarding me down his nose; his languid arms hung each side of the chair, they hung nearly down to the floor. "The times we were kids? Ferdinand-Marie Straße? Our first shared venture when we were five – that tunnel we dug under the wall between our bourgeois orchard gardens? Remember?"

He said it evenly, smoothly – I liked the bourgeois bit. Ah the tunnel, I thought, he said that to distract. Did he think he could sidetrack me?

"Of course," I answered. But I remembered.

"Do you remember too?" He had turned his head to Eva. She was still seated unmoving on my bed with her hands along her skirt, seated by my thigh. She nodded. She didn't smile. Sat tight and silent.

"We shared a lot in those days." Matthias was addressing me again. Complacent, in full control. "Remember the bombed-out ruins where we...?"

"Could we share again, do you think?" I asked. I said it directly, I spoke quietly too, I was trying to pull him back in.

He gazed at me. For the first time, his eyes wandered a moment. Then they came back. The door was shut; I saw his struggle. He was leaning his whole weight against it, against me, and raising his rapier again. He didn't speak.

I changed tack. "I appreciated the video." I made the jump intentionally, I lunged beneath his guard. Said it to assist him, and also to get to the heart of things – when he wished, Matthias could be painfully direct, he could also avoid the issue for hours if he chose. Reflections of Theo; they'd spent their time together planning demos, they'd been masters of the game.

I watched his reaction. He took it in his stride. "My good intention," he said. He swallowed; his pointed Adam's apple jerked.

I felt Eva's stare.

"You hinted at the future, and what we have in common." I paused, added: "If one reads between the lines." I glanced at Eva, met a hard and questioning gaze. Her eyes were accusing.

"That's what you always excelled at," Matthias said. "Like Tarot, like politics. That's why the message was mixed."

As I glanced away from Eva her eyes were now demanding an explanation.

"A little test for estranged friends?" I said to him.

"A litmus test." Once more he smiled that faint smile; he'd found his feet again. "To attract or repel."

I nodded. "It nearly succeeded in the latter," I said. I'd broken my rule; I knew it was a lie.

The trace of smile lingered. "I'm glad it was only nearly."

So there it was; what he found so hard to put in words – this poverty of his. He was offering the olive branch, he was seeking a renewal. Slowly I reciprocated his smile.

And inside I thought: oh Matthias, you kid yourself you need a male to sharpen your mental sword upon and you think you found your match in me – but in fact it was always the other way round, it was me looking up to you.

I had to look away. Is this why I'd missed him so much? Did I need the whetstone, or was it more – was there more to it all than this?

We had come closer. A glow was growing inside me. I was able to ask almost lightly: "Why the desert?"

"Why not?"

"I liked it, but why did you choose that?"

"Because you liked it." His eyes watched me steadily. What were they wishing to communicate? "Because you like deserts." There was that light in them again.

"And?" I said. I knew there would be more.

"And the symbolism."

"Sitting on a mountain of sand?" I smiled at his irony.

"With the desert at my feet." The light was beginning to burn.

I shook my head. "It struck me as almost religious."

"Religious?"

"Yes," I said. "Like a wise man, or a hermit. Like a prophet in the wilderness."

"Well, not a prophet, no."

"No?"

"And a different desert."

My turn to smile. "Am I getting warm?"

Those blue eyes were intense. He didn't reply.

"Is that what you've found, Matthias?"

"Found?"

"Or lost?"

Oh, the flame in those eyes. "Ah," he said slowly. "Now you're talking."

"Have you lost your old religion? The one with all that hate?"

"Hate?"

"Yes, Matthias."

He considered me. Unhurriedly. "Varying circumstance justifies varied response." His arms hanging down were quite still. Then he said: "Well, I see you've retained your over-used power of recall."

"Yes," I agreed. "Of all the other good things that are gone, at least I haven't lost that." I returned his gaze. We were on the same side of the fence now, we were looking at each other almost like of old.

A movement. At my thigh. The mattress jerked... Eva was standing up.

"Need a cigarette," she said. Her tone was tense, her expression unreadable. She glanced at Matthias, then at me.

"Are you coming back?" I said.

She was picking up her shoulder bag. "No."

"Come back." Matthias said it in a whisper, but it sounded more like a command.

"No, Matt." I watched her face; her eyes said what's the point.

He was tipping forward on the chair, his thin arms rose and laid themselves upon his knees.

I thought: this at least hasn't changed – he always would ignore her till she walked away.

"I'll ring you in a couple of days, Stef," she told me, swinging the strap of the bag over her shoulder. But she was looking at Matthias.

"Come back," he repeated under his breath.

She hesitated. She looked tired, almost haunted.

"I know a little *osteria* not far from here." His voice was easy, soothing.

I thought: how does he know that – does he know Nuremberg, then?

Still she hesitated, her fingers in a fist around the strap of her bag. Come on, little sister, I thought – it's time to kick him in the crutch.

"We'll spend the evening together before you drive back," he said. He said it like a prayer. I could feel the power of his persuasion – like the bands of a catapult stretching, like the pull of the moon.

"In half an hour?" he added.

Briefly she tipped her head back, condescended to give him no answer. And walked out.

Matthias sat there. Relaxed, not moving. You bastard, I thought – what else did you expect? We watched each other in silence. Then I said: "Are you still the hurting kind?"

He flapped a hand apathetically on his knee. "That's a long time ago."

"Is that an answer?"

"Don't judge me for the past."

"How else can one judge?" I said. "I don't have much else to go on."

His eyes didn't wander; he was taking it all in his stride. "I'm here, aren't I?"

"Yes." Yes, I thought, you're here – thick-skinned as ever, impenetrable, impervious to prying eyes.

"So that's a beginning. As we used to say, now you have the opportunity to paint a new picture."

"Do I, Matthias? Or is this all?"

"All?"

"All I'll be seeing of you. Or do you intend to stick around?"

"As far as one can look in the cards, I'm here for good," he said quietly.

Again we watched one another in silence.

After a pause I asked: "How long've you been back?"

"Is that important?"

"Yes," I said. "For you."

"For me?"

"For your honesty."

He shrugged indifferently. "Five or six years."

So long? I thought. Aloud I said: "You took your time."

"As we agreed, everything has its time."

I nodded. "And then you started writing little postcards. Postcards to your past." I didn't try hiding the sarcasm.

Slowly he lifted an arm from his lap, raised a nonchalant index finger. "One," he said. And let his arm fall.

I smiled – smiled to disguise my surprise. Then I said: "Wasn't even Eva worth a line?" and I wasn't smiling any more.

He frowned; he folded his hands in his lap again. That was his only reply.

"You hurt her, Matthias."

"That's going way back."

"You're getting repetitious. You dropped her like a brick, just dumped her."

"Yes." His eyes were steady, but they were far away. He didn't frown again.

"Now you've hurt her again." I meant because of the video, because now she knew where his priorities lay. But I didn't have to explain.

"Yes," he repeated.

I stared at him. "You're a bastard. You're still a bastard."

He shrugged phlegmatically, just a faint lift of the shoulders. "I have my reasons." A muscle ticked at his temple, not far from that little white scar; I saw I'd touched a nerve again.

"She understands," he added.

"She does? Well I don't."

"She understood then, she'll understand now."

"I hope so. I hoped she'd kick you in the balls."

He returned my glare, he didn't flinch. Suddenly he grinned. Wryly. "She left that one for you – she knows you're good at that."

I shook my head. I couldn't draw him. It seemed whatever I tried, I couldn't provoke.

"You're still bitter, aren't you?" he said.

I thought he was talking about Eva. "She's more than capable of fighting her own battles," I countered.

"No – I mean generally. About life."

"Yes," I said.

"And disillusioned."

"Yes." I left it at that. Didn't want to start long speeches. Not now. Perhaps another time.

"Welcome to the club," he said.

"It's not a club, Matthias."

"Of course it is."

"It's simply the state of human condition."

"It's about people who think like this, Stefan. And seek changes. Those who don't accept the status quo. Call it a club, call it a movement. That's what the sixties was all about. Remember?"

I watched him. Now it was he trying to pull me in; he was the one baiting, the one provoking now. I said nothing, refused to rise.

"It's about the fact that the more we learn of human frailty the more it sickens and fucks us up, and the greater our need to change things," he said. He said it neutrally, tranquilly, his tone belied the content of his words – there was no fury, there was no acrimony or fire. Was this the new Matthias?

"No, Matthias." I shook my head again. "It's purely the awareness of my impotence that I can't change anything. One's kicking against the pricks."

"Ironic." He paused. He smiled. Peaceably he crossed his legs, hooked his hands around a knee. "I used to be the one with a monopoly on bitterness."

"You're kidding." I couldn't let that one go. "You weren't just bitter, you were the one with a total lack of love in your life and you filled the hole with hate."

He took it standing up, he didn't turn a hair. "Accepted." He spread his hands temperately, clasped his knee again. "But it didn't last long – it was just a phase, then I saw the light."

"You did?"

"Yes. I got out."

"You did?" I repeated. I could hear my sarcasm coming through again.

"I got out in good time."

I lowered my eyes. I was thinking of Theo, I was looking at the list he'd shown me, the one from old East Germany. Was that what he called getting out in time? But I said nothing.

"Sure, in the early years we were wild and idealistic and we thought we had a dream," he said. "Everyone needs a dream, Stefan."

"Is that what you call it?" I looked up at him again. "Is that how you describe extremism and violence?"

"In the eyes of the beholder, an ideology is a dream." Gently he swung his hanging leg. "The same with a philosophy or religion."

"It all depends what kind, doesn't it, Matthias?"

"Of course. But as I just said, I distanced myself, I adapted. Don't confuse mine with the others. They got in a cul-de-sac."

"Hitler and Pol Pot had dreams," I said, ignoring him. I thought: if he thinks he can bugger about with me I won't let him off the hook.

Unruffled, he replied: "Gandhi and Mandela and Martin Luther King, too."

And I thought: you were about as far away from them as you could get. We considered one another in silence. Then into the silence I said: "Where did you go, Matthias?"

He shook his head. Said nothing. He stretched out his legs and leaned back, but his gaze didn't leave me: he lay in a line on the chair.

"Did you have to go far to find your distance?" I smiled. "To get away from your dream and yourself?"

His pale eyes were easy and clear. "Yes," he said laconically. "Quite a way." His cotton trousers hung loose from his legs and his feet were lazy there side by side; I could see his naked ankles, they looked brown and lean and fit.

"But that's another story," he mused. He smiled his quiet smile again. His lips were sensual and loose, and his mouth was as relaxed as his eyes, as his hands hanging down. "As we've already established, there's a time and a place for everything."

I was glad he said that. I was slipping – could feel tiredness trespassing into my limbs. I suppose, anyway, I didn't really want to know about it now.

Slowly he tipped a leisurely foot, tipping it on his heel. To and fro. "You're wrong about change," he said quietly. "It's going on all the time and one can play one's part. Little changes, positive changes, like the right kind of dream. Not revolution – I think recent history has taught most of us that's not the way..."

I held my peace, I closed my eyes...

"It's like democracy on foreign soil, and visions, they can't simply be implanted. They have to be nurtured and slowly grow, they have to grow from within..."

I sat there listening to him. And I was remembering – the way he used to talk: the staid Marxist workers-of-the-world-unite paroles, the inflammatory rhetoric and the angry ideological clichés. They were all gone now; it seemed he'd wiped the slate clean...

Then he changed the subject. Was glad about that, too. It helped me open my eyes. He'd made a big leap. We began talking of other things – of books and theatre and current affairs, of life and everyday things. Just like any friends do who meet regularly, who like to catch up on the news. Yes – it was almost as if we'd last met less than a month ago.

That was a good sign. Wasn't it?

I felt myself relaxing, letting go. My defences were falling. Had it really been twenty years? Despite my tiredness I felt an old glow growing deep inside me. There was a sense of nostalgia – about how close we had been, there was a thrill even, at the thought of how close we maybe could become again. I realised the extent to which I'd missed him.

Only one thing was odd: he avoided talking about himself. I thought: perhaps it's only reticence, the old dark horse in him. But still – after all this time one would've assumed he'd fill me in on one or two details of what he was doing now. So after about ten minutes, in one of the easy pauses, I put the question: "And what're you doing nowadays? – since you came back from wherever you went?"

And the air between us was suddenly still, the space had grown with a jump.

"This and that," he said. "Had to take my bearings first." He said it offhandedly.

"You said on the phone a new direction. Serious stuff."

"Yes." His eyes were sharp and acute. They considered me. Were they defensive? Then a faint grin reappeared; this time it looked almost sheepish.

"I've got my pilot's licence now."

That surprised me. "You're joking." Matthias as a pilot?

"I never joke," he said rapidly.

I shook my head slowly. The one who'd only laid emphasis on the intellect, on the brain? He'd studied law at university – wouldn't that be more his style? "What kind of pilot?" I asked.

"Civilian, of course."

"How many hours?"

He shrugged vaguely. "Quite a number."

I thought: so he's not talking about yesterday. Try nailing him down to specifics and...

"I've bought a farm."

I frowned. It sounded as if he'd said it to distract again. But at least it was some information. "Where?"

A ghost of a smile; it came and went. "Maybe I'll fly you down there some day."

Down? In the south – not in Germany, then? Seemed like he meant south of the Alps. Italy perhaps? I opened my mouth to ask...

"Close to nature," he said.

"You – a farmer?" I couldn't imagine.

"Good for the nerves. The quiet life. Sowing and watching the crops grow. Reaping what one's sown."

Why was he smiling like that – a slow ironic smile? Was he pulling my leg?

"No, Stefan."

No? He was reading my thoughts? He used to be able to do that. "Where?" I asked. "In Italy?"

"Away from the stink of cities, and corruption. Isolated and far away."

"Something small?"

"Not so small."

Something big? Where'd he found the money? "How did you finance a thing like that?"

"Inheritance."

From where? From his father? But Hermann wasn't yet dead.

"No," Matthias said. "Plus a loan."

Was he really telepathic? Or was he bluffing?

"Would do you good, too," he added.

I shook my head again, produced a weak smile. "Is that an invitation?"

"Isn't it?"

I raised my eyebrows. Felt the tug of the bandages – just a twinge up there, no sudden banging headache, no real pain now. I didn't reply. Matthias had never offered me anything concrete all his life.

"Or are you too inflexible, and disillusioned? That age-old apathy? I gather you've got pretty stuck in the mud."

So he'd enquired. I watched him. Well of course he had – Matthias always checked out the lie of the land thoroughly before he made a move.

"What exactly is involved?" I asked. I asked it carefully.

"Like I said." He gazed at me, ingenuously. "I plan and plough. I sow and reap. I spray my crops from the air to destroy the vermin, I do what a farmer does."

I tried to imagine. I tried to visualise this old friend of words and ideas working the land, or flying over the landscape, alone, watching the ground below slip by with nobody there to talk to. Had he really jumped over his shadow?

"Alone?" I said. It just didn't fit in.

"No, of course not. I employ a number of willing hands. Lads and lassies."

I just sat there. I didn't believe.

"Come and see for yourself. When you're better – when you feel maybe your life needs new meaning." He paused. Looked at me quizzically. Yes, he could read my thoughts. "When you have better things to do than messing with Moslems and Neo-Nazis," he added.

So he knew that too.

"Yes," he said.

He was too well informed; he hadn't lost his touch. "Maybe I will," I said. What else hadn't he lost?

He was looking at me. Penetratingly. Looking into me. As if searching for something, as if deliberating. It was a curious feeling – it was as though he were pondering a secret thought, wondering if he should share.

His lips parted. Then they closed again; they shut up like a clam. Maybe more than a minute passed. Neither of us spoke.

He was rocking a foot back and forth again, thoughtfully – his legs were still stretched out. Unexpectedly he chuckled. His arms rose slowly from his lap, he clasped his hands behind his head, gazing at me.

"Remember our blood oath?" His eyes weren't trying to penetrate me now, they were misty with recollection – it seemed the curtain had fallen. Obviously they'd put away whatever they'd been staring at, been prompting to say; perhaps they'd put it away for ever.

I just sat there. My tiredness was closing in.

"Remember?"

I nodded. I remembered. A silly game little boys play, with a knife. Most prick their palms or wrists and mingle a drop of blood, a symbol of brotherhood. We'd done it differently, for a different reason: Matthias cut me over my heart, he cut me deep, I cut him too. We pressed close together, naked chest on chest and swore the oath of silence never to divulge to others our secret adventures and thoughts on pain of instant death. We were nine years old; I still bear the scar. Though it's hidden now by a mat of hair.

"Yes," I said. "The games that children play."

"Yes," he echoed. He chuckled again. "It worked though, didn't it? Remember when we waylaid that car in the forest with catapults and I smashed the windscreen? You got caught and punished but never gave me away."

I smiled. I wondered: what made him suddenly think of that now? Memories came crawling into my weary brain, all the bad things we had done. But Matthias was reminiscing again – he jerked me back and forth, into our teens, into our childhood, into times at school, weekends in the mountains, our first conquests with the fairer sex... more memories – coming in a flood now...

Minutes passing...

We were far away. We'd gone back again, were laughing, I think it was at little Liza, our gawping at the wondrous attributes she'd agreed to let us peep at if we promised to smell as well as touch, for a packet of *Rolos* and half a *Mars Bar* in nineteen-fifty-nine. Yes, when the big door slid quietly open we were back in our early childhood, we'd returned to our roots...

Eva was coming in.

x x x

She smiled wanly at me, she was being followed by the nurse. I noticed: she had completed making-up her face now, her makeup was a mask. The instant he sensed her, Matthias twisted on the chair and rose, agilely, cutting off the conversation. He cut it like a knife.

The nurse behind her was saying sharply: "You must both leave at once or I'll get in hot water – it's way past visiting hours."

For a moment he and Eva stood there side by side. She was the small and tough one once again, he relaxed and thin yet coiled like a spring.

"Let's go," he said to her. "I want to seduce you." He looked at me with a wink.

"You bastard." I managed to let out a chuckle like a choke. And the cold in her face collapsed like a house of cards.

Then she was stooping to briefly kiss me goodbye. I saw the shadows in her face close up, her eyes said she was ready to take on the world again. "Keep in touch," I told her.

"I promise."

Matthias reached out, laying his right hand in my left. Our fingers closed, his cheek brushed mine. The smell of soap again. We kissed, both sides, just the way we used to do. "I'll keep in touch too," he said. And I wondered when.

We were parting. I lay there, uselessly, looking at them both. "Enjoy yourselves," I said. "Do everything I wouldn't dare." I thought: sometimes you have to dig deep to find your generosity; I was talking to myself.

They were turning away. I felt an unexplainable pain, a pang, that hurt, that left me empty. I didn't want them to go together but I didn't have the right to oppose. They were walking out the door. Matthias had one hand casually tucked in his linen jacket pocket, one thin erect shoulder close brushing hers; I knew they'd make love that night. I was happy for Eva, I wondered if it would work out this time. Then they were in the corridor beyond the windows, they didn't look back. They would have forgotten me by the time they reached the entrance to the intensive care unit – if they hadn't already.

Chapter 15

The rest of the week went by and my body slowly mended. The doctors said it was rapid, my power of regeneration good; it didn't seem that way to me. There was still no mention of my being moved to a normal ward – they said they wanted to keep me under observation a while longer, because of irregular heartbeat and because of the pain in my pelvis and lungs. My explanation that it should be put down to unrequited love remained completely ignored. They also said I was lucky: the pelvis had no fracture or breaks – no operation necessary, no crutches later on. One must always be grateful for things great and small.

My mother came to visit; it was, for her, an emotional and tearful affair. She left in her fox-fur stole in spite of the early summer heat, leaving a trail of her penetrative perfume in the sterilised air. I had tried to be kind.

Estella and George came by too, and another friend of sorts, each separately of course. George only popped in, had a bird on the hook outside and hated hospitals he said – hung in green, disappointingly for all the nurses no doubt, the drapes he'd donned hid the structural wonders of his limbs. Estella lingered though, how could she do otherwise: at her departure little flakes of her wisdom lay scattered on the floor and I was halfway back to being the man. That was the day they cut off the plaster cast: "We're giving you a Gilchrist sling." They hung it over my neck, bound my right arm to my belly, but I could move my still somewhat bruised hand a bit. I was pleased about that; my Heil Hitler pose was over and I could fill out a form with difficulty, and sign again.

The Kommissar visited briefly – he asked a few further questions and with spastic strokes of my fingers I signed a statement he had brought. They let in two reporters, too. I did my very best to conceal. Even Margareth turned up unexpectedly with all the children. They entered subdued by the strangeness of the place, but soon were tearing about till the Boss Nurse Barbara firmly stepped in. "Only two at a time," she said, "and quietly, please," but there was almost a tenderness on her north-German tongue; I was finding her more attractive by the day.

It was good to have the telephone, I used it now and then to reach people. But discreetly. They'd made a big exception. Annabelle called me each day which I appreciated with a devotion that was due – it bestowed upon me a sense of blessing; even down the telephone line our friendship began to flower.

One morning after breakfast my colleague Frau Bartenbach rang me, said could she come by that evening after work. I was glad to see her. She came in a businesslike working suit with her mobile switched on in her bag. The protective smock she'd put on back to front like a cloak – she looked even more wild and eccentric than the way she usually was. And she brought with her some very bad news. I recall: her mobile rang while she was with me and the Boss had cause to pounce again. Directly or indirectly I was getting a rather bad name.

It was from Frau Bartenbach I learned of the merger – our firm was being taken over, the deal had already been sealed. "I've got the chop," she said; I couldn't believe it. I shook my head. "No," I replied.

"I'll be gone before you're well enough to return to work."

My God, I thought. I thought of Eva. Was this plague contagious?

She sat on the steel and plastic visitor's chair, and I sat up in bed. Her thick wavy hair glowed like old gold, in fact everything about her was gold, even the eyes. And her backbone was strong as iron. She was dry-eyed and realistic; she was the number three, excluding the boss, she should've been number one. I always remember her for the maintenance of composure under pressure – when all around us was chaos, she continued to keep her cool. She was better than the best.

"Of course, I'm getting compensation, a year and a half at least."

"Do you have a lawyer?" I asked.

"You bet. It's a she, and she's very much on the ball."

"Screw them for all you can get." It was my only constructive advice. Inside I boiled. Not only did I like Cornelia Bartenbach, I held her in highest esteem. She ran rings round the rest of us; she'd never stood in anyone's shadow and never trodden on others to climb.

"Herr Heller's got the chop, too. He turned fifty-six last month, being put out to grass on a company pension."

"Like an old racehorse," I mused.

"Like a carthorse," she corrected. "Racehorses get shot."

I had to wince; she was my racehorse every time.

She observed me calmly, swept back her waves of golden hair. I thought: God, where does she find her courage and strength? I'd like to tap her source and catch some stray drops for myself. And then straight afterwards, I thought: what about my job? I'm probably the next on the list. And something sank in my stomach, turning into a stone.

"What are your prospects?" I asked her. I was thinking, my God how will she cope? She was already mid-forties like me. Didn't know much about her private life except she was divorced and had a son, had to fend for herself. And only knew that because we'd both got bored and roaring drunk at one of the office parties, let a few pussycats out of the bag. Otherwise our relationship was truly professional.

"Oh, they're pretty rosy," she replied. "You know my motto, Herr Falk, if you think positively, a phoenix always rises from the ashes and often you're better off than before."

I tried to look back at her clear eyes and solid open face without giving myself away. "Yes," I managed to answer. "It's one of the more pleasant ironies of life," but inside me was that sinking feeling like a ship going down, and the realisation I lacked the strength to believe my own words. I swallowed. I hungered for her courage like a dog for a bone.

I watched her unhappily.

"In fact," she continued, "my lawyer gave me an idea. Said I should set up on my own."

"I think she just hit the jackpot," I said.

"Aha." Her lashes were long, made of gold too; she appraised me like a friendly hawk. "Pleased to hear you say that – I lay a lot of value on your judgement, you know." Briefly she nodded. "Truth to tell, I've already made up my mind. I put my head together with an old industrial psychologist friend of mine. Between you and me, we're starting up together."

I smiled at her as best I could. With decisions she always was a fast one, but this was fast even for her. "I'm sure you'll make it a success," I said carefully.

I shook my head: within a few days of receiving the news she was changing the whole course of her life.

"I shall miss you," I added. And that I really meant.

"P'raps you won't have to." With both hands she cast back that thick hair each side of her face. "I want to make you a proposition, Herr Falk. How about coming on board with us?"

I took a breath. Inside I almost panicked.

"Just the three of us. Equal partners. We'll pool our resources. For start-up capital we'll need a loan. I shall put up my house as security, and Paul's prepared to do the same. Of course, at the start it'll be blood, sweat and tears – let's say the first three years. That's a fact of life, but nothing ventured, nothing gained."

I deliberated. Tried to hide my panic, hide my surprise. "I appreciate your trust," I began. I hesitated. The ship was sinking faster, and I was flailing to hold on. I cast about in my brain. For an instant I was looking at our firm; the offices, the corridors, the room where I worked, my room with a view – I'd been there so many years. "You're grossly overestimating me," I said.

"Oh no." Those golden eyes shone like the sun. "Like you I know who's good at what. It's not for nothing we've worked together nearly ten years."

I sat there propped up on the pillows. Procrastinating. "This is a bolt from the blue," I said. Defensively.

She smiled at me; there were red tones on the high bones of her cheeks. "Think about it in principle. We're thinking of a similar work line, but then branching out. Perhaps placement stuff and training for top managers, and over-forty-fives. And other things. We're working on new ideas – could use some of yours." Another smile.

"Okay," I said. Her courage was contagious.

"No hurry. Must think about your recovery first and foremost."

"You've given me food for thought."

She was standing up. I was sorry – I didn't want her to go so soon.

"However," I added, "regardless of the outcome, I want us to meet up just the moment I'm out of here and we'll share a bottle of champagne."

"We'll do that..." She was picking up her shoulder bag, the long strap hung down. "Back in a moment, I need a loo. I dashed out of the last meeting, had no opportunity." She laughed her warm infectious laugh again.

I watched her sweep out trailing the strap; her thick hair from the back was bedraggled as a mop.

I waited. Images of the firm came floating again. There was my desk and computer and conference table, and the high old windows. Across the open street city ramparts bathed in sun, trees on top from the castle gardens, the rumble of the trams. I thought: could I throw it all away – the security, the steady salary coming in? Could I really? Then the sinking feeling was back again – were they planning to sack me too, would the decision be taken out of my hands?

I stared into space. Stared at the glass wall and the corridor. In the nurses' station three of the staff: one was phoning, one writing notes, the Boss half-turned away reaching up to shelves, her thin body stretched like a rubber band. I glanced back to the corridor. Still no sign of my colleague, perhaps the way was long. Before me lay my body, they'd taken away the frame, my turned-up toes were tips in the sheet. I was dressed now in a loose white smock which hid my sling and bound-up chest. In fact my bandaged head and scalp without hair were the only visible outward signs to suggest I wasn't a fraud. That morning I'd inspected my pelvis while they changed bandages – everywhere was black and blue and yellow but the sown-up gashes were growing together, they said, and generally speaking there was far less pain when I sneezed...

Frau Bartenbach was back, slightly breathless, her eccentricity aglow. "Sorry about the delay, I popped down to the shop..." She was pulling her chair nearer, seating herself, bag on lap. Opening the clasp she dug inside, extracted two small labelled bottles which she held up smiling. "I decided we should strike while the iron's hot. We'll break open a proper one later." She lay her bag aside, unscrewed the cap on the first. A miniature champagne bottle. "I'm sure you're on medication and this is strictly forbidden. What d'you think?"

"I'd say not to think," I said, and added: "Spontaneity is a rare creature in my adult life and I'm sure it's to be encouraged."

Her smile came out like the sun again. She handed me the bottle. It wasn't more than a glassful anyway.

"You know, Frau Bartenbach," I said as she opened her own, "I'd like to suggest what I've wanted to for some time now..." Oh God, how formal we Germans can be, but we're enslaved by our language. "...Despite my chastened state and the captivating circumstance..." I indicated the bondage of my body with my humble left hand, "... may I make an offering at the altar of friendship as Stefan the broken man to Cornelia the new-born bride?"

The sun in her smile was burning still.

"Well, of course!"

She rose from her chair, sat down on the bed, reaching out. "About time you and I did this, my dear Stefan." She had switched to the intimate form.

"Cornelia..."

"Stefan..."

Holding the booze, we hooked arms, her right through my left, this was all I could offer, ah what a testimony to tradition. We kissed. And drank in a delightful physical tangle.

I'm sure it wasn't the displays behind me which gave us away; maybe Nurse Barbara was simply having an especially nasty day. Needless to say, Cornelia Bartenbach and I were both sharing a quiet laugh at something she said and I'd just taken another fizzy swig on the bottle when the Boss appeared unexpectedly.

"Herr Falk, how dare you!" she cried. She rushed me, her small tight body flying, her feet had grown amazing wings – her fury would surely have been an inspiration to the whole of her staff. Strong steely fingers extricated the bottle from my unhappy hand, and she startled me so much I nearly said: "Oh fuck", but just managed to bite my tongue in time.

"Ah, Nurse Barbara, just taking a little tipple." I tried the most crooked of my smiles.

"This is the *very* last straw." Oh that haughty Hanoverian high German, those thin hard lips, and blonde hair crisp and neat. With one hand on slender hip, she held up the bottle as if to inspect it, glaring angrily at me. How anger can sometimes be a source of such beauty.

"You are perfectly aware that your condition doesn't allow alcohol in the blood."

"Please put it down to the withdrawal symptoms." I made a gesture of submission like the beaten beast. "They were beginning to get the upper hand."

"All my fault," Cornelia said.

"All mine," I contradicted. I watched that little and capable hand; I prayed it'd change its mind about bringing the bottle down on my skull.

"How *can* a grown man behave in this manner." A toss of her head. It wasn't a question, that was clear.

"I confess to my juvenile sins." I bowed in shame; if I'd been in a position to I'd have crawled and kissed her feet.

She'd lowered the bottle, was turning to Cornelia and grasping hers too. "You really should have known better, you know. I must ask you to leave immediately."

"Don't take it too hard, nurse." A cheerful laugh. "This one could survive a magnum." She rose from the bed, hitching the strap of her shoulder bag, gave me her hand. "Think about my proposition." Her smile shed gold again.

I nodded. "I meant that about the jackpot," I said.

x x x

During the second week Annabelle returned to Nuremberg again to stay a little while; Margareth was holding the fort. She visited me twice a day, and I cherished each contact, I coveted the devotion she displayed. We would sit there in that room of glass talking leisurely about this and that, in small doses; it seemed by saying very little we managed to say so much. In between those conversations she would read to me out of the newspapers, articles on this and that, and in this way we discovered we had quite a number of interests and dislikes in common. Yes, I'd sit there watching her concentration and her hands as she turned each rustling page. I sat there listening to the sound of her voice, I was falling in love with that too.

My broken body mended fast.

While alone I now and then read from the book she'd brought me from my apartment, and did some work on the sly, by telephone, to keep in touch. I also thought a lot about Cornelia's offer. Was I gradually growing used to the possibility of upheaval, even of losing my job – or was it just the safety of distance and I was simply fooling myself?

Soon after, I was moved to a normal ward. I was extremely glad about that – I'd been beginning to feel like a genuine fraud. Goodbye to Nurse Barbara, goodbye to all that; she received the box of chocolates like a revelation. Thanks George for doing the shopping. But I suspect it was the yellow ribbon which helped heal my reputation. Perhaps that, and the little note. During one of our brief chats between all her chores she'd let slip the fact that yellow was the colour of her love. We took leave with perfect professionalism and I managed to say something nice.

Four strong arms lifted me to another bed parked alongside and two drove me off. I was out in the corridor I'd so often seen through glass. A strange feeling, a feeling of helplessness. Automatic doors, another corridor, strips of light on the ceiling flicking by, a very big lift – then new corridors with windows and sunlight streaming, other smells, staff passing, other patients, people peering. I felt a fool, lying there, being pushed around...

A new room, solid walls, a room for two. One window, outlook sorely limited. A stranger in dressing-gown sitting on his bed as I was wheeled in, pyjama legs hanging down. He was swigging from a bottle of mineral water, cackling at a television I couldn't help hearing but couldn't see. Light from the screen reflected in his heavy spectacles. The volume was turned up high. Sour smell of human sweat.

Oh God, I thought. I shut my eyes.

"*Grüß Gott*," the patient greeted me.

Sure, I thought, if I meet him, but the chances are fairly slim. Opened my eyes again.

"Schmidt." He raised his bottle in the air.

"Falk."

I was wheeled past, parked. The male nurse went out, came back with another. They levered me into the other bed, deposited a clipboard, folder and plastic bag of belongings at my feet. "Please get him earphones," I said. "At once."

When inside of half an hour at once didn't work I pressed the little red button.

x x x

Annabelle visited later that day; she'd been tied up with details of an exhibition in the morning. She came into the room, took one look, gazed at me. I put on my most pained and apathetic expression. She stooped close, kissed me the way she always did, the way no-one ever had – didn't say a word, quietly went out. I thought of Caesar: *veni, vidi, vici*; I hoped she knew her history too.

I was moved next day.

Single room, windows in two walls. Through one, the distant forest, through the other a roof terrace with trees like balls on poles in earthenware pots, American oaks beyond, and sky. Blessed be the meek, but also the mighty who believe in righteousness, blessed the woman who fought my battle for me – this was a naughty habit one surely could cultivate.

A room of my own, a room with a view; I appreciated Woolf and Forster anew. I spread my wings, felt the first sexual stirrings, I was on my way to redemption. It seemed that Annabelle sensed it too. Her contribution, and that of one other small but curious incident – an unsolicited visit from a holy one which remains in my mind because of the prophecy he purported to sell – are about all the revelation I recall of the following three weeks. The telephone beside me was activated without my having to make the request – I gave her a ring immediately, to express a sign of gratitude.

I was propped up in bed reading when she visited again – two doctors and entourage had just left. She came through the door like a queen.

"Hello." A murmur. That kiss again.

"Hello." Eyes meeting.

The mattress dipped, she seated herself, I could feel her sweet bottom through the sheet. Exchanging glances. Could feel something else, too. Wow. She wore pastel green, a simple summer dress – as plain as it was expensive, I guessed. It highlighted as much as it hid. Her thigh moved against me. I touched it, I traced a line; I was aware of my body again.

Nothing spoken.

She stroked me through the sheet. Oh God, that caress, those fingers like feathers, they lit a flame that had long gone out. Now she was opening her legs, her dress slipped like silk, she was letting me in. I touched her where she loved to be touched, I felt her liquid flow.

A little pressure in my side. I made room for her on the hospital bed; I knew all that I needed to know. She was lifting the sheet and turning around, she'd trapped my hand, I watched her beauty burrow and her head disappear, I was aware of the whole of her body too. Lips enclosing, soft and wet. I was in her mouth, her mouth was hot, I was very stiff, I was flying off, flying far away. Tongue tingling the tip, lips slipping along me, squeezing, sliding back and forth, I couldn't breathe – she'd swallowed me whole.

I was coming already. She floated above me, my hips were free, no weight, no pain, there was only her mouth and only me. I came. Bursting out of my core. An ache so deep, a burn, I turned inside out and her mouth received me without a sound.

We lay. She licked me, she ate me. All was liquid, I loved it all. I lay there and sighed, my hand still trapped between her thighs, wanted to eat her and lick her too. Could see only a bottom and freckled legs, the dress ridden high, my arm a thin sneaky thief snaking inside – the rest of her was just a slender mound beneath the snowy-white cotton sheet.

I loved her. I loved her with all my essence. And I hungered for her again, I wanted...

A knock...

I jerked, raised my head. Annabelle still motionless under the cover. More knocking – someone was rapping on my door. Quickly I shook my trapped fingers caught between her thighs, squeezing a warning, my other arm helplessly bound in the sling...

"Annabelle..." I whispered, panicking, at the top of my voice.

The door had opened. A man in grey smock stood in the doorway. He looked at me and I at him. Annabelle was stirring unhurriedly under the sheet.

"Er – *Grüß Gott*," he said. His eyes dropped to the moving mound in the bed. "Room two-one-oh-one. A Herr Falk?"

"Annabelle, we have company," I muttered. I tugged my fingers free. "Yes," I said to the man. I tried a feeble smile. Her head and shoulders were reappearing slowly from below.

"Arnold's Television Hire," he pronounced.

Calmly she gazed at the intrusion, dabbing her mouth discreetly on a corner of the sheet and placing her feet back on the floor. She managed it rather regally, I thought.

"Delivery of a set." He was glancing askance between Annabelle and me.

She swept at disarrayed hair.

"Ah," I said.

He nodded, turned, came backwards through the doorway pulling a trolley. "Where would you like it?" he asked. He said it now without looking at us, occupied with his task. "I'll park it here, okay? That's the best angle of vision for most." Stooping, he connected aerial and plug, switched on the set.

"Thanks," I replied.

Using the remote, he surfed rapidly through programmes, calling them out. Annabelle sat casually beside me, hands folded in her lap. Loose strands of hair hung like red ferns down her face, and her dress showed a lot less leg. "That will do fine," she said. She was in perfect control.

He finished testing, turned the thing off.

"Where do I sign?" she asked.

He held up a slip of paper and pen, stepped hesitantly closer. Annabelle signed. "Thank you for your punctuality," she said.

"*Grüß Gott*, ma'am." He laid the small black remote on the night-cupboard beside us. He put it down quickly as if it might bite – stepped smartly back, touching hand to a cap he didn't have on, turned and left the room.

I watched Annabelle in amusement. "You organised this?" I said.

"Mmm." A wistful smile on her lips. "So you don't feel lonely. It is for your Mickey Mouse programmes in the afternoons." She wiped at her hanging hair. "And, because I couldn't find all those wicked magazines you requested, naturally for your porno channels at night."

"Well I appreciate that." I cast her my most debauched of grins. "I certainly couldn't do without those." Let my eyes fall to her lap. I was shrinking, leaking – I could feel it on my leg.

"He'll spill the beans," I added to the valley between her thighs.

"Of course he won't. The poor man was speechless."

"My reputation's in tatters." I glanced up and rolled my eyes. "They'll take away my telly and teddy bear, and relegate me to a fifty-bed ward."

"Don't let that cramp you, they surely have curtains." Ah, that lovely lingering smile.

"I'll get a dishonourable discharge – they'll tear off my buttons and break my sword." I gave a dirty little chuckle.

"Didn't you know they break that off too?" Fingers caressing.

Rolled my eyes again, had to breathe rather heavily. "No more live sex in hospital beds," I sighed – only just managed to get the sentence out, the fingers had touched the tip once more.

"My poor starved one."

I laid my hand in the valley and left it at that; I yearned for her lily and her lips again.

x x x

Through fate and the force of circumstance, though, I had to wait five long days. She planned it like a general ponders his battle-plan, reconnoitred the lie of the land; she had my fortunes at heart, it seemed, as well as my repute.

And while she was pulling her end of the rope I did my little bit – practising with the hydraulic bed remote that raised and lowered various parts of the bed in rather fascinating ways. I even, craftily, on day three which was the Thursday, got one of the nurses to have a gallows installed above the bedhead with hanging grip, it helped me raise myself with amazing speed and without any staff aid; I rehearsed with the diligence of one who has all to lose.

Saturday came. Saturday was the Big Day.

It was four o'clock in the afternoon. Annabelle had laid the *Spiegel* magazine aside a while ago, we were discussing the contents of the lead article. An earnest subject: we aired our views, going into depth, we had the time. Three hours till seven. That was the plan: after they'd cleared the supper, during the change of shifts and the one-hour meeting they always held. I was starting to get nervous. Impulsively I glanced at my alarm clock on the little cupboard on castors beside the bed.

"You are not listening," she said.

"Yes I am." Only five-past-four. Oh God.

"You are looking at the clock."

"Yes," I confessed.

"And why, pray?" I could see that glint in her eye.

I wriggled uncomfortably. "Well, I've been looking at you for an hour and a half – so I was just taking a little break from your beauty."

"Liar."

"Well, half a lie, yes. The beauty bit was an untrue construction."

I received a dig just below my ribs – I'm glad it wasn't higher. "You are nervous," she stated.

"I am?"

"Penny for your thoughts."

Slyly I fumbled, found the remote for the bed. "Only a penny?" I said. I cocked my head on one side.

"I cannot imagine they are worth more." Chin lifting queenly, ah that superior stare down the noble nose.

I pressed the remote, experimenting. A little whirring sound. I said: "A man in his prime would offer a bag of gold in return for the secret." The mid-section of the bed rose where she sat, raised me in an uncomfortable hump too. Hurriedly I went into reverse, before I broke my back. "He might even offer a sack," I suggested.

"Ah. Dirty thoughts, then?"

"Quite the contrary. Beautiful aesthetic thoughts." I fiddled again, we rose again. What fun. I braked us just in time.

"Is that conceivable?"

I investigated the leg section and obediently it lifted; it tipped her towards me, her bag tumbled to my knees. I watched with fascination, I let us down again. "More than conceivable," I said earnestly. She had righted herself. I wiggled the toggle, jogged us up and down a few times, it did wonders to her loose-hanging breasts. I did it to show that I'd got the hang of it, I did it to show that I cared. "I was thinking of your holiest-of-holies," I explained. "Taking a little peep."

"My what?" The superior stare had become a smirk.

"You know. Deep in the temple." I laid the toy aside.

"How very instructive."

"Yes. I was peeping in rapture and wondering what her name is in Hebrew."

"Almost an intellectual wonder."

"Yes. I thought you'd think so."

"*Pamuschka*," she said.

I smiled to myself, returned her steady gaze. I savoured the word. "*Pamuschka*," I murmured. Let it roll over my tongue.

"Yiddish."

"Yes," I said. "Thought so. So German, so..."

"That is enough, now."

I gave another nasty chuckle. "So logical, so precise. Like..."

"Stop it."

"Like papa and mamma's Muschi, on the back seat of..."

"I imagined your tiny imagination would start getting the better of you again."

"I apologise for intellectualising..."

Too late, I received a second dig, a little higher. I gasped – that one hurt. Recovering, I asked: "Do tell me the Hebrew name."

"I shall not."

"Why not?"

"I cannot."

"What a big disappointment."

"Isn't it a shame. Mamma refused to elucidate." Green eyes slowly blinking. "And I omitted to ask all my academic Jewish lovers, too."

"All those sexy bronzed Israeli bodies...?"

"Far too busy for silly semantics."

I tried not to visualise. I took a breath; I had to know...

"No." Long fingers pressing on my lips...

"No?"

"No."

"Let me guess."

"God forbid." She was back to being a queen again. Ah, that lifted chin, that freckled and elegant nose.

"*Schlong*," she said.

"*Schlong*?"

"Mmm."

"How ugly."

"I gave you ample warning." She stirred.

"How unromantic of your race."

"Snake." She was standing up, smoothing her dress. Today it was speckled and rusty-red – like sunlight on autumn leaves.

"Ah." I tried to be erudite: "The eternal male mystic symbol." I looked up at her standing there. So graceful.

"I shall leave you now to your ruminations," she said.

"Ah."

"Till later."

That made me nervous again.

x x x

Seven o'clock. The moment had come, at last.

I sat there in bed, lowered the book. Amos Oz . Annabelle had brought me de Winter and him to give me some Jewish education. I'd chosen the less light one to get a good chew.

Five past seven...

I sat watching the door handle, listening for steps. Felt nervous as a kid. Raised the book again, read some more pages, caught myself watching the clock every few minutes. My nervousness grew.

How long had it been? With one eye on the door I counted the weeks. Nearly a month since we'd last made love. I sat there. Seven-fifteen.

No dip of the door handle, no sounds of activity outside. No sign of her. Was she doing this intentionally, to enhance my fancy, heighten my greed? Or had something happened – something gone wrong? I listened. No busy bustle, no sound at all except the tick of my clock and the hoot of a car far away; it seemed she'd been correctly informed about the change of shift. They'd collected my supper tray at half-past-six and said goodnight, since then it had been like a morgue.

I thought: I must occupy myself. Then straight afterwards I decided – I'll take a little walk, test my strength for the coming task; I'm sure that's what Don Juan would have done.

I peeled aside the sheet, and the thin feather duvet they'd given me for the nights, carefully lowered my feet to the floor. Curious feeling – a lack of strength, hadn't done this for weeks. With a wobble I arose. Then I was standing unsteadily beside the bed, leaning for support. My legs were like water, were a long way away. But it was grand to be vertical again. Holding on to anything I could, like a one-armed bandit fumbling through fog, I took a few steps, I made it to the door. Opened it a little, peering out.

A wide ward corridor bright with light, but silent as the grave. Blues and whites for decoration, a lattice of natural wood screening, a day-area with comfortable chairs on the open corner where two corridors met. Small tables with abandoned newspapers and magazines, a switched-off television set.

In the background, beyond a tiny glassed-in courtyard, I caught sight of a bent figure – a male patient in dressing-gown and slippers staggering along a wall, gripping the timber handrail as if clutching the last seconds of life. Nobody else in sight. No staff. No Annabelle walking sensually towards me.

I closed the door to a crack and stood leaning on the wall in the seclusion of my room. Enough of going for a walk, I'd grandly failed the test. My legs shook, I felt a bit sick, a banging throb beat in my head. This was the first time I'd stood upright since being delivered to the clinic feet first. No, I didn't feel too good.

Shuffling, I covered those four long unsupported yards to the table-edge, reached it, bent over it, taking a pause and peering dizzily ahead, planning the next leg back to base. Logic instructed me to avoid the TV trolley. Via the back of a chair, the next step brought me trembling and unsteady to the tall solid-looking clothes cupboard which I gratefully hugged with one arm. Too late did I discover that it also possessed castors and started to roll as I clutched it; it took on an unexpected life of its own and smartly rotated, managed to make it halfway to the bed with me. In an unhappy pirouette I was forced to let go – was propelled on forward falling flat on my face, crushing my cracked arm in its protective sleeve, and with amazing momentum shot ignominiously away across the slippery floor and under the bed, hitting my head with a thump on something very solid.

My body lay spreadeagled. And in that moment I remembered. Funny how the brain is wired to jump, to sometimes unhappily short-circuit – I remembered that duck and knew how he'd felt. There it was in a tiny flash... the winter lake, I was out for a walk, and down from the frozen white sky the lonely duck came in to land a bit fast, discovered too late the water had turned to ice. I'd laughed at the time, never before seen a duck skidding on its back at sixty miles-an-hour and doing a roly-poly at the end. But, ah yes, now I could appreciate.

I lay there; I gave myself up to the floor. It smelled of rubber and wax. The smell was overpowering, right under my nose. I thought: I'll turn over in a moment.

The headache beat loud as a drum I'd got trapped inside, perspiration prickled my temples. Disorientation. Postponed moving. No hurry. Shakily, gingerly, I rolled over. My pelvis flared like a flame. Flexed the fingers of my right hand in the sling. Only dull pain, seemed nothing new had got broken. Lucky there. And the penetrating reek of rubber was not so bad now. I opened my eyes. The underside of the bed had its points of interest, I suppose, for those who are mechanically minded. There were levers and hydraulics, a bright orange coiled cable snaked to the wall, and right next to my throbbing skull a white motor hung mounted on the lacquered chassis. That must be what'd brought me to a halt. I sniffed...

Oil. Now I could smell oil. I sniffed again. Yes, lubricating oil – sweet and pungent. Shut my eyes. Another jump, another flash, a memory exploding... Suddenly I was on the cobbles again, in the dark – there was that smell in my nose there too, mixed up with the smell of blood. Fingers of fear shrunk my skin for an instant, then faded. I lay there sweating. Take a little rest, I ordered myself.

That was the moment Annabelle chose to walk into the room.

I listened. Must be her. The footsteps stopped, inside, near the door. I could almost see her searching, hear her thoughts. I opened my eyes again, twisted my head slowly, now my cheek lay on the cool rubber floor. There – I had a better view of her through the construction of the bed. Yes, they were her legs and that was the hem of the swishy rust-red dress, and those were her elegant shoes.

"Stefan?" I heard her say. Then her feet turned to go out the door again.

"Annabelle?"

The feet paused, turned back.

"Stefan?" she repeated. This time her voice had a strange hollowness in it.

"I'm here," I said. "Cuckoo."

She came round the bed. And found me.

Still I could only see her legs, till she hunkered. Now I could see her thighs and face too. I lay there feeling a fool. She took in the situation, appraising it with her usual cool. She didn't say anything silly like what on earth are you doing, or what the devil's happened? She came down on her knees beside me, concern in her face. "Are you hiding, my nervous one?" She smiled faintly. "Did you get cold feet?"

"Something like that," I said.

"Are you hurt?"

"No."

"Do you think you can move?"

"I'm sure I can."

She helped me slide out from under the bed. I sat up, propped on hands behind me, taking a short breather. The ache in my head was better, the flame in my hips dying down, and from under the plaster of my right arm there seemed to be no pain.

"Tell me when you are feeling up to the next stage – or shall I call for a crane?"

I managed a smile, too; I think I managed it better than she. I rolled onto all fours, breathed in deeply, reached up to the bed above and began the long ascent. Wobbly legs. Her hands were under my armpits, I marvelled at her strength. She turned me – together we lowered my body to the mattress so I was sitting on the edge. I felt so faint and dizzy it wouldn't have troubled me had I started throwing up; my head was wagging like an imbecile and my arms had the quakes. Don Juan had just arrived back in all his potency and his glory on his favourite stamping ground.

x x x

It was the following Tuesday. That was the day of the prophecy, the day the High Priest came to call. I was feeling a great deal better and wondering how soon I could be discharged. He came unannounced, would turn out to be one of my last visitors. Midmorning. Was just enjoying a little time alone when there came a polite knock on the door. I called to come in but it was already quietly opening. A priest entered.

Benignly he greeted me: "I bring you God's blessing, and wish you the best of mornings." The beginning of a bow. He'd come in working clothes.

I nodded and thanked him. Inside I felt irritated at the disturbance, not the least because he was from the Catholic Church. "I think you've got the wrong room," I pointed out. "Not one of your flock."

He stood there complacently with folded hands, produced a quiet smile. "No, my son." He was chubby, rounded and rosy-cheeked, small curls of hair adorned his head. I guessed him to be in his early forties; he reminded me of a cherub. "It is my habit not to lay emphasis on denominations. We are all God's children, and at the second coming each will be judged in his own right."

I winced. The second coming? I fixed him with my favourite apathetic gaze. "I'm not dead yet, you know."

A little chortle. Still composure in those plump folded hands on the comfortable portly belly. "My name is Father Hubertus. It is my pleasant duty to do the rounds here once a week and bring comfort to those in suffering. Pray permit me five minutes of your time?"

I waved a vague hand of assent but already he was seating himself on a chair by the table.

"Are you a believer in the Faith?" he asked.

"No," I said flatly to disperse any misunderstandings.

He had crossed his legs beneath his dark austere garments, he regarded me kindly. "In what do you believe, may I ask, my son?"

I shrugged. "In myself," I suggested. "In the world about me, anything I can see and touch." I said it half-heartedly, I had no wish to be drawn into a discussion.

"In worldly and tangible things, that is?"

"Correct."

"And do you find that this belief suffices?"

"At least it saves my sanity," I said. "And enables me to survive."

"Survive." A gentle nod. Unhurriedly he savoured the word. "Do you consider this is our only purpose here on Earth? Simply to preserve our sanity and survive?"

"Yes."

"I marvel at your certainty." A twinkle in his eyes. "And your courage to go it alone." Smooth rosy cheeks aglow.

He looked almost heavenly, angelic, he somehow didn't look real – place a pair of wings on him and he could have been one of the cherubim just removed from a Ruben's oil painting. Perhaps he wasn't real, perhaps I'd dozed off, was having a little daydream.

"In my youth," he added pensively, "I must confess I lacked both these blessings."

Strange. He felled me there; it was almost as if he'd got inside me, almost as if he were teasing. I dropped my eyes. Black stockings, shiny black shoes peeping below his stern apparel.

"It led me to start searching for a meaning behind all these worldly visible things." He smiled. It was such a sagely smile.

I rallied, raised my eyes again, retorted: "And failing to find an answer you ended up with God." I tried to disguise my sarcasm, I wanted to get back to my book.

"I discovered God, indeed."

"What one euphemistically calls God."

"Yes, how we love attaching names. But He is the only answer, my son. The creator of Heaven and Earth, and Man."

"He's a figment of the imagination." I shifted impatiently. "God didn't create Man," I said. "Man created God to explain all the things he doesn't understand."

Patient eyes blinking. "If indeed Man had, that would make me very curious." Peaceable eyes.

"About what?" I said.

"Who, then, created the unexplainable?"

I hunched my shoulders – was my impatience coming through? I held my tongue, though. Perhaps that would help him go away.

"But here we would be getting into metaphysics, wouldn't we? I prefer to leave that to the atheists." His smile was almost sublime.

"You're right there," I agreed, and left it at that. We had reached a convenient full stop.

He didn't stand up though. I'm sure he was an expert on these subjects and practised them every day. I waited, wondering what would be the next trick he had up his sleeve.

"Don't you sometimes wonder, though, where all the wondrous things of our world come from?" he mused.

"Yes. But it gets me nowhere."

"And the purpose of life?"

"I used to," I agreed. "I gave up long ago."

He nodded slowly, observed me in friendly silence.

"Don't try and convert me," I said. "You'd be wasting your time."

"My son, conversing with God's sheep who have strayed from the path is never a waste of time." He continued watching me contentedly.

Strayed? I thought. "Have to disappoint you there," I said. "Was never on it."

"But indeed, my son." A quiet contradiction. As if he knew something I didn't.

I returned his pleasant gaze, I held my tongue.

"And death?" He popped it out. "Do you believe that is the end of everything for you?" I found that rather sneaky.

"That's it," I said. "The final curtain."

"Have you lost your concept of Heaven and Hell? Of an afterlife?"

Lost? I frowned. There he went again. Why did he say lost? I'd only believed that as a child because children, like the tortured, agree to anything if told often enough.

"No chance there either," I confessed. I meant it too. I chuckled. "No hope of salvation." I said it with tongue in cheek.

Still he gazed complacently. "Salvation of the soul and a place in Heaven are not for us to choose."

"Ah." That surprised me, hearing that, coming from a Catholic priest – didn't one automatically burn in purgatory if one hadn't subscribed to the club? What on earth would my brother Toby's wife Mathilda make of that?

Forgiving eyes, those round ruddy cheeks, yes he really looked like a cherub. Then, quite unexpectedly, he went and said it, something I wouldn't have expected him to say: "God's blessing be upon you. One day, my son, you will return to the fold and the joys of life after death will be revealed in all their glory."

He rose from his chair. "I shall pray for you, my son." He was crossing himself. He gazed at me, a happy comfortable unhurried gaze. Then bade me farewell with the lift of a hand, and was gone. Except for the memory of his face and those parting words he really might have been just an apparition; he left me sitting there in bed all alone.

Chapter 16

Six weeks after being admitted to the clinic I was discharged direct to a rehabilitation centre about an hour's drive from Nuremberg. Annabelle brought me a load of books and clothes from my apartment on the third day; that was the only time she came to visit me there. No explanations. I suppose she saw I was on the mend.

New routines: physiotherapy and water gymnastics, massages and craniosacral corrections, steamy herbal baths. In between, I'd go for walks or read in the shade, or simply relax with music. Since he visited me that evening on the intensive care unit, I'd seen and heard nothing more of Matthias. I often had him, and Annabelle, on my mind: because of the way I was built my mind was plagued with premonitions.

I pondered things too – for example Cornelia Bartenbach's offer; I decided to procrastinate. Late afternoons and at weekends, using laptop and mobile, I worked. Getting back in touch, getting back into the run of things again.

Apart from George Sunday, who popped in a couple of times with lanky limbs and dancing Adam's apple, and my old boss Herr Heller who'd got the chop at fifty-six and came to say farewell – except for them one of my only visitors of note was Estella returning again. Amongst other more pressing thoughts I recounted the conversation with the Catholic priest because I felt it might amuse her. I remember: she gazed at me with a faraway look and just smiled her smile full of wisdom then, mystifyingly, told me perhaps it was the turning of the tide.

Languid, lazy days.

But I knew those days were numbered – I was living on borrowed time. My strength was back, I was mobile; I felt like an impostor, a schoolboy playing truant. It was during the third and last week at rehab, in the middle of a conversation with an elderly patient, that an idea came to me; he'd been reminiscing about Italy. I rang my general practitioner at the surgery: "Hello Madeleine, it's me."

"Stefan! Recovering well?"

"Yes." I hadn't known she knew. She's a no-nonsense person, tall, dark and dominant – it even comes through on the phone. She's also a fairly close friend, in a practical sporting sort of way; we play squash together sometimes, she's pretty nifty with that racquet and beats me into the ground.

"The clinic faxed me their report."

"Ah," I said.

"Saw your picture in the papers, too. Did justice to an Egyptian mummy."

I chuckled. My less dirty one. "I guessed you'd appreciate the little disguise." Briefly I outlined my progress, ending: "Coming Monday they'll be sending me home." Then I asked her advice, and the favour – I needed to win another week.

"No problem." She told me what to do.

That was on Thursday.

I rang Annabelle; we hadn't spoken on the phone for a little while. I breathed in the sound of her voice, I indulged in my picture of her. We conversed. Then I told her that on Monday I'd be going home.

"I shall come and pick you up."

I thought: I can't imagine anything better. "I appreciate the offer, but far too far," I said. "George popped in again yesterday, said he'll do it because he has Monday free." He'd said it glancing away through glass – I saw he fancied the physiotherapist doing her stuff with balls with a group out on the grass.

"And will you be returning to work on Tuesday, my mended one?" Annabelle asked.

"That was the idea," I said. Well, it was in a good cause; it was less than half a lie. Delicately I enquired after her plans for the following weeks, I did it with great discretion.

"The school vacations have just begun," she explained.

"Ah. Naturally." Everything collapsing. A plunge into an abyss. "You're taking them on holiday perhaps?"

"Albert and Mimi have invited us all for August."

"How pleasant." I hit rock bottom. Had they already left? I was talking to her on her mobile, she could be anywhere...

"Margareth is driving the children down tomorrow."

Down was the Tegernsee lake in the mountains, Albert and Mimi her elderly grand-uncle and aunt. "And you?" I said, heart in stomach queasily. "Aren't you going?" Yes, she'd be following on the Tuesday – she had some things to settle first at home.

On shaky legs my hopes rose again. I'd take the risk, I decided.

I informed the administration and the lady in charge of my welfare and rehab programme, prepared myself for a premature departure. Then got on the Web, entered Florence, went through hotel homepages and whittled them down to two. It was also the afternoon I received a disturbing e-mail from Eva – I found it in my laptop, later, while tidying up loose ends connected with work. 'Something's happened (she wrote) need to talk but not on the phone. At home till Sunday. You switched off your mobile.' I couldn't reach her either; I e-mailed back I'd come the following evening.

What had happened? Something to do with her company, what she'd told me in the clinic? Had she lost her nerve and beaten up the boss, broken into the safe? Was this her way, a cry for help? I couldn't know it would be that bad.

I remember, too, there'd been another kidnap the previous weekend – I heard more of it on the news while packing, but I wasn't really listening. And I only recall it because the victim was an ex-politician suspected of corruption who'd earned my distaste years before when he used his connections to get himself off the hook. I confess: I experienced a sneaky feeling of satisfaction that this was punishment due.

Yes, that was the Thursday when several things started to happen; it was as if someone had pressed a switch and a motor fired into life. It was somehow symbolic, I would soon be back in the fray. Next morning I discharged myself, three days earlier than planned. George would be at work so didn't bother to call, just sent an e-mail cancelling Monday with thanks. The cream taxi crept up to the entrance, and I emerged like a moth from its chrysalis into the lowering, waiting world, unfolded my new-found wings. It was nine weeks since I'd got into that fight – nine weeks minus two days. And August hadn't quite begun.

x x x

My apartment was like a stranger.

I stood in the big living space saying hello. I didn't expect what I found – I hadn't dedicated much thought to it before. Although she hadn't moved anything, all somehow had the feel of Annabelle. All was tidy and clean, even the air was fresh. And in the middle, on the small round English table, was a beautiful plant in full bloom. If Annabelle does anything she never does it by halves.

There was a note, too, in the guise of a decorated card.

I touched it, turned it – she'd made it herself. It somehow reached out to me, lent me strength in what I had planned. 'Welcome home, my philosopher,' I read. God, how I hanker for the feminine touch.

I like to think, had I known the gravity of what had happened to Eva in Munich, that I would've postponed what I was about to do. But love is like a magnet, and selfishness a willing slave. So I didn't hesitate, in spite of Eva on my mind I popped down to the centre of town, to the owner of the travel agency I've often used.

I booked two flight tickets for the following day, Saturday, business class. Plenty of time, I thought – this evening for Eva, most of tomorrow for springing the surprise on Annabelle: spontaneity shouldn't be postponed. Then I sought and received advice and confirmation about the first of those two particular hotels, the converted Palazzo standing directly on the river with sixteenth century tower – it would seem to be appropriate for the replenishment of romance. Well, I'm a little finicky, and persuasion is one of the lady owner's finer points: she rang Florence, got the manager she knew on the line, clinched a deal for a little room at the top which was duly reserved in my name. I thanked her deeply and put the printouts in my pocket; I do so appreciate the dying sanctity of personal service.

On the way back up the hill my thoughts were already in my apartment. But something stopped me. I peered through the glass, decided on the spur of the moment; went in and bought the bonsai. A twisted dwarf tree with miniature pine-needle clusters – like a perfect Japanese painting, wouldn't it go well on that stand near her grand piano? Actually, though, it was the porcelain pot which had caught my attention – fine hairline cracks in pale Far Eastern green, and the green was the colour of her eyes. It was a bit heavy. I carried it in both hands; I carried it like a trophy.

In the hallway at the bottom of the stairs I had to invest another twenty minutes because Frau Maußer discovered I was back. Today she was in ravishing purple with a generous splatter of yellow spots; I found her bright green headscarf didn't match quite as well as it might. We parried and lunged like two fencers neither of whom want to give ground but, with consideration for the ticking away of the time, I felt it realistic and even gracious to allow her to win the last round.

I rang Eva at home to confirm she'd received my e-mail and that I'd be arriving at about five o'clock, but again she didn't answer, not even her mobile.

It was nearly 3pm till I was packed and ready to go. Then I was on the autobahn to Munich with fresh air coming in through the car window and the bonsai in the back. It had been raining quite a bit in the last few days, cooled things down, I was glad it wasn't hot. A lot of traffic, though – year by year it got worse and worse. Switched the radio on. Traffic service – the crackling was worse today too. I only caught a bit about a jam near Garching Süd near Munich. Switched it off again. Crossing the Altmühl river valley I steeled myself to the dust and destruction; the work on the tunnels and bridges for the high-speed train was progressing with ponderous inevitability.

At the Holledau rest-house I stopped for five minutes. Rolling hills and hop fields, the young hops were coming on. I tried Eva's number again. "Hello," she said suddenly. She said it so quickly I almost dropped the damn thing, I'd hardly got the connection.

"Hello Eva."

"Oh thank God." Her voice was dead.

"Thanks for the e-mail," I said.

Ignoring me: "Where're you now?" Her sentences were cutting corners.

I told her.

"Make it six not five," she said abruptly. "Okay?"

"Okay."

"Wait in the drive if you get there before me. In a meeting – don't know when it'll end."

The drive? I didn't understand. "In the drive?" I queried.

"Yep."

Had she muddled where we should meet? "Not at your flat then?"

"'Course – where else?"

The Schwabing town house where she lived, only a few blocks away from Annabelle, stood on the corner of two busy streets. Iron railings, pocket-handkerchief bit of green with a bush and a tree at the front; I could see her big Zen stones near the door she hid her key for her lovers and me beneath. Maybe she'd moved.

"Eva," I said carefully, "have you moved, then?"

"Sure. Thought I told you, or Toby did. Half a year ago."

Half a year? My God, was I so out of touch? I hadn't visited her in Munich for over two years...

"Gone back to our roots," she said. "One-oh-three." She said it as if someone were strangling her. The line went dead.

I sat there, adjusting. Ferdinand-Marie Straße? I shook my head. Tried to visualise, found it hard. Whatever made her go and do that? Funny feeling in my gut, queasy feeling. I stared at the hop fields. The sun had come out. It burned on my arm resting in the open window. The weather ahead looked better – blue sky, only scattered white Bavarian clouds. Switched on the old Mercedes' engine again...

Back on the road. The traffic jam started sooner than I'd expected, well north of Munich. Damn. Two lanes of standing vans and cars, the right lane full of lorries. Dead straight lines going into the distance, into haze, the overhead electronic signs switched to '*Stau*'. And far away, blue flashing lights. In the opposite direction only a trickle of vehicles. Suspicious, looked bad. Could be a pile-up both sides. I got out, stretched my legs, joined others doing the same. A helicopter was flying towards us along the line, flying slowly, another one high up, circling. People smoking, people talking into mobiles. I spoke to one of them, asked the cause, asked if he knew how long the jam was. "Seven kilometres. All we know. No info on the Web." He stopped, glancing up. The helicopter came close, clattering, passed us and rose in a curve. Wincing at the noise, I read the writing on its side – *Grenzschutz Polizei*. The man said:

"Looks like it's to do with the kidnap. Late this morning. Bavarian Finance Minister." A shrug. "Second in a week. Load of shit." A shake of the head, his eyes looking away. "Lovely old bird." Nodding at my car.

"Yes," I said.

"300 SE?"

"Yes," I repeated.

"Nineteen-sixty-five?"

"Sixty-seven." I walked away.

Sat behind the steering wheel waiting. Thoughts of Eva, what could be wrong? Thoughts of Florence creeping in between, queasy bump of excitement in my stomach. I expected the wait to last for hours.

But it didn't. Ten minutes later the rows of cars ahead began to move again, rolling forward like loose links in a chain being pulled tight one by one by a mighty hand. And after another twenty minutes or so we were crawling past the cause of the problem on the north-bound side – police cars and flashing lights and uniformed figures with automatic weapons at the hold filtering vehicles between rows of orange-and-white plastic hats, checking cars, searching some: I was on the lucky side, I was on the side of the inquisitive gawpers.

I arrived hardly late at Eva's. Strange feeling, coming back to the house where I'd been born, where I'd grown up. Had never intended to enter it again. At the tall gates to the drive I noticed once more the small changes I'd first glimpsed passing by in May on my way next door to search for a sign of Matthias: new bells, a shiny microphone, new nameplates on one of the stone pillars – and the iron gates smart with fresh paint...

"Hello, Stef," she said. Dark rings round her eyes. She looked a lot worse than that day in the clinic. Her tone was flat, her face a mask to match. She'd just opened our massive old oak front door. The door to our childhood. I didn't like it, felt uneasy, so many ghosts.

We kissed briefly – she held me close, didn't let go. Her small well-built body was stiff, as if she'd been bruised in a fight.

"Eva," I said in her ear.

"Oh, Jesus Christ."

"Okay?"

She nodded next to my neck, stepped back.

We were crossing the wide hall in the middle of the house. I glanced unhappily. One of the doors over there had glass in it now, and beside it was fixed a *Plexiglas* plaque with the name of a well-known insurance company on it – not Toby's though. Otherwise not much changed. Everywhere memories. Memories of Matthias, too.

The broad sweep of stairs. Evening sunlight streaming through stained glass in the high staircase windows above. I could hear our voices, from so long ago. Were we playing? The memory held no pictures, just the sound of our chatter. Oh God. I was home again; a circle was complete.

I heard myself say to Eva: "Never imagined you'd come back to live here."

"Did, didn't I?" A pause, a side-glance. Then: "Something was pulling."

We were ascending, side by side. The oak staircase was wide enough for four. She was saying: "When Tobias finally persuaded mother to let him convert and sell he naturally gave her first option on half the upper floor..."

I remembered. He'd rung me for agreement on the terms of sale and the five-way split, but I hadn't really cared.

"...said she couldn't bear the thought. So I took it."

We reached the first floor. New walls, new doors to the two apartments, everything modern and white. "Retired lady doctor," she said in monotone. She'd noticed me peering at a nameplate. Gone was half the generous landing where we used to race about. The stairs went on up to the attics, I suppose someone lived there now, too. LMU, I read – Munich University. Weird feeling. But Eva was opening her door.

We entered. There was the broad old central corridor lit by the window at the far end, doors left and right; things felt familiar again. Faintly I could smell smoke in the air.

She said: "I'm cooking us something small – okay?"

"Okay." I gave her the bottle of wine I'd stopped and bought, decorated with a thin green bow.

Modern lighting, everything freshly painted – even the parquet floor sanded down and waxed, a sheen like polished silk. The panelled Art Nouveau door to our playroom stood open, swooping brass handle shining bright. She led me in. Sunlight again, and a sense of spaciousness. Matthias and I were on our small knobbly knees playing with my wind-up trains; I had to look away. Half the wall to my bedroom next door was gone – it was a very big working kitchen now, with breakfast bar jutting into the middle and a comfortable living room visible beyond. The smell of cigarette smoke was slightly stronger here.

"Like it?"

"Yes," I said. What else could I say? Times have to move on, don't they? All was aesthetic, sleek, tasteful; I had to admit that.

"Sit down if you want." With her old lack of ceremony she crossed to worktops. A chopping board and gaily-coloured vegetables and fruits, a stainless-steel saucepan already stood on the ceramic-glass top of the very fashionable stove.

"D'you really want to bother?" I said.

"Yep." She was chopping rapidly.

"We could go out for a quick meal, you know."

A rapid glance over her shoulder. "What I've got to tell isn't for public ears." The knife was gripped in her hand.

She continued chopping – sharp clacking sounds. "Want to eat first, though." She wore tight jeans and a T-shirt, she had her back turned again; I could imagine many men found that behind to be irresistible, how often had Matthias found it recently too?

Through tall windows I saw the garden lying below. The ends of the lawns were visible, the two towering copper beeches, the orchard beyond. There was little Eva in green shade again, secretly touching Matthias – her mouth was wide open, her dress so pretty, his thin hand like a snake exploring underneath. The trees were so much bigger now.

I crossed to the breakfast bar, perched myself on one of the high, ultra-modern stools. I watched her slim back. My youngest sister was in no mood for surplus thoughts. She was turning; she put water on to boil. Because he still hung in my head, I said: "Have you seen Matthias again? Since the clinic?" Perhaps I said it a bit abruptly, perhaps I'd caught her mood.

She stooped to a pull-out rack in the cupboard near her knee. "No." She was picking things out one by one, concentrating. "And you?"

"No," I said.

"But before the clinic he'd already contacted you." It sounded like a rebuke. Another brief glance at me: her eyes were hard.

"He sent me a postcard."

"Just like that?"

"Just like that," I said. "After all those years, out of the blue. And enticed me down to Munich, got a friend of his to show me a video with a message."

She was busying herself, didn't speak.

"Said he wanted to meet again," I added. "But he didn't try, not till the clinic."

Still she didn't speak.

"And you?" I asked. "Did you relish that night?" I said it to provoke. I watched her pause. She was pouring oil.

"Nosey bastard." She'd stopped, was looking round at me again. "None of your damn business." She was reddening. The colour on her greyness was like the sun coming through.

"Be careful," I said.

"Meaning?"

"Don't let him hurt you again."

No answer. But for a moment longer the bottle of oil was forgotten in her hand.

More matter-of-factly I said: "Did he tell you he'd keep in touch?"

She nodded.

"But he hasn't."

Headshake. Nothing more.

"And do you have his address or number?" I said. "Can you keep in touch with him?"

"No."

She returned to the cooking. Put salt in the heating water, replaced the lid. Began warming the oil.

A silence between us. I turned my eyes away, stared out at the trees. The copper beeches were blood-red in the sun. Then, into the silence, she suddenly said: "I'm pregnant."

My skin contracted. I shut my eyes, shut them tight.

She'd said it so flatly. No emotion. But her words went right through me, they blurred in my brain. Like Margareth's news about her marriage breaking-up, here too I didn't know whether to be happy or sad. Oh God. So that's why she'd sent me that e-mail. I twisted my head, looked across at her.

"Eva," I said quietly.

She shook her head, her back to me, went on with the cooking.

Was the pressure so great, couldn't she wait? Hadn't she said she wanted to eat first? Oh Eva. Little sister. You career one – that's put a spanner in the works.

My feet were wriggling, my body uncertain and wanting to move, go hold her close – but something told me no. I stared at her, then glanced helplessly down at my hands on the breakfast bar. She was over there, all alone, standing there keeping it in; Eva always was an island.

The rapid clack of metal on glass. I looked: she was mixing salad in a big bowl, tossing it stiffly with both hands. Then she reached to the hood over the cooker. The click of a ventilator being switched on.

I had to speak. "Not planned," I said.

"Nope."

"From Matthias?"

"Who else?"

She had a wooden spoon, was stirring in the pan now.

Who else, I thought. From whom else would she ever have wanted a child? Yet – somehow there was a logic, somehow fate seemed to have played its hand. I took a quick breath. Had to tread carefully. I said: "It makes me happy. Does it make you happy too?"

"Don't know." She stirred rapidly, it was almost aggressive, her head was down.

Again I wanted to go over, still something held me back.

She let go the spoon. She swung round, stared at me. She looked defiant. As if fighting inside herself for which side would win. "Don't know yet." Fingers balled tight, two small fists, holding on hard to her feelings. Eva the fighter, the tomboy. Eva the woman against the whole world, the one who'd never given in.

I gazed across the kitchen at her. In another time and another place I could visualise her, gun in hand, knocking down all the enemies one by one. Why was it? It was strange – she had everything our father had lacked.

"Are you going to keep it?" I said to her. I was looking down at her body, imagining her womb and a tiny helpless foetus floating and curled; one should never take a life.

"'Course," she said abruptly.

Definitive. Consequent. That was my sister – had I had any doubt? She'd master it; she was the master of everything.

I nodded. "I'm happy to hear that," I said.

She returned my gaze. Her haunted eyes said a hundred things. She twisted back to the stove. But just stood there. "In my eighth week," I heard her say.

Then I knew — I caught the strangle in her throat. I got down from the high stool, crossed to her. Took her gently by the shoulders from behind. She let the spoon fall that she'd just picked up. Turned with a jerk and hugged me. Like our greeting just now downstairs at the door she hugged me very tight.

Maybe a minute passed. We didn't say a word. Her small breasts and tummy pressed firm, her body was stiff as a board. She had her arms high, fingers dug into my back, they were moving like a crab. I could feel the tips of pain.

Then she said: "Been on the damn pill all these years 'cos of one-night stands." Her breath tickled, she spoke to my neck, I was nearly as small as she.

"That's life, sister."

"Shouldn't've happened. Never did till now. Had some diarrhoea that week, though."

"It's happened," I said simply.

"P'raps it was meant to."

"Yes."

She held on a short while longer then let go. Twisted back to the cooking again, occupying herself. Her face was drawn but dry. No tears. I made space for her and leaned my bottom against the worktop nearby, crossed my arms, watching her in silence.

She started to say something, stopped — cleared her throat. "Used to dream 'bout getting pregnant from him," she said. "When I was a kid."

"That's what one calls fate."

"What I call bloody irony." She tipped noodles fine as hair into boiling water. "'Nother couple of minutes." They looked like Asian noodles.

"D'you intend to tell him?" I said.

"Over my dead body." She pushed at my arm. "In my way — go and sit down, brother." My tough little sister again.

I went back to the breakfast bar. After another pause she said: "Going to do this my way — never wanted marriage and all that crap. Men're all the same, Matthias too. All hot air and promises — parole, parole. When they've stuck it in a few times they bugger off."

I watched her across the room, waiting. But she seemed to be finished. So after a moment I said: "I'd like to do all I can to help. With the pregnancy, the baby."

Just a nod. She was turning noodles with big wooden tweezers.

"Just tell me, sister."

"Not necessary, ol' chap. You're never in Munich anyway."

"In the future I will be, perhaps."

"You don't say."

"I've got to know someone here." I said it carefully.

She was sieving the noodles. "Annabelle." She said it through steam. "Goldberg's daughter."

"Yes."

"Heard from Meg."

"Ah," I said.

"'Gratulations."

"Have to see. It's hot and cold." I fiddled with things on the bar-top. "We were talking about your baby."

In the wok she was tossing prawns. "Come and hold my hand when I go into labour. Okay?"

"Okay." Suddenly I remembered Judit, all the drama, all the pain. And little Andrea when finally she emerged.

"Like jumbos, do you?"

"Jumbos?" I jumped back. She was serving the prawns. Try, I thought. Have to break the strain. "You mean the ones with trunks?"

"Idiot – ones that swim."

"Sure," I said. Attempted a chuckle. "Anything that moves will do."

"Fine. Buy maggots next time, then."

She was coming over with cutlery and linen serviettes in one hand, salad bowl in the other. "Glad for you, brother. 'Bout Annabelle. Time you got off the masturbating track."

"Don't be vulgar, sister."

"Come on, we all do it. But the real thing's better, huh?"

I glanced at her sideways. "Sure."

She returned with plates and glasses. "What's she like?"

"A pearl."

"That's my boy." Gone again. "Spill the beans."

I said nothing. She came back with steaming bowls and chopsticks, placed them. "Suddenly still as the grave?" she said. She reached a small hand, waggled my chin. I looked in her eyes. Oh God, they looked dead.

She sat.

"Tell me..." I started.

"Open it?" She was pushing across the bottle I'd brought.

I took the corkscrew. "Is this why you e-mailed me yesterday? Because you're pregnant?"

"Jesus, no." She flapped a serviette open. "Only the hors d'oeuvre." Still those dead eyes. Then they blinked, were gone. She ladled salad onto plates.

I watched. I thought: my God, what else can there be? I opened the bottle, poured the wine. And as I did she added: "Matter of fact, didn't intend mentioning it. Not today of all days."

Of all days? Could feel the sinking in my stomach...

"Eat." She'd already started.

So I obeyed.

"Remember Ustinov?" She was holding up her glass.

I nodded. Conversation is the enemy of good food; ah, Ustinov had said so many good and amusing things. But I didn't feel like smiling now. We touched glasses. "To new insights, sister," I toasted.

By the time we pushed our plates and bowls aside the bottle was almost empty. Not a bad thing for what was to come; I guess it took the inhibitions from our tongues.

"Coffee?" she said. "Have it how you want, got a new machine."

I chose espresso. She too. While the machine steamed and did its duty into two small golden cups I replenished our glasses with the last of the wine, and she fetched another bottle...

"Remember what I told you in the clinic 'bout what's been going on in my company?"

"The discrimination." I nodded.

"You were in a bad state – remember all the details?"

"Yes."

I sipped espresso, she had lit a cigarette.

"'Bout the smug little Austrian bastard..." she blew a thin stream of smoke, "...the arsehole brought in over my head to eliminate me?"

"Schulz," I said. The wine was slowly going to my head but her seriousness kept coming to spoil.

"Yep." With a quick movement she stretched, pulled the ashtray nearer. "Well, that was a couple of months back. Meanwhile it's got worse. And not only for me. He started a hate campaign 'gainst two of the area managers I'd trained. My two best women. One's now seriously ill, the other threw in the towel. The arsehole's trying to worm out the best, keep the yes-men."

She tapped ash. It was a rapid jerk. She spoke in jerks, too. Not like the Eva I used to know. Now that she'd started in, she was tense – almost neurotic.

I said nothing.

"Handed in my notice too. Week last Wednesday. Took your advice, though – went to Karla first. Early June. She was great. And she referred me on to Dr Meier, just like you'd presumed."

I nodded again. This time she was making a pause, it seemed. So I said: "I'm sorry it had to come to this."

"Just you wait – hardly started." She inhaled deeply, frowning, poked the cigarette in the ashtray, playing with ash with the tip. "I'm in good hands with Meier. She's a finicky lawyer, tough as nails. Thanks, brother."

I spread my hands in silence.

"Got a mandate now from my two colleagues, too. I passed on the recommendation. Says it'll help in court, three cases against one – should we need it." She exhaled in a stream; she turned her head away to do it. It billowed in the evening sunlight coming through the windows.

I waited, didn't wish to interrupt; wondered what she meant.

"In a nutshell," she said, "that was the situation ten days ago." She hesitated – but only for a fraction of a second. "Then something dreadful happened." Her eyes were hollow, yes her skin had such dark rings. She stared at me. But she was staring through to somewhere else. "I was only told yesterday." She stopped again. "Stef, it's…"

Her mobile rang. Right next to us. Made me jump.

She reached over her pushed-aside plate, picked up the mobile from the bar-top.

"Hello?" she said… a brief pause; I couldn't hear the one the other end. "How you feeling?" Another pause. "Katie, listen, can't talk now – my brother's here. Got to fill him in. Okay? …Okay. I'll ring you tomorrow early. 'Bye."

She laid the mobile down. "My colleague," she said emotionlessly. "The one who's ill. In a clinic, had a breakdown." Again she inhaled; the tip glowed bright. "Schulz's had an accident.

In a coma, on the danger list. Happened last Friday. Two days after I gave in my notice." Again she stared into space. "He fell out of a window. Or got pushed. Jesus, Stef, it's horrible."

Brusquely she stubbed out the cigarette.

I sat there watching her.

She scrabbled at the packet, lit another. Her fingers shook. "Frau Daninger rang me yesterday in Italy just before my flight, gave me the news. She'd postponed doing it. I've been away all week, saying goodbye to my customers – she didn't want to disturb my plans."

"Frau Daninger?" I said.

"Schulz's secretary. Used to be my old boss's. We've known each other years – she's loyal to Schulz but upset by what he's done to me. Call it divided loyalties."

Still I watched her.

"And why does it worry you so much?" I asked. "This accident?"

"'Cos I'm a suspect. I'm plum in the middle." She was fiddling with the lighter; her fingers set it on its edge, turning it this way and that.

"Weren't you in Italy, then – when it happened?"

"No – I flew out Sunday."

"Was it you?"

"Don't be absurd." Dark eyes staring.

"Then what the hell. And if you have an alibi, all the better."

"I don't." She tipped back her head, exhaled another stream of smoke. "The police were enquiring after me, according to Frau Daninger."

"Have they contacted you, then?"

"Not yet." She frowned again. "They've another reason to suspect, too. 'Nother motive. Yesterday the company offered me Schulz's position plus a twenty-five per cent rise."

I smiled faintly at her. Into her tenseness. Said nothing.

Her fingers gripped the lighter tight. With cigarette hand she picked up her wine glass, drank, clacked it back on the bar. "Max himself called me on my flight back. Went straight to the office. He and Reubel were waiting. Didn't beat about the bush. Schulz's broken his neck, apparently paralysed."

"Well, well, well," I said. I said it noncommittally.

"So I'm the one who profits."

I shrugged. "Even if you do, which I doubt – the fact remains your hands are clean. The police aren't fools."

She didn't answer. In silence she continued smoking her cigarette. Her eyes jumped here and there.

I said: "And how did you react to the offer?"

"Rejected it."

"Good."

"Damage's done, isn't it." A statement.

I nodded.

"Anyway," she added, "they're only playing for time. If Schulz doesn't recover, Reubel'll replace him with someone new. Then it starts all over again."

We sat without speaking. She drained her half-full glass in one draught, stabbed the cigarette out. I'd never known her not savouring wine.

"Crafty buggers," I said.

"Yep." She fiddled with the lighter again, she had it in both hands. An expensive lighter – ebony and silver, had a slender flip-top. "Nipped my court case in the bud. Any judge'd laugh at me."

"Did they put the offer in writing?"

"Sure." She was reaching for the bottle of wine. "As you said, crafty buggers." I stopped her hand; it was shaking still. I replenished her glass, topped up my own. I wasn't going anywhere by car that night.

We drank. I just watched her over the rim. Her eyes were holes. She'd looked exhausted in the clinic, now she looked a wreck.

"Stef, I'm scared."

I sipped on my wine. Didn't react.

"Something not kosher 'bout what's happened. Mean with Schulz."

"No?"

"Nope."

"Things like this happen," I said neutrally, shrugging again.

"No they don't. Not like this."

I continued watching her.

"Frau Daninger said they don't yet know if he jumped or was pushed."

"Well you didn't push him." I said it to put on her brakes. "So dinna fash yerself." I said it to stop her boring too deep, her nerves were shredded enough.

"Don't block. Have to talk to someone 'bout it, someone I'm close to – don't know anyone more objective."

I shook my head slowly. "Okay." What else could I say?

"Wasn't suicide. That's for sure." Her small fingers shook another cigarette from the pack, lit it. The flame wobbled while she did. "Don't know why the hell they bother with that idea. Gets his kicks destroying others, not himself."

"Nasty bit of work, at any rate."

"No kidding." Behind the glowing tip her face bore testimony, wore a tired sneer. "Not 'nough to have *that* happen, though."

"Who knows," I said. I mused: "If he did this with you, probably he's done things like that in other firms before."

"No idea."

"Maybe he's got old enemies." I squinted at her, let my mouth sag down. "Maybe the mafia sent a hit-man."

"For Christ's sake, brother, don't bugger around. Being serious."

I spread my hands. "Just a little joke, sister."

She didn't react. Was frowning, concentrating, staring at the bar-top.

"Where did it happen, then?" I said, to help. "At his home? At your company?"

"*Four Seasons*, plum in the middle of Munich. Third floor window in a side street, they say. He fell on a parked car, 'parently."

"Ah," I said.

Blue smoke spiralled. Her eyes were lowered, hand gripping her glass.

"And why there?" I asked.

"Meeting a customer of mine. Nothing unusual. 'Cept that Schulz went himself. I do it regularly – pick them up there, drop them off, drinks at the bar, sometimes breakfast or dinner meetings." She stared at her glass. Her face was a mask again.

"Customer of yours?" I said. I watched her. "Do I detect deep bitterness?"

"Yep." Her head came up. "'Course." Anger in her eyes. "I told you – he took away all my best customers. Same little game with Eli."

"Eli?"

"Cohen. The one he went to meet. Stocky little Jew from the States. One of my biggest customers, we've known each other fifteen years. Subsidiaries in London, Paris, Barcelona. Schulz's had Eli's incoming calls to me diverted to his desk for months. Via

Daninger. Last Friday Eli was livid being blocked again, least that's what she said."

"Maybe he tried bumping off your boss, then," I said, tongue in cheek.

"Don't be absurd. He's hot-headed — but so're a lot in this business." She blew smoke, picked up her wineglass, drained it dry.

I drank some more, too. A warm fuzzy feeling spreading — now the wine was really going to my head.

"I imagine there must've been witnesses," I said. "Where he fell. It's a busy area."

"No idea. Didn't think to ask."

I refilled our glasses. I had to take care to aim straight. Pursing her lips she blew smoke up in the air again. Her cigarette was only half through; the air was getting thick.

I added: "And surely others in your company had a motive, too." I flapped a dismissive wave with my hand.

She was leaning sideways. "I'll check." With a jerk she picked up her mobile again, flipped it open. "See what she says." She pressed keys, held the phone to her ear...

"Frau Daninger, hello. It's me, Eva Falk. You're working late again."

Her eyes had gone out of focus. "Yes it is... You did? Well, in your capacity I'm not surprised... No, a company secret. Keep it under your hat, of course..."

A longer pause. She was listening. I watched her face. Then she said: "No, 'fraid not. Made up my mind..." Her face was hard, was set... "No. Any new developments? ...They were? Again?" Her cigarette was forgotten, it burned in her hand, a finger of ash. The smoke was getting in my eyes. "*Mordkommission?*" A flash of wildness in those tired eyes. "But... I see. The *Kripo*..."

I slid from the stool, went to the windows, opened one wide. Breathed in the clean evening air. As I paused there I thought: I must ring Annabelle later, just to check her whereabouts. Behind me Eva was saying: "Hang on a mo', I'm switching to conference... No, no — my brother, we're alone... No. Still as the grave, don't worry. Want him to hear — repeat that please..."

I was returning to the breakfast bar. She inhaled on her cigarette again — she must've noticed, she'd knocked off the ash. A woman's voice came metallically into the room: "Good evening, Herr Falk.

Frau Daninger." An efficient voice, very correct, pronouncing each word precisely – I guessed in the mid-fifties.

"Good evening," I called. I perched back on the stool, leaning to listen.

"I was saying to Frau Falk that Kommissar Müller has only just left. He was in our offices again for the third time. This afternoon he wished to question certain women colleagues and myself. It appears they have a new lead from a witness, a room-service waiter."

"In the *Four Seasons*," Eva prompted. "But please continue." She held the mobile away from her ear; she'd put out the cigarette.

"Yes. Directly after the accident a woman was seen coming out of the third-floor room. A call-girl, he said, I understand of the luxury class."

"Ah." I winked at Eva. "I'm sure they couldn't confuse her with you."

And Frau Daninger was saying: "The surprising thing was, the hotel room had been booked in Herr Schulz's name, not Mr Cohen's, and it seems it was also Herr Schulz who picked up the key at the reception. For that reason I had to be questioned again..."

Her voice broke off then returned, but upon the precise and polished tone a tarnish of fluster appeared: "Actually, Frau Falk, it was rather embarrassing. The police say that I, even if unintentionally, put a red herring in their way. So silly of me. I had taken what I believed to be Mr Cohen's call last Friday late afternoon and the man was so angry that I connected at once. Straight after it Herr Schulz cancelled an internal meeting and left in quite a rush and without a word so I assumed it had to do with Mr Cohen's call. The police checked, of course, and established my misunderstanding..."

A pause. A quick blowing of a nose...

"Apparently Mr Cohen was in the Far East and hadn't rung himself, rather had given orders to his Paris branch to cancel all present and future contracts with our company. I gather from the Kommissar that he wasn't very cooperative."

"Typical Schulz," Eva said to the phone. I saw her anger.

"I really am so sorry about this aspect too, Frau Falk," said Frau Daninger's voice. "Such a tragedy after all your successful business with him through the years." A brief hesitation. Then: "It was supposedly a woman who reserved the room for Herr Schulz, so naturally the police are now trying to trace her. I get the impression they suspect it must be someone from our company." Another small hesitation. "They enquired after you, Frau Falk, and of course I had to say you flew back yesterday and are probably at home. I am afraid they will be disturbing you soon, too."

Chapter 17

"D'you know what I think?" Eva said.

She'd ended the call just a few minutes before, cleared the meal things away and returned, perching her tight neat bottom back on the high stool opposite me.

I watched her, said nothing. The wine was warm in my veins. She was lighting another cigarette. She really ought to kick the habit.

"Think Matthias could've had something to do with it."

I considered her carefully. I thought: sister, you're losing touch with reality. Slowly I shook my head. She still looked so lost and vulnerable, though the news just now should've soothed. What happened to her defences? My tough little sister had shed all her shells, her common sense was in shreds.

"I consider that illogical," I said. I deliberately avoided saying paranoid, or absurd.

She drew on her cigarette; her hand shook still too.

I smiled a thin smile at her. I tried a different tack, applied a little humour – and I meant it: "You appear to be ignoring the rather obvious – the lone male sexual appetite." I chuckled drily. "Friday evening, the end of the stressful week, time to let the trousers down. To put it less delicately than this Frau Daninger just did, your Herr Schulz was simply having it off with a high-class whore in a high-class hotel befitting his income."

"That's clear." Her tired eyes stared back; they were haunted and bleak. "But what happened then?"

"Who knows?" I shrugged. Flippantly I added: "Maybe he lost his grip – maybe they were doing it on the windowsill for thrills. What do we know of his preferences or perversions? Maybe he took a running jump and missed..."

"Don't be so frivolous. This is shitting serious."

"But not for you," I said.

"'Tis – if Matthias had any hand in it." She played a finger on the rim of her glass.

"You think he was hiding under the bed?"

Wearily she shook her head. Tapped ash. Then, lost in her thoughts, went on nervously tapping the cigarette.

Whatever I tried, I could see she wouldn't let go. So I said nothing.

"Been thinking 'bout who was in the know," she said. "'Bout who'd have a motive." She was talking to the table. "Only told you and Matthias."

"Well, half your company knew the problem too, presumably."

"But only two 'part from me've been discriminated 'gainst."

"And they've probably talked to others."

She pulled on the cigarette, watched me through smoke.

"Like stones thrown in water," I said. "More and more ripples." I reached, touched her arm. "Stop torturing yourself. It's making you crazy. In a moment you'll think it could've been me."

A phone began ringing. Not her mobile, though. It was further away.

She was nodding dumbly.

"Forget it," I said. "Whoever it was, the police'll find out. Let them do the worrying." The phone went on ringing – she seemed not to have heard.

I shook her arm. "Shall I go?"

She slipped from the stool. Went through the wide opening where they'd knocked down half the wall; she went like a wounded animal.

"Falk," I heard her say. I blinked; the wine was working its way into my vision. I forced myself to concentrate, flipped open her mobile, looked at the time. Half-past-eight. I thought: I'll ring Annabelle, before she makes plans for tomorrow. Removed my own mobile from my trouser pocket and pressed keys to retrieve her number...

"It's them," Eva said. She'd returned.

I stopped.

"The police. They're on their way. Kommissar Müller."

I looked at her. That sobered me up a bit; I realised that, like Margareth, she could carry alcohol better than I. I put my mobile down. Her eyes were hunted, now.

"Seems they never sleep," I said. She really looked a wreck.

She turned away, crossed to the enamel sinks.

"Relax," I said to her turned back. She was rinsing things, stacking them in a dishwasher one by one. "As the secretary said, only a formality, they have to check everyone."

While she busied herself I rang Annabelle's mobile. It was switched off. I tried her apartment number but it rang till the answering machine switched in. I thought nothing of it, she'd said she'd be busy; didn't leave a message. Anyway I wanted it to be a surprise.

Eva came back to the breakfast bar.

"Okay if I stay the night?" I said. I'd drunk more than I had for months. Maybe, too, it'd be better if she had company.

"Presumed you would." She reached for her cigarette pack, then changed her mind. I'm glad she did that.

"Do you have a spare room?"

"Yep. But it's not made up. Can come in with me."

I produced a weak smile; Annabelle was on my mind again. "Thanks," I said. My smile was gone before she noticed.

She fidgeted. I'd never known her so nervous.

"Relax," I repeated. "Just take a deep breath, take it slow."

The doorbell rang.

She showed the whites of her eyes. I touched her arm again and stroked it briefly as she jerkily made to stand. "I'd suggest you just answer their questions but don't offer more," I said. "And of course don't mention Matthias – no point helping them bark up the wrong tree."

"Christ, not a fool, you know." Her small mouth opened, for an instant she stared at me. "Something else," she said. "'Bout Matthias. Tell you later." She gulped in breath, shot it out; it was almost a gasp.

The bell rang again. She turned away.

"Am I in the way?" I said. "Shall I go next door?"

She was shaking her head rapidly. "For Christ's sake stay." She went out into the hall.

Indistinctly I heard her speak into a microphone and receive a crackling reply. Then the press of a buzzer for the electric lock downstairs and the sound of her opening the apartment door.

I stared into space. Distant footsteps on the timber staircase... a deep, clipped voice was suddenly saying: "Hauptkommissar Müller, *Kripo* Munich – Frau Falk?" coming from her hall. Murmurs. The deep voice added: "And this is my colleague Hauptkommissar Schumann, *Mordkommission* Nuremberg..."

I sat up. Schumann? I turned, surprised – and in the same instant a tiny twinge of apprehension pricked through my stomach. What could he be...

The three of them were coming in. Introductions. A very big man, fifties, crumpled suit, no offered hand. And there was Kommissar Schumann, his faint non-committal smile, his small quiet way.

"Good evening. A small world indeed, Herr Falk."

"Indeed," I echoed.

We were standing. He gave me his hand; so flaccid, it scarcely squeezed. "A separate case brought me down to this neck of the woods." Steady pale eyes behind rimless glasses. "Had no idea you'd be here."

No? I thought. "Ah," I said. The way he said it I could only believe.

He twinkled at Eva. "It was the name Falk. I checked – what a coincidence. You are his sister. Confess it made me curious, thought I'd come along. Well, well." He flapped a hand. "I had the pleasure of questioning your brother after that nasty beating he took in May. Unfortunate business." Looking round at his colleague, he ended: "Sorry, Eberhardt – the court's all yours, dear colleague." I noticed, like me, he had to look up to meet the massive man's eyes.

Eva watched me. A taut puzzled gaze.

"Perhaps we could be seated," Kommissar Müller said to her.

"No objection to my presence?" I asked.

"No."

We sat round the breakfast bar.

"Apologies for the lateness of the hour," Müller said. His bulging eyes had swivelled back to Eva. "We'll make it as brief as we can."

We? I thought.

Eva reached for her cigarettes, I put on my mask of apathy which Annabelle so abhorred.

He set off in a dry monotone; his Munich dialect was thick. Without making notes he took Eva's particulars, explained why he'd come. I suppose he'd stored them in his head. Then he rumbled on ponderously – he reminded me of a hippopotamus, or an unstoppable Russian tank.

"You joined the *Portacus* company eighteen years ago?"

"Yep." Eva hadn't moved a muscle for two minutes, the unlit cigarette was stiff and still between her fingers. Now her other hand stretched to the lighter. But Schumann was already there. A paternal nod, as if to a wayward child. Calmly he snapped it, held the flame before her face. I watched him watching her as she dipped her head...

"And a week ago last Wednesday you submitted your resignation," Müller was saying. "Why did you do that?"

"Personal reasons." She blew a sharp stream of smoke up towards the ceiling. "Was being discriminated against."

"By your superior, Herr Schulz?"

"Yep."

"Who entered the company about fourteen months ago?"

"Yep."

"No love lost between the two of you, then?"

"Slimy little creep." She spat it out. "Was brought in to force me and others out." But I saw she was well under control.

"I asked, no love lost then?"

"'Course not."

"You hate him?"

She stared coldly over the cigarette. "Despise him. Hate's too strong a word." Her cigarette hand trembled. She didn't look at me.

"And last Friday Herr Schulz unexpectedly met with an accident. You know about that, of course?"

"Yep."

"How do you know?"

"His secretary phoned me yesterday on my flight back. Told me."

"Ah yes." Müller removed an electronic pad from his jacket, placed it on the breakfast bar, switching it on. "You've been in Italy on business." He was stooping, peering; his neck was so thick he had to tip his body, he hardly bent his head. "Since last Sunday. Correct?" The glowing display reflected in his heavy polished face.

"Yep."

"Was that the first time you learned of the accident?"
"Yep."
"From Frau Daninger?"
"Correct."
"You landed at Franz-Joseph about 2pm and went straight to your company offices?"
"Yep."
"Why?"
"Max called me on the phone ten minutes after Frau Daninger. Company owner. Said would I come straight by."
"Why?"
"Offered me Shultz's position."
"How very convenient, Frau Falk. In one foul swoop all your problems solved."
"No."
"No?"
"Refused the offer."
"Yesterday."
"Yesterday."
"And tomorrow? Or next week?" A touch of sarcasm in Müller's voice. "Your boss is certain you'll change your mind."
"He's a lousy judge of character."
"You're a dedicated career woman, I am told. This job's your life. It's a calling."
"Was."

Müller watched her unperturbed. "Curious chain of events, wouldn't you say? Discrimination, bitterness, your long career in the company destroyed, you hand in your resignation..." he intoned like a monk at prayer "...then a convenient accident and you're offered reinstatement with an even better position to boot."

Eva tapped ash, aggressively. "Life's full of unplanned twists and turns."

"Unplanned?" A wry expression on his powerful face. "You had motive and opportunity to incapacitate Herr Schulz, Frau Falk."

"Motive? P'raps in your eyes, not mine." She blew smoke. She blew it as if in disgust. "And opportunity? Poppycock. Not even if I'd wanted."

"One fact at a time, please. First, motivation. I am informed that before Herr Schulz came on board you practically ran the company. It was, so to speak, your baby. Correct?"

"Under Max's brother Alex, yep. But that's ol' hat now."

"Is it, Frau Falk? I am also informed that you're a fighter. You're not one to give up, take things lying down."

"Did fight back. At first. Just kicking 'gainst the pricks, though."

"Were you? We only have your word for it. Secretly you still harboured resentment."

"Sure. But didn't help a jot. Schulz's orders came from CEO Reubel and his came straight from new owner Max who can't stand strong women." Eva crushed out the cigarette with short sharp stabs. "'Gainst those odds end of the road's end of the road. Writing was on the wall."

"Resentment rankles, Frau Falk. As I said, we only have your word. And apart from possible motive you had opportunity, too." Müller tipped his body forward again unhurriedly, referred to his glowing display. "On the Friday of the accident you were on the company premises. Till when?"

"Late afternoon."

"When precisely, please?"

"'Bout five-forty-five."

"Herr Schulz left the building shortly before five-thirty. Did you hear or see him leave?"

"No."

"Quite certain? Your office is only two doors away."

"Yep. Was busy, in the last throes. Last trip to Italy to say my farewells."

"He apparently had an appointment. Did you know that?"

"No idea."

"Shortly prior to leaving he received a phone call from a man, allegedly from Paris, allegedly on orders from a Herr Cohen, an American. A very good client of yours. Do you know who this man could have been?"

Eva shrugged. "Probably Delon." Her small shoulders looked so thin.

"It wasn't. We checked. No-one from Herr Cohen's company rang yours on that day."

Eva was watching Müller carefully. For a moment she glanced at me. Those dark hollow eyes were unreadable. Then they were gone. Rapidly she retorted: "Check the number, then. Incoming calls're stored in our displays."

"We did. It was a no-number call. Ones from the Paris office are not anonymous, but ones from your company are. Were you alone in your office between five-fifteen and five-thirty on that Friday?"

"Yep."

"No male visitor? No company colleague? Did a man place a call from your phone?"

"No chance."

"Did you instruct any man to ring Herr Schulz at that time?"

"No, for Christ's sake." Eva jerked at the ashtray. It was gripped tightly in her hand.

"Did you place a call to the *Four Season's Hotel* the previous day, Thursday, and reserve a room in Herr Schulz's name?"

"You're kidding. He's got a secretary for chores like that."

"Yes or no?"

"'Course not, dammit."

I watched her. Anger had taken over from her anxiety and her fear. I thought: don't throw that ashtray, sister, you've been doing so well.

Calmly, imperturbably, Müller laid down his hands each side of the pad. "On the Friday you say you left the company at approximately 5:45pm. Did anyone see you go? Anyone who could confirm the fact?" His hands lay there like lumps of meat.

She shook her cropped head.

"No colleagues around, office cleaners? No caretaker?"

"Popped my head in to Frau Daninger to say cheerio. Mondays and Fridays always works late. Wasn't there, though. Lights were on – prob'ly in the loo."

"No-one else?"

"Didn't look. 'Cept to see that security weren't there. Prob'ly on their rounds."

"You left by car?"

"Yep."

"Where did you go?"

"Straight home."

"Home is here?"

"'Course."

"Did anyone witness your arrival?"

"Doubt it. Didn't notice anyone. Quiet neighbourhood."

"The insurance company on the ground floor? No-one see you?"

"Think they'd gone."

"Did you stop on the way home? Shopping, cigarettes, filling up with petrol, anything like that?"

"Nope. Was going on a business trip. Had everything."

"We're talking about witnesses, Frau Falk. Someone who can corroborate your story."

"Not a story."

"You know what I mean."

"Plain as daylight." She glowered. Finished fiddling with the ashtray, let it go.

"What time did you arrive here, would you estimate?"

"Friday rush-hour – took an age. Reckon best part of an hour."

"About six-forty-five, then? Would that be correct?"

"Yep."

"Did your route take you past the *Four Seasons*?"

"You're kidding." She balled her small hands. "No," she said, emphatically.

"Herr Schulz picked up an envelope and a room key from the reception around 6pm. At six-fifteen he fell from the third-storey window. About the same time, a woman was observed coming out of his room. You seemingly have no alibi for this period of time. Were you this woman, Frau Falk?"

"For crying out loud, no. Just said."

"Again – we only have your word for it."

Eva grasped her packet of cigarettes. "Listen, for Christ's sake. Most of them know me at the *Four Seasons* – reception, bar, doormen." Exasperation in her small fingers. "Go there regularly with customers. Someone would've recognised me." She played with the packet, glanced up, glanced at me, back at Müller. "Frau Daninger said on the phone she was prob'ly a call-girl. Do I look like a bloody call-girl, then?"

"Appearances can be deceptive," Müller said evenly.

"Poppycock. Got a face, haven't I?"

For a moment no-one spoke.

I cleared my throat. Thought I might be permitted a question. "Did she look like my sister?" I said.

Kommissar Müller turned slowly towards me; he twisted the whole top of his body. "For what little it's worth, the woman in question was blonde, slim, wore bright-red stilettos and black net stockings – and what are euphemistically called hot pants, colour turquoise."

He eyed me with his bulging eyes then just as slowly turned back to Eva. "Are you, or were you one week ago, in possession of clothes of this description, Frau Falk?"

"'Cept for the stockings, over my dead body," she told him curtly.

"Well, sister," I said, "and how do you like the insinuation that you're in fact a peroxide whore?" I peered myopically at her, cocked my head on one side.

Ponderously, Müller said: "A somewhat naïve observation, Herr Falk. Makeup and a wig can work wonders to alter a lady's personage." Sluggishly he turned his hands outwards. "Dress up ten ladies in the same garb and they look like ten peas in a pod."

He regarded Eva steadily. "Let us come back to the second troubling factor, Frau Falk – the man who rang Herr Schulz at five-twenty last Friday. We believe this call was the reason Herr Schulz unexpectedly cancelled a meeting and shortly afterwards left for the *Four Seasons* in such a hurry." He paused, watching.

She shrugged her thin shoulders. "How should I know?"

"You just stated that you instructed no-one to place this call. Let us assume you are telling the truth. Perhaps, though, unbeknown to you someone close to you was acting in your interests?"

"Just said, how the hell should I know?"

"A colleague, a friend? A relative? Someone in the know?"

She kept her eyes on him, stared back. Tossed her head. "All of sales knew what this little creep was up to."

"And outside the company? Who did you talk to about your unpleasant situation?"

"Hardly a soul. No-one who'd shove the bastard out of a window."

"Who, Frau Falk?"

"My brother here, and my therapist. 'Course my lawyer, too."

"Who else?"

"That's it."

"A girlfriend, surely. A woman always confides in her best friend."

"Nope. Couldn't go stressing her, has 'nough on her plate."

"A man-friend, then? You're single, I am informed. What about a boyfriend?"

"Nope."

"You have no boyfriend?"

"Did eighteen months ago. Gave him the boot. Englishman – hit the road Jack."

A slow stiff nod. Müller drew his pad nearer, a slender steel pointer poised in his hand. "The names of your therapist and lawyer, please." He listened, tapped keys rapidly.

Kommissar Schumann coughed politely. "Permit me to ask a question." He was gazing straight at me. "Where were you at the time of this tragic accident, Herr Falk?"

"In a rehabilitation centre," I said. "About equidistant between Nuremberg and Munich." I gave him the name.

"Doing precisely what?" The lenses of his glasses tipped, caught the summer evening sun; I couldn't see his eyes.

I considered. "I believe," I said, "sitting in the Jacuzzi surrounded by lots of bubbles and discovering with amusement the buoyancy of my knees."

"You didn't by any chance make a little trip to the *Four Seasons* that day?"

"I have to disappoint. The gymnastic classes lasted till four-thirty on Fridays to keep us on our toes, and the rules of attendance were rather strict."

"But naturally you had a telephone in your room, and a mobile?"

"Both."

"So you could place calls undisturbed."

"Which I often did."

"And all of which would be traceable to the numbers you dialled, Herr Falk?"

"I confess I hadn't considered the thought." I shrugged. "But no doubt you're right."

A quiet smile, a brief nodding of the head. "And when, if you have no objection to my enquiring, did you arrive here in Munich? Yesterday? Today?"

"About two hours ago," I said. I could see his eyes again, paternal and relaxed and pale.

"Just popping down?"

"Yes," I said.

"And back to rehabilitation when?"

"I discharged myself this morning."

"Ah." Another nod; the flash of sun came and went. "Anything remarkable about the journey down today?"

I spread my hands. "Till Garching Nord all was fine. Then lots of blue lights and all those little orange plastic hats."

"Ah yes. In your direction?"

"Northbound."

"Ah yes."

"Your colleagues looked quite busy," I suggested.

"Well, not quite our direct colleagues, poor chaps. We're Criminal Police and Murder Squad, you recall."

Müller had switched off his notepad, was closing it. I watched Schumann. Relaxedly he returned my gaze, he blinked like a satisfied cat. You're the quiet one, I thought. Still waters run deep. Thank God we've nothing to do with this business, you'll be the one to undo it all if anyone does.

x x x

They took their leave of Eva. Müller told her to keep herself available, he'd be in touch. It sounded like a threat.

I went down the stairs with them; had to fetch my things for the night. The air was clammy and close, felt like a storm, late sun behind trees – it would be gone in less than an hour. Warm, soft, pastoral light. From the north, though, black clouds were massing, rolling overhead. In the drive, not so far from my car, stood a large silver BMW – one of those very big ones. Kommissar Müller opened the left-hand driver's door.

"I'm glad to see that taxpayer's money is being spent on quality," I said to him. I said it with a serious smile.

With a grunt he got in; in spite of his bulk the suspension didn't seem to sag an inch. He left the door open. In fact he'd only half rolled in, one leg still hung out, one solid foot on the gravel. He was leaning, picking up a mobile phone from its black nest between the two luxury front seats. I stepped back. Then I saw it, and stopped. It gave me a bit of a start. It was dark grey, and clipped below the armrest on the inside of the passenger door beyond him – a submachine gun, a nasty looking thing.

"Well, I'll be saying farewell," Kommissar Schumann said quietly behind me. And I turned. Unusual to meet a man so small, he was scarcely taller than me. I thought: does he know how to use that thing? Could he grab it and point it, squeeze the trigger and blow people to pieces? He stood there, plain, inconspicuous – reaching out. Little spotted bowtie, white summer shirt; he must've left his jacket in the car.

Müller was speaking into the phone behind me.

Touching my arm, not shaking my hand, Schumann drew me away. And, almost as if as an afterthought, he said: "Are you thinking of going abroad in the next few weeks, by the way?" He asked it so blandly, as though enquiring about the weather or ordering an unwanted cup of tea.

"You must be telepathic," I said. Inside I thought: did you know or did you guess? You're a wily one, why did you go and ask that?

"Ah – anything specific?"

"Florence. A last breather before getting back to the grind."

"Ah, Florence. How very nice. Medici and wealth and courtesans, now ancient city of culture and luxury leather. Your sister's company deals in leather articles, too, if I'm not mistaken."

"You're not."

"In fact that's where she flew back from yesterday, I believe."

"Yes."

"Coincidence?"

"Purely," I said.

"Small world, to be sure. And when are you off?"

"Tomorrow afternoon."

"Driving down?" He was turning; his hand fluttered towards my parked car. "Lovely old lady – is she yours?"

"She is."

"Sixty-five?"

I blinked. I'd already heard that once before today. "Sixty-seven," I corrected.

"You going in her?"

"No. Too far. I'm..."

"They don't build them this way any more." A nostalgic look in his face; he was looking with love.

"She's just my getaway car," I said, to pull his leg. "When things get too hot."

"Too hot?" His eyes twinkled. They were mild and merry; seemed so harmless.

"The weather," I said. "I put down the hood, get away into the country, to shady landscapes and lanes, potter about."

He chuckled. "Well, I didn't expect you meant us hot on your heels, like Bonnie and Clyde." His mirth melted, but the mildness was still there behind those rimless little glasses. "Flying down?"

"Yes," I said.

"Alone?"

"No."

"Is she popping down there again with you? Your most attractive and what one might be permitted to call high-power sister?"

"No."

"Nasty business, discrimination. There's too much of it going on nowadays."

"Yes." I had to concentrate, to follow his turns – the effect of the wine had left me tired.

"Not my beat, of course. But my heart goes out to her, you know. I have a daughter, too. Don't know what I'd feel and do if the same thing were to happen to her."

"Well," I said. "I wouldn't advise you to push him out of a window."

He was watching me. Those kindly eyes. "What d'you think? Could it be revenge of some kind?"

"Sounds a bit like it," I said.

"It does, doesn't it."

"But my sister would never condone a thing like that. She's a woman of principle. And a realist."

"And you, Herr Falk? Are you that, too?"

"I'm just a realist."

"Yes – yes, that's what I thought," he mused. Almost sleepily. Then, more brightly: "Going alone, perhaps?"

I blinked. He was back to Florence again. "With a friend," I said.

"A male friend, if I'm permitted to ask?"

"A woman."

"How very romantic. For long?"

"I'll be back at the end of the week."

"That's fine. Just asked should anything else new crop up on that other case you were involved in and I need to get in touch." Behind his glasses his eyes beamed pleasantly.

I glanced at the brand-new BMW. Müller was still on the phone, speaking quietly, staring ahead, his powerful leg hanging out unmoved. His big free hand was raised now, though, gripping the curved edge of the roof while he spoke. I looked back at Schumann. I thought: have they planned this? They seemed to work together like a well-oiled team.

Schumann hovered there. Like a friendly ghost. He seemed in no hurry to go and get into the car. So I said: "Should anything crop up?" I asked it matter-of-factly.

"Well, actually yes. And something already has."

I stood there. My car keys hung from my hand. Something said to me: stop now, there's nothing holding you – get your things and go back up to Eva.

"Rather extraordinary, really," Schumann pattered on. "We never nailed those four nasty pieces of work, you know. Then out of the blue one of them gave himself up. Here in Munich, four days ago. Didn't you read about it?"

"No," I heard myself say.

"Scared as a rabbit, he was. Have you ever known a Neo-Nazi to show he's scared? Apparently prefers jail to the threat of a renegade crony from the scene. Sadistic bunch of characters. He wouldn't squeak, except to say his three fellow desperados from that night had made a scoot. Gone underground, as he put it. What d'you make of that, Herr Falk?"

I shrugged. No comment. What could I say?

"We grilled him, of course, but got practically nothing. Apart from one little slip. That night they beat up the Turks and you got in the way, something stopped them finishing the job. Appears this turncoat butted in. What d'you think, Herr Falk? Possible?"

"Perhaps."

I was going back, I was on the cobbles again, I was closing my eyes. "Somebody else," I said. Yes, I thought – there could've been. There was the nausea and pain again too, I was scared to death, I was peeing in my pants – the taste of blood, the stink of their sweat, the smell of my fear. And that glint on metal very close and that other smell, that reek of machinery, that reek of oil.

I opened my eyes. Sun in trees.

And Schumann nodding. "We now believe so, too. A fifth person, an ex-comrade turned traitor. It wasn't a V-man, we're fairly sure. We know of one character who deserted this group, but we'd assumed he'd moved further afield – Thüringen, or further east. Perhaps not, though, perhaps it was him."

"He had a gun?" I said. The thought just appeared in my head. Like the weapon in the BMW over there? Maybe that's what did it – the association. Yes, maybe that's what I'd smelt. I didn't remember much from that quarry in my schooldays, only what Matthias taught me about breathing and squeezing calmly, but the recollection of that smell on my hand afterwards as I handed him back his father's revolver hadn't quite gone – yes, it could have been the oil of a gun.

"A plausible explanation, Herr Falk. You told us there was a glint of light in your face for a second, from a knife. It could have been from the barrel of a gun, couldn't it?"

"There was a mechanical smell," I said. "A smell like oil."

"You omitted to tell me that."

"I omitted to tell myself. I failed to persuade myself. It didn't fit in."

"Is there anything else you forgot to tell, Herr Falk?" The voice was quiet and easy, there was no reproach.

"No."

"Quite sure?"

"Yes."

"Very good."

He was giving me his hand. Light and soft, hardly real. "I'll give you a tinkle should there be further developments. Who knows – perhaps the other three will give themselves up if they lose their nerves. Might require you for an identification line-up." A fleeting smile. "Franzi's one of them, remember? You heard the name."

I nodded. "Goodnight, Herr Kommissar."

"Herr Falk." A polite dip of the head. Glimpse of pale thinning hair.

His hand was gone, he was turning away. Then over his shoulder he added lightly: "Our friend's been charged, of course – it'll be coming to court some time late in summer. You'll be called as witness, naturally, and notified in due course. Only a formality, I imagine – not to worry."

I watched him walk quietly round the BMW and get into the passenger seat; he got in on the side of the automatic weapon, closed the silver door. And as he closed it I saw a shadow move on the back seat – someone was sitting there. I bent and peeped – the light was bad, but I recognised the face. It was the woman from the Mini.

I felt suddenly cold. I raised my eyes: the dark clouds had nearly covered the sky and the wind was getting up. In the west was a brilliant line of gold, the night closed down like a lid.

Chapter 18

Beyond the windscreen early sun streamed through wet trees. I stayed sitting in my car as Eva drove off. Wound down the window. Sunk in the old leather I rang Annabelle's apartment, waited for her to answer. My pulse was unsteady, my heart on my sleeve. I felt the thrill in advance.

There'd been quite a bit of rain in the night; the air was cool on my elbow resting on the chrome, the mugginess of last night had gone.

The ringing tone went on and on, then the answering machine switched in like it had done the evening before. I looked at the clock on the dashboard. Almost seven-forty-five. I hadn't considered that; perhaps a little early, she'd still be asleep. How late had she got back last night?

I left a brief message to ring me. Didn't say I was here in Munich. Ah – that element of surprise. She'd see the red light blinking when she arose. I imagined her standing there, naked, or in her ethereal gown, saw her stooping to press the button to hear my voice.

Still I remained sitting. Savouring the light on the leaves. No hurry. Plenty of time.

My thoughts wandered for a moment to Eva, driving over to console her sick colleague when it was she who needed a prop – then they jumped to Eva's words at the end of yesterday evening. "Something not kosher 'bout him," she'd said. "It's as if he's gone to earth again, as if he doesn't exist." She'd been speaking of Matthias again, and she wouldn't let go of the subject till I suggested it was time to go to bed. Her words undermined, I had to admit.

A woodpigeon was cooing. It reminded me of my childhood; it was such a soothing sound.

I decided: I'll drive over to Annabelle's place – I'll take her call on the way. Win half an hour, extend the morning with her, maybe enjoy a second breakfast.

I started the engine, let it idle. Deep and throaty in the quiet, sleepy Saturday neighbourhood. Relaxedly, leisurely, elbow still hung out of the window, I drove off along the sweep of drive. Turned into the tree-lined avenue, heading towards the centre of the city.

My mobile lay on the passenger seat beside me; I was ready for her call. Idly I watched the street ahead, looking for places to pause when the ring came. The streets went by, one by one – ten minutes passed, fifteen. She'll be awake now, I thought. Getting up now. Maybe taking a shower before going through: she'd pass the telephone on her way to the kitchen.

The weekend traffic was getting heavier the nearer I came to the inner city ring. I stuck in jams at every traffic light. Didn't matter – I had all the time in the world.

About forty minutes from Ferdinand-Marie Straße I reached the square in Schwabing with its small park where Annabelle lived. Plane trees, drying ground mottled with shade, empty park benches. Peering, I sought an empty parking space. I thought: it's early enough, I'll be lucky, it's my lucky day...

My mobile rang...

My heart jumped, thrilled. What perfect timing. Everything falling into place.

There...

I indicated, steered towards a free space. But another car, a little Mini from the opposite direction, braked, darted in before me. Cheeky bugger. I stopped alongside the row of cars. Full of anticipation, quickly picked up the mobile...

An SMS. The lighted display didn't say who. I thumbed the keys... the message appeared. Only an ad from my phone company.

Disappointment.

I erased the text without reading it. Glanced at the clock. Eight-forty-three. I put the car in gear, began moving off. At least she must be awake now – I'll simply go up and surprise her. Oh God... I braked hard... I was so distracted I'd nearly knocked down the young man emerging from between cars from his Mini. He grinned at me, I just shook my head and drove on slowly, looking for another free space. The morning was already warming up.

It took all of ten minutes.

Walking back along the side street with the bonsai, trickles of perspiration tickled my face – from the sun, from the exertion of parking a big old car in a constricted space. The heavy pot dripped a few drops of water now and then. I'd left the old metal tray lying on the car floor; I held the pot ahead of me out of reach of my feet.

Reaching her house, I traversed the small forecourt between pavement and portico, rang her bell. My feelings welled again at what was to come – I felt the excitement at the thought of her face.

No reaction.

I pressed again.

Still nothing. No voice crackling in the microphone, no buzz of the automatic lock. I stepped back, craned my neck, looking up. Stupidly. As if I'd find her four storeys up leaned on the terrace rails.

What to do?

I searched about in my head – for an explanation, for where she could be. Yes. Perhaps she was on the phone, hadn't heard the doorbell. Could be. Then ring her number and see. I set the bonsai over in the corner of the colossal portal in which the modern glass entranceway had been built, took out my mobile, called the number. Not engaged. It rang; I waited. A click – the answering machine started to speak again. The fragment of hope disintegrated.

Ring her mobile. I tried. Still switched off. Maybe she'd left very early to beat the traffic, gone shopping. Tentatively I pushed at the glass front door in its sea of glazing. It was locked, didn't budge. I stood there helpless, staring at my reflection in the glass, wondering what to do now. I'd just have to wait. But where? And for how long? Would she be returning soon, or later? Or had she settled everything quicker than expected and was already on her way back down to the Tegernsee lake and the children?

Well, no point standing here dithering. I retrieved the bonsai. Go to a café and wait – don't automatically assume the worst. I peered, tipping the big pot, looked at my watch. Not yet nine...

A curious cold sensation – on my trouser front. Awkwardly I glanced – oh God. Water had trickled out of the drain-holes in the ceramic pot. Crouching, putting it down again, I bent and wiped at the dirty wetness with my paper handkerchief...

And as I did the entrance door opened. Rapidly I glanced up. But no, not Annabelle. A dapper little sunburnt man of about fifty was emerging. Nip in quick, I thought – I grasped at the pot, hoisted it. A manicured hand was propping open the glass door for two white Pekinese dogs straining on leads, a slim body arched to let them march through.

"Good morning," I called.

A quiver of surprise, a high-pitched voice. "Oh hel-*lo*." Performing a neat pirouette and a wiggle, he twisted to avoid tripping over the leads and took me in from top to toe. Professionally, appraisingly. So did his two Pekinese: bulging eyes, silly sniffling things, both with pink bows on their heads.

"Falk," I said. "Friend of Annabelle Binoche. I wonder..."

"Oh my *dear*." A brilliant smile, disarming. "You must be the *lover*." He tittered – like a bird, like tinkling water. Released the door, fingers flitting through the air.

"Well..." I began, disconcerted.

"Oh *shame* on me, don't tell me I've made a teeny-weeny faux pas?" A delicate raised hand, the leads pinched between finger and thumb as if picking up a dead rat. The front door fell to with a definitive click. And the dogs were coming at me...

"No," I said. "I suppose one could..." A set of sharp teeth grabbed my sandal strap, sticky saliva smeared my bare foot, hot doggy breath on my skin. Excited snuffling and sneezing from the other one.

"How *abso*lutely delightful. Detlef told me *all* about you."

"Detlef?" I searched about...

"But darling, yes, the piano soirée with our a*dor*able Annabelle up on the fourth. Detlef had to go alone – I was *devastated* to miss it all, you know."

"Ah, yes." I remembered. Nasty little teeth still worrying at the strap. I shook my foot. Then the beast got me by the big toe, bit hard. I winced, nearly dropped the pot.

"De-*bor*a, what are you *doing*, darling – leave that gorgeous foot alone." He gave an ineffectual tug. And to my eyes another radiant smile.

Surreptitiously I gave a kick, contacted furry flesh. Little bugger, I thought. A sudden snarl, then snorting. But at least the teeth released my toe. Thoughtfully they transferred themselves to the sandal buckle instead, began tearing at it...

"I'm Georgie Poost – Georgie-girl to all my *special* friends. And you must be Stefan. How en-*chan*-ting."

"Stefan, yes..."

"So delighted." He held out a slender hand, like a queen. A golden chain dangled...

I could only offer a little finger. He touched it gently, stroking his palm along it. A snuffle. I peered down past the pot: the second Pekinese was inspecting my trouser leg intently.

"Nice to meet you, Georgie," I said. "I wonder if..."

A wet nose snorted and delved... then a tug, an unpleasant tautness on trouser cloth. I jerked – face half-buried in the bonsai I did a little dance, retreating...

"Debora, De-*li*-lah...!" A roll of the eyes, tugging twitches on the leads. "Girls, you absolutely *naughty* girls, come to mother at *once*." With *Ben Hur* chariot-race-like effort his slender body reined the snorting little bastards in. "Darling, I do a*polo*gise."

"No problem." I wriggled my toes to reduce the pain, glanced down briefly again. Both Pekinese were three safe feet away now, it seemed they were satisfied, seemed they'd had their fill. "I wonder, Georgie, if you'd be so good and let me in. It seems..."

"Oh my dear, of course." A flutter. "And such a *gor*geous bonsai. Absolutely *divine*! A little surprise for our pet Annabelle perhaps?"

"Actually, yes."

"How un-*beat*-ably divine! Oriental knick-knacks always win her heart." He let out a sigh, then his face puckered. "Darling, at the unpardonable expense of being an itsy-bitsy inquisitive, were you hoping to find her at home?"

"Yes. Actually I..."

"Oh how ghastly! I'm afraid I must be beastly and disappoint you. She was up with the lark in the weenie hours and out of the house at seven."

I swallowed. A lump clogged my lungs. With difficulty I said: "Did she say if and when she'd be back?"

"Oh tragedy, no! I only caught a teeny glimpse from our window of her driving off while I was busy squeezing Detlef's juice."

She's gone, I thought. I've missed her. She's off for the day – or driving back to the Tegersee. Everything was heavy, now.

"Oh, what *shall* we do?" He fluttered his free hand again. Like a mirror, his expression had taken on the colour of my anguish.

I found it hard to speak. Was this the end of Florence?

"My dear, I have to say she gave Detlef her spare keys yesterday – something about a little holiday. We play policemen for each other, you see. One can never be too careful nowadays, can one – with all these *horrid* weird people about?" His soft lilting words faded into a wince of pain. "Oh dear, oh dear, I fear..."

"Yes," I said. That's it, I thought. I sank deeper. "She told me she wouldn't be leaving till next Tuesday," I managed to mutter, but I was talking more to myself. "It seems she's..." My turn to give up the sentence. And the bonsai was getting heavy.

A brightening of his delicate face. "Oh heavens, but it's only Saturday! Then, there's hope!" Eyes widening, watching, picking up every signal and crumb. "Then I'm sure there's a weenie chance!"

What to do? Blackness closing in. Shit. I dithered. Stared down at the bonsai. Then back up at Georgie. Well – I was here now, so...

I decided.

"Listen, Georgie, I'll go up and wait for a bit. If you'd..."

"My dear, of course." He made another hurried little pirouette, tugging happily on the leads. Another burst of sneezing from the dogs. He crossed busily, waggling, back to the entrance door. "I'm sure there's much *more* than a weenie chance..."

I followed. He'd produced a key on a golden chain, was inserting it. The door opened, he held it wide. "Thanks, Georgie." I was passing through, craning my head downwards, watching out for stretched leads and teeth. "I'll let myself out..."

A scrabbling, a scuffle, one of the dogs rubbed dangerously close... "No, Debora – you're *not* to wee-wee here..." And then: "Such a pleasure, my dear. I shall pop in for a quickie to deposit the darlings in about an hour, then have to rush to a rendezvous. But later, if there's *anything* I can do..."

More sneezing and snorting... "Yes, yes, my little sweeties, you know I'm talking about you, don't you."

"Thanks, Georgie."

"Ours is the bell on the first with D and G in squiggly gold. Just give it three *tiny* tweaks and I'll know it's you."

I had paused, turned briefly. "Well, I'd be grateful for one small favour," I said quickly, round miniature branches and clusters of needles. "Should Annabelle not come back, may I put the bonsai by your door to be watered till her return?"

"Oh but of course, my dear. Don't forget – three tiny tweaks. Just our little secret. Detlef's at a conference so I'm all alone. Would so *adore* to help"

"Thanks Georgie."

"Toot-a-loo. So en*chan*ting..."

He'd let go the door; it zished, and closed. For a second I stood there in the hallway staring through glass: blinding sunlight, the trees of the square beyond, and the figure of Georgie wiggling away, feet delicately tripping as if traversing broken glass.

x x x

I crossed the elegant hallway; Italian marble with fountain in the middle, glittering glass and stainless steel, the generous curving sweep of the stairs. Took the lift to the fourth floor.

Sunlight streaming through sloping glass, the row of potted trees, the strip of carpet set in stone leading to her apartment door. With care I set the bonsai down. Inspected the front of my trousers – damp, pale-brown stains. Oh God. No tap, no cloth to expunge the worst.

I rang the bell again, just in case, heard its echo. Unanswered sound on listening walls. Pointless. I looked at my watch: ten-past-nine. Go to a nearby café? Or wait here? A café would be more comfortable, I could read the papers – remove the worst of the stains too, let them dry in the sun. But if I left the house now how would I get back in? Here I can't miss her – assuming, that is, a miracle happens.

I decided to stay put, give it a try.

I sat down, back to the wall, stretched out my legs. Wiggled my toes. The big one throbbed. I removed the sandal, inspected: nothing much, a few spots of dried blood, not swollen. Leaned back again, let my thoughts wander.

An hour passed.

I tried Annabelle's mobile again. Nothing. Still switched off. I stood up, stretching, rubbed my backside to restore circulation. Walked back and forth for a couple of minutes. Then leaned on the balustrade. Armoured glass, stainless steel tubular handrail clipped on top. I shook it: solid as rock. I peered over, looking down –

quickly stepped back. Sheer drop to the hall below, and the fountain; made me dizzy, I'm not good at heights.

Sat down again. Waiting again.

Was there any point? I shook my head. Where was she now – in Munich still, somewhere, settling things – or down in the mountains? If she'd set off at seven she'd be there already. Was she lying in the shade chatting to Margareth, or listening to the children play? Maybe she was looking down to the lake, glad to get away from it all – could one see the lake from where her great-uncle's house lay?

And here was I sitting here like an imbecile, not knowing. My God, why hadn't I told her in advance, why hadn't I played it safe? It was like a bad film – yes I felt such a fool...

A sound.

It echoed up from the hall – the distant click of a door snapping shut. And footsteps... feminine footsteps. My heart leapt, overjoyed. This could be her. The reprieve. I'd been too pessimistic, how stupid: patience always wins its reward. And we still had lots of time. I stood up, heart bumping, leaned gingerly over the balustrade, holding on tight. Could see no-one. I peered sideways: the spiralling staircase around the curved elevator core was deserted, too. Then... a yapping of dogs far below, and a high familiar voice shushing – the hum of the summoned lift.

I stepped back. Disappointment, disillusion; I think my whole being sagged. Instinct told me to give up, this was a losing game. But I managed to persuade myself: I sat down to wait again. Stared into space. Pity I didn't have my newspaper, something to read; stupidly it was in my hand-luggage in the car.

My eyes wandered, my mind wandered. For a moment it settled on Georgie again and I found myself thinking about him, his mannerisms and kindness and grace – but quickly his image got confused, it melted into that of George Sunday. And despite myself I had to grin. There was George my intrepid friend, the propper-up of bars and hero of the bed, dressed in drag for a dreadful fancy-dress *Fasching* party he'd insisted I accompany him to. This gangly chinless wonder had transformed himself into a slinky pink dragqueen and the way he walked into that party, the way he moved, he was Georgie to a tee...

I shook my head, hurriedly cast the memory aside in profound reverence to Georgie Poost. He couldn't help how he was, could he, just as I couldn't for what I wasn't. The memory of the waggling miniskirt was gone, so were the feathers and furs and the chorus of helpless laughter – but George's face was still there.

I frowned. No. Not that one... for God's sake don't start...

He was bending forward over a bar-top with a lecherous leer, we were both rather pissed. Beer and smoke, his gallows' humour and dreadful ditties, we'd been doing our very best to concentrate. His Adam's apple was going up and down like a golf ball as he spoke, what was he saying? – "...beneath the spreading chestnut tree the village idiot sat..." – a pause to politely belch, a glassy stare downwards at his bony hands laid flat on the bar – "...amusing himself by abusing himself, catching the drops in his hat." He cackled, swung bleary eyes to me but missed my face, nearly over-balanced from the bar-stool. "Wanna hear another one, real British one?"

"No."

Another cackle. "There was a young lady from Ealing who had a most peculiar feeling, she lay on her back and..." – he was gone, tipping backwards in slow-motion, still in perfect sitting position with those hands spreadeagled but now high in the air - "...opened her crack and..." and crashed to the floor. That was the night I had to get him to the clinic with severe concussion, I never got to hear the last line...

I forced myself to look away. No more George Sunday. Please, that's enough of George. Time to put my mind to more serious things. So I thought about Eva.

Slowly the sun rose. The shadows of the potted trees on the wall crept downwards; the sun burned through the glass on the top of my head. I heard Georgie leave, just as he said he would; I could recognise his footsteps now. There was nobody else. Nobody else came or went – it was as if the house were asleep, or dead. Only once did a sound make me start, bring a prick of hope. There was a click, a sudden buzzing noise, but it was only electric motors overhead, sun-blinds unrolling down glass. They bathed me in striped green shade.

I looked at my watch. Nearly eleven. She hadn't come.

What should I do? I was being punished, wasn't I? Punished for my presumption. One's not allowed to fool with fate. I could feel it in my gut, it wasn't going to work out.

Give it just a few minutes more. Then go.

I rose again, stretched again. My legs were cramped, my joints were stiff. I crossed to the stairs, sat down on a step, leaned sideways against the elevator core. Green light. The air was warm and close. Thoughts of Florence. Thoughts of how it might have been. My head felt heavy, I closed my eyes...

Must have dozed off. I awoke – orientating. I'd had a dream. I sat up with a start. Listening. Had I heard something? I concentrated, cocked my head on one side. Nothing. Still as the grave. What had woken me, then? The dream? What had I dreamt? No idea. The dream was gone...

I shifted my body. And then I realised – my bladder was full. Oh God, I needed a pee, and pretty desperately. Where to go? Hurriedly checked my watch. Ten-past-twelve. My heart fell into my stomach, lodged like a stone. Well, that was that – that was the limit anyway, the point of no return. I'd calculated backwards twice already: the flight left at three – an hour and a half for check-in and security, over an hour to the airport, at least half an hour for Annabelle to pack. Up till twelve that'd be running it close, later than that we'd never make it. I stared at my feet, at my shattered plans; I was a broken man.

I stood up. The Italian café, where we'd bought ices for the children, they'd let me use their toilet. I brushed at my clothes. Try her number quickly – just a very last try, perhaps... I tried. Only the mailbox. Of all days, why the hell had she gone and switched it off today?

I went down the stairs as fast as I could, at least it'd be quicker than waiting for the lift. Three-quarters down I remembered the bonsai – I'd told Georgie I would put it in front of his door. Go back up? Oh hell. My bladder told me not to risk it. He'd check, wouldn't he? Georgie wasn't like me, Georgie was a thoughtful guy.

The hallway was devoid of life. I crossed to the glass entrance-door, opened it. Was just walking out when I accidentally caught sight of the electric lock in the jamb. I stopped and stooped, inspecting it. My God, why hadn't I thought of that before? Yes – there it was, a tiny catch to release the latch. I crouched down...

My mobile rang. Made me jump. Jerking upright and blocking the door open with my bottom, I scrabbled in my hip-pocket, extricated it. The ringing cut off; I'd forgotten to secure the keys, unintentionally cancelled the call. Agitated, I retrieved the number. The sunlight was so bright I had to shade the display with my other hand, squinting and bending, craning my neck to read it. It was Annabelle's number. I nearly jumped for joy.

With labouring heart and nervous finger I called it back. Engaged. I thought: wait a few seconds. While I waited I stooped to the lock again, peering. My phone rang again.

"Hello?" I said.

"Hello, my philosopher."

How I treasured that sound, how I treasured the voice. "I'm glad you called," I said, a little quickly. "As a matter of fact, I..."

"Feeling nervous, old chap?"

"Me? Nervous?" I bent closer, placed my fingertip on the tiny catch, fumbling. "I'm a nervous guy."

No answer. Just a small laugh down her nose; her breath was a whisper in my ear.

I placed my fingernail in the almost invisible groove, clicked the catch down. "I was wondering," I said. "Are you down on the Tegernsee already, or..." I could hardly speak.

"In Munich, my jumpety one. Till Tuesday, as I told you. Why do you ask?"

Joy sparked again, my heart laboured with thrill. "I'm in Munich too." Still bending double, foot wedging the door, I stuck in my finger and tested the electric latch. It swung outwards – it was free.

"You don't say."

"Just on a whim," I ventured.

"A whim? My nervous one had a little whim?"

"Yes." She was teasing me now, wasn't she? I fiddled. Check it, just in case. I tried the spring latch again – it stuck. "Where are you now?" My God, I must get to that toilet.

"I'm very busy."

Excitedly I considered: if she's in the centre of the city, if she's not more than fifteen minutes from here, it's worth a go... "What are you doing, exactly?" I asked. And I thought: after all, I've got business class – couldn't we cut some corners?

"Now that would be asking."

"Ah." On the loo? In bed with some golden Munich male – lying on her back relaxing after the act? Frantically I wiggled the tiny catch up and down, bending lower, staring at it to see what was wrong...

"Actually I am having a short break in between things, and enjoying observing a rather attractive man, if you have to know."

"Ah," I managed. "A speciality of yours." I tested once more. The latch sprang back, was free again. I removed my finger; it was oily. "How about tearing yourself away from this pleasant preoccupation? I have a suggestion which might..."

"Oh but no. I rather fancy him, you see. He has an exceptionally sexy bottom." Another puff of breath close in my ear. "Especially from the back, when he bends low fiddling with locks and things, and sticking his foot in front doors which don't belong to him."

I stopped, and straightened. No, I thought. I turned.

She stood ten feet away. I shook my head, had to chuckle – it was one of those chuckles more like a choke. She was leaned casually on the portal, one foot hooked up behind her propped on stone. Her hair was unkempt; she wore old corduroy trousers, and a cheeky grin.

Chapter 19

We made the flight – just. We flew to Florence.
Coming in low, through the cabin windows, first memories like photographs: lazy Toscana hills in haze in the hot late afternoon, distant spires and towers and domes, the river Arno a silver snake. I still have those photographs, safely tucked away.

Then the hassle, the taxi ride.

Side by side we stood on the narrow old balcony up on the top seventh floor taking it all in. Hadn't yet bothered to unpack. My first thought was: is this balcony safe, is that rust in the iron of this balustrade? I concentrated very deeply on the view. Before us on the opposite bank the city a close panorama, to the right the Ponte Vecchio, below us the green Arno flowing sluggishly. I didn't remember Estella's last words.

"There is San Lorenzo," she said pointing.

Her slender arm, her naked arm – her body very near...

"...and Palazzo Vecchio..."

I followed her finger, squinting. She wore a simple tasteful ring, the stone was the colour of the Arno.

"Do you see the Duomo Santa Maria del Fiore, the big green dome? And the Campanile...?"

I saw. I saw, too, a sandaled foot up on wrought iron, a bent knee stretching her short dress taut, the clear line of her thigh; my thoughts stuck to her body like glue.

"It is like coming home," she said. "Did you know?"

There were those fingers touching my arm. And that ring. I gazed at the shimmering roofscape, and the sky and the birds.

"It's disgustingly romantic," I said.

I looked round at her face. Those clear green eyes.

Mature lines in pale skin, the cheeky freckles, the mass of red hair. She'd gathered it up, fastened it with a band and clips – there'd been no time for details.

She smiled a soft smile, looked away again; I suppose she knew she wouldn't get more. For a moment I watched her profile...

A nasty jolt. My thoughts had jumped – I was back in Munich sitting dejected on her stairs. It was so real, for an instant it nearly knocked me down; I stared at me sitting there, my mobile that wouldn't ring in my pocket, my heart like a stone in my stomach. Which was reality? Was I still there waiting, and fantasising, was it a trick of the mind – or was I really here in Florence?

I took her arm, I had to touch.

"Pinch me," I said. "Pinch me very hard."

She laughed. She took my face in her hands, shook it gently. "We are."

"Are we?"

She kissed me. Just a peck. "My insane one." She watched me. Then let me go, leaned her arms languidly on the old rail again...

She was phoning great-aunt Mimi on the Tegernsee, talking to Margareth and the children, making several other rapid calls. Then she was packing her case, there was a cosmetic bag open on the dressing-room floor. She required about three-quarters of an hour; I guess she took enough for ten weeks.

I leant forward, arms on the rail too, gripping my hands together. Clenching them would perhaps be a better word. We almost hadn't made it – I was kept on tenterhooks right till the end, even as we parked at the airport at quarter-past-two and ran for the lift I believed we were running in vain. Yes, there it had been again, that little raised finger wagging its warning; don't take anything in life for granted, boy.

I stood there, savouring my reprieve with the respect that was due.

Reflections in water.

Renaissance façades on the opposite bank, white and yellow. Black towers and tall steeples, hot red roofs shimmering in the sun. In the water, wavering mirror-images. Like a sponge I sucked it all up

– the architecture, the atmosphere, that special light; I let it cast its spell.

Now and then, lazily, she said something. Titbits about Florence, history and dates, the Medici and the world-famous works of art. Once she looked at me dreamily while she spoke; I disguised my ignorance behind a slow smile.

I felt the thrill. But, looking down, I felt my shrivelled body and my smallness too. I looked back at her and thought: touch me with your beauty, touch me with your mind, transform my ugliness. I was the serpent, she Eve, all I had was a rotten apple hidden in my sweaty forbidden hand. I beheld her face and her body and her grace – what the hell did she see in me?

Lulling moments close together, sharing sights and smells and sounds. Sharing touches, coming closer. Alone together with that view, no-one to disturb us, no hurry in the world; we had one whole week of stolen time. A satisfied feeling in my belly, I let my shoulder rest against her. Felt her warmth, felt her softness. Glancing sideways once or twice in between exchanging thoughts, I peeped. Secret glimpses – of the hollow in her throat, the long naked nape of neck, a pointed nipple poking. Things that tantalise, when one has the time.

How long did we stand there? No idea. Wasn't important. An hour at least – breathing it in, just existing...

Screeching. Like faint screams... swallows swooping, picking insects out of the air. We followed them as they flew, forearms leaned on the wrought-iron rail. I watched one diving towards the water, black on green, forked tail, tiny wings gliding, fluttering, gliding again, switching here and there, then turning in a long arc along the Arno. Beyond, Ponte Vecchio. Houses crowded on the old bridge, in the gap figures strolling. And beyond that, like a backdrop, the Galleria degli Uffizi stopping abruptly at the river's edge. I wanted more... twisted my head further – but the view got interrupted...

Annabelle's face, blurred, framed in out-of-focus hair.

She was watching me. I adjusted my eyes. Still she watched me. She'd turned her back to the view – slender arms folded beneath loose breasts, was resting her bottom on the rail. A dent in her dress. Long bare legs, a touch of gold on her sandal strap.

Those eyes. So steady.

Something flowing, flowing between us. She didn't speak, just watched me sideways – thoughtfully. Eyes far away.

I swallowed. Couldn't move.

Slowly she crossed one leg over the other, still leaning her bottom, still denting the dress. Her eyes came back from wherever they'd been. And then there, on that balcony halfway up to the sky with Florence at our feet, she went and said it. She said simply:

"Let's get married."

She said it calmly and quietly. Her lips were parted, her hair in disarray. She'd said it with such certainty.

I swallowed again. Get married? I think I twitched. My God, was she mad? I spread my hands. Was she serious – was she joking? Was she playing with me like she'd done so often before? I felt a thrill, though – it ran right through me.

"Well..." I hesitated. My God, she'd caught me on the hop. I cleared my throat, awkwardly. Maybe I should play along, just in case it was a game.

"Well, why not?" I said. I tried an apathetic grin. "Right now? Or do we have to wait till tomorrow?"

She was starting to smile. "I am proposing to you."

"You are?"

"I am serious."

"Ah."

Her smile was full now, her mouth was wide; it made her younger. "I realise it is not very conventional," she said.

"That might be one way of putting it." No more words came. But the thrill was growing, I felt dizzy, my senses revolved. After all the darkness, all the hot and cold and keeping me at bay – after all the waiting, she'd sprung it on me when I least suspected, done it when my back was turned.

"Well, my philosopher?"

I stood there like a fool. I said: "Well, I'm sure it's been done before."

That smile on her lips – so wistful, so wise. "You're in love with me," she breathed. The second of those simple statements – were there more to come?

Of course I was. "Annabelle..." I began. How could I say it? My heart bumped and lurched. Was this another trick of the imagination, just another nasty dream?

"Mmm?"

"I've been waiting nine weeks to..." Had to stop.

"Mmm."

"I felt it from the first day."

"I know," she said.

"In fact I..." Stopped again. Was I starting to spout clichés? I returned her green gaze. There was an air about her, an air of clear decision. But why this, why marriage? Why not: let's live together, see if it works out, see if we get in each other's hair? How can she be so certain?

"I know men, too," she said. Oh that knowledgeable lingering smile. "One has to test your true intentions."

"A deeply honourable infatuation." Now I'd made my confession, my honesty was complete.

She stirred. "How sweetly put."

So I'd said something right at last. This is it, I thought – this is what I've been waiting for, so...

"Well, my philosopher? And what do you say?"

Was I afraid of something? Beneath the thrill a small panic was rising. This was stuff of total commitment. For a second I could see Judit – why could I see her? Might it go wrong, might I hurt – would I get hurt again?

"Yes," I said, into space.

Did I sound convincing – did I sound convinced? I sat on the panic.

We stood there. Two feet apart. We didn't touch, didn't come nearer – we were so close.

"My philosopher," she said.

We just stood there. In a vacuum. All around, the sounds of silence.

x x x

I was stepping on cobbles five hundred years old, I was walking on air.

We'd slept till eight, made love sleepily on the antique bed. Crisp clean sheets, a white moulded stucco ceiling, Florentine glass on the old chest of drawers. Then we'd breakfasted on the balcony.

We crossed Ponte Vecchio, making our way into the city. I felt vital, alert, freshly showered and shaved – ready to take on the world. Annabelle hung her arm in mine. We were mercifully anonymous – knew no-one, and no-one knew us.

We strolled, paused, looking at things, strolled on...

Streets as narrow as alleys. Old palazzos and churches, residences of stone, some with high towers – everywhere elegant shops, trattoria and cafés. That was when I first saw him. At least, later, looking back, and despite deeper consideration, I supposed it must have been for the first time. Turning a corner arm in arm we almost collided with an elderly man. He looked distinguished, wore a thin linen jacket and bowtie; we halted quickly to let him by and as he passed, just for an instant his eyes met mine. Such bright and kindly eyes. Was there something vaguely familiar about him? It seemed not – he showed no sign of recognition. And, anyway, in those crowded streets he wasn't the only white-haired, well-dressed man.

We strolled on. It was very hot; the shadows were my sanctuary. I admit: mostly I was interested in the atmosphere, Annabelle in the history and shops. So here at least we possessed something not in common. But that was fine; one needs one's differences.

I had my camera with me, a rather ancient, clumsy *Canon Reflex*, heavy as a tank – when I hang it on my shoulder my neck aches like hell after half an hour as if I've been heaving a sack. Perhaps I'm old-fashioned, but it produces far more optical depth than digital ones starting to come onto the market. Very few and far between I would stop to take a photograph – once I needed so long getting the right angle I lost Annabelle for a quarter of an hour and only found her because she found me, with an expensive-looking carrier bag hanging from her hand.

"Oh, my philosopher, you look like a little lost professor trying to be a tourist," she teased. I didn't like the little bit, I showed the tip of a tongue.

We continued on our meandering course...

Via Por Santa Maria, Via delle Terme. I paused briefly to take another photo – had to wait because of people in the way. As they moved on, looking through the viewfinder, I was just about to press the shutter when I recognised the figure motionless before the newspaper kiosk. It was the same elegant old man with bowtie. He stood there so dignified, thin straight back and two books in his hand. I don't quite know why but the composition pleased. I stepped closer, refocused, took a shot.

We turned back along Porta Rossa. On the way, Annabelle bought leather gloves and a beautiful bag, I a pair of sunglasses.

"Now you look like a Mafia boss," she pronounced. "Shrunken after too stringent a diet." And I'd fancied I looked like a film star, or at least the sexiest man in town.

In Porta Rossa I also bought her a ring, an antique ruby set simply in gold. Just as a little memento. I thought: it glows like the sun shining through port wine, goes with the colour of your hair. In my bank account it tore a bit of a hole; I managed to appease my distress. It made her so happy I couldn't quite understand — I don't hold much affection for adornment. She kept it on when we left the jewellers; she wore it on her finger the way in that moment I wore my heart on my sleeve.

After two or three hours — or was it twenty? — I had to sit down. My brain couldn't absorb any more. My calmness and cool had given up the fight, I was wet with sweat, I'd completely lost track of time.

We chose an outside table at a chic café on one side of the Piazza della Signoria, drank the most costly latte macchiato of my life; I put it down to the splendour of the view. The square was large compared to the claustrophobia of the narrow alleys and streets, I could begin to breathe again. Gratefully I leaned back in the iron chair, linking my fingers on my lap and stretching out my legs. My feet ached, my tongue was tied.

Annabelle smiled at me. "Relax, my ancient one — we don't need to talk." Her wound-up red hair was muddled and unkempt, there was a sheen of damp on her brow. Her expression, though, was easy and gay, a revelation to wrecks like me. I hung out my tongue and rolled up my eyes; I nodded in relief.

Let my gaze stray.

The square was full — tourists and locals, colour and sound. People in pairs or groups and clusters, some standing talking, some walking, or stopped transfixed, craning necks with shading hands, cameras clicking, sometimes flashing in the brilliant sun as if the light weren't bright enough. Around us in the café a number of empty tables. People pausing, hesitating — then strolling on, perhaps they didn't like the look of me, perhaps because of the prices. The seated guests were mostly locals. I thought: maybe they only pay half.

I looked back at Annabelle. She'd removed her sunglasses, laid them on the table. Her eyes were far away. She looked so natural —

she looked so good I took up the camera surreptitiously and focused, released the shutter with a hollow clack. She started, startled, she'd noticed too late.

"Please, don't do that. I look dreadful."

"You look you," I said. "Sweaty and dishevelled." I curled my lip. "Except when you're naked, this way you look best." I laid the camera aside.

"And don't do that with your lip again."

"Do what?" I did it again.

She was tidying her hair with thin fingers. "It makes you look even crueller than you are." She stopped. Her hands gave up the losing game. Leaning, she squeezed my nose, stroked my face. "Stay sitting. Try and replenish your little energy reserve..."

She was rising. "Just going to pop round the corner to a couple of shops." She gathered her glasses and bag.

I watched her. I felt so good being with her, I felt more than twice the man. I sat there lazily, offered no resistance. She had put on the sunglasses, now – she looked cool enough to kill, she looked like a queen again. My God, was I really the male at her side, the one that she had chosen?

I followed her with my eyes as she walked away, I was looking at her body through her clothes, I was looking at her style...

A voluble voice from my left, rapid Italian. Sluggishly my eyes turned. At the next table a chic, young, over-dressed man was talking excitedly into his mobile, his free hand waving sunburnt circles in the air. A white laundered cuff, a glitter of gold. I winced at his extrovert show. Beside his elbow a glass of wine, an opened newspaper. In the headline I glimpsed in Italian the words *Death of a Terrorist*. Discreetly I leaned. My Italian is nonexistent; all I could decipher was something about a police raid in Germany.

My gaze slipped, wandered again; Germany was pleasantly far away.

Over the heads of the crowds, Ammannati's Neptune fountain three times the size of life. And beyond it Palazzo Vecchio, its mellow stones yellow in the sun, solid and severe as a bastion, its tower rising up to the sky; at least I liked the big clock. At right angles, the delicate Loggia dei Lanzi gracefully spread her three arches, old statues stood in shadows.

I opened my *Baedeker Guide* and looked up some names. Under Vecchio clock I read it was the pride of the Florentines and dated from 1353 – well, it pleased me we had that pride in common.

Sluggishly I raised my eyes from the book again and felt my heart labour for an instant... I was staring directly at the elderly man with the bowtie.

He sat hardly six feet from me at the table to my right. A few moments ago, I could swear, he hadn't been there. His head was lowered, he was writing in a small notebook open on the table top.

I felt an uneasiness. But why?

I watched him. The face was long and gaunt and lined, the hair silvery-white; those were fine sensitive hands. I put his age at late seventy, he had a distinguished air. So what was it that caused my unease? Simply the fact of seeing him for the third time in less than a few hours? That too. But no, it wasn't just that. There was an aura about him, an atmosphere. He sat there quite still, concentrating. Yes, the only movement was his hand taking notes. It was as if he were unapproachable, untouchable, almost like a ghost – yes, he existed yet didn't really seem to be there.

I think I stirred in my chair, uncomfortably.

Three times, and each time in a different location. Strange. Who was he? Was it simply coincidence? I shifted again. This time somewhat embarrassed...

He'd raised his head from his notes. He was looking straight at me.

What should I do? How should I react? Pale eyes, very pale, and penetrating. They returned my awkward gaze, steadily, almost with familiarity, almost as though they knew me. Curious somehow: they had a soothing effect. They smoothed the wrinkles of my initial unease.

I nodded, briefly, slowly.

Did he know me? Had we in fact, perhaps, met somewhere else? Maybe long ago? I cast my mind back, searching. But to no avail. Yet...

He was returning my nod. It was almost a slight bow.

...and yet somewhere inside me I experienced a sense of familiarity too. Just a feeling, which I couldn't put my finger on.

His eyes didn't leave me, he didn't speak. I cleared my throat. Again strange – I felt the need to say something. Unusual for me. I searched for words, but no words came.

"Skell," he said simply. "With a 'k'." The way he pronounced it, it sounded like shell.

"Yes," he agreed, as if I'd spoken. "Like a seashell." His voice was quiet yet resonant – clear as a bell. It almost took my breath away.

"Swedish. God forgive my sins."

I just sat there. I don't know why, I still couldn't speak.

Fleetingly he smiled. It was only a faint hint, tiny folds at the corners of his creased old mouth. "And who do I have the pleasure of addressing?"

I told him.

"So my assumption was correct."

Assumption? I thought.

"You are from Germany."

And only then did I realise that he'd been speaking German from the outset. "Yes." I nodded again. How did he know? I didn't look particularly German.

"Your *Baedeker*." His eyes dropped to my table, back to my face.

"Ah," I said.

We watched one another in silence. The silence, though, was not uncomfortable. He appeared to have the ability to put people at ease. Slowly my heart steadied and I could breathe more freely again.

"I beg your pardon for having observed you," he said quietly. "I fear it is one of my many bad habits."

"On the contrary," I retorted. "It was I staring at you." I couldn't help myself, I followed it with: "Do you realise this is our third encounter today?"

"Yes, of course." His answer came quickly and precisely. "I am pleased you are an observer, too," he added placidly.

"Well," I said, "something like this doesn't happen every day."

"Indeed no." He was closing his notebook, screwing the cap on an old-fashioned fountain pen. Laying them carefully aside, he asked: "Does it strike you as somewhat strange?"

I spread my hands. "Life's full of coincidences."

"It is?"

"Yes."

A lift of silver eyebrows, a deepening of wrinkles in the tall forehead. "Ah, but life is in fact full of wonders, you know."

Wonders? He made me stop. I considered a moment. "I'd stick to coincidence myself."

"Oh yes? Would you really?"

I watched him. He sat there so peaceably. His back was straight, his fine lined hands folded on each other upon the table. They lay there so still they might have been asleep.

"I beg to contradict." He said it quietly and precisely.

"It's a free world," I retorted. "You can't be so sure, though." I tried to reciprocate his calm. But it didn't quite come off. In my head a small voice had begun to whisper – and for an instant the image of Estella appeared, sitting in the Café Vienna in Nuremberg behind her glass of latte... then my sister Eva was hovering there too. She was in her old flat in Schwabing years ago saying the same thing.

"Oh but actually I can," he answered evenly.

Each time I spoke he simply turned my statements around. And each time I didn't he seemed to read my mind and answer as if I had.

"It is my job."

Job? I thought. It startled me.

"Indeed yes," he said. "One could venture to say, part of the tricks of my trade."

I suppose I showed disbelief. Or consternation. My tongue was in knots again.

With apparent amusement his pale eyes pondered, reading my reaction. He sat, still motionless, looking into me, through me. There was indeed something unusual about him. I felt my initial unease begin to creep back. Yes – he was a bit like an apparition: his presence wasn't quite real.

"Have I made you inquisitive?"

"You have," I said.

"Excellent! Would you like to venture a guess?"

I shifted unhappily in my chair. His eyes wouldn't go away, they hardly even blinked. Was I fantasising again – was that the explanation? Was he simply a figment of my imagination? Go and get him, I thought. Dispel the myth.

"Are you a magician?" I asked, tongue-in-cheek. "Or a spiritist, perhaps?" I said it without humour though. Inside, I felt my discomfort grow.

"Excellent!" he repeated. "You are getting warm! But perhaps spiritualist would be even nearer the mark." There came those small folds beside his mouth again. Otherwise no reaction.

I admit it: he made me uneasy – and made me nosey too.

"A padre?" I suggested. "A Catholic priest?" I was glancing at his clothes – the bowtie, the white shirt, the thin summer jacket. "In disguise?" I added. I said it with an unhappy smirk of sarcasm.

"As a young man I did consider that one, I readily concede." A wistful smile. "However, the Roman Catholic concept of wonders is a trifle self-serving, I fear. This and their teaching of Heaven and Hell, to mention just one of their failings, would have got me into hot water. Don't all those dogmas and the atavistic incense and Vatican pomp tend to bring out the heathen...?" His sentence trailed off, as though unfinished. Then he continued: "Heaven exists, naturally, and the underworld Hades, too – but Hell not, I suspect. And wonders?" The smile lingered. "Like a wicked gambler I wished to keep my options open." The smile spread. "I am sure, now, you have manoeuvred me into a corner and my mask has slipped."

I shrugged uncertainly. The water was getting too deep. I took another guess: "A protestant preacher? A Lutheran?"

"A logical conclusion, Stefan – I may call you Stefan, may I? Titles and surnames are rather clumsy, and according to the Christian teaching we are all God's children..." He was watching me, kindly. Had he stopped? His lips were still moving, though.

My mind had jumped. I stared at him. I'd heard that one just recently – the bit about God's children. For an instant I was back in the bed in the clinic, and the Catholic priest contentedly sitting there.

"...but actually, no."

I'd missed his words.

He paused. He blinked, minimally raised his eyes. A waiter with slicked-back hair had sidled over, bringing his order – hovered now before him, apathetically pouring water from a bright blue bottle into a glass. Patiently the old man waited till both had been placed on the table and the waiter had slouched away.

"Ah no," he continued. "Although Luther did an excellent job on those wicked dogmas, he had his little racial foibles too. And to don only one hat would leave Judaism and Islam out in the cold, of course, not to mention Hinduism, Buddhism and all the other fascinating 'isms'."

His eyebrows had lifted again briefly. "No, so I slipped on the renegade cloak of theology, you see, with a smattering of philosophy popped in." For the first time he bowed his head, his eyes were gone. Only his wizened hands rose and neatly adjusted the position of the fountain pen before him. "In my humble way," he added, "I teach and write and try to impart borrowed wisdom. Let us say I help others search for light in the dark."

"I see," I said.

His head came up again, he gazed at me penetratingly. "Yes," he said. "I believe you do."

I swallowed. It was as if the gaze went right through me. I thought: I wonder if I've ever...

"They are available in German translation."

I took a quick breath: he'd caught the thought in my head.

"In fact, I am engaged on a new little book at present," he continued. "Just a small tome."

"What's the topic?" I could hear the insecurity in my voice.

"Actually, I thought an appropriate title might be *Beliefs, Coincidence, and the Afterlife*." Another wistful smile, transient as autumn mist.

I couldn't explain it — my heart faltered again. And in my stomach came a queasiness.

"Coincidence?" I queried. "Put between those other two, it sounds like the fly in the ointment."

"Curious, wouldn't you agree?"

I had difficulty returning the gaze. I shrugged again, lethargically. I couldn't reply. I dropped my eyes, and found myself looking at his table — the bottle of water, the glass. Beside the notebook, the laid down mottled-green fountain pen with a ring of silver round the cap. And beyond it the two closed books I'd seen him holding before I took that photograph...

A movement distracted my eye.

But he was only raising his glass. My glance returned to his face. His lips sipped water. Those two bright, pale-coloured eyes. And a look of contentment, of inner peace.

"Allow me to indulge an observation." He said it so lightly, so politely.

"Please." Of course I couldn't refuse. But suddenly, some instinct warned me — said be careful, something's opening, like a window, or a door, you don't know where it'll lead.

"It is my humble experience, gathered through the decades, that this which we commonly describe as coincidence perhaps plays a not unimportant role in the development of our awareness of life on our path towards death, and of the possibility of what could lie beyond."

What nonsense, I thought. "At most a tickling of the fancy, I'd say." I shrugged my shoulders. "And an afterlife? I don't subscribe to that either, you know."

Again the wistful smile. "You consider yourself an atheist," he said gently.

"Yes."

"Ah yes." The kindly expression. "The denial. I went through that too, many of us do." A meaningful nod. "Until, of course, we get to the simple question of the flower."

The flower? I thought. I said nothing.

"Yes. The simple wild flower." Another slow nod. "How does one explain the creation of life, how can one explain the flower?" He said it so peaceably.

"I don't try," I said. "It just exists."

"Ah yes indeed. But I tell myself it must have come from somewhere."

"Maybe scientists'll explain it one day."

"Perhaps they will." His old fingers rested relaxedly round the glass. "And if they do, I sometimes wonder what they will have discovered. The secret of life perhaps, or a power beyond our imagination?" He spoke quietly, a hush in his voice. "Perhaps they will come face to face with God in their test tube, perhaps God is this secret."

"God doesn't exist," I said flatly. "More likely something following scientific laws and logic."

"Indeed, yes. And one may ask, who created the laws?" One of his fingers moved absentmindedly to the rim of the glass, stroking. "I often stop to think, isn't it all so wondrous? The flowers in the meadows, the birds in the sky, the dragonflies..."

Dragonflies? Instantly there was Estella again. What made him say that? The river flowed slowly by, there were dragonflies near our feet...

"Do you sometimes stop to think, too?" he asked. "Even as an atheist?"

I regarded him carefully. We'd been talking about coincidences down there by the river.

"It is, naturally, only an academic question from an inquisitive old theologian..."

"Occasionally," I said. "Of course I do. When I have the inclination."

"Ah, interesting." Another nod, a sagely nod. "And when you do, does anything in particular come to mind?"

"Of course," I repeated. But he knew, didn't he? He said he'd been through it all himself. Nevertheless I said: "I suppose I realise how insignificant I am. How little we all understand."

"Overwhelming, I find."

"So I don't think much about it, I just accept the way it is."

"Ah yes. How we humans do love brushing things under the metaphorical carpet."

"I'd call it being realistic," I retorted.

"A mite frightening though," he murmured, "how much we cannot explain, don't you think?"

True, I thought. But what of it? Each year research explains more and more. "I concede," I said, "thinking about it used to make me a bit insecure. But it doesn't bother me now."

"Indeed it can, can it not? At first." He lifted his glass slowly, sipped some more water. "I recall as a boy, on starry nights, sitting and looking up at the sky, gazing at the stars." He spoke lightly, almost nostalgically. But his eyes watched me steadily. "And when I looked through them, the universe beyond seemed to go on and on outwards into eternity. And I would ask myself, where does it end, it must end somewhere, and if it does what is beyond?" He paused and chuckled cheerfully. "It used to give me a headache." Still his eyes didn't leave me. Was he looking right through me again?

Yes, I thought. It seems he knows that too. "Used to make my mind boggle," I heard myself admit grudgingly. Why was I letting him draw it out of me? Old and mature and experienced, he sat there so calmly; he was leading me by the nose. Quickly I added: "Long ago, though."

He just smiled a small smile, continued watching me with those pale, almost colourless eyes. Then he spoke again. It stopped my mind in its tracks. He said what I somehow had an inkling he was going to say: "Perhaps it brings us closer to God, my son, an experience such as this. Perhaps as children we are nearer to understanding God than we as adults prefer to believe."

I'd heard those words before, too – long ago as a boy. I sweated. Was it coincidence? Was he telepathic? I was looking at my father. He sat beside me, one arm enclosing my small young shoulders, holding me gently as we stared up at the moon and the stars. He'd said exactly the same thing. And in those days I'd believed him, in those days I'd believed almost everything.

"You seem contemplative," said the old man quietly.

"Do I?" I shook my head, suppressed the memory. But a faint voice remained, querying. Had I lost my way? Had there been a way to lose? "Nobody can make that kind of presumption," I said. "Nobody can even prove whether God exists or not."

"In my humble opinion one should not discount that which one cannot disprove. And is it a question of proving?" Delicately he stroked a hand through silvery hair as if arranging thoughts. "Belief, naturally, is a spiritual experience which has been shared by a great many and cannot be measured with instruments."

"A human invention in my opinion. It's all in the mind."

"Ah yes? Well, if that should be the case, certainly a remarkably consistent and widespread one. One might recall that even Judaism reaches back over three and a half millennia."

I sensed the gentle taunt. "Okay," I said. "Even if he does exist, theoretically, then he does – and if not, then not." I shrugged. "It isn't important. No point wasting one's time puzzling over something one'll never know."

"Ah, no?"

"No."

"I have a tiny suspicion we all may one day. Though not in this earthly life..."

That stopped my brain, too. I struggled. Again the words were my father's, yet they came from the mouth of this man. Where did he get them from? I wriggled unhappily. Had I nodded off? Or was he really an apparition? Father stood in the garden, we were quite alone. He was suddenly confiding, speaking to me of an afterlife, speaking convincingly, his words falling on fertile soil; I'd just turned seventeen, it was ten days before his death. After he'd gone, though, the way he went, he dashed my dreams and stole my beliefs, he took my faith with him.

"Actually," the old man mused, "as a humble student of theology, I find it a rather pleasant pastime myself..." He spoke dreamily, philosophically, "...cogitating on this and other metaphysical themes..." His emaciated hand floated through the air, "...on life and death, on who and what we are, where did we come from, where are we going, is death the final act, the end of it all...?"

There was something about him that was compelling, fascinating almost – yet there was also something strange. I'd never met anyone quite like him before. His voice was lulling, it was wrapping itself round me, beginning to mesmerise – or was it just the heat of the Italian summer day?

Matthias and I had talked about stuff like this too, at the time of our life when everything was open, nothing seemed impossible.

"...ruminating on humankind's ancient antitheses of good versus evil, God and the Devil, Ying and Yang, how did they come into existence and what meaning lies behind them...?"

A part of me was fighting him still, but it seemed to little avail. The voice was so gentle, so calming, it was carrying me away like a leaf on a river, like a feather in the wind, I was swimming free in the eternal flux of life. It had taken a hold of me, was drawing me back... into my childhood, into my sickbed. I was five years old lying shaking with fever, my body pouring with sweat and weak and hot then cold, then burning again, my brain slipping in and out of consciousness... and there I was during the peak when people were murmuring and I could sense fear in the air but it wasn't my fear and an old doctor appeared, a wise old man I'd never seen before and his voice was soothing lending me courage and his ethereal hands seemed to lift me up yet without touching me and his voice was the voice I was hearing now...

"...and one is able to observe in the roots of all religions, however ancient and regardless whether possessing a godly pantheon or monotheistic, that from the earliest times man carried an image of an afterlife..."

I stared at him. His eyes still hadn't left me. Who on earth was he? How did he know, how could he sound like somebody else? How could he pick these things out of my past, out of my brain?

Take a grip on yourself.

I drew in my feet, changed position on the chair. My father faded, my father was gone. It's just that old trap, I told myself. Like those Tarot cards; you see what you want to see. Estella talks this way too.

I sat there and managed to return his gaze. I'd broken the spell. Slowly, trying to relax, I stretched out my legs again...

"Ah, these curious little titbits of facts," he said. "These eternal questions." That wistful smile again. With the speed of a snail he folded his thin wrinkled hands upon each other the way he had at the start. "And if I might be permitted to ask, do you nowadays ever pose them still?" The gaze was neutral, his eyes were twinkling. "When you have the inclination?"

"No," I said. But I had to lower my eyes. I'd broken the spell – yet a peculiar residue persisted in my brain; had he awoken something, had the damage been done? Had he gone and planted a seed? I stared at my stretched out feet. A thought appeared: was I afraid of him, perhaps?

Seconds passing...

"No reason to be, I assure you."

I looked up quickly again. That kindly gaze. Absurd. He couldn't really be reading thoughts.

"I wonder," the old man murmured. Then he paused.

I hardly heard, though – another thought had come into my head. A preposterous one. Where had it come from – something Estella had said? Or maybe in a book long ago?

He was nodding.

Why that? I suppressed the thought, sat on it hard. And watched him patiently waiting. But for what? His hand moved to the small blue bottle. Leisurely it poured the last of the water. A steady hand. An ancient yet agile hand. The bottle caught the sun; a flash of bright blue. He raised the glass. Then he said: "I wonder, might you like to ask a question of me?"

His suggestion caught me unsuspecting. I couldn't speak.

"After all," he added with another twinkle, "I seem to have been doing most of the talking."

I sat there, considering. Then: "Yes," I said.

"Feel perfectly free."

"Do you really believe in God?" I asked.

With no hesitation he replied, thoughtfully and easily: "I have come to believe. It took quite a little while, I assure you."

"And in an afterlife?"

"It is all one, you see."

"But you were once an atheist."

"Indeed."

"Nevertheless, you became a theologian of all things?"

"Allow me to put it this way. In my early period of denial in my twenties, somewhere along the path I discovered a vacuum. An emptiness, if you wish. Or possibly it was destiny coming to call on me rather than on my neighbour. You perhaps know the little old song *Is That All There Is?* Doris Day, I believe, or Peggy Lee. Somewhere back in your childhood, I fear, and not quite your cup of tea." Calmly his hands left the glass, laid themselves upon one another again.

"Imagine!" A sudden gaiety in his eyes, a raise of silver eyebrows. "A dashing young man who worshipped the ladies and all things material. And then, ah yes, that vacuum. I began to doubt my realism. And when denial turns to doubt, curiosity spreads her wings. Finally I slipped on my theological cloak. I confess, however, I was not yet a believer."

His hands were quite still – the sleep of repose, of concentration; they told me he wasn't quite finished.

"For some the path to truth is tortuous and can take almost a lifetime," he said. "I imagine, for my sins, that in my case it was ordained." He blinked benignly. "But regardless which, each footstep on the path reveals a new pearl of wisdom, each fresh step opens a door." He paused again, reflectively, gazing. Hollow, sunken eyes in the thin gaunt face.

A door? I thought. "A door?" I said. That's what Estella said.

"Ah, just a manner of speaking." The eyes were benign, too. "I believe an expression employed by certain therapists. How humankind loves its symbols." The eyes were old as the hills, misty and dreamy, as if they'd been somewhere and seen so much, and returned to tell the tale. "Let us simply say it all begins with the flower and the starry sky and they lead us closer to God."

I felt my irritation. He spoke with such certitude, as if it happened to everyone and couldn't be questioned, as if there were no other way. This incontrovertibility undermined.

"Okay," I said. "So you came to believe in God and an afterlife. That I accept." I said it impatiently. "That's fine for you, obviously it suits you. But it's not my cup of tea – never will be."

"Perhaps. Perhaps not. Possibly the choice does not lie in our hands."

"Indeed it does," I contradicted.

A trace of an introspective smile. "Ah yes. I remember thinking the same in my post-graduate days as I whizzed about Stockholm and Rome in my little Alfa Romeo. Canary yellow, I believe it was!" He chuckled again faintly. "And behold me now!"

"I'm mid-forties, not a student."

"It is never too late."

I spread my hands, I desisted. "As long as you want to believe," I said. I managed a smile, too. It was a dry one, though.

He pondered, watching me in his peaceful manner. "Are there perhaps any other questions you wished to pose?"

"No," I said. "I think that's about it."

He nodded slowly, his chin rising up and down, up and down. "I was mistaken, I do beg your pardon. I thought perhaps the proposed title of my present little book had possibly caught your fancy..."

And there it was again. That word. It jumped up — like a nasty jack-in-the-box. I stared at him, I didn't speak.

"Interesting," he murmured, almost under his breath.

Still I didn't speak.

"Yes. You asked two questions, did you not? About belief. In this case in the form of a God. And about an afterlife. But, curiously, not about my little thought, the naughty little catalyst, in between."

"No," I said. Left it at that.

"I wonder why not?"

"We'd covered that one." I was fighting again, I was blocking him, I wanted to change the subject. Again I found I had difficulty returning his gaze.

"Ah yes." He blinked. "So we had." His hands unfolded from the table, and his eyes were gone. He picked up his glass, held it high before his old face, as if inspecting its contents against the light.

"I do beg your pardon," he repeated quietly. "I believe I may have travelled too fast. I am sure that is enough of this subject for now."

For now?

I'd dropped my eyes: I forced myself to look back at him. He was slowly drinking the last of the water, leisurely, concentrating. Was he insinuating we would meet again? I watched him. His wizened old hands set down the glass, began slipping notebook and fountain pen in a side pocket and withdrawing a wallet from inside his summer jacket. He extracted a banknote, placed it under the glass, gathered up the books.

He was rising to his feet.

I felt a prick. Extraordinary, it was a stab of disappointment. Why that? After all, his presence had partly caused me discomfort, even unease, and seemingly awoken things in me I didn't wish to wake. Yet now that he was going I didn't want him to leave.

He paused before me, straight and dignified, thin as a rake. But steady – no wobble, no shake, no quiver of the hand or head.

"I enjoyed our encounter," I said.

"The pleasure was all mine, I assure you," he reciprocated. Politely, almost imperceptibly, he gave another bow. "Perhaps we shall meet again, in this world or the next." Again that faint twinkle in his eyes. "In a week I shall be blessed to have reached double your age..."

Ninety years old? But he looks...

"Everything has its time and place," he said placidly. "And for each there is a path. Take your time. There is no hurry. Perhaps one day a little copy of that book may fall into your hands."

He laid a small card on my table. I glanced down. Professor Dr Krister Skell. And two addresses with telephone numbers, in Stockholm, in the Toscana. Beneath was an e-mail address.

I opened my mouth to speak, but already he had turned away. I sat there. I was unable to move. I watched him go, making his way unhurriedly into the square...

"Hello my lazybones philosopher!"

I started. Gentle fingers on my neck, stroking. "Not fallen asleep?" I turned my head, looking up. Red tangled hair with long wisps hanging loose, radiant green eyes, carrier bags – and when I looked back, quickly, the old man was gone. He'd disappeared, as if he'd never been.

Annabelle was sitting down. I glanced at the table. Only the small yellow visiting card was left to remind me, left to confirm.

Her hand reached across the table to mine...

"My faraway one – everything all right?"

I raised my eyes again. "Yes," I said. I tried a smile.

"You look as if you had seen a ghost."

Chapter 20

Four days went by. Sightseeing and so much culture, good food, relaxation, taking strolls along the Arno. On the evening of the fifth day I sat exhausted in our room, sore feet in a big plastic bowl of cool water Annabelle had procured from house-keeping. A dreadful bright-pink bowl: in the water bath salts and the scent of perfumed oil. In the background, Annabelle on the phone to Tegernsee, talking to her children. She'd rung them twice every day up to now.

Sitting there, I leafed through the business *Capital* I'd bought at a kiosk. An article caught my eye; I began half-heartedly to read. But my brain was burnt-out and my eyes weary and dry. I dropped the magazine on the small table beside me, leant sluggishly back in the old armchair and closed my eyes.

"Stefan?"

The padded headrest was a haven. With effort I opened one eye, swivelled it. Annabelle was out on the balcony, summer dress flowing, seated in shade. I didn't answer. She leaned, peering, newspaper in hand. *Der Spiegel* lay open near her feet. "Do you think we can receive *Arte* here on the box?"

"Ah," I said. Closed the eye gratefully again. "Doubt it."

"Don't we have satellite TV?"

"Why?" I talked to the welcoming dark.

"There is a programme change, they are doing a special. Christian Beck is being interviewed at ten this evening."

Christian Beck? Ten o'clock? By ten o'clock if I had my way I'd be flat on my back dead-beat in dreamland. By nine o'clock more like.

"He is?" I said. My voice was blurred. "Who's Christian Beck – a politician?" I mumbled. "Or a wrestler, a boxer, a famous footballer?"

"A journalist."

"Ah."

"A friend of mine."

"Ah," I repeated. I mustered myself, managed to open my mouth again. But nothing emerged, except my flaccid tongue. So again I forced an eye open, groped a hand to the table, scrabbling feebly beneath the magazine and other half-read newspapers. Found the remote. Wasn't there a programme list somewhere? I fumbled, couldn't locate it. Switching on the set, cancelling the volume, I lethargically began to search. I sat there, wincing, squinting at the screen, shirt streaked with sweat stuck to my back, trousers rolled up and feet in foam.

Channel 1, 2, 3, 4... on and on... 17, 18, 19...

"Oh my Casanova, you are a pet." She was peering round the open balcony door...

...29, 30, 31...

...I found it. *Arte*. Channel 37... turned up the volume, German language not French. Winced again, silenced the set...

"Found it," I choked.

A flutter of her fingers. She'd turned back to her paper, feet stretched out on the opposite chair.

I pressed the button again but I was trying to stop... channel 38 sport, channel 39 porno, Italian style... channel 40 porno. My thumb stopped in its tracks, my eyes goggled like a fish... a quite remarkable swollen cock about as long as the leg of a chair was ramming in and out of a bloated vulva which bulged between a pair of magnificent buttocks bent over what looked like a fitness machine...

With glazed eyes I held out for fully five seconds, turned on the volume loud for another atmospheric five then, appropriate to my physical state of body, switched off the set with shaky hand...

"What on *earth* was that?" Annabelle peering briefly again.

I gave a weak and crooked grin. "Just putting in a spot of practice." Gratifyingly I closed my eyes again. Wriggled my toes in the soothing scented water, trying to bring them back to life. My head was heavy, my legs like lead. I did my best. I fought the beast, the blanketing tiredness, but it won the day. Slowly my head sagged forward, I gave myself up to the victor and slid into smothering sleep...

I was strolling through meadows full of flowers. Mellow sunlight. It seemed I was in Provence, deep in the South of France. There were larks in the sky, and over the meadows swarms of blue butterflies. Far away, up on one of the small hills in the rolling landscape, an old farmhouse stood. I felt happy, exhilarated almost, by the beauty. Suddenly I found myself on a stony track with mossy strip along its middle, winding up the slope between fields of waving red poppies. The farmhouse was much closer now. It was very old, red tiled roof, weathered grey stone half hidden by wisteria and creeper. Beside it there were cypress trees like dark green pencils – I counted them... five on one side and two on the other. And olive trees beyond, ancient and gnarled. I approached. The house attracted like a magnet, somehow I knew something important was waiting inside. I'd reached the front door. The beauty was overwhelming, ecstatic: the sweet heavy scent of wisteria filled my nose, overpowering, the special light just right. An old bell was ringing – I'd pulled on its chain. The green door opened. A woman appeared, middle-aged and severe, dressed in bright pink. I didn't recognise her but she seemed to know me, was beckoning me in. I clearly recall her words. She said: "You are late, give me your shoes. We are all here," and I wanted to speak but my jaw was a vice. I reached out, offering her a visiting card I held in my hand. She burst out laughing. I begged her to let me past, but she just kept on laughing, standing in my way, started shaking my shoulders...

I was awake.

I opened my eyes. Provence was gone, and the flowers and the farmhouse and the woman in pink. I was back in my chair in the hotel room. The dream was gone – it had been so real... I took an unsteady breath. Now I would never discover who had been awaiting me. I sat there. Sensed a sudden deep pang of disappointment...

The light was blinding. I winced, I blinked, tried to adjust my eyes – heard Annabelle laugh, felt her fingers – they were gently shaking me...

"Hello, my sexy Don Juan."

She stood there before me, bending forward. Her hair was wet and straggly, hung in dark threads. She wore a hotel bathrobe now, fluffy white flannel with golden coat-of-arms; the robe was undone, it hung half open, its secrets revealed, like curtains of sin drawn aside. A brief glimpse of a breast, a navel peeping, a tiny tuft of hair.

Struggling, I orientated, looked up at her eyes. Ruefully I smiled. "Hi," I said. My voice was a croak. I managed a cracked chuckle. Sat there sweaty and disgusting feeling a fool – feet still in water and trousers at half mast.

"A picture of German masculinity."

Nonchalantly I spread my hands. "Aye, aye, cap'n. Ready to do my duty."

"Seeing is believing."

Awkwardly I lifted my feet, flexing them. The skin of my toes was wrinkled as those of an emaciated old man. I planted them next to the bowl.

She was pulling my shirt over my head. I felt so sluggish. "Lift your arms." I lifted them. She skinned it off. "Stand up, Casanova." She tugged me out of the armchair. Deft fingers undid my belt, undid the button, opened the zip. My trousers fell down. She stripped me naked, grabbed me between my legs. "Up into the shower, my impotent one." Grasping it fast with strong slender hand, she towed me by it into the bathroom...

Hot water streamed in needles, they got in my eyes, they got in everywhere. In that generous shower closet she shampooed my hair, my sagging body, she showed no mercy, she soaped me all over, our bodies together... I was down on the tiles, I was down for the count, slippery skin, she sat in my lap, she knew just what to do, she slipped me in, holding my hair and leaning right back she nearly snapped it off... we came almost together, it didn't take long.

I have a little photograph buried in my brain. From when she was done. Steamy streaming walls of glass, the doors are burst open, I'm lying spreadeagled and crooked, legs in the air, my head stuck out panting and staring eyes, a stranded fish left high and dry.

x x x

I turned on the telly at one minute to ten; I'm still a punctual man.

A male voice was saying: "...since you were released from your ordeal seventy-two hours ago?" The speaker was seated beside a hospital bed, one could see him in profile, thinning hair, mid-fifties.

"The quacks, medical checks," replied the second man propped up in bed. He wore a pyjama shirt, looked about sixty, small and wiry with darting dark eyes. I recognised him instantly. "And my wife and children," he added in a flat monotone.

"And the federal police leading the investigation? Have they begun their questioning?"

"Briefly."

"Is the BND also involved?"

"I am informed the federal police are postponing further questioning until we receive the green light."

"Doctor's orders? The trauma psychologist?"

"One can assume so."

An electronic caption was running along the bottom of the screen... 'all scheduled programmes are running 20 minutes late: the interview with C. Beck begins at 22.25'...

"At which I should like to take this opportunity to express my thanks, Herr Minister, for your granting me permission to hold this interview so soon after your release."

"Not at all, Peter. In the public interest I am glad to oblige." The man in the bed lifted what seemed a weary hand to his chin. The movement rustled the tiny microphone pinned on his chest.

I glanced at Annabelle. "Interested? Or shall I switch this blather off till your pal comes on?"

She pulled a face. Then told me no. "That's Dieter Rosner, after all" she said.

"Our wizard and minister of infamy and economics."

"Don't be sarcastic."

I cast her a glaring wince. "He's more corrupt than most of the big boys." Beyond her stood the trolley with the remains of our room-service dinner. I suppose I should've parked it outside in the corridor. I shot her another barb: "The kidnappers should never've let him off the hook."

"All the same, I should enjoy hearing what he has to say."

"Well don't expect to hear any truths."

She leaned, poked my arm, laughing. "Just shush and let me listen."

I blinked benignly, returned my eyes to the screen. The interviewer was saying "...any prognostication about an early resumption of your duties of state?" There was a general shot of the room and I noticed a third seated person off to the side, pinstriped suit, his back to the camera...

"...or is the question simply too premature?"

A faint hesitation on the face of the politician. Then: "I feel in a position to emphasise that I have come to one or two conclusions. I have made one or two decisions in this respect."

"Would you be prepared to elucidate?"

"I think it might be wiser to await a press-release due to be made public later this afternoon." The sentence was stiff, like an automaton.

"Concerning your future?"

"Concerning more the private sphere of future plans."

"Would that be in regard to your immediate family?"

The eyelids in the face closed. Then the sharp sunken eyes were there again. The face was taut and drawn. "I believe, Peter, there is certain public knowledge about the state of health of my wife. The strain of recent events has not, of course, offered cause for improvement."

"I am quite certain we all appreciate that, Herr Minister. May I offer my condolences?"

A slow grave nod.

"Perhaps you would allow me to touch briefly on these recent events."

Another nod. A deepening of lines in the middle of the forehead.

"Your abduction lasted precisely eighty-eight days."

A camera cut to a close-up. The minister's face filled the screen for a moment. Harsh watchful eyes, hunted eyes. Was that a nervous tick in the skin?

"So I am informed. I myself counted eighty-four."

"You counted?"

"I did indeed."

"I am sure, under such circumstances, one can be forgiven for losing track of time."

"Not in my case. The discrepancy of four days can only be explained by the length of the journeys to and from my place of captivity during which I was rendered unconscious."

"Two day journeys?"

"The facts confirm this assumption."

"You were held here in Germany?"

"I was not."

"In a European country, perhaps?"

"It would appear not in Europe."

"May I enquire if you know where?"

"In a very hot country where Arabic was spoken."

"Are you aware which one?"

"I am not."

The interviewer seemed to pause an instant. Then: "Can you be certain it was Arabic? Not Farsi, or..."

"Definitively. I acquired a smattering during my times in the Gulf region."

"You appear, Herr Minister, to have retained a remarkably cool head during your ordeal. If I may say so."

"It was, certainly, an ordeal." A blank stare in the eyes.

"Whose outcome you naturally could not surmise."

"I was fully confident in the competence of our government, and in all individuals and services involved in such matters. And..." He raised his hand as if to interrupt the next question. "I should like here publicly to issue my grateful thanks to each of these persons and to all well-wishers whose greetings I have received in the previous three days."

He paused. A lift of the chin, a blink of the eyes.

"Herr Minister, before we come briefly to the period of your captivity, and although at the time the event was more than thoroughly covered by the media, I believe I speak for many viewers in saying I would be interested to hear in your own words your impressions of your abduction on that fateful Friday."

"Actually, hardly any." A lowering of the wiry thin brows, a darting of dark eyes as though they were searching. "My car entered through the gates to my driveway, the garage doors appeared to be defective, or at any rate they would not open. My driver was getting out when figures appeared. They wore uniforms. Thought they were our chaps."

Again a pause, brows frowning. "Everything happened exceedingly fast. One tossed a dark object into the front of the car where my bodyguard sat and it exploded, stunning us. It impaired my hearing and there was a pungent smell. I recall seeing something akin to a small dart in my driver's neck as he fell, then the gas or fumes or what not overwhelmed me."

"I imagine they are indelible impressions."

"Indeed." A frown.

"What were your spontaneous thoughts at that moment?"

"To be perfectly frank, Peter, I thought we three had met our maker."

"I am sure. Have you since been informed that they came to no harm?"

"Yesterday. It was a great relief to me to receive that news."

"May I ask, in retrospect, what are your feelings towards those abductors? Are there any particular emotions attached?"

"Emotions?" Another circumspect frown.

"Yes."

"Well – anger, no. Hate, no. They were professional devils, I will allow them that."

"Can you make any guess as to their nationality?"

There was a murmur in the background.

The interviewer was glancing sideways beyond the camera. He nodded, lifted a hand in acquiescence. The minister gazed blankly. Leaning back, relaxing, the interviewer crossed his legs, resting a notebook on his lap, addressed the minister again: "Do you retain any memories at all of how you were brought to your place of captivity? Sensations of an air-flight, drives in cars or jeeps or whatever, any particular sights or sounds?"

"None whatsoever."

"And when you regained consciousness, you found yourself in an Arab-speaking country?"

Another indistinct murmur could be heard.

"The possibility cannot be overlooked," the minister replied.

"And where were you hidden? In a building, a cellar?"

"In a mud hut."

"Could you describe it for us?"

"There was a hard, dusty, earthen floor with cushions and a small window with dirty glass. I was chained by one foot to a post."

"How were you treated?"

"I was treated in a simple but one could fairly say civilised manner."

"And to eat?"

"One cooked meal a day, always with rice, and bottled water. Breakfast was black tea and yoghurt and unleavened bread."

"You appear to have lost weight, Herr Minister."

"Eleven kilos."

Another close-up of his face, of his body in the bed. Hollows. Pale skin.

"Did the kidnappers demand ransom for your release?"

"I am informed that our authorities were not approached in the matter."

"Was a ransom paid?"

"To my knowledge there was no claim of responsibility for the act. The perpetrators remained anonymous."

"If not profit was there political motivation behind it, then?"

The minister stared steadfastly. "I would assume politics were not involved." The voice was heavy.

"Then could you surmise as to what?"

"Your guess is as good as mine." Said gruffly.

The interviewer sat still, his hands folded on one leg, clutching his notes. One of the hands opened and closed. It seemed it was deliberating. Then he said: "Minister, there has of course been a rash of kidnaps over the previous year. Would you consider yours to be related to the rest of the series?"

No answer from the bed. Just a faint lift of shoulders.

"By which I mean, in your opinion, was yours similarly motivated? Was it instigated by the same persons or group?"

"At this early stage such conjecture would be unwarranted."

"With respect, Minister, it is hardly early days. Since the first kidnap investigations have been continuing intensely for nearly thirteen months, and on your disappearance one of the largest manhunts in twenty-five years was set in motion."

"In these matters, patience and determination have first priority. Only a question of time till our highly efficient police forces and special units make a final breakthrough."

"To date, excluding yourself, two kidnap victims have been freed unharmed and ransom money subsequently paid in the form of donations by both individuals. There appear to be parallels here which indicate..."

"Unharmed, you say? Preposterous." The minister's dark eyes flared and darted. Was that flail of the arms under proper control? "Take our respected banker Manfred Schramm with whose case I am personally acquainted. Such was his psychological state on his release that his unfortunate subsequent decision-making forced him into early retirement. Unharmed? Brainwashed, that's what he was. Brainwashing is a form of torture."

"Was an attempt also made to brainwash you, Herr Minister?" Asked calmly, quietly.

A slight sag of the head, a droop of the shoulders.

A tall imposing man in white coat appeared at the edge of the screen, straight silver-grey hair combed back. A brief exchange of words, the doctor's almost inaudible. The minister signalled him away with a, "Thank you, Martin," and a regal wave. Staring the interviewer in the eye again, he said: "My dear Peter, as agreed, I am not at liberty to reveal any such details at this point."

A reciprocating nod. "Were there, let us say, at least conversations with your captor? Or captors, plural?"

"Plural. Yes there were talks."

"Were there many of these talks?"

"Most days."

"Of long duration?"

"Very long."

"Into the night?"

"More often than not."

"Were you deprived of sleep?"

The wave of a distracting hand. The minister stared. Alert eyes burning, sunken sockets. Yes, again they looked like hunted eyes.

"May one be permitted to enquire, Herr Minister, would you recognise your captors again?"

"I was blindfolded for the duration of each session."

"And between sessions?"

"There were short pauses without the blindfold. To eat and so forth."

"And these sessions. They spoke German?"

"They did."

"With accents? Without accents?"

Another murmur out of the background. Clipped and crisp, the words still inaudible, though. A brief shot, a general shot of the hospital room. The seated man in the pinstripe suit from behind and the doctor standing aside, both half in silhouette, a floodlight on a tripod and a second cameraman, the politician in the bed bathed in the light, the interviewer with his hands in his lap.

"Did you have, then, no visual contact with a single soul for all of those eighty-four days?"

"There were veiled women who brought my meals, naturally accompanied by guards. The devils had headscarves wrapped round their faces and Kalashnikovs and what not. All one could see were their eyes."

"Were there other kidnap victims in your hut?"

"No."

"And these weapons? You recognised them as Kalashnikovs?"

"Wouldn't you?" Again uttered gruffly. "One sees them often enough on the newscasts."

"Did they ever threaten you at gunpoint?"

"They did not."

The interviewer smoothed his hands on his thighs, still leaned casually back. "Any other memories?"

The minister blinked. His eyes went out of focus. Was he back to where he'd been? "The heat, the waiting," he mused. He puckered his lips. "Otherwise I imagine only small insignificant stuff. Sounds of distant shooting now and then, Arab voices." He blinked again, his eyes came back. "You know, Peter, under circumstances like these, one learns to appreciate the little things." He nodded slowly. "Time to reflect."

"And in spite of everything you didn't lose count of a single day?" The interviewer's voice was neutral. No disrespect, no hint of sarcasm, laudable neutrality.

"I did not."

"I am sure, Minister, it all involved a deal of courage."

"Oh, I wouldn't say that. There are men and women who show more courage in the face of far worse calamities."

"Nevertheless..."

A shrug. The eyes sinking into their sockets again. An empty gaze; the minister seemed to be shrinking.

The silver-haired doctor had approached the bedside. "In the interests of the minister's health you should be concluding now," you could hear him say near the microphones.

The interviewer was nodding. "Just one final question, Herr Minister," he said. He spoke clearly and easily, he appeared satisfied. "Is there any truth to the rumour which has been circulating in the previous twenty-four hours that you will be resigning your ministerial post, and to a further rumour stating..."

"As I said at the outset, Peter," cut in the reply, "it might be wiser to await this afternoon's press release." The tone was measured, mechanical.

"And is there perhaps substance to the rumour concerning your resignation from two posts in the industrial sector, effective as of the end of this month?"

"Posts? I possess no knowledge of any official additional posts."

"I am sure, Herr Minister, you do not deny your presence on the board of directors of a leading energy consortium and a major..."

"My dear Peter, you disappoint me..." A lift of a bony hand, a sharp jut of chin. "As public servant and chosen representative of the people, one is accustomed to becoming the target of scurrilous and unfounded speculation. You must further appreciate that the present circumstances in which I find myself are somewhat fatiguing, therefore I would seek your understanding in now winding up this interview." The hand turned outwards, dismissing.

"Herr Minister," said the interviewer smoothly, "we thank you again for granting us this opportunity to talk to you, and wish you a full and speedy recovery." He spoke as relaxedly, professionally, as before – neutrality still in his tone. And turned to the camera, talking briefly into it, signing off. Behind him one saw the minister nodding, leaning back his head. Then the picture faded.

I looked round at Annabelle. Her eyes left the screen, met mine. I waited, but she didn't speak.

"Corrupt bastard," I said quietly.

"Don't be so harsh." Chin on thin hand, elbow rested on the arm of her chair, she blinked demurely at me.

I cast her my sarcastic squint. But she merely blinked again, turned her attention back to the box. An announcer had come on, was saying something. Half-heartedly I listened...

"...Economics Minister was recorded in a Hamburg clinic earlier today. The following interview is being broadcast live from our Paris studio. Christian Beck, freelance journalist, began his distinguished career as Middle East foreign correspondent for the Berlin *Tagesspiegel* newspaper covering the civil war in Beirut, the nineteen-eighty-two Israeli invasion of Lebanon, and later the first Gulf War in Iraq. He is today considered one of the leading journalistic experts both at home and abroad, his most recent contribution being the lead article in the current edition of the political magazine *Der Spiegel*. Since the onset of the kidnappings which have plagued Germany for more than a year now, he has regularly published articles on the causes and effects of this phenomenon. Here now, Christian Beck. The interviewer is Theo Klaustaler, our chief political commentator..."

The screen went blank. Then a dot appeared in one corner. It grew to a tiny square, the square expanded, moving, till it filled the screen. A *Spiegel* magazine cover – a picture of computer keyboards overlapping printout lists of bank account numbers and bundles of high-denomination banknotes; a diagonal red rubber-stamp headline asked, 'Hacking at the Goodies?'

A cut. A transparent table, two steel-tube and white canvas chairs, two men in their fifties. On the table a carafe of water, two glasses, the same *Spiegel* magazine. The two were talking but the microphones were off, one couldn't hear a word. Just music. Then close-ups, a brief introduction.

The interviewer, Klaustaler, curtly: "You're here in Paris this weekend. Coverage of the elections?"

The journalist, Beck, relaxedly: "That's right."

"Thank you for finding the time at short notice." Klaustaler had a hard square face, a wiry clipped moustache, bowtie. The way he spoke, the way he sat there, he made an intimidating impression.

"Very welcome." A close-up of Beck's face; long and ascetic, tired, half-moon rimmed spectacles with the tops of the lenses cut and bare, worry lines each side of the mouth.

Klaustaler, indicating a monitor near their chairs: "Well, you've just watched the interview with Dieter Rosner. What's your interpretation of his kidnapping? The details familiar?"

"It would appear to follow the same pattern."

"As the Schramm and Biedenhof abductions, for example?"

An inclination of Beck's head. "Correct."

"They too were flown out of the country. Rosner likewise. Where was he taken? Middle East?"

"A possibility."

"The method of his abduction?"

"A new variant. But professional, as the minister himself mentioned."

"They're learning?"

"Yes. The progression awakes certain older reminiscences from back in the nineteen seventies and eighties."

"In Germany? In the Middle East?"

"The former. However, with more sophisticated weapons."

"Stun grenades, gas bombs, hypodermic darts? Sound more like James Bond." Klaustaler gave a mirthless smile. "Such stuff easy to procure?"

"Oh yes. If you know where."

"And where would be most likely? Syria, Lebanon, maybe? Eastern Europe? Russia?"

"For availability one might first look to Western Europe, Germany even."

"Well, granted, not your usual run-of-the-mill terrorist stuff – handguns, Uzis, Kalashnikovs and the like."

"No." On the journalist's face a contemplative expression. Then quietly: "Interestingly, there is also a subtlety and lack of physical violence not exercised a generation ago. As with each other abduction in this series, again here with Rosner no collateral damage. One observes the care taken to kill or harm no-one."

"What does this tell you? Different mentality?"

"Yes."

"The kidnappers German?"

"Yes."

"Then why use the Middle East? To date, the three victims who've been set free describe being held in an Arab-speaking country. Why smuggle them out there?"

"I wrote an article back in February suggesting the reasons."

"For the sake of our viewers please elucidate."

"There are two possibilities. By doing so they reduce the risk factor of the abducted being discovered during the captivity. There are a great number of places to conceal people out there. Or they have laid a red herring."

"A red herring?"

"A simulation."

"Of an Arab country?" Scepticism in the interviewer's face.

"A possibility. To distract the authorities and throw them off the scent."

"Of the various theories that've come from the media, you're out on a limb there."

A faint shrug of Beck's shoulders.

"Okay, let's assume for a moment you're right," Klaustaler pressed. "Can you make a guess where they're taken, then?"

"Almost anywhere. Or nowhere."

"Nowhere?"

"It is conceivable they remain in Germany. Or Europe. No border checks, or virtually none. To smuggle someone further afield even in a small private plane would involve additional risk. Subterfuge and bribes or blackmail, a willing pilot."

Klaustaler waved an impatient hand. "All three victims say they were flown out of the country."

"If one studies their statements carefully, with a toothcomb, one finds no direct evidence of this."

"The first kidnap victim, Manfred Schramm, reported briefly recovering consciousness in an aircraft."

"He was blindfolded, drugged and confused. Later he admitted the sensation could have been from within a utility vehicle on board a ferry or boat."

"And the Minister spoke of a two-day journey. You can drive across a number of borders or fly a damn long way in two days."

"Or drive only a short distance and keep the abducted unconscious for longer to mislead."

Klaustaler flapped a hand again. "An unusual hypothesis, Herr Beck."

"As I pointed out, it is merely a possibility. Naturally I could be barking up the wrong tree."

Both smiled. One impatiently, the other quietly.

"And what about the kidnappers themselves?" Klaustaler pursued. "Who are they?"

"We know nothing about them. Up until now they have issued no proclamations, labelled themselves with no catchphrase or name. They remain silent and anonymous."

"There've been only four arrests to date. Any leads there?"

"Hardly. As we know, one was in his fifties, a teacher by profession and terminally ill with cancer. He is the one who died four days ago. The second is a Green Party supporter and member of Greenpeace, a politically involved woman twenty-four years of age. The other two were released after questioning, cases of mistaken identity."

"The second's been charged. Driving a stolen vehicle in the Biedenhof case. Any connection to an organisation?"

"None."

"But she's an activist. House searches turned up masses of political pamphlets and e-mail addresses. What else do we have on her? And on the deceased teacher? Any new details?"

"My knowledge is no greater than yours. Neither carried a weapon or offered resistance on arrest, neither made a confession to involvement in any group or movement."

"Small fry, then?"

"It would appear so."

"Not your typical terrorist."

"No."

Klaustaler pursed thin lips. With a cynical tone: "Are they terrorists?"

"What is the definition of a terrorist? I would say not in the usual sense of the word. But the act of kidnap is a serious crime."

"And yet only two've been nabbed. Despite hundreds of police on alert, the roadblocks, the manhunts – despite the formation of a special squad?"

Beck spread his hands. "Past experience teaches us that it takes time, patience and a great deal of groundwork."

"Costing the taxpayers a packet."

"There is little doubt that a breakthrough will come one of these days."

Klaustaler without pause, with impatience: "This is all too airy-fairy – let's get at the meat, Herr Beck. You've made it your business to become a leading authority in this field and you've been closely following events since the very first kidnap. What's your personal opinion? Who's behind all this? How big are they, how're they organised?"

Beck sat there. A tiredness in his face. "As to who, your guess is as good as mine," he said quietly. "Activists at the very least." He sat unmoved, unmoving. "Research would indicate that perhaps a hundred or more are involved, possibly divided into separate groups. Each group may have a particular function, for example abduction, transport, operation of safe-houses, questioning during captivity, and so forth. And each group might be subdivided into isolated cells. The whole would appear to possess a classical structure as observable in any terrorist or guerrilla organisation."

"Ah-hah. And why? What's their motivation?"

"A socio-political philosophy."

"Political? In the interview just now the minister denied this."

"What is not political?" Beck smiled a small sad smile. "I am sure the minister had his personal reasons for such judgement."

"So what's this philosophy as you choose to call it? What're their aims, what the devil're they trying to achieve?"

Beck, pausing. "I believe, as many have correctly been doing in the previous months, that analysing the kinds of persons who have been abducted sheds light on this question. Let us consider – out of a total of eleven we have a judge, three politicians including a minister..." counting on his fingers "...a bishop and a priest, two bankers, the director of a charity and two influential industrialists. We are all looking for a common denominator."

"Which in your opinion is?"

Unflustered, Beck continued: "We observe that all are male, in positions of power in one form or another and, on detailed inspection, that all are or have been involved in scandals whether financial, political, social or moral. And furthermore that each will or has emerged unscathed."

"Ah-hah," repeated Klaustaler. "So you subscribe to this theory too. Now we're getting somewhere. These people're out to punish, then? Revenge? That what you mean?"

"I think not."

"What then?"

"I believe a form of correction."

"Correction?"

"A moral correction of ways, of attitudes."

"Through coercion? Through brainwashing?" The sound of sarcasm. "Like in a Stalinist or Maoist corrective camp?"

"Through a more subtle and professional form of brainwashing."

A curt jerk of Klaustaler's head. "You're in line with one or two others on this point."

"Indeed. *The Times* of London wrote an excellent article recently to this effect. As did the *FAZ* in one of last Saturday's *feuilletons*."

"Assuming you're correct – bit naïve of these radicals, wouldn't you say? What do they think they'll achieve even if they succeed in brainwashing a few individuals?"

"Considered superficially, I agree." Beck nodded. He nodded thoughtfully, sagely. "I believe, though, we have to delve deeper and pose different questions."

"For example?"

"For example, will the effect of these abductions a) create any wider and salutary ripples amongst others in positions of power, and b) accelerate the demands for stricter checks and balances already emanating from various quarters of our increasingly disillusioned society? Or, for example, should no long-overdue and deep-seated reforms be set in motion by the powers that be, is this phase of kidnapping all that these people have planned or only the tip of the iceberg?" Beck calmly raised his brows. "One could surmise, is this group just the visible hand of an as yet unknown grassroots movement?"

Klaustaler, watching sharply: "You aware of any?"

"There are indications."

"A grassroots movement?" A protrusion of the lips, a sceptical twitch of moustache. "You think there's more to these kidnaps than meets the eye, then?"

Seemingly unperturbed, and not losing his train of thought, Beck replied: "We are in the midst of yet another financial crisis, unprecedented national debt and increasing poverty. I am listening to all the small voices, to the students, to the man in the street with family to feed and lost job, the housewife trying to make ends meet, the wasted and unemployed youth. I hear their anger and impotence at immorally greedy bankers and capitalists, their disgust with the same old empty promises from politicians. I hear too their gut insecurities and fears. These are the sounds of unrest."

"The system breaking down?"

"No."

"A revolution brewing?" More sarcasm.

"Also no." Another tired smile. "We are blessed to live in a constitutional democracy, in the fairest form of political system known to man, of which there are tragically far too few in this world. The man in the street is no fool, he is aware of this. But our system has its faults, whose widening cracks have too long been ignored. What we are witnessing is a deepening unease amongst an ever greater number of people. They expect and deserve more than they are receiving from our society's so-called leaders."

"You paint a dismal picture, Herr Beck."

"A realistic picture, I believe."

"So what's in the works? In your so-called grassroots? What's behind the kidnaps?"

"I believe we are dealing with a possibly very serious movement, one intent on seeing that necessary changes are made."

"Who are they?"

"I have no details."

"Take an educated guess?"

A spreading of Beck's hands. "If we look closer at our society we observe that, apart from our political and industrial leaders, there exists a further influential group — that of thinkers and experts in various fields. Let us call them concerned and non-political citizens. Amongst these, it is my guess, are persons who have lost patience, persons painfully aware that certain fundamental reforms for the long-term good of our country can be postponed no longer, and that politicians are mostly only capable of short-term solutions and patching over the cracks."

"Assuming you're right, what're they intending to do?"

"Who knows? One hopes it will be in the democratic tradition."

"Like what? What's your opinion?"

"Setting more dramatic strikes and demonstrations in motion, for example." A gentle shrug. "Mass demonstrations with much venting of frustration and anger. They make good publicity and scare the politicians in power. And mass refusal to vote, perhaps. We have already begun to see first vestigial signs."

"Hardly ground-shaking up to now." More sceptical curling of lips. "These things peter out quick enough. Don't they? Storms in teacups. Aren't they?"

"In this country the average middle-class citizen is fearful, apathetic and conformist. Agreed. He yearns for stability and a leader, and the masses follow the herd. We are not France. We should, however, not underestimate the power of the people, if sufficiently provoked and well-organised. Social history teaches us that only upsetting the applecart forces the politician's hand."

"Think there's really any likelihood?"

A slow thoughtful shake of the head. "No." Again that faint philosophical smile. "History also instructs us that the people only rise up and demand change when they have a charismatic leader and nothing left to lose. Our present situation would appear to lack both."

"So the kidnaps, then? A pointless undemocratic start?"

"Well, they have achieved a groundswell of popular sympathy and support. They have informed, publicised and highlighted the depth of corruption and the unravelling of the moral fibre in the ranks of our leading class. This rankles a large majority. They therefore serve as a catalyst, one could say. A small beginning, perhaps. They might just conceivably lead to further demonstrations and civil disobedience. One can only hope the latter achieves the upper hand."

"Do I detect sympathy?"

"You do."

"Well, thank you, Herr Beck." Spoken forcefully. Klaustaler sat upright with a dismissive, interrupting jerk. "Looks as if you've given us some food for thought here, and maybe for future discussions. Which brings us..." he was reaching a hairy, muscular hand to the table before him, picking up the *Spiegel* magazine "...to our next topic."

A camera cut. A close-up of the cover again. One saw his thumb gripping, and his other hand tapping the title.

"Hacking at the goodies?" came Klaustaler's hard voice. Then he and Beck were back in view, a general shot. The journalist was sipping his glass of water, nodding.

Klaustaler followed abruptly: "Any connection with these kidnappers?"

"It is too early to say."

"Try another educated guess?"

"A possibility."

"Another bombshell?"

(Beck, equitably) "Another piece of the puzzle."

(Klaustaler forcibly) "A scoop though."

"That would be an exaggeration." A close-up of Beck's sensitive face.

"Too modest."

A light shrug of shoulders, nothing more.

"Is the story in every facet true?"

"Naturally."

"No risk of false information?"

"No."

"Who spilled the beans?"

(Beck, steadfastly) "We don't disclose confidential sources."

Klaustaler didn't blink. He came in on a different tack, speaking rapidly: "A hacker breaking into bank accounts – secret numbered accounts?"

"Mostly. Not exclusively. There are instances of coded names as well as original ones, for example, in association with trust funds."

"A professional hacker?"

"Or hackers, plural," Beck said. "Correct."

"They entered how many banks?"

"Let us say several."

"In how many different countries?"

"Three."

"They had insiders' help? In these banks and finance companies?"

"One cannot exclude the possibility."

"One recalls earlier cases of tax evasion. Discs sold to governments – to the British, French, and ours. Any connection?"

"No."

"Those were just bank clerks after reward?"

"Precisely."

Klaustaler's powerful fingers were flicking up, counting: "Secret slush funds, bribe money, tax fraud caches – the list of illegal nest eggs is long. All looted?"

"From those on the first disc, yes. Electronically."

"Minus a lump-sum tax deduction?" Hair-backed fingers turning again, hand stretching out palm up, as if beseeching. "Passed anonymously to the tax authorities?" A mirthless smirk on Klaustaler's lips again. "Sort of Robin Hood stuff? Stealing the cookies from the rich, giving them back to the people?"

"It would seem so. In a manner of speaking."

"Okay – now to the next one. You write that there're two discs. And on the second?"

"Also names, accounts and sums of money. These accounts were untouched."

"Why?"

"One believes the disc contains particular names of individuals and organisations, possibly of political or religious nature, and dates of transfers, and recipients of payment. Perhaps of interest to the powers that be."

"Passed on to whom? And when?"

"I am not at liberty to disclose this."

"But some while ago."

"Possibly."

"There've been no arrests, no charges made public. Why not?"

"Apparently not. This is my information, too."

"Why not?"

No answer from Beck.

"Cover-up?"

"Let us say there is the factor of security and the question of public confidence to be taken into consideration, certain boundaries which may not be crossed."

"For one known for directness you're unusually reticent."

"In this instance, yes."

"You been pressured?"

"No comment."

"Your scoop's stirred up a hornet's nest, though?"

"Yes."

"We still talking about the second disc?"

A nod from Beck, a silent nod.

"You mentioned individuals. Public figures?"

"Possibly."

"Including politicians?"

"I must pass here."

"And organisations. Political, religious? German Nationalist Party? Islamic?"

"Again, no comment."

Klaustaler seemed to hesitate an instant. His hand rose, touched the side of his head. Was that a tiny receiver tucked behind his ear? Switching, he said: "I gather you have more up your sleeve, Herr Beck."

"Of somewhat speculative nature."

"Ah-hah. A projected second instalment of your article's to be published in next week's *Spiegel* edition. This going to form part of the content?"

"This is, at present, under review. The timing has not been precisely set." Beck sat there calmly, a neutral expression.

"It won't then?"

"An editorial decision."

"So there is pressure, then?"

"There are certain factors to be considered."

Again Klaustaler paused. A fleeting frown, an almost non-existent nod. He backtracked: "Let's return to the first disc. These looted accounts – what quantities of money we talking about?"

Beck sipped water. "The approximate total is over one point two billion." He replaced the glass. "This is the figure we are aware of. It may be more."

"A tidy sum. Where did the hackers transfer it to?"

"All to one numbered account in a foreign bank."

"In the Middle East, you reported."

"Yes."

"From which that Robin Hood deduction was transferred back to the central tax authority?"

"About one third of it. Yes."

"And the rest — what — say over three-quarters of a billion? Still there?"

"No."

"Been what's euphemistically termed 'laundered'?"

"Correct."

"Where to then?"

"Untraceable."

"Could've gone anywhere?"

"Not quite anywhere. But the choice is great, shall we say."

"So how was the Middle East account located — by our tax people?"

"Via the central bank. And through the CIA."

"Yes, intriguing. You wrote, during one of their searches. For global terrorists?"

"For sponsors, yes."

"That where your tip came from? CIA?"

A faint smile on Beck's lips. "No."

"Where then?"

"A German source."

"BND?"

Another smile, fleeting, almost sad. "I am certain you do not expect an answer there."

"The CIA passed on the information to our people, then." A statement.

A nod from Beck, nothing more.

"Did they pass on more stuff than that? For other areas?"

"Of that I have no knowledge."

Klaustaler leant back. A creak of white canvas. Elbows on the chair arms, he steepled his muscular hands. "Three-quarters of a billion plus disappeared into thin air? These hackers hit the jackpot." His square chin pressed on fingertips. "Who are they, Herr Beck?"

"As I indicated, that lies in the realm of speculation."

"Young jokers? Do-gooders with perverse sense of humour?" His dark eyebrows lifted. "Or these kidnappers? They behind it?"

"I repeat. A possibility."

"Only a possibility, Herr Beck?"

Beck sat there quietly, returning the stare. Said nothing.

"There's a rumour, is there not?" Klaustaler pursued. "Read today's *FAZ*?"

"I did. Naturally."

"Talking about the piece by your colleague Landauer."

"Roland is a young and already excellent investigative reporter."

"So it seems. In a nutshell his article concentrates on other recent financial transactions connected to four of the kidnap victims and made by proxy in their names to charities after their abduction. Very dubious transactions, in the form of donations by close associates or organisations, including the Catholic Church and an Islamic society. Does one detect the hand of the kidnapers at work here?

"One should not rule it out until disproved."

"Or proved? Landauer also quoted from your piece here..." Klaustaler tapped the magazine on the tabletop, "...the names of all four of these victims are included on the lists from the first disc. An interesting fact, don't you think? Small world?"

"Indeed. And I am certain Roland Landauer's sources are impeccable." A smile from Beck again. It was warmer this time. "He is one step ahead of me there."

"Is he? You were previously aware of this fact too, of course?"

"No."

"No? He further hints that certain members of the press're aware of the identity of at least one of the kidnappers. How about commenting on this?"

"I am not prone to conjecture."

Klaustaler let his hands fall, gripped the tubular arms of his chair. "I'll phrase the question another way, Herr Beck. Believe you're very much in a position to air an opinion on the relationship between the kidnappers and hackers."

"It appears my colleague is better informed."

"But you have your informers too." Another statement.

"In my profession, lacking sources would mean impotence to discover and report the truth behind stories."

"You don't deny it, then?"

"No. But truths are often hidden in the undergrowth and hard to find. They do not grow on trees."

"To extrapolate your analogy then, you've got someone in the undergrowth here, at least amongst the hackers. So I repeat the question – they and the kidnappers part and parcel of the same phenomenon?"

"An interesting hypothesis which at this stage I can neither confirm nor deny."

"Landauer seems to know more."

"As I just conjectured, I would not presume to judge otherwise."

"If this be the case, this thing's growing. Is it a Hydra? What'll come next?"

"Again one could only speculate."

"Could one, Herr Beck? Only speculate?" Klaustaler leaned forward again, staring. "You and Landauer are not just colleagues, I hear, you're close friends."

"You hear correctly."

"In collusion on these stories?"

A relaxed blink of Beck's eyes. "Collusion is by definition a negative and, in this context, inappropriate word. Were you to mean collaboration, the answer naturally is still no. Privately we are friends, professionally we are competitors."

Again Klaustaler gave a curt nod, and dry smile. He was touching his ear again. "Unfortunately I hear our time's running out. Just two more questions, Herr Beck, and I'd be grateful for short answers..." His sharp eyes were watchful. "The logistics for this series of abductions must be highly complex and costing a bomb – put an approximate figure on it?"

Beck spread his sensitive hands. "With so many unknowns, an impossible task."

"Have a go."

A pursing of lips, a moment of consideration. "In case A, if the victims are being transported to and held in some foreign country, many millions in double digits I dare say. In case B, if hidden somewhere in this country or Europe, at least a million or two no doubt."

"So this way or that there must've been a number of generous sponsors up to now. D'you have any knowledge of where this financial support's been coming from?"

"No." Again that quiet, pensive, almost secretive smile. "Possibly my colleague Roland Landauer could provide an answer. Perhaps you should ask him."

And the prompt reply: "Maybe the cash flow's run dry and these people need a new source of revenue." A satisfied sigh, a grunt. "A three-quarter billion'd go a damn long way."

Klaustaler was gathering himself, reaching out his heavy hand. "Our thanks, Herr Beck..." Dark eyes moving sideways to the camera. "On this note we have to..." He spoke rapidly, clipped, signing off. Turned his gaze back to Beck "...and I'm sure many'll be awaiting impatiently that follow-up article of yours..."

Then, once more to the camera, gruffly: "That was an interview with Christian Beck, journalist and author. For more information on this evening's theme-programme please visit our website address now coming up on the screen. I'm Theo Klaustaler. We wish you a..."

I pressed the little loudspeaker button on the remote. The sound cut off.

Wincing apathetically, I looked round at Annabelle again. She'd curled up her feet, legs bent beside her, elbow propped, chin on thin fingers. Beyond her, the windows, the turquoise sky turning slowly to night. In silence she watched me, red eyebrows raised.

"Friend of yours, you say?" I said.

"Mmm," she murmured. "Of the family."

"Not a bad journalist." I squinted at her. "In fact quite a good one."

"Mmm-hmm." The tip of her tongue showed for a moment.

I chuckled. Glanced back at the screen. Beck and Klaustaler were still in view, sitting there at their table. Beck had crossed his legs, leaning back, hands folded on a knee. The fingers were long and fine; they reminded me of Matthias's hands. Slowly the camera was retreating from them. Klaustaler had said something, Beck was answering – his hands moved as he spoke; they were expressive, like a quiet extension of his speech. And before the picture faded I remember his eyes in that tired face, gazing...

"Want to watch more?" I said to Annabelle.

"No."

So I pushed the red button and the screen went dead. But although it was blank I could see those eyes still – bright and steady and blue, they gave away a dedication, a love of intellectual life. His world was also that of Annabelle and her father, the one she'd grown up in, in which she felt at home.

We sat there, side by side. Talking in the twilight. I hung a leg over the padded arm of my chair, twisted so I could see her better. I think we talked briefly about the contents of the interview but the subject didn't interest me greatly; what more could I contribute? They'd said it all.

And I was feeling sleepy. I recall her soon steering the conversation back to Christian Beck, Beck the man, and their past, her feelings about him. I recall too her facial expression as she spoke and the pang of jealousy it woke in my breast.

The last words I heard before my concentration completely deserted me were: "I should like you to meet him, I believe then you will better appreciate," and there was something catching in her voice which I suppose could've been a revelation.

Then my mind was wandering away, my gaze slipping sideways through the windows. Perhaps it was all the museums that morning and afternoon, together with the wine from dinner, or my sleepiness, or the effect that Florence had upon me – whatever the reason, an invisible force was now drawing me outwards, out of that room into the twilight of the dying day. And the earthly life with all its complexities and its discussions, all those erudite words, those worldly woes, were shrinking away, losing their importance. They seemed so far off now... I was drifting into the indigo sky and there were other voices, golden voices, and the face of Professor Skell was floating, his words coming clear... and I was rising up, I had no cares, I was feeling so good and thinking, could he conceivably be right, was there really something up there way beyond the dark and the clouds, beyond the reach of our powers of perception and would we one day discover the truth, discover what we were all about?

It was a curious sensation, but it didn't last.

Chapter 21

Another day went by and all was normal again. We spent it quietly; I was counting the hours. Then the morning of the seventh day dawned, our last. On waking, lying there in bed, we decided to make a trip out into the Toscana; we decided quite spontaneously. Just to relax, enjoy the scenery, follow our noses.

"We could head in the direction of Volterra," Annabelle said.

I contacted a hire firm via the reception, rented a car. On request they gave me an open-top cabriolet – I felt that would be fun. At about ten o'clock we set off. I went unwittingly, couldn't know what was waiting out there. Yes, I'd forgotten Estella's words.

After twenty minutes we were leaving the outskirts of Florence behind; I got off the main *strada* as soon as I could, heading sedately south-west. Country lanes, gentle rolling landscapes. Now and then a village or hamlet perched on a hill. The scenery was truly beautiful.

We drove leisurely, the roof folded back, the windows down – we just let the sun pour down upon us, the morning air was in our hair. In Volterra, up on cliffs, we stopped for coffee and strolled the narrow medieval alleys and streets for half an hour. Then continued our lazy way. Stretching open countryside, undulating, occasional clumps of trees, grasslands, fields of wheat and barley, now and then fingers of dark green cypresses, slopes with vineyards and grapes still green.

We passed a signpost. Had I read it correctly? I braked unhurriedly, reversed. San Gimignano. I glanced at Annabelle. She sat there relaxing, eyes half-closed watching me, one arm laid behind me on the back of my seat. A contented, uninvolved, you're-doing-the-driving kind of smile. I branched off, followed the signs, followed the road.

The little town came into sight up on its hill. We approached; even at a distance one could see its famous stone towers above the trees. I paused at the roadside, took a photograph. Outside the walls we parked and paid, a sea of cars, walked the short road up to the gateway. Old cobbles and stone houses, wooden balconies, throngs of tourists – and some of the towers extraordinarily tall. I aimed my old camera a couple of times; I still have the photographs. We explored small piazzas and alleyways, read the dates and histories of buildings, ate lunch in shade. Annabelle bought a picture in a quiet square higher up the hill. I like the watercolour; it reminds me. In fact I looked at it again recently while visiting. The artist packed it himself as the two of them talked of Italian masters. They talked in Italian; I just sat there in his studio in the background, a small insignificant figure silently lounging in the shadows amongst canvases, like an unseen voyeur – observing, watching her in pleasure, enjoying her joy, the gestures of her hands, breathing in her body and her beauty. Was I really the lucky man? Yes, I sat there indulging, the proud possessor of dreams. It was such a great day, no premonitions.

We were on the road again. In the mirror I watched the towers slowly receding. We had no further goal or direction, now we had half the day to ourselves.

It was mid-afternoon, the sun was still high, hot on our heads. I took a side-turning, then another. At random, with abandon. We were deep in the countryside again, on a minor road. Yes the sun was very hot. I accelerated to cool us a little; to catch more wind in our hair. I remember, Annabelle was leaned back, her face tipped to the sun, eyes closed, one arm hanging out over the side, fingers trailing. I glimpsed her sideways, drank her in, quickly looked back to the winding road ahead. She looked so good. Was she really there? Did we really belong together? My head was drowsy from the heat.

A fork in the road, languidly I took the right-hand branch. The minutes passed. I side-glanced again, at her relaxed repose. Was she sleeping? Was I too slipping into a half-dose? Maybe I should...

We passed through a copse, flickering light and shredded shade, mesmerising. Out into the sun again, into the open – began climbing a long, steep hill. Ahead, all I could see was the road and the sky – it was almost like ascending into heaven. I changed to a lower gear, sedately reached the top, came unsuspectingly over the crest... and had to brake the car abruptly, had to stare...

Before me, spread out below, a view to take the breath away – basking beneath the Toscana sun, as far as the eye could see, a patchwork quilt of meadows and fields and distant hills gradually melting into haze – a fantasy world, a carpet of colour, a fairy tale.

I stopped the car, switched off the ignition.

Annabelle murmured. I turned to touch her, turned to share. But her eyes were still closed, she was fast asleep. I gazed through the windscreen. I just sat there absorbing the scene. Five minutes passed, maybe ten; the beauty was almost overwhelming. A wave of happiness welled up inside, swelling, swamping...

Still Annabelle slumbered.

Sluggishly, as if half in a dream, as if drugged, I started the engine, released the handbrake, let the car roll slowly forward down the long incline into the view. A whisper of air on my face again. Meadows full of flowers in the mellow sunlight, slipping by... there were larks in the sky, and over the meadows swarms of blue butterflies...

I was about halfway down. A curious feeling was growing as I descended, a strange sensation, a sense of déjà vu. Somehow this was all so familiar. It seemed as though something was happening – what was it? For a moment longer, though, I didn't comprehend... till I saw before me the expanse of red poppies.

Then I remembered. And I knew where I was – yes, I'd been here before. I blinked, gripping onto the steering wheel. It couldn't be true. I blinked once more – I thought if I did my eyes would stop fooling me, the mirage would dissolve, the fantasy fade. But it didn't.

As if in slow motion the carpet of red poppies came closer. Now it was right next me, so close I could've almost reached out and touched it. I let the car come to a crawl, the colour was glowing, pulsing, intense. But I was looking for something else, I was peering, searching... then there it was – the winding stony track just like in the dream, between the poppies. And I knew, too, I only had to raise my eyes and I would be able to see...

There it stood.

The old farmhouse on its rise. And the track winding up to it. Even at that distance I recognised its form, its details – the faded-red roof tiles softened by lichen, the weathered grey stone, the wisteria, windows like eyes. And the cypress trees, dark, green pencils. I started to count them, but it wasn't necessary: I knew that already too. Five on one side, two on the other. And I could just discern the orchard of olive trees beyond, ancient and gnarled...

Where the track met the road I pulled the car onto the verge, switched off the engine again.

Absolute stillness. No tractors, no traffic, no drone of aeroplanes. Just the twitter of the larks and the hum of bees. The stillness pressed on my ears like an echoing drum.

The sun beat down.

Annabelle was fast asleep. Carefully, so as not to awaken her, I opened the door, got out of the car. Took a few steps. Wary steps. Stood a moment. The sense of happiness was still there, a kind of elation which buoyed me, carried me. Despite the hot sun I seemed light as a feather, filled with an energy I couldn't explain.

I began walking, slowly along the track.

Something was blocking my thoughts, stopping me from thinking, from posing questions, from starting to rationalise. The house drew me. Like a magnet draws. Thousands of red poppies, to right and left, their papery, ephemeral heads turned, glowing, lifted to the sun. Hazy, lazy blue sky above. I could still hear the larks, and the beat of my heart, feel the blood in my veins.

I was completely alone. I bathed in the beauty.

The track meandered, going up the rise, climbing the hill. Still I walked, unperturbed. The poppy field fell away, replaced by meadows sloping upwards – a mass of yellow buttercups, bright, almost blinding. And beyond, green and white and blue, going on as if for ever, moon daisies and cornflowers amongst long fronds of feathery grasses. My feet carried me onwards, effortlessly. A feeling of floating almost, of just existing. And all the while, up ahead, the farmhouse coming closer.

Small smooth stones beneath my feet, well packed from many wheels. Moss in the crevices. Left and right the brilliant yellow buttercups reflecting sun. I continued climbing up the slope.

Nothing moved, not a breath of wind.

And strange, the higher I climbed the lighter I felt, as though the air were becoming more rarefied. Closer now. The farmhouse mesmerised. It seemed to beckon. Its old roman roof tiles shimmered in the heat, its irregular windows, some small some big, deep-set hollows, their panes of glass watching me. What lay behind them – what was hidden there in the house? I remembered the dream: there were people waiting for me, expecting me.

Only a couple of dozen paces now...

The track swerved away towards a built-on outhouse like a barn with open doors and empty dark; a path continued straight up to the front door. Fifteen paces...

Flagstones in moss foot-worn and grey, a bed of roses. Beyond, a crescent of iron chairs, a marble-topped table. Against the wall of the house an old wooden bench. Another ten paces and I'd be there. Nine... eight... Everything was slowing down, the door coming closer frame by frame like in a film that's breaking down...

Suddenly my feet were turning to lead, a heavy blanket wrapped round my brain... five paces... four...

A glimpse of wisteria, thick-trunked and gnarled, silver-grey, like an ancient vine clinging to the stonework and spreading around the front door. Its blooms are pale blue – they hang like bunches of grapes, the scent is ecstatic... it is ecstatic, isn't it?

Now foreign thoughts were crawling in, intrusive thoughts – they ate at the happiness in my breast, like maggots, like acid. Where was that elation disappearing to? Where was the beauty, where was the dream? Why was that feeling of floating going down the drain?

I reached the doorstep. Stopped.

My heart was unsteady. I took a few breaths: my chest quivered each time I breathed. The carved wooden door was painted green just like in the dream – it was full of hair cracks and faded from the sun. The same green door.

No. Not possible. More thoughts were penetrating, undermining... a stone was getting in the works... this is just an optical illusion, a trick of the brain, just a little joke. My memory's playing games with me. Aren't I in fact still in the car? Drowsy from the heat haven't I too, like Annabelle, succumbed to sleep? I'm dreaming again. Dreams do have a tendency of repeating themselves, don't they?

Or don't they? Am I here or am I not? Tentatively I touched the door. It was solid and real. Is it remotely conceivable then? Could this be reality after all? Could the woman in pink be about to open the door?

I gazed at the weathered green panels. My fingers trembled. Hope was springing. If she opens it... but the hope wasn't strong. What if someone else opens it? What if the curious coincidence stops here and a complete stranger appears?

I dithered, uncertain. Began to panic. I told myself: curiosity killed the cat – be wise and just walk away...

Then I saw the bell chain. Old iron links, a ring at the bottom. I knew that chain – I'd had my fingers around it before. It hung beside the stone jamb, its upper end lost to sight in the gnarled tangle of branches and blue blooms. The heavy scent of the wisteria was overwhelming...

Shall I pull it? The bell would ring: I could still hear its jangle from the dream. Then she would open the door. She'd recognise me, although I had never seen her before. At least, she'd implied acquaintance – she had beckoned me in without enquiring after my name. "You're late, give me your shoes," she'd said.

Vacillating, I raised a hesitant hand. Touched the chain the way I'd touched the door. It too was solid and real. Why had I been late? Late for what? The chain was ancient, but not rusty. It hung there. It tempted. Yes, I'd been expected. "We're all here," she'd told me. We? Who's we? I'd never found out. I remembered the disappointment; I'd like to quench that thirst.

I pulled on the chain...

There. I could hear it. The bell tinkled in the depths of the house. No. It jangled – just the way I recalled.

I waited. I could feel my nervousness, my anticipation. The jangle faded. I stood there expectantly; I stood on the threshold, holding my breath, wondering when I crossed it where it would lead.

No sound. No movement, no footsteps.

I stared at the door, but it didn't open. Had they heard me? Should I ring again? Wait a minute. I waited. Then again I tugged on the chain. Again the bell echoing. No reaction. Nothing.

Disappointment began to creep back in. Was nobody there? Who should be there? How should I know? Whose house is it, anyway?

I glanced about for a sign, for a hint. There must be a nameplate. But there was none. I stepped back a few paces, looked up at the house, at the few irregularly-spaced windows in the thick walls above. No face, no-one peering down to see who had rung. I crossed to the ground-floor window near the old wooden bench, cupping my hands to the bright reflecting glass, peeping in. A large hall: vaulted ceiling, bare uneven white walls, big terracotta tiles on the floor. Just a grandfather clock standing dark like a sentinel, and an arch at the far end. No-one in sight.

I began to walk around the house. Turned the first corner. Lawns, the row of tall cypresses marching away, French windows. I peered in. A spacious living room, beamed ceiling: comfortable sofas with deep sunken cushions, a large open hearth, an old armchair. There was a pile of logs, lots of pictures on one wall – landscapes and portraits. Here too, no sign of life.

I turned the next corner. The back of the house. Another bit of lawn, then longer grass, the orchard of olive trees, ancient and twisted. The old house here on this side seemed to crouch, the eaves overhanging, the swooping tiled roof. Two windows. One was open. Slowly I approached it. Glanced about me; I had a sudden feeling of being observed. But no-one in view. Empty spaces, only light and shadows amongst the knotted trees. I reached the window. It opened inwards. Very carefully I peeped round the frame. Rapid, slightly guilty glances. A study. But there was nobody in it either.

The room was fairly big. Busy and cluttered: shelves from floor to ceiling like an untidy library, filled with books, some laid flat. More books in higgledy-piggledy heaps on the timber floor. Directly before me, in front of the window opening, an old oak desk with worn leather inlay and reading lamp, an old-fashioned swivel chair. On the desk piles of written papers and notes, newspaper cuttings, a granite pebble as paperweight and an inkstand, a small slender statue of bronze. On the corner near me stood a ceramic red goblet with black Roman figures which looked antique, full of pencils and pens. To one side, a book lay open as though only briefly abandoned and soon to be referred to again: strips of paper markers peeped from between thumbed pages. In the middle of the worn leather inlay, neatly placed in front of the empty chair, was another book, a paperback, closed. I knew the title before I read it. And beside it lay the small spiral notebook. And the fountain pen.

I stood there motionless, staring.

Then started again, uneasily. Yes, someone was watching me... I could feel the gaze. I turned, opening my mouth, about to speak, about to apologise...

But there was nobody there.

x x x

I saw Annabelle before she saw me.

She had stopped on the track leading up to the farmhouse, pausing to look at the poppies. She stood there, face turned away, a small figure almost lost in a field of blood-red.

Slowly I went down the long slope towards her; I think I trod uncertainly. Trying to rationalise, trying to grasp what I couldn't comprehend, yet knowing there must be an explanation.

Stones and moss underfoot. Dust on my sandals.

Annabelle standing in her sea of red, enraptured, frozen in time. I was coming on down. She turned and saw me, waved. I waved back, steeled myself. Her hand had fallen, she was continuing on her way again, moving in my direction. We came close; we met where the poppies met the meadows of gold.

"It is so beautiful." She was smiling softly; the beauty glowed in her eyes.

"Yes," I said. I tried to show that I shared her rapture.

She watched me. Then her eyes were gone, they took the beauty with them. She stooped to the mass of buttercups, picked one. Held it playfully under her chin, teasing, raising her head. "Do you see gold?" she said gaily. "When I grow up will I be rich?"

"You will," I assured.

"You're not looking."

"I don't need to."

"You have to look."

"I'm telepathic."

She laughed, let the flower hover. She was watching my eyes again. "That is cheating." She brushed my cheek with the buttercup, then held it beneath my own chin. "Now let us see if you will become rich too." She peered. "Oooooh!" she exclaimed. "So much gold. You will become the richest man in all the land."

"I am already..."

"Big-head. You are cheating again."

"From the moment I met you," I said. Did I say it too seriously?

"From the moment I met you," I tried again, "I gained that golden jaundiced look."

She tipped her head, her freckled face was close. "That counts." She ran the flower down my nose, and kissed me. "That was a nice thing to say." She threw the flower away.

Took my hand. My distant distraught hand. We turned together, began to stroll, side by side, back down the track towards the car. After maybe a couple of minutes I heard her say quietly: "I fell asleep. How could I have!"

"It's hot," I offered.

"I was so drowsy."

I liked the feel of her hand in mine. It reassured. It distracted. I said nothing.

"You should have woken me."

I side-glanced. "You looked so sublime."

"Wow, another compliment! But nevertheless."

"You always look sublime when you're asleep." I said it in a drawl to pull her leg. "The way your mouth sags. And the way you dribble when you dream..."

I choked, I coughed, I doubled up. That was a sharp elbow she'd jabbed in my guts.

We walked on in silence, poppies all around. The car in sight ahead.

She threaded her arm through mine. She was watching me sideways. "You went all the way up to the farmhouse? I didn't realise small men like you could walk so far."

"Thank you for your faith."

"Was it nice?"

"Pretty view," I said.

She stopped me. I returned her gaze as best I could, it wasn't time to talk. She raised a hand and stroked my brow. Was she trying to wipe away the frown? I shook my head; but I was shaking it at myself. Had Estella on my mind.

I needed time – until next day.

x x x

We were on the flight back before I broached the subject. I was sitting beside her, sunk in the aircraft seat, row four. I felt small, smaller than I usually do: my stretched-out legs didn't even come near reaching the Business Class seat in front of me. I sat there shrunken, my insecurity was a jungle, my uncertainty a cage.

I hadn't slept well. I'd lain awake in the dark, attempting to take my bearings, sort my thoughts, decide what I believed and what not, what was reality, what was dream. I tried to define the dividing line, the boundary in between.

I didn't get far. The facts were clear, they couldn't be denied, refused to be juggled; they contradicted the logic in my rational brain and permitted no explanation. There was no boundary, and certainly no blur or overlap – in fact there was a gaping gap, there was black and white and that was that. I'd had a dream, full stop. And the dream had mostly come true. Also full stop. There was a hole in the middle and nothing to connect the one with the other, at least not in my eyes, not in my process of reasoning.

It must've been after three in the morning when, exhausted, I came to the only conclusion I could: I'd adjourn the problem and talk to Estella about it just as soon as I was able. Estella – my shelter in every storm. Then I went for a pee, came back, lay down again and sank into a troubled sleep.

The plane was increasing altitude; there was a lot of haze, it looked a lot like I felt. I turned my head to Annabelle. My cropped hair on the back of my skull scraped on the *Lufthansa* headrest. She was reading, absorbed in her book. But the moment had come. Upon waking, my conscience regarding her had presented itself with more clarity. I discovered I'd changed my mind about first approaching Estella, had established the order of priorities. It was a question of allegiance: if Annabelle and I seriously were to become partners, I had to learn to share.

She turned a page, glanced up. I suppose she had felt my gaze. Our eyes met, she smiled. A slow, relaxed smile.

"Hello, my pensive one," she said quietly.

"Hi."

Fingertips resting on the open book, her eyes steady and clear.

"I need to talk," I said.

She nodded. Just nodded. "Mmm." She marked the page, closed the book, laid it on her lap. I glimpsed the bookmarker peeping out. A paper-thin gold clip, a *menorah* engraved upon it.

I concentrated. "I hate to disturb the bookworm in you, but I believe I owe it to you."

"Owe me?" She regarded me calmly, cheek on the headrest cushion beside me.

"An explanation." I paused. I was fumbling for the right words. "For yesterday. The hill, the farmhouse."

A faint smile, eyes soft. "Perhaps you owe it to yourself."

I shrugged. "Perhaps you're right."

She was watching. Said nothing.

"Something happened." I stopped. This wasn't easy.

She nodded slowly again. Nothing more.

"Couldn't tell you yesterday. Needed to sleep on it."

Her eyes were so relaxing, calming.

"I needed to try and find an explanation." I fidgeted my hands. But that green gaze was helping. Awkwardly I attempted a laugh – it came out strangled. "It's not often my tongue gets tied in knots," I admitted.

Another faint smile on her lips. Ah, those expressive beautiful lips. I watched them a moment. Unhurriedly they parted, and said: "My grandmother taught me that the little secret about knots is not to try undoing them all at once."

"Yes," I said. I was still watching those lips.

I took a breath. "Two days ago I had a dream," I started. I paused a second. Yes, that sounded better – that was a better beginning. "I dreamt I was walking through poppy fields along a track to a farmhouse on a hill..." Briefly I recounted the elements of the dream – winding up with the cypresses, wisteria, the green door and the bell. I postponed the last part about the woman in pink. "It was the same farmhouse we saw yesterday," I ended. "The setting was the same too – all the details. Even the blue butterflies." I watched her along the cushions. Her face was close, she didn't speak.

"It was absurd," I added, and lowered my eyes. Still she didn't speak. But I saw her hands – they were taking the book, tucking it into the seat pocket in front of her. And she was turning towards me, her legs twisting too.

I looked back at her face, deliberating. Then I said: "I thought I had a screw loose. This sort of thing only happens in the imagination. I thought, maybe I was dreaming again." I shook my head, wryly.

She sat there sideways, considering me. "My poor confused one," she said.

I spread my hands. "That's how I feel."

A thoughtful gaze, a silence.

"Am I going mad?" I asked.

"I am sure you are not."

"What's happening, then?"

Again that distant smile. Was she laughing at me? What should I say? I gripped my hands together, impatiently. She was reaching out, she touched my arm, stroking.

"Have you never experienced a dream which came true?" She said it so simply, matter-of-factly.

"No."

"Never before?"

"No."

"My poor one. Are you sure?" She was blinking calmly, gazing at me, blinking like a contented cat.

"Yes," I said. I suppose I said it automatically.

Again she was silent. Waiting, just watching.

So I cast my mind back just in case. I tried to recall other dreams, any at all I'd had in the past, ones of any significance. There was that recurring dream – I was being hunted, trying to run, my legs getting heavy, getting paralysed, my pursuers were catching up on me, cornering me, threatening... I frowned, sweating – an unpleasant feeling swelled. I suppressed it. That had never happened in real life, though. And there was that other dream, too, which kept repeating, that dreadful vertigo dream – I was on a cliff-face clambering, or on the façade of a building, getting dizzier, then looking down, oh my God, my fingers were slipping, I couldn't hold on, was starting to fall...

But no – those dreams also had never come true, thank God.

I frowned again. I used to dream of Judit too, that she'd come back. But she never did. And once I dreamt I was flying, like a bird, and woke up to deep disappointment. And...

And then there it was.

That other dream – that house, with all those rooms and all those doors. I was searching for something but I didn't know what and Matthias had suddenly appeared, confronting me...

"No," I said, correcting.

I was back in the aircraft seat, I was staring at Annabelle's hand on my arm. I looked up. "No," I repeated. "There was one maybe, a bit similar, but..." I stirred awkwardly. "A few months ago." I could scarcely breath, my lungs were a lump. "I dreamt of an old friend from my childhood, and two days later out of the blue he wrote to me..." There was that sensation again, the one I'd had on reading his postcard – that insecurity, and curiosity.

I described it to her, there wasn't much to recount – finished by saying: "The only connection between dream and reality though was the fact that both concerned Matthias. The subject matter was different in each – so it was really just coincidence..."

I stopped. Estella hovered. I could hear her voice now...

I shut out her words. Grunted. Sat there. Annabelle smiled upon me.

"Was it not a little strange, all the same?" she said.

I didn't respond.

"I don't believe in coincidences anyway, you see." Her voice was so certain, just like Estella's had been, like Professor Skell's had been. It seemed I'd stumbled onto a nest of believers.

I grunted again. "You sound like Estella," I said.

She gave a small laugh. Clean warm breath on my face. "Ah, your lamp in the dark!" More breath like a breeze. "I remember." She rearranged her hands on her lap, peaceably. "What you experienced yesterday, however, would not seem to leave so much room for doubt, would it."

Had that been a question? It didn't sound like one.

"It appears not," I said. "Nevertheless..."

She was waiting. "Nevertheless?"

I could feel it: she was handling me like one carrying raw eggs. I shook my head.

"Why are you fighting it?" she said gently.

"I'm not fighting it. I'm merely..."

"Yes you are, my stubborn one."

I shrugged. Again didn't reply.

"Don't you believe you could try to simply accept it? You might discover it opens up new perspectives."

Not those again. "No," I said. Did I sound too adamant? So I qualified: "I can accept that it happened, but not why. I'm not prepared to believe there's any meaning behind it or that one can read anything into it."

Another of those irritating cat-like smiles. "There is if one looks. These things happen for our benefit."

Nonsense, I thought. "Benefit?" I said curtly. Was I in a time warp? Again this almost could be Estella speaking, the way she had beside the river that day, and under the acacias in the Café Vienna.

"Mmm." Her green eyes blinked again, benignly. "Actually I would have thought you might consider yourself quite privileged."

"Privileged?" I cocked my head, gave her a squint, and a nasty curl of the lip.

"Mmm." Sovereignly she ignored me. "I imagine people don't receive dreams like this so often. I have read they are sent for a reason."

"From little green men from Mars, you mean?" I exaggerated the squint.

"Don't be so sarcastic."

"Don't be preposterous, Annabelle," I countered. "That's not a worthy explanation. Neither logical nor realistic – doesn't do justice to your intelligence."

"Oh no?" Another laugh, light and relaxed. "My poor puzzled one, there are so many things in our life we cannot explain. Isn't it better if we just accept that there may be more to some of them than meets the eye?" She reached a hand, shook my leg, then squeezed it playfully. She was stooping, peering up into my averted face. "My sceptical one?" she repeated.

I looked apathetically at her eyes, forced myself to grin; it was a sacrifice of great effort. "Who knows?" I said. I thought: am I being too serious, should I laugh at myself? And then straight afterwards I thought: well I ought at least to be honest, maybe I should tell her the rest – after all, I interrupted her reading and I wanted to discuss it briefly, didn't I?

I spread my hands. "It gets worse," I said.

"Your scepticism?"

"That too." I tried a very careful chuckle. "No – I mean what happened yesterday, and at the end of the dream."

Now she was silent again, considering me pensively. Ah, that sensuous mouth, those sexy freckles.

"That old bell-chain beside the front door – well I pulled it," I confessed. "Up to this point dream and reality were one and the same, but here's where they made an unhappy divergence." My hands were getting restless, I tried to steady them again.

"In the dream I rang the bell and a woman opened the door..." I described her appearance, and what happened then, ending: "When she shook me I woke up. When you shook me, too. I never discovered who they were, those people waiting. Rather frustrating."

I paused. Annabelle just sat there watching, neutrally. I was glad she did that.

"But yesterday I have to admit I was... I got a hint." Again I stopped. Had I formulated that wrongly? I returned her gaze, a little guiltily. Contrary to the laws I lived by, I was being forced to confirm what she'd said. "I rang the bell but nobody answered. So I went round the house and at the back there was a window open, to a study. On a desk there I recognised a book and a fountain pen which I'd recently seen."

I shifted awkwardly. "At a café on our first day here in Florence, at the next table." I had to stop once more. I lowered my gaze, I couldn't look Annabelle in the eye. I found my hands clasping each other on my lap, as if they'd never let go.

Calmly she said: "And you know who they belong to?" She said it about as simply as someone holding up some old socks or a pair of soiled panties.

"A theologian," I said. "A certain Professor Skell." I stared at my hands. "I fell into conversation with him. You'd popped off to do some shopping."

She made no reply. I looked up. Discovered her smiling. It was a soft smile again, full of sympathy and understanding – and patience, as if for the immature ways of a child; there was no smugness in it at all. Unhurriedly she said: "I wonder why you dreamt of him?" She said it in a dreamy way.

"He was a strange old bird." I managed a crack of a grimace.

"A theologian," she mused.

"Almost a philosopher."

"Like you, my philosopher?"

"Ah no." I shook my head slowly. "He was definitely from a far higher league."

"How unusual. In contrast to most other people, it would seem he left quite an impression on you, wouldn't it." Her voice was devoid of sarcasm.

"I can't deny that," I said. I was remembering. The memory haunted. I could see the old man: the wrinkles, skin like parchment, the silver hair, that ethereal voice...

"I imagined it must be him," she said.

"You did?" I queried.

"Mmm. His name was on the letterbox."

"Letterbox?"

"Beside the road. Where you parked the car."

"Ah," I said. So I'd missed that one.

"How lovely."

I frowned. Lovely? What an extraordinary choice of word. "Lovely?" I echoed.

"Mmm. I wonder what it means."

"There you go again." I twitched my eyebrows at her; I was feeling easier now – now that I'd broached the subject, got it off my chest. I suppressed a chuckle; she was, after all, thirty-nine years old, not a little girl who believes in fairies.

"Perhaps it was something you both talked about," she said. I sensed her stepping carefully, she was carrying those eggs again. Then she added: "Perhaps he awoke something in you."

Had he? He'd talked about God and the miracle of things, and what's behind it all. I pondered. I watched her with as much nonchalance as I could muster, decided to meet her halfway. "It was rather theological," I said.

She was gazing at me, a contented gaze. "I have a friend, a Hungarian. He is a parapsychologist. I think I shall introduce you." Her voice flowed like honey. Was that a shine in her eyes?

"You have so many appropriate friends."

"He says we should act on hunches and open our minds. He believes a hidden meaning can manifest itself and we are able to gain access to knowledge being offered us out of the subconscious."

Again I resisted the desire to mock. "My subconscious?" I hunched my shoulders, pulled a pained face. "I'd prefer to leave that safely locked away in its cage," I said. "I've got more than enough stuff manifesting itself up on the conscious floor." Had I spoken too glibly?

She smiled. Ah, what a magnanimous smile it was. She said: "He says the subconscious knows everything."

And that stopped me in my tracks. But only for a moment. I shook my head. "Preposterous," I said. How could it know everything? "Absolutely everything? In the past, the present and the future?"

The old theologian's face hovered. Why was it hovering? "You believe that too?" I said.

"Mmm."

I shook my head again. I could hear his voice, now, could hear his words...

Gentle fingers began stroking my clasped hands. "My disbelieving one."

...he was talking of the universe and the stars...

Her fingers stroked upon my skin, how soothing was their touch.

I sat beside my father, we were sitting side by side looking up at the moon and the night. And I could hear his words too, but it wasn't his voice, they were the words of the old theologian...

"...I recall as a boy gazing up at the stars, and when I looked through them the universe beyond seemed to go on and on..."

Annabelle's face was so close I almost had to squint. And the stars were still there.

"...how does one explain the creation of life, how can one explain the flower...?"

Overlapping, I heard her saying: "...would you not sometimes like to open your mind, my frowning one, don't you possess any inquisitiveness...?" But my mind was jumping, not opening, it wasn't opening was it? Her friend's sentence was echoing in my head and the old man's voice was whispering: "I sometimes wonder what scientists will discover – the secret of life perhaps, or a power beyond our imagination? Perhaps they will come face to face with God in their test tube, perhaps God is this secret."

I stared at Annabelle but I was only half there. Her face was retreating, or was it me? I seemed to be floating, in a daze, I was letting go or was I being pulled free?

There was something growing – yes, I could feel something growing. What was it? A pang? A hunger? A yearning for something. I was glancing at shadows, peering at faces, I was walking the streets of Florence looking over my shoulder... there – yes, there it was again, that hunger... He was seated at his table... speaking peaceably, his thin but straight back and his old folded hands, speaking of things I couldn't quite touch, as if he knew, as if he'd been there and seen them all...

I sat quite still on the aircraft seat.

The old man, the theologian. Is that what it was, was that what had drawn me... was that the meaning behind the dream? I looked round at Annabelle. She'd leaned back, but her head was still turned towards me. She smiled that quiet and thoughtful smile of hers. She didn't speak.

"I think I've got there," I said.

x x x

It was only another half an hour to Munich.

Then we would be back to normality again. She was saying, practically: "You will almost have forgotten what your office looks like – how long is it since you were last there?"

"Ten weeks," I said. I watched puffy white clouds beyond her face, beyond the cabin window. And I wondered: what little surprises are waiting for me there?

"Will you be driving back to Nuremberg today?"

"I think that would be wise." And I thought: it's Saturday already – only one day to prepare.

"Mmm," she said.

Shared glances, shared thoughts. I watched her eyes. And the strands of red hair hanging loose. Oh God, I thought, it's time for separation again.

"And you?" I said. "What're your plans?"

"I shall be driving down to the Tegernsee on Tuesday. I have one or two things still to sort out at home." She wiped at the hairs, sweeping them from her freckled forehead. "To the children," she added.

"Of course."

"I miss them."

"Of course," I repeated. I shall miss you too, I thought.

Her eyes creased slightly, on her forehead a small frown appeared. Had she read my thoughts, did I give myself away? Unspoken thoughts. I smiled a sardonic smile, turned my gaze. Watched those little clouds again. The sand was running through the hourglass.

"I think..." she began. Paused, deliberating. Was the pause a bad sign? "I think we should take a small break from each other," she said quietly. Oh God, yes, that had been a very bad sign.

"Small?" I stared at the sky.

"I think like a kind of sabbatical. To recharge our batteries, to take our bearings and take stock of our lives."

"Our lives?"

"Mmm. There are still old responsibilities there, aren't there?"

"You're doing quite a lot of thinking," I said. Did I say it emptily?

A faint crease of the crow's feet beside her eyes. "And you, my serious one?"

"I've been trying hard not to."

"I thought until the party."

The party. I'd forgotten about that. She'd mentioned it on the second day, up on the balcony on the seventh floor. In between other more pleasant things. "You're thinking again." I tried a grin. Was I still showing too much chagrin?

"On September the eleventh."

"Ah," I said. And today was only the seventh of August.

"You remember? It is our family tradition at the end of each summer, the last Saturday before the children's winter term."

"Ah, of course."

"That is only five weeks from today. I shall be rather busy, and you no doubt too."

"That's a very big small break," I said. "Sabbatical," I added. I felt myself sinking into darkness like an abyss. I rallied: "Sabbaticals that I know only last a weekend." I could hear the cracks in my humour. "A long weekend at the most." So I tried a smile.

"Don't be angry."

"How could I be that?"

"Disappointed."

"I shall miss you," I admitted. Now I'd gone and said it. I watched her eyes. Was I hoping? Waiting?

But she didn't reply. I'd prayed she would. A kind of confirmation of the same. Her eyes were soft – yet was there a little sadness there, too?

Our hands were touching. The sand kept on trickling through the narrow neck. Only twenty-five minutes to touch-down now. I was still sinking: I tried to prop myself up but my crutches were broken. I thought: it's happening again – we come together then it's time to part. When we're together we're close as two peas in a pod, we're like one, but when we're near for too long does she need to break out? I can feel it, she wants to get out as if it's turned to a cage, and fly free. Is she really made for marriage like we agreed upon on the balcony? Am I? Am I worthy? Or was she playing a game that day? Was I too? Do I want her too much? She's one of these women who seems built that way – is she really one to be tied down?

I looked at her eyes, so steady and mature and lined. They'd seen so much – what were they thinking?

Yes, it's coming soon to goodbye, it's the same old song, I thought – and I still don't know for sure, she keeps me hanging in the air.

Chapter 22

I dislike large parties.
I dislike them with an intensity they deserve. Can't stand crowds and noise. Small private dinner-parties are my upper limit of mass intimacy. I was therefore nervous; I put myself on my best behaviour. The evening of the Goldberg's garden party had arrived.

Since Florence, the intervening weeks had crawled by – too many thoughts of Annabelle, too little work to occupy, to distract. The summer slack, most clients on vacation. Only two highlights. The first an e-mail from Cornelia Bartenbach; she'd left the firm a month before, wished to make a concrete offer. The second was a flying visit from Annabelle late-August; "Hello, my hermit – my body made me change my mind!" On parting she gave me the official invitation; on parting she walked with sore legs, and my back pains were gone.

I drove down from Nuremberg in the afternoon, out of prudence I intended to be nearly punctual. 17:30 was printed simply in black on white. No curly letter-type, no decorative whirls. 'Frau Monique and Herr Elijah Goldberg request the pleasure of your company. Casual attire...' My name was hand-written in blue ink on card and envelope; it wasn't Annabelle's writing.

I suppose the unpretentious wording was what deceived me. Foolishly I thought: I'll take a feather from the cap of the infamous and arrive just fifteen minutes late. But only the strong are shielded by the divine – and the famous will always be forgiven. I hit a traffic jam north of Holledau.

I arrived over an hour and a quarter late.

The parked cars in the chestnut-tree-lined street proclaimed the first warning; they seemed to go on for ever. The second was the sudden late-summer shower – I could swear it came from nowhere. I reached open entrance-gates but a youth in uniform waved me away. At the far end of a row I parked. Had to wait a moment: big rattling raindrops splodging the dust on the windscreen, rain pattering on the canvas roof.

Is this an omen? I thought. Like the leaking pen at the start of the exam? Or like the ancient Greek priest at the sacrifice nervously reading bad entrails before the assembled warriors went off to lose the war? Should I take heed?

I peered upwards, craning my neck: blue sky and brilliant sun. But the downpour didn't stop. And I was very late.

I made a dash around the car to the boot. Rain staining my fresh shirt and light jacket like ink. Oh God – my good umbrella wasn't there, only the old one with two broken spokes. Snapping it open I ducked underneath – it sagged one side, limp as a damaged wing. Under its protection I retrieved the small wrapped present for Annabelle's parents and slipped it in my jacket pocket, left the second one in brown paper for later – too bulky. I locked the car. Silver needles of warm rain, sunlight reflecting off parked cars steaming from the wetness and heat, water dripping like grapeshot from splayed green hands of chestnut leaves onto my brolly as I ran. If they'd been plane trees this could almost have been Ferdinand-Marie Straße – but that was half a dozen streets away.

Through high gates. The uniformed youth lurked, keeping guard. Sports cars and limousines lining the driveway, ahead an austere, art deco villa with green and gold frieze beneath the eaves. Near the portico two dark oversized Mercedes Benz and a black BMW with official-looking number plate. There was still space, I noticed, for another couple of cars; mine would've fitted in with old-fashioned grace.

As I climbed the steps the rain stopped abruptly: had someone given it a signal? The front door stood open; I rang all the same. Set my face the way I do for such occasions, held the dripping umbrella away from me. Beside the door a silver Jewish *Mezuzah* set at a slant. I wondered what prayer from the *Torah*...

"*Guten Abend, Herr Falk.*"

An elderly man in butler's clothes greeting me.

"*Guten Abend,*" I responded. He knew me? We'd never met. It managed to unnerve me further.

"So glad you've arrived safely, sir. We were worried you might have met with an accident." A kindly old man, white hair, thin as a rake, pronounced stoop. This must be Wilhelm. And I'd thought Annabelle was pulling my leg.

"No," I said. "A traffic jam, actually. On the way down." A puddle was growing beneath the tip of the brolly.

"From Nuremberg?"

I gazed at him, flustered. "That's right." How ever much do butlers know? Before I could rearrange my official expression again, he asked politely but firmly: "Can I take your umbrella, sir?"

"Well... thank you." I glanced down, took a step away so he wouldn't get wet, began to shake it, flapping it open and shut several times like someone unsuccessfully trying to fly.

The sound of car doors slamming, the crunch of feet on gravel. I looked round. Two uniformed chauffeurs – one surreptitiously holding a cupped cigarette, the other stretching, a chamois cloth in hand. Beyond, everything steamed and shimmered, the sun burned down, the gravel stones already beginning to dry...

"Do let me do that, sir," the butler was saying.

I regarded him again. Stiffly he had stretched out both hands to take over. "I'm afraid not," I said.

"It's my job, sir."

Stubbornly I gave the brolly a last few shakes for the sake of precious carpets I expected lay within, but in doing so something snapped. "I'm afraid I'm programmed to do such things myself," I explained.

"That is frowned on in our household," came his prompt reply.

I smiled. "You must be Herr Wilhelm." I was attempting with some difficulty to close the umbrella.

"Not *Herr*, sir. Just Wilhelm."

"Well, Herr Wilhelm..." I struggled with the mechanism but the thing wouldn't close. "We'll do a deal, shall we? I'll leave off the *Herr* if you leave off the sir."

"I wouldn't dream of doing that, sir."

The broken spokes had given up the ghost, got in a total tangle. They poked out one side at right-angles under the dark-blue cloth and, somewhat inappropriately for the gravity of the hour, reminded me of the erection in my trousers when Annabelle had last come to call.

Firm fingers took it from me. With a few professional movements he deftly gathered the offending appendages in and twirled the brolly shut.

"I'd say the dustbin just earned an extra dinner, if you'd be so good," I said.

"I fear so, sir." He was standing aside ushering me in. "If you would be kind enough to follow me, Herr Falk." He turned; in his tails he looked a little like an ancient bent penguin.

I followed. I was crossing the threshold that divided the light from the dark, walking nervously – into the lion's den. For an instant I glanced back over my shoulder at freedom outside, caught a glimpse of all those expensive cars in the brightness, and the chauffeur wiping and polishing with his chamois cloth.

I was in a big hall lit from above: inlaid timber floor, broad staircase curving up to a balustraded gallery, an art deco chandelier: I had entered a rich man's world.

I said to the butler's back: "Tell me, Herr Wilhelm, how did you know I was Falk? Do you practise telepathy on the sly?"

"Oh no." He indicated. "This way please, sir. Miss Annabelle showed me a photograph."

"Ah," I said. Oh God, I thought. What photograph? Wilhelm waddled spritely past an exquisite ebony table with a gorgeous bouquet of flowers, I in frowning pursuit. That can't be true – the only photos she possesses of me are the two I gave her in fun from Florence where I'm pulling a face like Popeye in pain and spreadeagled naked on the bed.

"Well," I said drily, "hope I still have a few secrets left."

We had traversed the hall. Even from here I could hear the babble ahead, see a mass of silhouette figures through frosted-glass double doors. I steeled myself, I expected the worst: the Munich mafia – Munich society in all its catholic and arrogant nouveau-riche finery, its fashionable frills and coiffured curls, all its superficial faces and artificial blah-blah.

Wilhelm opened the doors with a neat flourish he'd probably practised for fifty years – and the cacophony of dozens of voices hit me like a wall of water bursting through a rupture in a crumbling dam. I winced, like one who's had acid squirted in his eyes, quickly hung a cold mask of nonchalance on my face.

Before me a sea of humanity standing about, glasses in hand, in groups large and small. An orgy of colour and noise. Deep voices, high-pitched voices, bursts of laughter – mouths moving or pursed or sipping drinks.

I stood there a moment, knees like jelly, feet nailed to the spot – but Wilhelm was already forging ahead, waving me into the heat of the fray. People parting. Glimpses of faces – handsome ones, beautiful ones, uglier faces, varying ages. A necklace here, a *Rolex* there, a naked neck, an earring catching points of light. We ploughed slowly through. My problem was, being small, I couldn't look over the heads; I was like a lost one in a swamp. A few faces I recognised here and there; a young actor, up and coming, a novelist I'd recently seen on the telly, one or two people who appeared in discussion programmes, even a tall, model-like anorexic apparition whose gaunt construction one sees on porno mag covers or was it in ads for *Vogue*?

We were making progress, coming through, moving diagonally now across the large room. Ahead, between men's shoulders and women's heads, I could see French windows thrown open, lots of light. The throng here was beginning to thin, people exiting into a garden, into the light.

Wilhelm steered us round a group of men. Summer suits, old-boy ties, one smoked a cigar, one wore a carnation – they looked like businessmen, or bankers, or from one of my seminars...

Then I saw her.

She stood in a circle of about ten souls. All elegantly dressed, some holding glasses. All young to middle-aged, the majority women; I noticed most had their eyes upon her. She was listening, though, not speaking, her head half-turned away from me. She wore a long, thin pale-green dress, almost ethereal, it clung to her body, hung down to the floor. Her red hair was coiled high, her arms and shoulders freckled and bare.

"May I wish you a very pleasant evening, sir." Said quietly beside me. Wilhelm was inclining his head.

I thanked him. And before I could look back to Annabelle, fingers touched my arm and she stood there before me. Exchanging glances. Nothing said. Her green eyes were laughing and gay. She was turning. The circle had opened. She stooped her head, brushed her lips briefly on my neck near my ear. I didn't dare to kiss her. Reaching her other hand, she laid it lightly on Wilhelm's shoulder preventing him walking away. Then she turned again. There was silence in the circle.

"This is Stefan," she said simply to them all. Her head was high, a secret smile; she smiled just like that queen I knew, the one I loved to know.

All eyes were on me.

Yes – elegant people, elegant attire. There were murmurs, and nods. The eyes were still watching, taking me in, summing me up. What were they thinking? So this is the little bugger? This is the runt? I felt nervous inside, but my mask of nonchalance was firmly in place.

"Good evening," I said.

I stood there blandly in the limelight, her dirty little secret.

And Annabelle, still smiling that special smile, calmly announced: "Well, my dears, we will see you later." That's all she said, no introductions; my gratitude was great.

Gracefully, unhurriedly, she turned her back.

She was drawing us away. Wilhelm too. Around us, as we went, a slow chattering exodus towards the French windows. I suppose it was only the shower which had driven them indoors. I was aware that the noise had reduced to a hubbub; I noticed, too, a long, inlaid table now visible, and chairs pushed back against one wall. So this must be the dining room...

"Wilhelm, I should like to introduce you properly," Annabelle was saying. She had stopped us. "This is Stefan Falk. He is not as nasty and dangerous as he looks. In fact he really can be quite human if he wishes." She cast me a wicked glance. "My philosopher, this is our faithful Wilhelm who I am very, very fond of."

I gave him my hand. "Herr Wilhelm."

He offered his diffidently. "Very pleased to meet you, sir, I'm sure." I squeezed it; his fingers were long and bony, surprisingly strong.

"Wilhelm, from now on you must drop this habit and simply call him Stefan."

"If you wish, Miss Annabelle." He bent his thin body to me in a slow stiff bow. "Mr Stefan."

I chuckled deep in my throat.

"And now, Miss Annabelle, if you will excuse me. I see Mrs Mimi has an empty glass, so I shall go and chivvy up one of the waiters."

I watched him go. He'd turned into a penguin again. The big room was emptying. Two couples strolled by, conversing, three faces glancing at me; one of the women stroked Annabelle's arm as she passed. I felt a touch. Annabelle had hung her hand gently on my shoulder, arm behind my back, standing beside me – was watching Wilhelm's retreating figure too.

"We owe his family so much," she said quietly. "Father wouldn't be alive today if it were not for them."

"Sounds rather dramatic," I said. I felt her slender hip pressing on mine.

"Mmm." Her fingertips wandered, as if absentminded. They stroked the nape of my neck. Were they pondering?

An elderly pair was going by; she fluttering fingers, he nodding his head.

"Perhaps I should tell you."

I had no idea what. So I said nothing.

"Yes I will – just a little."

The deliberating fingers were still. "We don't speak of it often, you must understand. It belongs in the past and should remain there. It is nobody's business now. But when you meet father it will perhaps help you not to judge him too harshly."

Thoughtful fingertips again, distant fingertips. They rested on the nearly shorn hair on the back of my skull. I just stood there. We were almost alone in the room now. Could feel her body, my hip against hers, her thigh on mine...

"Father is Jewish," she began. "One hundred percent, that you know. The name alone..." She didn't bother completing the sentence. "His parents were German Jews, his forefathers assimilated generations ago. Before the War his father owned the bookshop *Goldberg's* in Rosenstraße here in Munich and had four children, two boys and two girls." She was still speaking in a subdued tone, but there was no-one near to listen anyway.

"In November nineteen-thirty-eight the Nazis ransacked his shop and shortly afterwards arrested him and the whole of his family, with the exception of the youngest, Elijah my father. He was three years old. At the time of the arrests he was down in the kitchen of their town house with the cook and the chauffeur. While the Gestapo were upstairs searching, the chauffeur hid him in a cupboard. The chauffeur was Wilhelm's father."

She stopped.

She had spoken in a calm monotone, no touch of emotion. Still I stood there, still said nothing. Perhaps there was more to come. In the background I glimpsed Wilhelm beyond open doors to an adjoining room.

She caressed my skull. "Wilhelm's father came from a village near Munich, and was a widower. His wife had died giving birth to Wilhelm, and he lived out of wedlock with another woman. The two of them took Elijah in and registered him as illegitimate. Wilhelm, then thirteen and ten years older than my father, naturally became privy to the secret. Through the war years they grew up together as brothers till he was called up and sent to northern France. In nineteen-forty-five Wilhelm's father and stepmother died in the last air raid on Munich, Elijah survived."

She sighed. I stared into her coils of hair, was trying to visualise.

"...Wilhelm was serving as a young soldier in the defence of Berlin when informed of their deaths. In the chaos of the last war weeks he deserted the *Wehrmacht* and made his way home to search for my father and take over responsibility for him. He risked his life doing that. Wilhelm, like his father, is a courageous man – he is a chip off the old block."

She stopped again. I thought she was finished, but what could I say? As I cast about for suitable words, she said: "And his faithfulness didn't end there. During de-Nazification he was interrogated by a British officer with Jewish blood and persuaded him to send my nine-year-old father to England. Here in Germany people were dying of hunger. A Jewish family in London adopted him in autumn nineteen-forty-five."

Her fingers rubbed over my stubble.

Still I could find no words of wisdom. I could only ask: "Did his parents and brother and sisters perish? Were they murdered?" Hadn't Martina said they all died?

"In Buchenwald and Auschwitz. Also his grandparents. The only other survivor was his father's youngest brother Albert." Her fingers slipped, she turned me, arm round my shoulders – she turned me in the direction old Wilhelm had taken.

Past the few remaining persons in the room where we stood and through the open sliding double-doors Wilhelm was no longer in sight. Looked like a living room beyond, with sofas and armchairs and figures seated.

"There is Albert on the sofa to the right of the fireplace, with the white hair and the stick. He turned eighty-three last month..." She was pointing "...And next to him is Mimi his wife, my great-aunt. She is from an old Jewish family in the north of England, a marvellous old lady. I should like you to meet them."

I felt the light pressure of her hand. We were moving forward, walking slowly.

She said: "Grand-uncle Albert emigrated to the States in nineteen-thirty-three and avoided the Holocaust. He studied geology and later worked in Argentina and Brazil, in fact he has been wandering most of his life. He married his third wife Mimi at the age of fifty-two. They have no children. He has, however, an illegitimate son who is a farmer in South Africa, but whom I have never met..."

We'd reached the doors, were passing through.

A spacious drawing room. Cool. Pleasantly cool – could it be it was air-conditioned? And more French windows, with light pouring on Persian rugs and parquet floor. A tasteful room, few decorations – two oil paintings on pale, wallpapered walls, a slender bronze sculpture like a Brancusi over in the corner standing alone.

Annabelle had taken my arm. Her thin fingers guided firmly; on one finger, the ruby ring. Memories of Florence. I concentrated. About a dozen people were seated in a crescent, only a few couples standing talking or stooped to those sitting. All looked middle-aged or older: quiet relaxed conversations. Annabelle's free hand giving small waves as she passed, or trailing across people's shoulders, not disturbing; most conversations didn't cease. Ahead a marble fireplace, an open hearth – on the mantelpiece in the centre a French clock beneath glass dome, and left and right a porcelain figure, a gold *menorah*, photographs in frames. We approached...

The elderly couple sat on their sofa; with tipped-back head the old lady was chatting to a woman propped on the padded sofa arm. The old man was thin and gaunt as a skeleton, cheeks and eyes sunken hollows, a jutting jaw. He gazed into space, lost in thought, dinner jacket hanging loose on wasted body, knobbly hands gripped on each other on a silver-topped stick wedged between his legs – was he gazing into eternity?

"Grand-uncle Albert is rather deaf," Annabelle said. Her lips brushed my ear; I could feel their warmth. "He refuses to wear his hearing aid so one has to talk loudly."

"Ah," I said, eying him critically. "Too much disco?"

She kissed my ear, and breathed: "Cheeky bugger." I thought: I'm a bad influence – she's catching my vocabulary.

We'd nearly reached them. Her grand-aunt wore an evening gown and glittering necklace and tiara. Were those diamonds at her throat, and in her silver hair? Her old wrinkled eyes turned in the middle of a sentence. They widened, they sparkled, there was adoration for Annabelle in the gaze.

"My darling!" she exclaimed. In one hand she held a champagne glass, the other she stretched out to Annabelle.

Annabelle took the glass from her. "Stay sitting. Mimi, this is Stefan. Stefan, my adorable Grand-aunt Mimi."

I stooped too; I was glad of the absence of ceremony.

She took my offered hand in both of hers. "My dear," she smiled, "I'm so delighted." Husky voice, slight English accent. And genuine warmth.

"I am too," I said. "I'm afraid I can only reciprocate."

Beside her, her husband had turned his head, was looking at me. He had very big ears and strands of white hair. Vague, faded eyes, vacant stare. It seemed to say: all these worldly things, so immaterial, such a bore, think I'll go for a piss.

I concentrated on his wife. She was leaning forward, drawing me closer. Yes, those were diamonds everywhere. "Annabelle has told me *all* about you." Said conspiratorially. She patted my hand; a merriness upon her lips.

"Ah," I said. I returned her smile. "I hope you didn't believe a word."

"Oh, but of course, my dear." Patting me again, she released my hand and leaned close to her husband. "Albert, Stefan wants to say hello," she said in his ear. "Be nice."

He adjusted his gaze; he fixed me instead with an impatient glare. "Who?" he said very loudly.

"Now don't get stroppy." That was in English. She tapped his thin and bony leg. And in German again: "Stefan. I told you. You remember, Annabelle was in Florence with him."

He stared at me. "Florence?" he called at the top of his voice.

"Yes dear."

"Venice is a damn sight more romantic." He gave a guffaw, jogged his eyebrows up and down. They were white, too, and extraordinarily thick and bushy.

Annabelle had come round from behind me. She bent, snaked an arm over his shoulders. "This is my wicked Grand-uncle Albert," she said to me.

"I heard that," he pronounced. He didn't say it petulantly, though.

"You were meant to," she retorted, and stroked the high dome of his head.

His fingers flexed, opening and closing on the cap of his stick. Again fixing me with a withering stare, he shot out a hand, took mine. He held it like a vice. "You're late," he bawled.

"You're right," I said. I returned his stare, nodded.

"Heard about you. You're Johannes' boy, aren't you? Bloody tragedy, that." His hand still had me in a stranglehold.

I nodded again. I sat on the memory. Why did he have to go and say that?

"Welcome to the club, my boy."

I just watched him, didn't reply.

"Always late myself, don't you know. Hate parties. You hate parties too?" His voice reverberated round the drawing room.

"Yes," I bawled back. "Like the plague."

"That's my man." His faded eyes widened, brightened, his bony hand shook me, released me at last. "Parties cramp a man's style, my boy." A flare of mischief in the eyes. "Best women're the ones in the bars or the jungle, not at these cocktail stiffs."

"Sssh, my wicked one." Annabelle's lips were at his ear.

"Prettiest ones're always there to be had." With a jerk he inclined his old head at her, his stare still on me, roguish now. "Caught a big fish there, my boy. Bet your boots not at a cocktail do."

Bending, I brought my face closer, one hand supporting me on my knee. "You'd never guess where," I said seriously. And gave him my favourite sardonic grin.

A crack of a laugh. He stamped his stick, waggling his emaciated head.

"That's enough of your nonsense, Albert dear." His wife shook his leg, affectionately. And to Annabelle she said: "Now off you two go and have some fun."

Annabelle, straightening, was patting his shoulders. She leaned and touched her elderly aunt's arm. "And you stay here where it is cool, Mimi. I will come and fetch you later when it has cooled down outside."

"Till later, my dear." They kissed.

Old Albert was peering up at me. He clutched at my cuff, gave it a brief tug. "Bring along some broads," he shouted. His bushy eyebrows were twitching again. "Meet you at sundown with the boys at the bar."

Annabelle was taking my arm. I nodded my head at them both, then we were walking away.

She said: "I am very fond of them. And they are devoted to one another." She was steering me past the last of the seated people, back towards the dividing doors.

"They're real characters," I said.

"Albert is an old Casanova. He has seen the world, and possibly been acquainted with most of its women. But Mimi managed to tame him."

"Your father's only surviving blood relative?" I said.

"Mmm."

Out of three generations, I thought. I shook my head.

Her hand hung lightly on my arm. "It is nothing to get sentimental about, my secretly sentimental one. My father taught us to forgive and forget. And our family was not the only one."

We passed through the open doorway – beyond, in the dining room, only half a dozen people still stood about. She was adding: "It does make Albert rather precious, of course. And through him, naturally, Mimi, too." She smiled a wistful smile. "Aeron and I used to nickname him the Lone Ranger when we were small."

She had stopped near the first French windows. I stopped too. Could feel her fingers through my jacket.

"Aeron?" I said.

"My brother."

Sunlight from the windows fell across the floor.

"You have a brother?" I watched her. She stood before me, calmly – she hadn't let go of my arm.

"I had a younger brother. He drowned when he was eleven. A canoeing accident." She spoke quietly. "That is also a long time ago."

A dead brother. Like Matthias. It seemed they had more and more in common. I glanced sideways at the others in the room, but they were occupied with their own conversations, they were far away.

"You never told me," I said. Did that sound like a reproach?

"You never asked, my silent one."

Faintly I shrugged. Why hadn't Margareth told me? Or was it possible she didn't know? I frowned. Annabelle stood there quietly smiling upon me. How could she be so calm?

"Do you have any other questions, my frowning one?"

"Yes," I said. "Your father was only nineteen, then, when you were born?" I watched her eyes again.

"Twenty. You have been doing your little mathematical sums?" The smile lingered.

"Yes," I said again. "So you were born over there? In England?"

Her fingers stroked slowly along my jacket sleeve, through the cloth, through to my skin. "In Germany."

"How come?"

Ah, that wistful smile. Still quietly she said: "I was conceived in London but entered the world here in Munich. In actual fact, so mother explained it to me, the conceptual act took place on a Jewish sofa in a drawing room in Bedford Square. She was twenty-two, and father two years her junior."

"But why did he leave England? And at such a tender..."

"Oh, my suddenly inquisitive one!" She raised a hand, rested her palm on my cheek. "He had been planning to later, anyway. But that was nineteen-fifty-five. British Jewry would have been scandalised had it found out. Mother and father were forced to marry in a London synagogue with my mother three months gone, and they simply decided to emigrate straight away."

"Simply?" I said. "To Germany of all countries? He must've hated us." I could smell the perfume from her hand.

"He hated Nazism, not the Germans." Her fingers traced a line up my face and over my brow – were they trying to wipe away my wrinkles? "German was his mother tongue, too, and language is his life."

I thought: a twenty-year-old Jew in post-war Germany? "How did they survive?" I said.

"Oh they did. Father's adoptive parents assisted with the fares and a small lump sum to tide them over the first few weeks. Otherwise, though, no-one was there to help. Mother's parents had perished fleeing Strasburg at the start of the war, and she had lost all trace of her uncles and aunts."

Annabelle stopped. When she didn't continue, I said: "I meant, how the hell did they manage it? Germany was in ruins."

She rubbed my nose. "So many questions, my inquisitive one."

"You make me nosey."

"But you know about these times. Everyone was in the same boat."

"How many Jews went and did that, though?"

"Because father is a fighter." She considered me peaceably. "He found jobs as journalist and translator, and studied at night. In nineteen-fifty-nine he earned his degree. And two years later founded his own publishing house." Slowly she ran her fingers over the stubble on my skull, gracefully withdrew her hand. "Father is a stubborn one, and tough as leather."

She stopped again. This time it seemed final. There was silence between us.

"Ah," I said. I tried a grimace. "So that's where your genes came from."

She laughed. She just tipped back her head, shaking at her piled-up hair, and laughed that gorgeous gurgle of a laugh. "So you appreciate now, I am a complete mongrel," she said. She slipped her hands inside my jacket, coming closer. "I am one quarter French Alsace Jew from my mother's side, one quarter Polish Jew from my father's and half German Jew from both."

I could feel the heat of her body; her stomach was resting on mine.

She laughed again: "And a red-headed Jewess to boot."

"Yes," I said to the laughing green eyes. In spite of myself I had to smile. "I think it was the hair and the freckles which won me."

I wanted to kiss that mouth, those lips – I wanted to reach round her and feel her bottom soft and warm, press her to me. But everything around us said no. We stood there watching each other, beside the long windows. Not speaking.

A middle-aged couple strolled by, hand in hand, coming from the drawing room. I glanced briefly, felt suddenly awkward, almost ashamed. The woman was smiling at us. I looked away.

Light flooded.

There was music in the background. And a babble of voices. I glanced again. Through the French windows bright sunlight, a terrace, a crowd of people...

"All right, my pondering one?"

"I suppose so," I said.

Her face hovered. "Let us go out now and meet my parents."

Oh God, I thought.

She kissed me. Very gently, on my lips. "Don't be a coward."

"There're a great many people out there," I pointed out. "About a thousand. Two thousand..."

"They won't eat you." She laughed again, but softly. "As a matter of fact you could probably eat most of them."

"There's brutality in numbers."

"Come."

I eyed her. "I noted your emphasis on that word probably and your certainty concerning only most." I gave her a wince and a sagging lopsided mouth. "I readily concede my cowardice." Then, returning my face to its usual apathetic state of normalcy, I proclaimed in a flat hoarse whisper: "Give me my armour and blindfold me, Sir Harry, send me into the breach."

Chuckling, she let me go, stepping back – and poked me lightly in the stomach. And as she did Wilhelm waddled past balancing a silver tray, accompanied by two guests. He didn't bat an eyelid.

Annabelle was taking me by the elbow...

"Stop," I said, watching Wilhelm's retreating back. "Weren't you going to tell me..."

"I believe we agreed no more questions." Her grip on my arm was so firm she must've got one of old Uncle Albert's genes mixed in there too.

"Indeed we didn't," I said.

"Indeed we did. Come."

"About how Wilhelm..."

"Too late, my procrastinating one, that will have to wait."

Her fingers were insistent and her profile, when I peeped, had adopted the iron poise of a stern and noble queen. She propelled me forward towards the open French doors.

"Ah, there is the breach," I said.

She slipped her hand into mine; we were stepping out into sunlight, I was panicking again.

Chapter 23

People. People everywhere. And a string quartet.
I readjusted my face to deadpan; don't think I managed it any too well. Glancing, taking in the scene. Green sun awnings cantilevered along the whole back of the white plastered house. Beneath them tables in shade, each big enough to seat a dozen or more, between the tables the long French windows and climbing vines. Other tables too, placed about the terrace under big white sun umbrellas.

People sat relaxing, people stood about – small groups, large clusters, couples content alone. Young people, older people, there must've been near a hundred. A few strolling on lawns below. Children down there playing, too, at least a score or more. Bordering the lawns, far away, stretching flowerbeds, a mass of impressionist colour, trellises with climbing roses – and in the background, trees.

Annabelle led me unhurriedly along the terrace. Conversations, chatter, laughter. She'd slipped her hand inside my arm again, I crooked mine like a tin soldier. Between pools of shade the sun beat down; my God, it was hot.

Passing tables, skirting standing groups. I counted four or five *kippas* amongst the crowd – they stood out like sore thumbs. Nods and smiles, but not for me, here and there hands lifting or fluttering, greeting her. Old flagstones beneath my feet. Dry as a bone – had I only fantasised, had it only rained on me? Moss in the joints. On empty chairs at some of the tables, summer shawls discarded, hanging stoles, small handbags lying, jackets draped. And on all the tables bottles of wine and carafes of water, assortments of glasses large and small, some empty, or half-filled, some with cocktail sticks. My God, what a noise.

We wove our way. I looked at faces; recognised a few from the dining room. Found myself sometimes nodding too; I switched on a sardonic smile. I felt so small, Annabelle beside me half a head taller.

A squeeze on my arm; Annabelle was changing direction.

There. Had we nearly made it? That must be it, over there, the lion's den. A glassed winter-garden built onto the villa, jutted out. And in the angle between it and the house, the last sun awning in the row, the very last table. Shady corner, almost secluded. The noise wasn't too bad here either – I could hear the strains of Haydn from the string quartet again.

We were crossing over.

Oh God, I thought, here we go. The crowd was thinner, we'd nearly reached the fringe. I peered – past the last of the standing people. Sun canopy, telescopic arms embracing. The long table, at right-angles to the wall, tubular chairs looking like ones from the thirties, green shade. We were still too far off to see the details: seated figures, I counted the heads. Nine – no ten. I tried to pick out Annabelle's parents. Nervously I wondered: who'll be the illustrious invited guests? Politicians, chief rabbis, kings and queens? Quickly I corrected my mask for cracks...

Coming closer now. Oh, thank God – I recognised Margareth, with relief. And left of her sat Benjamin Cohen the concert pianist, the one who'd come to play that night, and at the far end of the row against the wall a man I didn't know. Things were getting a little better. Then on Margareth's right I saw, to my pleasant surprise, the journalist Christian Beck. Inside, I began to relax a bit more; things were looking up. And the other side of Beck a woman leaned on her elbows, brunette, about thirty, big bangles on raised arms, very attractive – could she perhaps be Beck's girlfriend or wife?

We approached. I let my eyes dart. Annabelle's father must be one of the ones with his back to us, then. The stocky one this end of the row? Probably. Then that'd be Annabelle's mother next to him. And next to her, the elderly man, those clothes? I almost chuckled – yes, it was a rabbi. Well at least I'd got one of them right. And the last two, near the wall? Rapidly I scanned their backs... no – it couldn't be...

...that woman's prim hair-do with its stern little curls, and that bottom, tight and pert, perched on its cushion – I'd recognise that bum from any angle, anywhere. My sister-in-law Mathilda. So the almost bald pate on the big man beside her hugging the wall could only belong to my elder brother Toby. My first fleeting thought was, he's lost more hair since I last saw him – and the second: how the hell had they managed to get themselves invited?

Margareth caught sight of us. She raised a hand, waved, cigarette between fingers. She looked great, she looked so much better. I thought: are they all here, then? Where's Eva, where's...? Glanced briefly at the next table: a gaggle of pretty women, fluttering round the young actor, all just sitting down, laughter and giggles – those already seated were strangers to me too. No, Eva was not there – and my mother also not. Well, it'd only been a thought...

We'd nearly reached the end of the long table. Several conversations in progress. One or two faces turning. Before us four empty chairs, gave the impression of expectation... yes, they were 1930's style. Annabelle's father, half-turned away, in energetic discussion, gesticulating with stumpy hands. But beyond him his wife was rising... More talking interrupted, more heads turning...

A rapid glance along the table: I acknowledged the family faces with a nod. Primly pretty Mathilda fluttered her fingers in slow-motion, pompous Tobias dipped his heavy head. Over her burning cigarette Margareth just winked...

"Eli," Annabelle's mother whispered, tapping his arm. And louder: "Oh my dears..." She had pushed back her chair. She was tall and elegant, wore a white evening gown. Over her shoulders a silver silk shawl was draped.

Calmly her husband continued to the end of his sentence before unhurriedly twisting towards us.

Annabelle said simply: "Mama, Papa – I should like you to meet Stefan Falk."

Her mother came round behind his chair, her hand reaching out to me. "Good evening, Herr Falk, you are very welcome." She stood before me, noble and erect, as tall as Annabelle, she had direct searching eyes; were they making comparisons? With her daughter's first husband? With the long list of suitors who'd probably followed? How long had that list been, how elite? Intellectuals and professors, lawyers and doctors? Surely more suitable bastards than a mongrel like me.

"Thank you," I nodded. I had given her my hand. "Good evening, Frau Goldberg." In an old reflex, in spite of myself, surprising myself, I gave a slight bow. Was it the memory? Old Albert just now had gone and jogged my brain. And all this here reminded me... of days long ago, of my own parent's private parties, of Munich society smugly gathered in – till the bankruptcy, the horror, till our world collapsed like that house of cards. There... At the back of the garage my father hung from the cobwebbed beam, they were cutting him down, and day turned to night in our childhood lives, stranding us outside the closed club door. Did we still carry the mark, was that the reason we were shunned like the plague, were we contagious?

Chairs were scraping on stone: everyone was standing up.

Next to his wife, a good half-head shorter, Annabelle's father watched me steadily, eyeing me the way an expert appraises a horse he doesn't intend to buy...

"How good to meet you at last," her mother was saying. Wasn't that a tinge of French accent? Rather attractive, almost seductive. Her hand was firm – wrinkled and sinewy, lightly browned and flecked like the skin of her face. She looked all of her sixty-three years.

"Thanks for the invitation," I said formally. "I apologise for being late."

"Don't give it another thought. You are not the last."

Ah – I'm not? I thought...

"Annabelle has told us a lot about you." She smiled at me, a practised smile, not too friendly, not too flat.

I thought: well, she told me nothing of you, she's got me tapping in the dark.

"I hope not too much." I smiled back politely.

"Oh, I wouldn't presume to judge." Her mouth was wide, the lips thin, a little hard – they looked used to holding their own. "May I assume you have nothing to hide?" A quick lift of the eyebrows, another smile. She was quick, she was intelligent.

I watched those frank eyes. What was she thinking? Was once bitten twice shy? They seemed to say: For the record I'm reserving my judgement.

"I must confess," I said, "I haven't yet met anyone who didn't."

She watched me intently. She was still holding my hand; she squeezed it and laughed. "My dear Herr Falk, I am certain I am no exception."

I tried to return her laugh with a little one of my own. But I was nervous – mine came out more like a belch. I cleared my throat. "Perhaps this evening, Frau Goldberg, you'll allow me to complete the counterpart of the picture your delightfully dishonest daughter omitted – so you don't remain too prejudiced in my favour."

She didn't blink. Was that a glint of humour in her eye, was she preparing a rapid repost? But Annabelle said blithely right next to my ear: "I warned you, Mama." And, her hand still tucked beneath my arm, she turned me calmly. "Papa... this is Stefan Falk. Stefan – meet father."

My heart staggered unhappily. I turned my eyes quickly to the small stocky man. In the first instant I thought something positive – I thought, thank God at least he's as small as I.

We shook hands.

"Pleasure," he said flatly. It was very abrupt. His expression seemed to say: Sweet Moses, look what the cat's brought in. His handshake was feeble and brief. I returned his gaze as best I could. Yes, he had eyes like a snake – he had cold bulging almost colourless eyes.

"Reciprocated," I answered in kind.

He wore smoking jacket, crisp white shirt, black bowtie – was nearly bald, just hair at the sides in two wild untidy tufts. I couldn't refrain: I was glancing at old photos of Ben Gurion. He stood there with stumpy legs placed apart, compact and tough, it looked as if nothing could bowl him over.

"Hear you intend marrying my daughter." He spoke rapidly, his sentence clipped. Apparently a man with no words to waste.

I nodded slowly. "You hear correctly." His manner antagonised. But at least he came straight to the point.

"So, so." Calmly he assessed me. "I have no say in the matter?" He was solid and certain, he had presence; one saw he expected to be listened to every time he chose to speak, was used to being obeyed. He had fixed me with that horse-trainer's eye again.

"No," I said. I thought: if he takes me by the chin to check my teeth, I'll kick him in the marbles. Aloud I added: "When two consenting adults of our age come to such a decision, I believe that's the general rule."

"Never played by the rules all my life."

"So I heard," I said. "Neither did I." Don't give him any rope, I told myself – he'd hang you by the slack.

A grunt. "Heard that from my daughter too."

Was that a sudden, faint flaring in his eye?

"Ah," I said. "Sounds as if you'll be saving me brushstrokes, then. Seems Annabelle gave you the better half of the picture, too."

"Forewarned is forearmed." He chuckled, unexpectedly. He was raising the hand he'd withdrawn – patted my arm. "So now we'll both at least jump over our shadows with respect to the rules of etiquette." His fingers gripped my arm robustly now, all the weakness of the handshake gone. "Mustn't keep these good people standing about like troops on parade."

His hand swung me towards the elderly rabbi, his other extending like the perfect host, starting the introductions...

"...trusted friend, father of light and keeper of my unorthodox soul, Rabbi Abner Singer..." A lined but kindly face, grey suit, a plain black *kippa* on the head... "Abner, meet our protagonist Herr Falk from the heathen camp..." A soft hand, an exchange of greetings, politenesses...

Then – Annabelle still at my side and hand on my arm - we went round the other side of the table, going down the row with her father ahead, expansively, the master of the ceremonies...

"...Mona Dohm, artist of the very Modern, also known as 'Mona Mo'..." Hot hazel eyes seen now from close-up, I'd only ever seen them distantly on TV, that brunette hair twisted back and fixed with sticks on the sinewy nape of a neck – the gold bangles jangled as she gave me her hand, her red-orange dress almost blinded... I tried to say something appropriate: I fear her reply fell on stony ground, she'd cast her pearls before the swine...

And next to her, there he stood, the man I'd seen on the television screen "...let me introduce you..." A stumpy sweep of the arm "...a good friend and humble fighter, bearer of the eternal torch, Christian Beck..."

There were those drawn and quiet features again, and the worry lines running deep – there too the half-moon spectacles, discarded now, hanging loose at his chest on their chain. Long sensitive fingers, our hands were touching...

"You remember..." Annabelle murmured contentedly in my ear...

"Ah," I said. "Let me guess."

Eyes meeting, holding, compatible eyes, something flowing, so much in their depths, sadness and humour side by side flowing outwards, this was one who'd seen the world...

"Do I detect here connotations of fame?" I mused. I could feel it coming; I was going to tease her just a bit. "A well-known novelist? Or Hollywood?" Fingers tweaking on my backside, a tiny warning pinch. "Bearer of the eternal torch, ah yes – *Columbia Pictures*?" I suggested, brightly. "That lady in Yankee Grecian dress and radiating rays of light? You're perhaps a movie star?"

Across the table a harrumph of disgust – one didn't need to look, that was Tobias. In those tired blue eyes before me a tiny flame was lighting, and on those lips a little crack. Such expressive lips.

I smiled slowly, let it linger. "I see I'm getting warmer."

A chortle, full of fun: Annabelle laughing in my ear. "You cheeky one." She pinched again.

"I second that." Tobias, loud and pompous. This time I glanced. My big brother didn't seem amused. He was puffing up his massive chest: "For your information, little brother, Herr Beck is one of our best-known and respected journalists." Ah, how importantly he spoke, with what genius he tinged his words with awe.

"Aaah." I cocked my head, blinking. "You don't say."

Raised square chin, gazing aloof down his magnificent nose, he expounded further: "He writes regularly for the *FAZ* and *Süddeutsche*, the *Spiegel* too. For Heaven's sake stop displaying your ignorance."

"Thank you, Tobias." I bowed my head towards him. "Whatever should I do without your boundless erudition and bottomless humour." Mathilda was whispering into his tipped ear.

"The *Spiegel*, ah yes — heard of that," I said. "But what were those other two? Thought the *Bild Zeitung* was the only one read nowadays..."

"My embarrassing one, that will do." Annabelle slapped my bottom; her father regarded me quizzically. Beck just watched with those steady blue eyes.

"Sorry," I said to Beck. "Always goes to my head, meeting one of a dying breed." I gave a watery grin. "Our frail sword of democracy, last ditch in a losing fight." His hand and mine were still touching, I pressed it a little firmer. "Falk. Stefan Falk. Don't expect you've heard of me either."

"On the contrary." Said quietly. "Annabelle thoughtfully warned me too." The introverted eyes were calm. "I should enjoy hearing more of your views on that subject, in the course of the evening."

"I'd much more appreciate hearing yours," I said.

Our hands were letting go. He turned his head, an inward trace of smile. A chuckle from Annabelle's father beside us. Beck said to him flatly: "A comrade in arms, Elijah?"

"Possibly, possibly," came the gruff reply. The pale eyes trained on me were unreadable, though.

Around us a few laughs, relaxing laughs. One was Margareth's. And beyond her the pianist's too, and the other man's, still waiting to be introduced. Herr Goldberg gave my shoulder a firm pat.

"Hear you're already acquainted with our close friend from Tel Aviv..." He was drawing me by the arm past Margareth, relishing his role as host again. I watched her face as we passed – her painted red lips gave a devilish grin behind another just-lit cigarette; I gladly reciprocated.

"...our genius of the fingers, Benjamin Cohen..."

Annabelle was renewing her faithful hold of me on my other side, together they had me in an able grip.

The pianist took my hand in those musical fingers – he was dressed in long flowing clothes, all folds and frills; he looked eccentrically elegant and perfectly at ease as he said: "What a pleasure it was to learn that your friendship has borne fruit in this delightful way..." His voice was like a symphony.

"It took a bit of watering," I agreed. We exchanged a few more pleasantries...

"And it is my honourable duty to introduce you..." Two guiding hands left and right propelled me on "...to Benjamin's companion and composer Mark Swayne, originally from London and now, to our greater benefit, resident here in Munich..."

A dainty touch, a thin twitchy man with jumpy eyes. We greeted. He spoke. I listened; he spoke delightful lilting German with cockney accent. I recall almost nothing of what he said, with one exception – in response to my attempt to purvey a few English sentences, he confided with a spontaneous guffaw in his unleashed mother tongue: "Done yerself marvellous there, your fiancée's a right smasher," summoning up in my mind's eye a picture of Annabelle devastating porcelain and men and all things fragile in her passage through life, and instigating the start of my reply:

"Funny that you mention that, Mark, you should just watch her demolishing..." before another vice-like grasp from Annabelle's fingers forced me to wince in unspeakable pain...

We'd made the rounds.

Some were sitting down again, some not. Herr Goldberg was saying: "Well, now we've got the formalities out the way, pray excuse me I have to go and attend to things." He returned to his place, waving like a windmill at one of the waiters. And Annabelle was good enough to open the vice and let me loose on my family.

First Margareth. She was the closest. She stooped, stubbing out her cigarette. Dominant fingers on the nape of my neck, deep brown eyes, those red lips kissing left and right of my mouth, a thumb wiping the imprints away; the smell of smoke and nicotine, the powerful scent of perfume. Standing holding each other, exchanging glances – then I held her at arm's length.

"You're looking great," I said. She'd put on a bit of weight again.

"Thanks."

Yes, her face was fuller, her body fuller, her eyes had that old lustre again.

"Tegernsee did me good. And Mimi and Albert were grand."

I nodded, still held her. A waiter in black and white stood at the end of the table receiving instructions.

"How're things with Heinrich?" I asked.

"He can't accept."

"He'll have to."

"Yep."

"Does he pester you?"

"In spurts."

"He'll have to learn," I said. "We all have to learn, don't we." I paused. "We men seem to have this little problem."

"You've solved yours now, it seems."

"Have I?" I said. "Yes, perhaps I have." I watched her. "Or have I merely plastered over the cracks?"

"Don't know about that. But you've sure bitten off more than you can chew."

"I'll keep on chewing."

We laughed.

And talked for another minute or so. Then Margareth said: "We'll talk later, okay?" She had glanced away. "Sure you're just dying to meet Tobias again after all these years. Looks so happy, looks as if he feels the same. Mathilda's already crouching to pray."

"Pray for or prey on?"

We laughed again, briefly. Let each other go. Then, unexpectedly, she stepped close and gave me a hug – she did it with breasts and stomach and all. Was that for the second time in her life? "Don't be too nasty to them, Stef," she whispered near my ear.

We were separating. Then I said what I'd forgotten to say: "By the way, Meg, in this horrible gathering of the clans I'm missing two faces..."

"Yes, I know."

"Where...?"

"Mother's in Morocco on a camel – got a new flame."

"New flame? Oh God."

"Some Graf von Hammerstein or something – tell you later, if you want. Eva said she'll call by if she can."

"Ah..."

And she turned away before I could nail her.

I skirted the table, keeping my distance. Rows of heads, conversations. On crisp white linen half-drunk glasses, open Bocksbeutel bottles of *Frankenwein*, two silver branching candelabra, candles unlit, discreet bouquets of flowers. The waiter had gone, and so had Herr Goldberg. Someone else had occupied his chair, was chatting to Annabelle and her mother. All were seated now, mostly conversing with one another – I was safely back out of the limelight, thank God...

Tobias and Mathilda broke off talking, they turned their heads as one. Warily they watched me approach; they watched with the whites of their eyes. God forbid, the Good Lord protect us, the same procedure as last time – one could read it in their stares. They began rising as I neared, Tobias behind her his hands on her shoulders, holding her like a shield. And as she stretched erect to her prim little height of four-feet-nine he was still rising, and seemed to go on upwards for ever.

"Hello, Stefan, congratulations," she said sharply. She said it like lightning, said it far too quickly, I hadn't even reached her; she shot it out as if it would stop me, keep me at bay.

"Yes, mine too," echoed Tobias, and his voice was a hollow bass drum rumbling over her head.

I nodded, acknowledging. They hadn't yet forgiven me for my first divorce, how happy they must be with me now. I stopped in front of Mathilda. Too much makeup seen up close, those tight blonde little curls aerosol-sprayed stiff as wood shavings, a trace of exotic perfume which she might have confused with incense.

"Hello Billy," I said to her, sniffing the scent like a bloodhound, breathing heavily. My God, was that *Shalimar*? It simply didn't suit her – or should I say, she couldn't quite do it its due. Not any more. How people change; was this the tragic final fragment of her former self? The last dying ray of that gay, giggly girl from our teenage clique playing Minigolf with me out of sight of the others, letting me press my fingers on her private place in the soft warm crutch of her skin-tight jeans, the girl whispering to me and panting to please, at the same time kissing the erotic zone beneath the lobe of her ear as I stood close behind her, chin over her shoulder revealing the secrets, showing her how to putt the ball up the spiralling ramp at hole number four? Could it really be she – this superficial silly woman, mother of five, indestructible pillar of the Holy Roman Church? This prickly, prudish lady whose passions were now restricted to rosaries and incense and lighting endless candles to illuminate her dark?

"Oh Billy," I sighed.

"Don't call me that!" Mathilda hissed it in a suppressed whisper and her small sharp round eyes glanced about, but nobody was listening except Tobias and me.

I chuckled. I remembered: they'd returned from their honeymoon Big-Trip-To-Australia and thrown a party, and Eva and I had got drunk and couldn't resist. All those slides and the didgeridoos and *Waltzing Matilda* playing in the background – we started raucously singing along with the song and in the middle she broke off to remark vulgarly far too loudly in my ear: "Wanna know a secret, brother? Thissis Toby's new signature tune 'fore sex, sittin' waitin' till 'is pretty li'l billy boils." And I, in an unusual burst of inebriated poetry, picked up the song at full volume: "An' Toby sang as he sat rubbing up and down his billabong, who came a-waltzing Matilda's billy before me..."

"Only our private joke," I reassured her. "Cross my black heart I'd never spill the beans." I reached out my hand.

Unwillingly, tentatively, she extended hers, as if afraid her wrist might return without it. Hastily Tobias let go her shoulders, stepping back, flexing his big hairy hands – seemed he'd lost his last line of defence and was preparing himself for close combat.

It was time for The Kiss. Stiffly she jackknifed the top half of her body forward, a quick peck on each of my cheeks – then we were coming to the clinch I'd forcibly introduced upon their engagement over nineteen years ago, the part she always prays I'll forget, the part I love the most; a kind of paralysed tango with both hands in play, she jerking backwards and stepping back, I faithfully following, body on body while she does her best not to be touched. Her fingers flailed, mine ran down her spine and pinched her prim Catholic bottom.

Face flushed, greeting completed and her duty done, she waited tensely to be released. But wasn't today a special day? And wasn't it years since we'd last met? Naughtily I dipped my lips to the *Shalimar* nest between neck and ear and nibbled her erotic zone.

"You devil," she whispered, squirming.

I gave her a sultry grin. "Don't be a silly-billy," I breathed. "Those hungry Catholic eyes lead a man into temptation, bring the billabong blood to the boil."

We separated. I was stepping back a pace. On a more serious note I said: "How are the children?"

"They're fine." Her flustered fingers fussed at her hair. "Rebecca, Maria and Robert are in the Waldorf school now." She completed the preening, clasped her hands before her. "They're doing very well. Priscilla is a mite slow and Dan has more of a practical bent." By which I guessed she meant they were dim. Her voice was nearly back to normal...

It was Tobias's turn now.

"Toby," I said in greeting. Tobias my brother, my mentor of the frailties, churchgoer supreme, pompous defender of dwindling faith; Tobias, with his dirty little secret...

"Hello, Stefan." A rich baritone from far above me. His glance was dark, furtive, watchful – like someone expecting a nasty blow but not certain from which direction.

I followed his big manicured hand coming out to mine; tufts of black hair on it, and on the backs of the fingers. He'd nearly made it. The fingers were sliding into my palm as if it weren't there – felt like jelly or rubber wrapped in fog, floppy and flaccid and feelingless; Tobias didn't like touch.

"Long time no see," I said. And it had been – at least three years.

"It is, isn't it?"

No hug, no kiss. I watched his discomfort, let him go. Could hear sister Eva's tart remark at the fifth christening: "How our big brother managed to rise to the occasion five times borders on a Catholic miracle, like walking on the water or turning water into wine – 'spect Billy was forced to light up the thorny path to her fanny with lots of blooming bright candles, or, failing that, grabbed the devil by its horns and rammed it in herself." I remember – Eva wore a rather attractive hat that day.

"How are you, Tobias?"

"Fine." He towered above me. "Things are going well. With you too? Good." He stood there so stiffly, arms hanging down, one hand flapping open and shut. "As a matter of fact we're in the midst of a reorganisation, so pretty busy. But of course, it's..." He was beginning to distract already, to waffle, so I stopped him.

"Actually, I meant your health, Tobias."

"Oh that? Fine, fine."

"The heart trouble?"

"Absolutely no problem. My cardiologist's rather satisfied, don't you know."

Which is not what I'd heard from mother, but then she gets things from the horse's mouth. "And your asthma?" I enquired. He'd had it since his childhood, could never participate in sport.

"Better." A hesitation. "These sprays and what not work wonders, you know."

I thought: shall I, shan't I? But Mathilda made it easier; she helped me to decide. "You must've got a bad attack three months ago, though."

"Attack?" He stopped in his tracks.

"You sacked five hundred souls. Half a year after that take-over. The media justly kicked you in the backside for that."

"Oh that."

"Yes that. When those camera teams caught you at the marble entrance I feared you might choke to death."

"Bad business." His eyes shifted, fluttered away above my head. "Regrettable but necessary."

"If nothing else, you're good at treading on others then running away and slamming the door." You bastard, I thought. You CEO arsehole with size forty-seven feet of clay, you dwarf in giant's clothing. "Not good for your health, Tobias. Not good for a lot of other people either."

"Crass simplification." He pumped up his six-feet-four frame, glared down at me imposingly. "Company decision. The board of directors..."

"Crap, Tobias. They do what you and your ilk dictate. You should think more of your health, brother, and less about profit and shareholders..."

"Stefan, *stop it.*" It was Mathilda. Her voice was bright and brittle; it went so well with her eyes.

But she was right. So I stopped.

"This is *not* the time and place," she added.

"Ah, Mathilda," I said – I left off the Billy bit to give her the benefit of the doubt – "when the subject's morality and hypocrisy, one asks oneself when is not the right time and place?"

"Don't be insulting. Toby's the most devout and upright man I know."

"Sorry, Mathilda. His actions can in no way be equated with the Christian ethics he, like you, purports to live by."

"Well that's rich," she retorted. "Coming from an atheist."

"Hear, hear!" Tobias echoed.

But I noticed his bluster had frayed at the edges, and his brown eyes watched me with care.

"I don't deny it," I nodded. "As a matter of fact..."

A cork popped loudly behind me, startling me. So I began again: "Matter of fact, I know quite a number of atheists whose behaviour at the workplace as well as in private life's more morally upright than my brother's."

Toby's eyes were glazing now, more furtive now, his mouth was a grim sealed line.

Mathilda eyed me viciously. "That's an untruth." She let it out like a hiss. And she believed I was only talking about his work ethic. Little hurt Mathilda. Eva had told me, she had no clue about Toby's naughty Thursday indiscretions.

"Mathilda," I said quietly again. She hadn't deserved this. Yes, I felt a pang of sorrow; was I showing what I shouldn't, was I giving myself away? So I kept it more neutral, merely said: "Isn't the Christian code of ethics something to be practised every day? Or in the Catholic Church is it limited to Mass and only recited like a parrot before one rises from one's knees?"

Tobias was clenching fists, pressing them stiffly at his sides. He cleared his throat and said importantly: "I won't tolerate any more of this, or any slights on our belief." But his bluster wasn't just frayed now, it sounded torn to shreds.

I lifted my eyes to his face, I didn't bother to reply. He was very still. I could see he was checking the chances of whether or not I knew. And in my brain sister Eva was saying in her so succinct way: "Reckon it'll cost him 'bout ten thousand Hail Marys an' a permanent seat in the confessional, assuming the Good Shepherd doesn't decide on that worst-case scenario with one-way ticket to purgatory. Anyway, open your ear flaps an' listen, going to tell you 'bout our jolly ol' fiddler an' oh so Righteous One so you don't go 'n' put your nasty undiplomatic foot in it by accident one of these merry days..."

Another cork popped. Someone laughed, someone quietly clapping. Mathilda's head was turned and raised, she gazed devotedly up at Tobias, a picture of perfect wife...

"...Mondays to Wednesdays..." (Eva had rapidly and deadpan recounted) "...are his work-late-even-if-you've-nothing-to-do-for-Christ's-sake-don't-go-home-yet days, but boy're Thursdays hallowed. That's the Holy Amateur String Quartet night. He strokes chastely all evening with quivering fingers an' rolled-up eyes upon his faithful ol' 'cello wedged 'tween his thighs — but boy, when midnight strikes an' number three an' four call it a day, does the fiddling properly begin an' rise to frenzy. It's the slinky female second violin with long hair an' legs sliding fingers and fanny along his billabong an' Leading it into Temptation. According to the Gospel of mother it's been going on all of five years, and she got it from the male first violin she lays monthly and he ought to know..."

A third cork popped, and Mathilda had taken Toby's hand in hers. The babble of conversation at the table was reducing.

I said to my brother: "Take the advice of an embittered old atheist and..."

"Herr Falk, my dear chap..." The gruff voice was raised, almost cheerful, made me turn my head. "...come and assist me with the honours, please do." Herr Goldberg stood stocky and square at the far end of the table, two raised champagne bottles in his hands and an array of partly-filled glasses before him.

"Of course," I called. And to Tobias: "Take my advice, brother, and live by the Word in your Book day and night and not the heathen hypocrisy practised in the Vatican and company corridors of power – I'm certain it would improve the world and maybe even redeem your imperfections on Judgement Day."

But he wasn't listening – and Mathilda beside him was holding him hard, beaming sublimely into space. His big brown lapdog-like eyes had lifted, too... not to me but to the congregation around the High Table, and a celestial light burned deep within them as if he'd been saved by a heavenly bell.

x x x

Toasts were made and glasses held high, and the glasses rang together like happy chimes with Annabelle one side of me and her father on the other, and everyone standing saying things appropriate to the occasion.

"Elijah," Herr Goldberg said to me.

"Stefan," I said to him.

Stolidly he shook my hand again. Hooking elbows and dipping heads, we sipped from our champagne glasses like two puppets on tangled strings. Good old Germanic tradition. For a few seconds our faces were close, I could see the start of stubble on his cheek and chin, smell his aftershave; his pale bulging eyes steadfastly scrutinised mine.

"Elijah," I repeated. Let his name roll over my tongue.

We embraced. His body was compact, rigid as a wrestler. For an instant we clung, chest on chest. We were two small men from two different worlds – only the body of his daughter had brought us near.

"Welcome, my friend."

I nodded. I felt nervous again.

He chuckled. Was drawing his wife to his side. Her thin wrinkled fingers rested on my arms. "Monique." She smiled. "Stefan, my dear. You don't know how happy you make me." She took me in her arms; we embraced too.

"No," I said. "I fear I don't." I breathed in her aura, and her oriental scent. "But if it's ten percent of what your daughter does to me, there could be worse starts."

She kissed me carefully, three times, graciously – left, right, left. She did it with her eyes closed. And as we separated I thought: I suppose now's not a bad moment. I reached towards my pocket. But a hand took my arm...

"Let's take a stroll." It was Annabelle's father, and his hand was certain and firm.

Chapter 24

"They're my passion," he told me, flatly.
We were strolling alone. Lawns like a putting green. Further away, children still scattered about. I recognised little David and his brother, and Marcel too, playing football with the boys.
"...apart from publishing, the only one I possess."
He was talking about his gardens. I followed his pointing finger. Flowerbeds ahead – big and long and piled high with blooms in rank and file.
"The summer colours are still rather elegant."
I side-glanced at him; he was watching me. Steadily, unblinking. It was clear from his expression it was my colours he intended to see.
He steered me nearer his passion. We passed a middle-aged couple, also strolling, deep in conversation. Grass gave way to flags of stone, a wide walk between the flowerbeds. Three women in smart party clothes went by, one nodding, one listening, one talking; they received a small bow from Elijah. All around, beautiful flowers, some for me exotic flowers. And I'd never seen such enormous dahlias. He told me names as we went.
I only half-listened – I was looking at this small ugly Jew and thinking: my God, what's he been through, from a childhood under the Nazis...

"...the carnations there, *Dianthus barbatus*, and *Erysimum cheiri*..." He indicated; they looked like mother's wallflowers to me. "And those Pampas grasses're *Cortaderia selloana*..."

...his family murdered, an orphan of war who returned to the country with his family's blood on its hands and worked his way up, then lost his son – how can he walk here talking about flowers?

The path widened. A round pool with stone surround, water lilies, a fountain, a statue made of bronze. We stopped. Two curved, wrought-iron benches. A pleasant quiet spot; a place for meditation. But he didn't sit down. In the background distant strains of the string quartet. Abruptly he said: "I hear my daughter holds you in high esteem."

He faced me. Was here where the confrontation was to be? I didn't reply.

"Well don't expect the same from me. I respect hardly anyone – that's how I got where I did."

"I didn't plan on expectations in this regard," I said. "You can take me or leave me."

He nodded. A brief jerk of his head on the thick neck. Then: "People love to hate me, you know."

I tried a smile. "Yes," I said, "that I can imagine."

"Can you now?"

"Presumably they're jealous. Isn't jealousy the main motivation for hating Jews over the last two thousand years?"

"Correct. Plus propaganda. Do you hate Jews?"

"If you're trying to provoke me, you'll have to do better than that."

"Well?"

"Have to disappoint you there." I shook my head. "No more or less than I do Christians or Moslems or Buddhists or atheists. Or any other human category, for that matter. Although I will confess, for hypocrisy Catholics might top the list if there were one."

"Uh-huh. What's your religion, then?"

"Avoiding religion."

"Ah-hah. The atheist breed."

"And you?" I asked. "Certainly not orthodox."

"Unorthodox." He gazed at me a moment, a neutral stare – this was obviously one who gave nothing away. "Reform with scepticism, if anything," he added, and his voice was dead. "Once a Jew always a Jew."

"I'm not surprised," I said.

"About what?"

"After what you and your family went through. Your God didn't precisely spread his protecting wings."

His gaze became colder, harder. "That subject's taboo." He shot it out.

"So I hear."

"Oh you did, did you? And how much did you hear?"

I shrugged. "Not enough to put on a postcard."

"Then we'll keep it that way. Past's past. A load of crap."

He was treading on my toes. "The past's what's made us what we are," I said. "It's about all we have."

"Cliché. There's more to it than that, maybe you'll learn that one day. G-d moves in mysterious ways." He hunched his compact shoulders, swept a stumpy dismissive hand. Had the master decided? Was the subject now at an end?

I watched him. Yes – he gave nothing away. He stood there returning my gaze, stable as a block. Then something caught his eye; he looked down. A tiny frog was hopping past. He stooped, picked it up – his seemingly clumsy hands did it with perfect care. Leaning, he set it on a lily leaf, remained bent a moment, observing the pond. "*Nymphaea candida*," he indicated the lilies.

Water fell from the fountain, splashing on stone. Wet ferns and moss in crevices. Reflections of light. The white water lilies looked crisp and perfect, in their centres small glowing crowns of gold...

"I knew your father Johannes."

He'd straightened again – I hadn't noticed, I'd been peering at the perfection.

"Yes," I said.

"G-d bless his soul."

I nodded at him. "If he does bestow a blessing he'll be the only one – no-one in Munich did."

He regarded me in silence. Unexpectedly, he produced a gruff chuckle. "You're a chip off the old block, my boy. But you lack his sovereign touch."

"Unfortunately it didn't save him from the dogs."

"I warned him about that mill."

He was talking about the paper mill father'd built in South America. Again I said nothing; this was my subject to dismiss as taboo.

He pursed his thick lips. Gave my arm a brief tap, turning me. We walked on. Unspoken thoughts. A clump of firs, a big bamboo grove – tall graceful stems striped yellow and green, luscious, exotic...

"*Phyllostachys vivax*," he murmured, noting my glance.

You could've fooled me, I thought.

"Grow to a maximum of twenty-five to thirty feet..."

"You don't say," I said. They reminded me of northern Laos and Vietnam.

Beyond them, the corner of the gardens: a greenhouse, a potting shed, and a stretch of seedling beds. We'd reached a high brick wall with coping stones on top, it stretched away – the boundary to next door. The stone path curved between birch trees then we were back on lawns again.

And again, too, music in the distance, but the children closer now. Shouts and squeals and laughter. There was Martina with the girls – pretty party dress.

He said suddenly: "When're you two intending getting married?" He was looking sideways at me.

"Did Annabelle tell you?"

He stopped again. "That's a very Jewish habit." Another short chuckle. But it had gone in a second. He was peering down.

"What is?" I said.

"Answering a question with a question." He trod with his shiny patent leather shoe, pressing an undulation in the perfect lawn.

"Ah," I said.

"Well when?" he demanded.

"We thought in autumn."

"Which autumn?"

"That's a very good question." I smiled vaguely, but I was smiling to myself. "At the expense of borrowing from your heritage again, what has Annabelle told you?"

"My daughter tells me nothing. And what she tells her mother is apparently no business of mine." He said it with controlled irritation; was that a kind of confession? "You don't appear to lay any value on the date."

"Well... I wouldn't say that," I said. I decided to leave it at that.

"From whom came the idea of marriage, anyway? You or my daughter?" Said brusquely.

"Annabelle, as a matter of fact."

"Uh-huh." He stared at me. "Should've guessed." Pale penetrating eyes. "And you? You really want to marry my daughter?"

"I'd lose her if I didn't."

"That an answer?"

"I'd say the best," I said. "Anyway the best you'll get. She's an all or nothing woman, I'm an all or nothing man. Like you."

He watched me in silence. Didn't give a hint what he was thinking. I thought: if you were a poker player you'd eat me for breakfast, you'd surely always be one of the winners.

I said: "It took about two seconds." I decided it was time to try to pull his leg.

"What?"

"For me to decide."

"To marry her?"

"That took one second. No – to suggest we marry next day."

"Uh-huh."

"She felt that would be pushing things a bit, though. And we were in rather Catholic Florence at the time. Up on a balcony overlooking the Arno, as a matter of fact."

"Don't try taking the Mick out of me."

"Doubt I could if I wanted to."

"If you had a daughter you'd be damned careful what kind of potential son-in-law you let over the threshold."

"I do have a daughter. And I can appreciate your concern."

For the very first time his guard came down. Just for a second. "You do?" Was that a chink in the armour? Was that a glimpse of surprise?

"Didn't Annabelle choose to tell you that either?"

He hunched his shoulders again. Stiffly, heavily. "You divorced?"

"Five years ago."

"Other children?"

"Just one daughter."

"Where's she now?"

"In the States. With her mother."

He regarded me carefully. "Any more skeletons in the cupboard?"

"If you'd been filled in there wouldn't be any, would there? I'm sure she had her good reasons, though. Forearmed and so forth?" I smiled — a faint rueful smile. "She did the same to me concerning you, too."

A grunt. Slowly he nodded his head. "About all my communicative daughter divulged was your name, age, profession and her intention to get married again."

Sounded like name, rank and number. "Was she under torture?" I allowed a humourless crack of a grin.

Another grunt. "If you want to know, my boy, she sold you as badly as she could. Dry, nasty, with a dangerous and sarcastic philosophical bent. The only saving grace was you appear to please her intellectually and sexually and she professes to love you, whatever that overwrought word's meant to mean."

I stood there, didn't respond. Now it was my turn to admit surprise.

He said: "And you? You in love with my daughter?" He said it drily and expressionlessly. He was the most unsentimental of men.

"I'd kill for her."

"I imagine that won't be necessary. So far as I know, she's not in need of a Paris or Hector." That seemed to satisfy him. Then he came at me again: "She said you're poor as a pauper, too."

"I see she did her best to impress." I managed to match his dryness. And inside I thought: careful, he's presumably onto papa's favourite subject now...

"How're you intending supporting her?"

"I'm not."

"You're not? She's used to a high standard of living. You erroneously expect me to foot all your bills?"

"Not mine."

"No?"

"I'm not after your money if that's what you mean."

"Talking about your financial responsibilities. It's a man's duty to support his wife."

"I'm fully aware of my duties and responsibilities." I spread my hands. "All I can offer her is who I am and what I earn and possess. We've no conception of each other's financial situations — never talked about it. She appears to have sufficient to live well, so do I."

"Time you began, then."

"Let's be direct," I said. "Is Annabelle independent of you?"

"Ask my daughter."

"You broached the subject. I'm asking you."

He stood there before me. Pondering. "I foot the bills."
"That I assumed."
"Did you now?"
"Only since her husband died?"
"Since before, during and after her marriage." He'd clasped his hands behind his dinner jacket, stood there stolidly.
"And her husband's bills? Those too?"
"Those too."
"Ah." I returned his gaze. "Yes," I said. "Understandable."
"What's understandable?"
"You think I'm after your cash."
"I didn't say that."
"I have a suggestion, then."
"Which is?"
"I'll put my cards on the table with Annabelle sometime soon. See how many of her bills I can afford. All of mine is hers. What's left over to cover is your and her affair."
"You find that sufficient?"
I watched him. Was that the Jew in him coming out? "It's all I have," I said. "Unless I sell a holiday apartment I bought in the mountains as investment a few years ago."
He regarded me. In silence. Then slowly turned away. Was that a brief shake of the head? A glimpse of his back as he began walking: black smoking jacket arms, crisp white cuffs with cufflinks peeping, powerful pink clasped hands.
I followed.
"How old's your daughter?" He'd made quite a jump.
"Twelve."
"Miss her?"
"Yes." We were strolling on grass again, side by side.
"How often do you see her?"
"Not once in the five years. Her mother managed that rather well."
"Bad. A daughter needs a father, too. Your first wife remarried?"
"I'm not sure."
Ahead a summer house.
"Your daughter. What's her name?"
"Andrea."

"An-dre-a." He mulled the word; the way he said it, it sounded almost classical. "Greek," he said. "The valiant one, the courageous one."

"Yes."

A brief pause. Then: "Annabelle tells me Martina and Marcel call you uncle."

"I like that," I said. I noticed: that was the first time he'd called Annabelle by her own name.

"They're fond of you, I hear."

"I believe so." Now I knew where he was heading.

"And you?"

"I'm fond of them, too," I said. I glanced at him but he was looking ahead, hands still comfortably behind his back; I watched his profile. And I thought: he's got this conversation fully under control, he goes only where he wants to go; this is a wily old fox.

Another jump. But smaller this time – he was drawing the net tighter and tighter. He said: "Are you and Annabelle living together?"

"No."

"You're still in Nuremberg, then."

A statement, not a question. So I didn't bother to reply.

"When're you going to?"

"Going to what?"

"Come together. Not till you marry?"

"I think so," I said.

"Where?"

Where? I considered that one; I'd pushed it aside for weeks. "In Munich," I said. I could see my flat. My faithful nest, that womb. Would I be able to tear up my roots?

"Where in Munich? Her apartment?"

I knew I couldn't do that, couldn't just move in, like a travelling salesman without his wares. He'd got me now. I said: "We haven't decided yet."

"Uh-huh."

I added: "Whatever we do, the children's wishes will be respected more than mine." And I meant it. That was the trouble.

"Correct."

A clump of larches, swooping feathery branches. We'd reached the summerhouse in the other corner of the gardens. It was built of timber, open one side like a shady arbour. A David's cross on the lintel, painted in gold; on one of the benches a couple smooched. We skirted it, picking up a path leading back towards the terrace.

"Think you can do it?" he said beside me. "Made of the right stuff?"

"For what? A second marriage?"

"Not just that. You're taking on a wife with two kids."

I'd given it much thought; that was no problem, in fact that was an added incentive. No – the problem was me. Could I rip up those roots, could I make the jump from A to B?

"They're the icing on the cake," I told him.

He shook his head, thoughtfully. "In truth?" Was watching me sideways.

"I miss being a father." I paused. "My first wife took that away."

A nod – a very slow nod. A silence. Then he said stubbornly: "They're not your own, though."

He took a breath, his voice changed. "They're from my blood. My own stock. They're Goldbergs, you understand?"

I smiled faintly: he'd said it in Yiddish. It sounded suddenly so intimate, it suited him – and he'd said it so I understood.

"Annabelle is like my own blood," I said.

He stopped. He regarded me in silence again. Before us high iron hoops, climbing roses, like a tunnel yawning. "I like the sound of that." He spoke gruffly. But was that a lessening of the hardness in those cold pale eyes?

We continued strolling. Were entering the tunnel. Filtered light, sun and shadow, a profusion of roses, cooler here; the scents almost intoxicated.

"My special passion." His voice was hushed. And pointing: "Albertine, introduced in nineteen-twenty-one, cultivated by Barbier." Deep pink blooms. "And here..." White roses, now, touched with pink. "...New Dawn, English, nineteen-thirty, scent like apples, can you smell it...?" His voice intoning like a religious chant.

"Yes," I said.

He paused. A cluster of yellow blooms hung near his head. "Maréchal Niel, an old stock from eighteen-sixty-four, Pradel – you don't find a scent like this often now..." He reached up, cupped a stumpy hand round one gently, fondling it. He touched it like lovers do.

The tunnel was long. We followed it.

"So you'll be starting a new life here in Munich." Another statement requiring no answer.

"But your work's in Nuremberg. How'll you equate the two?" That turned head, those eyes again, watchful, measuring, calculating – was that how he'd survived? And the old hardness was there again too. Up and down; this conversation with him was like a roller coaster. I wondered where it'd land.

"I'm working on that," I said. But it was true. Cornelia had an intriguing idea, and she was down in Munich now. Should I let her succeed in seducing me?

"A weekend marriage's no marriage at all."

"I agree." I nodded my head.

"And the children need a full-time father."

"I realise that, too."

"So?"

"I'm working on it," I repeated.

Trellis by trellis we meandered, along his tunnel of love. Yes, the scents were overpowering...

"You're a dark horse," he said.

"Am I?"

"And stubborn as a mule, I'm told."

I glanced at him. "So're you."

Another faint chuckle.

The music was getting louder. And I could clearly hear the babble of many voices again. Patches of blue sky above. Between them, the roses and the leaves and the thorns. The sunlight was losing its strength, I saw.

He didn't continue. The pause, though, wasn't brittle. "I have a question," I said.

"Fire away."

"D'you think we could learn to tolerate one another?" I felt I should keep it brief.

He came to a standstill again; that was the last time he'd do it on that walk. He stood there beneath his trellises of roses and there was sunlight on the two wild tufts of white hair.

"What's your opinion of me?" he countered. Ah, there was the Jew coming out again.

I thought about it; was the answer important to him? "I would say, humility," I said carefully. "For what you've achieved in your life.

And for what a daughter you've produced – she's once in a blue moon and half of her is you."

He took a step, moved out of the ray of sun. Steady gaze; his thick lips were ruminating. "Think I could learn to like you, my boy," he said flatly. "Like how you tick – in fact you're a bit like me."

"I hope not."

He laughed. It was a genuine chortle, rumbled up from his stomach. He patted my arm. Was turning me. And then, unexpectedly, as we went, he put an arm round my shoulder.

We emerged from the tunnel. Were walking side by side, nearing the terrace, and his arm was gone. Hands in pockets, jacket unbuttoned, he was chatting about his garden again, just as he had at the start. It was on the steps going up that he quietly said, with hardly a change in tone: "Never mess about with her, will you – if you hurt her you hurt me," and although his voice was neutral the warning was crystal clear.

x x x

Not a great deal more of note happened at that garden party – with one exception: Eva's little surprise.

Elijah Goldberg and I returned, traversing the terrace. Tables being laid: white cloths, cutlery, fresh glasses, bottles of red, white and rosé wine. Most of the guests were sitting now. Babbles of conversation everywhere, but the music had ceased. The string quartet was packing its stands and instruments away, being replaced by a handsome young man in silky glittery clothing and locks which looked like a wig, wheeling a steel trolley piled with electronic paraphernalia.

Midway along the terrace waitresses and waiters all dressed in black and white were setting up a long buffet. Silver dishes, terrines on legs over methylated spirit lamps, large graceful sculptures carved from blocks of ice...

Elijah hung an arm around my shoulders again as we passed. Perhaps it was a signal for anyone who needed to see; I felt awkward, but didn't let it show. He was speaking to me, in Yiddish, telling a Jewish joke, chuckling now and then. I had to concentrate to understand and our heads were fairly close.

The sunlight slanted. Longer shadows cast by the big sun-umbrellas now; the heat was going out of the day. Glancing, taking in small fragments of the scene, I have to confess it was all rather elegant, and the company surprisingly compatible and civilised. Was this a good omen? Was this a part of Munich society, too?

His arm was still around me and the joke had come to an end; I could feel the warmth of his body, and its compact and muscular strength. As we approached our table I saw it had already been laid, and that the great-aunt and uncle had come out to join the fray. I saw, also, that Annabelle was watching us with a calm expressionless gaze.

They'd mostly changed places – as though they'd been playing musical chairs. Others had joined them, remained standing: the chairs stood higgledy-piggeldy, various clusters of conversation. Christian Beck stood too, back turned, talking to two elderly statesmen in dinner jackets, talking discreetly. Only Annabelle and the rabbi remained unmoved near the head of the table where her old uncle and aunt had been placed. Her mother was no longer there.

She rose.

Exchanged glances, unreadable glances, between her and her father. He'd patted my shoulder, let me go. Then he said to her: "Off to do the rounds – join your mother. You hold the fort, will you?" He stolidly drew out a pocket watch, clicked it open, peered at it. "Twenty minutes, then I'll do the speech." Snapped it shut again, tucked it away.

"Ten, father. We're all ravenous."

Expansively, his short arms raised, he capitulated. "Ten it is."

He stumped off, nodding, small and sturdy and in command, completely in his element.

x x x

It was two hours later.

A hot glow on the horizon going into indigo; the sun had set. Strings of lights like pearls along the house and all around the terrace. Hung from the awnings and sun-umbrellas, paper Chinese lamps, and on the tables clusters of candles.

Had been a good speech: erudite, short, to the point, punctuated with quotations and wit. He'd held it at the other end of the terrace using the disc-jockey's microphone, and at the close proposed a toast to Annabelle and me for the future in a paternal jovial way. The buffet had been excellent too – I didn't eat much though. During it I'd enjoyed talks with Annabelle's mother, with Christian Beck and a journalist friend of his, and with the rabbi.

Discarded soiled linen napkins, empty pushed-aside plates. Two waiters were discreetly clearing. Empty glasses, refilled glasses, in the background modern music chosen by the DJ, not too loud from where we sat – a comfortable, mellow mood had descended on those at our table. Relaxation, lazy gestures, faces aglow in the light; the candles flickered over the tablecloth, it was like a shimmering pool into which people dipped their hands.

Schnapps, brandy. Elijah offering cigars around. Legs stretched out, streams of smoke blown into the night, bodies leaning back. Halfway down the table Tobias savoured his Havana importantly, puffed up like a buffoon, prim disgust in Mathilda's eyes – I with empty hands slipped one secretly beneath the table, relished Annabelle's slinky thigh. Sideways glances; she was answering mine. The Bavarian Minister-President sat with us now, a late arrival, we'd all just been introduced. He was seated beside Elijah: with him had come a bodyguard, nasty cold piece of work who stood inconspicuously in the shadows against the wall between our table and the next – tall, athletic, summer jacket open and tieless white shirt, a pair of sunglasses pushed up onto a shiny shaved skull, eyes continuously on the move. Wasn't that a tiny receiver at one ear, a short spiralled cord going out of sight? Now and then I idly noticed, while surreptitiously stroking Annabelle's gorgeous thigh, the head would dip and the eyes would dart, the lips murmuring soundlessly into a lapel. So presumably there were two, unless he was chatting to his mum.

The Minister-President, Dr Gustav Breitenbach, was speaking; a heavily built, gravelly and direct kind of man with a dry and gritty voice – along the table people leaned forward to hear, people hung on his every word. With honest undistinguished face and bright enquiring eyes, he spoke fluently and down-to-earth. I'd never seen him in the flesh before, but regularly on TV: in the hallowed and lonely arena of my ability to admire, he was also the first Bavarian President from down the decades I'd ever enjoyed listening to, ever wanted to see. Brilliant, blunt and incorruptible, an exception proving the rule – a rough diamond, an oak amongst so many saplings.

When he had rounded off his topic and opened it up to general discussion, I leaned to Annabelle, whispered: "D'you fancy the Minister's goon?"

"Mmm."

"You noticed him, then?" She noticed everything.

"I have noted him down on my list of future lovers."

"I feared so."

And a little later, after the talking had broken up into separate groups again, I bade the thigh briefly farewell and drew the small present from my jacket pocket and laid it quietly before her mother seated beside me.

"Oh Stefan, how kind." She was gazing down. "But you know you shouldn't..." Ah that lilting French accent again.

I'd wrapped it in a piece of parchment, which seemed appropriate, tied it with brown string. And the beneath the string I'd pressed and tucked a leaf.

"How did you know?" Her bony fingers touched the leaf. "The oak is my favourite tree."

"That I didn't know," I said.

With care she laid the leaf aside, undid the bow, opening the wrapping. As she did so she turned her head to me. "Oh but you did, you see." For a moment her eyes looked into mine. It was strange – although they were grey with specks of brown I had the feeling I was looking into Annabelle's eyes; I was gazing at eyes I knew.

"I simply thought it might serve as decoration."

"Nothing is that simple, Stefan."

Her eyes were gone; she was once more concentrating on her hands. They had peeled open the paper, revealed the old book.

"Oh Stefan, I'm overwhelmed. This is beautiful."

Annabelle's shoulder brushed mine as she looked. The other side of her mother the rabbi politely looked too. And beyond him her father, mildly inquisitive, peered with lips pursed. I'd meant it as a surprise; isn't that what a present should be?

I watched her mother Monique's face. It was tipped towards the book, her fingers dipped into the opened wrapping. They stroked the worn leather indented with gold, tracing the words of the title tenderly. I stared at the book. I could see my father's hands now – could see his study, him seated at his desk. He'd touched it that way too...

She was opening the book slowly.

Screwing up his eyes, her husband Elijah Goldberg queried: "Heinrich Heine?"

"Yes dear. His *Reisebilder*." She paused, not looking up. Her wrinkled finger turned the faded flyleaf, pressed it gently flat. Then she read aloud: "1826. Düsseldorf."

There was a snap. Elijah had clapped a spectacle case shut, was setting small gold glasses on the broad bridge of his nose.

"Twenty-six?" he said. "That's a first edition, then."

"Yes dear."

"Which volume?"

"Volume one."

The Minister-President said: "My dear Elijah." He gave a small hollow laugh. "Am I correct in recalling a first lecture of yours in the varsity debating society? Nineteen-fifty-eight?"

"Indeed, Gustav, indeed." Goldberg was ponderously reaching a hand past the rabbi. "May I, my dear?" His shirt-cuff stretched out of his dinner jacket; there were those cufflinks again. Small, gold, David's star on black. His fingers flexed – was that a hungry hand? He took up the book from his wife. But I noticed he suddenly handled it with care, the way he did his roses, as though it might disintegrate, or as though it were holy – all his power and impatience were gone.

Annabelle's lips touched my ear. I tipped my head to her, thought she wanted to whisper something, but she just nibbled me cheekily with her teeth.

"A little gem," her father muttered. He was studying it through his spectacles down his nose. He cradled it, turned a page, then back again. Nodding, lowering his head, he peered at me over the gold rims; his pale eyes were professional, his gaze hallowed with respect.

"This work was published in four volumes," he said. "Eighteen-twenty-six to eighteen-thirty-one."

"Yes." I nodded. I recalled the dates – had only recently read them. But that was all I recalled. It had been my father who knew much about Heine.

"A masterpiece. The first modern feuilleton. Harry Heine was his Jewish first name in those days, till he felt forced to convert to the evangelical church because of the damn bourgeoisie." He turned the old book. Turned it in his hand. "Hundreds of copies were destroyed by our friends the Nazis. Ignorant, illiterate bastards. Pure sacrilege."

He paused, considering. Then added: "Very thoughtful gift. You must've searched quite a while. Can't be many left."

"I suppose not," I said.

"Where did you find it?" He was handing the book back to his wife.

"I didn't." He asked so directly I couldn't lie. "I inherited it from my father."

"Johannes? Well I'll be damned." He removed his spectacles. For a moment he stared at the table before him as if staring at the past. Then he raised his wineglass, drained it, savouring it.

And his wife said, laying a hand lightly on my arm: "Stefan, then I appreciate this even more. You really ought not to have given us something quite so cherished."

I smiled. Said nothing. The other three volumes I'd get from the boot, give to her later.

"You couldn't have found anything more suitable." Wistfully she smiled back. "In fact, when Elijah proposed to me in London after the war, he did it in writing with a quote from Heine..." She bowed gracefully forward. "Do you remember, Eli?"

Gruffly he answered: "Long time ago." Then he closed his spectacle case with another snap, and chuckled. "Don't you go giving any more trade secrets away, my dear." He rose, pushing back his chair with his legs, stockily but slightly unsteadily, picked up two bottles of wine. As he did so, the Minister-President began to recite a poem. Ironical satirical verse. I didn't recognise it. And when he stumbled on one of the lines Elijah, red wine in one hand and white in the other, picked it up and continued – and in between made pauses to pour, on his way around the table.

Finishing the circuit, bottles still in hand, he announced: "'*Gedichte*' from Heine's pen at twenty-five years old – am I right, Gustav?" and the Minister nodded.

"One can imagine the scene..." Christian Beck was speaking now, quietly, assuredly – was this the journalist's eye? "...it's eighteen-twenty-two, candlelight, plush bourgeois drapes, a literary gathering in Rahel Varnhagen's salon, and there in the middle is young Harry reciting, sharp as a knife..."

I leaned back in my chair. Close beside Annabelle.

I'd found that thigh beneath the table again. Felt the thin silk slipping on skin. Christian was describing the scene still – like an artist, bold brushstrokes on canvas, filling us in on background; and Elijah and the Minister adding details here and there... I sat there distracted, only half-listening... erudite men, cultivated men, sure of their subject, then after a few minutes changing the subject, leading and jumping, thrusting and parrying, dipping into their intellectual depths, losing me...

Surreptitiously I began stroking her thigh again, following her eyes as she calmly followed the conversation...

"I recall, Christian, an article you penned to that theme..." That was Elijah...

Her head turned slowly, regally, she looked at me like a queen again. Those green, green eyes, those cheeky freckles, that sensual mouth – the most beautiful woman in the world. I was hungry for her, even hungrier than her father for Heine...

Hello, Miss Goldberg, I said with my eyes.

Hello you randy devil, hers greenly replied.

x x x

Elijah, Monique and the Minister-President were rising; Elijah said to the gathering: "You'll please excuse us? Time to do the rounds again."

As they left, I glanced at the bodyguard: he was talking rapidly now, head ducked, holding his lapel to his lips. I leaned to Annabelle, whispered: "Back in a jiffy, have to have a pee, and have to fetch something from the car."

"Uh-huh." She gazed, one of those gazes which go through me. "You are not intending to do a scoot, I hope?"

"Ah," I said. "How do you always see through me?"

"I believe I will accompany you, then, just in case." A piercing stare.

I was standing up. Could it really be she hadn't smelled the trap? As we set off she said: "I notice you are hardly drinking."

Ahead of us the Minister and her parents were skirting a standing cluster of guests, making for one of the tables. The bodyguard had discreetly moved too, hovered at a distance, like a shadow that's lost its host. Beyond, at the far end of the terrace, the disco was in full swing, figures dancing in a flood of light.

"No," I said neutrally to Annabelle.

"Is my nervous one afraid of losing his self-control?"

"My self-control?" I smiled slyly at her. The trap was closing, soon we'd be out in the street, alone together, away from it all – already I was touching the flank of her slinky dress, trailing my fingers...

"On second thoughts," she sighed, "not such a bad idea." She threaded a thin hand through my arm as we went.

"One shouldn't drink and drive," I explained.

"Drive?"

"Later."

"We have a bed for you."

I glanced sideways again. Smiled again – but this time a lecherous one. "A bed?" I queried.

"Mm-hmm. And don't look at me like that. It was mama's suggestion."

"A small, narrow single bed, or perhaps...?"

"Naturally with shackles for arms and legs, and a big padlock on the door. On the outside of the door."

"How could mama be so cruel?"

"She's an expert on men."

"You inherited that from her too?"

We were passing the tall bodyguard; my head nearly reached his chest so I had to stretch. On tiptoe I called loudly to his lapel: "Mayday, mayday..." and peered about sneakily but in vain for the one clutching his eardrum.

To Annabelle I said deadpan: "So now I can get drunk?"

And that was the moment when I saw him. I tensed. He was emerging through one of the French windows, with Eva. They walked close together but not touching; no fingers tucked in an arm, no holding hands – that'd never been Matthias's metier. Old Wilhelm was accompanying them. When he saw Annabelle he indicated her with a stiff raised arm, let them pass and withdrew into the house again.

We were headed for the same windows. Annabelle saw them and waved; we met between the tables. Eva greeted Annabelle, they kissed – so it seemed they knew each other. Then she kissed me. She kissed me full on the lips – a small, soft, warm cushion on my mouth for a brief moment. Since Florence we had only talked on the telephone, I'd rung twice to give support and keep myself informed;

up to now no new developments. I glanced down at her body, it looked so slim, no sign yet of her pregnancy. I wondered if Matthias knew. She was still close: she smelled of alcohol, cigarettes and perfume. And something else. I think she smelled of Matthias. She gazed directly into my eyes – was she trying to tell me something?

But I had no time to ponder, Matthias was standing there. Quietly, gauntly. Almost sensuously. My God, he looked fit.

"Matt, this is..." Eva was introducing him to Annabelle...

I could feel it. At once. That instant attraction. My senses jumped, went into high gear.

Matthias and Annabelle. Their hands reached out, touched – I watched them watching one another. I knew Annabelle, I sensed the change. It was subtle, camouflaged, but it was there; for the initiated like an aura suddenly glowing, like a searchlight switched on – I knew her too well. I thought: even a blind man would notice. And Eva?

But if she did, she didn't show it.

My turn now. His eyes – steady, blue, he'd turned them slowly away from Annabelle. His hand in mine, his lean body coming closer. We embraced; he kissed me on both cheeks – he embraced me as he had in the clinic. Yes, I could smell his Cologne, he'd left it on Eva like a cat leaves its mark.

"Matthias," I said.

"Stefan." His eyes so clear, penetrating. He looked into me, through me – but not like Annabelle did; he looked through me like a knife.

We were separating. The four of us. Standing there. Eva was talking – to Annabelle, I think. I could feel something else; it'd followed straight after the first feeling. But it was inside me, not Annabelle. Powerful, deep, like acid – the cut, the burn of jealousy. I tried to suppress it...

Had someone else spoken? I looked up...

"Stefan?"

"Yes?" I said.

It was Annabelle; a flash of those green eyes. "My pondering one?" Fingers stroking my arm. "I want to introduce Eva to..." She mentioned the name of a woman from the fashion world – a girlfriend of hers. "After the car you won't be scooting, will you?"

A voice was singing, singing very distinctly. It came from over by the disco where people were dancing – mournfully singing an ancient oldie *Fool on a Hill*. Was it George, or Paul? I'd never been sure. The timing was most inappropriate. Yes, that song. No doubt Rosi would know — I must ask her next time she called in for a renewing dose when her pimp wasn't there.

"Yes," I said to Annabelle. I bared a grin.

"We will be over there." The fingers squeezed, were gone, were indicating.

"Ah," I said. Leather meets fashion, I thought.

She was drawing Eva with a graceful hand, touching Matthias too; walking between them. Why did she have to go and touch him? For an instant I glimpsed him. He walked beside her, just a little taller, walking like a cat. And they looked so good together.

x x x

I returned from the car very quickly. Near the gates, lurking between trees, one dark shadow amongst many, I glimpsed bodyguard number two. And in front of the house another big BMW with chauffeur was being backed up to the steps. It had a little flag on one wing.

Back through the hall, past Wilhelm on duty — I gave him a small salute, and the three books in brown paper to look after till later — through the empty dining room. The terrace beyond. Dozens of voices, different music, dancers jazzing it up. Flickering lights. Nearly dark, in the western sky only a faint green afterglow.

I joined them again. They stood at a table: the three women were talking and I saw that Eva was hitting it off. Matthias was bored. He didn't show it, but he'd put on his ingenuous mask, the one we used to share. We exchanged a few words, then after a couple of minutes, hands in pockets, I said to him: "Let's go for a walk."

And Annabelle, glancing, said: "Could you postpone it till later?" She excused herself to the two, took our arms, turned us away. I thought: from the back could a stranger differentiate her lover, would a stranger know who was who? And Annabelle added: "I should like Matthias to meet a few people." She was walking between both of us now; was I mistaken? I thought I could hear her hormones on the gurgle.

"Fine," he said. That's all he said; he was looking at Annabelle not me.

We were making for our table again. I saw her parents and the Minister hadn't returned to their places, perhaps they were bidding farewells. Margareth, Mathilda and the rabbi were also nowhere to be seen. But Christian was still there; a small group had gathered around him, mostly men – some were seated, tipped back relaxedly, some standing propped or sitting on the backs of chairs. I saw Tobias had managed to get in on the act too.

Christian was one of those standing, in that instant talking to an elderly man.

We approached. And then something curious happened.

Christian caught sight of us and hesitated a fraction. In mid-sentence. Was that a flicker of surprise in his eyes? It was gone again quickly, and he glanced away, continued speaking. But I saw: he'd been looking directly at Matthias. Perhaps his defences were mulled by the wine, perhaps his professional reflexes lulled – wasn't that, though, an instant of recognition?

"Christian," Annabelle said. "I should like you to meet an old friend of Stefan's."

And he was turning to us again. Matthias stopped before him, Annabelle did the introductions, and I watched Matthias's profile. He showed nothing – if there was indeed anything to give away. Formal greetings. He offered his hand the way one offers it to any stranger. And Christian did precisely the same.

x x x

The rest of the evening passed pleasantly enough, and the evening turned into night. I continued to keep off the drink. I also stayed close to Matthias and Christian for the half hour while they conversed: they neither of them showed their true colours, except in an ironical political way. One noticed, though, they were on the same wavelength, they both had very sharp compatible minds.

And afterwards, too, I stayed close to Annabelle when Matthias was floating near. Just to dampen the atmosphere, just to keep an eye on his box of tricks. There was something there, all right; the right chemical mix. They danced together once; my God, yes, they made a fine pair.

I had a little dance with Eva and learned that she'd rejected outright her company's offer, had decided to form a company of her own. She said Schulz was out of the coma now and had apparently confirmed that a prostitute got nasty and pushed him out of the window.

I never got that walk alone with Matthias – not on that particular evening.

The party went on into the early hours. Matthias and Christian didn't approach each other again. And Eva was never far away. But later, with the benefit of hindsight, I thought I was able to see it more clearly: on that evening things were coming together, the threads were drawing in.

Chapter 25

An e-mail from Cornelia awaited me upon my return next day: yes, she had a grand idea, made me a clear unambiguous offer. I mulled it over, nervously, wrote back.

Met her in Munich at the end of that week. Our discussions lasted fifteen hours in all – starting Friday evening, not ending till late Saturday afternoon. At the close I rang Annabelle, found her at home, agreed to call by. I noticed a reservation in her voice. It took me over an hour and a half to reach her apartment in Schwabing.

"Protest march," one driver told me as we stood paralysed in a side street in yet another traffic jam. I arrived impatient, tired and unnerved.

We had supper. Almost a curious feeling, just the four of us; Margareth had moved out some weeks ago, she'd found an apartment to rent. After supper Annabelle put Martina and Marcel to bed. They'd played us up during the meal – school term had just started, they were jumpety and in exhaustingly high spirits. Perhaps that's why even Annabelle lost her cool. No sooner were we alone than she said: "So that was Matthias."

We were still in the kitchen, at the table – at the table where she'd first let me touch her those four long months ago.

"Yes," I said. At once my sensors went into high alert; I studied her carefully, secretly I watched her like a hawk.

"Eva had told me about him."

"She did?"

"Mmm."

"I didn't know you knew her that well."

"Through Margareth."

"Ah."

"He nevertheless wasn't what I was expecting."

"No?" I said. "What were you expecting?" Yes what — less attractive, less fascinating? Were her hormones still on the boil?

"It is what I wasn't which is more to the point."

"And what's that?" A heavy blanket was descending, it started to blur my feelings and my thoughts. Had she fallen for him? Was there going to be an affair?

She hesitated. Sipped at her red wine: it wasn't like Annabelle to hesitate. Then she said: "You and he are very old friends," and she was speaking in a roundabout way which also was unusual.

"Since our childhood," I agreed. "Then he faded from the scene." Still I watched her carefully — yes, there was something in the air. Oh God. "You recall," I added flatly. "I recounted it to you when I was in the rehab."

"Mmm." She gazed at me over the glass. "And what is your impression of him now?"

"Now?" I shrugged. "He's changed. He's lost that old wildness. More regal, more mature." I was trying to be generous, in spite of myself. I feared I knew what she was getting at: was she about to push me out into the cold?

"Is he?"

What could I say? I shrugged again. Said nothing.

"He is very intense." She stared at me steadily. "Very animal."

Animal? I thought. Oh, for Christ's sake, what's coming now? The gorilla bit with the massive chest and beating on it with hairy paws — the call of the wild uncontrollably tickling her fancy? I held my breath; I was sinking fast.

"I don't want to hurt you," she said. "He is a very close friend of yours. Or once was."

This is it...

"Say it," I said. I could hear the coldness in my voice — or was it purely anguish?

"He makes me afraid. Insecure."

"Afraid?" I echoed. What was she hinting at now? Afraid of herself, of her feelings for him?

"Yes." She just sat there, holding up the wineglass but not drinking.

"I don't follow you," I said. For God's sake, get at it – let's stop beating about the bush. "I noticed you found him attractive," I challenged. Or irresistible? I thought. In my tone I could hear aggression now.

"Oh yes. That's the animal in him." She suddenly sipped her wine again. "One has to be very careful of a person like him, even if he is a friend."

You mean you do, I thought. The darkness was closing in. "One does?" I queried. I fear this time I said it with sarcasm.

"I want you to be careful, too."

Oh you do, do you? What the hell can I do? Go and tell him to bugger off – keep his hands to himself?

I started to speak...

But the door opened and little Marcel came in – he was crying, small fists balled in his eyes, he'd had a bad dream, he moaned. Annabelle took him up in her arms. And was gone.

x x x

The evening had started badly and it went on that way. I suppose I should've stood up at that point and gone; it's wise to listen to the whisper in the bones, it's like that cheese that's going mouldy one side – don't eat the rest because the threads of rot go deep. When she returned she changed the subject and refused to be drawn. She was reserved, preoccupied, and it left its footprint on me: I'd been going to tell her about Cornelia's offer, but now was anything but the right moment. I procrastinated, didn't mention that on the first of March in the following year I would be coming in as partner. As we sat, Matthias kept creeping into my head; even when we retired he was there, kept walking between us. She lay close to me in her big bed but I had the sensation she was only half there; we didn't make love that night.

I remember: that was also the night one of the demonstrators was shot dead by police. There'd been marches and disturbances in several large cities, especially Paris and Berlin, but it was in Munich that the worker Horst Schneider accidentally went and got shot. Well, as the press expressed it, at least it put Munich on the map. I heard it on the News, on my return to Nuremberg, depressed, on Sunday afternoon. It was the spark which ignited a flame.

At the end of September, with somewhat heavy heart, I jumped over my shadow and wrote a letter of farewell to my firm: my contract demanded six months notice. It took all of three lines. Tragic, I thought – after nearly twenty years seventeen words is all it takes including my name, there's nothing left to say. My resignation was promptly accepted. It was signed by someone I'd never heard of, on paper with the new letterhead; half a year previously my old boss would've done it, and personally. But he'd got the push already, hadn't he, and ten years too soon – put out to grass like an old carthorse, with compensation as indemnity and 'all the best old chap'.

Times were changing, nothing stands still.

The days lengthened into weeks. I had my hands full preparing seminars. Annabelle and I telephoned regularly but she was busy organising another exhibition, she said. In late October the financial crisis had got no better and new tax laws were pinching the poor and the not so well-off: I recall that on one or two demonstrations in Berlin bottles and stones had begun to fly. That's all I recall, though – I was too involved with work. And I knew, anyway, it would all blow over soon, however bad things got, just the way it always did. What concerned me the most was Annabelle; I suffered from her distance, was disquieted by her cool.

Then unexpectedly, on the tenth of November, something happened to sorely distract my mind. From out of the past somebody else suddenly re-entered my life – a little the way Matthias had done. With an e-mail though, not a postcard, and female this time not male. I remember the date because that was the morning I had to appear in court as witness to that business from May, and ironically it was also the day a further kidnap victim was released in northern Germany. It was in all the papers, a kidnapper had been killed; they reported that the security apparatus was tightening the noose.

I remember, too, what the message did to my heart: a heavy horrible jolt.

I peered at the Notebook screen, disbelieving, then pressed the key to print. As the white tongue of paper emerged I was thinking: I'm imagining things again. But there it was, black on white, the brief text: 'Hi Stef! How're you? Coming over 12/1 with LH, landing NUE 22.50. Andrea accompanying. Will you pick us up, put us up? Judit.'

My hands were unsteady, my heart in labour and my body weak. Was this a nasty joke? Judit was coming? And little Andrea, too? It had been six years now. No phone calls, no letters, no news – and now, suddenly, this...?

"Herr Falk?" A nasal pushy voice.

I looked up in a daze.

A tall young secretary stood before me the other side of the desk. Chewing gum. "For you." Her eyes were glazed with disinterest.

I tried to reorientate, concentrate on her. Obviously she wanted something, but I didn't want her. She was new, looked like sweet sixteen, young enough to be my daughter. Had she forgotten to get dressed? Poppie, I think they called her. Glancing at her remarkable body I could see what they meant. Where was the old one, then? Doris – the one who'd been part of the furniture, and looked like the furniture too. My God, everything was new, everything was different now.

She was holding out a folder. Yes, everything popped out everywhere.

"Thanks," I said.

"Signature."

"What?"

"Got to sign."

"I never sign for anything."

"Orders of the boss."

"I'm one of the bosses too, you know." I glowered at her. A pretty thing, very long naked legs that seemed to go on for ever, and the residue of what used to be called a skirt. Signature? So that's new too, I thought. It's time to say goodbye. What extraordinary breasts, how did she get that T-shirt on? There was a picture of some pop star's face screen-printed on the front, his pupils neatly coincided with her nipples, his eyes swollen out of recognition by the volume of the breasts...

She was bending forward. "Here." The eyes bulged, wobbled, squinted inanely down at my desk, and the cheeky little golden loincloth rode up her bottom at the back.

I signed.

"Should I know him?" I said. Just to be friendly, just to show her the over-forties still belong to the human race.

"Huh?" Chewing gum being rapidly chewed. She'd straightened again but the minimal skirt at the rear didn't seem to have bothered to notice the correction.

"That one there." I pointed at her magnificent mammary glands.

"Oh him." She puffed them out, dug chin into chest, inspecting them for all of a second with nearly as much enthusiasm as a vegetarian in a slaughter house. "That's Elvis. Real cool."

Elvis? "You're joking," I said. And I'd thought I'd recognise him anywhere.

"He's in."

"Ah." Well, certain bits of him begged to differ, but I didn't wish to contradict. "Hasn't he been dead for decades?"

Her jaws were in a frenzy, she masticated like a horse. "Comeback." Chomp, chomp. "Just for Saturday night." Chomp, chomp, chomp. "At the *Bull's Arse*."

"The what?"

"Disco."

"Ah."

"Like Bull's Eye." Chomp, chomp.

"You could've fooled me," I said.

"*Affengeil*."

A squelching sound within her mouth, a pouting of goldfish lips; I prayed she wouldn't blow a bubble, bubbles are known to burst.

"Ah," I said again. I find it so invigorating talking to the young.

She was walking away. Yes, a remarkable fragment of skirt like a crinkled gold band, it went so well up there with the broader belt around her waist. The colour of the G-string I couldn't quite determine because there wasn't enough of it to see, but the colour of the buttocks had been greatly enhanced by over-exposure to the sun.

Ah yes, the times they are a-changin'. I was sorry my friend George Sunday wasn't present, he did so appreciate these kinds of new direction in fashion.

The door closed. Alone once more. I steeled myself; my heart was unhappy again.

I re-read the text of the e-mail. Trying to read between the lines, trying to find what wasn't there. Then I read it again. I shook my head. Judit of all people. Why on earth was she coming, what the devil did she want? And on 12/1. Twelfth of January? Or first of December? Must be the latter, the American way. Or had she adapted the date for my sake? But whatever – did I in fact wish to see her again? No, not really. Yes, the answer was no. But why – was I afraid something might stir again? No. And if she'd changed her mind, wanted us to come together again and started to seduce me – would I say no? Yes, of course I would. But...

But – wasn't I inquisitive? Just a little? To see how she'd changed, how she looked now? Better not, though. But...

But then there was Andrea – that was a different kettle of fish. Was Judit using her as bait? She'd just turned thirteen now. Oh God, how I yearned to see Andrea again.

The telephone rang. I was forced to stop.

It was an hour later till I was able to start thinking about Judit again. And I found the interruption had helped. If I wanted to know why she was coming then the best thing was to ask her. She'd given no phone number but her e-mail address was there with the text on the screen. I formulated a reply; it took several false starts and over ten minutes. It read: 'Send me a telephone number. Stefan.' A delicate situation like this has to be thought through thoroughly, has to be handled with care. As I tapped 'Send', it occurred to me: where did she get my e-mail address? I'd never given it to her.

There came no answer. Not even next day.

I thought: maybe that's an omen, maybe she's changed her mind already, I wouldn't put it past her. But still, there was a question mark. So I went to the oracle. I recounted it to her briefly. It took quite a time, though, because we hadn't spoken together since before Florence and she wished to be filled in. I obeyed: I just left out the bit about the dream and the theologian and farmhouse. Even oracles, I felt, shouldn't be confused by too many issues at once. At the end of it all I came back to Judit: "Estella," I said, "what would you do?"

And her response, overflowing with wisdom, came forth thus: "What's written is written, shouldn't she come, what will be will be." To dot the i's and cross the t's she even expanded on her pearl with: "Isn't this another of the doors?" She really overtrumped Delphi's Oracle that day.

Having received The Prophesy, and still tapping in the dark, I went home and secretly began to search the Web for inspiration. Lacking city, state and zip code reduced the choice of help pages but I had, after all, her Christian name and from her e-mail address could assume Powell was her new surname. I'd only been paging for a few minutes and getting hits in several larger cities when I received a message: E-mail from Judit. My heart made another nasty jolt. I opened it, read it. A phone number, nothing else.

I looked at the clock. 10:25 pm. Thought: what time is it in the States? West Coast, East Coast? At least six to eight hours earlier. Private number, work number? Probably work, so I can't trace her home address – will she be in the office now?

I took a breath, taking my bearings, felt suddenly nervous again. Tried to think about what to say. What does one say after six years of nothing? Keep it short, I ordered myself. I tapped in the number. My hand was shaking. The ringing tone was like in Hollywood movies – it purred, relaxed as a cat...

"Judy Powell's secretary," said a smooth male American voice. "My name's Wilbur Yeats, how can I help you?"

My word, I thought. I paused a fraction; was I waiting in case he added darling? That was a very gay, feelingful voice.

"I am sure you can," I said, mustering my best English. I gave my name, asked for Judit.

"Oh, Mr Falk, hi. It's a pleasure to connect you."

A click, a pause, no ringing tone... Then Judit's voice came on the line. Across the ocean, across the years, there was her voice again...

"Hi Stef. Fast mover." She spoke German – with a taint of American. The accent made me wince.

"Hi Judy," I said, mimicking. "Forgotten? I was always fast with the ladies."

"You're kidding." That was in English. A rich laugh, that cut out quickly. The same laugh.

"Long time no hear," I said.

"Yep."

I felt it already: I was building a wall, hiding behind it, wanting to take pot-shots at her.

"Things okay?" she asked. "How's life?"

"Well..." I hesitated. "I think one could say it's treating me better than I deserve."

That laugh again. It rippled along the line, into my brain, mixing with memories. Was this natural? Maybe it was.

"You haven't changed," she said. She said it like a reprimand.

"Have you?"

A heavy breath. Was it a sigh? Or was she smoking one of those old cigarillos? "Maybe on the surface."

"Ah," I said. "Your makeup?" Curious, my nervousness was nearly gone. Like having at last arrived in the exam; one finds one's left the fear at the door.

"Still love your little word games, I note." Another reprimand.

There was no nostalgia. I thought: is that natural too? After all the hurting – perhaps. She's the one who left. I decided it better to say nothing.

"What's your status?" she enquired neutrally. "Married?"

I could hear her breathing in my ear. Like a whisper now. "No," I said. "And you?"

"Was. Busted up. Year ago."

"Number two?"

"The bastard beat me up. Had to throw him out."

"You've had a little practice there."

"Thanks for nothing." A brief pause. "Tried to fuck Andrea. What'd you have done?" She said that in English as well.

Andrea. Oh God. "Kicked him in the balls," I said, "then cut them off." I could feel sudden anguish, feel the pain – it almost strangled my throat. I corrected myself: "No – would've cut off his prick with a carving knife. Or with a big, blunt, rusty saw."

"That's my boy."

"And Andrea? Did he try raping her?" My heart was in my mouth.

"Yep. Close shave. She scratched his fucking face and nearly tore out an eye. Wish she'd scratched out both." Also in English.

"Good girl." Thank God, I thought. "Sounds like a chip off the old Judit block." My turn to sigh now.

"Left its mark." She'd reverted to German again.

"Shit," I said. I gulped some air. "Well, of course it has. Did you get professional help?"

"Sure."

"And?"

"Lady therapist was great. Half a year long. She helped."

"And now?"

"The scar'll never quite heal, she warned. But Andrea's made of the right stuff. Could be okay in the long run, have to wait and see."

"Shit," I repeated. And then: "Why the hell did you go and bed down with such a bastard?"

"Was sugar-candy and bronzed angel till he'd got what he wanted."

I shook my head. "Well," I said, "take more damn care with number three."

"You kidding? Never again, brother."

I stared into space. I was thinking of Andrea. "Men're all bastards and dogs," I mouthed; I was talking to myself.

"You included." She said it flatly, though.

"I know."

"Oh? You do?"

I was gazing across the living room. "I do my best, that's all." There was the rocking-chair where she used to sit. "At least you taught me that."

A brief silence. Into it I said: "Is she beautiful?" Time to raise the carpet again and sweep the dirt back underneath.

"Yep."

"She's thirteen now," I mused.

"She's a real little lady."

"Tell me."

Another silence, a bit longer. Does it take so long to find the words to describe one's own daughter?

Then: "She's got my hair, my mouth, and my body – reminds me of me when I was her age."

I was trying to imagine; it wasn't hard. "Did I mishear you, then?" I said. "Did you say she's a real little lady?" Just having a shot at humour.

"Yes I did, you bastard." Another of those rich short laughs. "I could be, you know, when I wanted."

"Past tense?"

"Past tense."

"I'm sorry to hear that."

I waited a moment. And when she didn't continue, I said: "And her eyes? Are they your eyes, too?"

"No." A sniff. "And she's got your cheekbones."

"Ah." That pleased me. "Well I'm glad you allowed her something of me." I added a little gauntness, and painted in the two discs of speckled grey eyes on the face I held before me; the image was coming clearer...

"She's got my laugh. And that habit of mine with the hands, expressing things. Remember?"

How could I forget? "Yes," I said. Was there a slight thickness in my throat again? Suddenly? Watch it, I ordered myself. Give nothing away.

"She's got your character, give you that."

She has? Well thank God for that. The way Judit said it, though, it sounded remarkably like another rebuke. "That's tough on her," I said, tongue in cheek.

She ignored me. "When she wants, she shuts up like a clam. Just like you. Drives me up the wall."

"I'm glad to hear about that too – I was getting worried you'd managed to cheat the genetic laws and passed on ninety percent."

"Snide bugger."

A pause.

I cleared my throat. Made my confession to the queen of cruelties. "I miss her," I said. "Missed her for six years." And left it at that.

But nothing came from down the line.

I thought: time to get this over with. "Why're you coming?" I asked.

"Because of Andrea."

"Why?"

"Give her a small dose of Germanic culture."

I waited. Again nothing forthcoming. So I said: "Do I have to keep on asking why?"

"She's getting too Americanised."

"Well what did you expect?"

"Thought I could offset it, let her get the best of both. Okay, she's got school influence and Yankee friends, but we only talk German at home and've got several German friends, too."

"But she was only seven when you took her out. Formative years, and so on."

Another pause.

"How long were you intending to stay?" I asked. I formulated it diplomatically.

"Just through Christmas vacation. You'll put us up?"

"Just like that?"

"Want to shunt us into a hotel?"

What did I want? I was still thinking about it when her voice came again: "You made other plans already then?"

"No plans."

"It's for Andrea's sake." She sounded insistent.

"Not yours?"

"Not mine."

"Does she want to come?" I said it straight out; I had to know. "Or are you coercing her?"

"Fifty-fifty. I'd intended spending the time in Berlin. She said okay to Germany, but only if it's Nuremberg."

I could hear the disappointment in her tone; she was never a big one at hiding emotions.

"I see," I said.

"Nothing else doing. Used to be home for her, didn't it? What she remembers, where she was born."

"Does she wish to see me, then?"

"Yep."

"After all this time? She must think — I made no contact..." I stopped. Perhaps I should've said: you broke off the contact and made damn sure, you were the one who cut me out. But I didn't. I felt no recriminations, not any more; too much water had flowed under the bridge. "She must believe I'm a bastard ignoring her all these years," I said. "Are you certain that's...?"

"Yep." Loud und clear, no hesitation. "You're the bait," she added.

Me? I thought. "I'd imagined she was your bait to persuade me," I said carefully. Inside, my heart beat faster: so Andrea really wanted to see me again?

"Bit of both."

I considered a moment. "Have you thought this through carefully, Judit?"

"Sure."

"Yes? Thorough weighing up of facts was never one of your strengths."

"Thanks for the roses."

"I'm thinking of Andrea." And I was feeling so happy at the thought.

"Who else?" she retorted.

"In the apartment it'll awake old memories. Of the three of us, I mean. Wouldn't they upset her?" I stared across at the rocking chair again. And the table where Andrea used to sit drawing and messing around with crayons. Sheets of sketching paper were lying about and she leaned there, concentrating, the tip of her tongue peeping at every move of the pencil in her tiny perfect hand: she'd inherited that from me too...

"She's not a fool," Judit said in my ear. "She knows that."

I summoned up the picture of Andrea again. The new one. Had I painted it right? I wanted to find out – no, I yearned to find out.

"Okay," I said. I drew the calendar closer on my writing desk flap, was stooping. "December the first."

"Right."

"A bit early, isn't it?" I was thinking quickly.

"Early? For what?"

"I mean, school holidays in the States. Presumably don't start so soon, do they – like over here?"

"Talked to the school director. He knows me well."

"Ah." I wonder how well?

"He appreciates what she's been through. I convinced him."

"I'm sure you did." I'm sure she could, she'd always been good at convincing. With those hot, temperamental, burning eyes, those big hungry breasts, that sultry mouth – and those volumes of words flowing from it. Judit could sell steel to Krupp if she put her mind to it. And her body.

"We're calling it a kind of sabbatical."

"You are?"

"She needs the longer break."

I nodded to myself. She'd convinced me too. "Okay," I said again. "I'll pick you both up."

"Great."

"I don't know about that." I'd have to work a lot of the time till the twenty-third – at least during the day.

Another sniff. Did she have a cold? "Coming via Frankfurt," she said. "I'll e-mail you or ring if the flight's delayed or rescheduled."

I straightened from the desk. I'd made a note. "I'll be there." I thought: try a little humour, just once more, to show there's no hard feeling. "I'll be the one with the folded newspaper under his arm," I said deadpan, "and the carnation in the buttonhole. Just so you recognise me."

That laugh came back. Was richer this time, fruitier. Was like it used to be in the old days, the few times it was pleased with me.

"See you," she said.

"See you."

The connection cut off. I was left standing there, phone still to my ear, a lot of dead things in my head.

x x x

But the dead things were stirring.
Had they only been dormant? Just been suppressed, just asleep? They were like maggots, though. Were eating their way out of my subconscious, into my woken-up brain.
I set the telephone back on its base; it chirped its thanks like a bird. Glanced at the clock again, 10:40. Late, but not that late. A voice in my head said: get out, go down to the bar. So I listened to it and obeyed. Pocketed my wallet. Maybe Rosi's there. She can exorcise any man's devils, she'll kick you in the butt. Hadn't seen her in a while, not since she last called by for the usual, just to take her mind off things. Rosi the tough one, the hard little nut, with language to make a bricklayer blush but born with a soft and lucrative spot: our acquaintance was seriously unprofessional, we were pals in a platonic sort of way, in as far as a man can be pals with a whore.
But she wasn't there. Only Prickle her pimp. The place was nearly empty.
I sat down at the bar on one of the high stools. Ordered a double whisky, and asked after her. I asked Prickle, of course – always go to the heart of things. His eyes darted to me, flicked away: an ice-cold little specimen of man with a work ethic worthy of a razor blade and manners and charm to match. "F'gettit," he spat through a slit of a mouth. "Three hour job, plus."
Slick bastard. Was that bulge in his jacket a gun, or the result of good pickings? Maybe I'll ask him one of these days. So that was the end, already, of our enriching conversation. He turned his back, standing there, pressed a number with thumb, talked into his mobile. And a minute later snapped at his glass, swallowed his bitter lemon, and left.
Old Sammy the barman set my whisky before me, exchanged a few words as he always did, and sidled off to the two Boys at the other end of the bar. Morose type. Not precisely my cup of tea – especially for tonight.
I stared at the mirrors behind the shelves and the bottles, stared at my reflection: I didn't like what I saw.

The bar was tiny. It was the one on the corner fifty yards from my flat, the one jutting out with leaded glass windows and hanging bottles outside. Yes, it was like a short corridor. Eleven stools and that was it, no space for chairs or tables. It's for pick-ups, and people like me – and sometimes George Sunday of course: it's Rosi's beat where she and her colleagues work the five side streets going up to the old city walls and down to that hotel where the guests come and go very often.

What to do? I drank down my drink, ordered another. I wasn't going anywhere else that night. Call Estella? Or Lars even? No – categorically no. Well, what about George? George was grand for distraction. Yes: and he was always game, if he wasn't in bed with one of his chicks or out on assignment for a Customs razzia. Give him a tinkle, on the off-chance. I reached to my trouser pocket. But I'd forgotten my mobile.

So I went to the wall-phone. It hung between the door and the start of the bar top. In winter it's totally hidden because in its generosity it shares the space with the jackets and coats – but this evening it hung nearly alone. I picked the receiver from the hook on the side – it's one of those delightful old contraptions which you dial with a disk engraved with dirt with the tip of your finger, or with a pencil if you're one of the fainthearted. It's that kind of bar.

The apparatus was dead. I'd forgotten. I called old Sammy. He sauntered nearer, threw a switch on his big black box under the bar top, squinting Scrooge-like at his meter – what he charges per unit probably used to finance his twice-yearly vacations to Thailand, including extras for little girls under twelve, until the advent of the mobile phone. More recently, I have noticed, he extorts ten minutes for a ten-second call.

I received my dialling tone, rang George. Dirt of ages on the tip of my index finger when I'd finished, dust falling like fluff. I only had his house number in my head. If he wasn't there I'd have to go and fetch...

He was. "Will do," he said – I warned him not to come by car and not to bring his wallet, this one would be on me. He just cackled; I could imagine that golf ball of an Adam's apple jerking in his ostrich neck. Funny how he gets all the girls.

He was still cackling when he walked in through the open door. Gangly, chinless Casanova, blessed with a body his colleagues call the structural wonder and a tool, they say, to thrill the very biggest of the girls. He'd known Judit well and hated her guts, which surprised me because normally he went after anything with curves as long as it wore a skirt. I'd chosen with natural wisdom, it seemed; after Rosi he was the very next best. With his barbed observations and bottomless wit, he got Judit out of my system that night although it took till 3am.

Chapter 26

The moonlight turned the fields and trees rushing past the car windows to white; it was so bright it might almost be day and so cold one had the feeling the frost had frozen the sky.

A November night.

I'd been attending a lecture in Erlangen, at the university, was on my way home. Normally a half-hour drive. At short notice Annabelle had had to decline my invitation to drive up and accompany me, stay over till morning. Martina had mumps. Never mind. She'd popped in twice spontaneously since our unhappy evening in September, and I'd spent three weekends with her and the children in Munich in between, taking only a little of the time out for Cornelia. She didn't once mention Matthias. Things were on an even keel again, in fact we were back to being our cheeky, ironic selves: she now knew my plans about Munich and the deadline at the end of the coming March. That had lifted the barrier, I suppose. She also knew about Judit's scheduled visit, hadn't turned a hair. Yes, that reverent basis of trust was fully re-established; as was appropriate, she now had a key to my apartment, and I one to hers.

My eyes slid hither and thither, from the Franconian landscape to the straight monotonous intercity autobahn, and back again. I was tired. Very little traffic. I think I was thinking things like, why couldn't I snap my finger and find myself in bed, and if I switched off the headlights I could probably see just as well by the moon. I slowed a bit, my speed had crept up well over one hundred kph –

that wouldn't have happened in my old Mercedes. I was in George's car; he'd lent it me for a few days, mine was in for repairs. Nice car, a big Audi – but it lacked the character of yesteryear. Got a good backseat for the babes, he'd said as he handed it over, and had let out another little cackle. I reduced back down to eighty. I'm a bit nervous, anyway, driving someone else's car.

The dazzling full moon followed me along a line of trees...

Something going on up ahead. I braked again, gently, because of possible ice. Blue flashing lights. A tiny panic – just for an instant I lay on those cobbles and could feel the pain. The court case had opened the wound, I suppose. Would this accompany me all my life? A police car on the hard shoulder, blue beams sweeping the white trees and fields. Traffic jam warning. A red Porsche roared past, a black Mercedes in hot pursuit. Then both braked hard. I slowed to a crawl. Shortly after, a parked motorbike with a policeman in green like a frogman sitting astride it, his blue light on a stalk flashing too. Beyond him two more uniformed men standing, sub-machineguns at the ready. Slowly I drove past. Florescent hats cordoning off the left-hand overtaking lane, more to the right along the shoulder. We were being filtered into a line. Checkpoint, I thought – this appears to be getting to be a routine. Red tail-lights, a row of waiting cars, exhaust fumes like cotton wool in the frosty air.

The moon disappeared behind a cloud.

We crept forward. Armed figures walking up and down. It took about twenty minutes till I could see what was going on. Police van in the middle of the road, our queue being directed in zigzags to one side or the other. Police stooping to opened windows, weapons shouldered, flashlights, papers being checked. The Porsche and Mercedes went left. A gloved hand held me up, waved me to the right. Not so many cars this side – floodlights and uniforms: I didn't like the look of this row. A helmeted figure peering through the windscreen at me, the silhouette of a gun. Shit, I thought. Before me, in the glare of lights, opened boots and hoods, opened doors. A bang on the window. I fumbled about, needed several seconds to find the right button to press. A cold draught of air, a peering face; I could see his breath. Then the moon came out again.

"Switch off the engine."

I switched it off.

"Get out, please." The policeman was stepping back. I saw he wore no gloves, but that's not what I had on my mind. I got out. I was shaking already: I have this silly reaction to law courts and police.

"Hands over your head."

I did so.

"Face the car." I looked unhappily at him. In one hand he steadied that sub-machinegun, it hung by a strap from his shoulder – his naked finger was on the trigger and the muzzle pointed at me. He was very young. He was very nervous, too. But not half as nervous as I because he was the one with the gun – the proximity of such a lethal weapon made me extremely insecure, did he have the damn thing on safe?

I leaned ignominiously, spreadeagled against the car. My God, the body work was cold. My knees quivered and I thought: I pray I won't wet my pants. And straight afterwards, as the hand professionally patted and searched my body and clothes: I'm glad Annabelle was forced to decline the invitation and isn't being subjected to this...

The whole procedure lasted only about five minutes including a thorough search of the car by two of his white-gloved colleagues, but all they turned up was a half-empty box of paper tissues and a used contraceptive under one of the seats. An extraordinarily magnificent specimen, actually, when they held it up between finger and thumb to the light – I fear I would've fitted in three times. The little fact that the car wasn't mine somewhat complicated the issue. George is a thorough man, though, he'd put the papers in the front pocket alongside an interesting collection of spiky rubber objects which might have made even a beauty queen blush – and it seemed the officers were linked to computers because they used a mobile to check.

I was waved through. On the road again. Moonlight.

I drove sedately, trying to calm my nerves. Then more blue lights. Another road-block in the opposite direction. I reached the outskirts of Nuremberg...

Sirens. Sirens everywhere – in the old city centre on my way in, too. I parked in the underground garages. Positioned the Audi carefully to avoid the old patch of oil. I'll have to cancel the lease here soon, I thought. And the apartment as well. A pang. Why did I feel so much regret?

I walked the short walk to home that would no longer be home in less than five months. Feeling very tired, now. I pushed at the ancient front door, it yielded with a click. Turned the switch, put on the lights, began climbing the old timber stairs. I counted them one by one to avoid the four treads that creaked like hell so as not to wake Herr Eggenhofer and the others. They smelled of stale polish, seemed to go on for ever. Funny that, I noticed the smell particularly this night, I hadn't been aware of it for years: was I starting to get nostalgic?

Above me the stairwell was dark. Was the damn light bulb broken again? I reached the last but one landing, I'd been careful to make hardly a sound. Tomorrow old Eggenhofer would have no cause for complaint. I turned the corner, I was on the last flight of stairs...

I stopped.

There was a shadow in the dark. Someone outside my door. I hesitated, peering; I suppose tiredness takes away surprise.

"Matthias," I said quietly. I could only just make him out. He sat there unmoving. He was sitting propped against the plastered wall almost lost in the gloom. Yet I knew it was him – how did I know?

He didn't reply.

I climbed the last of the stairs, walked along the short landing towards him. One of his hands was out of sight sunk deep in a pocket, his legs stretched out. He wore a brimmed hat and long autumn coat; he looked a picture of repose. But there was something unnatural in the way he sat, and his stillness – perhaps he'd been asleep.

I paused in front of him, my eyes slowly adjusting. Behind me the staircase wound downwards into light.

He drew his hand from his coat. It was black like his coat – was he wearing gloves?

"Open the door, Stefan," he said in undertone. His head was back, he stared up at me; he didn't offer his hand.

I nodded, unlocked the apartment door.

"Go in alone and turn on the lights," he told me. "Draw all the curtains. Behave naturally and do what you normally do." His quiet voice was tired and tight, authoritative; it was like an order.

He made a small movement. I saw him wince. There was something wrong. And the way he continued sitting there so still, he acted like a cornered animal.

"I only have blinds," I said. "Never close them." I spoke quietly, too.

"Then take off your shirt and trousers, and close them. Tonight's an exception." His hatted head was falling forward, collapsing.

"Matthias..." I began. I was beginning to understand.

"When you've done that, please come back here," he said to his chest. "Don't waste time."

I went down the hall and into the living room. Light from the street streamed in, the moonlight bleached the houses opposite, silver on the roofs, ghostly – the chimney stacks threw black shadows. I turned on lights, taking off my clothes, let down the canvas blinds. My body was tired and sluggish but I made my brain wake up. Something told me I was afraid.

When I returned to the landing I found Matthias standing. There was light – the bulb burned brightly in its shade again, it swayed to and fro on its flex. He leaned, thin and stooped, his back to the wall, one arm hung stiffly. His face was white, there were lines of grey; he looked ten years older. His long coat was open showing a dark suit – he looked chic, looked like any businessman. Except for the pain he projected.

"Can you walk?" I asked.

"Don't touch me. Just hold me under this armpit." He indicated which with a faint nod. "And bring the case." I looked down. Where he'd been sitting, a metal attaché case stood at the wall. It must have been behind him when I came up the stairs. It reminded me of airports, of flying crews.

"Wait," I said. I could see I'd need both hands. I picked up the case, put it round the corner in my hall, came back.

I had to help him; he walked like a broken man.

"Bathroom," he said.

We had to change direction. I wondered in what way he'd been wounded, I feared that he'd been shot. His movements caused me concern. My God, I thought, what the hell do I do?

"Get a chair, would you?"

"Sit down first," I told him. Yes, now I saw he wore thin leather gloves. I closed the wooden toilet lid, held him, lowered him. He legs shook as he went down. He leaned back on the tiled wall, head raised. Stared ahead; eyes half closed. They were dead, devoid of emotion. He stared as if he couldn't see.

I fetched a chair, a wooden one with a wicker seat. I brought a cushion for his comfort too. Helping him stand, I pulled off his hat and his gloves, began removing his coat. He'd shaved all the hair off his head.

"Slowly," he said. Very unsteadily. He was leaning his weight on the washbasin, he only had the use of one arm. The coat was not of thick material, and when I'd taken it off and it hung in my hand it had a heavy lump. I assumed it was a weapon. Carefully I removed his jacket as well. I saw my hands shake like his legs. I sat him down in the chair. He sank onto the cushion gratefully, his head fell forward again. He wore a waistcoat. With feeble fingers he was trying to undo the buttons, doing it with one hand.

"I'll do that." Gently I took his hand, put it in his lap. His waistcoat was open now; I could see the first stains on the shirt. And there was a brown patch on the left sleeve of the arm he didn't move.

"Lean forward," I said. I had to remove his waistcoat. He obeyed. The movement made him moan. His shirtfront was covered in pale wet stains like sweat. It puzzled me that there was no sign of blood.

I stopped. "Matthias," I told him quietly. "Tell me where the pain is, so I can avoid making it worse."

He just shook his lowered head.

I stood looking down at him for a moment, then bending, undid the front of his shirt. Gingerly I peeled it back from his shoulders; I was apprehensive at what I might find. I glimpsed bandages full of the same stains. His back was pressed on the back of the chair; I didn't dare touch his shoulders.

"Try leaning forward a fraction again. Got to take off your shirt."

He sighed, not more. I winced inside; I'm not good confronted with broken bodies and blood. I drive past accidents on the autobahn as fast as allowed with my gaze fixed straight ahead. Gently I pulled back the shirt. It caught on something, went taut and he quietly cursed. There were bandages over his shoulders as well as most of his chest, all covered with those strange yellow stains. I drew the shirt down the good arm and slowly from the other. I saw it was bandaged too. He bowed like a Buddha over his lap, silent as the grave.

The bandages hadn't been well applied, were unevenly wound round and round his body, and here and there roughly knotted. Everywhere fluid was seeping through.

"It looks bad," I said. "What happened?"

"Accident." His voice was a faraway whisper.

"What kind of accident?"

He shook his head to himself again.

"What happened?"

No reply.

I thought: save your breath – you'll get nothing out of him. Better listen to the News later. So instead I asked: "What's that under the bandages?"

He was hesitating, his breathing unsteady.

"What?" I repeated.

Still no reply.

I stared down at his suffering. Shit, I thought. "Okay," I said quietly. "Just tell me what you want me to do."

His head rose. "Change the dressings." His words were laboured, he had difficulty speaking.

"All of them?"

"Yes."

"I don't have enough fresh ones."

"Get my case."

I fetched it from the hall – it was heavy. Laid it at his feet, tried opening it. It was locked.

"On my lap."

I placed it across his knees. He bowed again, peering at it, raised his good arm and tapped a code on numbered buttons, snapped open the metal lid. I stared at the orderly contents: rows of small cardboard boxes, long and short bundles in plastic bags, a wad of banknotes bound with a band. Was I staring at a terrorist's tools of the trade? The only other objects I recognised were two mobile phones and what looked like the shape of a gun wrapped in cloth.

His thin hand moved deftly, like the fingers of a piano player. Drawing out two white plastic bags, he looked up and said: "Should you ever be interrogated, you never saw me, never saw this case." His eyes were half-moons, they were steady and cold. Then they were gone and he gave me the bags.

"Start with this one." He nodded his chin at his right arm bandaged from shoulder to wrist, closed the case and made to heave it off his lap. I heard him gasp, his head sagged.

"Don't be stupid," I said. "Sit still." I removed the case, began on his arm. I couldn't undo the knot; I cut it with my nail scissors. Slowly

I began unwinding the bandage. Each time round when I reached the wet stains, the cotton stuck like glue to wads of dressing beneath and I was forced to pull carefully. It must have hurt like hell; he didn't make a sound.

I reached the end of the bandage. Above the elbow was badly bruised. Otherwise the whole surface was sodden; each side of the wide dressings it came away with blistered skin and I could hardly bear to look. Chemicals or acid? Burns? The smell was unpleasant, the sight made me sick. I glanced at his face; it was prickled with perspiration, his head was raised as though he were staring ahead but his eyes were shut. I couldn't speak. I looked back at his shredded arm again. He must've raised it to protect his face from a fire or a blast or something.

The gauze dressings I'd exposed were held with strips of plaster – someone hadn't applied them well, they must've been done in a hurry. Had he done it himself? I needed several minutes to remove them; my hands shook more and more.

Matthias moved his head; he was inspecting his arm. He did it clinically, objectively, as though observing something not part of himself. I interrupted the work, turned away...

"Where're you going?" he demanded. His voice was weak but his tone harsh.

"Back in a minute." I returned with a plastic bag and began dropping the used dressings into it. He stopped me. "Flush them down the toilet."

It'd block the old drains. I cut them up smaller, did as he said.

"What next?" I asked.

"Remove the rest."

"What, these ones? You sure?"

"Yes. You got a mirror?"

I gave him my small round one with a handle. Started removing the bandages round his body beginning at one shoulder. They crisscrossed diagonally over his chest. He watched my progress in the mirror.

"Keep the bandages. They can be washed."

They were long – over two yards, and patchy and wet like those from his arm. I put them one by one in the bag. As I progressed, some of the dressings underneath fell off of their own accord taking yellow clots of skin with them, others stayed stuck, and as I peeled them away I saw raw, suppurating areas of red. The sight turned my stomach, the smell nauseated.

"Incendiary," he said matter-of-factly, as though talking about the weather. "The bastard," he added.

"Oh," I said neutrally. Oh God, I thought. What the hell's happened? I must watch the News as soon as I can. Or maybe there's more on the Web. I stared down at his body, that once beautiful body; it looked horrible. One didn't need to be a doctor to see the damage was very serious.

"You have to get to hospital, Matthias. At once."

"No chance."

"I mean it."

"So do I." He laid the mirror down, dropped his head. "You fool, they're obliged to report cases like this." His voice was a whisper, his strength going down the drain.

"I'm serious," I repeated. "Better than dying."

"I'm not dying. I've got ointment. Do your best."

"Are they burns?"

"Yes."

"I'm not a doctor." I'd seen a documentary long ago... "To survive you probably need a saline bath."

"Crap. I've known cases worse than this. They survived."

You have, I thought? I wonder where.

With his good arm he indicated the bags of medicine I'd laid in the washbasin. "Don't waste time."

In one there was a variety of tubes of ointment, and tins and rolls of tape – in the other, dressings and packets of cotton wool and bandages.

"The blue and white tubes," he murmured.

Gently I took his burnt arm by the hand, rested his palm on the edge of the bath and told him to keep it there. I felt his body stiffen but I had to do it so it wouldn't press on his side. I started gingerly smearing and dressing the mess of leaking skin. My hands and my head were doing things I'd never done in my life before; as he said, I could only do my best.

Halfway through, the phone rang.

Matthias tensed, his head came up. "Answer it," he said. His eyes were glazed with pain, but his voice came clearly.

I was already straightening up, glancing at my watch. "I always do when it rings," I told him flatly. Shortly before eleven. Unusual for someone to call so late. I went along the hall towards the living room. The ringing cut off just before I reached the phone. I turned away. As I went back to the bathroom I heard it start to ring again. After three times it stopped. I cast about in my mind; who would do a thing like that? I stood considering, uncertain. I admit it made me inquisitive, but nervous too. Maybe...

The telephone began ringing again.

"Falk?"

"Stefan, it's me," said Eva. "Did I wake you?"

"No." A sudden thought befell me. "Hello Eva." I listened intently for some sign. Was the situation making me paranoid? Or could it be someone might be eavesdropping on the line?

"You sound on edge," she said.

"Possibly," I agreed. "Went to a lousy lecture this evening. Got under my skin."

"So you haven't heard the news?"

"News? No."

"Another kidnap attempt. In Nuremberg this time. Something went wrong though..."

"Ah," I said, interrupting. "I heard sirens. And there were roadblocks on my way home." So that was the cause — now I knew for sure. Was he the brains, or just one of the boys?

"They used violence this time, that's something new," Eva said.

"How do you mean, violence?"

"There was an explosion, they say. One of the kidnappers was badly burnt."

"Was he caught, then?" I asked. I tried to make it sound offhand.

"Yep." A brief pause, a sigh. "He's on the danger list, it seems — not expected to come through. It's all very horrible. Can you imagine?" She paused again. She was trying to tell me something, wasn't she? Trying to communicate without giving it away. She was breathless; I sensed the anxiety behind her words.

"I can," I said. She was thinking of Matthias, wasn't she? She was suspecting what I now knew. But evasive, no details or names; she feared it was he who'd been caught. Had Matthias perhaps trained her? He was always so careful.

"Well, don't let it get under your skin," I said. "It's not who you think." I couldn't say more. "And all these troubles'll die down one day, you know."

Again I could hear her breath. "I'm in Bamberg – a seminar. Can I call in tomorrow?"

"Afraid not." I had to say it, had to lie. And it hurt. "You've caught me on the hop." But I wouldn't have told her even had we been alone together in the middle of nowhere. For her sake, the sake of her sanity – and for his damnable sake, too. "Got something planned I can't postpone," I added. "Please try and understand."

"Pity."

"I'll ring you as soon as my commitments allow." How long would that be? How long does one need to force someone like Matthias into a hospital under such circumstances? "Then I'll come to Munich," I promised. Or would he die on my hands?

"Okay." Her disappointment strangled; it was like a tight shoe.

We said goodbye.

Matthias sat where I'd left him, head bowed low.

"Eva," I said before he could ask.

"What did she want?"

"She's worried about you."

He said nothing.

"How much does she know?" I said.

With difficulty he looked up at me. "Nothing."

"She suspects. As soon as you can, reassure her."

He didn't react.

In silence I continued applying dressings and bandaging him. Then I removed the rest of his clothes. He was naked now. I took his temperature – he had a fever. As best I could I bathed the parts of him which sweated and were accessible, and afterwards got him into night clothes I fetched from my drawer. While next door I spread out a thick layer of towels over the sheets of my bed and turned the radiator on full. When I'd finally finished doing everything I thought I ought to do, I helped him to the bedroom, put him in my bed. It all took time; he hardly had strength to move now, I had to half-carry him.

He lay there like a corpse. "I need my case," he said in a dead voice.

I brought it, set it down beside him.

"Give me my coat, too."

"You don't need your coat."

"Do as I say."

I went and checked the pockets. In one a mobile phone, in another a gun and two extra clips wrapped in paper. Unpleasant objects. Smell of metal and oil – there it was again. Nothing else in any of the pockets. I imagined that was all he wanted so I just returned with those and laid them on the case.

"Thought you'd turned over a new leaf," I said.

"Give me them," he ordered.

I did so.

"And a rag or cloth."

I found one, laid it in his hand. Laboriously, meticulously, he wiped the clips and the gun. "Don't touch them again." He put them under the sheet beside him. Had he wiped away my prints?

He lay on his back, he'd closed his eyes.

"Wait," he said. I was half through the doorway. "I need information." His speech was slurred.

I waited.

With effort he began asking questions – about my apartment, and the house, who lived there, about entrances and exits and the old fire escape here at the back, things like that. Considering the state he was in I found it all superfluous, but I granted him my ear. When I thought he'd finished and was turning away, he started off again, telling me procedures should anyone ring the bell or phone me, and made me repeat every word. He was very thorough; I marvelled at his mental strength, his physical courage. His last sentence was: "Wash the bandages at ninety-five degrees."

The first thing I did in the living room was turn on the television, keeping it quiet. I surfed the main German and English-language News channels without much success, decided to wait for the late-night News. In my address book I looked up a private mobile number and dialled. I let it ring, but Dr Duchac didn't answer – she also hadn't switched on her mailbox so I couldn't leave a message. Going over to my jacket and retrieving my mobile I stored the number for future use. Then I tidied the bathroom, flushing small quantities of dressings at a time down the toilet; I hoped the old drains would cope.

When the News came I sat down and watched. It was a condensed version, however. All I learned was that a kidnapper had been shot dead, two had escaped apparently unharmed without their victim and a fourth had been discovered badly burned a few hundred yards away. Apart from footage of the two scenes of crime

I gleaned nothing more of interest. I visited several News websites but gained only the following snippets: the abduction had been foiled by the victim's bodyguards who had possibly received prior warning – the small explosive charge which nearly killed the fourth kidnapper could have been detonated by accident – the timing of the two incidents had been almost simultaneous – the identity of the arrested kidnapper was being withheld...

I switched off the laptop, continued sitting before it.

No mention of a further person who might fit a description of Matthias. Or at least not yet. I gazed at the dead screen. You're sheltering a terrorist, I told myself – you know what that means. How deep does friendship go?

I raised my eyes. Sounds of sirens in the night. I listened. Were they coming nearer? If you were to get caught, that'd be the end of everything.

The distant sirens went on and on.

How far from my apartment had the kidnap been attempted? Maybe two miles? It'd been in the north-east part of the city, they said. And Matthias – how had he got here? On foot? In a car? Could he have made it in this condition? And had someone seen him?

I stared into space. My body was folded in the old office chair. What exactly had happened? And who'd bandaged him, dressed him in fresh clothes? And where? Or had he done it all himself? I could feel my fear.

Suddenly a siren screamed loud and close. I panicked. I started forward... was it coming up the street? Was it one of those special units – they were brutal, weren't they? Had I been under observation, had they followed him to my flat? The siren grated on my nerves. Then cut out, was gone. The distant ones were still there, though. Several of them. With different pitches.

I sank back into the chair, still as a mouse. Listening...

Would one hear them when they came? Could one? Didn't they come on rubber soles, using hand signals? Did they ring the bell before breaking down the door – they burst through windows too, didn't they?

I raised my head.

All the blinds were pulled down, I couldn't see out. Somehow it still seemed stupid; only people with secrets draw blinds. I arose, let them up. Peered out. From what I could see, the usual scene. I opened one of the windows, leaned over the sill, looking down. Just civilian parked cars, a few people walking, dark shadows, pools of light. God, it was cold. I could feel its bite on my face, I could see my breath.

Then I thought: the fire escape. Of course, they'd use that, so easy. It went right down to the courtyard at the back. My fear flared again. Go and check. I left the blinds up, turned out the lights. In the hall, though, I paused. I stood quite still behind my apartment door, listening. I could hear my heart, it was far too loud. Were there black figures poised the other side, out on the stairs, out there right on the landing? Were they on the point of breaking in? I stared at the door. It was solid as oak. But didn't the panels in it look weaker?

Unsteadily, with nervous hands, I opened the heavy door. Nothing.

A small touch of relief. Okay, now the back. I went in to Matthias. All was still, he seemed asleep, just the dimmer-light burning. My God, it was still so cold in here. I crossed, raised the big blinds which went down to the floor. I saw my faint reflection in the glass. I looked like a ghost, oh God I looked bad. I peered through cupped hands. Silhouettes of the wrought-iron balcony and balustrade, the opening where the steps spiralled down into the night. And naked branches of the almost leafless chestnut tree.

Nobody.

I thought: what about... But my fingers were already turning the handle on the glassed balcony door. It stuck, I pulled at it. I opened it so seldom — only when Frau Maußer came to clean the windows for me. I tugged — it clattered open.

Matthias murmured from the bed. I turned my head to speak, to reassure. He lay on his back, but his eyes were still closed. Sweat prickled his face, the sheets were in disarray. Was he in a coma?

Oh God, I thought. My panic returned. Would he die? What the hell was I doing — what was I going to do? I had to get him to hospital...

I stepped out onto the fire escape into the ice-cold night. All around, the shadowy backs of houses, a few lights shone in slits through closed shutters. I leaned over the handrail: the courtyard below a deserted black abyss. No sounds, nobody. I went back in, washed and undressed, went to bed — beside Matthias's prone form.

Chapter 27

Predictably, I didn't sleep well. Matthias shifted restlessly; he could only lie flat on his back. His breathing was fitful, irregular, it disturbed me. Sometimes he snored. In the early hours I was awakened for about the tenth time. I'd been dreaming, a pleasant one, actually; waking caused me shock. Reality rushed in – I lay panicking in the dark, kept asking myself the same question, what shall I do?

Matthias breathed heavily beside me, and the air was sour with sweat.

My thoughts revolved dizzily, viciously. I knew I wouldn't sleep again that night. I twisted and switched on the dimmer-light next to the bed, turning it on low like the evening before so as not to wake him. With a linen cloth I lightly dabbed his face and brow to absorb the running sweat. Carefully I kneeled, peeled back the thin crumpled sheet. The shirt I'd lent him was damp and stained where it pressed on the bandages, and some of the patches were yellow. His fever filled me with alarm. I felt myself start to sweat too.

I had to get help.

Still kneeling, I leaned on my hands gazing down at him. It was like a film, like a nightmare. I kept thinking of movies, of wounded cowboys, or gangsters on the run, and what their helpers had done. I deliberated taking his temperature again – in his mouth, or under his arm? Then decided against it, in case it woke him. Carefully I took his wrist and measured his pulse instead. It was weak, it fluttered – it was very faint but fast, just under a hundred and twenty. And where I'd wiped his forehead it prickled with perspiration again.

Was there something gravely wrong?

I had two hours. I showered and shaved, made coffee, drank several cups. Gradually my thoughts steadied. I felt washed-out, hollow. I sat in my kitchen considering all the possibilities, going through combinations, trying to establish a strategy. I also had to win myself time. The office doors unlocked at half-past-six, and Angelica the new receptionist was one of the first to arrive.

I stared into space, I waited. At quarter to seven I rang her.

"Hello Angelica, it's Falk."

I told her I wasn't able to come to work, had to go to the doctor. "Would you tell Personnel, please?" She was agitated, I could tell from her tone. But she did her job well enough and waited till I was finished. Then she said: "Have you heard the news? About the kidnap, I mean. Isn't it dreadful? Right on our doorstep! I could hardly sleep last night." There was thrill on her tongue.

"Yes, I heard," I said.

At shortly before seven I rang Dr Duchac again. I'd never called her at home so I didn't have her private number; had to use her mobile like the night before. She didn't answer, but her mailbox was switched on. After the bleep I said: "Martha hello, it's Stefan Falk. Could you ring me back at the following number as soon as possible? I need advice." I gave her my number.

Briefly I went in to Matthias with a fresh bowl of cold water and a clean cloth, bathed and dried his head and neck. He still slept, didn't stir.

I waited by the phone but it didn't ring.

At eight I rang the mobile again. Still only the mailbox connection. So I rang her surgery. The number was engaged. Using the repeat button I tried several times – I couldn't get through for twenty minutes...

"*Praxisgemeinschaft Duchac und Dornbaum,*" a young women's voice said efficiently in my ear. I recognised the voice.

I greeted her, gave my name and asked for Dr Duchac.

"Oh, Herr Falk. Long time since we've seen you here. She's not arrived yet. Tell you what, soon as she comes and has a moment I'll ring you back. You in the office?"

"No," I said. "I'll give you..."

"Already noted. In my display."

Ah, how I appreciated efficiency.

"Till later," she said rapidly.

"As soon as possible," I corrected.

"Will do – *Tschüß.*"

I put down the phone, went into the kitchen. Matthias ought to drink, I thought. He's lost a lot of fluid. I was boiling water to make herbal tea when the phone rang in the living room...

"Falk."

"Hello, Herr Falk, me again. Putting you through to Dr Duchac..."

I began to thank her but she was gone...

"Duchac."

"Martha, hello, it's..."

"Stefan! Long time no hear. Fully recovered?"

"Yes thanks."

"Told you to come for a check-up and cup of coffee after rehab. Don't you like me any more?"

"Martha, I'm sorry, I have..."

"No problem – how're things?"

"Well..." I hesitated. "Let's say a bit off colour in the soul."

"You and your soul!" She laughed heartily; she was a sporting woman. "What's up? Need a sick note?"

"No," I said. "I need some advice."

"Medical, or succour for the soul?"

"Medical."

"Keep it short. Can it be done on the phone right now?"

"No... it's..."

"Then come round to my surgery tomorrow. Today's a bad day – the waiting room'll be full till I drop. No – better the day after. Wednesdays I've only got the clinic. Could find an hour or so. Can it wait?"

Again I had to say no. "Could we meet for half an hour in your lunch-break today?"

"Lunch-break? You're joking! Haven't had one of those since medical school! It that urgent?"

"Yes."

"Mmm..." She paused. "You at home or at work?"

"At home."

"Uh-huh. Tell you what then, got my house-visits today between two and four — I'll try and squeeze it in and pop by. Can't promise though. Okay?"

"Martha, unfortunately..." My turn to pause. Have to avoid her coming to call, mustn't involve her directly. "I need longer than a few minutes," I said. Was it possible — was my apartment being watched now? I mustn't endanger her, or her livelihood. "And I won't be home at that time," I ended feebly.

"Make a suggestion," she ordered.

There was pressure in her voice. I heard a woman's voice whispering in the background. "Yes, yes," she retorted impatiently.

"Could we meet this evening?" I said. As I said it I sensed my panic come back; the whispering nurse in her surgery awoke a whisper in my mind. I sweated, felt the prickle on my neck. Was my phone being tapped? Oh God, I'd forgotten — was someone eavesdropping, recording every word that was said?

And Martha was saying: "No chance, my dear. Concert tonight — Peter and I've got tickets from friends. Haven't had an evening alone with him in weeks."

"And afterwards?"

"What? After the concert?"

I said nothing.

"It so important?"

"It's urgent and it's rather personal."

This time there was a silence on the line, not just a pause. I could almost hear her thinking, of how she had no time at all, of how to best say no.

Then she simply said: "Where?"

And I said: "Where's your concert?"

"*Meistersingerhalle.*"

That was south of the city centre. I thought rapidly; I saw the concert hall and the bars. And the hotel lounges next door. No privacy, bright lights, too many people. In my mind I traced the route she'd take going home to her posh residence in Erlenstegen on the east side of town. Don't take her too far out of her way...

"There's a bar five minutes by car from your concert. First right turn after St Peter's Church." I told her exactly where and the name.

"I'll find it. Ten-fifteen or thereabouts. Okay?"

"Thanks Martha."

"Got to go."

x x x

She arrived late but I was glad; I could adjust to the atmosphere, collect my thoughts. It wouldn't be an easy task. Shit you, Matthias. The bar was unexpectedly full, and loud, however, there was no-one I knew. I hadn't been quite punctual either, because of Matthias. He wasn't in good shape, I'd had to bathe him in the bed a second time at short notice and change one of the bandages again.

With a sixth sense, too, he'd suspected my going out so late. "Where're you going?" he'd demanded decisively, although only half-conscious.

"I'm meeting someone."

"Who?"

"My nightlife's my business."

"Who?"

"A woman." Only in the omission lay the small lie.

Under half-closed lids his eyes were cold. "Be vigilant. Guard your tongue."

"For me that's nothing new..."

These were the things which had held me up. Dr Duchac arrived. It was ten-thirty-five. She came in like a gust of wind wearing long leather coat and a fur wrapped round her throat. She was easily the tallest person in the fuggy room; her self-assurance stuck out like a thumb.

"Hello there," she said matter-of-factly, extending her hand as if it were a weapon. She had to speak up; the music and voices were loud. She slid along the padded seat opposite me, opening her coat and unwrapping her fur but not removing them – she gave the impression she didn't intend staying long.

"Bit late, I'm afraid." She swept her hands, scooping up hanging strands each side of her thick, piled-up auburn hair.

I shook my head.

"What're you drinking?" She wore mascara and bright-red lipstick, was in her early fifties. Her face was long and strong, her gaze direct; from the very first time we'd met she'd reminded me of some bird of prey.

I told her which wine.

"Dry enough?"

I nodded, slid the green-stemmed glass towards her. "Try a sip." The stem was woven like a vine.

She laughed, tossed her head. "You never were a conventional one."

"You too." I managed a faint smile.

"Probably what attracts us." She tipped the glass, sipping. Then cocked her head. "Uh-huh – not bad." She glanced round. The barman over the other side was standing drying a glass. She raised two fingers, pointing at my glass. She didn't say a word. He dropped his cloth as though he'd been shot. Me he'd kept waiting five minutes and reacted as if carved from stone.

"How was the concert?" I only asked out of politeness.

"Fabulous. We need a fun evening now and then – pulls us out of our ruts."

"Yes," I said. "I recently read that somewhere."

"Never said it was original." She observed me with her bold dark eyes. Her undone coat hung open, revealed a bright-pink blouse just about half-covering very big breasts.

The wine came. She glanced up. "Thanks," she said to the girl in the dirndl.

She raised her glass, leaned towards me. Yes, they really were magnificent; I was used to her white coat, I'd never seen them on display before.

"What shall we drink to?"

I watched those wide-open, deep brown-black eyes. "Perhaps to my power of persuasion," I said.

"So?" They didn't blink. Like all black eyes they gave nothing away. "Then I'll drink to that."

We tapped glasses.

Gold bangles on her arm; they clacked. They somehow reminded me of Peru. "You've hooked me," she said. "So start persuading."

I stood there on the end of a springboard, the water lay far below. I glanced at my hands and my glass, felt her eyes boring into my brain. With a woman like Martha one can't beat about the bush.

"Martha, we've known each other many years..." I began; in my mind I was opening up the notes I'd begun to prepare in the kitchen. "Although we've had little opportunity to get closer and dig down under the surface, would you say I'm a serious kind of guy?"

Expressionlessly she returned my gaze. "My God, what a question! What d'you expect me to say?" She was forewarned; she was on her guard.

"Let me put it another way. Do you consider me the sort of person who might be prone to doing things he'd regret?"

Her dark brows raised. She drank some wine. Her bangles rattled again. "If this were the nineteenth century the only thing I'd think is, this guy's attempting to propose to me and can't spit it out."

I tried a feeble grin. "Actually that's not what I had in mind." I fiddled with my glass.

"You're far too damn serious. And over-cautious. That's the cross you bear. That what you wanted to hear?"

Oh God, I thought, I have to tread carefully. I picked up the wineglass, took a sip. "We once had a conversation about the late-sixties – the riots in Berlin. D'you remember?"

A frown. "Possibly," she replied curtly. "What of it?"

"You told me you used to sympathise with what was going on."

"Long time ago. Yep."

"And you mentioned you had a younger brother who took part."

"Correct."

"You spoke at some length about him..." I remember: she'd spoken with a hidden passion like a fire that hasn't gone out.

"Did I?" She stared at me, direct and intense. "Then I did."

I watched her long, strong fingers steepled under her chin, watched her face too – the frown had come back again. Had I touched a nerve? That's what I'd wanted to do.

"What're you getting at, Stefan. Spit it out, man."

"Just one more question. Hypothetical, but I'd like to hear your answer. If your brother had become more radical, and..."

"Which he didn't."

"No – but supposing. And had he gone underground and in an emergency turned to you for help – would you 've..." There was sudden loud laughter behind me, it grated... "would you 've been prepared to help?"

"Didn't catch the last bit. What?" Martha was tipping forward. Framed between the long leather lapels her heavy breasts fell forward too.

The raucous laughter subsided, the hubbub of voices rolled in again swamping. I repeated the sentence.

"What sort of help?" She was watching my eyes.

"For example if he were wounded," I said.

Another burst of laughter. She pursed her lips, impatiently. "Stop beating about the bush."

I glanced around at those nearest us, then returned her gaze as best I could. "I'm in a similar situation." I spoke as quietly as I could. Above the noise I thought: nobody's interested, nobody can hear. "I need your advice, Martha."

"What kind of advice?"

I leaned closer, all the same; I spoke to her eyes: "About how to treat someone who's been hurt."

"How hurt?"

"Burns."

"Can this someone walk?"

"Hardly."

"Who is it? That brother of yours?"

"An old friend from my childhood."

She watched in silence, calmly. She picked up her glass of wine. I felt her beginning to close up. Then she said: "Would it be stupid to suggest that this friend be taken to a clinic?" She asked it coolly.

"Yes," I nodded, "it would." I added: "He turned up unexpectedly last night, he's been badly burned. I need to know how to treat him – got to buy the right medicine."

"Last night," she repeated. She made it sound like a curse; she stared at me over her glass. "Yesterday there was another kidnap attempt."

"Yes."

"We talking about the same lost cause?"

"Yes. And lost it is."

She didn't blink. "Don't touch it."

"I have to."

"You're kidding, it's criminal. I hear one was shot dead, another arrested. Also with second and third degree burns."

"I know."

"You're talking about a terrorist."

"I don't know if that's the right label. I'm talking about a friend."

"Doesn't matter two hoots."

"I'm going to help. Made up my mind."

"Then think again."

"It's too late, Martha."

"It's never too late."

I said nothing.

She put down her glass with a clack. "You're a bloody fool." There was bitterness in her voice, in her fingers. "You're playing with fire."

Again I said nothing; I just watched her.

"What d'you expect me to say, except, not on the cards."

Carefully I answered: "I expect nothing, Martha. I'd just hoped, that's all."

"Hoped what?"

"That you'd listen to me, let me describe his symptoms, give me a guide how I can help him. And perhaps give me a prescription."

She regarded me, coldly – with disbelief, almost with arrogance. "How badly burned? How much of his body?"

"His chest, neck and arms."

"Hands?"

"No."

"Face and hair?"

"No."

"The whole thorax? Chest?"

"Yes."

"Are all the burns bandaged?"

"Yes."

"And his condition? How'd you describe it?"

I considered. "He could only just walk when he arrived. He's weak, only half-conscious." I described his pulse, his shallow breath and the sweating.

"Have you tried cooling him?"

"I checked on the Web. They said use wet sheets, so I did. But he cooled down too much so I stopped. Then I bandaged him again."

"That's okay. Has he nausea? Did he vomit?"

"Twice this morning."

She paused, deliberating. She shook her head, her gaze was hard. "Know what you'd need? A prescription long as my arm."

I dropped my eyes, unhappily.

"Alone the prescription'd arouse enough suspicion to warrant the chemist to make a phone call."

"To the police?"

"In the first instance to me. My name'd be on it. After that most likely the authorities."

I cast about, grasping at straws. "One could perhaps write several small prescriptions. I could call at different chemists."

"No go. They'd all land at the same health insurer. Doesn't take long to add up two and two."

"I have private insurance." I spread my hands. "In this case I'd simply destroy them."

"My books are vetted too. It's not the good old days, there's lots of cross-checking."

I shrugged my shoulders. We watched one another over the table, over our wine. I said: "You can't help then?"

Her chin was raised. She said acidly: "I'm a doctor. My Hippocratic oath commits me to save life." Her strong fingers clenched. "But within the law. I'm obliged to play by the rules."

"And if theoretically you were to help? You'd automatically have to report it?"

"Naturally."

"Could you tell me what to do?"

"I'm telling you what – his condition sounds serious. Get him to the clinic, and pronto." She was answering mechanically, just like a machine.

"They'd notify the authorities too, though."

"After yesterday's fireworks..." She pulled a wry face. "Sure, they're on the alert, bet your boots."

"Could I bluff?" I said. I was desperate now. "Say it was an accident at home or something?"

"What? Like he lit a cigarette in the gas oven, or something?" Her sarcasm was thick. "Forget it. That was an incendiary charge, I read this morning. There'd be telltale traces. D'you think burn specialists are fools?"

I returned her hard stare. Inside, my panic squeezed my stomach and crushed my heart; one by one she'd closed all the doors. "Then there's no other way," I said resignedly. "I'll have to treat him in my flat."

"My God, you're stubborn."

I shrugged faintly.

"Drive him to emergency in Klinikum Nord or Süd. Take him tonight. If he's in bad enough shape they'll fly him to the nearest Burns Centre."

"He refuses to go."

"To procrastinate's aiding and abetting a crime – carries a stiff sentence. Want to land in the cooler?"

"I'll have to take the risk."

She sighed loudly; it hissed through her teeth. "From what you've described, he's in a very bad way, and deteriorating."

I shook my head. What else could I do?

"He's losing body fluids. He could die on your hands."

Oh Jesus Christ. I gulped for breath, couldn't respond. Instead I took out the tube I'd brought. I laid it beside her hand, hiding it from prying eyes as best I was able.

"Where did you get that?" She didn't bother touching it.

"He had it with him. Is it suitable for burns?"

"Yep. Not the best, but it'll do for a start. How many d'you have?"

"Another three."

"You're kidding. That's hardly enough for twenty-four hours."

"Can I buy it without prescription?"

"Nope."

"Is there anything similar on the market prescription-free?" I had turned my head to put away the tube. There came no reply. I glanced back at her. Found her gazing at me, a distant unreadable look. Her expression had changed, the hardness had melted round her mouth.

"Okay," she said. She drank the remains of her wine in a couple of gulps. "Let's go." She called the girl in the dirndl. I swallowed down half of mine, left the rest; I made her let me pay.

Outside in the cold she told me: "We'll go to my place. I'll sort out the stuff you need." She stood there a whole head taller than me.

"Thanks," I said simply. I asked for her address in Erlenstegen.

"Better come with me."

"Got my car round the corner."

"Come with me. It'll avoid complications."

Complications? I spread my hands; I didn't enquire. As I stooped to get into her car I glanced back along the street. George's Audi was still there. Nobody in sight. No-one had come out of the bar.

"Well, Sherlock Holmes – we being followed?" She started the engine; that unmistakable sound, one I normally only heard overtaking me going twice my maximum speed. Was there nothing her eyes missed?

She drove a black Porsche, she drove extremely fast. Pressed back in my seat each time she accelerated I seemed to be lying more than sitting – I'd never been in a Porsche before. The difference between it and mine was the difference between her and me.

"D'you secretly like playing with fire?" She screeched calmly round a cobbled corner.

"No," I said. I clung on hard, still scrabbling with the seatbelt.

"Some do. Gives them a kick."

"I fear a Porsche would already be over my limit." I managed to fasten the belt.

We zigzagged through side streets, emerged onto one of the main arteries leading out of the heart of the city.

"You're a damn fool, Stefan."

"Maybe."

"He's one of these kidnappers."

"So it seems."

"You're not sure?"

"I am since last night," I said.

"Thought he was an old friend. You seriously didn't know?"

"No. Somewhere along the way I suspected, that's all – we've hardly been in contact since our student days."

"He just turned up? Like a bad penny?"

"Yes," I nodded into the night.

The tyres drummed over more cobbles, rattling my teeth. A brightly-lit petrol station swept by. Then she said: "You don't approve of what these terrorist guys're doing?"

"No." I felt I ought to qualify that, so I added: "But at least they avoid violence, don't kill people."

"They're brainwashing the bastards, isn't that enough?"

The bastards? I thought. Did I detect a grain of sympathy? I was about to ask, but she continued: "Form of violence in itself. Most of them've come out of it psychological wrecks – meek as lambs. Made public confessions they'd never've dreamed of prior to the act. Implies torture even." She spoke the way she drove.

"I sometimes wonder," I said, "if that's worse than the way these big boys treat people and rape the democratic process." What was I saying – was I starting to defend Matthias and his ilk?

She was silent. She braked for a red light, my head and body lurched forward; the seat belt had me taut in its grip, thank God.

"And you?" I asked, with a touch of guilt. "You condemn the kidnappings out of hand, then?"

She revved the dreadful throaty Boxer motor, foot on the clutch and in first gear. "I condemn a lot of things including the mores and morals of the kidnapped bastards."

"Ah," I said. The machine vibrated through my pants; felt like a hungry hyena on a very tight chain. I shifted nervously. I ventured: "Sadly this whole business'll change nothing at all."

"Naturally not." The orange light came on under the glowing red; with a roar she shot away before it turned green. "It draws attention..." she began. My skull was knocked back on the headrest like a ball that's just been kicked; I was glad I had no false teeth, I surely would've swallowed them. "...draws attention to the woes though, I'll grant them that. When the pressure gets too great the human animal needs its safety valve..."

Second gear, a whining scream, still second gear, we were going over seventy – I grabbed the handgrip, panicking, stamped my foot on the brake that wasn't there... another red light. Then she braked too, did a hair-raising zigzag into the left lane – wasn't it too late? An instant of lightness, almost like flying; I was physically lifted from my seat.

"Makes for grand publicity if nothing else." She sat there so calmly in her bucket seat. We'd reached the Business Tower – a silly, ugly cylinder with a sort of run-over cartwheel on top.

"Grand?" I queried. I'd landed on my private parts, it wasn't very nice. I wriggled, freed them.

"Brought a lot of dirt to light. Good for the man in the street to learn a few unpleasant truths."

The traffic light changed – she was off, a sharp left turn on the major crossroads before the opposing traffic had thought of getting into gear, accelerating in the curve over slippery threads of frozen tramlines; I was thrown against the door.

Wide straight road now, she was getting out of first gear. Lighted houses being left behind.

"Memories are short, Martha," I panted. I righted myself, wriggled carefully again. "That won't change anything either."

She flipped the short gear stick – thank God, she'd made it into third, my intestines had seemed pressed back into my spine. We roared down into the river valley, onto the long, curving concrete bridge. She had her foot down, had reached nearly ninety in about a second. Wasn't there a speed limit here? Silver crash-rails on black flashing by, trees in the night, slithers of silver on the river below.

Another silence. I could sense an anger, read her thoughts: I guessed they were back to me again.

"Sorry to involve you," I said. I said it with penitence. I really meant it.

"Damn fool," she repeated.

Yes, I thought. You're dead right. I'm endangering you, endangering me. But what else could I do, what else could one have done with a friend? Turned him in? I glanced sideways. "What'd you do in my shoes, Martha? If it was your brother?"

Her strong face was red in the glow of the dials. She changed gear, another flick of her hand. "Damned if I know."

We were climbing out of the small valley on the other side. Bright lights ahead, houses, side streets. Then a main intersection, more traffic lights, cars creeping in the cold. She turned right into Äußere Sulzbacherstraße, didn't accelerate like before… sauntering in second gear. Wide road, tree-lined, buildings beyond, lots of space to overtake. With a car like that did she know where all the speed cameras were hidden? We covered 200 yards, 300 – then there it was, but not a camera…

Police check. Blue and yellow flashing lights, a long line of waiting cars.

"Damn," she said.

She slowed, stretched past me, flipping open the locker at my knees. I couldn't help it, my mind had jumped…

"Your identity card," she said briefly. Her hand was searching.

…I was in an old film, black and white, what was it's name, wasn't it from Godard? I took out my wallet… Belmondo reached into the glove compartment, pulling out a gun – beside him, in French sunlight in open-top car, cropped-haired Jean Seberg in T-shirt and jeans looking sexy, looking cool…

Martha had laid an 'On Call' sign on the dashboard behind the windscreen, was fumbling in her handbag between us. She accelerated, warning blinker lights switched on, overtaking the line of cars the wrong side of the row of hats. Armed uniformed figures blocking our path. One stepping aside, stooping, gloved hand, machinegun barrel pointing. With a soft whirr her window opened.

"Duchac. I'm a doctor. On call."

She flapped her identity card at him, took mine from my hand. "And Falk. Patient."

A torch beam in our faces, then sweeping the small space behind our seats. "Sorry, orders. Open the bonnet and boot, please."

She clicked them open. Bending figure, flashes of torchlight.

"Okay." He lowered them, snapped them shut with a jerk. Waved her through. She'd probably saved us half an hour or more.

× × ×

I sat in her cellar, if one could call it that. Swimming pool with view to the garden, sauna, bar, fitness area; her house was a villa in the best part of town, built into a slope. Most of the well-to-do live in Erlenstegen. Even the large storeroom she'd led me to had two small windows with bars high up.

"Describe your pal's burns precisely as possible."

She sat on the packing table beside me. She'd taken off her coat, and the fur wrap from her throat, her long legs and big breasts hung down; undressed to her slinky concert clothes in the brightness of halogen lamps, she displayed her body in all its splendour.

I told her in as much detail as I could. All the time she sat there gazing down at me. Now and then she asked a brief question. When I'd finished, she nodded. "Okay," she said. "Won't be a mo – then I'll tell you precisely what you're to do." Her expression was unreadable.

I watched her unlocking cupboards and peering at shelves, removing boxes; there was a whole wall full of medical supplies.

"Why d'you have so much here at home?" I said.

"Alfred, not me." Alfred was her doctor husband. "Since his stroke he works his practice two days a week from here. Private patients."

She placed a pile before me, went back for more. While I waited I let my thoughts wander. I could still see the second checkpoint and the thoroughness with which they'd searched even her doctor's bag. They'd stopped us on our way up the hill to where she lived two minutes after the first control down on the main road. Side streets had been cordoned off. "Because of Judge Horlamus-Stahl," she'd said as our papers were checked again. "The one they tried to kidnap. Lives two streets from my place." I wondered: my God, will they search us again on the way out?

I tried to suppress the thought. Followed Martha's movements instead.

The other wall near where she stood had shelves full of bottles; it looked more like an off-licence shop – whiskies, cognacs, liqueurs, schnapps...

As she returned to the table, to distract myself, I said: "You planning on opening a liquor store?"

She glanced. "Oh that. Patient gratitude. Help yourself – we hardly touch the stuff any more."

"Do you have a wheelbarrow?"

She had dumped another load of boxes and packets on the table. "Here." She slid a pad and biro over. "You'd better write everything down." She propped her bottom, folded her arms, leaning against the tabletop. Her gaze was calm and professional. "Now's your opportunity to play burn specialist. The training only takes eight to ten years."

"You make me nervous."

"Good."

For perhaps five minutes she gave me instructions. I noted down the essentials. Then she showed me how to take the blood-pressure, the best way to apply dressings and bind bandages, how to use a throw-away syringe. She also showed me how to check the heartbeat and lung functions using a stethoscope; she made me use her as a guinea pig. We started on different places on her back. With her blouse untucked from the waistband of her skirt and drawn up high to her shoulders, she explained when to tell Matthias to cough and what to listen for. Her long back was brown and sunburnt, with moles.

Then came her chest. She was turning to me, still standing erect, opening the front of that tight bright-pink blouse. Her remarkable bosom lay not so far below the level of my eyes; yes, she was an extraordinarily tall woman. Oh God, I thought, this is getting a bit near the bone.

"Lower," she ordered me. I was nervously holding the diaphragm as near her heart as I dared.

"Here! Since when was the heart up on the collarbone?" She pressed my fingers firmly on her ample left breast swelling out of the bra. My hand shook, it wobbled her flesh. I thought: I hope to God her husband won't choose this moment to pop down to the basement for a midnight swim or another forbidden bottle of gin...

"Can you hear it now?"

I could mostly only hear the massive palpitations of my own heart, I felt extremely uncomfortable. Through the white cotton gauze the dark areola was big as a brown bowl with the nipple a finger poking out. The dirty dog in me was having a difficult time.

I forced myself to concentrate. Yes – there it was like a hollow drum; in contrast to mine, her heartbeat steady as a metronome.

"Yes," I said obediently.

"Good. Now place it here... okay? And here. Deep breath and hold it..." Her body swelled wondrously, took my whole hand with it "...and make him cough like I told you." She coughed. Her breast shuddered, my fantasy too. We'd reached her magnificent pendulous right breast now – there was another cheeky black mole on the lower slopes.

"Well?" she said. "Doesn't it arouse memories of all the checkups you've had through the years? This is what one hears."

Rousing things it certainly was. "Not much," I said. "I was never on the listening end."

"Okay, you're doing fine."

I tried to keep concentrating, but the beast in me was feasting on the joys of the view. I'd never seen such large and beautifully formed breasts on a willowy woman before; in fact I'd never conceived it biologically feasible...

"And now, lower thorax..."

Matter-of-factly she lifted the opened front of her blouse over her bosom, wedging it with her chin. One of her hands guided mine, the other unceremoniously scooping her breasts up out of the way, while her mouth calmly instructed: "Deep breath, hold it, let it out... deep breath..." Her chest rising and falling. Flat smooth stomach bronzed like an Amazon, ah what cute little moles. I could smell her skin, feel her heat, didn't dare peep – these surely were sights to uplift the fainthearted...

"Keep your mind on the job, Stefan boy," she ordered calmly.

When we were finished she asked if all was clear, did I have any questions? I shook my head, relaxed my shaking hand.

"So..." She surveyed everything on the table, looked up, looking pensively at me. "With this stuff you can't go wrong." She was pointing at the ointments, her voice was practical; was she trying to reassure? "And the bandages here – how many've you already got?"

I told her.

Without a word she crossed to another cupboard, returned with more. Then: "Back in a mo."

She was gone. I sat there staring into space: my fears got the upper hand. She came back with a rucksack and some folded cotton shopping bags. I helped pack everything into them. While we did she told me succinctly: "When it's all blown over give me back everything – stethoscope, blood pressure gauge, empty packages, tubes and all." We put the bags into the rucksack, then she was pulling on her coat. I did the same. "Okay?"

"Yes," I said.

We were back in the car. She had to take the same route through Erlenstegen to get out, but was waved through the control on the hill without being stopped again. Thank God for mercies, great and small. I tried to relax a little. After that she made a detour through side roads and avenues to avoid the main checkpoint, then retraced our route, rocketing down over the river.

To distract myself, to desperately seek some cool, I said conversationally: "How fast can this little pop-pop go?"

"About three hundred kph."

"Ah really." Tree silhouettes streaking by, lights blurred in wavy lines. "I imagined over two-fifty it would tend to take off."

"Sure. Over undulations and crowns of hills it does." Somehow my cool wasn't in her league.

"Ah," I said again, holding on tighter. I squinted ahead looking for hints of unevenness.

Three or four brutal minutes went past in silence, my stomach in vertigo, my private parts on the block. Without mishap she made it back to my car. I told her where and she paused beside it. She said suddenly: "Where do you live?"

I glanced at her but she was staring ahead. "Why?" I asked.

"In case I lose you." The motor throbbed throatily.

"No, Martha."

"Where?"

I told her. I added: "I can manage on my own now."

"Like hell you can."

No, I couldn't do that, couldn't endanger her any further. "Too risky for you, you said so yourself."

"I'm getting cold." She flexed her leather driving-glove on the gear stick. "Hop out, Sherlock. I'll follow you. Leave the rucksack with me."

How could I argue? I felt a lightness, I felt such relief. I touched her arm, I squeezed it, my gratitude revealed. And hopped out. Bending and craning my neck just before closing the door, I said: "I'll drive slowly so you won't lose sight of me." I don't think she bothered to appreciate the joke.

Sedately I drove the short distance into the centre, along the ring still busy with cars outside the old city walls, and into the Altstadt at Neutor using the hotel access to avoid the area they cordoned off at night. The hulk of round medieval tower was still floodlit so it couldn't yet quite be midnight. At the entrance ramp to the underground garages I waved my card at the sensor and the red-and-white barrier obediently rose. I accelerated hard; the Porsche followed me smartly, stuck to me like a leech, just made it before it closed. I signalled her into my parking space, took a reserved hotel one for myself.

I carried the rucksack, she her fat black doctor's bag. We walked up the narrow cobbled alley behind the city wall, round the corner of Albrecht Dürer's house and down the hill along Bergstraße where I lived. Almost no-one about, the usual handful of residents' parked cars; I checked each one as we went, nobody sitting watching, on the other side opposite my apartment nobody either. We entered the open archway that led through the house to the inner courtyard, I opened the old front door.

We were climbing the stairs – I showed her where not to tread, if she could. Frau Maußer would be asleep, thank God, she always arose at the crack of dawn. We went like mice; I could hear my joints creak.

I unlocked the apartment door.

Black as night, no light. We went in without speaking. I switched on the hall lamp. My bedroom door was open. Was he waiting behind it, was he in bed? Was he dead?

"Hello Matthias," I said. I didn't want to get shot.

No answer.

I entered the bedroom; I didn't know what to expect. With Matthias one never knew. He lay in the dark, motionless, still didn't speak. I stooped, turned on the halogen light next to the bed. He was flat on his back the way I'd left him – except that his arms were now under the sheet. His eyes were closed, he appeared not to have heard me. Was he asleep? Was he unconscious? I was so relieved

Martha had come. He looked sickly pale, there were lines drawn deep in his face and the grey skin was still sweating with fever.

Beside him, at his insistence, where I'd put it before I left to meet Martha, sat my small portable battery radio. It's aerial stood up like a silver wand. It was turned off, it didn't seem as if he'd touched it.

Yes, he looked ghastly; was he going to die? That was my first thought as I gazed down upon him. Or had I spoken aloud? Martha had removed her coat. She walked past me, placed her case on the floor and sat down on the edge of the low bed next to him.

"No problem," she said. "He's been in shock — coming out now." She said it matter-of-factly.

I set down the rucksack, removed the cotton bags and opened them. Remained standing, watching. One of her hands opened her case, the other was at his throat, I suppose checking his pulse. He opened his eyes. He looked ahead, but didn't focus, didn't seem to see.

She peeled back the sheet, exposed the unbuttoned nightshirt and his bandaged chest. Next to his thigh lay the gun; it had slipped from his hand. Martha simply picked it up and tossed it away near his feet. I took it carefully; it was a long time since I had handled a gun, I didn't know much about these things. But even I could see it was on red, not on safe. Quickly I secured it. It was anthracite grey, a nasty looking weapon, had the letters HK USP on the barrel and the butt — I suppose it was what one called a semi-automatic.

"Better wipe the prints, Sherlock," she said calmly. "And remove the exhibit, please." She was still facing Matthias, stethoscope in ears. She'd tipped him left and right, taken off his shirt.

I obeyed. Oh God was I glad. How could she be so calm?

When I returned, I found her examining him. I watched and waited. She was very professional; her movements and her hands were quick but not hasty, she knew exactly what to do. After a few minutes I asked if I could help.

"Just do what you're doing, that's best," she said simply. "Observation's a good teacher."

So I continued observing.

Very seldom did she speak, and then only to show me how to apply ointments and dressings, or to tell me to help her sit him up or turn him to a different position. Matthias seemed gradually to become aware of what was happening, of the fact that somebody else was there, that it wasn't me touching him. I'd expected problems, fury, recriminations. He made and showed none. I took it as a sign of the condition he was in. His half-focused eyes turned now and then from Martha to me and back again; mostly they remained closed.

Then, unexpectedly, he cried out — it wasn't loud, it was a horrible stifled sound, ending in a gurgle.

"Fetch two bowls and a kettle of boiling water," she told me coolly. She was working on his arm.

I needed a few minutes. I returned.

When she came to remove the last of the bandages from the arm she didn't turn a hair at what she found. Matthias moaned, bit off the sound and shook his head like a dog, shifting in pain; I felt nearly sick. Unfazed, she continued her examination.

In all, her visit lasted less than an hour. And it was only during the last few minutes that she talked to Matthias. "You're a cat with nine lives," was one of her first comments. She spoke directly to him as if he could comprehend.

He opened his eyes. So he'd understood.

"I'm a doctor. Friend of Stefan's. Don't know your name, don't want to. I won't report your case. Okay?"

He stared ahead. That was all.

"I said, okay?" She said it clearly, firmly.

His eyes turned; he was looking directly at her. "Yes," his mouth said. Then his gaze slid down, it was searching. His fingers too, feebly. "Where's the gun?" he asked. His voice was scarcely audible. Now he was looking at me.

"In the kitchen," I said.

A faint nod, nothing else.

And Martha was saying: "Amongst other things, you're badly burned — third degree. But if you do what I advise you'll survive."

He nodded again, slightly.

"As a doctor it's my duty to inform you, you belong in a burns clinic. At once."

He gazed at her. "No."

"Yes. And pronto."

He was gathering himself. "I stay here."

"If you ignore me there's no guarantee of recovery. You're endangering the both of you."

"Yes."

"Yes what?"
"I know."
"Well?"
"I stay here."
"Your decision. But you'll..."
"My decision."

Emotionlessly she was gathering in all the used tubes and empty packaging, stuffing them in one of the cotton carrier bags. "Now listen to me. There's only stuff here for the burns. Okay?"

Again he nodded. "Okay," he repeated mechanically.

"But that's not enough. You..."

"How long?" Matthias's voice was quiet. But it penetrated.

"How long what?"

"Till I can walk about, use my arms?"

"Two or three weeks at least. Depends."

"On what?"

"On your good luck holding out. And on your arm. I have to operate on it. I need X-rays too."

He was still staring at her. His eyes were slightly alive now. Where did he find the strength? They burned unmoving in deep recesses; they were almost intense like they used to be. "No possibility," he said. His voice was flat and monotone.

"You want to lose it?"

"How great's the risk?"

"There's a risk."

"I'll survive."

"You know why I'm telling you, don't you?"

He didn't blink. He just stared. "Yes," he said.

With her finger she drew a brief ragged oval in the air above his left arm and up to his shoulder. "These splinters are causing serious inflammation. I have to..."

"They've been removed."

"Some of them. Extremely clumsily, too. What did you use – an old kitchen knife or a dirty pair of pliers from the garage?" She shook her head. Tapping one of the bowls on the bed, she added: "Here are three more I found – metal and plastic. There're more still in there, I found the points of entry. But they're deeper. I have to establish how many, how serious, and extract them."

"They stay in. I'll take the risk."

"It's not a question of if, but how soon. In the clinic I'd do it at once, here it's undesirable to move you for thirty-six hours."

"No."

Martha straightened her back where she sat. "I suspect you have a fracture of the humerus, too." She raised her hand, tapped his right arm lightly.

Matthias took a sharp breath, half closed his eyes in pain. The perspiration on his face was running.

"Listen," she told him coldly, "I don't care a damn what you decide – if I never set eyes on you again, that's okay by me. But I'm a doctor, it's my duty to save life, so I'm informing you what you have to do. In forty-eight hours your condition will become critical. It's your life."

He had opened his pale blue eyes again. They watched her; they were unreadable. But somewhere inside he must be weighing the facts, deciding, should he override his instinct, jump over his shadow, or not?

"Wednesday afternoon my surgery's closed. I'll be alone. You come then, two-thirty. How you get there's your affair. Yes or no?" She stood up, put on her coat.

He blinked slowly; he followed her with his eyes. "Okay," he said simply.

I thought rapidly: Wednesday, that's a bad day, Frau Maußer's always at home – I'll have to get him out in her lunch hour when she's busy in the kitchen.

Martha Duchac stood there tall, turning away, as if she were ignoring him or hadn't heard. She'd picked up the bag full of rubbish, her heavy workbag was in her hand. Signing me to follow, she walked out of the room without a further word. I believe that was the first time I'd ever witnessed Matthias lose a round, meet his match.

In the hall, before the apartment door, Martha paused, put a stern hand on my arm. Only for a moment did she melt enough to tell me with lowered voice: "He's got guts, I'll grant him that – if he comes, there's more than a fifty-fifty chance of good recovery." She faced me, expression hard again. "But armed, no dice. Even in his present state he's dangerous. Could use you as hostage if they trace him here. Get rid of that gun."

"I will," I said. And thought: both of them.

Already she was back to being professional – she gave me a few more instructions about his treatment, about what to do if he went into shock again. I remember she also said practical things such as: "He's lost a lot of body fluid through the burns – see he drinks plenty of water, and especially strong coffee and black tea," and, "He'll have no appetite for a while, try some thin soup tomorrow." Then she reminded me to measure his blood pressure mornings and evenings. "Before you bring him to the surgery check it too – if it's down to eighty-sixty or almost not measurable, give him an injection like I showed you. It's as easy as falling off a log."

"I'll remember that." I opened the door for her. "The exit barrier opens automatically," I said, talking about where we'd parked. She just nodded curtly. Her last words were: "In thirty-six hours he can take a few steps on his own – this guy's got remarkable reserves." How the hell did she know what I was thinking? Could she smell my new panic?

We were shaking hands. She was warning me with her eyes, she didn't have to say it twice. I thanked her as best I could; I gave her both my hands.

Chapter 28

I lied to Matthias next day.
About his two weapons. I said I'd thrown them in the river, which was only half a lie because that's what I intended. He'd come out of a troubled sleep around noon, collared me at once to describe procedures should anyone come calling, then right afterwards demanded I bring him both the guns, feebly confronted me. When I told him, he didn't show the aggression I'd expected. He simply said: "Don't bugger about with me ever again," and his tone had turned to ice. Then he closed up like a clam. A pillar of steel could've communicated more. But he did one thing – he reached for my wrist. He was extremely weak, I think even thinking caused him pain. I will never forget that grip.

He switched on the radio, one of the News channels. Lay listening.

I made him strong coffee, forced him to drink. Then I warmed some soup, offered it. He drank a little, sip by sip, shaved head propped in my hand. His shadowed sunken eyes watched me all the time, did he suspect I'd put poison in the pot? I returned his gaze, furtively. I thought: you're touching a wanted terrorist, you're aiding and abetting – if you get caught how many years'll you get? Martha's right, are you mad? And in that instant, returning his unreadable gaze, I felt it. It hit me like a brick: he'd kill me if he had to, wouldn't he – if I endangered his chances of survival, if I messed about, stood in his way again?

Afterwards, I brought him a fresh bottle of water and took away the empty he'd drunk in the night. I also brought the portable television in to him as he demanded, plugged it in the aerial socket like I sometimes do if I watch in bed when I'm tired; it was old but had about thirty channels — I guessed that should be enough for him.

He made me fetch him newspapers, and my town map as well. He kept the radio. After the injection I left him to his own fevered devices, took up the umbrella again, went out and moved the Audi back to my own parking space before it caused complications. Then briefly went shopping. It wasn't so cold now, but windy and teaming with rain. Typical November.

On my return I went in to Matthias where he lay. He was spreadeagled, unmoving; he looked like a dying man. With the remote control clutched in his hand he was trying to watch TV.

"How're you feeling?" I said.

He just turned his eyes. "Could be better," he murmured. It was hardly a whisper.

I made him drink more water. Sat down on the bed to watch too. Every now and then he pressed with a thumb, kept jumping the channels — I think mostly the local stations, he was searching for latest News. All I gleaned was a utility van had been discovered abandoned near the scene of the crime and forensic experts were analysing it and its contents.

"Yours?" I said. I received no reply.

I stuck it out, his switching and surfing, for nearly half an hour, then it got on my nerves. I retreated to the kitchen, taking one of the newspapers with me. Sat there reading...

My mobile rang.

I glanced up. The clock on the beam said half-past-two. Quickly I went through to the living room where my mobile lay, checked the crystal display. It was Annabelle. I picked it up. She was so full of energy; I found it hard to speak. After a brief exchange she said: "There's something wrong, my philosopher. What is it?"

"Let's just say I'm feeling under the weather." There I was, lying again. I frowned; I didn't like that, especially not with Annabelle.

"Is it something serious?"

"No," I said.

"Shall I drive up?"

"That isn't necessary."

"It would be no bother."

I took a long and unsteady breath: I'd just remembered something — she had a key. Oh God. Carefully I said: "I prefer to creep into a corner, be alone till it's passed. Know what I mean?"

"Mmm."

I managed to curtail the call, before I gave myself away. At the close I heard her say: "Promise you will be sensible? Go to the doctor?"

"She was here yesterday." And I added: "She gave me all that I need." Well, at least that wasn't a lie.

There was silence her end of the line; I could hear her concern. "I'll ring you Friday," I promised. We rang off.

I stood there. Maybe it was because of her, and the key — suddenly I thought of something else too. My heart fluttered, my panic renewed. Judit. Oh my God, how could I have forgotten? She'd be flying over on the first of December, that was in less than three weeks. I'd have to get rid of Matthias before then. What if there were complications? What if his recovery took longer?

I left the living room and, on some whim, checked the guns and ammunition in their hiding place in the kitchen, but they were still there. Tonight I'd have to get rid of them. Then I crossed the hall corridor. Matthias lay with his head still propped up on pillows. Thankfully he'd turned off the sound on the TV, though. The city map was opened on his lap. He was white and shaky. Had Martha misjudged? Was he using up his last resources?

"Who was that?" he demanded. Light flickered on his face from the screen.

I told him.

He nodded. "Sit down." He wanted to talk about next day, about Wednesday. But Wednesday seemed so far away.

"Save your strength," I said. "Do it later, get some sleep first."

"Listen carefully," he said, ignoring me.

So I listened. He was tense; it seemed he'd done quite a bit of thinking. He'd planned it all, even alternative routes. After at least ten minutes he was still speaking with laborious effort and making wobbly references to the city map with index finger when the doorbell rang...

The sound made me start. It was shortly before three. I wasn't expecting anyone.

"Who is it?" said Matthias.

"No idea."

"Concentrate." He was stiff, quite still; how could he be so alert?

"Could just possibly be someone from my office," I said. "They think I'm sick at home." Or the police? I thought. Or a special unit? Have they located him? My heart was contracting again, my stomach a stone.

The bell peeled again. Impatience in the tone.

Abruptly he breathed: "You know what to do."

Was this it, the end of the road? I looked at him; I was more nervous than he. Hurriedly I got off the bed, my legs were shaking – went through the routine he'd taught me: checked the fire escape, listened at the apartment door, surreptitiously checked the street on the living room side. Nothing. No police cars or vans or snipers behind tanks, nobody standing with craning neck peering up. Began to relax slightly again. Whoever it'd been had maybe given up and gone away...

Back into the hall, listening at the door again just in case... Oh my God. I jumped, nearly out of my skin... a clack, a rattle, right outside. Dear God, they're out there – was that a weapon being primed, or a battering ram on the backward swing? My legs went weak, I felt very faint – nearly peed in my pants. Quick... open the door before they smash it down...

A fist – or something – struck the oak panel. I leapt back in total panic, I couldn't breath, my bladder sprung a little leak...

"Hey, ol' shit, it's me – open the fucking door." A female voice, coarse and sharp.

I stood stock still a second. I knew that voice – through a thousand cries, through the screams and horns of a football crowd, through a thousand storms I'd know that voice. I relaxed; I could breathe again.

I opened the door. It was Rosi. Little Rosi the hard one, Rosi the whore.

"Hi," she announced. "Fucking Ada, took yer time, din'ya?" Toss of the head, black-painted fingernails tearing though short, blonde, damp hair.

"Hi Rosi." I almost had to look down; Rosi was even smaller than me.

She stood there barefoot in all her glory, she was wearing her winter working clothes: black net blouse and white string stockings with sexy suspenders garnished by puffs of fur on the poppers, silver miniskirt that managed to half-cover that tiny tight bum – and those ghastly shoes. She'd shed them, they hung from her hand with that cute little bag, those steel stilettos she called heels, thin as pencils...,I could well appreciate her point of view that they hadn't been designed for climbing stairs...

"Knew you was here." She jack-knifed, revealing all, picked up a small bright-red plastic mac dripping wet. "Fucking pissing with rain, bad for business." She brushed me aside unceremoniously. "Need distraction from me pain." No handshake, no kiss, no contact; that's the way it'd always been, that's the way we wanted.

She was past me now, too late for me to turn her back.

"How did you know I was home?" I said, loudly enough for Matthias to hear. Already she was wiggling towards the living room. Ah what a sight for sore eyes.

"Yer weirdo pal's limo's still parked in yer space."

"Ah." I followed her meekly. "Another car job?" Her euphemistic name for sex in clients' cars in the hotel garage. I left out the screw bit; I like to try to keep things clean.

"Fucking Mini. Jesus, here stinks like a bleeding 'ospital! You sick, or something?"

"Yes," I said. Damn Matthias, he was making me lie right down the line.

"Phewww. Shit and arseholes. Catching?"

"No."

She was round the corner, a tiny tough angel going into the light.

"Like the usual?" I said. Had to accelerate things today. "Cappuccino?" She was on the sofa, legs crossed, arms up left and right. She'd dumped red mac, stilettos and little golden bag on the floor.

"'Spresso. Just a quickie – Prickle the prick said twenty minutes, or lick his arse."

"Oldies?"

"Yeah. Thanks pal."

I crossed to the deck, slipped in one of the old, old cassettes I'd mixed myself that turned her on, the one she liked the most. Love wasn't part of her vocabulary.

I went to the kitchen, made espressos in my ancient machine, a double one for Matthias too. When I returned, Rosi was still on the sofa but bent forward, concentrating, dabbing at her thigh. Narrow shoulders, neat little knees, tiny feet. The Everly Brothers were singing.

I put down the small cups. Sat down in one of the armchairs, looked out at the rain.

"I'm over here, mate."

I glanced at her, just to be kind.

She'd raised her small face, was still dabbing with the tissue. Her little bag for contraceptives, *Kleenex* and lubrication lay open near her thigh, like the crinkled mouth of a golden clam enjoying the front row view.

"How's Annabella-bella?" she asked, concentrating.

"Fine. Things are going well."

"Yer kidding?"

"No I'm not kidding."

"That's why yer sick. Look sombre as a screwed-up bishop what's missed his turn in the barrel."

"Well thanks, Rosi."

"Yer 'ere, she there, a fucking autobahn in between. Yer want a quick poke, she's not there – she wants a good fuck and where's yer prick?" She was applying something from a tiny tube now; I looked away again.

"At present it suits us," I said. I hadn't yet told her about my plans, and I wouldn't do it now.

"When was yer last bang?"

"About a couple of weeks ago."

"Jesus." Her bag snapped shut. "Poor Bella-bella – she'll be getting a sore finger."

"Sorry?" I looked back.

"Sitting alone with her fanny, masturbating." She had sat upright again, wriggling the miniskirt; it almost reached to her intimacy.

I chuckled. In spite of myself. "I doubt that," I said. "She's not the type to..."

"Wanna bet? Course she does, all broads do, cradle to grave." Oh, those ice-cold eyes; the pupils were black pinpricks on blue. "Yer get down there next weekend, soon as yer better, screw her Friday through Sunday – broads like Bella-Bella need it a lot."

Well I guess a woman like Rosi should know.

We sipped our espressos and the oldies played on. Buddy Holly, Elvis, Beatles, Stones... I felt very on edge because of Matthias; I suppose in her eyes I was getting more and more like that bishop.

We'd changed the subject, were talking books. She mentioned she was into Molière now: Rosi never ceased to astound. For about another ten minutes we continued conversing. I'm fond of Rosi – she's had a hard life, was abused by both father and nuns as a child, she once told me. She has to survive, she does it by doing the thing she knows best, but she has her secrets. Which we share. I've been told, too, it's good to give so I give her all I can whenever she calls, whatever she wants, it's not much anyway.

x x x

Early that evening I disposed of the weapons. While doing so, something slightly weird happened, though. I took a tram not George's car, in case of police checkpoints, rode out of town going east, alighted and walked away from the houses down into the valley to the seclusion of the river and trees. It was 7pm, dark and deserted, most people would be having supper, I thought. Last faint lights diminished, left behind. Was drizzling still, too. On the path only one jogger, a bedraggled shadow puffing past.

I know the area, it's where Judit and I often walked. There are two small humped bridges, the river divides, is deeper, and the current is strong. Ducks in the dark, quacking vulgarly, too black to see. I reached the bridges, left and right, crossed one and walked on a few paces, peering, listening. Nobody. Back to the narrow bridge. From the cotton bag I hurriedly withdrew the tight heavy ball full of loaded clips and boxes of bullets I'd bound round and round with adhesive tape in thick plastic so nothing could float away – it was heavy, I pushed it over the top of the broad and solid wooden balustrade, I was glad to say goodbye. I heard the splash, ducks flapped water, quacking louder. Oh God, had anyone heard? Frantically, I upended the sack to tip out the guns, get it over with; I couldn't see, could only feel. I fumbled. My hands were shaking again. A clack on wood, another splash – something hit my foot. A clatter, a sudden pain. I crouched, groping with my fingers, found it. One of the guns lay on the footbridge not far from my shoe. For God's sake get rid of it. I scrabbled, picking it up. The scuff of footsteps... was that a shadow on other black tree-shadows? It was coming closer, coming my way...

Still crouching, I panicked – for a moment held the gun tight in my hand. It'll make a splash. Don't... The footsteps louder, grittier now... The gun was cold, was heavy. Somehow horrifying, fascinating...

Quickly I stuffed it and the empty cotton sack in my winter-coat pocket. I was sweating in the cold. Legs jittery too, now. Get up for God's sake. Start walking, can't just stand here in the rain looking suspicious...

I rose and turned, striding off. A snuffle in the blackness. A dog? A little snort – a snout poked my leg...

"*Guten Abend.*" A gruff voice. The sense more than sight of someone going by.

"*Abend,*" I echoed. Going down the ramp away from the bridge, the asphalt path widening. The shuffling footsteps fading. Give him a minute, then follow – got to chuck the damn thing away. I stopped, waiting. A clump of trees, I knew them so well, vague silhouettes against the darkened sky, the little river fifty yards beyond. Thirty seconds, forty... no more sounds to be heard. Began retracing my footsteps. A beam of light...

I stopped again on the start of the ramp, panicking again, fearful, quickly turning my head and peering past the tree-clump... No, two beams, parallel beams – bright and penetrating, coming slowly along the other path beside the river, coming in my direction... long black shadows cast on brilliant white, moving shadows, the beams lit the night, they came from a car... But this was a nature reserve, the ways they'd laid here were purely for walkers – so it could only be a police car...

My panic was complete. I ran up the steep slope towards the shelter of the planked balustrades of the bridge, the gun bumping clumsily on my thigh. The pitch-black shadows and the lights were turning, following... had they seen me? I reached the top of the hump, cast a rapid glance backwards. The car had paused down there beyond the trees. Yes, it was the police...

Walk slowly. They can't drive over the bridge – too narrow. I went down the other side, I did it as slowly as I dared. No megaphone, no slamming doors. I walked on...

Twenty minutes later I was in the tram again, the number five, travelling back into the centre; I sat there still shaking. The gun I'd transferred to the deep inside pocket of my coat, before I reached the houses and the lights, before another jogger went by. Oh shit, oh shit. I stared at my reflection, the tram trundled on. I felt like a fugitive.

xxx

It was Wednesday, one o'clock; I was in a nightmare, I was nervous as hell.

I'd washed and dressed Matthias on the bed, given him an injection. He'd planned it all, gone through it with me half a dozen times – like a general in war, like a battle-plan, he'd done it in meticulous detail. Get the car, drive the three routes, return and park it outside the door, check via the inner courtyard that Frau Mauẞer was busy in her kitchen. So far so good. Had to half-carry him down those flights of stairs; I suppose my fear lent me the strength. His he found in sheer courage and will, he made the last steps alone.

It's a curious habit of life: when I'm expecting the worst and see everything black, things invariably turn out far better. The reverse is equally true. That afternoon, thank God and our lucky stars, the habit stuck to its rule. We didn't make it back to my apartment till well after six, though – because of time for recovery and Martha's pepping him up, because of the darkness and dinnertime, too. Frau Mauẞer was cooking again and, by the smells on the stairs, probably the rest in the house were as well.

I helped Matthias to bed; he was out like a light almost before he hit the sheets.

I watched the evening News, there was nothing new, then tried to read, gave it up. Sat in the dark on my own with my thoughts. I let the last three days run through my brain; they rolled before my eyes like a horror film. It must have been about ten o'clock, in the midst of the chaos of images suddenly something Estella had once said came back to me – she'd been on her favourite subject again. I remembered, she'd said: "There's a protecting angel looking after each of us."

I thought about it, mulled it over in my mind. I'd laughed at her at the time, told her if I had one he must have lost his grip. But could there possibly be a grain of truth in it – did I have one too? Under the circumstances, after all the risk, I suppose I was damn lucky to be sitting here.

I put on a lamp, sat down again, gazed into space. Then found myself staring across the room at my big antique *Biedermeier* writing desk with all its little drawers and nooks and crannies and hidey-holes; I was staring at the gun. And more words of Estella's jumped into my head. "Everything happens for a reason, Stefan, understanding why simply depends on our level of awareness." I was on the humpback bridge: why didn't the gun fall into the water like the other? Was there a reason, wasn't it just my nervousness? And when I was about to try a second time – why did the man with his dog have to appear just at that moment, wasn't it coincidence? And the police car?

I shook my head. No, it was just my bad luck. I'd have to try again as soon as I could, be cleverer next time. Nevertheless, academically it might be interesting to tell Estella and hear what she thought. Would she really say there was a reason behind it? But I couldn't, could I? I couldn't talk to anyone. I stared at the desk. The simple fact was I hadn't managed to dispose of it. Go to bed, then. Tomorrow you've got to work.

I dithered. Something nagged. I felt washed out, I wanted to share; I felt so very alone.

x x x

A week later Martha came to call. And the gun still lay there.

Ostensibly on a house-visit for me, she came to check Matthias's progress. It didn't look good: on the day after she'd operated he had collapsed in the bathroom while I was at the office. I'd rung her at once; I followed her advice. For three days he lay in my bed half in coma.

The day she came I took a day's holiday, but after a quarter of an hour's examination she said she was satisfied. "Be back a week today – ring again if necessary." And she left.

I had to duck out of my seminars that following weekend – my right-hand man took my place: I couldn't leave Matthias alone for three days in a row. Tuesday came, then Wednesday. As agreed, Martha called by again. It was the 27th of November. He'd picked up a lot in the interval, thank God, could even take the few steps to the loo on his own five or six times a day. His appetite was getting back to normal, too. "Another ten days and you can kick him out," she pronounced. I was counting the days: in four Judit and Andrea were due. I stood there sweating – what to do?

Only one thing was realistically possible unless I rang her to postpone, and I didn't want to do that because of Andrea: I booked them into a hotel. It took a bit of wangling – all the hotels were booked solid. What d'you expect, I kept hearing, the Christmas Market starts in two days. But little *Burg Hotel* put me at the top of the waiting list because they knew me and the clients I sometimes placed there, and a cancellation within twenty-four hours brought a double room for the first three days and a move to a suite for the rest. I guessed they could slum it there together till he'd gone.

That Wednesday evening while cooking, I noticed a kitchen knife was missing. I waited till he was on the toilet, searched the bed, found it under his pillow. I left it there, though – if I hadn't he'd simply have taken another, found a better hiding place. Better the devil one knows...

x x x

The *Lufthansa* flight from Frankfurt came in only twenty minutes late.

I waited. I was on tenterhooks. I stood there in Arrivals beside the enormous *Ficus benjamina* tree that went up two storeys almost to the glass roof. Thoughts of Judit and Andrea. They flooded my brain. Was I imagining all this – after so long would I really be seeing them again in just a few minutes?

The passengers had started coming through in dribs and drabs, pushing their luggage trolleys. Greetings from people come to pick them up. Cheerful cries, and hugs and kisses. Ah, Andrea... soon I'd be doing that too. Could feel the thrill already churn my stomach, creep my skin. I waited, watching those sliding glass doors from Customs like a hawk each time they opened. The crew came through. Fifteen minutes. The hall was emptying. Twenty minutes. No sign of them yet. I waited. The hall nearly deserted now. On the electronic board there were no more flights that night. Still I waited – till no-one else came. And even another five minutes just in case – till the Customs and Excise guys emerged too through their side door: Andrea and Judit weren't on the flight.

It was quarter to midnight

The *Lufthansa* counter was closed. Checked my mobile. No messages. I rang Frankfurt. Sorry, against regulations – no names on passenger lists can be disclosed. Can you just say yes or no – were they on the list New York to Frankfurt? Very sorry.

I checked my mobile address book, but I'd forgotten to store Judit's telephone number. Must be a simple explanation – probably they're stuck in Frankfurt, missed the connection, Judit used to be so scatterbrained. Strange, though, no message or call. Dejected, I drove home.

x x x

Matthias was awake. He'd been waiting too.

"Okay?" he said. "Joyous reunion? They in the hotel?"

I gave him the news. "Get some sleep." Went into the living room. I began to do all the things I suppose anyone would do in a situation like this: I rang the hotel to keep the room, explained to the night receptionist what had happened, that they'd be coming a day late. I hoped. Then I checked my work mobile for SMS and my laptop for e-mails. Nothing. On the off-chance, I even called Judit's home number, it was only early evening New York time. No answer. I left a voice message. Went to bed. A feeling of helplessness, a sense of loss.

Next day I awoke early. Matthias slept fitfully. Still no messages.

At 7am I rang *Lufthansa* at Frankfurt again, explained the situation. The woman was kind: I learned they hadn't been on the flight, the tickets had been cancelled at short notice. Why? I thought. Had she changed her mind, got cold feet – or was Andrea perhaps ill? Why hadn't she called, then? That's the least she could do.

I had to wait till well after midday to ring the States again, because of the time lag. I called the work number again. Unexpectedly, like a machinegun, a woman's nasal American voice answered.

"Judy Powell's secretary my name's Ester Larue how can I help you?"

"Hello," I said. I gave my name, and in my best British-German English: "Could I speak to Judy please?" I thought that was the simplest way to begin.

"'Fraid not." There was a brief hesitation. "In what connection? Maybe I can help?"

I explained.

More hesitation, awkwardness this time. Then: "She won't be coming. Sorry to say she's had an accident."

An accident? My heart fluttered; fear came first, then disappointment. "Is she badly hurt?" I asked carefully.

"Sorry Mr Falk. Can't tell you more."

"A car accident?"

"Yeah."

"Is she in hospital?"

"Sorry, not permitted to say more. Company policy."

"Look," I said, "I am calling from Germany. I need more details. I have got to get in touch with her."

"Very sorry. Give me your e-mail address and I'll enquire how much we can write you."

"My daughter Andrea was planning on flying over with her. Is she hurt too?"

"No – that much I can say. She's fine. Wasn't in the car."

Thank God, I thought. But still my fear was increasing, it was like a lump in my lungs. Then I remembered. I asked: "Is Wilbur there? Wilbur Yeats?"

"No, 'fraid not. He's indisposed till Wednesday."

"Would you give me his number please."

"Sorry. Also company policy."

"The number of the hospital, then? Or anyone who can give me information."

"Sorry."

Damn it. I cast about helplessly. "Could you reach Wilbur?"

Another hesitation. "That depends."

"Would you give him my number and ask him to call me?"

Silence down the line. Then she said: "Sure."

I gave it to her, and my private e-mail address. "Beg him to contact me straight away."

"Will do. Decision's up to him, though."

I thanked her and was about to ring off when she said: "Really do apologise for not being allowed to help you, Mr Falk. Guess you'll understand."

With heart like lead I replaced the receiver; there had been something else embedded in her tone.

I didn't find out Judit was dead till late afternoon.

x x x

"Thanks Wilbur," I said. "I much appreciate that you rang."

"If I can do *anything* else, Stef, you just call me." He was still sniffing, speaking in anguish. "Too dreadful. We're all *horribly* shocked."

"Yes," I said. The emptiness in me had deepened, the coldness endured.

He'd given me the details of the accident, but I mostly had Andrea on my mind. Judit had been on the way to pick her up from school and she was now in Reading Pennsylvania with friends, four or five hours by car from New York. She was in great hands, he said, she was being taken very good care of. He'd supplied me with names and addresses and numbers, too: the family, the lawyer, the attorney.

"I understand your grief," I told him; I think it was greater than mine. Wilbur was full of emotions which seem lost on most of us mortal men. "I look forward to meeting you at the cremation," I signed off. Why did I feel, for Judit, only cold?

Via the Web I procured a flight ticket, two-way, tourist class, coming back in four days — it still cost a bomb. Using my surplus points they graciously gave me an upgrading to Business. While I was doing so, an e-mail arrived. It was from Andrea, the first I had ever received from her, the first contact in six years: *Mama's dead, apologies for writing too late, can't come.* Very short, very sad, poor Andrea. For her, not Judit. I held the e-mail in my hands; I held it like a jewel. My heart hurt. With tense fingers I replied, said I was flying over, and when; signed it with love.

I rang the hotel to cancel, then Annabelle, told her what had happened and about my plans and when I would return. That was the first mistake I made, I think — I shouldn't have mentioned the date, and afterwards only had myself to blame. Down the phone she tried to give solace but she didn't quite succeed — my thoughts were so much with Andrea. For once I didn't tell Estella I'd be away, because of Matthias of course. Frau Maußer also not; she'd recently been snooping around with intensified voracity, wondering why I so often wasn't at work.

And Matthias himself was the least of my worries: he was mending gradually, his survival no longer at risk. In spite of much pain he could move his body a bit, it'd be enough to get him to the kitchen to heat soup and ready-made food in the microwave once or twice a day, he'd even be able to eat fresh bread from my freezer if he remembered to thaw it in time. No, I hardly spared a thought for Matthias after what he'd done, he could crawl on his damn hands and knees for all I cared. Now the danger of discovery seemed to have passed I was only left with anger.

I went shopping for him one last time before leaving, though, including lugging crates of mineral water – and I bought a little present for Andrea...

I sat down alone in the living room, put my feet up. My small bag was packed, everything was done. I glanced at my watch. Still a couple of hours. I let go – I let my thoughts wander where they wanted, let them off the leash. That's when it hit me. I'd been so busy, and my only concern concentrated on Andrea, I suppose it was delayed reaction. It was then it suddenly jumped at me: Judit really was dead. I'd never be seeing her again.

My mind wound backwards, from that last telephone call, memories invading, all the things we'd done, right back to the beginning – it was curious, it was like a review in reverse. My God, she's dead. I sat there stretched out, staring at the past. Time ticked by, the room grew dark. It felt like a hole; she'd simply been snuffed out, like a candle, just like that. How quickly these things can happen. But it was only a hole. Yes, there was a sense of loss, a book half-finished, a film that's broken – yet there was no sadness, I'd gained enough distance, it was devoid of sentimentality.

I rang for a taxi.

x x x

From Kennedy Airport it took me nearly two hours to get out of New York. The traffic was hell, I lost my way; it was early morning rush-hour local time, my body told me I ought to be eating lunch. The flight from Frankfurt had been badly delayed. Freezing fog.

My head was hollow, my arms like dehydrated sticks, I'd hardly slept on the plane. I drove the limousine carefully. There was sufficient space at the front for a family of ten, and for one and a half more at the back. I drove, shrivelled and small, lost in one corner.

In the centre of Reading I asked after the address and was directed back out to the edge. I passed a small hotel – thought, I'll call there later for a room. Had to stop and ask the way twice more. My heart was starting to get out of control now; I was getting closer to Andrea.

In an avenue leading along a rise fringing a forest of maple and firs I found number eight. A well-to-do residential area, lots of open space between each house, clumps of trees and lawns, no walls or fences or gates. I left my bag in the extravagant automobile which I'd parked in the drive beside a little red Porsche. Rang the bell...

"Hi, you got the side door!" A short slim woman, short dark hair, dark eyes, holding out both hands. "Don't tell me – you're Stef." She said it very warmly; she looked extremely attractive.

"Yes," I said.

"I'm Samantha Bernstein. Call me Sammy. Great to meet you."

"You too."

"We've been expecting you since breakfast – where're your bags?"

I explained about the hotel.

"You kidding? No deal – you're our guest."

I politely resisted... "Well, you fetch them in after..." I was being ushered in... "Saul's in court. My husband – he'll be along for dinner..." Later I discovered Saul was a lawyer, had done all the paperwork for Judit and had some more for Andrea's benefit if I would like to agree, yea or nay. I'd learn, too, they were both German Jews.

Getting very nervous, now.

Through a big lobby at the end of the house. I saw what she meant, I'd picked the wrong door. "Well, you come right along through – and excuse the mess. There's a very sad but excited young lady just waiting to get reacquainted..." Freezers, high sloping roof, stuff for horse-riding, coats and boots and shoes en masse...

A whisper: "And boy is she on edge..." A fluted glass door opening... I thought: well that makes two of us... A big family kitchen right across the width of the house, sloped ceiling too, and pale grey rafters up there...

Andrea.

There she was.

She sat at a scrubbed pine table – straight-backed, wide-open eyes. Eyes meeting...

"Hi." Another girl next to her, nearer me, greeting: "I'm Rebecca, the daughter – call me Becky."

"Hello. I'm Stef."

She stayed sitting. A small computer with flat-screen switched on sat on the table between them. I held out my hand – she said: "Hi," again, she said it coolly. But I only had eyes for Andrea.

Six long years.

She was rising, carefully, as if in slow motion, as though she'd been hurt. Jeans and T-shirt, her body already had the start of a figure that might soon become like Judit's. I just stood there. She was thirteen years old – she looked a little older. Already she was nearly as tall as me. I walked towards her; it was like crossing an ocean. I stopped again.

"Andrea," I said.

Six long years: an enormous tear torn in time. She was waving from the steps of that plane and Judit was turning her, pulling her in...

"Papa."

She said it so simply. I could feel my tears. Had she really said papa? I'd dreamt of hearing her voice say that a thousand times just the way she used to. I smiled gently, as calmly as I could. Inside I was dancing for joy, I was nearly breaking down.

She was crossing towards me. I held out my hands. She stopped too. She stood proud and straight, chin raised, long thick hair piled up like a goddess, looking much too mature for her age.

She gazed at me. They were my eyes. She gave a wary smile – it was my smile, too. Judit's hair, though. And Judit's nose. She was holding back – did she feel like me? Was she holding her breath counting to three very, very slowly? Or was she thinking with youthful disdain: Jesus, who's this bastard who never wrote me or came to visit, who's this stranger?

Carefully, very carefully, I opened my arms. Would she come, would she reject – should I go to her? Then before I'd quite realised, I was reaching out and touching her shoulders, we stood at arm's length. In her eyes there was such a mixture of emotions, now – in her eyes, in her face. The pride was fading, there was diffidence, almost fear. And puzzlement and pain. Was that a frown of confusion, too? She was hesitating; was she thinking that's close enough? Or was she on the brink, the tips of her toes poised on the edge? Could she jump – or was it too far down to make that leap?

I couldn't help it – I took the step, took her nervously in my arms, I was drawing her nearer, enfolding her. Hair at my throat, on my cheek; it smelled so clean, freshly washed. We stood there like statues. No kisses. We just stood there quite still, touching – and only then, after more than a minute, did I sense her raise her hands, snaking arms behind me; tentatively she hugged.

Oh what a feeling.

I wanted to kiss her smooth skin, those perfect cheeks, but I didn't dare. So I just leaned back my head and looked at her. No, she didn't have my nose, or my body or hair – Judit had dominant genes, Judit was strong. But she was half of me, I was half of her; she had my silences. Did she have my character, too? My guarded soul?

Silence stretched.

Those eyes that were my eyes watched me. Grey with funny specks of brown. They were dry, there wasn't a tear. Like mine just managed. Did she know what I was thinking, too?

"Andrea," I said. I'd gone and said it again. I didn't know what else to say.

And then she did it – she closed those eyes for a second, gave me a slow, small peck on the cheek. It did something to me, dislodged something. All of a sudden; it released a brake, it turned a key.

"You look lovely," I said. I said it in German.

A tiny smile. "And you, Papa?" she answered. "You look tired." Also in German. "And you need a shave."

Those were our first personal words.

They were followed by others. Just a few. Holding her at arm's length again I said, full of pride, admiring her: "You were just a pretty little girl when mamma took you on that plane. Now you've turned into a beautiful young woman." And I meant it.

"I'm still me," she said.

"Yes." I nodded. "Of course." I tried a feeble grin. "I'd have recognised you in any crowd – even a Yankee one."

I'd tried a grin, she tried a laugh. A small squeezed sound. I sang inside: she had my laugh too.

I let go her young shoulders; I didn't want to, but thought I should. Thought I ought not to prolong, to overdo it. Then I didn't know what to do with my hands. I stood there, a little awkward. My fingertips itched; I wanted to hold her, hug her for a hundred years – I the defender of all that's unsentimental, how could I feel this nostalgia now? Yes, suddenly I prayed to turn back the pages, watch her grow up again, relive every lost second of those six long years...

What was this? I glanced down: Andrea had taken one of my hands. Didn't press it, didn't squeeze. Simply took it in one of hers. A neutral touch. I stood there gazing at her. Her eyes were neutral too, now. They'd emptied. She began to turn me... my God, I thought, she displays more maturity and presence than me. We faced the other two. Sammy smiled quietly. She had crossed her arms, there was a light in her eye – I suppose she'd just been watching, waiting. She said: "I guess you folks need some personal time." Then repeated unexpectedly, in Yiddish with a strong American accent: "*Schein, mir wil losn eich alein.*"

At the table her daughter stared at her computer screen, tapped a key. She seemed to do it pointedly.

"Becky honey, let's scoot."

Another quick tap. Then the girl was rising, grudgingly, scraping back the chair with her legs. She was somewhat plump, not like her mother – a bit moody, a bit jerky, but she looked the same age as Andrea. She avoided my eyes, only glanced at Andrea – they appeared to be close friends; for her, then, I was also an intruder.

Raising an arm, I said in English: "I have a suggestion." I looked at Andrea. And still in English out of courtesy said: "How about a walk? I think I need some fresh air."

Andrea just watched me. So serious. What was she thinking now?

x x x

Along the avenue, wearing winter coats; chill in the air.

Neither of us spoke. Now and again I glanced at her, and she at me. She walked straight and stiff, she moved like me but so much about her reminded me of Judit. There was a track ahead going up the slope through trees.

"Shall we go up there?" I suggested in German.

A shrug.

We climbed. Moss and dead leaves beneath our feet, naked winter branches, the occasional firs and a pine, thin skin of powdered snow higher above. A frail sun, pale-washed blue sky.

"You never wrote me," she said suddenly. She said it in American; she had no accent.

The reproach struck me like a rock. It hurt. We'd reached the top of the hill. I stopped, regarded her.

"Yes I did, Andrea. Often." I answered in English. Said it quietly. "I never got them."

Up there was open ground, it was lighter, the trees away below.

"It was your mother's wish." I thought of the presents Judit had returned. But I didn't speak.

"She had no right to do that."

No, I thought. I kept watching her young face, I could glimpse Reading in the distance down beyond the tops of the trees; ah that beautiful milky skin.

"You didn't phone either."

How often had I requested it in writing? But Judit never gave me a number.

"I expect she wanted to help you make the break quickly," I said diplomatically. To say it in English, for me, was a struggle. "I am sure she meant it well," I added.

"That was cruel."

For both of us, I thought. But I said nothing. I simply nodded, slowly.

She stared at me, her eyes haunted. There was nothing in between us except the air and the sun and the sky.

I held out my arms. She hesitated. I could see her pain. Then she came half-heartedly towards me. I held her close again. "I've missed you very much," I said. I had to speak in German now, I hoped she'd understand. "You left a hole nothing could fill."

She stood so stiff. And silent. I couldn't see her face. Only after a minute or two I heard her say: "Papa, I'm so horribly unhappy." She'd said it in German too: at least I was glad about that.

"Yes," I said.

She sniffed. She was crying.

I stroked her neck, I stroked her hair; I tried to sooth. Why didn't I feel like crying too? Oh God, I'd forgotten, when had I last cried?

"Try not to think badly of us," I said. "Marriages sometimes go wrong, we human beings are weak."

She sniffed again, tossed her thick hair. Again her face was gone. "I shan't make that mistake," she told my shoulder. "Never going to marry." Her German was all still there, but there was a touch of American twang.

I nodded beside her head. "Maybe later you'll let yourself change your mind." I stood there, hugging her, stroking her hair, trying to purge her unhappiness, trying to soften her pain. There was something stirring in me somewhere, why couldn't I feel where?

Then she said: "Mama's dead." That's all she said.

"Yes." All I could say.

"It's horrible, I can't believe it."

"I can't either."

"She's dead and'll never come back. Never ever." The way she said it haunted me – I knew I had to speak.

"When someone close dies," I said, "it's like losing half of oneself. But they say with time the half grows back again."

"It's horrible, horrible. On Friday she called to say when she'd pick me up and on Saturday she was dead. Papa, just can't believe it."

"However hard at the start, Andrea, we all have to learn to live with loss. We learn to live again."

She was sniffing at the tears.

I said quietly: "I'll help you if you like."

She coughed. "Last night I dreamt we were in Florida together. She promised and promised me she'd take me there but she never did. Now she never will."

"I'm sure she would have. Your mother never broke her word."

Her whole body shook, she cried into my neck.

I waited.

"Would you like me to take you there?" I said.

A pause. Then: "Sure thing. Uh-huh." That was in American. She stopped. I suppose she was considering. Then she shook her head, it rubbed my cheek. "Wouldn't be the same." German again.

"Glad about that."

Another pause. She tipped back her face, her skin was wet. "Why d'you say that?"

"I hear it's a dreadful place." I pulled a face. "Full of the rich and retired, and high in humidity – that's where the dogs go to sweat and die."

"Yes?" She stared at me. "But all my friends say it's cool."

"Then you go there one day. You paint your own picture." I smiled down at her speckled grey eyes. "And when you come back, write and give me your opinion."

Her eyes squeezed shut. Oh God, I'd said the wrong thing. Tears oozed beneath those perfect lashes, the tears trickled again.

Moments passed. I clasped her gently, watched the sky.

Then I heard her say: "Papa, I'm terribly lonely."

She reached me with those words, those were words I knew. I was staring at myself six years ago after they went away. I took a breath: I wanted to share it, to explain that I knew what she meant, that each of us is alone. But you can't tell a thirteen-year-old that – can you?

I leaned back, held her face between my fingers. "I'm here," was all I said.

"But you'll be gone soon, won't you?" Brimming eyes, agonised eyes. Oh God. That gaze went through and through me.

I kissed her forehead. "Would you like to come back with me? To Germany – like you and mamma planned?"

The gaze contemplated, went out of focus.

What was she thinking? "Or for ever, if you wish." I just popped it in – I'd given it no thought up to now.

She raised an arm, wiped her tears with the back of her hand. "No," she said simply.

"That's okay." I sighed inside. "If you change your mind you know where I am. For Christmas, or any time in the future. I'd come and fetch you."

She sniffed again. Had to break away to blow her nose. "All my friends are here."

"Friends are very important, I know."

"And Sammy. And Saul."

"Yes," I said. I watched her. "Are you very fond of them?"

"Very."

"Do you know them well?"

"Sure." Another slip into American. Then back again. "Mamma got acquainted soon after we arrived here. We come over most weekends. They're our best friends."

"And where do you and mamma live?"

She stared at me. "You don't know?"

"No," I said.

"New York. Near Central Park. I hate NY."

"And Sammy and Saul? They looking after you now?"

"They want me to move and live with them here, be my guardians if you agree."

"I'll agree to anything that makes you happier."

"He's a lawyer, you know. And all that."

I nodded. "If that's what you'd like, I'm certain that's a good idea."

Her eyes fell down. Oh God yes, they really were my eyes.

"But what about your school? I imagine it's in New York, isn't it?"

"Sammy says I can go to Becky's one instead if I want. They'd arrange it."

"Would you like that too?"

"Think so. Becky's my very special best friend." Again her eyes fell away, just like mine do when I'm unsure.

I said: "And your other friends? Are they all in New York?"

She nodded: a small jerk of the head. She bit at her beautiful lip.

"Wouldn't you miss them?"

A shrug. She looked back up at me. "I can see them in the vacations, can't I?" Was that defiance in her tone? "And maybe at weekends now and then."

I waited. I didn't speak. She had to think it through herself.

Then she shot out: "Chuck's in NY. Never want to go near that sod again." Spat out with bitterness, with venom.

"Chuck?" I said. "Your stepfather?"

"Mamma's number two. She booted him out, but he's still around somewhere. Tried to rape me."

The bastard. "Yes," I said. "Mamma told me on the phone..."

She drew in a sharp breath. I felt her body shake.

"Andrea," I held her fast, "forget the bastard. He'll never harm you again. Everyone will see to that."

She clung. Her body was so stiff.

"Never again," I repeated. I thought: I'll kill the bastard if he comes within a mile again.

She made a jump: "I wish Germany wasn't so far away, Papa." She said it in a small tight voice. I was very glad she'd managed that jump.

"Only six hours on a plane." I tried to make it sound light.

She was watching me; she'd tipped back her head. She said nothing.

I waited. Don't rush, I thought – this is all too much for her. Then I said slowly: "As I said, if you'd like you could fly back with me for a few days – or a week or two. Or come on a little later just for Christmas. Like you'd both intended."

"It was Mamma's idea."

"Ah," I said. I peeped at her, cocked my head on one side. "You didn't want to?"

Another little shrug. "Don't really know."

I felt disappointment, like a pang. But I sat on it, on my selfishness; I didn't have the right. "Don't worry," I said. "It was just a thought. Maybe we'll do it next year if you suddenly want."

Still she watched me. Those perfect lips, that perfect nose – and those eyes red from crying.

"How long can you stay, Papa?"

Oh God, I thought. I wrapped her in my arms again so she couldn't read my face.

"Not till after the funeral," I said.

x x x

That evening I got to know Saul.

After dinner, at his invitation, we sat alone together in his study. A mass of papers and documents; but Saul was a tidy man. He told me about himself and his family to put me in the picture, I suppose to reassure. He did it in a typical short, dry lawyer's manner. Then we spoke exclusively of Andrea.

Near the close I sought his opinion regarding the immediate future, whether I should stay on longer, maybe give her a little holiday somewhere in the States to distract her troubled mind, or what did he think? His answer was a thoughtful smile. Then: "Distraction, yes. But not in the States." Saul understood her, it seemed, very well – he'd make an excellent legal guardian.

So I asked about the plane tickets Judit had bought for Germany.

"*Lufthansa* was great," he said. "They refunded hers. No problem."

"And Andrea's?"

"No." He twinkled at me under thick bushy brows. "I put that on hold." Then he gave me a tip, made a suggestion. His eyes were kindly, but very alert; Saul was a man of few words, but a big jolly bear of a man.

x x x

The funeral was scheduled for 11am Saturday, not the Friday as Wilbur had said. I learnt this, also, from Saul, had to postpone my flight home – was lucky to get a seat on Sunday. I was sitting at the computer in the big kitchen, Andrea beside me; she'd helped me with the English. As I was about to exit she stopped my hand.

"Papa?" she said.

I waited. She was staring at the flat-screen. She reached over my arm, tapped keys. "Still two seats available."

"Yes," I said. "I saw."

"Changed my mind. Can I come with you? Just for Christmas?"

I looked up at her. She was watching me, cautiously.

"Of course," I said.

She left the kitchen, returned. Had a ticket printout in her hand. Her old flight ticket. I vacated the chair, let her take my place before the screen. She called up the form, started going through the steps, her fingers tapped so quickly.

"Andrea?" I was leaning over her shoulder. My heart was light, it had grown wings like a bird; and I was thinking of Saul.

She paused, looked at me; our faces were very close.

"You make me very happy," I said.

"Yes, Papa?"

"And I'll try and make you happy, too."

Her eyes were blank, as bright as stars; I couldn't read the message.

x x x

Those three days went by fairly fast.

They were partly filled with practical tasks giving appropriate due to the funeral and, in between, the Bernstein's hospitality. I also managed, in spite of the Christmas crowds in Nuremberg, to find a small hotel room. Few details stand out – except for one: a short exchange with Andrea.

We had just come back from the preacher, from giving him details of Judit for graveside words. Andrea was very still, her thoughts turned in, introverted. I remember: we stood alone in the spacious living area, at the window, looking out.

Into the silence I said in German, not realising it would ignite a spark: "I'd imagined it was to be a cremation." It would've been somewhat simpler.

Andrea turned to me, eyes suddenly wide. "But of course not," she gasped. Also in German. There was almost a hallowedness in her voice.

"Of course not?" I echoed.

"Never, never – that's not allowed."

"No?" I was puzzled.

"The body must return to the earth from whence it came. One must never cremate a body, that means eternal fire and damnation." She paused an instant to draw a quick breath – there was indignation now: "It's against the faith."

The faith? I watched her shocked eyes; I wondered, what faith? Catholicism, Evangelism? Or Judaism even?

I nodded. I felt it better to say nothing.

But Andrea wasn't finished. "Sometimes the soul doesn't leave the body right away, it could perish in the flames."

"Ah," I said, and left it at that. The soul? I thought. Where did she get that one from – the preacher, a priest, some sect...?

"That's why they open the windows when someone passes away," she pronounced categorically. "So the soul can fly out. Some depart very quickly."

...Or had she possibly got it from the Bernsteins? Well certainly not from Judit; Judit was into more esoteric stuff, mysticism, Buddhism, Tarot – and in her circle of cronies turning that old bottle with sheer willpower and spelling out creepy names...

"Ah, the soul," I murmured diplomatically, imagining for a second it flapping off on fluffy wings. But suddenly little Eva was in my head, that time when we were kids and grandmother died. And the grin in my brain faded.

"It's like reincarnation, really, but it only happens once." She said it very seriously. "The soul receives only one new body of course, and it lives on for ever in Paradise."

Is that so? I steeled my nerves, let my eyes glaze over. I recalled snippets of Christian teaching from my childhood: naughty souls being sent to hell or an underworld, only faithful souls being stored in Heaven till the second coming or the Final Judgement, the good Book of Life being opened, the lucky guys getting a new body and eternal redemption, the bad guys getting the chop...

"Ah," I said again. I thought: well, she's gathered herself a grand old mixture here – almost enough to please them all. I kept a perfectly straight face.

She was calm again. "Do you believe in the soul too, Papa?"

She'd put me neatly on the spot. "Well..." I didn't wish to provoke or undermine. I took a measured breath. "It's a noble concept, naturally. But..." And there was Professor Skell the theologian, the wise old man from Florence – without any warning he just entered my head.

I think I blinked. I'd not seen or heard of him since Florence a quarter of a year ago – although I'd tried to make contact on my return he hadn't answered my e-mail; yes, it was really as if he'd never been. Yet here he was now: I could see him so clearly in my head, I could see every detail. He didn't sit at his table, though; he stood there before me in my mind's eye surrounded by nothing. Could hear his voice too, he was talking about the flower again, and the stars, and the existence of God – he was talking so quietly but I could hear every word. I thought: why's he telling me all this again – is Andrea going to ask me next if I believe in Him too?

"You know, Andrea..." I paused, got to head her off, "...I met an old theologian a little while ago, a very wise old man. It was an interesting conversation..."

He was speaking of the soul, now... his voice had changed its tone, it was as though he stood right there in the room, it tinkled like a bell: "What is a soul, Stefan? What is in a word? Would you not say that each of us possesses a source of energy, a special character, a very individual Me not definable in terms of a material body? You might consider that one, might you not?"

Energy perhaps, I said – but energy is energy, when people talk of the soul they're talking about something else. Do you honestly believe you possess such a thing as a soul?

There came no answer, though. It seemed that just as suddenly the old man was gone. I chuckled quietly. Eyed Andrea. She watched me. She looked so innocent, so certain.

"Yes," I said. I ended: "He tried to guide me towards the truth, but I confess for me it's not an easy subject." I stopped.

And it seemed to satisfy her. No more questions. Not even that sixty-four-thousand dollar one. I was extremely glad about that. All she said was: "Mamma told me it's not that easy for her either. You adults make everything so complicated, it's so simple really."

"Ah yes," I agreed with caution. "The most beautiful things often are."

"She was into Hinduism and Buddha, and all that. Really horribly complicated."

"Yes," I said. I could see Judit now, cross-legged on her regulation mat. All those chants and mantras, all those little bells. "I found that too," I confessed.

Her clear thirteen-year-old eyes still watched me. Ah, so pure and innocent. Then they brightened even more, they turned, they were looking at something across the room...

"Papa, come and see."

I followed her. Yes, from behind, her hips were on the path to Judit's hips, they were beginning to swing like Judit's, too.

A deep recess in the wall at the back of the room, hung with black folds, a shelf and black cloth, the faint hint of an object upon it. A click. A halogen spot switched on – in the narrow beam of light a small jade Buddha glowed green in the dark.

And I smiled inside. What unorthodox Jews to put a Buddha in the place of honour. Ah yes, I thought – Judit had lots of little Buddhas too.

"Mamma's present to Saul last *Hanukkah*," she breathed.

I side-glanced. She regarded it, she was gazing in rapture. And then I thought: so she's into that, too – maybe one day she'll embrace Zoroastrianism and Islam as well, then she'll pretty much have them all in the bag.

Secretly I observed Andrea's profile; I suppose, really, we're all just squirming worms on a hook.

x x x

On the Saturday I became acquainted with Wilbur, but not very well. A very feeling person; the world would no doubt be a better place were it filled with more of his kind. Of the funeral I remember almost nothing – except the coffin down there in a hole bearing a corpse I once used to hold, and when they threw the first earth and Andrea the first flower. That's about all.

Chapter 29

We landed in Nuremberg, stood at the belt waiting for the luggage. It was only early afternoon. Andrea immediately started sending SMSs, tapping little messages. From my mobile I called Matthias as agreed – three rings, stop, one ring, stop, then phone again; he'd insisted on the code. Who was I to question the ways of the wanted? I stood there, head cocked, phone to ear, one eye on the belt. I hadn't bothered to call from the States about the one day's delay. He wasn't a child.

He didn't answer.

Has he had another fall? I thought. Collapsed? Or maybe he's on the toilet. Give him ten minutes.

My modest bag came through first. Then Andrea's two suitcases. I had to smile: she'd inherited Judit's luggage gene too. She pushed the trolley out to the taxis, I phoned again. Still no answer. Strange. Then an unpleasant thought crept in. Had he perhaps been discovered? Had they raided my apartment, was he under arrest? Oh God. Could it be the police were waiting for me?

I told the taxi driver which hotel; we both sat at the back. Andrea was busy looking at all the changes beyond the Mercedes' windows, said little. My brain had no distraction, it worried at the possibilities like a dog with a bone. Was it possible Frau Mauβer had observed me leave in the taxi, knew my apartment must be unoccupied and had heard sounds from within? She so loved snooping at doors. Or maybe Herr Eggenhofer had heard movements through his ceiling and mentioned it to her? After all, the old floors were only of timber. Had Frau Maußer tipped off the police?

We reached the hotel. It was only a couple of hundred yards from my apartment. Went into Reception. The room wasn't ready, would we like to leave the luggage, come back in an hour? I tried to be decisive, said "Yes." And to Andrea: "Let's go down to Henkersteg, walk around a little – I'll show you places you may remember, ones which haven't changed."

She stood there looking at me, then round at Reception. Was that a reproach in her eyes? Because of the hotel? Driving to Kennedy I'd briefly explained a friend was ill, staying at my place, contagious, the hotel would only be for a few days. Yes, on that flight I'd decided: regardless of his condition, I'd push Matthias out in four days. But that was eight hours ago, I hadn't known something might happen.

And now?

Andrea turned to me again, with those eyes which could've been my eyes, with an expression that could've been my own. Hurriedly I hung a mask of fatherliness on my face – could I disguise my fears?

I said to the receptionist: "If you'd please arrange for the luggage to be brought to the room, we won't be back till six or so."

We re-emerged into the cold and grey day. Narrow cobbled street, old timber-framed houses. Began strolling down the hill towards the main marketplace.

"Look, Papa, there's the fountain my ball fell in." She said it in German.

"Yes," I said.

"You rolled up your trousers but they still got wet, d'you remember?"

I nodded. Of course I did. I tried to smile. We walked on by. And a minute later: "Papa?"

"Yes?"

She'd stopped, was regarding me. "What's the matter?"

I stopped too. "The matter?"

"You're far away."

I shook my head. "I'm sorry."

"Are you sad?"

"Sad? No, Andrea." I shook my head again.

"Are you worried about him, then?"

"Him?"

"You're friend who's ill." She watched me so seriously. Did I look at people like that too?

"Well," I said, "actually he was on my mind, yes."

"Was it he you tried to phone? I thought it was the hotel. D'you want to pop in and see if he's okay? Is that what you're thinking?"

How did she guess? I hesitated. I felt torn, I felt so bad.

"No," I said. "Of course not. He can wait – you're much more important."

"He didn't answer the phone, did he?"

I frowned.

"I don't mind, Papa." She stood there quite straight, her thick hair fell together from the cold damp air, just like Judit's used to do. "I'll walk around a bit. You tell me when and where we'll meet, and I'll be there."

She was making it easy for me.

"No, Andrea."

"Don't be silly, Papa."

We stood a yard apart. She tossed her head, lifting her arms, she was tousling that hair. She shouldn't have done that; I remembered Judit again.

I rescinded. "Okay," I said. "I'm so sorry about this."

"Don't be. Where shall we meet?"

I thought: where would she remember? Museumsbrücke, Frauenkirche, Heilig Geist Spital? No – with the Christmas market on they'd be far too crowded. "Schöner Brunnen?" I suggested. As a three-year-old I'd had to lift her: she'd loved turning the ring, making her wish. "Be a lot of people around – I'll be the one in the funny hat, and the red bobble nose."

She giggled, squeezed fingers on my arm a moment.

"You recall the ring?" I tried another smile.

"Sure."

"And *Christkindlesmarkt*?"

"Oh yeah."

"Well, we'll do that of course – but maybe another day, a bit later when it's dark? More romantic."

"Okay Papa. And meet when?"

I looked at my watch. Ten-past-two. "Shall we say three?"

"Fine."

Then I thought: what if something's gone wrong, what if they arrest me?

"Andrea, give me your mobile number. Just on the off-chance I have to get a doctor for him or something, and it takes a little longer." I took out my wallet, wrote it down.

"You'll have to dial via the States," she said practically.

Thirteen years old and she knew it all. "No problem," I said. Ah, youth's on the ball.

We parted ways.

x x x

As I walked up the steep hill all appeared normal.

No barricades and black Marias, no machinegun nests, or whatever they do when they come to get you. I'd gone via the hotel. Now, with bag in hand, I tried not to hurry, tried to keep calm. I reached my house number. In the big archway no-one lurking in the shadows. Still all seemed normal. I went in, crossed the hall, began climbing the wooden stairs...

"Herr Falk?"

I jumped. Frau Maußer. She'd opened her door from the ground floor flat, stood looking up. Today she had donned a delightful smock of shocking-pink with pineapples – a forceful concoction fresh from her new Winter Collection, perhaps.

"Just back from your travels, Herr Falk?"

"Ah Frau Maußer, *Grüß Gott*," I said. "Yes, that's right." Had she been waiting for me, watching and waiting?

"There's someone in your flat." She sounded flustered.

Oh God, I thought. That's that. Inside I panicked. "Someone?" I queried. For God's sake keep calm.

"Yes. I don't know who – missed seeing him arrive. Herr Eggenhofer's taken poorly so I've been out and about a lot fetching things for him..." She spoke so rapidly, she didn't seem to have to pause to breathe like mortal men "...was up with him yesterday cooking a small something in his kitchen, it must've been about one o'clock and then I heard something above..."

Oh my God. Trust Frau Maußer to hear everything – she had the sharpest ears in town.

"Something?" I said. Had I said that neutrally enough, casually enough?

"Sounded like footsteps." She stared at me.

I stared back. Footsteps? I thought. That can't be – Matthias is far too careful. Could it really have been someone? Maybe it was a mouse or a rat, we had enough of them, or maybe simply her imagination, she had more than enough of that too.

"Ah," I said carefully. "Perhaps it was a rat."

"I know the difference between rats and men, Herr Falk." A hard glint. Was she thinking of her husband?

"Yes, of course," I agreed. The difference, though, must be rather fine.

Was that suspicion in her stare? Or accusation? What was she thinking in that brilliant brain? Was she dying to get in there, take a snoop around, was she hoping perhaps to break up a terrorist cell or my stash of lucrative hookers, or count the hordes of illegal immigrants I smuggle to make ends meet? Had she smelled a rat?

"Perhaps you imagined it," I ventured.

"Oh no I didn't." Indignation now.

I thought quickly: so she doesn't know who it is. And she hasn't rung the police, thank God – that would've been the first thing she'd have told me. But why didn't Matthias answer the phone?

"I went up to your door ever so quietly and listened." Her hands picked at the pockets of her smock in agitation. "But I couldn't hear anyone. If it was burglars I would've. Do you have a visitor, Herr Falk?"

"A visitor?" I stood there, holding the bag, looking down the stairs at her; the bag was getting heavier. Don't put it down, I ordered myself – if you do you'll be here all night.

"There was a car, too..." She was off again "...it was there for hours, parked opposite. Lucky he didn't get a ticket, the time on the parking slip ran out at quarter to one..."

So she noticed things like that too. And no doubt noted down registration numbers. Perhaps in this special case she'd even prised open the bonnet and checked the engine identification as well.

"...it was gone at about four, must've driven off while I was busy sweeping the yard at the back..." Disappointment in her voice, mixed with a shot of self-recrimination; her fingers plucked the dazzling front of the smock "...never seen the car in this area before, one of those ugly big foreign ones. Wonder if it had anything to do with it?" Then at last she took a brief breath.

I blinked. How penetrating her voice was, especially in enclosed spaces.

"Munich number plate..." Her little round mouth was off again...

I swallowed. My mind speeded up. At once I thought: could it be Annabelle's? "Was it a silver Volvo?" I asked with hollow voice.

"That's right! That's what it was!" Already she was reciting the registration number... "You know it?"

Oh my God. Yesterday. So she'd discovered Matthias; she had her key.

"Yes," I said, weakly.

"Not your nice lady friend?"

"Yes."

"Frau Goldberg?"

I nodded dumbly. How on earth did she guess?

"She's from Munich? I didn't know that, she doesn't have a Munich accent..." I could see her storing away the titbit in the vast archives of her hungry brain. "She has a key?" A sharp piercing stare, a reproachful stare; her small beady eyes were going right through me.

"Only for emergencies," I reassured.

She gathered herself, puffing up her portly figure like a party balloon. "So you see, Herr Falk, I was right, wasn't I? I wouldn't mistake footsteps anywhere."

"Ah yes, Frau Mauẞer." What else could I say? "How could I have doubted one as astute as you?" I caught her glance; perhaps that wasn't a word she heard every day. But there was no time now for vocabulary lessons – I had to go. "Thank you so much, Frau Mauẞer, for your care and concern." I braced myself to fade away...

"If there's anything else I can do, Herr Falk, you just..."

"So kind..." I glimpsed her as I turned away; the pineapples had collapsed again, back into their fields of bright pink.

I continued up the flight of stairs.

I was very nervous now. I reached the top, unlocked the apartment door. Stood listening, peering behind me – Frau Mauẞer wasn't following. I entered, closed the door and locked it. Paused again, listening again. No sounds here either, it was silent as the grave. I set down the travelling bag, apprehensive, expecting the worse, went quietly to the bedroom. No-one. The room was empty, the bed had been made. No portable television, no radio. I retraced my footsteps to the hall, whispering his name quietly. Bathroom and kitchen doors open the way I always left them, no-one there either. Hesitantly I approached the living room...

But nobody. No Matthias, no Annabelle.

On the small round English mahogany table, a beautiful bouquet of flowers in a vase. From Annabelle? No note. But yes – from whom else? Her taste, her colours. Had she brought them to welcome me back? Come all the way up from Munich just to do that? And had found Matthias not me? What had she thought, how had she reacted?

I'd half-expected that I might find her here too – that she'd just moved the car yesterday to a more permanent place and come back. So she hadn't. But Matthias? Where was he? I glanced about – then it occurred to me, and I knew. Of course: he was hiding. He couldn't be sure it was I who'd just arrived. He'd think, if Annabelle has a key, God knows who else has one too.

I went through the whole apartment again. He must be somewhere, he'd be hiding well. I told myself he was hardly in a condition to go anywhere let alone travel on his own. I'd already decided when I pushed him out I'd take him in my car to wherever it was he needed to go. Where else can I look then? The fire escape? But the bedroom windows and glass door were locked. I looked anyway. To no avail. Then I thought of films, what people did – squatting up in rafters, or hanging from gutters by their fingernails. I even looked there too. No sign of him.

Matthias had gone.

x x x

Why wasn't I glad then?

Why didn't I tell myself: good riddance? After all, it was what I'd wanted; at last I'd seen the back of him, the risk had paid off, the danger was passed. And now I didn't have to keep Andrea at bay any more, now I could call in at the hotel on my way down to fetch her, could cancel the reservation and apologise, pay what I had to pay.

Yet unexpectedly I experienced a different kind of feeling – of something missing. Yes, another of those holes. I was left hanging in the air again. I'd received no explanations, pursued no clarifying conversations – he'd been too sick, too badly burned for me to even think of that.

There was a question mark. There was so much unanswered; why was this old friend always surrounded by question marks? Was he my friend, still? Or my enemy now? Yes, now that he was gone a part of me wanted him back.

I stood there in the middle of my living room. Beyond the windows the day was so grey.

Then another thought occurred: was it possible that he'd left two or three days ago, that when Annabelle arrived he was already gone and she'd never discovered him? He had a sixth sense, had it served him here too? But if so, then how? Alone, unaided? And if not, perhaps with Annabelle – was it conceivable she'd taken him with her? Had she been the one to tidy everything up, had I unwittingly got her involved? Oh God.

I must ring her at once.

I was looking at the flowers over there on the table. Must ring her anyway. I glanced at the clock. Not much time – Andrea would be waiting. I rang Annabelle's mobile. It was switched off... 'the person you're calling is not available right now, you can leave...' I rang her at home.

"Goldberg." She'd come to the phone very quickly.

"Annabelle," I said.

There was silence down the line. Then: "Where are you?" Her voice was cold.

"I'm in my apartment. Only just got back."

Another silence. More brief. "I called in yesterday." Oh God, yes her voice was so cold. And distant.

"Yes," I said.

"Did he tell you?"

Tell me? She must mean Matthias. She'd found him there, then. "No," I said. "He's gone." So she hadn't taken him.

"Thank your lucky stars."

"Yes."

Another silence. I could almost hear her thoughts. Then she said: "I warned you."

"Yes."

"You didn't listen."

I said nothing. What could I say?

"You are a stupid fool."

"I know."

"I wish to have nothing to do with this."

"Of course not."

"You are endangering the children. And me." Voice like a haughty queen, like disinfectant.

I thought about that one. "It wasn't my intention. That'd be the last thing I'd wittingly do."

"You have, though."

"I realise."

"Totally inadequate."

I took a breath, let it out. "You're very angry."

"Yes I am."

I could find no more words. A blackness was closing in. The silence down the line stretched.

Her voice came again. "Are you involved?" The voice was so hard, so controlled. I'd never heard her this angry before, not even that first time as a stranger in her bed when she caught me with lust in my eyes.

"Involved?" I said.

"In what has been going on here in this country for over a year?"

Oh God, how could she think that? "No," I said.

"Are you lying to me? Did you lie about him?"

"Naturally not. I would never lie to you."

"I cannot believe you."

"You must." The blackness was all around me now. What was she saying? Was it all over – was this her way of saying goodbye?

"Annabelle..." I began.

"I am listening."

Oh that deathly coldness. Like the blanket of death.

"He just turned up."

Yet another of those unbearable silences. It pressed on my ears, it compressed my brain. Why didn't she speak? I had to say something. Into the silence I said: "I thought he was dying."

"You should have handed him over to the police."

"He's my oldest friend."

"A friend, did you say?"

"Yes."

"Are you aware of what true friendship really means?"

I walked into that one. "I think so." I had lost my balance, lost my touch. All was black.

"And true friendship to me?" she said. "I offered you my opinion of him, did I not?"

"You did. But..."

"But what? I told you he was dangerous, I warned you not to go near."

"Yes," I said.

"I felt it in my bones."

"Yes."

"And now it has come to this."

Come to this? It sounded so final. I could read her thoughts now, read between the lines. She was thinking of her children again, wasn't she? She'd sacrifice anything to protect – she was a lioness with her cubs, she sensed danger, she'd even sacrifice herself, and me.

"Annabelle, I'm very, very sorry..." I began. I was searching desperately for the right words, I was on the ropes, I was fighting now. "You see, I was torn in half, between..." I stopped. Started again. "I had this hope, I was trying to be faithful to an old dream."

Again I stopped. Then ended: "He's gone now. It's all over." I shook my head; that sounded so pathetic, cowardly, sounded so weak.

"Is it?" she said.

Yes, I thought. But for some reason I felt my skin contracting. "Yes," I said. I said it firmly. Was I convinced, though? Could I be so sure?

"How do you know?" Her voice was quiet. Yet was there a menace in it?

I suppose it was instinct: just for a second I was looking at Matthias. I saw his guns, my kitchen knife, he was the snake in my bed – I'd offered him my hand, tried to help, he'd bitten me. Now he was destroying the most precious thing in my life – except Andrea.

There was that silence again. It coiled tight around me, it was strangling me.

"I have to talk to you, Stefan," she said. "Not on the phone, though." That was only the third time she'd ever called me by my name, never heard her say it so harshly.

What else could I say? Nothing came – had I said it all?

"Okay," I said. I was falling now.

"Come next weekend if you can find the time. On Sunday."

On Sunday? "Of course I can," I said. "There's nothing more important than this." Sunday? I thought. That's not for seven days. My God, seven whole days of not knowing? She hadn't even offered

Friday evening, or Saturday like we'd always done. Just an hour or two at the end of the weekend, then boot me out? For good?

Then Andrea was there again...

"Annabelle?" I said. I said it quickly; I thought – she won't say goodbye, she'll just put down the phone. "Annabelle – there's one thing I must tell you."

She was still there. She said nothing, she was waiting; I felt helpless, insignificant, small as a worm.

"Andrea's flown back with me. She's here in Nuremberg till after Christmas."

A pause. Was that a hesitation? Then her voice: "How lovely for you."

For me, only for me? She didn't care? How could her voice still remain so cold? I took a breath, was about to say then maybe it'd be better if I came alone, when her voice was in my ear again: "You can bring her too, if you believe it wise, if you think she would like that. Come for lunch."

That stopped me dead. If I believed it wise? What did she mean?

But before I could ask she had put down the phone. I hadn't even thanked her for the flowers.

x x x

I hurried down to the hotel.

Gave a short explanation, a longer apology; they'd been very patient with me. They were kind, too, altogether just charged one night without breakfast. Then I met Andrea – more explanations, equally brief. I think she smelled a rat. But her joy at unexpectedly being able to go back right away to the house of her childhood, the place of her birth, overwhelmed any vestigial query. I took her via the hotel. We each carried a suitcase. It had begun to drizzle.

In the hall we nearly made it, but unfortunately I forgot to warn her and Andrea spoke one or two words. In a flash Frau Mauβer was out through her door, bucket and mop in hand. Or was it Frau Mauβer? For a second I stared. Had she had a little accident or something, had her famous red bucket untimely tipped its contents where they shouldn't? Gone were the pineapples on pink – she had done a quick-change into azure-blue-on-turquoise with blood red buttons. She stopped in her tracks, puffed herself up; she looked like a peacock on display. She glanced between the two of us, didn't recognise Andrea and shot me a glare fit to kill and a frown which said you dirty old man, you baby-snatcher.

I told her who. She nearly dropped her pail.

"Well, I don't believe it, I just *don't* believe it!"

The gushing bombardment began.

Twenty-five minutes later we succeeded in extracting ourselves; my nerves were nearly in shreds. Nevertheless, as we turned to the stairs, I managed to compliment her on her remarkable taste in her latest smock. I surely gained a badly needed plus point for that.

We climbed the old stairs, entered the apartment.

Surreptitiously I watched my daughter; she stood there motionless in the hall beside her suitcases – she looked like a bird just back from migration alighting in its old preserve and carefully checking the lie of the land. Discreetly I withdrew, deposited the suitcases in the bedroom – this would be her room for the duration, I'd get the spare bed up from the cellar for me later or maybe simply sleep on the sofa tonight. When I came out she was just going through the open doorway to the living room; she went in as if walking on eggs. I thought: leave her to it, that's what you'd want in her shoes. I began busying myself in the kitchen checking the pantry and fridge, considering what to cook us later for dinner. No fresh vegetables or fruit – no matter, I'd pop down to...

An exclamation from next door. Sounded unhappy.

I shook my head, I'd been half-expecting it, I knew the reason why. As casually as I could I sauntered in. She stood in the middle of the big room – almost on the spot where I'd stood half an hour before weighed down by thoughts of Matthias's departure, distraught from Annabelle's call. But, unlike me, she was gazing up at the rafters in the sloping roof high above.

"Oh Papa – the Crow's Nest has gone!" Her expression was the disappointed grimace of a child, a small child that's lost its toy.

"Yes," I said carefully. "Sorry about that."

"And I thought I'd be sleeping up there." Her dismay grew, her face downcast, she clutched her hands tight together in front of her unbuttoned winter coat.

"I'm putting you in the bedroom." I produced a wan smile. "You're the guest of honour."

"Oh no – in yours and mamma's bed?" Round uncertain eyes.

"You're a young lady now, you're the princess who needs her privacy." I watched her, added: "And I've bought a new bed since then." Yes I watched her, but I was looking through her, and I remembered the mattress: I could see the old one, the sag in the middle, that broken spring — Judit the wild one, the almost insatiable, on the bed and outside... how often she'd taken me by the tool and towed me there to make a little change from her cupboard or chair; one time I thought she'd snapped it off, she cut the corners too fast, she couldn't wait, how could she always come so quick and then come back for two or three more?

"But why Papa?" Andrea was saying.

Quickly I cast Judit aside, refocused my eyes.

Her neck was craned, she stared at the empty space and the old brick wall rising into the roof. Her fingers were gripping frustratedly now.

"I only built it for you," I explained. "Then you both went away." I'd constructed the gallery up in the rafters, together with a wooden ladder, when she got too big for her cot in with us over by the bedroom window. I'd done it myself with a little help from George and we christened it the Crow's Nest — I'd haul her up in a basket on the end of a rope till she was old enough and, later, she never fell once when climbing. Andrea was a fine climber even at four.

"I kept it nearly three years," I confessed, sheepishly. Feebly I smiled at her. Don't get sentimental, I ordered myself. And don't dare...

But it was too late... like a film unfolding, like an unfurling flag, Judit was coming, she was there again. She'd put Andrea to bed, was coming backwards down that ladder, backside a bell so broad and so fine, and I had to look, I looked up her flimsy loose pink linen skirt...

Andrea was eying me, unhappy still. So I added helplessly: "But then mamma and you didn't return, you know — so..."

Judit was glancing down to watch her step, she caught me peeping, she caught my eye. Her naked feet reached the floor, that flippy skirt being lifted high, *Bhagwan* knickers an orange flame on full display, the swell of female belly exposed, swollen bulge between her thighs — she was coming for me with hungry thumbs hooking, peeling off her pants. Ah, that bushy beard of wiry black hair once more revealed, a hand ripping open my zip and reaching inside grabbing the goodies — I was cast to the floor, just made it to the rug thank God. I was flat on my back, she lowered herself like going to the loo, her squatting body opening wide like she'd practised in Poona for a thousand guys, fertile Artemis in all her fruitfulness parting her wonders and getting astride, impaling her pussy on the best of me or what she held out for the best. She was wriggling and squirming and stirring it around, now bowing forward, now arching back and, on his little string hung from her neck swinging in time with those heavy breasts, *Bhagwan* rocked to and fro staring me accusingly in the eye...

"Oh Papa..." Andrea laid her young hand on my unsteady arm. "Poor Papa."

She gazed at me, she didn't have to gaze up far.

I reached out, Judit was gone, I drew her to me – I hugged her tight.

"Very sorry about your Crow's Nest," I repented into her hair. Yes I hugged her tight, then hurriedly released my grip, didn't want to overdo it. She stepped back, her eyes were dry. And said simply: "Papa, now I want to explore."

Trauma laid to rest, she cast off her coat, continued her prowl in slow-motion round the room – peering, peeping, lifting objects, touching tree plants and orchids... "Oh my, how this one's grown!"... gazing at pictures on the wall and photos in frames, stroking the few things Judit had left, and the new and old things of mine from my travels...

I popped down to the market.

Later that evening, after dinner, we were on the sofa relaxing – me sitting, she curled up against me just the way she used to do when I read her stories as a little girl. I'd got her to ring Sammy and Saul in Pennsylvania to say she'd arrived safely, and then had been discussing some plans for the impending three weeks with her, a few ideas I'd thrown together. Now we fell silent; it was a pleasant silence though. She sipped at her diet *Coke*, I stroked her hair, and I thought: she and I here, it's just like the old days, it's as if a wheel has turned in our lives, as if a circle has closed.

Chapter 30

The following week went by quickly, despite Annabelle being on my mind. The days were well-filled, which was one reason, and my thrill at having Andrea there another. My planning seemed to please her: visits to the *Christkindlesmarkt* to imbue the Christmas atmosphere, going shopping in stores and boutiques, walks around the city reviving her childhood memories. But I think my surprise for her went down the best – behind her back I made contact with the parents of her favourite little kindergarten girlfriend Louise, discovered to my pleasure that the two of them had been pen friends, by letter and by Internet, through the intervening years; secretly I arranged a reunion in a with-it café for the young. Yes, it seemed that turned out rather well. The café bit too.

Next day she only had thoughts and eyes for Louise. Beginning right after breakfast, she was glued to her mobile – messages being sent frenziedly to and fro, they wanted to meet up again at once. So I showed her the way to their meeting place, left them to their own devices.

Back home, I rang Eva.

"Hi," she said. She sounded so good; she'd got all her bounce back. She talked for five minutes non-stop: how the business she'd set up was progressing, how many of her old clients were placing contracts with her now, all the details and the technical side. I only interrupted once with: "Be careful there."

"Why?"

"Your competition clause from the old company forbids you..."

"Deleted. My lawyer forced it through. 'Cos of the extenuating circumstances."

"They'll regret that."

"They're not stupid. Got a new man who's sweeping clean. Cheap leather products from China, different market."

"A new man?" I queried. "What happened to Schultz then?"

"Compensation. They pushed him out, didn't I tell you?"

"You only told me he'd come out of the coma, recovered well."

"Is it important?" she said.

I stopped. Why was I asking? It was like a small voice in my head. "No," I said.

She was off again. I had to wait another five minutes; she was so full of plans, she wanted to share – I was glad she'd landed on her feet. Then, when she was finished I asked: "How's Matthias? How're things there?" I asked it neutrally.

"They're not."

"What d'you mean?"

"Not seen or heard of him."

"I see," I said.

"Have you?"

I hesitated. Didn't answer.

"Well?" she demanded.

So I said: "I'll be down in Munich at the weekend. Will you be at home?"

A pause down the line. I could almost hear her thinking. Then she said: "Something happened?"

"Will you?" I repeated. "Could you find the time?" I'd decided – I was going to tell her.

"'Course I will." She stopped as well. Said nothing else. She had got the message; could she hear me thinking too?

"We'll talk then," I suggested.

"Okay," she agreed.

"I'll bring someone with me."

"Yes?"

"Andrea. You remember little Andrea?"

"You're kidding!" Of course she remembered.

"She's come over for Christmas."

"Don't believe it." Her voice was changed; the impatience evaporated, the hardness had gone. Eva had a soft spot for very few people, but Andrea was one of those few. And even more important, Andrea used to be very fond of her. Was the bond something which might grow again?

"After so long?" she said. "What brought on the change of heart?"

"Judit's dead."

"Jesus."

I didn't speak.

"Well? Do I have to pick it out of your nose?"

I shook my head to myself. "A car accident. I was over there for the funeral last week."

"And?"

"Let's talk at the weekend."

"When?"

"Would Friday afternoon be possible?" I said. "And stay two nights? I'd like to show Andrea around Munich, and give her a bit of time with you."

"Sure."

"But your hands are full, aren't they?"

"Let yourselves in – you know 'bout the key. This is something special. Be back at seven, then I'll cook us some dinner."

"Let me invite you."

"Saturday night you can."

We signed off.

That was Wednesday. On Thursday evening Andrea and I sat at the dining table in my apartment. We'd just eaten. She was pensive. We stayed sitting there; I lit some candles. She stared at the flames, she had something on her mind.

I thought: don't disturb her. I was about to rise to clear the plates, to leave her alone...

"Papa?"

I stood there, looking down at her.

"Does she love you too?"

She was talking about Annabelle. I sat down again. Pushing plates aside I reached across the table, took her hands. "Yes," I said, "I think she does." And I thought: does she still?

She nodded slowly. Simply nodded. Watched me. Her face was very serious; I tried to read her eyes.

After she'd returned in high spirits from Louise the day before, I'd told her about Annabelle's invitation and who Annabelle was –

and about going down to Munich to stay with Eva. She'd agreed at once, showed nothing contrary.

But that was twenty-four hours ago, and now was now.

I held her hands – didn't try stroking them, just held them in mine: twenty-four hours is a long time for people like me, to ponder, to ruminate, to let pennies drop – and Andrea? Had she inherited this from me too?

Carefully I said: "What d'you think about that?"

A small shrug. "Don't know." Still those eyes on me. My eyes.

"Does that make you unhappy?"

"Not sure."

I watched her. Gently I squeezed her hands. "Well I'm glad you're not sure," I said.

She blinked. Looked down at the table.

A long silence. The candles wavered; wax ran down one, ran down to the candlestick. It was windy outside, and wet.

She was frowning.

I knew that frown – it was just like mine.

I said: "Andrea?"

"Yeah?" The eyes lifted to me. They were deep and distant, and sad.

"Would you prefer not to meet her?"

She said nothing. Just looked at me. That look went through me. Was it hurt, was it accusing?

Still she said nothing. She was deliberating, I could feel it. She was thirteen years old, she could have been thirty in that moment. Then she said suddenly, and her voice was controlled: "What's she like?"

And I knew what she was thinking. I knew she was asking something else.

"She's quite different from mamma. Nearly the opposite in fact."

"Is she?"

"There's no-one else like mamma, Andrea." Oh God, what else could I say?

"No?"

"No."

She pursed her lips. Or was she, secretly, biting them inside? No words emerged.

"Listen," I said gently to her. "let's forget about that visit, shall we? We'll just go and have a good time with Eva, and maybe go to the cinema and the dolphinarium and things like that. Okay?"

Those cool grey eyes speckled with brown rested on me, observing me, looking into me and beyond.

"I'll come and meet her, Papa," she said.

"Okay," I agreed.

Then we changed the subject, we turned a page.

And a little later – we still sat at the table, we were peeling fruit, she was a child again – she asked out of the blue: "Papa, could I see the home movies – the ones you made of mamma and me when I was a kid before we left for the States?"

I suppose she saw me flinch, and misunderstood.

"Oh please, Papa."

And I smiled weakly at her. I'd watched those old videos for nearly three years, three long unimaginable years, time and time again. I must've watched them twenty times or more, I'd tortured myself on every frame, at every gesture and every smile...

I shook my head. "I'm sorry," I said, "I don't have them any more." Now it was my turn to stare at the table: I hadn't the heart to divulge the detail, that after a long walk with Estella one autumn afternoon I'd gone home and simply destroyed them.

"Oh gee." A spark of American, a flash of disappointment.

"Yes, I really am sorry," I said.

I glanced up, I tried to brighten, knew before I'd said it, though, she wouldn't be interested: "All that's left is a folder of photos and an album somewhere, I'm afraid." I thought: she's of the computer generation, everything rapid and moving, still photographs would be something she'd never condone.

But she said: "Of you and mamma and me?"

"No – mostly only of you both, you remember?" I looked at her, added in English: "I was the dude with the camera."

"Oh Papa, let's look shall we?"

So I left her sitting there, alone with her thoughts, alone with the candles that were burning low. I went down to the cellar, opened that cupboard I hadn't touched for many years. I'd stored them as far from me as I could; the cellar was the furthest away I could get. There they lay on the top shelf, the album of snaps of her as a baby and Judit as proud mother, and the big folder with its sheets I'd mounted larger photographs on.

I removed the album, flipped its pages: glimpses of Andrea in a pram, on her potty, ah that cute summer bonnet where she sat in the sand. And of Judit holding her high over her head and both of them naked, and crawling with her, oh I shouldn't have taken that one from behind, and Judit breast-feeding her on the rocking chair at the window, how soft the light fell over her shoulder, over her thighs...

I snapped it shut.

There was another album, too – smaller, much older, standing in the corner at the end of the shelf – the one from my own childhood; would Andrea be interested in that? Surely not. What photos were these? Were they the first ones I'd ever taken with that *Leica*? I took the album down from the shelf, I'd forgotten about it, it smelled a bit musty; opened it half-heartedly, leafing the black pages. There was my father at his desk, there was Margareth with Eva both on ponies, there was Matthias on his bike, and Tobias mowing the lawns, Ferdinand-Maria Straße, mother with parasol and father in deckchair. I turned the pages – Tobias and Matthias at athletics, even one of me; I leafed more quickly, then the album fell open on its old binding... I stared at the photos – Tobias in the choir with those silly clothes, in the school orchestra looking so grand, and me on the stage for the school play, me as the soldier and Matthias the...

My eye stopped. Matthias in wig dressed as a woman, dressed as the queen.

I peered. And I remembered. He'd been so convincing, he'd fooled them all, no-one could tell; he was so good he'd almost fooled me too...

My mind made a jump and I was looking at Eva, hearing her voice – the accident, the hotel, Schultz pushed from a window, they said it was a woman who went to his room...

I stood there staring and that little voice was there again.

x x x

"Hey Papa, that's cool – you've still got Herr Eggenhofer's!"

We were in the underground garage, Andrea had just spied the old car.

"Of course," I said.

Right from the start, even as a little girl, she'd insisted a car has to have a name. So for want of anything better I'd nicknamed him that. She stroked the chrome, touched the hood, a wistful smile on her face. It was good to see her smile.

We dumped our overnight bags in the back, got in; sedately we set off for Munich. Rain on the windscreen, the whirr of the wipers. The weather got worse going south.

That evening Eva cooked us a fine meal, although I could see she was tired. She was six months pregnant now, her body swelling, she wore loose clothes. Andrea warmed to her quickly, wanted to know all about pregnancy and helped her in the kitchen while I sat on the sidelines observing – no chance to talk to Eva alone. They both chatted a lot, laughed a lot – in fact they got on like a house on fire. It was very good for Andrea, was good of Eva. She even, on reticent request, let Andrea come in with her to sleep in her bed. And told me next morning Andrea had cried in the night and held her close, had whispered how much she missed mamma.

Oh God, poor Andrea.

I felt so bad; first with Judit, then fate, now with me, we'd pulled her this way and that, we'd torn her apart. I wondered: what would be best for her now?

After breakfast I phoned my mother briefly, and Margareth. Both were in. Then, on a whim, I rang Annabelle as an afterthought, feeling more than a little on edge. I rang to mention we were in Munich already and whether she'd changed her mind. She was at home too, it seemed a good time to reach people; she was still subdued but did I detect a little more softness in her voice? "Why not come around tomorrow at ten, if you would like?" It surprised me, her bringing it forward two hours – was that perhaps a positive sign? She had to go, she then said, I'd caught her on the hop, and again her voice was neutral, there was no hint about how she'd greet me next morning, about what she'd be going to say.

That day in Munich was a domestic day, a family day – for me enjoyable because of Andrea at my side, and our conversations, and coming closer, sharing things, but for outsiders I'm sure it would've been very boring. We followed behind Eva in the car to her new offices, she showed Andrea around for half an hour, explaining everything – and I noticed Andrea hung on her every word. Then we left Eva to herself, she was very busy; I drove us into the city. Next to me she sat absorbed, thumbing SMSs. I parked in the centre, and from there we went sightseeing on foot like the previous afternoon. I took this opportunity to buy some small presents. It was cloudy and cold, but at least the rain had stopped. We met Margareth and the children, Henri and little David, for lunch. It was my intention to draw Andrea back into the family as far as I could, but although Henri was the same age as her and they'd been friends in their early childhood, they'd grown far apart with the years. There appeared no resonance between them. Was this to be the first nail in the coffin of my secret wish? During lunch Margareth filled me in on local news, that her divorce was going through, that the flat she'd rented in Schwabing not far from Annabelle had worked out well, that David was not getting on at school. Afterwards we all went to the zoo and the dolphin show, and on to mother for tea. That was a mistake. Despite the fact that mother had brought us four children into the world she'd had little time or use for us then, had let nanny take over her role, and had even less for her grandchildren now. I could see it upset Andrea.

Was this the second nail?

Oh God, and I hadn't yet dared broach the most dangerous subject — of my moving to Munich in March. Was I a fool to hope? Was there even the slimmest of chances she'd decide she'd come back here to live?

In the evening I took her and Eva out for a meal in a restaurant Eva recommended and often frequented. All I really remember of that evening is what Eva told me. She said it in her chopped abbreviated way, but quietly, in the moment we were alone, while the restaurant owner was standing at the big aquarium with Andrea telling her the names and origins of the water plants and exotic fish. Eva said: "The police were there again — Kommissar Müller. Because of Schultz. I had to go for a line-up. They haven't found the woman seen at the *Four Seasons*. They made us dress up like whores and put on blonde wigs, they forced me to walk to and fro and speak a line — they suspect it was me."

I watched her across the table. Her face was set. I thought — a weird coincidence; I didn't mess about. "I think it was Matthias," I said.

Steadily she returned my gaze. Her eyes were haunted again. "Why?" she demanded.

I told her about the album.

"Jesus." She nodded with a jerk of her cropped-haired head. "What I've been reckoning for weeks."

I glanced over at Andrea. Still absorbed. She was bent, bottom poking out, hands clamped between knees, peering.

"Listen," I said to Eva. Rapidly I told her about Matthias, his turning up in the night, his burns. I avoided all details, didn't bother mentioning Annabelle as the reason why he'd left; I spoke with one eye on Andrea. After a couple of minutes I was finished.

Eva sat there opposite me. Quite still. She didn't speak, showed no surprise. Only her eyes gave her away – a disturbing mixture, of anger, of fear.

So I added: "He's in deep, sister."

"Yep."

"You knew?"

"Suspected." Her voice was dead.

"Maybe he's dangerous too."

"Only if he's cornered." She said it with such certainty.

I shrugged, glanced at Andrea again. "Well, he's in danger, that's for sure."

"What I'm scared of. I've got to stop him."

"You can't do that," I said.

"If they corner him, he'll resist. Then chances are they'll kill him. So I've got to stop him – no choice."

I shook my head. "No chance." She knew Matthias well enough.

"You've got to help me."

"No," I said. "I..." I was thinking of Matthias – his resolution, his iron will. Then I thought of Annabelle. "Listen Eva..." I stopped again. Andrea was coming back.

We had to wait till near bedtime. Andrea was in the bathroom taking a shower – she took one every day, I'd noticed, and sometimes two. I described to Eva how Annabelle had discovered Matthias the day before I returned from the States – I felt it necessary now.

"Shit." She sat there drinking the last of her wine.

"Precisely."

Then I told her about my subsequent telephone call to Annabelle, and her fury. "I'm in her bad books now."

"Shit," she said again.

"She says I've endangered her and the children."

Eva didn't reply.

"What will Matthias do?" I said. "What should he do? His cover's blown as one so poetically puts it."

"Nothing."

"Nothing?" I queried.

"Depends on Annabelle, doesn't it? If she goes to the police she's in the clear and goodbye Matthias. Goodbye you too." She stared at me, coldly. "Does she want to lose you? Thought she loved you."

I shrugged. "If you'd asked me a week ago..." I shrugged again. "But now?" Disconsolately I shook my head. "How well does one really know anyone, sister?"

Chapter 31

Sunday came.

I paused at the big glass front door to the street, key in one hand, cotton bag in the other, Andrea beside me. I glanced at her. She was eyeing me sceptically, uncertainly – like she did at the spoon as a child about to be fed nasty-tasting medicine.

Into the lioness's den, I thought nervously. And to Andrea I said: "She's a kind person – you'll like her." Was there a hollowness in my voice?

Her head was cocked slightly on one side. No I won't, said her eyes, I'm only doing this for you. Oh, how she reminded me of me.

I rang the bell. My God, why did I do that? Did I feel we'd drifted so far apart? Hurriedly I unlocked the door, let us in. We crossed the hall. Behind us I heard the electric lock buzz. I headed for the stairs.

"Not the elevator?" she said.

"Stairs are good for the health."

Grudgingly she followed me. Ah, the modern youth. I omitted mentioning about the fourth floor. At the start of the third she said: "Hey Papa, how many more?"

"Just one after this," I panted. My thigh muscles had turned to lead. She flitted ahead, agile as a mountain goat. At the top, though, she waited, hanging back, well away from the apartment door.

We approached. The door stood ajar. I tapped, pushed it open.

"Hello," I called with apprehension. My heart beat fast, but not because of the climb. My God, I felt so on edge.

Andrea still held back. I put an arm round her. "She won't bite," I whispered. I tried to smile. She's going to bite me though, I thought.

But she didn't. Not right away, at least.

We had entered the long hall, Annabelle was coming towards us with Martina at her side and little Marcel trotting close behind. They were coming from the kitchen. Faint smell of fresh coffee. Oh how gracefully Annabelle moved. Nervously I watched her face, her eyes, watching for all the warning signs. But her smile was inscrutable, gave nothing away, it was more the smile of a queen greeting guests come to court.

A slender arm reaching, fingers lightly stroking my cheek. A flash of her eyes looking into mine, green and bright — what were they saying? A kiss — brief but warm, moist lips on my mouth. Could that be a redeeming factor? Then quickly she withdrew, her attention turned fully to Andrea, and her hands too. They took both of Andrea's in hers...

"Andrea," she said softly; she put so much warmth in the word. "I'm Annabelle." They held Andrea's a moment more, just long enough, not too long. No attempted kiss, no hug, no overwhelming.

Andrea stood stiff. Like an animal cornered, not daring to move. All the world could read what went through her head. With set expression she looked at Annabelle, glanced at me, back to Annabelle.

"Hi," she said, clipped American style. Resistance in her gaze, and on her tongue.

I watched Annabelle smile, I was wincing inside — there was warmth in her smile too, it was quiet and understanding. She touched Andrea, just for an instant, on her arm, just like she'd touched me. Then she was turning, saying matter-of-factly: "Andrea, meet my daughter Martina."

"Hello," said Martina. She wore a very pretty dress, one for special occasions. She held out a firm, friendly little hand and Andrea, looking down her nose, coolly, diffidently took it.

"Hello," she answered.

"I'm Marcel," said little Marcel, tripping forward. "Andrea, Andrea."

"My brother," explained Martina like a miniature adult. Then, reaching up to me and standing on tiptoe, she gave me a big hug and kiss. "Hello, Uncle Stefan." Another hug.

Andrea watched. Her eyes were unhappy, lonely, like a stranger left out in the cold. Uncle? they said.

"Hello, Uncle Stefan," echoed little Marcel. I had to stoop lower this time for the greeting, for that big wet kiss I always received on one cheek. "Are those presents?" he asked coyly. Inquisitive eyes, a tiny tug at the bag.

"Don't be rude," Martina ordered sternly, pulling him away.

And Annabelle said gently to Andrea: "Give me your coat, my dear."

But Martina was quicker: "I'll take it," she pronounced, busying herself. And to Andrea, businesslike: "We take off our outside shoes here too, you see. I'll give you slippers." She was taking charge, taking Andrea by the hand, leading her – quite the little lady. At the big antique cupboard I heard her say: "You get special slippers because you're one of the family, because you're Uncle Stefan's…"

Annabelle was shaking her head in silence. I just stood there helplessly.

"Do they fit properly?" Martina, like a small mother hen.

"Sure."

"Come along then – now I'm going to show you around."

"Martina." It was Annabelle. Firmly.

Martina looked round.

"I'm certain you mean it well, little snail, but you should ask Andrea first what she would like."

"Sure," said Andrea again. She spoke to Martina, didn't look at Annabelle. "Let's go."

And off she went, expressionlessly, being drawn by a six-year-old hand.

"I want to come too," said Marcel.

"No, Marcel." Annabelle again. "You come along please with Uncle Stefan and me."

Disappointment. A downcast frown in the little face.

"Marcel?" I said.

The start of a tantrum just round the corner. Defiantly: "Yes Uncle Stefan?"

"You guessed right." I held up the bag. "I've got something for you."

"Oh you have, you have!" A rapid change of expression like a slate wiped clean, big excited eyes, a joyous smile – Marcel jumping up and down, clapping his hands, then tugging at me.

We went into the kitchen. "Sit yourself down with Uncle Stefan," Annabelle said.

He did so obediently. Fidgeting, more excitement. I noticed she'd left the door wide open. I rummaged in the bag, peering into it, glancing at Marcel, rummaging again, making a game of it like I knew he loved. Till I drew out the toy he was almost in a frenzy.

Annabelle returned to the table with a latte and a glass of water, set them beside me. Then stood there behind us, hands leaned on our chair backs, watching little Marcel. He had the sealed cellophane undone in a matter of seconds, he had very quick, nifty hands – and he found the switch to activate it with no help from me.

"Oh, the football one," he cried. "It's number three, I haven't got number three!" Small fingers pressed at the keys, figures were flashing onto the tiny screen. It was one of those children's electronic games. They'd promised me in the store on pain of death it was one which didn't beep or bleep or jingle or jangle or any of those things that fray the nerves of people like me...

Deft fingers tapping, little head bowed, fascination in his face – the pure concentration of the very young. I watched a moment, amused; at four years old he was mastering the game already. I'd have probably taken half an hour reading the instructions before beginning to comprehend.

"Marcel?" Annabelle was walking fingers through his mop of fair straight hair. No reaction. "Marcel?"

He side-glanced, frowning. Glowing screen between his small hands.

"Haven't you forgotten something? What do you say to Uncle Stefan?"

Focusing eyes. Wriggling fingertips. Then comprehension jumping in. "Thank you, Uncle Stefan..." He twisted, ducked towards me, his little face burrowed into my shirt. "Thank you, thank you." Muffled. Then an impatient jerk – he'd returned to his game...

Annabelle was sitting down the other side of me. My nervousness leapt. "Good of you," she said.

I just nodded slowly. Tried a slight smile.

She blinked. Those clear green eyes; a spark of kindness glowing. She had swung her chair to face me, was leaned back, legs crossed. Wide-cut loose trousers, tight at the top, big floppy roll-neck pullover hiding their secrets. I looked back at her eyes –

wanted to reach out and touch. But I didn't dare. What was she thinking now, what should I say?

I decided: say nothing. Wait and pray.

"So he has gone," she said.

I swallowed. She was talking about Matthias; she was getting straight to the heart of the matter, she was never one to mess around.

"Yes," I said.

"When?"

"I imagine soon after you left." I shifted on the chair, crossed my legs too. "I suppose that night. Before I returned from the States."

Her eyes were staring, the kindness had gone. They were neutral now. She didn't speak.

"Thank God," I added.

"Thank God?" Eyebrows raised briefly, thin lines. She'd plucked them again, like she often did. Funny habit.

"Yes," I said.

One of her arms lay on the table. It was naked nearly to the elbow; the pullover sleeve had ridden up. She said flatly: "Recount to me what happened, please." She spoke in a normal voice, not loud, not quiet, ignoring Marcel.

Was she giving me a chance? Did she really want to hear? I glanced over my shoulder at Marcel, noticed my latte standing there still. But he was busy with his game, only had eyes for the flickering screen, lost in an electronic world. I suppose, though, he wouldn't have understood us, even if he'd wanted to.

I drew the latte and water closer, turned back to Annabelle. She was sitting there waiting, patiently – she looked so composed. Would it make any difference what I said?

I sipped at the latte. Then briefly told her what had happened, just the essentials. When I stopped I kept watching her, forced myself not to glance away. She looked grim, didn't speak.

So I said with penitence: "You came to welcome me home." I meant the day she discovered Matthias. "That was very good of you – you even brought flowers. Circumstances distracted me from thanking you."

"They know about him, they have been searching for him for weeks." She had ignored me. "It came on the News while you were over in the States."

That made me sit upright. Oh God, was that true? Why hadn't Eva told me?

"I didn't hear." I said it humbly. This was it – this was the subject to be treated with respect, handled like eggs. I knew everything depended on how I spoke, what I said – was my future hanging in the balance? "What did they say?" I asked carefully.

"Enough to condemn you." She sat there so still, she sat like a rock. "On the night of the kidnap in Nuremberg somebody else was also severely burned. It appears this someone was a bodyguard, not a kidnapper as at first assumed. This person is now recovering. According to the press he was able to give a description of your friend to the authorities within days of the attempt." She paused for a second. "You placed yourself and others in even greater danger than you imagined."

"I see," I said. Again said it carefully, guardedly. And I thought: did Matthias know – did that bastard know the odds were so...?

A gurgle of laughter from Marcel. More faint rapid tapping of keys.

"You appreciate what that means?" She said it calmly. There was a coldness coming into her voice like the coldness I'd heard on the phone.

"I do."

"All the time you were hiding him they knew about him and they were not far behind, they could have traced him to you. Then you would not be sitting here now."

I nodded. Dumbly.

"And they still could, Stefan. No doubt they are continuing their enquiries. And if they receive a lead and are successful?" She paused. Her thin eyebrows had raised again. They made wrinkles like waves on her forehead, on the colony of freckles, they rose up to her perfectly combed red hair. "It would create a domino effect. You will fall, this doctor also, and I by association for concealing the fact. And through me the children would then suffer." Her chin had risen, she stared down her nose. "Do you see what you have done? Your foolish action has turned us into accomplices to a crime and we now carry a share of the guilt."

Still she spoke calmly; the coldness was plain to hear. But, in contrast to that telephone call, there seemed no anger now. Had the intervening days helped her take bearings – was she offering an olive branch, was she considering whether to let me off the hook?

I nodded again slowly, said nothing, tried to return that steady green gaze.

"You have placed me in an impossible position. Were I to do my duty as my conscience dictates and notify the authorities, I should automatically incriminate you, not to mention this doctor. If I do not, however, in principle I face the same dilemma as you. In order to protect someone I am forced to break the law."

I spread my hands. I said: "Annabelle, I really am sorry..."

A triumphant little cry from behind me, a chortle of glee. "I won, Mamma, I won!"

"Good, Marcel," Annabelle said. "You're a clever boy." She didn't even glance away.

"Can you forgive me?" I began.

"I shall try level two now, Mamma. Uncle Stefan, do you want to watch?"

"Not right now." I didn't look either. "Perhaps later."

"Is it a question of forgiving?" she said.

"I hope so." I shrugged. "Unfortunately I can't put the clock back, I can only express genuine regret for my thoughtlessness."

"Isn't it more a question of the future?" she asked. So serious, so stern. And it didn't exactly appear like a question. "We have to look forward and learn from this mistake."

That sounded very wise.

"Yes," I agreed. I think I would've agreed to anything to get myself off that hook. "What do you suggest?" I watched her, still nervous.

"I would say we ensure that it can never happen again."

Again she'd said we; it sounded like sharing. There was such generosity in the word.

"It never will," I said sincerely. I really meant it.

"No?"

"No." I changed position on the chair, crossed my arms, it was hard to return that gaze.

"I want us to be sure."

On the table her arm moved; she was slowly leaning forward. "I do not intend to lose you," she said. A hand was reaching out.

"No," I said. I swallowed. How sweet were those words. Was she really offering me a reprieve?

"He could still cause us damage. I told you, people like this are of the destructive kind. Don't you understand?"

I glanced down at her hand coming close. It was pale, almost white, there were the patchy freckles I'd learnt to love dotting its back.

"Of course," I said. "I've known it since he and I were young." I shut my eyes...

She was touching me. I could scarcely believe it; her fingers lay on my folded arms. They were back again, just like I'd prayed. Oh God, I felt so small. "He wants to change the world," I said, talking to my lap.

"He never will."

The fingers were firm, they played on my flesh. Her voice was strong too – she was so much stronger than I.

"I want you to promise me something."

"Anything," I said. Again I said it with the humility which was due; I'd do anything to win back the trust.

"Do not let him threaten our lives again."

I forced myself to raise my eyes. "How can I do that?"

She didn't reply. She just watched me, and her eyes said you'll find a way.

I sat there. She was touching me again, that was all that mattered in that moment, the worst of the burden had fallen away. Imperceptibly I nodded. I was thinking of Matthias now. And then I thought of Eva; I remembered her words. I sat there cross-legged, Annabelle's arm rested in my lap – I felt as weak as a child.

Seconds passing...

Nothing spoken. Sounds of little Marcel fiddling with his toy. And thoughts of Matthias again. How can one stop a person like that, doesn't he have to stop himself? Can the devil be led into temptation too, can a serpent eat its own tail?

A small squeeze on my arm. I concentrated.

"Tell me, how did things go in the States?" she said. Change of tone; she'd made a jump.

I shrugged. "About as expected."

"And with the funeral?"

"Depressing. It rained." I shrugged again. "I hate funerals – they remind me that nothing stands still, that life can be very short."

"Mmm." A pensive smile. Another squeeze, gentle, considerate. I sensed a reservation still, but weren't things looking up? "That sounds like my philosopher again," she said.

And I thought: yes, thank God, and that sounds almost like the old you.

She was releasing my arm. But she left her hand on my lap. She knew what I was thinking, didn't she? Was glad about that.

"And what about Andrea?" Her eyes didn't leave me. "How did she take everything, how is she coping?" She had lowered her voice now.

"She was wonderful." I nodded. "She's being very brave." I began to speak more quietly too.

"I am relieved." Another distant, thoughtful smile. "I am sure you are contributing a great deal."

"I don't know about that."

"You are the most important person for her now."

"You think so?"

"I know so."

"I fear not..." I hesitated. "She's already decided to return to the States at the start of January."

"To where? Where will she stay?"

"With good friends of hers and her mother's, in Pennsylvania. Saul and Sammy. They're taking over legal guardianship till she comes of age."

"You made his acquaintance?"

"Yes. And Sammy's. They're both good reliable people. Saul Bernstein's a lawyer. He's..." I paused: I nearly stumbled. "He's like a father to Andrea."

I watched Annabelle. Watched her slow knowing nod. She said:

"When did Andrea decide she will only be staying till January? Before she flew over with you?"

"Yes."

She stroked my lap. "That is fully understandable, isn't it?"

"I suppose it is."

"Oh it is, poor child. She has to take her bearings, she needs time." She watched me. "Who knows what the future has in store?"

"She's spent the last half of her life in the States. That's pulling her too."

"I am sure."

"And the Bernsteins have been close friends for years, it seems."

"Friends are friends, blood is blood," Annabelle said.

That startled me slightly. Like her father. I watched her; was that the Jew in her speaking?

"Give her time, my philosopher."

I just nodded.

"I reiterate – you are the most important one in her life now."

I shook my head. I shrugged.

"And she is the most important person in yours," she added. A calm steady gaze.

"She's very important, yes," I said. "But you're..."

There was a sound outside in the corridor. I hesitated, turned my head. Martina and Andrea were coming through. And Andrea had stopped. I noticed she was holding Martina's hand, and Martina's hair looked different. She stood there – looking at me, looking at Annabelle's hand on my lap, a stern expression on her face. Or was it hurt?

I felt embarrassed. How much had she heard? We'd been speaking quietly, but...

"Andrea, Martina." Annabelle was turning too. "Come along and join us."

But Andrea remained standing, let go the hand.

Annabelle spoke again: "Andrea, I was asking your father about you and your home in the States because you are the most important subject..." She spoke so openly, directly, it was so refreshing. "Are you angry at me?"

Andrea stared at her, at me, back to her. Her expression lost a little of its hardness. "No," she said.

"I am glad. Now come along and join us if you want. Little snail..." she turned her eyes to Martina, "...first show Andrea what we have to drink, please, she might like something. We will be starting the lunch in a minute."

Unhurriedly she withdrew her arm from my lap.

The two girls were behind the kitchen island at the open refrigerator. I heard Andrea speaking. Martina giggled. A rattle of bottles and tins. They seemed to be getting on quite well.

I glanced back at Annabelle. She smiled a subdued smile, nodded briefly. "Time is a good healer," she said.

"Healer for what?" That was little Martina, sharp as a knife. She was crossing to the table carrying two cans of diet cola, followed by Andrea with glasses and straws.

"For everything, little snail," Annabelle said calmly. She was leaning back on her chair. "Now that looks pretty." She held out a hand as Martina came past her, and gently took her by the arm, inspecting her hair.

"Andrea did it for me." Martina stood proudly, turning around, a pleased smile on her small self-confident face. Drawn back hair, bundled behind her head and pierced with what looked like chopsticks.

"Very artistic, Andrea my dear."

Once more Andrea held back. She cast a glance at Annabelle, cool and brief — I'm not your dear, I want nothing to do with you, said her eyes.

Annabelle just smiled, a wistful smile, leaning back again. And Martina continued her way round the end of the table.

"Well, and what else have you two young ladies been occupying yourselves with, apart from hairstyling?"

Martina, somewhat bashfully: "We looked through all your cosmetics and stuff on your dressing table."

"Uh-huh. So you snooped round there too, did you, little snail?"

"Was that all right, Mamma?"

"That was all right."

"And Andrea helped me with my homework." Martina pulled two chairs out, seated herself. "You can sit here," she said to Andrea, patting the seat, looking self-assured and quite the little lady, although only half the age. And across the table: "She's very clever, Mamma."

"I am sure she is." Annabelle nodding seriously. "She has a very bright father, and her mother was too, from what Uncle Stefan has told me."

Andrea shot her another look, a quick intensive stare, unreadable. Said nothing. The hiss of cans being pressed open, *Pepsis* being poured.

Annabelle said: "Thank you, Andrea. That was very sweet of you."

Andrea just gave a curt nod, sipped at her straw, watching me over the glass. I saw she was still doing her best to ignore Annabelle. Then she dipped her head to Martina and quietly asked her something. I didn't quite catch it.

Martina answered importantly: "He's not my *real* uncle, of course. But we've always called Auntie Margareth that and she isn't an auntie either, so Uncle Stefan said I can call him uncle." She sucked the straw, holding it with both hands, concentrating on what she was doing.

I watched Andrea sitting there upright and stiff, staring at Martina for several seconds. I wondered: oh God, what's going through her head? Then she said, unexpectedly, in an almost adult voice: "That's okay by me – I'm sorry your papa died, I know just how you feel." And she laid an arm over Martina's small shoulder. So they've been talking together about things like that too, I thought. Seated there a good head taller, displaying that sudden tenderness, Andrea looked almost maternal, older than her years...

A small cry. Followed by a moan. Marcel's little fists drummed the table in fury. "It beat me, Mamma, it beat me."

Martina's head turned sharply; she seemed to notice him for the first time. "What's that you've got?" she demanded, jumping to her feet, Andrea's arm forgotten.

"A present, a present – from Uncle Stefan," Marcel said in his tiny sing-song voice. "For *me*," he added, pointedly.

Martina stretched over the table towards him, lying on her tummy but still not quite able to reach. "Let me see."

"It's not for you." He gathered the gadget, pulling it closer.

"What game is it?"

"Football Three."

"Oh, that." A grimace, disgust. She wriggled back, righted herself, straightening her pretty dress; her eyes were now like searchlights pointed powerfully on me.

"Uncle Stefan?" Said coyly. She hadn't sat down again.

"Yes, Martina?" I looked across at her. I tried my best look of innocence.

"Do you have a present for me too?" She tugged at her puffed cuffs expectantly. Oh those eyes. They could melt the hardest heart.

"A present?" I echoed.

Beside her Andrea looked cool again, and withdrawn.

"Oh," I said, and attempted a crestfallen frown. "Actually, I thought you and Marcel might like to share the..." I let the sentence trail off.

"What, *football*?" Repugnance and disappointment.

"Little snail?" Annabelle was leaning towards me again. "That is impolite. One may not ask for presents, you know that perfectly well."

"But Mamma..." The searchlights swept away, and fell.

"Now sit down please, and don't be greedy."

Annabelle had lain a hand softly back on my thigh.

"You're smiling," Martina said accusingly, staring at her again. "Why're you smiling then? That's not fair."

"I said sit down, please."

Obediently, but with obstinacy, she seated herself. Cast me a glance fit to kill.

I stooped to the bag on the floor. "Oh," I repeated. "What on earth is this?" I withdrew the book I'd bought which they'd wrapped in the store as a present, half-rose and handed it over the table to Andrea. "Just a little something," I said to her.

"Oh Papa." A slight softening of her cool stern countenance. "You shouldn't have."

"Shouldn't I? But I wanted to." I didn't dare glance at Martina.

Her fingers carefully opened and removed the wrapping paper. "Oh Papa, no." She picked it up slowly, like something she'd lost and never thought to find again, pressed the big book to her breast. "You noticed," she said simply.

I just smiled across at her. I'd seen her pick it out in the bookstore when she wasn't watching while I sought a book for Martina, I'd seen the look in her eye.

"Thank you." She smiled a small smile at me, chin on the edge of the book.

I rummaged under the table again, taking my time; Annabelle was stroking my thigh. "Ah, what have we here?" I said quietly. Took out the book of horses, also wrapped, placed it on the table before me. "Now I wonder who this could be for, for Annabelle perhaps?" I peeped at Martina, still sitting in silent frustration.

Oh those big eyes opening wide again. A rapid glance at her mother – then she leapt up, pushing back her chair, ran round the end of the long table, stopped next to me.

"Oh thank you, Uncle Stefan, thank you!" Excitement, anticipation; a small impatient hand, fingers itching to grab. But she didn't – had she learned her lesson? – she waited, side-glancing at her mother, like the athlete tensed at the line waiting for the gun.

"Little snail?" Annabelle didn't stop stroking my thigh.

"Mamma?" Hopping up and down.

"Patience is a virtue, virtue is a grace."

"Yes, Mamma." Trying to stand still. Like a coiled spring.

"And will you remember Mr Manners in future?"

"Yes Mamma, I promise."

I was picking up the book for her. Annabelle smiled and nodded, giving her tummy a gentle poke.

Marcel had been quick, but Martina's hungry fingers were faster; they ripped off the wrapping before I could blink and grasped hold of the shiny book. Like two other young girls in her circle of friends she adored anything to do with horses, was just coming into the phase...

"Thank you so much, Uncle Stefan!" Book gripped in hand, she hugged me where I sat, overwrought with happy relief; I received a lingering kiss on each cheek. Then, in new haste, as she freed me and turned her head in a whirl, a chopstick almost picked out my eye.

"Look Mamma, it's my favourite series." The book was joyously waved in Annabelle's face.

"Slowly does it, little snail." Annabelle patted her bottom as she danced past – then rose from her chair, withdrawing her hand from my thigh. "All right folks, I am going to start the lunch..." And to Martina plonking herself down next to Andrea again: "Ten minutes, then I want you to please come and assist me."

"Can I help too?" I asked.

"Stay put please." Said over her shoulder.

As soon as she had walked away Andrea stood up; I watched her coming round. Opposite me Martina was engrossed in her book, turning illustrated pages, and next to me Marcel continued playing with his game.

"Papa." She hunkered down beside me, put her arms around me, cheek on mine. "That was a lovely present, thanks a lot." Her mouth was very close to my ear.

"I didn't know you were so keen on tennis."

"Sure. I play every weekend, and Wednesdays. All winter too in the halls." Arms still round my neck, cheek on cheek.

"You must be good then," I said.

"Not bad."

"How good?"

"Well – my pro says I could take it up seriously."

I pressed her shoulders, drew her face away so I could see her. "That's great, Andrea. Congratulations."

"He says he could find a sponsor."

"Would you like that?"

She stopped and rose, she let me go. "Mamma said no."

"Why?"

"She said too much stress, because I have my schooling too."

I noticed: she spoke of Judit in the past tense for the very first time. Was that a good sign? "That's right," I said. "You shouldn't neglect that." I watched her serious eyes. "And although you're already thirteen, you still have lots of time to discover what else you like and what you're good at."

"I like ballet and theatre."

"Hey," I said. "That's great too. To participate in, or just to watch?"

"I do ballet classes once a week, and I've acted in all our school plays."

I smiled at her, at those earnest eyes that looked so much like mine...

"I go to ballet school too." It was Martina, talking over the table. She'd glanced up from her book.

"Little snail, you are not to interrupt people in the middle of their conversation." Annabelle calling from across the kitchen.

"But Mamma, I wasn't interrupting."

"Yes you were." Called again. "Anyway I should like you to come and help me now. You have lots of time later to read your book."

"But Mamma..."

"No more buts."

I winked at her, turned back to Andrea. "So you see," I said, "you have talent in several fields – mamma was right about tennis. How would it be if you don't tie yourself down to any one thing to the exclusion of others too soon?"

"That's what mamma said too – she said I might be good at acting one day."

Then that was that. She'd dropped her eyes, turned away.

I nodded. Ah yes, I thought – typical of Judit to say that. She would've made a good actress herself. Bet my boots she'd have played all the most dramatic roles like *Who's Afraid of Virginia Woolf* and *The Taming of the Shrew*...

Andrea was round the other side again, she'd gone back to her book.

Little Marcel beside me still tapped at his keys, so I swung my chair to him and watched him play, but I wasn't really looking too hard.

The lunch preparations continued, and halfway through, unsolicited, Andrea put her book aside and helped Martina lay the table – after which she started helping with the food. Surreptitiously I observed her now and again: she kept her distance from Annabelle, ignoring her, but Martina she showered with attention, showing patience and even tenderness. I didn't know why, but like big sister with small sibling she had taken Martina under her wing. Perhaps it was from loneliness, or because she was an only child.

We ate at midday.

By which time I had just about managed to master the secrets of Marcel's toy that he had grasped in five minutes. I believe experts call this the new wiring of the youthful brain; I imagine mine must look more like barbed wire.

That lunch was not a very happy affair, thanks to my daughter Andrea. Wherever Annabelle could she drew Andrea carefully into the conversation but in return received only curt over-polite replies and eye contact reduced to absolute minimum. I attempted the same with hardly more success. Effectively Andrea drove an icy wedge between us and her.

It irritated me. But I kept my mask in place, disguising. Behind it the insult stung me, or was it a sense of loss? Annabelle felt it though; she knew me too well. She continued smoothing corners, doing it with grace – she behaved like the professional mother who understands the moods of the young, who knows that nothing lasts. In fact the only distraction I experienced during lunch was created by her too, when I gave her Rousseau as a small present; her pleasure radiated like a lamp.

"*Emile*," she said. Smiled. I thought: so dry and intellectual. But Annabelle was the intellectual one. She held the book in her hands: "Did father tell you?"

I shook my head. "A little bird." I'd not found the title some while ago when going secretly through her ordered bookshelves; that was the only reason I knew.

The meal came to an end.

Andrea at once took up her mobile, began thumbing keys – and Martina leaned close to her, watching in fascination. Marcel switched on his electronic game again; it had sat all the time beside his impatient hand like paradise postponed.

"Espresso?" Annabelle said to me.

I nodded. "I'll do it." I got up, went round behind the island. And while I stood fiddling with the machine I heard her telling the children they should feel free to do and go where they wanted. Murmurs, then scrapes of chairs.

I returned with steaming cups. The children were gone.

"Thank you, my philosopher," Annabelle murmured. She still sat at the table, was holding up the book. "I have a great respect for Jean-Jacques Rousseau." She kissed me. I found it hard to smile.

She watched me, frowned. And laid the book aside. "You are irritated."

"Yes," I said.

"Why?"

I shrugged. Said nothing.

"Because of Andrea?"

"Because of the way she's behaving toward you."

"It is quite natural," she said.

"I find it rather childish."

"She is a child."

"She's old enough to know insulting you is not on the books."

"She is not insulting me – of course she isn't. Now stop this."

So I stopped. I shook my head.

She leaned on an elbow on the table, chin in palm, calmly considering me. "She is a little jealous, that is all. She wants all your attention for herself."

"That I suppose I can understand," I said.

"But it will pass. When the novelty wears off she will be able to accept me and share you again. It is a learning process, you see. I should not be surprised even if she later changes her mind about staying in the States."

No. I couldn't believe that – she'd just said it to sooth. "This is my aspiration," I confessed. Yes, this was my dream. "But not my expectation."

"Then be patient."

I bowed my head.

"You have done everything excellently up to now."

"I thank you for your generous words," I said.

She watched me. "Have you also told her you will be moving to Munich?" She was watching my eyes.

"No," I said. That was the coward in me. "Should I have?"

"There is no hurry, is there?"

"When should I?"

"I am certain you will sense it when the time is ripe." She took a calm breath. Then, without a pause or change of tone, she said: "When shall we start house-hunting?"

I blinked. House-hunting? I had to adjust to the jump. We'd touched on the subject late September, not returned to it since. I stared at her. She was serious? Despite Matthias, was the situation sufficiently out of the danger zone, then?

"I should say soon," I said slowly. "After Christmas?"

"In early January when Andrea has left, perhaps?" She made a tiny pause now, produced another small smile. "If she leaves," she added quietly.

"Yes," I said neutrally.

"And when we do, we shall keep Andrea in mind. Enough space to accommodate her too, a room of her own."

Ah, I thought: so she didn't make a jump after all. I returned her gaze, nodded again.

She sat there beside me; she was sitting on the very same chair she had been that first morning, that fateful Friday. I thought: my God, how much water has flowed under the bridge since then. I tried an unsuccessful chuckle: I didn't know what to say.

She leaned forward – she was taking both my hands in hers. She said: "My philosopher, don't be so pessimistic."

She'd seen through me again. So I tried a smile instead, but it came over crooked. I held my tongue.

"This has been a shock for you too, do you realise? The fact of Andrea re-entering your life. You have to take your bearings, just like her."

"Yes," I said, carefully. "I believe, in your wisdom, you're right." How good those hands felt – it wasn't long ago I'd thought I'd lost them for ever.

"And it is a big responsibility for you."

Had to reply to that one. "Actually I don't see it that way. Responsibility, yes – but not big, not a load." For God's sake don't take your hands away.

"It means she will be partly taking you from me for a while, of course."

Taking me from her? I thought: God, what does she mean by that? I said: "Well, only till early January. That's not long." Is she hinting that Andrea will drive us apart, is she wishing to soften the blow? I watched her, waiting for some revealing sign, or a word of clarification, praying for redemption.

But none came. This time it was her turn to maintain silence.

Beneath her gaze my eyes fell away. I turned my hands and held hers fast. Thin strong fingers entwined in mine. My brain was on the move again, leaping, whirling, searching, looking at all the possibilities, peeping in all the cracks...

Rapidly I glanced up: she had asked a question – something about suburbs. Could it really be she was back to the subject of where to live, could it be my mind had simply been overly self-destructive?

"Yes," I said. "That sounds like a grand idea." I produced a worldly and nonchalant smile.

"And we could rent or buy, depending on the offers, wouldn't you say?"

"I would," I agreed. Right now I'd readily agree to just about anything.

She was taking her hands away, her fingers slipped out and were gone. I offered another ingenuous smile, I managed to convince myself she'd only done that because she needed them for scratching herself or smoothing those trousers along her thighs, or maybe for gesticulation.

That was the last time that afternoon she touched me, until we came to say goodbye. We left about five, Andrea and I, she walked us to her apartment door, and the echo of her words about Andrea, and about Matthias, were only there in my brain for a moment. We held each other, and kissed, it was just like before, just like the way it had always been. It was, wasn't it? I watched her eyes in that second, I could feel her feelings meeting mine, they were like a mirror – yet, was it only my imagination, or in their reflection could I detect a tiny crack?

Chapter 32

I was right; I'd felt it in my bones. She didn't change her mind and on the second day of January Andrea flew back to the States.

My telling her of my plans to move to Munich had, of course, tipped the balance – assuming there'd been any balancing in her head to do. Even the New Year's celebrations, so typically German and which she'd adored as a child, hadn't seemed to awake any nostalgia in her now worldly thirteen-year-old eyes: hot *Glühwein* in mugs warming cold hands, snow on the old pitched roofs, thousands of fireworks public and private at the stroke of midnight lighting up the whole of the sky. She'd loved the kids' torchlight parade, though, to which her girlfriend Louise had invited her – flickering flames, burning pitch smoky in the night, the crocodile of children winding through the medieval streets and up the hill to the castle ramparts, while Louise's parents and I admired things discreetly from a distance. I'd felt fatherly, full of pride, standing there, breath clouding the air, praying she'd change her mind.

Yes, two days before, there'd been tears in her eyes as I told her I was moving to Munich. And I realised: she doesn't like changes, just like me. But nothing stands still, even for ones like us; even the most beautiful fruit if left hanging too long on the tree gets overripe and falls.

In fact, up to the first of January, the chances hadn't looked quite so bad: her German was improving steadily and she began to sound like a native, she was also spending more and more time with

Louise, staying overnight with her at whim, and making other new friends. We both grew closer too, I even thought I'd won her heart for good – I treated her and Louise to a trip to Stuttgart, the Planetarium then live ballet in the evening, driving over and back on the day getting home very late, and afterwards she hugged me the way she'd never hugged me before.

Despite all this, though, she flew back as planned. It left me lame, another hole. My God, how I missed her.

I gave in my notice in writing for the apartment and the parking space. I did it with a stone in my belly. A little voice in my head said don't do it – stay. It also said: you don't want to lose Annabelle, but couldn't you keep her and live on alone? I was too late to catch the quarterly deadline at the end of March, had to accept continued tenancies till halfway through the year. I'd procrastinated, should've done it before Christmas. Had I perhaps also subconsciously been keeping a tiny door open in case Andrea decided to stay? What would I have done had she said: "Papa, I'll stay here for ever if you stay in Nuremberg"? But she hadn't, had she? So that bit was academic now.

Time passed.

January went, the first week of February too. I was fully occupied – winding up the work at the firm in Nuremberg, setting up new programmes with Cornelia in Munich and giving moral support to Eva who was now in her ninth month of pregnancy – and on top of that looking at apartments and houses with Annabelle; it all helped fill the hole. I heard from Andrea from the States only sporadically at first, then that petered out; it was a bit like those years ago with Judit when she left, out of sight out of mind, it was back to business as usual.

Baby Daniel arrived three weeks prematurely on the 14th of February, without any complications, and I was there. I played proxy father with pride. Eva returned home from the clinic several days later; she had already organised a day-nanny, a contact of Margareth's, and was back to full-time work within twenty-four hours. She looked thin but fulfilled, Daniel looked gorgeous. I think he liked that breast-feeding.

Annabelle and I had found one or two properties up for sale which might have been worthy but were either in neighbourhoods which didn't appeal or too far from the schools. We inspected several houses up for rent too, but the landlord owners were all demanding exorbitant terms. I decided to involve Eva because she had good contacts and also knew Munich so well – she had, though, very little time to assist: apart from Daniel she was still busy building up her clientele and training two new staff. It seemed finding the perfect home wasn't going to be so easy, so we prepared ourselves for the longer haul.

This all involved a deal of shuttling between Nuremberg and Munich, between my old life and new. It did, however, mean that all the driving time on the autobahn gave me opportunity to think, to ruminate, to let things go through my head. Apart from developing further ideas for two areas of consultancy Cornelia and I had agreed upon, I started to consider the subject of Matthias again. I'd promised Annabelle to undertake this task, to somehow reduce or rid us of the danger he could possibly present in the future and had merely postponed it because of those other priorities. But a promise is a promise.

So I began to mull it over. It was anything but easy. There was a sense of helplessness, my thoughts turned in vicious circles, how can one get a grip on someone like Matthias? After a number of fruitless attempts I came to the conclusion there was only one thing possible: I had to talk to Matthias.

That evening I rang Eva. She was my only connection to him. I explained the reason for my call and she told me to come round. I regret very little in my life, but my regret regarding that visit, because of where it led, still runs deep even today. I remember: she was stressed and impatient, irritable, there was snow blanketing the lawns beyond the windows and hanging heavy in the trees. I asked her to give me a telephone number where I could reach Matthias. She refused. And not only that. My question opened a floodgate. She said angrily: "Talking'll achieve nothing, waste of time, what the hell d'you think I've been doing?" She snapped it out, and her anger was a storm. "We've got to *do* something."

"What then?" I asked. "Have you an idea?"

She hadn't. "But it's got to be bloody soon," she demanded, "he's still involved. Soon as he'd recovered he disappeared again."

Ah, I thought. "Have you still got contact?" I said.

"Once. On the phone."

"When?"

"Two months back."

"You seen him too?"

"Christ no. Not since the party."
She lit a cigarette. I watched her. I'd noticed: before the birth of Daniel she'd cut down a lot. Again I wondered if Matthias knew about the child. Then she made a jump, said: "'Nother kidnap six days ago."

"I know."

"His signature."

"Signature?" I echoed. "They all sound the same to me."

"Nope – different patterns. Been studying them. Different groups." She grasped my arm, and ash fell. "Only a matter of time till they corner him, for Christ's sake. Or kill him."

"Give me a number."

"No."

"You have one though, don't you?"

"Changes every time."

"You have one though."

"Maybe."

"Then tell him to ring me."

"Not as easy as that."

"Tell him to ring me," I repeated.

She didn't reply.

It took only two days. On Monday afternoon he called me in Munich. I should've been back at the firm in Nuremberg that morning; was it just luck that he caught me? It was early March, the snows were melting. The call came through in our new offices – I sat at my laptop next to Cornelia, we were in the middle of a discussion about our homepage, and it came directly to the phone on my desk.

"Well?" he said. That's all he said, but it was his voice.

"I want to talk," I said.

"Why?"

"I want to talk." I didn't glance at Cornelia. She sat so close she could probably hear his voice.

"Okay." No dithering, no hesitation. "I'll ring you back." Nothing else. The line went dead.

It was nearly two weeks till he rang again. Different hour of the day, and to my mobile this time.

"Hello?" I said. Snowflakes falling again outside, but big and wet.

"Next Friday, 9:30pm. Station car park in..." He named me a town, out in the countryside, some distance from Munich. "Okay?"

"Okay," I said.

Friday came. I drove there by car; I'd wondered why a railway station, had briefly considered taking the train but cast the thought aside in case it got too late to get a connection back. Since the telephone call I'd wondered about other things too – like why on earth there, why not in Munich, why this particular town? And I'd also considered with growing apprehension: had I made a mistake, was there any danger, was I getting out of my depth?

Because I wasn't familiar with the area I had set off overpunctually to allow myself ample time, didn't want to arrive late, find him gone. The cold spell had passed, a little milder now. Slushy snow on the verges, mud in the lanes near farm turnings. Had to drive carefully. I got there too early. It was dark, isolated, outside the small town, the last houses two hundred yards away. I parked, sat waiting. The car park was nearly empty, lay at the side of the country station parallel to the railway lines. Four dim old orange neon lights in a row, a ghostly gloom, only five other parked cars and no-one in sight. Beyond, too, the little station building was ill-lit, seemed deserted. I could see, for his purposes, Matthias had chosen well: not a bad place for an anonymous talk. But cold though. Only about ten degrees.

At nine-fifteen I started the engine to warm the car for five minutes. At twenty past, car lights in the distance, coming closer. A vehicle drove past on the country road outside. Didn't turn off though, didn't stop.

Punctually at nine-thirty more lights approaching. But it was a train, a local one, two carriages. It pulled in at the station, a little chain of lights. No-one got in, one person alighted, came in my direction, opened a car, drove off. I watched its receding tail lights.

Then headlights, far off. There were hardly any trees. Just silhouettes. I could see the vehicle coming nearer. It turned off, was big, powerful lights, looked like a Land Rover. It steered in an arc, paused, reversed, came to a standstill next to me. Its headlights still burning, the engine running. I peered. Could discern a hand from the driver's side flapping at me. I had to look up, yes the vehicle was big. I wound down my window. A pale face in the dark. It wasn't Matthias, it was a woman, an emaciated face. Heidi Prell.

"Get in," she said. Turned her head away, her window was closing.

I locked my old car, went round behind the vehicle because its lights were so bright they hurt my eyes. One wing was dented and battered, the sides and the back spattered with mud; even had I wanted to I couldn't read the registration plate properly, it and the light illuminating it were half splashed with dirt too. I reached the passenger door, opened it. She glanced sideways at me, didn't say a word. I couldn't see anyone else, she seemed to be alone.

I got in, had to climb up. Shut the door. Cosy and warm, glowing dials in the dark, smell of diesel and hay, the smells of a farm.

"Seat belt."

I obeyed. And as I did, something came from behind. A pad or a cloth over my nose, over my mouth, my head was forced back to the headrest. I couldn't breathe, a sickly sweet sensation. I suppose I struggled but my arms were held fast. The last I remember is those four dismal orange neon lights tipping, falling, and going out.

x x x

It was very hot. But not humid. A dry heat, like in an oven, like in the desert.

I opened my eyes.

Daylight. Bright. Not direct sunlight, though. Had to blink my eyes. Mouth and throat dry; I needed something to drink.

First impressions: a mud hut, not very big. A small window, dirty – very pitted and smeared, the view beyond blurred. And a doorway, roughly rounded dried-mud corners, and set in its opening an old door, crudely constructed, planks of wood painted green, colour flaking, long rusty hinges. On one wall hung a picture in a frame – a man's face, dark skinned. And under the picture a recess with an oil lamp standing, blackened glass chimney.

I looked down.

I lay on my side on a hard lumpy mattress, on a rickety old iron bed. Beneath my head a solid elongated sausage-shaped cushion covered in a cloth of stained yellow and gold. It stank of sweat. I peered over the edge of the mattress. Bare sand-coloured floor, looked like dried mud too.

I looked up.

Trunks of small trees spanning between the walls, lying horizontal, serving as rafters, looked like poplars. Thin branches and twigs on top laid crosswise, bits of straw poking through. From a hook a flex hung down, a naked bulb, but not switched on...

A donkey brayed. Not loud, though – must be some way off. There was the occasional cluck of chickens too, and voices. Sounded Arabic. The hut, the sounds, they reminded me of other huts, other places on travels, in Oman and Yemen and Iran. And didn't they ring a bell in my brain as well? But I was confused, couldn't put a finger on it. I looked across at the doorway, the door stood slightly ajar. A big drawn-back rusty bolt, a latch, and a loop of coarse string.

I thought: sit up. Can you sit up or are you tied?

But my hands were free, my feet too. I swung my legs to the floor. And started, startled. A sudden sound of shooting far away. An automatic weapon. Made my skin contract. But that's what did it, that burst of sound: I remembered – the minister, the interview, the description of his captivity.

I panicked. I thought: where've they taken me, have they flown me out somewhere? On Monday Cornelia and I have appointments. I sat up. Stayed sitting though, propped on my hands, feeling helpless, feeling scared. Over against the wall of the hut two plastic bottles of water stood – blue and white labels in Arabic. I stared through the crack of the door then out of the small window. Looked like a yard outside, strewn straw, bounded by a mud and stone wall. And beyond the wall, visible through the old glass pane, indistinctive, shimmering, sand and steppe, and in the distance a line of low hazy mountains.

My God – where the hell am I? In some Arab country? Can't be. And that's daylight. What day is it? Saturday, Sunday? And what time is it, then?

I glanced down to my watch. But my watch was gone. Then I realised: my pullover and jacket and my socks and shoes were gone too – I sat in trousers and shirtsleeves, bare feet.

It was quiet now. Quite still. Even the voices had ceased. Just this intense heat. Must drink something – is that water for me? The crook of my arm itched. I scratched at it through my shirt, my fingertips caught on something which tugged at fine hairs on my skin. I peeled up the sleeve. A tiny plaster. I tore it off, I was panicking again. Two tiny red marks on the vein, slightly swollen. So I'd been given injections. I rubbed my right arm. Nothing, no plaster there. I thought: for God's sake, how long have I been unconscious?

Is this a nasty joke? I only wanted to meet him for a short talk. My panic grew...

A movement.

Someone had walked past the window. Then a shadow at the door. Matthias?

An Arab woman entered. She wore long flowing clothes, a mixture of colours, a headscarf and veil. I could only see her eyes. How old? Couldn't say. Four small paces and she'd reached me; I could just glimpse sandals and bare toes. The nails were painted dark red, scratched. She stooped, placed a round cheap metal tray on the floor, hunkered. On the tray two glasses, and a blackened copper pot. The spout had a beak like a bird...

Another shadow...

Matthias walked in.

He walked in casually, unhurriedly, crossed over. Stood a moment, nodded down at me. Just nodded – no offer of a hand, no smile, completely neutral as if we'd only taken a brief break, had been together ten minutes before. He wore normal clothes, western clothes: a thin long-sleeved shirt, jeans, normal shoes. I hadn't seen him since December in my apartment. I peered. Scars were visible only at his throat and on the back of one hand. Then he sat down, cross-legged, beside the tray on the floor.

The woman was holding the pot, filling the glasses, raising and lowering her hand, pouring accurately from quite a height. The liquid frothed a bit, looked like tea.

Matthias said something to her, speaking rapidly – sounded so guttural, was it Arabic? Didn't sound like Matthias at all. She put down the pot and went to the wall, returned with one of the big bottles of water, gave it to him.

"Water?" he said.

I nodded. Took the bottle. The plastic cap was tight, I twisted it, breaking the seal. Drank. I was glad about that seal. Luke warm water; wet at least.

The Arab woman had turned away, was going out.

I stared at Matthias. "Is this a little joke?" I said.

Slowly he shook his head.

"Where am I?"

He considered me calmly. "Tea?"

"Where?"

He handed me a glass. "You expect an answer?"

"Yes."

He shrugged.

I sipped. It was black tea, hot and sweet. I don't like sweet tea. But I drank some anyway.

"You really want to know?" he asked.

My turn to shrug. I wasn't going to beg. "I suppose natural inquisitiveness," I said.

No answer.

I watched him. Decided to try: "I suppose they all ask that."

"Yes."

"So this is where you keep them."

"A few of them."

"A few?"

"Yes."

"You have other places too?" The glass was hot, I put it down on the floor. Where was I?

"We," he said.

"We?"

"There are a lot of us."

"Ah." I just nodded, uselessly. What had he said when he visited me in the clinic — he'd bought a farm, had a pilot's licence? Had he flown me out, was I on the farm? But I'd guessed it would be Italy at the furthest, and this must be the Middle East or somewhere similar.

"We have several other places," he said.

I thought: he trusts me enough to tell me that? Does he really trust me?

"Yes," he said "I trust you."

Suddenly? I thought — just like that? I thought he stopped trusting me in our youth. I suppose I showed surprise, for he added:

"I have my reasons." He sat there so peaceful, legs still crossed. "But you don't trust me." Said quietly.

"No," I agreed.

"In fact you've started to hate me."

"Hate's a very strong word," I said. "I wouldn't call it hate."

He considered me slowly. Then: "So you want to talk to me?"

I hesitated. I spread my hands. Yes, I thought. But only because of Annabelle, now. And Eva. It was only because of them, wasn't it?

He watched me steadily. He said: "You've wanted to since I sent that postcard — nail me down, get down to basics."

"Wasn't it natural?"

"Surely."

"Well..." I shook my head. "Yes, I guess I did at the start." I allowed that as a concession. "I tried in the clinic to..."

"You tried very hard."

"Yes," I said. "I thought it was important."

"You weren't in a fit state."

I ignored that. "I had a dream, Matthias. That I could find you again, go back to our roots. I wanted to try. Later too, when you nearly copped it, when I took you in – but then you were in no condition either." I paused, then added: "Before my anger began."

"Fate kept getting in the way."

"Is that what you call it?"

"I felt it, though – your dream."

"You felt?" I retorted. "You are capable of feeling?"

He didn't blink. He let that one go by.

"You blocked," I accused.

"Wrong."

"Not wrong."

"It was more the force of circumstance."

Was it? I paused again a moment. Yes, I thought – that's true too. "Ah," I said, "your commitment."

"It has priority."

"It always did." My anger simmered, my disappointment was king.

"Your anger's understandable."

"Is it?" I said. He was looking through me again.

"I turned up like a bad penny, then endangered your life."

Something slipped inside me. You endanger your own, I thought. "Yes," I said. How can he be so calm? He's an extremist, isn't he? How can he talk with such equanimity?

"I turned to you because we're friends."

"Is that what friends are for?"

"I couldn't warn you."

Had to contradict that one. "Yes you could have. I thought you possessed enough trust."

"I had to take the risk first to find out. To be sure."

"And now you are?" Was that sarcasm in my voice?

"You wouldn't be here if I wasn't."

"You're fooling yourself, Matthias."

"Am I?"

"If you turned up again I'd turn you in."

He smiled. A very faint smile. Shook his head.

"I'd turn you in," I repeated.

"No," he said. So much assurance in his tone. "There are some friendships that go too deep, Stefan."

"Friendship?" I sounded harsh, I sounded like Annabelle now.

"Yes, Stefan."

He continued watching me. Sipped his tea. The heat was intense, it was getting at me, crushing me.

Then he said: "And you're inquisitive."

"I am?" I wasn't, was I? Wasn't I more afraid?

"You want to know what's going on, what we're doing."

"You're wrong there."

That trace of smile again. That unshakable confidence. "That's why you wanted to meet and talk."

"I purely wanted to talk about you."

"One and the same."

"No, Matthias." I was still certain, wasn't I? I was here for the others, not me.

We sat there staring at each other, I on the edge of the bed, he on the hard dry mud floor. I could see he felt quite at home sitting like that, felt more comfortable than me. His knees lay flat on the sides of his feet, he looked lean and fit once more. Did he train every day, exercise, did he do yoga too? And his eyes – they were so steady, clear, pale blue. They were eyes which could mesmerise. I had to look away.

I stooped, picked up the glass, drank some more tea. Yes, the heat pressed down on me, it was blurring my brain.

"Go ahead, then," he said. "Now's your chance."

I looked back at him. Gathering my thoughts. It was hard to believe: we were meeting face to face at last. We were alone together, really alone, this time no distraction, nothing standing in the way. I was glad. Secretly I was glad. How could I be so naïve as to believe I wasn't here for me? It was like nearly a year ago, after his postcard came, started awaking old memories – there were still a thousand things I wanted to ask yet not one found its way to my tongue.

He was waiting.

Again I shook my head. "Absurd as it sounds," I said, "I scarcely know where to begin."

Slowly he nodded. "I know that feeling." He raised a sunburnt hand. Lightly he punched my knee. He did it with intimacy.

"You do?" I queried. "You never used to – you used to be the master of rhetoric." How I loved that touch – his touch could always weaken me.

"And you the one with fast ripostes. The guy who always tried shooting me down."

"It didn't help though," I said.

A silence. Watching each other.

"You're mistaken there," he said.

Mistaken? I thought. Had I influenced him somewhere then, after all?

Another silence.

I was casting back. I found a memory – he was twenty-three, saying icily: "That's sentimental crap, politics carry a higher priority than friendship, but who knows? Maybe one day..."

I stared at the memory. Is that what he was talking about now? Yes, I decided. That's it – that's where I have to begin.

"You stumbled onto the word friendship just now," I said. "And the notion that some go too deep to be destroyed by anything. I'd like to come back to that, because it's a concept that could be misunderstood."

He nodded. Just nodded.

"You really believe that, Matthias?"

"Yes."

"Because it's convenient? Because it suits your circumstance now?"

"No. Because I believe it's true."

"You used not to."

"I was wrong."

"You changed your mind? Are you capable of changing your mind?"

"I am now."

"Ah," I said again. "That's ironic." The glass of tea was still in my hand. I drank some more, put it back on the floor. I'd found the right words now. I said flatly: "You used to say friendship was expendable, that it had its limitations."

"My politics got in the way."

"Yes they did, didn't they? And you also used to say friendship is a sign of sentimentality – that needing someone emotionally was a form of weakness, a flaw in the personality. Remember?"

"Yes." That subtle smile was there once more.

"Well I have a little confession to make. When that postcard arrived it awoke a flaw in my personality again. I realised I'd missed you, I realised our lost friendship left a hole I couldn't quite fill."

"I'm heartened to hear that."

"Are you?" I said.

"It isn't lost, Stefan."

"Isn't it, Matthias?"

"It was simply a postponement. We just went different ways, that's all."

"You went. Not me."

"Fate dictated it. But it doesn't alter the fact of the friendship."

"Well, that's interesting. Because despite my sentimentality, and missing you, I have a feeling in my bones something essential died."

He rocked to and fro. Gently. "You and your bones." The faint smile traced his face again, came and went. He didn't say anything else.

I watched him. Watched that smile. Ask him, I thought. So I asked: "Why did you send me that postcard?"

"To make you curious."

"Well it made me that," I said. "At least it did that."

"And to rekindle our friendship."

"So you could use me?"

"I didn't intend that." He shook his head again. His face was open, his eyes still clear. "I've missed you too."

I leaned back on my hands. The mattress was prickly – was it full of straw?

"Nothing's died, Stefan. That's just your wounded pride at work."

My wounded pride? He'd ended the friendship like a light switched off, like a guillotine falling – no explanation, no goodbye.

"Friendships were your *non plus ultra*. When I buggered off you were like a child that's had its toy pinched."

I considered that one. Thoughts of Estella. I didn't speak.

"I had a purpose and direction in life," he said. "You didn't. Friendships were your substitute."

Hadn't Estella told me something like that, too?

"Time's the litmus test, Stefan. Twenty years can be like yesterday if the threads are still there."

Defensively I said: "Are they still there, Matthias?"

"If they weren't you wouldn't have taken me in that night."

I thought about that one too. Yes, he'd got me there. I shifted position on the bed; my bottom sagged between scratchy lumps.

I said: "You're stretching those threads." I indicated the hut we sat in. God knows where he'd brought me.

"Next time we'll meet somewhere simpler."

I wondered: would there be a next time? I held my tongue.

"This little game's not for much longer. Not in this form."

"Ah," I said. "Is it a game?"

"A deadly serious one." Those calm, calm eyes. "But necessary. A first step."

"To quench your thirst for danger?" I just said that to provoke.

"No, Stefan – to start a necessary ball rolling. I quenched that thirst long ago."

"Did you now?"

"Put more precisely, it was quenched for me by others."

"How?"

"In a dirty little war. It destroyed my naïvety, it exorcised my devils."

I sat there quite still. That rang true. I watched him watching me. Was he starting to open up at last? I waited. But he'd stopped speaking.

So I said: "Where did you go then, Matthias?" I said it because I wanted to be quite sure.

He considered me, carefully. For several seconds. Then: "Jordan, then Lebanon." He smiled that faint smile again, but this time the smile was tired.

"You're joking," I said. Yes, his honesty surprised me, was his trust really complete?

"I never joke."

"The civil war?" I asked.

"The dirty war. I helped the wounded. And with logistics."

"You were crazy, Matthias. You always had that crazy side – you could've got killed."

"I was fighting for a cause – at the start. A cause is like a shield."

Was that an answer? I shook my head. "Well, you always had enough of those."

"Better than none," he retorted evenly. He swept that sunburnt hand through the air, that golden hand calm and controlled. I could see its strength, it fascinated, I could sense the animal in him. It didn't touch me this time, though; how I wished it would touch again.

Then he murmured, distantly: "The bastards were corrupt on both sides, all the factions, I was in the wrong game. I learnt my lesson there."

He stopped.

His head sagged slightly, his eyes turned down. "When the Israelis came in, I got out." He was nodding slowly; I wondered what his eyes could see. "They're tough cookies, those Israelis – you don't mess about with them. But at least you know where you stand." His thoughts seemed to have gone off at a tangent, got trapped. He nodded again to himself, it looked almost sage.

"It's the old story," he said quietly. "The best fighters are either highly motivated or have their backs to a wall. Those boys have both."

I waited. But he didn't continue. Was he still out there seeing things? I said: "They'll survive. If you read your bible they're God's chosen people – they've truly got God on their side."

He pursed his lips, his eyes remained unfocused. Then he caught the thought, said drily: "If you read further they'll have to change their politics should they seek redemption." His eyes had come back again.

"Those who live by the sword," I suggested.

"Yes, I learnt that." His eyes didn't stray. "It extended my education."

Did you really learn? I thought. That was it, wasn't it – that was the critical question.

"Tell me," I said, expecting nothing.

And he told me. Very briefly, unemotionally. He took me through the streets, the boulevards, the shell-shocked houses. He showed me the ruins of Beirut where so many people lived and died, he walked me behind and along the green line and into the minds of the people.

"I saw a lot of good guys go down. Moslem and Christian." His eyes had clouded once more. "Such a terrible waste." Then they refocused. "But I learnt another lesson too, Stefan. The root of evil in this world is poverty and desperation – that's what fanaticism feeds on."

"Well I agree with you there," I said. "I'm glad we've got something to agree on."

But I don't think he was listening for he went on: "I've seen hopelessness in people's eyes close up, you know. And watched radicals and self-proclaimed saints leaping in to take advantage, peddling hope like candy on a stick for little kids. Sometimes they spouted pure propaganda, sometimes perverse religious crap – they always found their foot soldiers for the cause, though. And they always will, till one gets to the root to break the vicious circle."

"You're right," I said. "But you didn't need the Middle East to teach you that – we talked about this at eighteen."

His eyes considered me. Were his memories failing him now?

"I know." A dip of the head, acknowledging. "But practice leaves a better print. Your words, if you recall."

"I believe they were." My turn to smile weakly.

He spread his hands. Those golden hands. The subject was dismissed.

I sat there on the mattress, he squatted cross-legged at my feet. Contentedly he gazed up at me. Yes – here he was very much at home, the crusader come back from the wars with his cross, the lion laid down to rest.

"So you got out," I said. I wanted to know.

"Yes."

"With all those little lessons in your pocket."

"Yes."

"Where this time?"

"East Germany."

Ah. So Theo had got it right. I didn't speak.

But neither did he. After a pause I asked him: "They took you in?"

"Of course."

"Just like that?"

"My enemy's enemy is my friend."

"Were you the enemy, Matthias?"

"In fact not. But how were they to know?"

"How indeed."

"And I had an immaculate letter of introduction. In one of my other pockets."

"From the Lebanese?"

"From Damascus, actually."

"What the hell did you do in East Germany?"

"Laid low."

"Did they use you?"

"They were singularly unsuccessful. Then the Wall came down. Went to South Africa. It's a good place to learn farming."

"I imagine."

"Pleasant climate." A slow grin.

"That where you bought your farm?" I was trying to steer him.

A slight shake of the head. "I tell you..." He was back to South Africa again – he started describing the life there, in neat brief brushstrokes, taking his time... was he blocking, was he getting reticent now?

I listened. Until he said: "But their politics aren't my politics, their cause isn't mine..."

And I took up the cue. "So then?" I said.

He stopped. His eyes considered me. "Then is the present tense."

"Farming? Flying?"

"Yes. And this."

I returned his gaze as best I could. "Ah yes." I glanced past him, around the hut. "You've picked up the banner again."

"A new banner, Stefan."

"Meaning?"

"You read the newspapers, watch the News."

"Yes," I said.

"So you know what we're doing. Close to home now."

I shook my head. "Kidnapping a few of the big boys?" I said it with sarcasm.

"Just a few of the biggest and baddest. A small cross-section."

"Big or small, a kidnap is a criminal act."

"Correct."

"Well?"

"Regrettable, yes." Placid tone, relaxed gaze. "There are certain situations, though, where the end justifies the means. Like police raids with force, Stefan. Like war."

"Is this a war, Matthias?"

"No."

"What is it, then?"

"We're talking about the act of picking up criminals protected by intentional loopholes in the law, then setting them free again."

"They're well-known guys." I shrugged apathetically. "They're foundation stones of the establishment."

"That's the idea."

"You out to change the world again, then?"

"Not the world, Stefan. And not the fundamentals. Democracy's the best system the human animal ever created, but it's coming unravelled. We aim to correct the flaws."

Was I hearing right? Twenty years ago he'd been advocating anarchy, aiming to topple it all – and with a leftist jargon and communist inspired clichés enough to numb the brightest brain, like someone firing an automatic or bashing on a drum. I said derisively:

"By kidnapping?" I flapped an impatient hand. "This'll alter sweet nothing."

"Isn't the overriding intention."

"What is, then?"

"To create a scandal," he said.

"That all?"

"Yes. Draw attention in order to inform. First one has to inform." A slow relaxed blink of eyes. "People love scandals, keeps them focused, it makes them nosey."

I said nothing. Offered nothing.

"Scandal gives the media opportunity to reach mass audiences and go into juicy details, tell millions of people what sort of devils these household names really are. Tell them what's going on behind closed doors in this country."

"Is it worse than in others?"

"Only partially. But is that justification for doing nothing?"

I shrugged.

"Too many people are tired of it all," he said. "Sick of corruption, sick of the rich getting richer and the poor poorer, and politicians' empty promises. We're informing, and helping to focus their frustration."

"These things are human nature, Matthias. You can't fight human nature."

"That's your apathy talking."

I shrugged again.

"There's anger too – people want changes, Stefan. Real changes."

"I've heard that one before."

"This is different. There are more very angry. This time around things are going to get changed, we intend to make sure. It's a different game, different people behind it."

"By kidnapping?" I repeated. Let my sarcasm off the hook now. "You can't change things that way. You could brainwash ten thousand and another ten thousand will step into their shoes, power and corruption go hand in hand. And the masses? Memories are short. Till it comes to the next elections..."

"Just step one, Stefan. Then we help them let the anger out."

"Ah, the anger," I echoed. "And how? Start a revolution?" My turn to smile a small smile. Mine was weak and bitter, though.

"Rallies and demos, serious civil disobedience. Put on the pressure. Politicians only panic and wake up when the people get out on the streets."

"Well, we've had some of those already. What've they achieved? Two deaths and even more anger, and just political papering over the cracks."

"We weren't in on those, they just happened. We're beginning the programme soon. I'm talking about mass demonstrations, very well-organised and coordinated."

"And more violence? More deaths?"

"Strictly peaceful. We'll deal with the rowdies, we know how to isolate."

I wondered: is that his next task then, when they stop these kidnaps? Applying violence against violence? Well – he'd be good at that, wouldn't he?

I watched him in silence. Inside I thought: a load of crap.

"I know what you're thinking," he said. He said it peaceably, patiently – like an adult talking to a child.

"What?"

"That it's all old hat. That it'll get out of control then peter out like all demos do, given a month or two."

"That too," I confessed.

"This time it won't." He looked so contented, sounded so sure. How could he be so sure?

I waited, in case he intended to explain. I had no inclination, though; I was here for a purpose, wasn't I? I was here to stop him.

But he didn't continue.

I could feel myself sweating – my God, it was hot here, where the hell had he brought me? I stooped and picked up the tea glass again, drank it empty. Felt his eyes. I bent low once more, put the glass back on the tray at our feet.

"More tea?" he said.

"No." I shook my head. "No thanks."

But how the devil could I stop him? Could I persuade him? How does one persuade a man like this?

I looked back at him. "When does this kidnap business come to an end?" I said.

A steady gaze, a pause. Then: "In my cell, one more."

Cell? Is that what he called it? Is that where I was – in his group, in his cell?

"They're after you," I said.

"Yes."

"The net's closing, Matthias."

"Yes."

So calm, so collected. Didn't he care?

"Do you really know what you're up against?"

That transient smile again. "Of course."

"The whole weight of the State. They'll corner you."

"Who knows."

"And if they do?"

"Well?" He shook his head gently. His stare was intense.

The way he talked, the way he thought, on the surface he seemed to have changed. But was he still the old Matthias deep down inside, was he still the dangerous one?

"Will you give yourself up?" I said. "Will you go quietly?"

"Depends."

"Depends, Matthias? They'll kill you."

"Don't be immature, don't be melodramatic."

"You have to stop. Get out."

A casual shrug.

I was kicking against the pricks, I was wasting my breath. Uselessly I said: "Don't you care?"

Evenly he watched me. Those steady blue eyes. "I care very much."

"Then get out while the going's good."

Another of those smiles. "This thing's far bigger than me, Stefan."

I returned his stare. I was giving up. All I could reply was: "Now who's being melodramatic?"

Unhurriedly, legs still casually crossed, he leaned back, propping himself on his hands behind him on the mud floor. "Have you no conception about what's involved?" he said quietly.

"Only what I read."

"And what have you read?"

"I imagine you mean this movement – this new political wing?"

"Yes."

"You part of it?" I said.

"Will be later. No connections, not yet. Logical."

I watched him. Shook my head slowly again. "A political movement kicking off with kidnapping?" I said. "Are you all completely out of..."

"Of course not." He gave a tired grin. "The political movement began later, an entirely separate entity. Didn't you read about that, too?"

"Somewhere, I suppose."

"As a reaction against the kidnap scandals. It condemns the kidnaps, but picks up on the disclosures. It's been carefully orchestrated to put the horse before the cart."

"The truth'll come out one day."

"What truth, Stefan? All that'll emerge is a manifesto from the kidnappers, that they're an extremist left-wing faction bent on abolishing the capitalist state. The new political movement will simply distance itself and emphasise the democratic process."

And I thought: but doesn't truth always surface in the end? I cleared my throat – it was rough from the heat and croaky again.

"Yet another party?" I said, lethargically. "Haven't we got enough of those?"

He watched me unhurriedly, nodding at me. It seemed he was in no hurry. Then he said: "Apart from the Greens, all old hat. All steeped in dogma and the dreary status quo. And the Greens...?" A vague shrug. "They've moved to the middle and their platform's been pinched by the bigger parties, they're establishment now."

"They've achieved a lot."

"Ecologically, granted. We're not talking about ecology now."

"And this White Party? Come on, Matthias, it'll never work. Regardless of how clever they think they are, they're being naïve."

"Anything but. Their platform's clear. The areas to reform have been well thought through. Tax system, education, integration, health service costs, lobby politics..."

"It'll never catch on."

"It's catching on fast."

"On the Web?" I allowed myself a small chuckle, nasty and tight. "That's kid's stuff." Careful, I thought, don't play into his hands. He chose to get onto this one, he's trying to draw you in – don't let him draw you.

And Matthias was saying: "It's got the best minds behind it. Intellectuals, experts, thinkers, journalists, and they know what they're doing. They're simply on the ball, Stefan, they're moving with the times."

"It's hardly a step above social networking crap," I retorted.

"Wrong. And it's working. No party's ever attracted members so quickly before."

I shook my head sadly. "One needs substance not speed. They're almost all young people, it's merely a fad."

"Then go on the Web and read for yourself. The political programme – have you studied it?"

"I have."

"And?"

"Very crafty." I spread my hands. "Got all the ingredients to attract the disaffected and young. That's not the basis for a sound movement, Matthias."

"The disaffected are the ones sick of empty promises, and the young are concerned about their future."

"That's nothing new," I said.

"Are you aware what numbers we're talking about?"

"Yes – a small minority at most."

"Not so small. And growing. Nobody wins majorities nowadays, Stefan."

I spread my hands again. Get off this subject, I ordered myself. And didn't reply.

Quietly he said: "All one needs is clearing the five percent hurdle, then one's in. We'll build it up from there."

"That's a very big hurdle. They won't make it."

"The polls say otherwise. Over double."

"The polls." I tutted my tongue, cocked my head on one side. "It's half a year till the next bi-elections. A voter's as fickle as the wind and the weather." I gave him my favourite apathetic squint; this was a fine place to stop.

But he calmly countered: "Don't underestimate the Web as a weapon. We have homepage representation in every town, real people, real faces. For voters it's all about speed and communication and personal involvement, being able to ask questions on the Web and get answers. It's spreading fast, Stefan, it's like a fire."

"Wait and see," I said.

"Oh yes." He just sat there contentedly, nodded his head.

Sidetrack him, I thought quickly. What should I say? I took a breath...

"The eternal pessimist!" Still leaning back, propped on his hands, he grinned casually at me.

I dropped my eyes, had to attempt a grin too.

"You always were, weren't you?" Another grin.

"Yes," I confessed.

"The man who stares at the shadows, sees everything black. The friend who never found a meaning in life."

I didn't reply, didn't react.

Lazily he leaned forward, bowing, stopped propping himself. He was pushing the tray of tea aside...

Is that it? I thought. Is that it already?

"Water?" He indicated with offered hand.

I glanced down briefly at the plastic bottle. "Is the charade at an end, then?" I said.

"It's no charade, Stefan." He slid the bottle closer. "But if I'm boring you, you're free to go whenever you want."

"I am?"

"Just say the word."

"You've got the plane waiting out there?" I was trying a little irony again.

"There's no plane, Stefan."

"Ah. Really?" What did he mean by that? That I'd be going by camel or donkey or something?

"You wish to leave?" The eyes were candid, relaxed.

My turn to smile. Emptily. I spread my hands. "I'll give a little whistle when I'm ready."

"Do that."

Yes, he looked so relaxed. So perfectly in his element. I reached down to the bottle. Gratefully drank several gulps.

He'd folded his hands back in his lap. "Listen," he said quietly, and his head came up, his blue eyes were there again. "I'm going to tell you something, put you straight..."

He rocked gently, almost imperceptibly, to and fro. And began to speak.

I sat there, listening.

He had changed the subject, returned to me, now. He was talking about me, and my life, and things which were important to him, things which used to be important to me too, that we used to share... he talked slowly, philosophically, he went down deeper and deeper, he was reaching into me, getting under my skin...

Still I sat listening.

It hurt, what he said, it hurt very much. He did it carefully, though, because he knew me so well, I think he intended to help and to heal. Then he came to where I suppose he'd been heading for. I steeled myself, raised my defences; he'd reached the part of me that had died.

"Matthias..." I said. I couldn't say more.

"It didn't die."

It was me bowing now, I had dropped my head. I found I was hugging myself too.

He continued on. I couldn't bear to hear.

"Don't," I said. That's all I could say. My father was standing there in my mind, he was hanging from the beam and I wanted to go, life had turned pointless in all its filth, I wanted to be there with him...

Matthias moved, I sensed it. He had stopped speaking. I raised my eyes. He laid a hand on my leg, and left it there. Thoughts passing between us. No need of words.

A minute passed.

I could feel the warmth and the strength of his hand, his touch, and the heat of the hut; how I loved that touch.

Then unhurriedly he began to speak again.

He had made a jump, a big one. He'd left me alone, withdrawn the sword, left me alone with the wound – he had changed the subject again, he'd gone back to the world...

"...and during all this time our planet's been shrinking," he said. "Countries are coming closer together, whether they like it or not, global economics are binding us fast and the hermit kingdoms can't hide any more." His voice was a murmur, calm and resonant, a golden glow...

"We in the West have learnt some lessons too, haven't we? That religions, like dictatorships, aren't solving basic problems and evils in this world, in fact sometimes propagating them. We've also learnt that the charter of human rights is universal, doesn't depend on politics and race and creed, is not negotiable. And we're learning how to help the oppressed everywhere, using the Web. It can't be blocked for long, we keep one step ahead, it reaches the people who need to hear and at the same time creeps into the chambers of the mighty and robs their sleep. Our world is changing, Stefan, and a lot of it is for the better. Power blocks are shifting, there are new ones rising, there's new affluence where poverty and ignorance used to be king. Affluence demands more knowledge and freedom, it forces ideological dogmas aside and breaks old chains. When the struggle merely to survive is overcome and the yoke of oppression gets too heavy, the human animal yearns to be free..."

His words flowed over me. Was he trying to sooth – or did he have a different goal? I sat there on the edge of the bed, wondering, and his hand was a lifeline I didn't wish to lose.

"Yes the world is changing, Stefan, life is a flux, one can't stop the clock. There are going to be those who get left behind, archaic structures and beliefs and failed states, old religions like fossils which don't reform. What happens to them when the world overtakes them and stops paying their bills, what happens when their poverty explodes and the oil runs dry? Will they try to destroy what they can't comprehend...?"

He wasn't finished, he continued on. I watched his eyes, his gaze didn't leave me while he spoke. Was he talking about Heaven and Hell on Earth, was he speaking of Armageddon? He'd returned to religions now, to the different faiths and their influence on civilisation, that motivation all boiled down to belief. Halfway through he withdrew his hand from my leg to quietly gesticulate, to emphasise a point, then laid it back on his lap. "Islam is Christianity minus its love, Christianity is Judaism robbed of dogma and hate, only the Christian tradition and teachings finally led to the charter of human rights and the deepening of democracy – not Hinduism, not Buddhism, not Confucianism or Islam..."

I watched his body, too, lean and fit – watched its strength, its decisiveness. His voice remained calm, certain, didn't once raise – he knew what he was talking about.

I listened till he stopped, waited a moment longer. But it seemed he was through. His last words had returned to the subject of democracy, that democracy was what it was all about; he'd come back to the beginning, he'd come a full circle.

He regarded me placidly in silence. Then I said: "Are you seeking confirmation, Matthias? Of the human condition, of how you view it?"

"No."

Of course not, I thought. But what then? "To convince me?" I suggested.

"To reach you. To remind you of the priorities."

"I see."

"And to pull you back in."

"Pull me in?"

"Jog your conscience, re-awake your interest."

I said nothing.

"To re-involve you, Stefan. Give you a direction, offer you a purpose in your life."

"Ah."

"We could use someone with your experience."

"No thanks," I said.

"You have excellent contacts."

"I do?" So he'd made enquiries, been researching, he knew about those. "You know about them?" I said. He'd done his homework thoroughly, then.

"You could help recruit fresh blood."

"You believe an eternal pessimist would be appropriate for that?"

"To put your pessimism to constructive use."

"Recruiting fresh activists for the front?" I said. I only said it with very light sarcasm this time, though.

But he took it easily in his stride. "And bring back meaning to your existence," he replied evenly.

I shook my head. "No," I repeated.

"You're still looking for that meaning, Stefan."

Am I? I thought. I returned his gaze. "You're wrong, Matthias."

"And you'd still like to see some of the wrongs in our society put right."

Well that's true, I thought. But I'm not the man to do that. "Count me out," I said.

"Here's a chance for you."

I shrugged, didn't respond.

"It's an important cause, Stefan."

I watched him. I stopped a moment to think about that one. Then I thought about Eva again, and the kidnaps, and the part he was playing. And I knew what I had to do...

"Our country's being led by the peevish and short-sighted and corrupt," he said. "And it's got to stop. A lot of committed and well-informed people are very concerned. You're concerned too, and there's a place for you. It's time for serious reform."

"I'm not your man."

"Yes you are. Think about it. It's what you've been waiting for, I know you're going to think about it."

"Listen, Matthias..."

"No, listen to me..."

"I haven't come here to be persuaded," I said. "I'm..."

"I know."

I stopped. He gazed up at me, and the enigmatic smile touched the corners of his lips again.

"Eva sent you," he said quietly.

I shook my head, I lowered my eyes. So he'd known all along.

"She's sent you to try and stop me."

"She wants me to, yes." I looked back at him. "But I've come on my own initiative, it's my intention to persuade you, too."

"You never will."

A silence between us. We stared at each other.

"She's afraid, Matthias."

"No need."

"I am too."

"Tell her," he said.

"What?"

"To trust me. In four months it's all over."

Four months? I thought. My God, four whole months? "She's scared you might get killed," I said.

"I won't."

"Or kill someone else."

"No chance."

"In self-defence then. Or by accident."

"I don't hurt by accident."

I spread my hands, shook my head again. "You know what the hell I'm talking about."

"Our rules are strict and straightforward. No-one gets hurt, each of the kidnapped is set free. Four months, tell her that."

I shrugged. I was wasting my time. Stooping, I picked up the plastic bottle again. I was thinking of Annabelle, too. I said: "And if something goes wrong again, like it did in Nuremberg? You planning on hiding at my place again?"

"No."

"Don't even think of it."

"You're moving, anyway."

So he knew that too. I sipped water, watching him over the tipped-up bottle.

"Relax," he said. "I shan't endanger you again. Not Annabelle either."

Was there anything he didn't know? I lowered my eyes. I felt relief, at least in that respect.

Another silence between us. A longer one. Then I saw him slowly uncrossing his legs, begin to stand up. He rose like an athlete after a rest, rising refreshed for the start of the next race. But he wasn't going anywhere. He stood before me looking down, pausing – and seated himself on the mattress beside me.

His body was close.

He said: "So you're returning to your roots." He had taken the bottle from my hands, it hung between his knees. "Munich."

I nodded. His face was close too, that lean, handsome, sunburnt face.

"Found somewhere to live yet?"

"Still working on it."

"With Annabelle."

"Yes," I said.

"And the two children."

"Yes."

His eyes were so clear, gazing into me. What was he thinking? Was he just making conversation, catching up with the news like old friends do – or did he have an ulterior motive?

The pause lengthened. Then he simply said: "She's quite a woman." Suddenly he grinned.

I relaxed again. "Yes she is," I said. Managed a grin, too. And added: "A celestial queen."

"Your Jewish goddess."

"Who would've thought," I mused.

He put down the bottle. I gazed into space.

"Good move, Stefan."

We sat there, side by side. Could feel his thigh on mine. And I remembered: we used to sometimes do that as kids, didn't we? Sitting on the window ledge legs dangling side by side up in his nursery...

He'd snaked an arm round behind me, laid a hand on my shoulder, his elbow hung down. We were very close now. And he was speaking again, but I didn't hear – I was drifting away, going back, I was happier now, I was crying inside...

Something had broken, unexpectedly, in my brain. I turned my head and looked at him, watched his profile while he spoke. That feeling ate its way through my mind, into my gut, beginning to overwhelm me, a ghastly premonition. I sat there watching him, watching us both, as if from a distance, I was outside myself. And the feeling became a certainty: I'd never see him again.

He was talking of our teens, he'd gone back too, I think still on the subject of women, the girls we'd known, the first one he'd laid. I began to listen, I wanted to scream. Were these some of the last words from his lips I would hear? Oh God, Matthias, for Christ's sake, why can't you get out before it's too late? I wanted to reach out my hand, mask his mouth, to silence him, to tell him what I knew. Questions were rising up, in my panic, so many questions, there was so much I still wanted to share. Serious things about the past and the present and the future... and silly things, too, like had he saved me on those cobbles, had he been following me? And had he really believed he could save Eva's future, alter fate, by shoving someone out of a window?

I don't know how long he continued speaking on that bed, but I know I hung on every word – all that was important was we were together, we were like one, no-one could take that away. At some point I started slipping; I was very tired, could feel myself falling. Was it the heat? How long was it since I'd last slept? I sensed his arms, his muscles, healthy and strong, supporting me, setting me upright, I must've tipped over...

"I'll give you a bed for the night."

Wearily I thought: a bed? Not this one? I opened my eyes. For the night? The sunlight outside the mud hut was bright. He was gathering me in. I shook myself awake.

"Can you walk?"

My God, it was still so hot, what the hell had he done to me, where had he brought me?

"Yes," I said.

He helped me stand. My legs were sluggish, my body a load.

"Just tired," I told him.

"Sure. It's four in the morning."

I managed to stand alone. Looked blearily out the dirty little window, through the cracks of the door, looked at the sunlight.

"Where am I, Matthias?"

Was that a faint laugh? It was so far off...

I glanced. That quiet smile on his lips once more. Would it, too, be for the very last time? I felt sick: it strangled my throat, it shrank my soul. He said nothing. He indicated the door with his hand.

I followed him. The door was opening, he was passing through; I followed, hesitantly, uncertainly, what would I find? I felt my nervousness growing again, felt insecure.

Through the doorway, out into the yard – or what I thought would be a yard. It wasn't, though. We were still enclosed inside a building. The dusty straw on the floor was real, so was the stone-and-mud yard wall over there, but that was all. Above the wall rose a blank surface, like a cinema screen: there was the steppe, there were the hazy mountains and the vast expanse of sky – I suppose it was back-projection. No hens, no donkey, just tripods with powerful arc lights. I glanced up: we seemed to be in what looked like a barn. Old timber beams and broad planked flooring far above my head, a modern steel ladder reaching up to a hatch, big silver tubular hot-air ducts. Out here it was even hotter.

At the corner of the mud hut whose walls were strengthened by diagonal supports and struts, Matthias stopped briefly before a trestle table. A console and snaking cables. His index finger extended, pressing – whether keys or touch-screen I couldn't determine, didn't care. All the arc lights dimmed, the wafting hot air from the overhead grilles cut off, the scenery faded from the screen...

Chapter 33

On the last day of March I gave a small party for everyone at the old firm; I wished to leave with grace.

Then the following week I moved to Munich. Annabelle and I were still hunting for a suitable house, but with no success. So I left all my furniture and most possessions in the flat in Nuremberg, just took some clothes and a few books, went to stay temporarily – and somewhat unwillingly – in her Schwabing apartment.

Psychologically, however, I'd reached the decision in my mind, pulled up my roots, made the jump: I'd moved to Munich to live again, had made the move for good. It was a strange feeling. After twenty years here I was back again. Another circle closing?

All this time Matthias preyed on my conscience, he was permanently in my thoughts; twice I dreamt about him, once that he was crippled for life, once that he was dead. From that weekend after we'd said goodbye and I'd been returned the way I'd arrived – after that farewell, regardless of where I was, I made sure to listen to the News every morning, waiting for the worst. But day after day, week after week, no catastrophe came through.

Over Easter Annabelle and I took a few days off, drove down to the Dolomites with the children; it was their school vacation. There, south of the Alps, isolated in nature, we missed the News: several Easter marches in Paris and Barcelona and Rome had got out of hand. In Germany, at the Brandenburg Gate in Berlin, another demonstrator died, a police officer was badly wounded – and in

Munich a government building was vandalised and set on fire. When finally I learned about it, I thought: well at least it wasn't a synagogue and there was no burning of books. I thought of Matthias too. He haunted me.

Also during April one of my estate agents found a buyer for my small holiday property on the *Schliersee* lake and the formalities were clinched within weeks. Despite the worsening economic crisis and bursting of the housing bubble, he sold it for over double what I'd originally paid. The place had, anyway, only been a financial investment to rent out to holidaymakers; there was no pang of nostalgia, no sense of loss. That, if one's lucky, is what nest eggs are for. And I needed the money. Half I ploughed into the new firm, a little more than agreed in the contract with Cornelia, the other half would go towards the new house. But still we couldn't find one.

The first of May, Labour Day, was a black day, I remember. In Germany it's always a traditional time for demonstrations anyway, but this year, they said, was the most angry and bitter on record. Many of the marches turned nasty during the morning, and by late afternoon the violence had increased, continued into the night with fires and riots and several dozen people hospitalised. Yes, I recall: Cornelia and I were in our new offices taking advantage of the bank holiday – we could hear chanting and megaphones and breaking glass although the demos were two blocks away. I'm a coward – it made my skin creep. And I thought of Matthias again.

Still no word of a new kidnap.

x x x

It was in late May that I received a private phone call at my desk. Eva's voice. "Got a plan," she said. She sounded impatient, under pressure. It was becoming quite a habit.

Since reporting back about my visit to his farm I'd been avoiding the subject of Matthias with her, had pushed it out of sight: I'd had too little time anyway, Cornelia and I were having to work like dogs – seminars, lectures, industrial psychology therapy groups, training unemployed managers and helping to place them. Annabelle hadn't mentioned him either, I think she understood.

"Got to meet this evening," Eva said.

I tried to postpone. Was unsuccessful – with Eva, when her eye's on a goal, it's like biting on granite. So I cancelled an appointment and drove over.

We sat at her breakfast bar, alone. Baby Daniel was asleep in his room next door; the day-nanny had gone home. She didn't beat about the bush. "I've nailed him down," she pronounced.

"You have?" I said. Oh God, I thought. But I didn't know what was coming.

"Thought I'd have to wait till my birthday, but he agreed. Matter of fact, said it would do us good, well overdue."

"What is?"

She wasn't listening. "It's this coming Saturday."

My heart stumbled: oh God, I thought again. She made me nervous, I shut my eyes. Mentally I peeped in my diary: Annabelle and I had something planned. "Shit," I said. Her birthday wasn't till the thirteenth of June – that would've given me a breathing space...

"With Matthias everything's short notice," she retorted. Her cigarette burned between fingers.

"Tell me," I said. I balled my fists, I waited for the worst.

She told me. A weekend in the mountains, climbing the Zugspitze, the easy trekking route. And even while she spoke, rapid and precise, I realised that something was wrong, that something didn't add up.

"Not kosher," I said.

"What?"

"He'd never agree to doing this. Not yet." Matthias knew well that Eva was frightened, would do anything to stop him. I told her. And ended: "He'd smell a rat a mile off."

"Forgot to tell you..." She stubbed out her cigarette; she did it with a single stab, she did it the way Margareth does. "I confronted him. Made him tell me too. He confirmed in four months it's all over. He promised. So I said okay. Even said I'd help him if it came to the crunch."

I shook my head. "He's not a fool. He wouldn't believe you."

"He believed me. I know him, know when he's lying."

I shrugged...

But she was hurrying on: "You know the route, it's on the south face. You did it with him a couple of times as a kid, and he took me once."

"Long time ago."

"No problem..."

That mountain, I thought. It made me go cold.

"And you know the hut halfway up," she said. "Where you stay the night. Remember?"

"Yes."

"And 'bout another hour up there're like natural steps in the rock. And after the steps comes that narrow ledge round the rock face with a drop to the right."

I remembered that too, could see it still. An unpleasant place, a dizzy place for people like me, how could I forget? I'd flattened myself, crawled inch by inch, both times it'd made my stomach squelch. All very well if you're good at heights, I'm the master when it comes to vertigo. She's crazy, I thought...

"Eva, no..." I began.

"'Course you do." She'd misunderstood. "Where the ice cracks like gunshots when the sun's coming up and you have to watch out for falling rocks. Told me 'bout it yourself."

Falling rocks had been the least of my problems. I stared into space; I was feeling giddy and sick already. Deeply unhappy, I nodded. "Yes," I said. I was contradicting myself now.

"We'll be reaching it 'bout ten Sunday morning. After the other groups from the hut're well past. I'll find an excuse so we leave late. Okay?"

I said nothing. I was watching her. She had it all worked out, didn't she?

"You get there 'bout nine-thirty just in case. You do it the easy way with the cogwheel train and cable-car to the top, you come down from the summit and hide. Got to help me, case anything goes wrong."

Help her? Goes wrong? I shook my head helplessly, already I was shaking inside. I guessed what she was going to say.

"I'll be behind him, push him over the edge. The slope's steep, he'll break some bones, get lacerated..."

"Eva, you can't do that – that's madness."

"'Course I can. He'll have the rucksack, it'll pad him a bit."

"He might get badly hurt."

"Not a sheer drop, silly. Long way down but there're boulders in the way. He'll just smash his legs or an arm. Put him out of action long enough till..."

"He might split open his skull."

"No chance. He's fit. And he knows how to fall."

Again I shook my head. "My God, Eva, it's far too risky — what if he gets wind of..."

"Don't play chicken — promised to help. When the deed's done you call the Rescue people and we'll get down there, wait with him." She lit another cigarette, determined fingers, determined face.

I spread my hands. What the hell could I say? "This is madness," I repeated. "It'll never work." I cast about, grasping for straws. "Why not simply turn him in, that way he wouldn't..."

"He'd get fifteen years, mate. Don't intend waiting fifteen bloody years till he gets out of the cooler..."

"At least he'd..."

"And Daniel needs a father — not a dead one or behind bloody bars..."

But I was up on the mountain again, trying to visualise. I had another go: "He's like a cat, Eva, he's got fast reactions. It's too dangerous — he might take you with him when he falls."

"That's 'nother reason I need you, silly."

So she'd considered that one too. I sat there.

"Got to help me," she said.

I bowed my head, stared at the bar top. What else could I do? "Okay," I said.

x x x

That was Wednesday. On Friday afternoon Eva rang again.

"It's off," she said. "Forget it. Bloody shit."

"Off?" I held my breath.

"The weekend. Just called me, can't make it. Said sorry, some other time. Fucking damnation."

I closed my eyes, I thanked my lucky stars. "Ah," I said. Tried to say something to console; but inwardly I realised. Why had I been so stupid — I'd known it couldn't work out, hadn't I? I'd already seen him for the last time.

I did what I could to calm her, her disappointment was like a knife. It cut into my ear: "Had it all planned to a fucking tee. Got to bloody start from scratch again now..."

"Eva..." I couldn't tell her about my premonition, about the certainty in my bones. Instead I said: "We'll have to wait it out, be patient — only another eight weeks..."

"No we bloody won't..." There was fear underneath her disappointment as well, and anger coming through. "Your fucking turn now. You think of something."

"But what, for God's sake?" I could see Matthias as we said goodbye, he'd held me close and kissed me, there was something in his eye. Had he known it too?

"How the fuck should I know? On the thirteenth, p'raps. He might find time on my birthday. Got to get him alone, though – and it's got to be somewhere nearer."

"Yes," I said, dejectedly.

"Won't work in the mountains again, he'd prob'ly only have a few hours. Rack your own shitty white cells for a change, and ring me back."

Oh God, I thought, what's the point? Can one really change the course of things, can one stand in the way of fate?

"Okay," I said, to stem the tide, to calm her fear. I told her that I would.

Abruptly the line went dead.

I did my best. I'd promised. At the first opportunity I left the office to clear my head, walked the streets in Munich rain. One hour. Two hours. But no solution presented itself. That evening I tried again, and next day too. Still nothing.

A week went by, June began. I'd given up now. And then it came.

I was on the autobahn driving north; had to pick up files I'd forgotten in Nuremberg. The rainy patch had passed, the late afternoon was warm and bright, early summer everywhere. Was crossing the Old Mill Valley. Maybe subconsciously Matthias still hung in my head. They'd finished tearing up the valley floor, were making progress on the long bridge and embankments between the tunnels being bored in the hills both ends; it still hurt me to look. And there it was: an old memory woke – the one that had been dislodged a year back but wouldn't quite materialise. I slowed the car and briefly turned my head, glancing over my shoulder. I was staring up at that cliff – and the open space along the high shoulder before the forest began... the forest, yes... But it was the cliff which had done it; that was the first thing I'd noticed in the night, looming and ghostly, as Matthias drove us by...

The memory from twenty-three years ago came suddenly clear. I could see Matthias, see the three of us up there, driving deep in amongst the trees. He'd asked me to help: in the wildness of his youth he'd turned to me. I the traitor, I the coward. They'd buried it up there somewhere, hadn't they? Had he wished to bind me?

My apartment smelled musty, like a museum. But it was a museum now, anyway – full of the past, full of me. After sorting the files I got out a couple of my maps of the area, then another better one, the Ordnance Survey with more details, sat in my old armchair at the window studying it. There were the hills and the three river valleys cutting through them, converging – and where they met there was Schellenburg Hill rising up steep and dramatic at the end of the long ridge of rock, and the patches of forest and the paths were clearly marked.

An idea began to form.

I checked the calendar at my desk: her birthday was on a Tuesday. Not a good start, the weekday traffic would be bad, would waste time, hold us up. And if summer vacations were starting? ...traffic jams, even worse. I turned the calendar, looked at the lists on the back. The first one, in Saxony, not till ten days later. That at least was good. I considered a moment. Tuesday... Tuesday. Well, on the other hand, there'd be no groups or hiking tours up there during the week. So the place should be fairly quiet...

During the following twenty-four hours I went over and over the idea, looking for holes, looking for snags. The main ones seemed to be the weather, and how to draw Matthias. Next day I decided: give Eva a tinkle, see if she's got time today or tomorrow to meet. I reached for the phone, but it started ringing. It was Eva; she'd beaten me to it.

"D'you want to hear some good news?" she said rapidly, before I could speak.

"Always," I said.

"Well, you may be interested or you may not, so pin back your lugholes..."

She was calling about something quite different, about my house-hunting. "The house administrator just called. The ground floor flat under me'll be vacant soon. Interested?"

I sat there, the phone to my ear. I stared into space.

"Hey, you still there?"

"Yes," I said.

"And?"

"Well, that's unexpected news." Ferdinand-Marie Straße. Oh God, no. I was gazing at the old house, at the front door portico, the ground floor rooms, the gardens beyond...

"Interested?" she repeated impatiently. "Have to know soon 'cos the admin's got several clients who'd snap at it – so he says."

"Well..." I began.

"Our family's got first option till Saturday – in the agreement Toby drew up when he sold the house."

"Ah yes," I said neutrally.

"So?"

"Well I'm just thinking."

"Don't fall asleep over it, mate."

I was procrastinating. I thought: should I, shouldn't I, give it a chance? "When will it become vacant?" I asked half-heartedly.

"September, officially. But the tenants'll be gone end of June. It's *Munich Insurance* – they're closing half their branches pronto, cutting their losses after the fiasco."

"Is there an option to buy?"

"Only rent."

"Okay," I said. "I'll mention it to Annabelle." Maybe she'll simply say no, I thought, take the thing out of my hands. "D'you have the admin's number?"

"Got a pen?"

She gave it to me. Then: "Name's Koch. He said viewing evenings only."

"Okay," I said again. So I'd have to move fast, have to leave Matthias till later. "Thanks," I said.

Just in case, I paused waiting, expecting the obvious, but all she added was: "Keep me posted." No new tirade, no mention of him.

I replaced the phone. Rang Annabelle, passed on the news. She sounded inquisitive. I tried to dampen it, only made it worse. She started asking questions: "Your old home, my reticent one?"

"Yes."

"How large is it?" She meant the ground floor.

"About thirty percent larger than your apartment."

"That's a bit big. And..."

"Yes," I quickly agreed.

"And the garden?"

"About an acre."

"An *acre*?"

"Lawns, trees. And an orchard. Far too big, too."

"Does it go with the ground floor?"

"Well there's Eva upstairs," I said, "and an elderly doctor. And in the roof a flat rented by the *LMU* – I believe a visiting professor now and then. So I presume one would have to..."

"Oh I am sure that would be no problem." A brief pause. Then: "What do you think, Stefan?"

Now she'd put me on the spot. Carefully I said: "I suppose one might have a brief look."

"We only have till Saturday?"

"Yes."

"Have you time this evening?"

"I'll make time."

x x x

It was a curious feeling standing there in the spacious old drawing room. Memories, ghosts. I tried to suppress. Visually it had changed: modern office furniture with long table, tasteful new lighting, the open hearth clean and unused, the walls hung with modern graphics and all painted white now. The firm had turned it into a conference room. The atmosphere was still there, though. Annabelle seemed occupied inspecting the parquet floor and the fixtures. I stood there, stiff...

My mother was saying: "And woe betide those who forget, Adolf Hitler did more for our country from the very start than all the *Weimar* wimps of politicians put together..." Her voice was raised, indignant and heated. I watched her; I was thirteen years old. Small and attractive in fashionable cocktail dress, she steered the conversation, led the herd – her blonde hair coiffured, her index finger wagging to her words. Weren't those acquiescing murmurs from a number of the elderly guests?

I turned. There was my father tall and erect over by the marble fireplace, ignoring, playing the distinguished and perfect host, but I knew he'd heard every word. And Annabelle said: "So this is where you were born and grew up, my silent one."

"Yes," I said. I could scarcely nod, I had to get out of that room.

We walked slowly through the rest of the ground floor, opening doors, peering: another very large room, the dining room where those grand dinner parties had once taken place. Then the smoking and billiard room, father's study, the laundry area, utility rooms, the maids' day room — plus what had once been the kitchens, WC and pantry. Everything spick and span and bright as snow, everywhere old installations and cupboards torn out, renewed, desks with flat-screen computers and chairs and charts, new toilets, even a fitness room with training machines. Details and traces wiped clean as a slate. But the memories pervaded, hanging there, no-one could take those away. Annabelle appraised all with professional eye, the windows, the curtains, the orientation of spaces...

Finally, through the French windows of the old study, we went out into the gardens. Soft evening sunlight. I stood staring, blind.

"What lovely lawns," Annabelle said. "Oh look, that's an old copper beech over there." I tried to look, but all I could see were Toby and Margareth playing badminton on the grass court, the ping of feather ball on thin rackets back and forth — and Eva up a tree with a book.

"Yes," I said. There was my mother again, a tea party, a circle of chairs, the chink of china, latest hats. I had to look away.

Annabelle was taking my hand. "Now I can imagine you all better, my philosopher — now I can imagine your roots." She was gazing at me.

I shouldn't have done this, I thought — shouldn't've even thought of coming. I made a non-committal noise; I couldn't look her in the eye.

"Don't turn up your nose like that!" She squeezed my fingers, I managed a glance. But she'd turned her head away. "It's lovely. The children will adore it."

Will? I thought. Had she already decided?

I had to nip it in the bud, had to head her off. "It's absurdly large," I said. I waved a negligent hand; I could hear the weakness in my words.

"Oh no, my philosopher, this is just what the children require." Her hand had gone, it was indicating the garden. "And the ground floor has potential."

"The bathroom's far too small," I said. "And anyway we need two. I find..."

"We will make it for the children, and put in another one for us."

"We'd have to start major alterations. I ask myself if the place's worth it."

"My critical one." She was laughing. "What is the matter?"

I shrugged. "I simply find it all rather impractical."

She was watching me. "Does it remind you too much?"

I shook my head. She'd seen through me. "A little," I confessed.

"Don't worry." She laughed again, took my hand again. "It will pass quickly enough, wait and see. I know you."

Did she? Did she really?

She stood there before me so tall, so elegant, so beautiful. We'd made the decision to live together some while ago, now here was somewhere she liked, here was the chance. I hovered on the brink, procrastinating. We'd said we'd get married too, didn't we? But we hadn't – not yet. I'd postponed and postponed...

I gazed away at the trees. Eva the bookworm was gone. I thought: will it pass? Could I really live here again? Is another circle closing, is it meant to close?

x x x

We returned to the hall. On the way she made one or two suggestions, practical and precise, pointing things out to me, but I hardly listened – I was concentrating on those memories, those voices, trying to block them out.

Outside, beneath the portico, we stopped. Spoke briefly together, then descended the steps. The administrator, Koch, was waiting for us in the drive; he leaned on his big white Audi talking into his mobile. When he caught sight of us coming over he ended his call abruptly.

"Nice property, isn't it?" he said. "Nice area." He was young and smooth, a nasty bit of work. I ignored him. I'd met his father once long ago, an estate agent – a pleasant, correct old gentleman.

"Let's talk conditions," I said. "We may be interested." How could the son be so different?

"Well, I'm not the least surprised – would quite fancy the place myself, as a matter of fact. Just fire away then."

"How high's the rent?"

He told me. Added, as he noted my reaction: "Of course, because you're family, so to speak, we could consider coming down a hundred."

"Another two-fifty," I retorted. I watched his practised wince. Quickly I calculated: "Still fifteen percent above the average hereabouts."

"That would be a little too much."

"Take it or leave it." I had a little ace in my pocket, I knew what Eva paid per square foot.

A pained expression. "Well, perhaps we could stretch our rules here."

"And a five-year lease with first option for a further five."

"Now that would be a distinct possibility. Naturally I shall have to ask the usual three-month commission. Administration costs, don't you know, and so on."

"One month," I said. "Lease beginning first of July."

He eyed me calmly, suavely. I could see him doing a few little calculations of his own.

"If you prepare the contract pronto, we'll sign on Saturday," I said. "Conditions as just discussed."

His eyes were dark and sharp. They regarded me a moment in silence. He smoothed the jacket of his corduroy suit, adjusted his natty silk tie. Then: "I believe we could agree on that." His eyes looked pleased with themselves. And why not? We'd saved him a lot of time and work.

"Settled." I nodded. "We'll e-mail you all our particulars tomorrow morning. I have your visiting card."

Annabelle slipped her hand through my arm. "And Mr Koch, don't forget the inclusion that the first five-year lease is on a fixed-rate basis, with subsequent increases coupled to the current rent scale."

He blinked his eyes at her, trying to express more pain. Then expansively: "I should say that would be on the cards."

Behind my back Annabelle gently, cheekily, pinched my bottom. I gazed apathetically at Koch: good for her – I'd gone and forgotten that one.

x x x

"You're looking at your new neighbour," I said, deadpan. It was Friday evening, I'd just called in on Eva; baby Daniel lay cuddled on her lap. No beating about the bush: first the news, I thought, then briefly the idea.

"You're kidding." She dipped her head, kissed Daniel's head. "Hear that, Danny?"

I spread my hands in uncertain silence.

"Never b'lieved you'd even reach the starting line."

"No?"

"Nope – not with all your hang-ups. And 'specially not 'cos of your 'mazing ability to take ten years to reach a decision, shall I change the broken light bulb or not?" She watched me, head cocked on one side. "Do I smell a bit of friendly persuasion from the fairer sex?"

Feebly I grinned a crooked grin.

She laughed – drily. The laugh cut off. "And when's the big day?"

I told her. "Of course," I added, "till Annabelle's honed everything to perfection it'll probably be the Christmas after next before we actually move in." My grin this time was laconic.

Then I switched – to the subject of Matthias. I explained my idea. She didn't break in once till I'd finished. When I stopped, she rose. "Wait a mo'." Left the room, returned without Daniel. Sitting again, she tipped back her head, her eyes fixed on a spot far away; her stare looked full of scepticism.

But I was mistaken. "Got something going for it," she said after a few seconds. "In fact..." She reached, pulled a cigarette out of a pack, lit it, left it a moment in her mouth. "In fact not bad."

"You haven't changed your mind then?" I queried.

"'Course not." She plucked the cigarette from her lips, blew smoke upwards. "Could work."

"More risky than your plan," I said. "Not so isolated." Hurriedly I started to try to pick holes – perhaps I could dissuade her.

She interrupted: "Said yourself, on a weekday almost no-one about. And the cliff's high."

"D'you remember it, then?"

"Remember the ol' ring wall from the Celts or what not up at the top."

"The cliff isn't so steep," I said. "Not like that place in the mountains. And there are trees below."

"Jesus, I don't intend killing him, mate. Just incapacitate."

"There may be rock outcrops."

"Same applies as my ol' plan."

I watched her, I felt insecure. "And Matthias? How will you persuade him?"

"It's my birthday. Promised he'd manage to find time for that."

"But Schellenburg? How're you going to entice him, get him up there?"

"Don't panic." She sat, frowning, considering. Then: "Sex at sunset and all through the night." She nodded. "Yeah. Surrounded by mother nature – likes it that way."

"You don't have to drive halfway to Nuremberg to find a quiet spot. Maybe he'll say he knows somewhere closer."

"Won't tell him till we're nearly there. Be my birthday secret he's to obey. Just to please me for once in a bloody blue moon."

I shook my head, wasn't so sure. Matthias never went blind into anything, he was the very careful kind. "He'll smell a rat," I said. "He'll want to know in advance where he's heading."

"Not with me. Likes my surprises, always did." She shrugged her tough little shoulders, took another puff.

I said: "I'll give you a tip. If you have to tell him, just say Schellenburg."

"Would anyway."

It was suddenly night... "But nothing else," I reinforced. "Just the name." I could see us – Matthias and me and Molotov Theo...

"Uh-huh." She exhaled smoke again, watching me through it. "Why?"

"It might make him nosey." The path was steep, we were driving up it in that forestry jeep they'd stolen for the purpose. Endless pines in silhouette, a bit of a moon, the long rutted track between the trees. They'd only taken me because it was heavy and three could dig faster, and because they still trusted me in those early days, and I was too scared to say no...

"Nosey?" she queried. "Why?"

Was it still up there? Or had they removed it long ago? "Just say it," I said.

She tapped ash, shrugged again. "Okay, brother. Will do."

I stared at the bar top, stared at my hands. Late evening sunlight streamed through the windows, fell upon my skin. That reminded me. I looked back at her – she was gazing directly at me.

"What if it rains?" I said.

Her cigarette end glowed red, her eyes considered me over it. Then she tossed her head, said: "What's the problem, mate? Never done it in the rain?"

I spread my hands. No, I thought; not even Judit had stumbled on that one.

"Thought I'd tell him to take along a tarpaulin?" A touch of sarcasm. "Make him fuck me under it?"

"Don't be vulgar, sister. Be serious."

"Am. *That* wouldn't be the first time either, if you have to know."

I ignored. "Okay, so assuming everything works out up to here, d'you think you can get him near the edge?"

"Well, not the way you 'magined, that's for sure, me going for a jolly little stroll over there and saying cor' blimey ol' chap come and look at the gorgeous view."

"How then?"

"Let that be my problem, I'll think of something."

But we had to work this one through. "What then?" I demanded.

"How should I know?" She waggled her head, stubbed her cigarette out irritably. "How 'bout me balancing on the edge of the precipice and bending over, pulling down my knickers and saying come and get it?" She stuck out the tip of a tongue.

"Don't fool around."

"Well stop all these bloody whats and hows." Impatiently she switched position on her barstool; her jeans were sexy and tight. "I'll threaten him, of course – what else?"

"Threaten? With what?"

"I'll procure it."

"What?"

"A gun. I'll bring a gun."

I gazed at her, unhappily. Oh God, no. "You're joking again," I said.

Her chin went up. "Never more earnest, mate. I'll stick it in my bag."

"You can't do that. Far too dangerous."

"Yes I can."

I swallowed. Hunched my shoulders. "You'll procure one, just like that? You think such things grow on trees or something? Come on, sister, knock it off. One can't..."

"Wanna bet?"

"Too damn dangerous," I repeated.

"Got a better idea?"

I dropped my eyes. I was thinking fast, how to head her off. But nothing came.

"Settled then," she said. She said it so determinedly.

I couldn't let her. I shook my head, looked at her again. Slowly I said: "No Eva."

"Yes."

"Forget it."

"No."

Shit, I thought, I'll never persuade her. I felt afraid. Resignedly I said: "Okay."

"Good."

"But I'll do it."

"You?" She watched me.

I said nothing.

"Now you're kidding, brother."

"I said, I'll do it."

"Yeah? Know someone?"

"But I'll keep it. I'll bring it."

"You?" she repeated.

I returned her gaze, again said nothing.

"You couldn't shoot a sheep," she accused.

But you could, I thought – couldn't you? If you had to.

I said: "No-one's going to shoot anyone, sister, if they don't have to. Just threaten, like you said."

"If the chips're down, think you really could?" Sarcasm. "Really think you'd fool him?"

Could I? Would I? I was panicking inside. Fearfully, I looked her in the eye. "I'll have to, won't I?" I couldn't let her have that gun.

She stared so steadily, but she didn't speak.

"This whole thing's crazy," I said.

She just continued staring; I could read her thoughts.

So I added: "I want you to do something for me."

"What?"

"We'll check the place out together, be on the safe side. See what you think, if it's too risky – maybe I've overlooked..."

"Tomorrow. We'll go tomorrow, okay?"

My God, she was so fast, so under pressure: my little sister's impetuosity. "Only if it's in the afternoon," I said.

"Pick you up at two, okay?"

I knew it was a waste of time, knew it wouldn't work. But I'd thrown in the towel now, I'd resigned myself. "No, I'll pick you up," I said. I'd done my best, though, at least I'd kept my promise.

x x x

Next day was cloudy, with rain. Before Annabelle and I went to sign the contract I rang Eva, asked could we drive in separate cars, meet direct at Schellenburg.

"Sure," she said. "Why though? Don't find your driving *that* nervy."

I gave a strangled chuckle. Explained I had to go on to Nuremberg. I didn't mention why.

"Okey-doke."

"Meet at the parking spot up on the hill," I suggested. "D'you know the little road that...?"

"Parking?" she queried. "Jesus." I could hear a sudden small worry in her voice. "On the hill?"

"Not at the top," I reassured. "Just a patch of grass two-thirds up, save us a climb."

But she didn't know the turning; so I gave her a simpler rendezvous. We agreed on 3:30.

x x x

On the autobahn, alone, heading north. Time to collect thoughts. The rain had stopped, clouds clearing, the sun coming through. The traffic was heavy, but no jams; in just over an hour, slightly late, I was on the long incline dropping down into the Old Mill valley. That's where her little silver Mini overtook me, going much too fast for the eighty kph allowed. I flashed my lights to warn but there were cars ahead of me and she didn't notice; was she sunk in thoughts too? The speed camera caught her, must've been a pretty picture. She braked too late, accelerated again.

On the last stretch down, the green valley below me coming into view, speckled with cloud-shadows and sun. Like a festering wound in flesh, the broad line of new rail tracks under construction was already clearly visible. And poking up the other side like the head of a dragon, rocky wooded Schellenburg hill with its bumpy forested back stretching endlessly away to the left. A minute later I took the turn-off.

Eva was parked before the *Gasthaus* in Enkering next to the road as planned. I made her jump in with me; we left her Mini standing. Through the village, past the little church, then left, up the narrow winding track between trees – they'd asphalted it now. The old Mercedes engine laboured, had to change down to first. Above the tree-line we emerged into the open: just grass and sky. We parked. Although weekend, only one other car.

On foot we set off along the open saddle leaving the forest to our rear: short coarse grass beneath our feet still slightly damp from the morning rain, big billowing grey clouds to the south, the sun warm on our heads. Left and right longer grass disappearing out of sight down the steep slopes full of early June flowers, a mass of pink and yellow and white. Nice view, had to admit, but my mind was busy somewhere else. Ahead the steady incline, rising up to the head of the hill a quarter of a mile away. Faint traces of tyre tracks on the slope, could they be from forestry trucks? Or something to do with the railway and tunnel below? Never seen them before.

I cast a glance back over my shoulder, remembering, and slightly concerned. Was it less isolated up here than it used to be? Beyond the two cars in the distance, the fringe of forest dark green, almost forbidding, hiding its nasty little secret. But that was all.

Climbing more steeply now. A man with a dog, strolling down towards us, passing us, brief nods, brief hellos. We reached the grassy ditch and defensive earth wall built by man I guess thousands of years ago, weathered by time, a cut in the middle. Stony, mossy path. We reached the plateau. It was loud up there, far louder than where we'd parked: a distant roar of traffic from the autobahn, hammering and noise from the construction sites. We walked on. Scattered bushes, clumps of trees, grass under foot again. A small modern hut, new to me, nearby an antenna rising high. To do with the railway too?

We veered left, approached the cliff where it was steepest: near the edge, bare silver-grey rock, big thick bushes of broom with bright yellow flowers, thick scrubby heather not yet in bloom. And all around us only sky.

Side by side we both peered down. She didn't turn a hair; she was good at heights. My stomach went queasy, had to step back. But I'd caught a glimpse: a dreadful drop, tops of pine trees growing from crevices, weathered rock, heather clinging. Went down on my knees, felt better then, leaned out, peeping again. There was shiny new chicken wire down there too, stretched taut on the cliff face where rock showed through, I suppose to stabilise, prevent falls of stone.

Unhappily I peered.

It was steep, but not sheer. It went down and down: there were not many outcrops, but lots of trees. Was it too dangerous? I didn't like it at all. My stomach turned over again at the thought. At the bottom, on a line directly under us, I could see the new bridge stretching away, the half-finished tracks, the autobahn, two of the river valleys flowing into one...

I retreated, stood up. Unhurriedly Eva stepped back too. We were looking at each other.

"No," I said. Nothing else.

"No what?"

"We can't do it."

"Simple."

Hammering again, from below, and sounds of a circular saw.

"Just push him?" I shut my eyes.

"Yep. I'll give him a shove."

I stared again. "My God."

"Don't start that crap again. Told you, he knows how to fall."

My breathing was uneasy, constricted now. "You'd have to get him right to the edge."

"My job."

"And if he smells a rat? He'd watch you like a hawk, you wouldn't have a chance."

"If he does, which I doubt, then I'll see he's got his back to you. You hide there." She pointed. "You come up behind. I'll distract him – know how to do that. If I can't, then you just push him, mate."

"He'd hear me." I was trying to imagine, I was panicking again.

"What, on grass?" Said with a sneer.

"He's trained, sister – he's got eyes in the back of his head."

"Well, even if he did, so what? Then he turns on you and his back's to me, he'll jump out of his skin when he sees you. You've got the gun, so threaten him. *You* distract him and I'll shove him over."

"And if he tries grabbing you?"

"Won't. Jesus Christ – use your nut! Shoot at him near his legs, he won't take his eyes off you for a single bloody second, he'll know you mean business. Don't have to hit him." She tossed her head, her little hands were fists. "I'll yank him backwards and that's that. Simple."

Simple?

Oh God, I thought. I stared at her – at her steadfastness, her determination. And right afterwards I thought: just look at us – two naïve, untrained, unprofessional fools kidding ourselves we could really do such a thing to a man like Matthias.

She was turning away. I watched her small athletic back. And I wondered: if we ever manage to get this far, which one of us, in fact, is going to get hurt? Eva? Me? She was going ahead, I let her go. I gazed down the hill the way we had come, across the long grassy open shoulder; the car that had been parked there was gone. It seemed we were quite alone.

x x x

The e-mail came through as I sat at my computer.

It was weekend again, Sunday afternoon, I felt tired and stale. The four of us were at home in Annabelle's apartment, I was using her workroom as I had been now most evenings for a couple of months. They were busy times. For Annabelle too — involvement in a new exhibition for young artists in Munich, and planning the alterations for the house. She'd found us an architect, was working up her ideas with him. I felt like a monk; we hadn't made love for a week.

I pressed the key, called up the e-mail. Andrea. I awoke at once, my heart made a bump.

Briefly I read it, then read it again more carefully, trying to steady my breath. There were only four lines, short and sweet. Just like me, I thought. And just like me had she maybe taken an hour then deleted ninety-nine percent? Laconically I chuckled. The apple doesn't fall far from the tree, does it?

'Dear Papa (she wrote). Miss Mamma, miss you. Sammy and Saul super but not the same. Not quite. Get me? Living here in R since Jan. New school OK but NY too far. You in Munich now? With HER? Tell me what shall I do, please, please. Hugs and love, Andrea.'

I sat there, work forgotten. My heart refused resuscitation. Read the text once more, bent forward in hallowed concentration, this time attempting to read between the lines. She was toying with the thought of returning to Germany — oh God, was this true? Was she really unhappy? Did she mean, though, that Munich with Annabelle was out of the question? She sought my opinion — a cry for help? Or a hint perhaps. If I were still in Nuremberg, alone — would she come without asking my point of view?

With the sloth of a serpent, and with a supplication, a thrill slid through my being, failed to subside. My God, was I dreaming? What should I advise her – come back, I feel the same way, I miss you too? Could I extend the lease on my flat for another quarter year, give her time to find her feet and get to know Annabelle better, become acclimatised to the concept of Munich? Just to think: Annabelle and I and our three children, all together, all under one roof, Andrea back in my life again. A new chapter starting, another circle closed? The serpent glided, crept, the thought seduced, I tried to imagine...

But would that be right? Right for Andrea? Was that circle meant to close – or was it all too neat?

She had roots in Nuremberg, but in the States too – younger and stronger. Did she really want to pull them up? Maybe this was just a mood of hers, maybe it was only a momentary hole. She was in adolescence, a difficult time, a phase of life full of uncertainties, full of change. If she stuck it out a bit it'd probably turn her head again, her roots would get deeper. Then she'd be glad, in retrospect, that she'd stayed.

Slowly, hesitantly, I drafted a reply. After a number of corrections and deletions I wrote:

'My dear Andrea. I received your lines with deep appreciation. Yes, since April in M with Annabelle G. Greatly miss you too. But don't wish you to jump the gun, then regret. Suggest you wait a year or two, might be best for **you**, might answer the question whose answer you seek. Love and hugs, Papa.'

I read it through carefully, twice, sent it.

Within five minutes the reply came. So she'd been waiting: 'A year's a lifetime, Papa.'

She'd passed the buck; I knew she was waiting still. It tore me this way and that. I yearned for her to come, I knew that she shouldn't. With due consideration for the earnestness of the hour, I tried a subtle feint – it took me only ten minutes:

'We've found somewhere bigger to live, here in M (I wrote). Probably from September. There'll always be a room waiting, in vacations or otherwise. Love, again. Papa.'

It seemed to do the trick; my e-mail in-tray remained dormant. At least she had food for thought. I returned to my work. At least I tried to. But Andrea kept intruding like the testimony of the righteous, like a thorn in my side. Now it was I who was waiting.

Chapter 34

It was the day before Eva's birthday. I was getting very nervous. I watched the weather forecast that followed the breakfast News. Today: continuing sunny and warm. Damn. Tomorrow: starting bright, a low moving in from the British Isles at midday bringing a drop in temperatures and heavy rain. I stared, almost unable to believe – had my little prayer been answered, was He smiling down on me? Would it mean perhaps too heavy for even tarpaulin weather?

I thought: shall I ring Eva? Decided against. And left for work. She rang about ten.

"Change of plan," she said. She sounded tense.

"You heard then?" I gave a little wink to the one up above, I thanked my lucky stars.

"What?"

"Heavy rain tomorrow," I said. "Beginning late morning." I stood up to do a small dance. My heart fluttered free, I'd been let off the hook.

"No. Didn't." She inhaled sharply. Oh God, those cigarettes. "He just rang, put it forward to this afternoon."

I stood there dumb. My nervousness shot up again, stabbed me like a pain. "I see," was all I could manage. I thought: oh God, has he done this for her, did he hear the forecast too?

"Have to drop everything..." she was saying.

Goddamn it...

"He's picking me up at four."

So early? My heart staggered, my hand shook. Have to cancel two appointments as well. "Picking *you* up?" I echoed stupidly. Shit, I thought. We'd planned for her to take him and park on the hill.

"'Nother change of plan."

Shit, I thought again. I tried a few deep breaths, tried to slow my heart. "Four o'clock, that's very early."

"Can't help it, mate."

"Okay," I said. "I'll leave at two."

"Take my Mini."

"I'm taking mine." Had she forgotten already? If he got badly hurt we'd need the big back seat. Had her panic made her forget?

"Take it," she ordered. "If he parks down in the village yours's too bloody tell-tale, might see it."

"Too small, Eva, for God's sake."

"We'll take his, stupid."

She had a point there. Would he use his Land Rover? Did she know that too?

"Okay," I repeated.

"I'll drop it off at your office, give you the key."

"When?"

"Half an hour."

I glanced down at the time on my computer screen. Ten past ten.

"Hide it bloody well," she said.

But I couldn't react, couldn't speak.

×××

I remember the intense scent of the yellow broom, like warm honey almond, and the luscious green needles of the big thick bushes against the blue sky. Larks were singing, there were bees humming, and peacock butterflies too.

Four-fifteen.

The constant roar of the traffic rising up from the valley. Hardly any noise from the building sites, though. I crouched at first, but I needn't have bothered – I was far too early, they would only just have set off, wouldn't be here for nearly an hour. So after a short while I drew the wrapped gun carefully from the baggy calf pocket of my old trousers, laid it in the shadows. Sat down on the grass beside it. Weathered rock near my feet, grey almost silver, moss in the cracks. And between the bare rocks, thick tousled clumps of tough-looking heather managing to hold their own. I was only a few feet from the edge of the cliff.

I waited. Queasy sinking in my bowels.

Four-thirty.

Went over and over in my head how we would do it, how it would feel if I had to fire. Now and then, just in case, I leaned sideways and peered to the right, observing the opening in the grassy rampart a hundred or so yards away. Between it and me stood a few trees. Birches and pines. Couldn't see any further than that opening, though, couldn't look down the slope beyond to the open saddle, or further down to where we'd parked ten days ago, it was too far below.

Five o'clock.

I unwrapped the gun. Wouldn't be long now. Oh my God. Breathing getting blocked and jumpy again. The gun was heavy. A nasty-looking piece of work. The barrel was worn, one or two scratches – I wondered for a moment how often it had been used, and where and on what. Had it ever been used in hate? I released the safety, switched it on and off, and on again, practising. Removed the clip from the butt, clicked it back in. I'd done it several times in the apartment in Nuremberg too, uncertainly, not knowing about these things – I'd even counted the row of shells, fifteen of them in all. Horrible. And that smell of oil. Then finally I switched it back to fire, laid the gun delicately down and stuffed the cloth in my pocket so I couldn't forget.

I stood up, stiffly, glancing about – nobody in sight. I noticed my hand was shaking like it had been on the phone. Looked down, stooped, picked up the dreadful weapon again. I stretched out my arm, gripping the gun, finger loose on the trigger, aimed into the bushes. The muzzle wobbled and wavered. Tried holding the butt with both hands the way they do in the movies – not a great deal of improvement. Oh God. I prayed I wouldn't need it.

I sat down. Another half hour went by. Still no sign of them.

Sudden bursts of drilling and hammering, competing with the distant roar. Twisted my head. From where I sat, glancing over the cliff edge, I could see only the tops of three fir trees, though, and beyond them the far side of the valley lazy in the sun. And as I turned back, out of the corner of my eye, I caught sight of a movement. Oh shit... I scrabbled closer to the protecting broom, peeping. In the distance a man and a woman with a dog strolling along the grassy rampart wall. I stared, concentrating. Yes, that was the Labrador and the same old man Eva and I had seen. I kept well hidden, watching. But I needn't have panicked – they pottered down the ramp away into the cutting, their backs turning, disappearing.

Another quarter of an hour passed.

For God's sake, where were they? I began to seriously worry. Had something gone wrong? Or had Matthias changed his plans once more, changed his mind about where they'd go? Or were they caught in a traffic jam, perhaps? What had happened? They should have got here by five-thirty at the latest. I looked at my watch again, for the second time in thirty seconds. Nearly six-fifteen. Well, I thought, if they come this late it'll at least be quiet, most locals will be busy with cooking and supper now. And if they don't?

I stopped. Then that's that – I'm off the hook. In the midst of the worry a tiny speck of relief popped up, began to grow.

I crouched there, watching the cutting. Nothing. Had she tried to ring me? Shall I risk switching on my mobile and check? No. Not yet. Or the rampart? Shall I creep over there, have a look if they've even arrived, if they've parked? Could do it stealthily...

I decided. I bent to pick up the gun.

The sound of a voice. I crouched, absolutely still, listening. My body had tensed, suddenly petrified. That queasy feeling back in my gut again. Could hardly breathe. The sound repeated. High pitched and clear, like a bird. Some way away. Very slowly, carefully, I peered through the broom over towards the cutting. No-one.

A laugh. Short and brief. The voice again. Again I listened, intently. No, it was coming from the other direction, the other side of the plateau, beyond the clearing. I shifted position, still crouching. Through the succulent stems and bright yellow flowers I could just discern the solitary pines standing there in the open, and the hut, the antenna – and two figures approaching. Matthias and Eva.

I crouched lower, heart and stomach heaving over. I panicked. Couldn't breathe at all now, everything cramped. Oh God, oh God... this is it. I hunkered, helpless, paralysed with fear. My brain seized up. I couldn't do it – I simply couldn't. But my hands... they were moving, as if of their own volition, they were moving... they weren't really my hands, were they? I watched them fascinated, horrified, half-mesmerised: they picked up the gun. Where it had just lain I could see each blade of bent-back grass, I could see each detail of the deep green shadow at the base of the bush, see a shiny black beetle scuttle – I followed the fingers as they checked the safety...

The two of them were coming closer.

I could hear Eva's words now, louder, every single one – they were like a laser painting its target, like a searchlight guiding me in.

Closer and closer.

Coming round towards my left. I moved in slow motion, keeping the bushes between them and me. Couldn't see them, only hear them – words, serious words, being printed indelibly on my brain, prelude to what was about to come... would I remember them the rest of my life?

They were stationary now. Words of affection, words of remorse, she was preparing the way, they hung motionless in the warm air. I dared a peep just for a second. They faced each other, they were right at the edge, maybe a dozen paces from me; she'd done just what she'd said she'd do. Matthias had his back to me, a small khaki rucksack on his shoulders, Eva's hands were on her hips. I could see it clearly in that instant: she couldn't push him if she tried – he was looking directly at her, not at the view.

So it was up to me.

But my God, he was a bit too far away... I rose stiffly, horrified, mechanical as an automaton, gun held tensely at my side, finger intentionally not on the trigger. Came round the bushes into view.

Yes, maybe a dozen paces...

Eva didn't blink an eye, she just stepped away, pointing off at the view, distracting him, Matthias still with his back to me, saying something. Concentrate on him, nothing else, I ordered myself. Eleven paces. Ten... I approached as quickly and quietly as I could... Nine paces. My brain was screaming, I didn't dare think, fixed my gaze on his back where I'd have to shove him... don't stumble... wiry stubbly grass beneath my feet... a bit of flat rock, a fractional glimpse, no for Christ's sake don't trip... patch of moss, wild stone-carnations... strike him hard just above the hips... I'd raised the gun, I was in a dream, still he didn't turn, Eva several feet from him now.

Eight paces... seven...

I had both hands raised, a fist and a gun, was leaning forward, my whole weight tipped to increase the blow... in four or five seconds I would reach him, then it would all be over – would he go like a skittle bowled over the edge, would he get badly hurt... was there just a possibility he would die? Oh God, oh God, I was completely crazy, what the hell were we doing? We both were...

"Hello Stefan," he said.

Said quietly, it was just a whisper. It hit me like a club.

I went into spasm, I was six yards from him, his back was still to me. I stopped dead, terrified, all my muscles blocked solid... he'd said it before bothering to even turn his head... I froze up, I shrank back. Dropped my arms, nearly dropped the gun.

He was slowly twisting, no surprise in his movement. How could he turn so unhurriedly? He was facing me now. There were his eyes, steady and pale blue. They were the animal in him.

He watched me, standing there thin and tall, he was hardly five feet from the edge. A dreadful silence. He wore jeans and a T-shirt and light summer jacket unbuttoned, it was open, hung loose. His hands were empty, his arms relaxed at his sides. Everything told me he was in his element, he was in control; oh my God he looked so good.

"Stefan," he repeated. So calm, so quiet. That's all he said.

I stood there helpless as a child.

"Matthias." Only just managed to get it out.

Behind him Eva stared.

He glanced down at the gun, with unconcern, didn't react – looked back at my eyes. Eva was signalling to me.

I stepped back a couple of paces, lifted the gun. We were seven or eight yards apart. Yes, his concentration was totally on me just like she'd assumed. He watched me calmly.

She sprang at him, she was like a cat, full of fury, tried to knock him backwards. But he reacted so quickly, went down on one knee almost before she could hit him. She stumbled, fell sideways towards the cliff – he grabbed her, held her fast, set her safely upright. For a moment he gripped her in both his hands, gazing at her... then released her, gently pushed her away... did he know I was going to have to shoot, did he want to protect her if I missed?

My arm was stretched out, I was horribly afraid, I wriggled my finger onto the trigger and aimed, I aimed down low – along the dark-grey barrel I could see one of his thighs, but it came and went. Aim further away, for God's sake don't hit him. My whole body shuddered, I was losing control...

"Shoot," Eva cried sharply. "For Christ's sake shoot."

I raised my other hand, I'd forgotten to do that. Oh God my muscles were like water, they wouldn't respond...

Matthias just stood there. It completely unnerved me. Aim higher, I ordered myself – near his head, but to the left, make him duck, maybe we can...

"Put it down, Stefan," Matthias said quietly. He was watching me so peaceably.

Eva ran at me, keeping out of his range, she came at me, moving in an arc. Calmly Matthias's hands were disappearing, sweeping aside his loose open jacket, reaching out of sight behind his back...

"Shoot, you damn fool – he's got a gun..."

He had, too. Was casually drawing it out, I suppose it'd been tucked in his belt. His arm raised, straight and true, the muzzle pointed at my face.

I the coward, the chicken, the incompetent one – I just stared mesmerised like before. I thought: he's going to kill me – from that distance for him no problem, he could hit me exactly in the middle of my mouth or between the eyes, wherever he chose.

"Put it down," he said quietly again.

But I didn't. I didn't even lower it; at least I didn't do that.

Eva had reached me, oh that anger in her eyes, she was grabbing at my arm, my hand, fingernails digging in my flesh, it weakened my grip – I was scared out of my wits it might go off, I knew I mustn't let her get the gun. Panicking. A glance at Matthias – what would he do? He was lowering his gun, deliberating, I could see that look in his eye, what was he thinking?

Could feel her tugging, her nails tore at me, she was using both hands, I could feel her strength... she had hold of it now, extricating it, was wrenching it free. She turned to face him, small and compact, determined, she was raising the gun and walking towards him closing the gap...

"No, Eva," I shouted. Was that my voice, was that my shout? She was pointing the gun at his legs and I knew she'd do it, wouldn't miss...

For an instant he watched her, taking her in, then his gun was gone, his hands sweeping up the jacket out of sight again, fast and practised, tucking the weapon in behind his back... was that the mistake, was that the move that would break his spine?

"Eva, for God's sake don't," I bawled. And she hesitated...

He let out a laugh, it was brief as a sigh, went to a crouch, quick and sure and cool – he always was so quick. He was ducking, weaving, hands free and prepared, arms stretched ready, twisting towards the cliff...

It happened so fast, it was just a glimpse, but it comes back to me in the dark of the night in nightmares over and over, and the image is there clear and fixed like a photograph: a sandaled foot caught in tough heather, a thin sinewy sunburnt body suspended for a second in the air. Then he was gone; he went head forwards over the edge.

There was one little detail though, which afterwards when I saw his lacerated hands and lost fingers that turned my stomach, made me throw up – one detail I knew I'd been wrong about: I thought those arms were stretched out wide as he went, not flailing but seeking balance to successfully break his fall like a cat with nine lives always lands on its paws. That's what gave me hope in the three or four seconds of silence that followed – seconds like an hour and a half I prayed would go on for ever and confirm the picture in my mind's eye that he'd managed to hold on safely to a treetop down there somewhere or at least was controlling the fall.

Then came the sounds – a body falling, crashing through branches, rocks and stones rattling. In an instant Eva and I were on our knees at the edge, peering over. Treetops, the valley floor far below, I felt quite sick. Nothing to be seen of him, though, except a ghost of dust to mark the passage. Above the distant roar of traffic, birds screeching their warnings. That was all.

x x x

We had to go down on foot, didn't have his car keys. And were forced to go around to where it wasn't so steep. We took the shortest route we could, from the open saddle out in the sun, turning right as near the trees where he'd fallen as possible. I'd stuffed the wrapped gun back in my trouser-leg pocket; it banged on my calf as I ran, irritated, but I couldn't risk carrying it in my hand. From the top up there, before descending, I could see his parked vehicle in the distance at the edge of the forest. A Land Rover, but not the one Heidi Prell had transported me in. This one was white.

There were two other cars standing close by it, but nobody visible. I asked Eva, just to make sure.

"That's it," she said curtly.

We scrambled down the steep grassy slope, zigzagging so as not to trip and fall. Pretty flowers. Directly below us, the little village of Enkering where I'd parked the Mini, almost a bird's-eye view. It was a sharp incline devoid of paths, the long, dry grasses were slippery, sometimes I lost my footing, had to grab at tufts or cling onto small bushes of broom to prevent myself slipping down the hill. Eva was nimbler; from all her fitness training, but I think also from anguish. We went in silence. I guess all her thoughts, like mine, were with Matthias and what we might find.

We needed nearly five minutes to get three-quarters down. Then, scrabbling carefully, diagonally, we dropped lower and entered the thick pine-wooded slope near the bottom of the cliffs. Cooler here, filtered light, treacherous deep beds of dead needles and buried boulders it was hard to keep one's footing on. From ledge to ledge, using branches and tree trunks for hold, we clambered and skidded, losing height all the time. Sweet smell of pine resin, thick pine-tree roots clutching in crevices, the steep cliffs like a leaning wall rising up through trees to sky.

Still seemingly quite a way down, glimpses of the new bridge – we were almost vertically above it now, where it met the tunnel bored through the rock somewhere beneath our feet. We began searching; if he'd fallen as far, he'd maybe have landed around here. But no sign of him. Between rock outcrops, here and there, were small slopes with standing Scots Pine which might have caught him – we scrabbled about, working our way lower. Still nothing.

Ahead of me Eva had stopped, head tipped back, craning her neck, gazing upwards. "Wouldn't've fallen this far," she called.

"I disagree," I said. "I fear he could've landed further down." I was glancing at the bridge underneath us, could see its details now. It was built of concrete, unfinished – in lines along its surface clusters of reinforcement rods stuck out; the rail tracks hadn't yet been laid. I thought: oh God, if he'd fallen that far he wouldn't have stood a chance. I leaned out nervously, peering, gripping onto the bough of a tree. Could see the mouth of the tunnel now, a graceful white concrete arc about thirty feet below me, cantilevered out towards the bridge. But there was no object to be seen – no Matthias, no body.

"I'm going up, waste of time here," Eva shouted. "He'll've grabbed onto branches much further up, they'd've broken his fall."

"Okay," I said. Moved up higher, towards her.

We separated, left and right, began climbing again, searching again. Still we couldn't find him.

After a minute or two Eva called: "Reckon he's beaten a retreat, or's hiding till we give up." She stood, hands on hips, looking down at me. "If he hasn't broken both legs he'll've sneaked off back to his vehicle."

"I fear he's broken more than that, sister." I'd muttered it more to myself than her.

She heard though, and retorted: "Fucking crap." Her anger was back, I could hear its heat; but I knew it was against Matthias now, as if he were to blame.

"Face it," I called. "He tripped, didn't he." I didn't say it like a question. "Just look up there, Eva, it's a good two hundred foot drop – nobody simply walks away from that kind of fall."

"Matthias could." There was bitterness too.

I ignored her. "I'm going to keep searching."

She shook her cropped head. "Okay – five more minutes." Said half-heartedly. She turned away.

"He'll be lying somewhere, may be hard to see," I shouted to her back. "Maybe unconscious."

"More bloody likely lying watching us, laughing his guts out."

More likely half-dead, I thought.

Well she was wrong about him. Eva saw him before I did. We'd hardly been hunting a further two minutes.

"Stefan!" She said it in a suppressed whisper; we were less than thirty feet apart. I looked over. She was pointing, small jerks of her tiny hand. Then put her finger to her lips, beckoning. She was crouching down, not moving from the spot. She beckoned again. "Ssh," she hissed. Flapped her hand for me to crouch too. Doubled up, I went towards her.

"Give me that gun," she whispered. "May be one of his tricks."

You're joking, I thought. I peered where she'd been pointing. There he lay, face down, twenty feet away.

"Give it me." Barely audible.

I shook my head, went over to him.

"Matthias?" I said.

He lay strangely crooked, like a puppet someone's dropped, his clothes half-covered in pine needles and dust and dirt. His small rucksack was gone, his jacket torn, his jeans ripped open, there was blood coming through.

Oh my God, I thought. I stooped. His head was twisted sideways, couldn't see his face. Had he broken his neck? "Matthias," I repeated. I wanted to touch him but I didn't dare. Eva was coming over. She stood staring down.

"Jesus Christ," she said. She knelt the other side of him, shook his shoulder.

No reaction, no movement.

"Don't move him," I said quickly; at least I knew that.

"'Course not, stupid." Her small fingers were at his neck, pressing.

"Is there a pulse?" I said.

No answer for a moment. Then: "No." She shifted position, ducking her face very close to his, keeping still. "He's not breathing, Jesus bloody Christ."

He's dead, I thought. I knew it – I'd known it all the time. I gazed down at his body, in utter horror. Memories flooded... they swamped my brain. We were being introduced, two and a half years old, shy and suspicious, I could see his expression, feel my feelings concerning this stranger, this intruder into my world – but how could I? I'd never had that memory before, I couldn't remember that far back. A jump: we were children still, but strong and wicked and five years old, digging under the garden boundary wall between our parents' properties, he from his side and I from mine, meeting in the middle with dirty clogged hands and filthy faces and full of glee...

A voice somewhere was screaming, was accusing: he's dead, he's dead, you killed him you bastard, you killed him, you killed your oldest friend...

Our blood was mingling, we pressed chest on chest... he was on that stage receiving the ovation like a god above such mortal praise... we were high in the mountains all alone, we'd reached Valhalla and, my God, did it feel good. He was always leading in battle, I the follower trudging behind – he the fearless, I the funk. And now here he lay, that hero of old, that invincible body reduced to a smashed and thrown-away doll...

My throat was thick, I could feel the tears — I swallowed, I wanted to scream, I bowed down to his body, my forehead almost touching the blood...

"Stefan, Stefan..."

Eva's voice, small — constricted.

Oh God, what a sound, like pain within pain, it tore at my heart. I raised my head and looked at her.

She was still kneeling. She was gazing at me, fists balled on her lap, lips compressed but in control — dry-eyed. But that gaze went through me like a knife, I knew what it was saying.

"Yes," I said. I forced it out, my throat was a vice. We'd carry this burden the rest of our lives, but was hers even heavier? She'd helped destroy the only thing she loved.

"No," she whispered. It was louder than the loudest cry. "Got to do something, for Christ's bloody sake."

The memories were gone, a flame snuffed out. They'd come again, though, I knew that for sure — they'd come back to haunt me year after year. I shook myself: I was back in the present, back by the corpse. I made myself think, concentrate — I thought: what do we do? Ring emergency services, ring the police?

Eva was bending over him, listening to his heart, she was pulling at his clothes like an animal in pain, stroking his face and kissing his shirt, what was left of it — then she reached to his wrist, I suppose to check his pulse there too, just in case. Was she praying, like me, that there'd be some sign?

"Oh Jesus!" she uttered. "Bloody hell, look at that..."

But I'd seen his hands too, at the same moment. Tops of fingers missing, others torn to the bone, one visible palm bloody and shredded, all the skin scraped away. And from the way the arm lay so unnaturally, it looked broken in more than one place.

I stared. Began to retch; hurriedly turned away and threw up. A sour, acrid taste — cramps in my stomach. I was squatting, head down. I spat out the last of the bile, wiped my mouth with tissues, tried to rinse away the bitterness with saliva, spat again. And when I turned, Eva was kneeling still, fingertips on the side of his neck again, uselessly trying again to find a sign of life. I watched her. Tough little Eva, size is deceiving, she was one of those people who never gives up.

I hunkered. The wrapped gun in my pocket dug into my leg. I took my mobile out, had to start phoning...

"Wait!" She held his face between her hands. "Matthias, Matthias..." Twisted her head to me. Back to Matthias, whispered in his ear: "You can hear me, know you can hear me. Give me a sign, for Christ's sake."

I laid the mobile down on the pine needles, leant over him, peering at his face too. Eyes closed, just a few scratches and smeared dirt, that was all. His expression looked so peaceful, was that even a faint smile on his lips?

That's when something made me: I reached out hesitantly, squeamishly, touched him for the first time. The skin was still warm. Ought to check. I lifted his eyelids, carefully; only whites, the eyeballs rolled up. Eva was pinching him. Still no reaction. She pulled off a sandal, fiddling with the buckle, then jabbed the sharp point into his flesh over and over again. Pinpricks of blood.

Still nothing. Matthias was very dead.

"Eva," I said gently. Tried to draw her away. Picked up my mobile again, switched it on, thumbed in the code. As it jangled, she sat upright with a jerk...

"Bloody fool – stop!" She snatched it from me. "I've got to do it, for Christ's sake." Fumbling, she switched it off, threw it down next to me. "I was alone with him, see? Was an accident, you weren't here." She stared at me. Despair and fear in her eyes. Then one of her hands dropped rapidly to her jeans.

I swallowed, nodded. Shit, I thought. Knew she was right – but didn't want to leave her in the lurch, wanted at least to share the burden.

"Have to ring the police," I said.

"Emergency," she curtly retorted. She was standing up, already on the phone using her own. She stood there small and efficient, giving name and location – despite her state she was very professional; one would think she did this kind of thing every day.

"...climbing accident, yes. Be damn quick, might be dead, not hundred percent sure..." Listening into the mobile, then: "Above the tunnel mouth where the bridge goes in..." A pause, craning her neck. "Bits of sky, yes, but lots of trees. Shall I get down, stand on the bridge...?" Hand gesticulating in the air. "...Okay – reckon 'bout fifty feet the way the crow flies, maybe hundred feet up..." Her eyes were wide with worry, with impatience. "How long? Jesus Christ, make it quicker..." She dropped her hand holding the mobile, pressing Cancel, for a moment staring at me, through me.

"How long?" I said.

"'Bout fifteen minutes, he said. Air rescue 'copter." Her eyes focused. "Better bugger off quick, brother."

But I was panicking again... in anguish was thinking: can't leave her like this, what the hell can I do, is there anything...? And I remembered his rucksack... oh God – what was in it, would they find it... had it...? Then, suddenly, I thought of his gun...

"His gun," I said stupidly.

I pushed back, still on my knees – touched his body, his twisted jacket, felt the lump, lifted the jacket free. It was wedged half-hidden under his belt inside the jeans. His T-shirt was ripped out, torn and grimy. Wincing, I carefully removed the gun, it was still warm; wanted to be sick again. The skin underneath was indented, broken, an angry red, but there was hardly any blood. I stared at his body for a moment, wondered if he'd struck a rock, wondered what the gun had done. Then rapidly looked away...

"Sweet Jesus," I heard Eva saying.

I checked the gun was on safety, shaky hands, awkwardly stuck it in my other calf pocket. Buttoned the flap...

"Give me his keys. Can't touch." Her voice so tight. "In his back pocket."

I reached in, still warm there too. Could feel the muscle of his backside through taut denim. My tears were coming, my throat was thick. Handed them to her.

"When they pick him up I'll follow in his vehicle." Said coldly. "Switch your mobile on then. I'll call."

I was getting up, she was too. A last glimpse of Matthias. That broken corpse. Shut my eyes. Oh God, how could it end this way? I gripped her shoulders for a second, squeezed. Eyes meeting. She gave me a push...

"Get the fuck out of here, brother."

x x x

I reached her Mini in about ten minutes. Had gone fast, taken the shortest route I could: diagonally down, scrambling till I got out of the trees, then parallel along the grassy hillside out in the sun. Slid down the last steep slope on my bottom, picked up the path into the village. But even before I'd arrived at her car I could hear the helicopter.

I drove as quickly as allowed, out of the village along the country road the few hundred yards back towards the half-built bridge. Craning my neck and peering up, still couldn't see it though. A motorbike had stopped beyond the bridge, and two cars; people getting out. Arms raised, eyes shaded. I pulled onto the verge, parked at a discreet distance. The sounds of the helicopter were loud here.

I opened the sunroof, a press of a button, a little whirr. I looked up. Then saw it. Orange and red, like an insect. It was hovering, clattering, against the cliff above the trees, and a winch had been lowered with a man in red in a harness hanging there, a pack on his back. He was looking down but didn't move his arms or gesticulate; he wore a helmet, maybe he had radio contact. I couldn't see the details.

Other cars were stopping...

I stayed in the Mini. Switched on my mobile.

The helicopter moved slowly this way and that, searching. It couldn't have been more than twenty feet above the steep slope, above the treetops. It paused, hovering again. Made a correction, hung there again directly on an axis with the bridge. The man on the winch was being lowered, like a spider on its thread, disappeared into the trees. Had he found her? I thought: fantastic how they do it. Then my thoughts were only with Eva – I could imagine her standing there on the pine needles, beside the body, all alone, looking up at the man coming out of the sky. Be brave, Eva, be brave...

A siren.

And a blue light flashing, revolving, coming round the curve from the autobahn beyond the bridge. It stirred that memory again, just for a second; I sat on it. No cobbles this time. A police car, silver and green, a BMW traffic patrol car – and behind it, another, a police van, just green. They braked, and parked right in front of me on the verge. Two men dressed in dark overalls, and leather boots, climbed from the side of the van, stood staring upwards. The first was looking through binoculars using both hands, the other hitching a large pack over one shoulder. They seemed to be conversing. But both had their backs to me.

I looked where they were looking. The winch was being lowered again with a stretcher on its end; it must have left the man down there on the ground. And the helicopter changed its position slightly...

A motor revving. I glanced. The BMW patrol car was reversing, turning, driving off the way it had come – and the two policemen in black were crossing the road heading for the steep wooded incline and the cliff. They looked very business-like; I felt insecure.

It took several minutes, then Matthias was coming up through the trees. They raised him slowly, steadily. He was harnessed to the stretcher, the man in red suspended beside him. Up, up they went – to be received by the hovering machine. I watched in anguish, my horror was complete. The helicopter rose, gaining height with a rattling roar, banked and flew away. In seconds it disappeared behind the hill. Matthias was gone.

I started the car again, turned, drove off; I think I was the first to leave. Went back towards the village. But I hadn't even reached the *Gasthaus* to park and wait before my mobile rang. Eva.

"He's dead, Stef. He's dead." Strangled voice, strangled breath.

"Yes," I said. What else could I say?

Silence down the phone. Could hear that breath, it tore my heart. Then she said: "Been told to wait. Police're coming, have to check everything, take a statement."

"Two are coming up to you," I said. "From the road."

"Jesus."

"I'm sure it's normal procedure." Said it to calm.

"Could take bloody ages."

"Doesn't matter. I'll wait." I told her where. Then I said: "Where're they taking him?"

"Dunno. Said maybe Ingolstadt, depends. Want to try and revive him in the chopper on the way. They'll..."

"Revive him?"

"What he said. I begged him. Said it's standard anyway."

Ah. I thought: well, let's pray. I didn't speak; I don't believe in miracles – and people rising from the dead. Not in angels either.

"They'll call me."

"Okay," I said.

"I'll keep you posted."

"I'll wait," I repeated. "I'm coming with you."

"Thanks, brother."

I cancelled the call. Sat a moment. I reckoned I would have the best part of an hour, depending on what the police had to do – time to get rid of these dreadful things. I moved off, driving west out of the village on the small country road away from the autobahn, took several turnings right and left... five minutes passed... ten. Small hills and dips thickly wooded. Eva rang again.

"They just called me from the chopper. Taking him down to Munich. *Klinikum Großhadern.*" She stopped. Was that a break in her voice, a tiny spark in her darkness?

I slowed the car, I didn't speak. Waited – keeping my eye on the minor road.

Then her voice returned: "Said he was clinically dead, then suddenly came back. Just a bit. That's why Munich, see. Faint brain activity, they got his heart going again. But very faint too." Yes, I could hear the spark.

I halted the car. Couldn't believe. Why was my heart still so heavy? "This is wonderful news," I said quietly. I thought: if he's really come back, for how long then? He'd be a cabbage wouldn't he, wouldn't his brain be destroyed?

And Eva was saying: "They said it happens sometimes. But couldn't explain it really." She stopped again, I waited again.

When she didn't continue I asked very carefully: "What are his chances?" I spoke the words like one walks on thin ice.

"Practically nil." Another silence down the line; was her spark going out again?

"But this is an excellent sign," I said. I tried to cheer. "If he can rally once he can do it again. He'll be in good hands in Munich." Why did I see it differently then, why couldn't I believe?

Her voice was back. Suddenly practical, sharp. "Got to go," she said.

"Yes." I could hear the voices in the background too. "The police?" I asked.

"Yep. Call you bit later."

I set off again. Picked up the little meandering river. Sometimes sunlight, sometimes shade. Must be after seven, now; the sun was still relatively high though – in a week would be the longest day. Following the river for a few minutes. Then I found a good spot. I parked and walked through the woods till I was completely alone. Threw the two guns into the river, retraced my footsteps.

In the car, halfway back to the village, my mobile rang again.

"They found the rucksack," Eva said. "They're fucking thorough."

"Just doing their job, sister." I took an uneven breath. "What was in it?"

"Wine and a corkscrew wrapped in a rug. And his mobile. That's all."

"Well I'm glad to hear that," I said.

Another of those pauses of hers which made me unhappy. Was she finished, maybe? So I asked: "You rang just to tell me that?"

"Christ, no. One's on the way up near the cliffs, the other's gone down – fetching their van. Told me to take a safer route, wait for them up there where he fell. Jesus."

"Just going through their procedures, you know."

"They'll do a reconstruction."

"Tell them he was just assing about, playing the fool. And tripped."

Silence her end of the line; I could almost hear her thoughts. "Keep it cool, sister. You're doing a grand job."

Another pause. Was that a sigh? "For Christ's sake don't wait," she said. "This'll take half the bloody evening. Go to him and be there. Meet you in Munich at the *Großhadern* clinic."

"Sister, I'll wait here for you all night," I said.

Chapter 35

We got to see Matthias's body, but were only allowed to view it through glass – and not until two days later.

We were told he had undergone two operations, one to the spinal cord, had been placed in an artificial coma. They also said his condition was critical, he was on the danger list.

I wondered what condition they were speaking of. A vegetable? A paralysed cabbage? Oh God. Would he ever walk or talk again? He was dying, wasn't he? He was dying a second death...

"He's alive," Eva whispered.

"Yes," I said. He looked dead to me. And I knew: he'd want to be should he ever wake. I watched her staring through the observation window and asked myself, is she thinking the same way too?

But at least, finally, they'd let us in to see him.

They were very strict here, in this intensive care unit, in this white and sterilised world. Only next-of-kin, and one by one, so it ruled us out. But his old father was very ill, couldn't be moved, the private care home informed – and they failed to reach any of his few relatives. Eva, however, had supplied them with all necessary details about him, had been very helpful. So here we were in there together in the corridor after two long days of waiting. We wore green gowns, head protection and stretch plastic covers on our shoes.

We had five minutes.

That was more than enough, though. What was there to see? A motionless corpse, with bandages, attached to tubes, lying there, head and shoulders slightly raised. His eyes were closed, his skin was taut and bleached; despite that sunburn, how could he be so pale? There was a grimace, too – horrible, like a death mask. He'd had a little smile when he died, hadn't he? Was he aware of pain, then? Was he suffering, somewhere, wherever he'd gone, wherever his mind had wandered? Was he even capable of thought, or was it purely instinct, a reaction of the muscles, just a reflex?

I stood there behind the glass. And felt almost nothing. No more tears, now, not any more, just the emptiness – not even a thickening of the throat. Seemed it was too late for those sort of things: yes, that was all I could feel – the chapter had ended, the book was slowly closing, he was on his way down to the underworld already, descending that lonely path you walk alone. Could he see the boatman waiting there? Should I knock and simply go in, slip a silver coin between his teeth?

He'd've liked that. Just a little gesture.

x x x

Eva went in first; she had to go alone.

It was three weeks later, and I'd been mistaken – with Matthias I'd so often been wrong. Just one at a time, they said, and don't touch. They only gave her ten minutes but she took twenty anyway – I was very glad about that. When she emerged they stood in my way, wouldn't let me in. Eva had taken my portion of time: I was grateful I could give her something. Tomorrow, I was told.

So we went and got ourselves coffee from the automatic vending machine, and sat outside in the sun on some stone steps that weren't too near.

"He's changed," she said. She was staring into space.

I didn't speak, didn't wish to interrupt.

Then she added: "It's not Matthias," and turned her gaze to me, and I didn't understand. Still I said nothing, though.

"It's someone else." She was frowning. "Someone else talking, Stef." But her voice was soft, not dramatic, there was nothing mysterious, nothing negative or untoward. In fact there was a relaxedness coming out of her, and a glow, which I hadn't seen since she was a girl.

"You mean his brain's been damaged?" I asked. "He's a cabbage?" I was just trying to be practical.

"No. Not in the least." Slowly she shook her head, she was staring into me. "Matter of fact he's unbelievably coherent, knows precisely where he is, what he's saying. Simply changed."

I returned her stare, patiently. But she offered nothing more. So I ventured: "You're speaking in riddles, sister."

"Simply telling you how it is."

"What did he say then?"

Very faintly she shrugged. "Talked 'bout the future. That it's going to be okay. Said the slate's been cleaned now and there's no looking back; said if one did there'd only be regret. That's not Matthias talking."

No, I thought, she's right there.

I said: "Did you ask him what he meant?"

"Yep. Simply said ahead of him's a straight line, it's all become clear, and I can stop worrying 'cos I was right all the time."

I watched her.

"Well," I said, spreading my hands, "isn't that just what you wanted to hear?"

"That's just it – not Matthias." But her calmness was still there, she exuded relief, happiness even. Yes, she really was a new person. Like Matthias?

I shook my head. Tried to seek some better explanation. Perhaps he fell on his head, I thought. Concussion maybe. Perhaps he'll need a little time to get over it all, to get back to his normal self. Or maybe it's the drugs they've given him, the painkillers – side effects can be a nasty business...

"And he's paralysed," Eva said.

Oh God. I started. She'd said it out of the blue, her words banged on my brain. Paralyzed? I shut my eyes. No-one had told us that.

"From the waist down."

"Oh God," I said. "Are they sure?"

"Yep."

I thought: can that bring a change of heart? Is that what's done it?

"You won't b'lieve it – he said it so damn peacefully. Like someone chatting 'bout the weather."

I raised my head, looked at her. She'd said it so calmly too.

"Matthias in a wheelchair?" I said. "Oh my God." I was trying to imagine.

"He said it's the way it should be – said it's perfectly logical."

Logical? I thought. What the hell's he talking about? Aloud I said: "Well, Matthias was always full of surprises – maybe this is one of his little games."

"Isn't."

"No?"

"Got to see for yourself."

"Such a change?" I watched her. The composure, the calm. Like a metamorphosis. Yes, that was happiness breaking through. Was she really talking about the only man she'd ever loved, the one who'd never walk again? "You seem to be taking it pretty well in your stride, sister."

"Told you – got to see for yourself."

I shook my head. I thought: he's pulling the wool over her eyes. I said: "Did you ask him why he's had this change of heart, then?"

"Yep. Said it was given to him."

"Given?"

"Yep. Said I should just accept it, that I don't need explanations."

"Nothing else?"

"No." She turned her eyes away. Sipped her coffee.

"And can you?"

"Yep." Sipped again, gaze far away.

I sat there beside her in silence.

Then she looked back at me briefly. "He did say one other thing, though – that you wouldn't accept, that you wouldn't understand. Said he'd like to talk to you."

I stared into the distance. Well, I thought – at least he wants that. Yes I stared into space, but I was blind to everything else.

x x x

"I was watching you," he said quietly.

I didn't understand. There was so much I didn't understand.

"Watching?" I echoed. "What do you mean, watching?"

I'd only been admitted to him two minutes ago, I sat on the only available chair. He lay at a slight slope, straight and stiff; his hands were bound in white like two big balls. They'd shaved his gaunt face, it had a bit of colour now – they'd shaved his head too, I could see that, at least the part of his skull that showed. We were talking about the accident, and the place where we found him at the bottom of the cliff. Smell of ether, of bandages — lots of medical smells.

He smiled. Not vaguely — it was a soft and introspective smile. That was something new too.

He said: "It's quite simple. I was there looking down on you, the three of us — Eva and you, and my body. It was slightly surrealistic."

Another faint and thoughtful smile. "It was a good feeling, though — there was no more pain. It was like floating in water but there was no water."

I shifted uncomfortably. He was pulling my leg. "You're joking," I said.

"I'm not joking."

I shook my head. Eva hadn't mentioned this. "You mean you imagined you left your body?"

"I didn't imagine, Stefan. I left it." He blinked. His body was totally still. He didn't move a muscle, just calmly closed his eyelids in those hollow sockets, then opened them. His pale blue eyes were there watching me again. "I was glad to leave it, you see. Before I did, there was only pain and darkness and hell — I couldn't take that threshold of pain."

My God, I thought, who could? "I thought you were dead," I said. My little contribution to bring him down to earth.

"Perhaps I was. My body looked dead, didn't it?"

I didn't reply to that one — didn't wish to look at the memory again.

"Is that why you couldn't touch me?" he asked. Another fleeting smile. "You didn't touch me for quite a while, did you?"

No, I thought. That's true. At least not till...

"Not till you put down your mobile and touched my skin and my eyes. And afterwards when you lifted my jacket and removed the gun."

I watched him watching me.

"And my car keys."

I swallowed. He couldn't have known that. Again I didn't speak.

"And you threw up too, didn't you?" His voice was so calm, so relaxed.

Still I didn't answer.

"You and Eva saw what was left of my hands, and then you threw up – you hunkered there and then wiped your mouth with a tissue, remember?"

He couldn't have known that either – Eva must've told him. He'd been lying face down in that bed of needles with his head turned away...

"You don't believe me, do you?" he said quietly, equably.

"Eva told you that, didn't she?" He couldn't fool me.

"No, Stefan. I have to disappoint you. We didn't talk about things like that because it wasn't necessary. Eva understands, you see."

"What does she understand?"

"About dying, and the transition. And being sent back."

"Transition?" I said. Had to pick it up. Never heard him use a word like that before.

"The crossing between life and death," he said. "Or afterlife, in fact."

I shook my head again. This time I shook it irritably. "Oh, come on, Matthias. Cut out that crap."

"What crap, Stefan?"

"You know damn well – you must've read some of those books," I said. "Seen documentaries too."

"Sure, I didn't believe them either."

"Well of course you didn't, because they're just a figment of the imagination." I could feel impatience, too. "Doctors disproved it all – it's the chemicals in the brain, there are physiological explanations."

His blue eyes considered me, peaceably. "But I left my body, Stefan."

I stared at him. "Crap," I repeated. I knew he was lying. But why?

"That's the reason I wanted to talk to you," Matthias said. "To help you understand..."

"Understand what?"

"And to take away your fear."

"Of what – of dying?" I retorted.

"Of everything. You're afraid of everything, Stefan, you always were. You're blocked. Don't you see how restrictive it is, how it puts you in a cage?"

"You're afraid of death too," I accused. "We used to agree it's a healthy basic instinct, the survival instinct. Helps keep us on our toes." I knew that – at least I knew that.

"I used to, that's true. But not now." Another trace of that patient smile. He lay, still stiff, still unmoving.

I gazed down at him. "Just because you fell down a cliff?" I flapped a derisive hand.

"Sarcasm doesn't become you."

"And dreamt you could fly? Come on, Matthias – you can do better than that."

"You're being rather aggressive." Said tranquilly.

"Because you're probably going to tell me..."

"You should ask yourself why."

"You intending to spout all that nonsense about a tunnel and light at the end, and heavenly choirs?"

"Don't you think you might ask yourself why this subject makes you so aggressive?"

I stopped. Yes, that made me stop. Shades of Estella again. I could hear her voice, hear her words getting at me, getting into me... I sat back, crossed my legs. Took a breath.

Silence between us, stretching.

Then he said: "I will never lie to you again, Stefan," and he said it very seriously, and even quieter than before. "I confess there've been times in the past I've told you only half-truths, but half-truths are half a lie. And sometimes I've confronted you with silence and silence can be a lie too. I regret this – I regret a lot of things in my past. I've been sent back because it was too soon, and now I intend to make amends."

Yes, there was that other weird expression he'd used just now. So alien, so absurd. "Sent back?" I said. I tried a chuckle. It came out cracked.

"Yes," he said.

My God, so earnest still. It was as if he'd passed through some invisible valley, some filter, as if he were untouchable.

He continued: "It's a fact, Stefan. I left my body – I don't know for how long, but I left it for a while. There was no sense of time. I hovered above you both and could see your concern. I could hear your exchanges of words and watch Eva snatch your mobile, call for help with hers. I wanted to stop her and tell you both, no point, it was too late, that I was fine and didn't need my body any more. I called to you but you didn't hear. I just looked down on it and it seemed such a broken useless thing. Extraordinary, don't you think? I was impotent to communicate."

He paused. Inhaled unhurriedly, exhaled slowly too. But his eyes didn't leave me.

"Then I was rising up and you were gone, the trees were gone – there were dense clouds or a fog, it was rather confusing..." his eyes took on a sudden sparkle "...no tunnel or Chopin, Stefan, no choirs, or angels flapping about..." a sardonic grin that came and went "...I remember the light getting brighter and brighter, and I remember the feeling of ecstasy, the freedom from pain. I can't describe how good that was..."

He continued on; was he recounting? His murmur was like a river...

"...there was a voice, too. It was in my head, clear as crystal, guiding me through my life..."

The river flowed on...

"...were people I recognised, beckoning... and the light wasn't just light, it was alive, it was so intense..."

...and on...

"...I wanted to come closer to these people, these friends, but suddenly someone else materialised, a very old man, standing before me and saying he was a guardian. He started imparting knowledge, speaking to me about love and hate and good and evil and how it all began, and his voice was the same voice I'd just heard in..."

Ah, I thought – my sarcasm was breaking through again. I thought: the eternal themes, just up Matthias's street...

"And he spoke, too, of the universe and stars going on for ever..."

I sensed a slight giddiness. The stars – the universe? No. Imagination. Anyone can talk about those. Carefully I uncrossed my legs, though, and placed both feet firmly on the floor, and a breath touched my skin...

Matthias's voice continued intoning where he lay on the bed – his mouth and face and eyes were all there were of him, the only thing alive, his body just an empty shell...

"...sitting at night looking up at the stars and the endlessness of it all..."

I was falling. It was almost like in a trance. The floor and Matthias and the walls were falling away.

"We were in a magical garden and he was pointing out a single flower..."

I was far away now, drifting... so why was Matthias's voice still here? I was in Florence again – the old theologian over there, at the next table, thin, wrinkled, ascetic hands folded one upon the other, his mouth moving; I was driving sedately, the hot Toscana air wafting through my hair, there were larks singing, and blue butterflies, and fields of blood-red poppies each side of the track rising up the slope to the farmhouse on the hill...

It felt as if I were in space – I was, wasn't I? And yet I knew I floated close. I thought: if I open my eyes it'll all still be there. So I opened my eyes – and there were the walls once more, and the bed, and Matthias.

"I felt happy, Stefan."

"Yes?" I said.

"I've never experienced such happiness, I realised that I'd arrived – I was drinking from a cup and I wanted more and more. I told him that, this guardian, this wise old man."

"You did?"

"We still stood in that garden, and beyond him was an even lovelier landscape and I wanted to walk on. But he gently barred my way."

I was holding my breath.

Matthias stopped speaking. His eyes were clouding over. There was something wrong, there was pain flowing in – he was frowning, seemed to be struggling to find new words.

"He told me it wasn't time yet, it was too soon, and I had to go back. I didn't want to, Stefan, do you understand? Going back meant back to a wrecked body and all that pain. I fought against it. But I was going back in, then out, then in again. I fought damn hard. He was very persuasive..."

He stared. Hollow eyes in sunken sockets. "So here I am. I've been sent back – in his wisdom he showed me the way."

His sight was clearing, the muscles of his face easing again – and a slow smile came suddenly creeping, as if he'd just remembered something which amused...

"A very old man, distinguished and white-haired, with eyes with no colour as though faded by time..."

The smile was sparkling now, like sun after rain.

"He sends his regards."

x x x

Matthias had unlocked something; I was seriously undermined.

I rang Estella in the hope that she would have the time, but she was packing to go on a painting tour in the Camargue, was leaving tomorrow for the coast. We fixed a date, though, when we could meet – I thanked her like a good friend does, for the guidance which might come.

I sent an e-mail, too, to Professor Skell: I told him what had happened and what I couldn't see. Like the last time, however, I didn't expect to receive a reply. I even thought: perhaps he doesn't really exist. I guess I simply sought a safety-valve, my desperation was complete. But surprisingly an answer came within a matter of hours. It read:

'My dear Stefan, I thank you for your communication regarding your friend's revelation. My humble apologies for not responding to your first letter. I sincerely hope you may forgive, and appreciate my intention now. One says there is a time and place for everything, the great as well as the small. And lo and behold, in accordance with this eternal truism, water has flowed beneath the bridge and your two communications have turned to one.

'A wise teacher once told me that for us mortal souls there are many paths which lead to God, but only one is destined for each. Perhaps your friend discovered his that day and came nearer to Him than you might care to believe. To lend him an ear might not be amiss. Knowledge, like love, is a universal spring waiting to be tapped. And revelation shared is a blessing in disguise, is enlightenment embraced.

'I am wondering, might not a second visit to my humble Toscana abode possibly be propitious? In the season of falling leaves I have made the observation that each leaf floats to earth in its own individual way, following the laws of God and completing the cycle, returning to whence it came. We humans are but a leaf.

Sincerely, Krister (Skell).'

x x x

It was the end of August.

The apartment was finished, we'd just made the move; a little party was deemed appropriate. So we invited some people – just a few good friends, and family. I invited Estella down too.

I'd done the rounds. We sat now in the garden, the two of us, a little apart from the others, there was lots of space; I felt oppressed by the heat.

"It's quiet and tasteful," Estella was saying. "Like her." Very slight pause. Eyes like searchlights, china blue. "Conducive to opening the senses." She was speaking of Annabelle's conversion of the ground floor. Was she also playing with words?

Lethargically I turned back my glance from Matthias over in the shade on the terrace. I'd only been unfaithful to her eyes for a second.

"You think so?" I questioned.

I twitched my shoulders. Thoughts returning sluggishly to Annabelle. Yes, she'd done it to perfection, she'd nearly erased the traces, yet I still didn't feel I belonged. Where did I belong? I needed her, just needed her – but not the where and why. Did I simply belong in her shadow? We still hadn't made the other move, either, towards the decision to marry. I'd kept on postponing, and she gave me room – was there a danger it might lead to distances, though? I was her knave, she was my queen, without her I was lost. I'd follow her to the ends of the earth if she left, without her I would die. But marriage kept raising a small warning finger – was I afraid of strangulation, would I repeat my mistake, was I afraid of what Judit had done?

I'd panicked a week ago. My work had brought me to London for three days: lying in that hotel bed the first night I panicked and thought: when I return will that be it, will she have said goodbye, will she have pushed me out? So I'd sent her a message I prayed she'd keep tucked away beneath the cushion of her throne to peep at whenever her nerves got frayed, to replenish her faith when belief wore too thin:

'Annabelle, you're the book I can't put down,
you're the film I don't want to end.
I'm just so scared of strings. S.'

"Isn't her aesthetic good for your senses too?" A little twinkle in Estella's eye.

I was back in the garden and the sun was high. Was she thinking what I was thinking?

"It hasn't quite banned the ghosts," I said. God, I was in a negative mood.

"You and your ghosts!" A toss of that storm of wild wavy hair. "They're simply in your mind."

I waggled a foot. She wasn't giving me any rope.

"They'll go away," she said. "Just as soon as you let them go."

Will they? Well, maybe she was right.

A movement, at the corner of my eye. A movement which hadn't been there just now. Eva strolled into the background, Daniel in her arms. She was speaking to him and showing him things; she exuded that glow again, moving from shade to shade...

A laugh. Rich and uninhibited. I knew that laugh – I'd know it anywhere. Another brief glance at Matthias. Christian Beck still sat relaxedly beside his wheelchair; Annabelle had joined them. She stood stooped behind Matthias, leaned over his shoulder. A languid arm hung down his chest, her laugh hung in the air. Yes, I thought – they look like lovers again. I thought it with a twinge.

Returned my eyes to Estella.

"An unusual man," she said.

She was talking about Matthias, wasn't she? I could see that look in her eye. Again I glanced. Couldn't help it. Every time I saw him he reminded me, it made me insecure. I'd visited him each day in the hospital, I'd tried to catch him out – but the more we talked the more he'd sucked me in.

"Yes," I said.

How good he looked, he wore a panama hat on his shaven head, he was mending now. A cripple, yes, but a cripple with a cause.

"A wonderful aura."

"Yes?" She could really see it then? Estella could see so much.

"The postcard man."

Had to submit a chuckle for that one, but it came out stifled, it didn't come out too well.

"Where it all began," she said.

I held my peace.

She gazed at me. Ah, that Estella gaze.

A silence. Not particularly comfortable. Then she said quietly: "What has happened?"

"Happened?" I echoed. I looked away again; I hadn't yet told her. "You mean to Matthias?" I queried.

"No, Stefan. To you."

"Ah." Had to turn back my eyes. I regarded her unhappily. "Yes," I said. She could sense it, couldn't she? She always could. Still I felt so disinclined, so blocked. Was she breaking the ice for me?

"Matthias fell from a cliff and nearly died," I said. I had to force myself, had to begin somewhere. "I visited him in hospital and he told me something absurd. Said right after the accident he was lying unconscious and left his body." Is that what was holding me back – was I afraid of receiving a confirmation?

"Said he hovered there looking down at himself," I added feebly.

"Is that absurd?" she said. Said thoughtfully – but without pause to consider, without any surprise. Did she know already, then? Had he told her? They'd been conversing together half an hour ago, and for two people who've only just made acquaintance they'd conversed in a rather intensive way...

"Well?" Penetrating eyes, strong smile.

I hesitated still. "Well..." I began uncertainly. And I thought: coming from the mouth of any sane man isn't the absurdity perfectly clear? And yet...

"That's why I wanted to talk," I said; I said it like a confession. Meekly I spread my hands.

Another smile. It was slow and bountiful; it bestowed itself upon me like a holy blessing. Would she help me through the thicket, would she somehow help me to come clear?

"Did he tell you about it too?" I asked. I'd be glad to know what not to repeat.

"No." A tiny shake of her head.

"Nothing at all?"

"No, actually we only talked about me, he wished to learn who I am." Those bright eyes held me like a spotlight. "He is a very good listener, this old friend of yours."

"Yes."

"And observer."

"Yes." I dropped my glance, I knew what was coming; I had to begin.

"Is that all he told you, Stefan?" I heard her say. "That he left his body?"

She was leading me in. No turning back now. My gaze had alighted on her lap, on one of her hands. "No," I said. The fingers lay on her dress along one thigh. Wasn't that the dress she'd worn as we sat by the river that fateful day? Light glittering like diamonds on the water, mesmerising, and round the rushes, dragonflies? Yes, that was the dress that showed so much thigh.

I set off. It was like a journey. I started to tell her what he had told me, I concentrated on her hand. It wasn't as hard as I'd expected, and the block in my body began to ease, the oppression in my head to lift. His sentences were still burned in flame, like the writing on the sky his words were branded on my brain, I couldn't forget a single one – they described a state which didn't exist, a world which couldn't be…

On the fingers of that hand she wore five rings: four were simple silver, plain or plaited bands. The one in the middle was different though, while I spoke it caught my eye. A big rock crystal squatted there, and in its depths, catching the light, there seemed to shine a star.

I concentrated. And it aided my concentration. I described the strange noise, and the darkness through which he'd shot, and that light beyond compare; I told it just like he'd described, I dwelled on each little detail…

It dazzled, it transfixed me. It was as if the star were very private, as if it were only there for me. I heard myself say: "He said a warmth and love was emanating that words just can't describe. He said something spoke to him without speaking and his body was a blob. He said…"

The star blinked, radiated – it was as though the star almost were guiding.

"He said his life was reviewed but in a flash, just all those things that he'd done wrong, they entered his mind. And the thoughts were communicated with clemency and kindness – he used the word compassion…"

I saw its flourish, saw its flash.

And sometimes I was thinking while I spoke, it broke on through: he must have been delirious, he must have simply been dreaming. And each time I found I was thinking too, or a voice was there: he didn't lie, he couldn't lie about these things, he'd been sent back and here he was. But back from where, and where did all this leave me?

The star sparkled. Clouds were drifting, clearing, but there were more clouds beyond. The star beckoned. I was going in, crawling to the temple, I was down on hands and knees. I could hear the sounds and smell the incense, smell the smoke, was the goddess of the mysteries drawing back the veil?

"He came back changed," I said.

Estella stirred; I felt the move... But she hadn't said a word.

"He spoke of love, and having found something. He said it had been given to him – like a present, like a precious gift, he said like a Holy Grail."

The star was gone, the hand had moved; the dress and thigh revealed.

I raised my eyes. I was going weak, I was breaking down, my resistance had started to crack. Estella sat there, and smiled, legs stretched out; her arms seemed to embrace the world. I said to her: "He said he'd found the essence and it illuminated the path ahead. He said he has to follow it until he's allowed to return." Return? To where he'd been? Where had he been? He was too much of a realist to fantasise. Wasn't he? Could it be there was something to it all? Estella was still silent, still listening, just that generous smile. It was I who was speaking, passing it on; I was talking to her, to myself, I was talking to air – but somehow it did something, opened something, somehow it brought me solace. There were a thousand voices like thoughts in my head... where had the universe come from, who really created the heavens and the stars, who created the flower? I could hear Matthias recounting it, describing the light and the dark and where he'd been, his sentences factual and precise, yet now and then with gaps in between where he groped and failed to find a word, gaps I'd never known afflict him before. How could a man like Matthias fail to find the right word, were there places and things which belied description? I could hear Krister Skell the theologian, and that Catholic priest, could hear my father beside me as we gazed at the sky, even Eva from our childhood looking up to the corner of the room where grandmother's corpse lay cooling, and Annabelle too when I tried to communicate, and Estella's voice down by the river... they were all there, flowing together, could it be they were saying the same thing – was there really something out there, outside this world, was there more than meets the eye?

x x x

Sometimes I feel there are strings pulling us, invisible strings. Maybe there are, maybe not – and if it's true maybe there are times they even prevent us drifting off too far, they haul us back before it's too late. Is that what Andrea felt too?

A week after the little party I received an e-mail from her. It was very adamant:

'Papa, I'm coming back SEPTEMBER. Saul and Sammy in agreement, they'll be writing you. Can I live with you in M? Glad you moved from HER place. D'you have the room in F-M Strasse? You promised. Please. Hugs and kisses, Andrea.'

Isn't happiness like a shot in the arm, like getting drunk? I felt drunk all day.

Chapter 36

I had a strange dream the other day, it was almost like a déjà vu. I was in a building I'd been in before, everything was so familiar yet so far away. I was looking down from high above, had I come to say goodbye? I rose up stairs, passed through walls, and finally alighted. I was back in my old apartment in Nuremberg walking through the empty rooms – but hadn't I done this a quarter of a year before? All my furniture was gone, there were decorators in white overalls, painting the ceilings and the walls. Everywhere were echoes.

Then, unexpectedly, in one of the rooms I was confronted with myself. I saw me standing in the big kitchen at the heavy scrubbed-pine table. That was the only object left – except for the expanse of pinboard hanging, still adorned with all those newspaper cuttings and forgotten photographs.

And except for the postcard.

It lay there on the naked table. Had Frau Maußer handed it to me – had I put it there myself? I watched me stoop, draw it closer with a finger so I could properly see. Pretty picture. Green flowing hills going into the distance, a meandering path that wound on for ever, puffy-white fluffy clouds...

There was my hand again, turning it over in order to read. Neat precise handwriting: 'My friend. The captivity and the exodus are passed, ahead of us lies a promised land. Let us share it together. Sincerely, M.'

I could see him writing it, the way he had written. That was a pen in his hand, he was reaching out, he'd shed the last of his masks. I watched him float across the floor; there were footsteps I couldn't hear. Then he and my fear were gone. A clock was chiming; the time had arrived for the end of regrets and my confusion had flown away. It was like that feeling of redemption for those waiting on the mount, or pulling the cork on that vintage reserve to pour the sacred wine. Or like the wound that's finally healed.

I could see them: my hands were moving again, they were picking up the postcard like picking up the past. No shadows now, no ghosts. They hung the card on the pinboard with a drawing pin that was free: just a little signal that its duty had been done. I liked that. Rather pleasing somehow.

I hovered, waiting – what was I waiting for?

Nailed boots on naked timber boards. Two decorators were entering the kitchen, gesturing, and I was nodding assent. They lifted the table with some difficulty, carried it out, came back. Tore down the pinboard including its contents, broke it in rough pieces, carried them out too. Such a good feeling, a curtain lifted, goodbye to it all – a sense of lightness pervading.

The room was deserted now like the first day I ever set eyes on it, before Judit and I moved in.

I was moving through space; I was following me out into the hall, nothing left of mine, nothing left to show that I'd once been – no more cobwebs any more. There was that doorway, though, that golden frame of flaming sun containing my old secrets. Would it whisper them when I was gone, to the next one passing by? I watched me crossing the living room to the other side, hollow footsteps on the wooden floor – could see the houses opposite across the street. Window shutters were clattering up to greet the new day. There was the busy housewife putting out the bedding as she did every morning, fluffing the feather duvets over the sill in the cool fresh air. And there was the old lady, her neat net curtains tweaked aside, looking out at the world – had she been looking out for over a year?

I was lifting up, I was slipping inside me again, inside my envelope of skin – and into the tabernacle of my thoughts. Would Andrea really come in September? Would I maybe take up the offer of the Toscana when the leaves started to fall? There was such a lightness, like the soul flying free; it seemed another circle had just been completed and another was about to begin. In the house of my life more doors were opening, and now through the windows there was light streaming in – a bright, a beautiful, a clear white light.

THE END